Praise for THE TIGER CLAW

The Giller Prize Finalist

"*The Tiger Claw* is a first-rate spy thriller and also first-rate literature. Set in the 1940s in Occupied Paris with haunting similarities to the world today, this is a novel that reminds us that sometimes only fiction can really tell us the truth. . . . The story of one woman's courage in the face of racism, betrayal and hypocrisy on one hand and the evils of war on the other. It is also a love story between Muslim and Jew told in a language that resonates with mysticism and romance—yet it is brutally honest in its assessment of motives and ambiguities."

—Giller Prize judges

"Baldwin finds a Muslim woman who has much to teach our own time. . . . She becomes more ambitious with every book. . . . Years of careful research on three continents, as well as extensive contact with her subject's extended family, result in a portrait of Noor Inayat Khan that explains why she did what she did in compelling, convincing ways."

—*The Globe and Mail*

"A stirring tale of love and betrayal in a foreign land. Like the troubadour, [Baldwin] has the natural gift of pinning you to the window of her imagination until you hang by her each word and every twist and turn of the tale, begging for more."

—*India Today*

"*The Tiger Claw* brilliantly reveals the shifting sands of allegiance in times of war and the duplicity required for survival when all who are operating underground are interdependent but no one can be trusted fully."

—*The Gazette* (Montreal)

"I only had to read the novel's first line to know what was in store. . . . A fascinating portrait of a legendary woman and a novel that, in turn, examines love, religion, nationalism and sacrifice."

—*The Sun Times* (Owen Sound)

"It's a fiction closer to truth than any authorized account. . . . Baldwin's ability to bring her characters to life has never been in question and it reigns supreme now."

—*Outlook* (India)

SHAUNA SINGH BALDWIN

THE TIGER CLAW

A NOVEL

Vintage Canada

VINTAGE CANADA EDITION, 2005

Copyright © 2004 VICHAR

Published in Canada by Vintage Canada, a division of Random House of
Canada Limited, Toronto in 2005. Originally published in hardcover in
Canada by Alfred A. Knopf Canada, a division of Random House of Canada
Limited, Toronto, in 2004.
Distributed by Random House of Canada Limited, Toronto.

Vintage Canada and colophon are registered trademarks of
Random House of Canada Limited.

www.randomhouse.ca

Library and Archives Canada Cataloguing in Publication

Baldwin, Shauna Singh, 1962–
The tiger claw : a novel / Shauna Singh Baldwin.

ISBN 0-676-97621-2

I. Title.

PS8553.A4493T44 2005   C813'.54   C2005-901306-0

Text design: CS Richardson

Printed and bound in the United States of America

2   4   6   8   9   7   5   3

For
David J. Baldwin

Remember, even though I have done terrible things
I can still see the whole world in your face.

—RUMI (KULLUJAT E SHAMS, QUATRAIN 1110)

*Two hands, two feet, two eyes, good,
as it should be, but no separation
of the Friend and your loving.
Any dividing there
makes other untrue distinctions like "Jew"
and "Christian" and "Muslim"*

—RUMI (KULLUJAT E SHAMS, QUATRAIN 321)

AUTHOR'S NOTE

The Tiger Claw is inspired by the life and times of Noor Inayat Khan and the non-fiction accounts of many other resistance agents of WW II. Many historical people are mentioned in this book, but no living person is portrayed. A few new characters have been substituted for historical persons and some names have been changed. Most transliterations are from Urdu, some are from Arabic.

The first non-fiction biography of Noor, *Madeleine*, was written in 1952 by Jean Overton Fuller. William Stevenson summarized and embellished this account in *The Man Called Intrepid*. Later non-fiction writers commented on Noor's story, like Rita Kramer in *Flames in the Field*. Noor's brother, Pir Vilayat Inayat Khan, offered his tribute to Noor in his book *Awakening*. Noor is mentioned in footnotes to biographies of Hazrat Inayat Khan and discussed in books by retired agents of the Special Operations Executive (SOE). Recently, her story was presented with more context in *Women Who Lived for Danger* by Marcus Binney.

For me, these non-fiction accounts raised more questions about Noor than their facts could answer.

My depiction of Noor begins from fact but departs quickly into imagination, bending time, creating characters around her, rearranging or inventing some events to explore as if through her eyes, to feel what may have been in her heart.

THE TIGER CLAW

PART ONE

CHAPTER I

Pforzheim, Germany
December 1943

DECEMBER MOVED IN, taking up residence with Noor in her cell, and freezing the radiator.

Cold coiled in the bowl of her pelvis, turning shiver to quake as she lay beneath her blanket on the cot. Above, snow drifted against glass and bars. Shreds of thoughts, speculations, obsessions . . . some glue still held her fragments together.

The flap door clanged down.

"Herr Vogel . . ."

The rest, in rapid German, was senseless.

Silly hope reared inside; she reined it in.

The guard placed something on the thick, jutting tray, something invisible in the dingy half-light. Soup, probably. She didn't care.

She heard a clunk and a small swish.

Yes, she did care.

Noor rolled onto her stomach, chained wrists before her, supported her weight on her elbows and knelt. Then shifted to extend the chain running between her wrists and ankles far enough for her to be seated. The clanking weight of the leg irons pulled her bare feet to the floor.

She slipped into prison clogs, shuffled across the cement floor.

A pad of onionskin. A scrawl that filled the whole first page. It said in French, *For Princess Noor—write children's stories only.* Signed, *Ernst V.*

She had asked Vogel for paper, pen and ink, but never expected to receive them. "Everything in my power," Vogel had said.

She tucked the pad under her arm, then tested the pen nib against her thumb. She reached for the glass jar. Dark blue ink. She opened it, inhaled its metallic fragrance.

She carried the writing materials back to her cot. She lay down, eyes open to the gloom, gritting her teeth to stop their chattering. Mosquito thoughts buzzed.

Do it. Shouldn't. Do it. Shouldn't. Do it.

Use initials, think the names, use false names, code names.

She caterpillar-crawled to the edge, turned on her side to block the vision of any guard and examined the leg of the cot. A pipe welded to the metal frame. Hollow pipe with a steel cover.

If I can hide some of my writing, I will write what I want.

She pressed a chain-link against the steel cover. Was it welded? Cold-numbed fingers exploring. No, not welded. Screwed on tightly.

Push, push with the edge of her manacles. Then with a chain-link. She wrapped her chain around the cover like a vise. It didn't move. She pushed and turned in the dimness for hours, till she was wiping sweat from her eyes. She froze whenever she heard— or thought she heard—a movement at the peephole.

Deep breath. Attack the hollow leg again.

Night blackened the cell. Baying and barking outside, beyond the stone walls of the prison. Twice, the rush of a train passing very close. Noor grimaced and grunted on.

Finally, the steel cover moved a millimetre along its treads. By dawn, it loosened. She lay back, exhausted. Then, with her back to the door, she rolled up half the onionskin, poked it down the pipe-leg and, with an effort, screwed the cover on again.

Above her, the window brightened.

The guard was at the door. She unchained Noor's manacles so she could use the toilet. Did not glance at the bed. Did not shout.

The flap door dropped for Noor's morning bowl, sawdust bread. A single bulb lit the cell.

Begin, "Once upon a time there was a war . . . ?" No. She would write *une histoire*, not the kind her captor had in mind, but for someone who might read her words in a time to come:

I am still here.

I write, not because this story is more important than all others, but because I have so great a need to understand it. What I say is my truth and lies together, amalgam of memory and explication. I write in English, mostly, English being the one language left in the ring. Other languages often express my feelings better—French, Urdu, Hindustani. And perhaps in these languages I could have told and read you stories better than this, your mother's story. But all my languages have been tainted by what we've said and done to one another in these years of war.

When the flap door dropped that evening, Noor dragged her chains to it and placed two sheets on the open tray. On one she had written the Sufi tale about the attraction of a moth to a flame, on another the one about the young man who came knocking at his teacher's door and when his teacher asked, "Who is there?" cried "It is I" and was told, "Come back when you are nobody."

She could see the guard glance at the English writing then thrust the sheets in her pocket without examination. The pad of onionskin lay upon the cot behind Noor, but the guard didn't enter to count its remaining pages.

So, the next day, Noor wrote another paragraph, and another:

With that first creation of Allah—the pen that Vogel has allowed me—poised over the ink pot, then over the page, I wonder what to call you. Little spirit never whispered into this world—une fée. In Urdu I would call you ruh. Feminine. Ma petite ruh. We all begin feminine in Al-ghayab, the invisible, before we enter our nameless bodies.

I imagine you, ma petite, nine years old, looking much like me and as much like Armand, expectant and still trusting. Encourage my telling as any audience encourages a teller of tales, though I may tell what you may not condone, what you may not believe, or what you cannot bear to know. I write so you can see me, so Armand will appear again by the telling.

CHAPTER 2

Germany
July 1945

AGAINST THE FLUME and smear of a dying sun, the silhouette of a motorcycle rider rose over a ridge of dirt road. The sharp engine roar dropped and levelled. The rider's gloved hands downshifted to avoid the scorched remnants of a tank blocking his way. The bike bounced over ruts and craters as Kabir swerved the pod of his sidecar around the shell-pocked hull. The Tiger tank was canted over its cannon, its mud-caked treads stilled in a ditch.

Kabir didn't stop to examine the tank, or let thoughts of the Germans who must have died inside cross his mind, but goaded his rattling steed past. Showers sprang from spinning rubber as he furrowed a puddle. He shot a glance through spattered goggles at the jerricans bouncing in the sidecar and, gritting his teeth against flying mud and wind, headed into the darkening horizon.

Out of Strasbourg, Kabir had raced over a makeshift pontoon bridge crossing the Rhine with a moment of wonder. Only a few months earlier, before the Germans surrendered, crossing the Rhine at any point was unthinkable.

Faster, faster.

Past the Rhine, the road crumbled in patches, as if the very soil had soured beneath the tar-skin pasted upon it. Kabir's Triumph sagged into valleys, zoomed past forests of pine. Detour upon detour drove him south to Freiburg im Breisgau, a city he knew only as a target objective last November, now almost conjured out of existence by Allied bombs—his bombs. As he drove through its high canyons of scorched rubble, the sight of a tiny, ragged girl foraging alone with a wooden bucket amid a mass of crushed possessions and twisted steel brought the Al-Fatiha surah to his lips:

> "' . . . master of the Day of Reckoning,
> To you we turn to worship
> and to you we turn in time of need.
> Guide us along the road straight,
> the road of those to whom you are giving . . .'"

Now, as he sped past these patches of green and gold, it was difficult to believe he had just seen Alsatian hamlets like Gérardmer flattened to the level of its glacial lake by the retreating German army, seen the abandoned barracks, the gallows and gas chambers of Natzweiler-Struthof camp near Strasbourg, or the stone skeletons and smoky ghosts of Freiburg. The putrid stench of death at Natzweiler, mingled with the bomb-smoke and rain of Freiburg, lingered in his nostrils, saturated his lungs, an all-pervasive odour that the scent of lavender blooming by the roadside could not erase.

This was his first time on the ground through Germany. In his childhood, his father's savings were reserved for passages "home" to India, not European excursions. And since 1933, Germany, though literate beyond Indian nationalists' wildest dreams of progress, had become the sick core of Europe whence refugees flowed into France. Hitlerland was the omnivorous devourer of the hapless, the racially impure, the non-Gentile, the circumcised. But these beautiful forests, hills and fields of Germany seemed unblemished by German actions.

The motorcycle rattled past a sign—*Stuttgart: 120 km*—and approached an improvised checkpoint beside a maze of oil drums.

A young American military policeman sauntered up, obviously expecting a courier on the motorbike. Noting Kabir's rank, he snapped to. "Can I help you, sir?"

Kabir returned his salute and held out his pass and ID booklet. The MP studied the pass and looked uncertain. A lieutenant approached; they exchanged salutes.

Kabir raised his goggles, unbuckled his helmet, peeled off his gloves, while the lieutenant took the documents and read the pass aloud.

"'This is to certify that the bearer, Flight Lieutenant Kabiruddin Khan of the Royal Air Force, is proceeding through Germany to locate his sister who was held in a German camp.'" He paused, glanced up at Kabir.

Kabir was intent on the road beyond the barrier, fist clenched about his gloves.

"'It is requested that British, French, American and Russian military and civilian authorities assist Flight Lieutenant Khan in his task, and make such housing and mess facilities available, as well as radio, press and all other means which can help him locate his sister. A further request is made to permit his sister to cross the border with him on his return to his home in France.'" He again examined the signature and date on the pass for what seemed like an eon. "Which camp are you headed for, sir?"

"I don't quite know. All I know is that my sister was deported to Germany."

The lieutenant's opinion of Kabir's chance of success was expressed with a sigh, but Kabir was long past listening to the opinions of uniformed officials. He knew the odds were slim. Folded in his pocket he carried a list of the known concentration camps between the Alsace region and Berlin. And this list, without any German prisons, was three pages long. Officials of the International Committee of the Red Cross and UNRRA, the UN Relief and Rehabilitation Administration, had reminded him every day for weeks in Paris: one in ten people survived a camp. Searching for one woman among the millions displaced might be futile. But this was not just any woman. This was his sister, Noor.

Immediately after Germany surrendered, Kabir had obtained permission to return to Paris, where he waited for the transports bringing deportees and prisoners of war home to Paris. For weeks, in deepening amazement and horror, he met trains arriving at the Gare de l'Est each morning with hundreds upon hundreds of hollow-chested, shaven-headed returnees. Every day, at UNRRA headquarters, at welcome centres for returned deportees and at the Hôtel Lutétia, he examined and re-examined the cards and notes tacked to bulletin boards covering every wall, coming to realize with ever-mounting dread that while he was looking for one woman, many were searching for entire families. A lucky break had come a week before when he recognized an UNRRA worker. A former theosophist, she'd studied Sufism first at his father's feet, then at Uncle Tajuddin's, in the now-haloed years before the war, learning about the oneness of Allah and all other names for God. Straight away, he wheeled a list of German camps now under Allied control right out of her lacquered fingertips, requisitioned a motorcycle from an RAF base, obtained three weeks' leave and a high-level pass, and came searching.

"Try Munich," said the lieutenant, handing Kabir's papers back with heavy finality. "There's a collection centre there, run by UNRRA."

"Thank you." Gloves back on his hands, Kabir adjusted his helmet and goggles and gunned the engine.

"Good luck, sir." The young MP waved Kabir through with a salute of triumphant camaraderie.

A short distance further, four men and two women carrying bundles and suitcases were climbing slowly into a Red Cross lorry parked along the road, facing Kabir. These anonymous survivors of the terror, weak from their time in the camps, still wearing their sacklike prison attire, were the liberated—"displaced persons," or DPs—on their way to somewhere they once called or could now call home.

Kabir slowed, scanning their faces as they passed, searching for one familiar face, one woman's face. Sympathy blended with revulsion. Noor—petite, gentle Noor—might be in such abject condition at that very moment. As they trudged past, a sob of desperation surfaced in him. He pushed it away. Insh'allah, Noor was alive. He began another *du'a* to add to all the others he'd uttered during the last few months, calling on Allah's mercy for her.

Speeding to high gear again on the rutted road, a dust cloud lifting in his wake, he tried to recapture the bravado that had filled him like poppy-fume when he volunteered for the RAF, returned from flight school in Canada and began to fly bombers. Back then, in England, he was a refugee after the fall of France, and his British Indian citizenship gave him what he wanted most—the chance to fly. The destructive actions he justified multiplied daily as his tenets and personal code of conduct were suspended, superseded by the obligations of war.

Flying over Germany once in daylight last winter, the spiky pines bristling from snow-covered slopes were like the bayonets of Great War soldiers buried alive in the trenches of Verdun. From twenty thousand feet the world had looked flat but for mountains, giving no indication of the 23.5-degree tilt affecting the experiences of each person below, or the ferocity of emotions that curdled all co-operation and compromise. And nothing below had presented the jigsaw of warring countries, delineated any boundaries or coloured parts of the soil Occupied. The surface flowed instead from grassy field to knoll, ridge, escarpment, cliff, sea.

But now, what had looked like green explosions erupting in sudden abundance beneath his wings had expanded to three dimensions—dense foliage flashing past his careening motorcycle.

Kabir acknowledged his motives, acknowledged that he would have, and had, killed for the joy of flying ever more wonderful machines, almost as complex as birds. How he loved that swift, fragile Mosquito whose engines and high-octane fuel propelled him across the Channel and back, through searchlights and puffs of ack-ack, almost as fast as the rotation of the giant planet beneath. Flying, he felt ever closer to the infinite Allah, ever conscious of the hidden Orient hemisphere, regretting only that he could never gain enough altitude to see it. Later in the war he had thought of himself as a birdman carrying seed, and the scattered markings on the fuselage of his Lancaster the coefficient of Indian bravery. High in his metal bubble, the lure of gravity had been his most pressing problem, gravity operating even in the aquamarine depths below, saving fish from sloshing away into space. The probability of Messerschmitts sharpened each reaction, increased his impetus to prove his role in the drama of Europe's war.

It came to him now, as he saw these displaced people, that after each night's sortie, while he could — *allhamdullilah!* — retreat to safety across that tiny moat heaving as if with uneasy dreams between the crone face of England and the sea-encrusted Continent, he'd been far above the sight and smell of blood, the effect of his work, that he'd been spared a single scream of the dying. While he feared only the blaze of sudden fall and a living cremation, or capture, the lives of the landbound had been a string of long moments of dread and privation.

And yet. Some intangible element within him and the survivors was indestructible; it had demanded of all of them that they survive these terrible years.

If Noor hadn't survived, he would never forgive himself. If she was wounded or worse because of his bombs — Damn it, why had he bragged about Noor to Boddington? It was Kabir who introduced Noor to Nick Boddington — a journalist, so he'd thought — whom he met perusing *The New York Times* in the circular reading room at the British Museum Library. How anxious he'd been then to prove his loyalty to Britain, how anxious for Noor to prove hers too. It was 1942 — must have been June, for it was shortly after Premier Laval said "I desire Germany's victory" and broadcast his latest madness, a program to exchange six French workers for each French POW held in Germany. One of Noor's stories for children was to be broadcast over the BBC, and he'd mentioned it to Boddington over a pint at the Café de Paris in Trafalgar Square. Surrounded by a babble of languages, including the halting, lilting English of refugees from all over Europe ordering themselves into old hierarchies, he'd enumerated Noor's accomplishments: multilingual, children's writer, pianist, qualified nurse, wireless telegraphist. Impressed, Boddington wondered out loud if his sister might be amenable to doing a little "liaison work" for King and Country—"very hush-hush and all that, could bring in a bit more pocket money, if you get my drift." And Kabir said, "Yes, of course, but of course," and gave friendly Nick Mother's address where Noor could be reached.

And just why was he so anxious for Noor to take any position Boddington offered? Admit it now: was it that Boddington's very hush-hush job brought in a few pounds more than a telegraphist's pay, more than any nurse or secretary in London earned, and those few pounds more would help him support Mother, Dadijaan and their young sister Zaib? No, no, that wasn't all. Admit the real reason: he meant to spare Noor the remotest chance she might be ordered to clean bedpans, swab blood, tend strange men. War be damned, at the time, he couldn't stomach the idea that if Noor became a nurse on active duty, she, his sister, his unmarried sister, would touch, hold, bathe men's naked bodies—unrelated men.

He could imagine Noor, gentle Noor, as a wireless operator for the Nursing Yeomanry, as Mother, Dadijaan and Zaib believed, but not as a secret agent. He couldn't imagine his sister flying the Channel to France tucked in the gunner's end of a Lysander.

Because Kabir still thought in French, preferring the solid logic of its verbs to the exception-dense mutt-quality of English, he could have asked to be assigned to the no-less-dangerous path of the Lysanders carrying guns, ammunition and operatives like Noor into France; bilingual pilots were in high demand. But like some other RAF men, he thought the Lizzies a mere bus service and remained with Bomber Command. When his bombardier released the four-thousand-pound cookies that stung the distant surface, none of them knew if the bombs had found their targets. Wind and speed affected their downward trajectory, and Air Marshal Sir Arthur Harris and his officers at Bomber Command had to wait for aerial reconnaissance photos taken in daylight, and coded dispatches from wireless operators like Noor, to determine the extent of enemy damage. Noor had sent such damage reports, reports on enemy strength, troop and supply movement, arsenals, artillery the Allies would encounter across northern France and beyond.

Brother and sister are tethered at the ankle, always running together in a three-legged race, striving to match one another's stride, leaning on one another even as they pull away. Younger by two years, he'd leaned on Noor from the time he was ten and his father, Abbajaan, went "home" to India and never returned. All of them — Mother, Dadijaan and Zaib — had relied on her; so he was, well, affronted that she hadn't leaned in similar fashion on him.

He was in charge of the family, and had been in charge since they all arrived in London. She should have consulted him when someone from Boddington's hush-hush organization interviewed her! Instead, she just upped and volunteered to go overseas. In fact, she told no one she was being sent back to Paris. Until the fateful War Office letter, the entire family believed Noor was stationed in North Africa.

Noor could have, should have, confided in him if no one else. Forget the damn secrecy. Not a single letter from her since she left for France. Not one letter to Mother, Dadijaan, Zaib or himself in two years.

As dusk faded to darkness, the engine sputtered. Kabir slowed to a stop, dropped his foot to the verge of the road and dismounted. Coming around the bike, he stayed on tar to avoid land mines. He hoisted a jerrican clear of the sidecar with greater force than was warranted by its weight and used a rubber hose and metal funnel to pour the last few pints into the tank. He doffed his goggles and helmet, took a welcome gulp from a canteen, and swept the back of his hand across his moustache and stubbled chin. Then, chilled by some vague premonition, he reached into the sidecar for his RAF jacket.

Distant bells, rusted from five years of silence, sounded wavering tones against the evening air. They announced food and a place to rest nearby, raking Kabir in like a marker drawn across a map to a plotter's magnet.

He was loath to stop, but stop he must. Besides being low on petrol, he was stiff and sore from long hours of riding, and needed information — if nothing else, confirmation that he might somewhere in Munich find a card or file with Noor's name on it.

He guided himself by the tall steeple needling the sky, through the town's brick-lined streets to the central square. Everywhere, the dispossessed shuffled and limped, helping the wounded or carrying their meagre belongings.

He stopped two Frenchmen in faded stripes and showed them his most recent photograph of Noor. They stared at her serious face, arrested by her direct gaze. Vibrant eyes, Kabir told them, black and fiery, just as in the photo. Her hair — long, wavy, jet black. He demonstrated her height at the level of his chin, no more than five foot three. Petite, he said, very petite; from a distance you could mistake her for a child. Perhaps they knew her by her Western name, Nora Baker? or her code names, Anne-Marie Régnier, or "Madeleine"?

"*Non. Désolé*," they said. The Frenchmen had been held in a POW camp, not a concentration camp. They questioned Kabir in return about their loved ones. Kabir listened carefully, compassionately, but sadly shook his head as he had so many times before.

At a dry stone fountain before the church a peasant woman sat alone nursing a baby, a small basket beside her. Past her, thin, rough-looking men clustered around a small fire, cooking. Through the broken light from the remains of stained glass set in

Gothic arches, Kabir saw a file of the forlorn thronging the centre aisle inside the church.

Dismounting, he wheeled the motorcycle to an alley around the back. He switched off the headlamp and began searching for a place to secure his bike.

Light glowed from an open door. A stable. A stable crowded with hollow-faced men and women, spreading jackets and saddle blankets on the straw in the stalls for the night. Polish or Russian flowed between them—he couldn't tell. A few stared in hostile silence, some in frank curiosity. He moved on.

Ten paces past the stable stood a weatherbeaten garage. Kabir pulled a torch from his pocket and wrenched the door open. Flicked the torch on.

Someone gasped, and a ghost hand shot into view, palm raised, fingers splayed as if to halt him. The torch beam jerked in an arc. Another hand rose before him, then another. Kabir lowered the beam: half a dozen frightened faces below the forest of surrendering arms. German soldiers moving homewards, hoping to surrender to the British or Americans.

"*Restez tranquilles,*" he reassured them, and backed away from their visible relief. They were boys. Or maybe they just looked like boys to him. This damn war had aged him far beyond his twenty-nine years. If he spoke German, Kabir could have explained they had nothing to fear—that the Russian army was nowhere near this tiny town, that British, French and American troops had thousands of German POWs now and were no longer interested in surrenders, except of Nazis and other war criminals.

Did those boys realize that their suffering was the outcome of arrogance? that the battles of Paris and London, the bombing of Coventry and Dunkirk, made this necessary?

Necessary. How much retaliation had really been necessary?

In the alley, he switched on the headlamp again. Shadows loomed and shrivelled against the church walls—tattered scavengers sifting through rubbish. The beam illuminated an iron hitching ring embedded in the church wall. Kabir mounted, started the bike and guided it up to the wall in low gear. He took a fastening cable from the sidecar, looped one end around the frame, the other into the ring of the post, then snapped a Masterlock through both ends. The empty jerricans couldn't be secured, but were hidden beneath the black button-down cover.

Why had it been his hands that guided a plane to where it could drop its payload on the most people? Women, like that one looking at him with deadened eyes. Children, like the street urchin looking like a starving beggar-child from India.

Kabir entered the church through a side door, fighting the urge to pull his collar to his nose against the reek of flea-infested, unwashed humanity. In Paris bistros before the war he'd played lighthearted games with friends, identifying the origins of tourists fed on buttered scones, kielbasa, sauerkraut or paprikashed goulash from their sweat—so different from people raised on wheat and brie. But here the pores of each man, woman and child excreted a common animal odour of rot, dirt, disease, feces and fear, indistinguishable in origin.

So many years since he was in a church or mosque, he'd almost forgotten the silence such places inspire. A U.S. Army chaplain stood near the altar with Red Cross workers dispensing hot soup in place of the sacrament, ladling it from a great cauldron to outstretched metal bowls. What of the German parish priest? Probably interned long ago in some Nazi camp.

Every inch of the church was covered by ragged travellers of all ages, kneeling, sitting, lying anywhere, everywhere, in pews, on the stone floor. Some sat, some lay pillowing their heads on rotten shoes, many coughing and spitting. Children wailed or played. Money-changers operated in the shadows, turning Reichsmarks and American military scrip to dollars and pounds. Money passed from hand to grasping hand.

As he had in other villages, Kabir queued with the rest, hoping the steaming cauldron was full enough to contain a share for him. Hushed voices rose and fell in a dozen languages and dialects around him:

"How far is the border from here?"

"Which border? Of this zone or of France? Maps change every day."

"Please, is there an orphanage? This child is lost."

"Did you hear Herr Truman came to Berlin, now the canals are clean? *Ja*, the Russkies made the Nazis haul out the dead first."

"Pétain will be tried next. Oh, let the Maréchal reveal his 'double game' now. Perhaps he'll be found dead, like Hitler and his whore."

"Hitler dead? Not so—I hear he gave a speech on the radio."

"My village is in Poland. Is there any Poland now?"

Someone clutched at his arm. "I have sister—she is pretty little virgin, she love officers," said rotten teeth and a cunning smile.

Kabir shook the ghoul away in horror. His gaze flitted from face to face.

Noor, dear sister—where are you?

Kabir reached the front of the queue. The American chaplain sloshed lukewarm liquid into his bowl.

"Better than water soup," rasped a shaven-headed scarecrow. His toothless grin made him look ancient.

Kabir's hunger pronounced the soup and slice of Wonderbread worthy of Maxim's.

He rinsed his bowl and spoon in a drum of scalding, soapy water, dipped it into another drum of boiling hot water and joined a queue for the slit trench at the back of the church. After a wash from a jug of hot water, he climbed to the second storey, spread his jacket as a prayer rug and did namaaz, hoping, as he had since his tenth birthday—the day Abbajaan transferred his mantle to his shoulders— that the prescribed motions would open the invisible connection to the Divine and leave in its wake the deep, abiding faith in the will of Allah that Abbajaan always had.

But on this night, as on every night, nothing moved within him. When he had completed each motion and prayer, he was still alone.

Someday your heart must awaken, he told himself sternly.

Oh, for the luxury of faith! But since the German invasion in 1940, when the war truly began for France, for Kabir and his family, he'd been awkward with Allah, finding it impossible to believe the Most Merciful would will the Western world into this state of barbarism.

Faith would rise because it must. The hiatus of war was over. Abbajaan's followers would be among the displaced making their way home from concentration camps. They would return for Kabir's blessing, his assurance, as Abbajaan would have given them, that Allah would recognize their sacrifices. He could not, like Edward VIII, say, "I hereby declare my irrevocable determination to renounce the Throne for myself and my descendants," for he had no physical throne to renounce. The warrior in him balked at abdication, like the philosopher Jiddu Krishnamurti, when so many needed Kabir as their organic link to the late Inayat Khan. *Hazrat* Inayat Khan. To tell them Abbajaan's blood was no guarantor of continuing faith or understanding of Sufi thought would be cruel indeed after all their suffering. And Kabir and his family relied on the donations of the faithful to the Sainah Foundation—all of which meant that any such misgivings or crises of faith must, simply must, be quelled.

Suddenly overcome with fatigue, he returned to ground level and found a length of stone slab on which to lie, rolled his jacket into a pillow and used his cap to shade his eyes from the too acute angles of the Gothic arches over his head.

He dreamed Noor sat writing at a table suffused with light. Yes, that was Noor, not his sister Zaib or his girl Angela—black hair strayed about that oval face. She paused, nibbling the end of her pencil the way she often did. She looked far past him down the way he had come, and wrote again, as if writing his deeds in the Book of Judgement. He floated between her and the light, and now he could read over her shoulder. She wasn't writing in Persian script. No, she wrote in English. And in the language that was not Abbajaan's, not their heritage, she wrote cruel truths about

Kabir. Guileless, she wrote Kabir had betrayed her, sent her alone into harm's way.

Kabir woke, heart in spasm as if a bugle called him to another freezing sortie over Europe. He sat up, quickly spitting to his left side, in case the Noor he'd dreamed of was the recorder of his deeds. If she was, there should be two of her—twin angels, the Kiraman Katibeen, pious writers writing diligently in the Book of Judgement. Couldn't he even dream it right?

How is a man to know these days which deeds will finally be recorded as good, which ones as evil?

Light slivers of cobalt and scarlet filtered through shards of stained glass and stilled Kabir's dreams the next morning. A shave, a cursory wash, a tin mug of coffee and three slices of unbuttered bread eased some of his stiffness. More refugees filed in, and the second storey came alive with crying babies and children as exhausted knots of people found places to rest. So Kabir gave up his space and jogged smartly up the bell tower's hundred and six stone stairs for his Fajar prayers.

At the top, a small iron balcony suspended him over the central avenue of the town like a mullah in a minaret about to call the faithful. In the distance, fields amber with wheat rippled beside the road he'd travelled the previous evening. To the west, undulating hills rose to meet the Black Forest. He faced towards Mecca, towards Munich, and did his remembrance of Allah, praying this day to find Noor or, insh'allah, some clue as to her whereabouts.

Heartened with new resolve and urgency, he descended into the church again, thanked the chaplain for his stay and asked directions to the nearest U.S. motor pool for petrol. The chaplain drew a map locating it a few kilometres from the church and, yes, Munich might be a place to continue his inquiries about Noor.

In the cool sunshine of the alley outside, refugee women were removing their shoes and socks to wash clothes under a water pump. Except for their dresses they looked like poor women he'd seen in India.

He unbuttoned the canvas shroud covering the sidecar. Fumes were released from the remains of the petrol when he opened the jerricans. Not much left in them.

He put on his gloves and goggles, strode smartly around the motorbike, unlocked and released the cable, swung his leg over the bike and kick-started it.

Nothing.

Kabir swore softly in Hindustani and kicked the starter again. Still nothing.

He swore in French. Kicked downwards again.

A cough and a backfire, then nothing.

Kabir dismounted. "Bugger it!"

A smart metallic report as his boot hit the wheel rim.

Delay, delay. Nothing to do but button down the damn canvas, retie the bloody fastening cable, relock the damn Masterlock, and set off on foot through the cobbled streets clogged with refugees to the U.S. Army motor pool.

An hour of walking and a ride in the back of an army truck brought Kabir to an officer to whom he presented his letter of authorization—possibly the most harried man in Germany, juggling transport and maintenance demands for several units.

"Motorbike? Not my specialty—but there's a sarge back there who claims to know all about them. Guy with three up and one down." His fingers traced chevrons on his sleeve. "Behind the deuce-and-a-half."

In search of the lorry Kabir wended his way past soldiers in grease-streaked OD fatigues, through an obstacle course of vehicles in stages of diagnosis or dismemberment, past a field where bewildered British soldiers were learning baseball. He spotted the staff sergeant's chevrons, three up and one down, under the open bonnet of the lorry, where he was teaching a private more about cussing than mechanics. A thoughtful, rotund face emerged, and a husky six-foot-three snapped to attention and the reflex of a salute as Kabir approached.

"At ease, sergeant."

Kabir returned the salute, then explained, pointing back to the village. The sergeant nodded and sent the private scurrying for spare parts, a tool kit and some cans of petrol. Then back to the harried officer for permission.

"I should make you walk like us infantry," the officer bantered with jovial disrespect. "But you RAF guys sure put on a helluva fireworks display for Hitler, so I guess old Uncle Sam should loan you a Jeep." To the sergeant, "You get your black ass back here ASAP, get it?"

"Yes, sir!"

A Jeep pulled up and Kabir swung into the passenger seat beside the sergeant. They bounced back to the gate, past a guard-house and back onto the road.

"Where're you from, sir?"

A question Kabir detested.

He could have said he was from London, where he'd sported his British India passport through five years of war. He could have said Baroda, the tiny kingdom in India where his grandfather's ancestral home was presumably still standing. He could have told this Dravidian-faced GI the name of any city in the world and, given people's ignorance of geography, the information would have the same non-effect.

But Kabir had lived in Paris most of his life. Other men kept their beloved girlfriends or wives before them as they fought, but not Kabir. For him, Afzal Manzil—house of peace—the house Abbajaan left to him and the Sainah Foundation, was sacred ground worthy of battle. And so, because he had most to claim and most to lose in Paris, he answered, "Paris."

Paris. Paris and all of France, abandoned but fixed in still life for four years in Kabir's memory, had been held hostage by the Germans. His city had endured unspeakable deprivation, pain, secrets and shame. But he'd "done his bit," as they said in England—by bombing its marshalling yards when ordered.

"But you're in the RAF? 'Scuse my sayin', sir, but you don't look English."

"My father was from India."

The sergeant appeared either confused or unenlightened by this. Kabir tried again.

"You know, the place Christopher Columbus was looking for."

The sergeant swerved to avoid a pothole. "Columbus was a Wop, wasn't he, sir? Like Mussolini—no sense of direction." He squinted down the macadam road. "Never met anyone, and anyhow no officers, from India."

"And I've never met any Negroes to talk to."

"Yeah? Lots of us in London, sir."

Kabir shook his head. There were swing clubs in London where, to the chagrin of their British mothers, women lily-white as Angela went dancing with Negroes, but he'd never frequented them.

"I saw Indians in London, sir, but if you'll 'scuse my sayin', you're not real dark, and you don't wear a turban. I did figure you was too polite to be American."

"My mother is American," said Kabir. "From Boston."

"Uh-huh! Thought so. You're a mulatto."

The Jeep tilted into a decline, then accelerated again. Kabir accepted the label warily, never having applied it to himself before.

The sergeant said after a while, "Must be some lady, your ma, marrying your pa."

Kabir smiled polite assent.

"No, I mean it—that's one gutsy lady. You ever see your white folks in America?"

"No," said Kabir. Mother's family was opaque to him, absent from her spoken recollections, which always began from the day Miss Aura Baker packed one portmanteau and a hat box and caught a steamer from Boston Harbor to London town, arriving at the Sufi Music Centre, which was at that time Abbajaan's only doorstep, and proposing marriage. Family lore continued that Abbajaan had warned her he was a dervish, that bread and water were to be her lot, but it didn't deter Mother. And for eight years, while Abbajaan tried to perform Indian classical music to ever sparser audiences in England, she said he'd been right about the bread and water.

"And 'scuse my sayin', sir, but I don't believe you ever will see them."

"Why's that, sergeant?"

"Heck, sir—when your father's a coloured man, that's real tough for white folks to swallow. Where I come from, there are laws against it. Your pa could get lynched for less in my hometown."

The Jeep made a detour between the drums of an unmanned roadblock set up to slow traffic. The sergeant kept his eyes on the road.

"Most unfortunate," said Kabir.

Lame response—as if fortune were to blame for man-made laws.

His kaftaned Abbajaan was brown, not "coloured" or "black." Kabir was nine when he first learned that the United States had only two classifications, white and black, for all people. Abbajaan had returned from a performance tour to the States, annoyed by reviewers who devoted more inches to "the lightness of his coloured skin," his "exotic dress and accent," than to the music he so cherished. America, said Abbajaan, had the strange idea that what it called "freedom" was possible without justice in society. Pity had surprised Kabir, a pity he'd never forgotten, imagining Abbajaan's discomfort in the midst of his moneyed white followers in San Francisco, Chicago and New York.

"He'd be a Hindoo, like that Mr. Gandhi, right?" The sergeant was speculating again.

"A Muslim," Kabir corrected. "Like Mohammed Ali Jinnah."

"Oh, I get it, like Elijah Mohammed. A heathen, anyways, for your ma's white family, right, sir?"

Kabir acknowledged this, though Mother had converted to Islam immediately upon marriage, whereupon the words "infidel" and "heathen" became applicable to her blood relatives, certainly not his father's. Yes, it was possible, indeed probable, that Mother's family saw Abbajaan and himself as heathens.

Still, it was no business of this stranger.

"You don't speak like a Negro, sergeant."

"'Scuse my sayin', sir, but you don't either." A giant guffaw followed.

Kabir smiled thinly, holding on as the Jeep bucked and slid sideways beneath him. When he was five, Abbajaan had sung a few anti-Raj songs that drew the attention of British authorities. He'd been obliged to flee London, like the Prophet to Medina, and so the family had moved to Paris. The sergeant's comments were making Kabir glad Abbajaan had chosen Paris over Boston. In Paris, among Abbajaan's rentier followers, blood distance from royalty, even petty royalty, was the measure of excellence, while skin colour went unnoted.

"I talk white, like you, sir," the sergeant confided with pride. "Been working on it a few months now."

"You have?"

The sergeant nodded. "When I got to London, it hit me right away: the enlisted men in the British army talked in their different accents, but their officers talked like they're all on the BBC. That got me thinking. I started noticing how I talk. Realized that on the telephone, on the radio, even when they couldn't see me, they could *hear* the colour of my skin. So I figure I'll just talk different—fool 'em whenever I want."

"Been here a long time, then, sergeant?"

"A little over a year now. I was with the Red Ball Express, hauling gas and ammo from the depots to forward airfields. Got assigned to the pool afterwards—I'm a natural with machines."

The sergeant had supplied *le sang rouge de guerre*—the red blood of war—when the Allied armies sped past their supply lines in late 1944. His endless hours of driving in convoys and each five-gallon jerrican he hauled had saved Allied forces from stalling on their way to the Rhine.

"How long before you go home?" Kabir asked the question foremost in every serviceman's mind since Mr. Truman had declared a Day of Prayer throughout America and diplomats were back in split-tailed splendour on both sides of the Atlantic.

"Don't mind if I never go back, sir, though I'm a native son. Think I'll just settle down anywhere there ain't no Whites Only signs. Not Germany, even though the women are real easy pickin's here now we're allowed to fraternize. Many of them have never seen Negro Americans like me. We tell 'em we're night fighters and they all doggone believe it! I'd live in Paris, maybe. Negroes do well there—I'll have a club of my own. Can't do that in Mississippi without a Colored sign, you know, sir. But then again, maybe you don't know, seeing as you pass."

"Pass?"

"Pass for white, sir."

The Jeep ploughed past a scorched, roofless cottage. A sagged-faced woman shouted after them, pointing to her cart filled with pots, pans and clocks for sale.

Kabir kept his face impassive and looked away. His aspirations had so far been better served by identifying with Mother's race than with Abbajaan's. No reason to admit this to a stranger. And "passing," as the sergeant called it, only takes one so far: Kabir wasn't entitled to American citizenship, since Mother had lost hers by marrying an Asian Indian. American laws expressed the wishes of Mother's family perfectly. An occasional letter arrived when a relative died, and once, a parcel had sailed across the Atlantic from an aunt in Boston.

"Right now, I must get to Munich," he said, showing the sergeant his photograph of Noor. "I'm searching for my sister. I know she's still alive."

"Amen, sir. She's about your colour; don't you worry—she'll be just fine."

The spire and bell tower of the village church came into view. The Jeep closed in on its destination, dust barrelling in its wake.

"Can I ask you a question, sir?" said the sergeant as they turned into the village and bumped into the central square. "You have any trouble with the white folks in your unit?"

"In the beginning," said Kabir, "but after a while the important thing is flying, fighting and bombing, and how well you do it."

He wanted to add, "You have to fly better, do everything better, be more anxious, show more courage, and shout louder for King and Country," but he was an officer, and such confessional remarks would establish an equality he wasn't sure he wanted.

Kabir never imagined himself, and certainly not Noor, fighting for England. England was too full of lords and ladies still posturing and preening in clubs while mocking the French for their defeat and betrayal of democracy, and Indians for their non-violent struggle for independence. His equal presence in the officers' mess had required an effort of mental inclusion that was beyond his fellow British citizens, the normal hazing, mocking and teasing that would have broken formality becoming an extension of imperialism in the hands of the hazer, so that they and he all found themselves playing roles in a very old script.

It didn't help that he couldn't fit their image of an Indian—too tall, too fair, not Hindu, not Gurkha, not even Sikh. A Muslim. A Sufi Muslim, they sniggered—"sounds delicious." And Kabir would explain earnestly and proudly. Uselessly, too, for not one, if questioned, could have repeated anything he said over tankards of beer. He became accustomed to this. It gave him the freedom to indulge in reverie out loud, to reminisce, pontificate, even pray, without concern his words would change anything or be remembered by his mates. In place of friends he gathered followers, as Abbajaan once did, prolonging his own life and career by showing unstinting appreciation to his flight crew and those who maintained his aircraft.

"You're right, sir—I always say, if you've got the grits, serve 'em."

Kabir pointed the way to the alley behind the church. The sergeant shifted to second gear and turned. The Jeep approached the motorcycle against the church wall.

"And the white misses, sir? Would they go out with you if they find out you ain't really white?"

Actually, the few English girls he knew would do what their mothers never dreamed of. Especially Angela. She listened to Kabir, loving his strangeness—his dark, wiry moustache, slim hands with tapering fingers, his straight white teeth. Angela listened as he vowed, when the war was over, to return to France and spend the rest of his life like a travelling curator, exhibiting Abbajaan's Sufi ideas: peace, love, tolerance. Above all, tolerance—the simplest idea, the most difficult to teach.

And damned difficult to learn.

"No," he replied. "But it made no difference to my girl."

"You got a picture?"

Kabir snapped the catch of the locket on his watch, showed him Angela's rose-touched, dreamy smile. Angela's coquettish eyes, so unlike Noor's direct gaze. Kabir could all but see those lashes fluttering. Fine rippled locks—light grey in the photo, but the sergeant had made a mental correction to gold.

"She gonna marry you, sir?"

Kabir closed the locket with a broad smile. "Haven't the faintest idea, sergeant. I'll ask her when I return to London."

The sergeant grunted sceptically. Kabir jumped off the Jeep as it slowed to a stop. The sergeant heaved his bulk out and took his tool kit from the back. He squatted and stared solemnly at the motorcycle engine.

"Just think, sir," he said, "you and I gotta go to all this trouble because a bunch of Kraut, Eye-talian and Jap white folks wanted to take over the world from the other white folks."

Kabir nodded, though he'd never thought of the Japanese as white. And the war with those chaps was far from over; the U.S. fleet had just begun bombarding the main islands of Japan. In three weeks' time Kabir would have to report for duty and could be sent to the Far East to bomb Japan. At least he wasn't a fighter pilot who'd be called on to intercept those suicidal lunatics strapped into their bomb-loaded planes. What did they call themselves? *Kamikazes*.

His view of the war was rather different from those of his fellow officers. As a colonial, born in Britain of a father from an Indian princely state subservient to the Raj, he felt Britain's historic lust for power and its rule in countries it occupied to be only slightly less virulent than Germany's, and scoffed internally at the English view of themselves as being less racist, more humane than Hitler. Over the last four years more than three million Indians—many Muslims like himself—died of starvation in British India, thousands in the streets of Calcutta, from deprivation far worse than any he had witnessed riding through the villages of France or Germany, many times worse than privations in blitzed and bombed London. After the bombing of Chittagong and Calcutta, Churchill's "Rice Denial policy" and "Boat Denial policy" diverted rice from the people to war-related industries; and in London, when only the tiny expatriate Indian community had protested and shouted "Famine!" it was Churchill, demigod to Kabir's fellow officers, who refused to extend UNRRA's war relief to His Majesty's brown subjects. So Hitler caused the deaths of yet-uncounted millions by his actions, Churchill by inaction.

Was there a difference, Kabir wondered, *excepting opportunity and method?*

A ragtag band of blond-haired waifs gathered around the Jeep, the youngest about five, the oldest fifteen. Holding hands, whispering. He didn't have to know German; they were debating what could be filched or begged.

The will to survive is amoral.

These children and every other survivor had a tale. Stories the newspapers could not know. They'd tell them someday, in pubs and bistros, in beer gardens and boarding houses, to anyone who would listen.

Kabir was as responsible as Churchill for the rain-filled craters in German cities. Somewhat responsible for the lost stares of these children. But now that he was on the ground, on the Continent, a single line from Mr. Gandhi's prison cell resonated louder in Kabir than all the stentorian speeches of Churchill. When asked his opinion of Western civilization, Gandhi said, "It would be a good idea."

Small errors compounded. The German interpretation of Darwin, and the loss of faith all over Europe, that loss of faith of which he too was guilty. Errors hardened into assumptions that clogged the arteries of intelligence, scarred the sensitivity of synapses, till European minds travelled only pre-grooved pathways. Infidel armies were drawn into battle, each fighting for their collective hallucinations and territories.

Kabir's family had the misfortune of being caught between them. Hitler first outlawed Sufism in Germany, whether practised by Muslims or anyone else. Then, when his armies swept through Holland, the Sainah Foundation at The Hague was raided by the Gestapo and Abbajaan's followers were arrested, thrown into camps. Before that happened in France, Kabir and his family escaped, and soon he and Noor found themselves fighting "for England."

The motorbike stood motionless, and Kabir, in a fever to be on his way, paced the alley. Children followed like dogs sniffing at his ankles. Eventually, the sergeant, using wrenches, spanners, swear words and new spark plugs, completed surgery.

Some other time, what my Indian half shares or cannot share with the heritage and experience of this helpful, generous black man must be discussed. But now I can only ask Allah's blessing upon him and hurry on, for Noor's sake.

The bike sputtered and fired back to life. The sergeant exchanged three full jerricans for the empties in Kabir's sidecar, handed Kabir a few K-rations and diverted the children by tossing a K-ration packet across the street. A brown hand engulfed a darker one briefly, warmly, before the Jeep swung away down the alley.

The motorbike thundered away from the village milling with woeful, bargaining refugees, and headed in the direction of Munich.

Kabir placed a trunk call to Zaib from the Messerschmitt factory at Gablingen Kaserne, now a U.S. military base. He'd been in this area in 1942 — one of his first operational raids, and against a military target, the Augsburg MAN plant. In daylight, at very low level. Seven of the twelve Lancasters in his squadron were shot down, his own severely damaged.

It was soon after these early raids that city centres became Sir Arthur's targets. City centres were all one could see and hit at night—was that Kabir's fault? Harris called it terror bombing. Rays from searchlights criss-crossed as his plane screamed over them, and the cities became caskets of jewels as his bombs exploded.

Banish the image.

"Dr. Zaib-un-nisa Khan, please."

Zaib might be the very first doctor in their family. Definitely the first woman to become a doctor. Still unmarried—probably touching unrelated men, wounded soldiers, every day.

Her voice, so much like Noor's, kindled a painful ringing in his inner ear. "I've been on the telephone all day, talking to the Central Tracing Bureau of the Red Cross, the War Office, Miss Atkins. No one seems to know anything. They keep mentioning the Official Secrets Act and all that."

"And Boddington? Did you talk to Boddington?"

"Yes. He says he last met Noor in Paris in July."

"July? This is July. Or did he mean last year, before the liberation of Paris?"

"Non, non, Kabir. Écoutez! July of '43."

Two years ago! Information like starlight—it told you the star was alive light years ago, but was that star still pulsing?

"Did you ask if she sent any letters? Any that may not have been forwarded to us?"

"Of course I did. He said there were none."

"And then?"

"He was vague after that. I got the impression he wasn't at liberty to say."

"Damn it, Zaib, the war is over. Why the secrecy now?"

"Don't swear. Where are you now?"

"Augsburg. On my way to a refugee collection centre at Munich. How's Mother?"

"She doesn't eat much. Dadijaan isn't even arguing with her. The two of them are sitting together in the drawing room."

"Together?"

He couldn't remember Mother and her mother-in-law, Dadijaan, ever sitting together voluntarily, not since Dadijaan first arrived in Paris in 1938. When Mother married Abbajaan in 1913, she received a Muslim name, and it was assumed she would uphold her husband's religion and traditions. So whenever there was a chance of Kodaks and photo bulbs, she dressed up in a sari. Abbajaan would send the resulting family photo "home" to Dadijaan in Baroda. And all through Mother's sole two-year visit to India as Abbajaan's widow, she had worn saris. And so Mother completely and unwittingly misled Dadijaan to believe she wore saris every day, all day, as did Dadijaan. In Paris.

The discovery, on arriving in Paris, that her daughter-in-law, her son's widow, Rukhsana Begum née Aura Baker, habitually bared her legs beneath a dress evoked Dadijaan's deep and abiding suspicion. From that moment, Mother, American though she was, began to personify the East India Company, the British Raj, the marauding West and all its depredations. Mother remained oblivious, continuing to wear dresses every day and saris as fancy dress in Paris, and then not at all in war-tossed London. Dadijaan's distrust had never abated. And it didn't help that Mother often forgot namaaz if she was working or the cinema beckoned.

Zaib gave a small laugh that turned into a sniff. "Yes, together. And it's Sunday, but Dadijaan hasn't gone to Hyde Park."

For two and a half years Dadijaan hadn't missed Speaker's Corner in Hyde Park on Sunday, not to listen to speeches in English, which she understood perfectly well, but to make her own passionate denunciations of Mr. Churchill, in court Urdu mixed with Gujarati. Standing on a box six inches above English soil, she could shout what she knew: that Churchill was denying rice to the hungry, denying boats to fishermen, that his policy was to starve His Majesty's subjects in India into submission for the

English war. That it had no effect was Mother's main objection; she liked actions to have quick and measurable outcomes.

"I told Dadijaan the Khans are a hardy lot. Right, *bhaiya?* I said, see how many missions Kabir flew, and he's still alive."

"Subhan-allah. Did it help?"

"Oh yes, she told Mother all about the Tiger of Mysore again." Kabir allowed himself a small laugh.

Damn brigand Tipu Sultan—not an exemplary ancestor. Tiger or not, he still wound up dead, his children taken hostage by the Brits. Mother needs stories with better endings.

"Mother never understood a word," said Zaib.

"Poor Mother," he said. "You'd think she could comprehend elementary Urdu by now."

"She doesn't have to."

Zaib had never learned Urdu or Hindustani for the same reason—she didn't have to. Like Noor and Kabir, she could read Arabic enough to read the Qur'an, but learning other languages had to be linked either to sticks or carrots; she didn't feel anything was worth learning for itself. If Zaib had known Abbajaan, and hadn't come of age when Uncle Tajuddin ruled at home, and then during a war, she'd be different.

All of us would be different, but for the war.

"Zaib, before I left Paris, I called U.S. Military Command several times and asked if any of Noor's names—Noor Khan, Nora Baker, Anne-Marie Régnier or Madeleine—appear in files from Gestapo headquarters at the avenue Foch. I thought perhaps the Nazis didn't have a chance to destroy them before they fled Paris. Call them again."

"I did. They said the Americans have the files. The ones from the avenue Foch and the rue des Saussaies."

"Where did they take them?"

"Top secret, they said. They're going to find all the Nazis in Germany and try them. Don't want the same chaps in power again. Determined to replace the entire bureaucracy of Germany with new people. Prescription for anarchy, if you ask me."

"I'll call you soon."

"Allah hafiz."

As he replaced the black earpiece on its hook, a wave of anger welled up so high that his hands trembled.

Why is it Noor? Why not Zaib?

Dreadful thought! And about little Zaib, their baby sister. Zaib, who didn't barge through society's norms like Noor but worked at helping people cope with them. Daily, Zaib encountered pain and disease to be healed; she left philosophy, symbols, spirits and significance to Kabir. But she could be relied on to keep up appearances. And she was as determined as he to find Noor.

Noor. Abbajaan's favourite.

Abbajaan was open and warm with Noor in a way he never was with Kabir, teaching her the veena, allowing her to massage his feet when he returned from touring, serve him warm salt water for gargling after a day of speeches. But then, Noor loved Allah and worshipped easily and naturally, whereas Kabir could see beauty in the poetry of the Qur'an, but . . .

Long after Mother had put him and Zaib to bed at night, young Kabir listened for the periodic clink of chess pieces, Abbajaan's childlike laugh, then Noor's low murmur to see if they would embark on another game. By the time he was old enough to play chess, his Abbajaan was gone.

Once, when Kabir was fourteen and Noor sixteen, he dreamed Noor was lying on the grass. And in the dream, he, Kabir, was glad at her dream-death. Glad! The self-knowledge released by that dream still filled him with horror. How could he resent so beloved a sister at one and the same time as he felt himself willing to die in her stead?

Envy? Noor was the only one in the family who could join Abbajaan in the loneliness of his experience of India, the experience Abbajaan never could communicate to Europeans. The only one who could play the veena with him. When Mother, desperate for money, moved the family to Baroda for two years after

Abbajaan's death, Noor absorbed India naturally, as if born there, whereas young Kabir was painfully aware that though he knew his Qur'an better than any of his Indian cousins, he wasn't Indian enough; the cousins all dubbed him a lousy batter and an even worse bowler.

And he didn't need Mr. Freud to tell him what the dream meant: hatred for the part of Noor that was most like himself. Yes, it had taken Kabir years to name it, but he knew it now. It was the shared part that was "too damn Indian." Today he could even name the source of his gladness as a child wandering in that dream: with Abbajaan gone and without Noor, his family would now be European, look European in every way.

It was just a dream; he could also refuse to remember it.

And besides, even if Noor was older, Kabir was the eldest son, the son on whom Abbajaan bestowed his mantle. Abbajaan *chose* him to bridge the gulf between earth and heaven for his followers. Of course, that choice followed the Sufi silsila tradition, but the memory of his initiation ceremony was still comforting.

Kabir searched the K-rations for a vitamin biscuit—a "cookie." He replaced the chocolate bar, chewing gum, cigarettes and lima beans in the sidecar. Perhaps he could barter them for information in Munich.

Large drops wet his jacket like spit from the sky.

He mounted the Triumph and took to the road again.

On his way to the U.S. Office of De-nazification in Munich, Kabir rode right through the ground floor of a shattered building, unable to see any difference between the scarred outside and the building interior. Stalagmite shapes loomed over roads reclaimed by grass and the buzzing of insects. The reverberation of a single scream might bring every brick and stone to knee level.

The cathedral was completely gutted. A place referred to as the Brown House was damaged badly but not destroyed, and the priceless collections in the Pinakothek had received a direct hit on

a date matching an entry in Kabir's flight log. Everywhere, clearing crews of Nazi prisoners and large-boned women in scarves
were loading rubble from gargantuan fallen monuments at a
steady pace, but anyone could see it would take years to restore
what bombs had destroyed in an instant.

A peddler jiggled the tray suspended from his neck, calling,
"Eggs, eggs!" as Kabir approached the Rathaus, the richly orna-
mented town hall in the Marienplatz. The mechanical clock
began its glockenspiel performance as he climbed the stone stairs
inside. Soon he was shifting his weight on a hard wooden chair
sized for a child, in a modest room with the scrawled label *U.S.
Office of De-nazification.* There, a very young-looking captain
from Chicago to whom he'd been referred by Zaib listened to his
story without comment, then laughed with a cynical timbre that
placed him closer to Kabir's own age.

"Find her in three weeks? Christ! Lieutenant, you sure set
yourself one helluva task."

But if Kabir didn't leave Munich tonight, he couldn't report
for duty in Paris on schedule. Upper echelons would believe he'd
delayed or even deserted, fearing confrontation with the Japanese.
It would match their prejudices against Indian men and confirm
their worst opinions of refugees from France.

So he must, he had to, return on time to Paris.

"Know how hard it is to find a single person?"

"I know," said Kabir.

The captain's eyes were bloodshot from sleeplessness or drinking or both. Kabir knew his own eyes had the same crazed look
from days of filling in international tracing requests, quizzing
forced labourers, former POWs and other refugees at the
Deutsches Museum, sending telegrams and telephoning Zaib
from the American base.

"You'll need months of leave, buddy. Maybe years. Tell me,
how many camps can you go to? How many prisons? How many
mass graves can you search?" The captain rose and turned to the
map of Europe on the wall behind his desk. "You saw the buildings

of Natzweiler, right? Wasn't that discovered by the French? The Russians came upon this place—here." A forefinger alighted on a single, tiny red push-pin. "It's called Auschwitz. You wouldn't buh-*lieve* me if I told you what they found. And you Brits liberated Buchenwald and Belsen in April. Then we stumbled over the horrors of Ohrdruf."

Jab, jab, jab.

Kabir had seen photographs in the newspapers: piles upon piles of skin-and-bone dead. But he could not, would not, believe Noor was among those people.

"Then Dachau. And Dachau wasn't just a camp for Jews; it was for anyone the Nazis disliked—Poles, Russians, Gypsies, Catholic priests, homosexuals, and dissidents of any kind. It goes on and on . . . For three months we've been uncovering primary concentration camps, sub-camps and work camps, and prying folks out of civilian prisons."

Kabir leaned closer. The entire map of western Europe behind the captain's desk was prickled with a constellation of tiny red and blue push-pins. He sat back, stunned.

"We're just trying to clean out the Nazis in Munich, but there's too many of them and we're awful undermanned."

"I was told your office has the files captured at Gestapo headquarters in Paris."

"I haven't received any. Pleased to know I can expect some, though." He paused, then continued in a kinder voice. "Look, pal—flight lieutenant, I mean. If your sister was an agent for the British, the Nazis would have labelled her 'Nacht und Nebel.' That's a 'Night and Fog' prisoner. She could be anywhere in Germany. God forbid the Russians have moved her to one of their camps. There were many—no, I'd say mostly—French and Italian Jews among the prisoners liberated from Auschwitz, and many of those are still DPs and haven't arrived home yet, coz guys like you did such a great job bombing bridges, railroad tracks and stations across Europe. Or they can't find rail cars or . . . I dunno, there's always some darn Limey, Frog or Russkie excuse."

Kabir's arms and shoulders felt like rock, ready to attack this destroyer of hope. The captain tore the wrapper off a pack of Lucky Strikes and propped a cigarette in Kabir's direction, as if to soften the impact of his words. Kabir raised a hand, refusing on principle.

"Some DPs aren't well enough to travel, two months after liberation. If she's still alive, Lieutenant Khan, she might be in a prison, in a camp or under medical care. You don't know, do you? You can't know."

It wasn't "if" Noor was alive—she must be, she must be. But if she was, surely she would contact him, send word to him in care of the RAF? A Red Cross message, a phone call? The captain's words rang true. Kabir rested his elbows on the desk and clasped his hands at moustache level, desperate to unite thoughts and body.

The captain continued in a kinder tone. "The Nazis weren't ordered to keep records of Night and Fog prisoners, but that don't mean squat. Amazing how much the bastards wrote down 'bout what they did and to whom. Always afraid some bigger bastard might raise questions, accuse them. Here—" He pushed an index card across the table at Kabir. "Fill it in. I promise you, if we find anyone matching her description, or anyone who can tell us about her, I'll contact you personally. Immediately. Best I can do."

The captain was asking Kabir to acknowledge and accept powerlessness in the face of chaos. Passivity. Fate.

Hope crumpled beneath the weight of reality, then turned unaccountably to anger.

Noor, you brought this on yourself; you are responsible.

Noor wasn't his only obligation. He had three women to support on his pay: Dadijaan, who sent all the house money she could get her hands on to Muslim charities for the millions starving in India; Zaib, for whom he should arrange a marriage with some Muslim who could be persuaded to overlook her tending unrelated men—and soon, or she'd follow Noor's example and ally herself with some totally unsuitable man and commit the same mistakes;

and Mother, who, since the letter from the War Office saying
Noor was missing, had lost her legendary organizational efficiency,
energy and optimism.

If only he could be all places he was needed at once.

Kabir managed to fill in the card, shake the captain's hand,
salute and mumble thanks that sounded grateful. Outside the captain's office, he threaded his way between desks. Shoulders
cradling telephone receivers each bore the flaming crusader
sword insignia of the Allied Expeditionary Forces. Outside, their
businesslike, optimistic drawls yielded to the calls of street ped-
dlers vying for attention from passing hausfraus. A Rosenthal
lamp, a dinner jacket, a music box—scavenged and looted goods
to be bartered and sold. Even fresh eggs, here and there. Shirts,
shoes, a pair of patched trousers. One hawker balanced a lone
tomato on his palm, loudly boasting its matchless beauty.

*Survival of the fittest often means survival of the loudest, the
most bumptious.*

Neither term described Noor.

What more could he do but report for duty on schedule? He'd
call Zaib, Mother and Dadijaan on his way back to Paris. He
would say: Noor must be alive, insh'allah she'll return home to
Paris, she'll telephone, she'll write. He wouldn't wonder if Noor
might write to someone else if she was alive—to her friend
Josianne Prénat, or that Jew Armand Rivkin.

He would try not to remember the meeting with the Jew, five
years ago, that meeting he hadn't mentioned to Zaib. Climbing to
Rivkin's apartment on a cold spring day, a weight in his pocket. Just
before the May invasion, before the battle of northern France,
before the fall of Paris. Holding that envelope out, saying, "Leave
my sister alone." Try not to remember the packet of money that
never changed hands. He couldn't imagine where Rivkin was now.

Zaib wouldn't give up, of that he was sure. She'd continue
writing letters and telegrams of inquiry.

Of course, if Kabir was sent to the Far East, he'd go. But if,
insh'allah, he was demobilized, there was Afzal Manzil to be

reclaimed in Paris. He would restore it, bring his family home from London. After that, he would decide whether to reopen the school. Could he muster enough faith to preach Abbajaan's beliefs? Perhaps. That is, if any in Europe would pay to learn again about tolerance and love.

No recourse at present but to endure, wait, watch, hope, pray, write letters—women's pastimes. But there was also work to be done.

Kabir skirted the edge of the crowded Marienplatz, made his way through a tent city sprouting behind the Rathaus, and returned to the Triumph and its passengerless sidecar.

PART TWO

CHAPTER 3

Surrey, England
May 1943

INTERMITTENT SPRING RAIN had eroded the topsoil from Glory
Hill, exposing tree roots like ribs rising under famished skin. May
sunshine speared tangled foliage, revealing more than a dozen
young women in the khaki uniform and shoulder patches of the First
Aid Nursing Yeomanry. Pale faces drenched in sweat, they waited in
the underbrush. At the signal, an all but unnoticeable flutter of a
white handkerchief, the women broke into a trot, then into a run for
the slope, using the roots as stairs, climbing in purposeful silence.

Noor grabbed at the roots with gloved hands, lungs expanding, buttocks tensing alternately in coordinated rhythm.

Quiet, quiet!

She pulled herself up, glancing sideways to check she was
level with the others. A few yards off, another crouching figure in
FANY khaki turned for an instant. A tweezed sandy-brown eyebrow
arched in Noor's direction. A few more strides uphill, her strength
renewed by Yolande's unspoken challenge.

Noor threw Yolande a quick smile.

Now the crest was in sight.

Look for black uniforms. Wait.

Breath sounding too loud.

Hold that breath. Listen!

That was the owl hoot? Some atrocious imitation.

She rose and scaled the last few yards.

Over the summit, she dropped to a squat and held out her hand to Yolande.

"Ouch, my bum!" said Yolande in a stage whisper. "Three times up and down that hill today!"

Noor's regulation black shoes half slid down the slope. With the hill behind her, Noor pulled a miniature pair of binoculars from her pocket and peered at each clump of foliage at the edge of the woods. Not a leaf stirred, so she signalled an all-clear to the next pair of FANYs and emerged from cover with Yolande. The taller girl slipped her arm through Noor's as they stood in the clearing. Yolande, her competitive yardstick, was breathing deeply too.

"I thought they might be doing that 'sorting out' today, but that was easy," said Yolande. "We pass! Together to the end!"

Noor laughed. The others were emerging from the woods.

"You might have thought they'd ambush us here, now," said Yolande, wiping her face with a mud-stained handkerchief.

"They did that yesterday," said Noor, pulling her hat off. Warm hair tumbled about her shoulders. "It has to be unexpected," she said, tying a ponytail.

She could match Yolande in endurance, score as high on the shooting range and transmit Morse faster, but she could never match Yolande's unstated assumptions of not only surviving but thriving. Unlike Yolande, Noor hadn't learned German at a Swiss finishing school. But her French was excellent.

Someone she was three years ago had felt the collective terror of the French, joined refugees fleeing Paris, moving south in a frenzied stream of bicycles, carriages, automobiles and pedestrians as the jackboot of the Germans descended. In June of '40, the head of their family, Uncle Tajuddin, steamed his way back to Baroda, and Kabir drove their old Amilcar voiturette south out of Paris. Noor and her family joined the refugee stream, with the stuffed bedroll Dadijaan brought from Baroda lashed to the roof. Dadijaan sat with Zaib almost on her lap, moving her prayer beads and muttering the *Tasbeeh*. Mother, wedged in the back seat, cheeks whiter than usual above her chinchilla collar but sharp-sighted as ever, tapped Kabir's shoulder to point out the muddy cowpath wide enough to take a car. The Amilcar bumped off the road just seconds before Stuka-rained bullets raised screams from hapless refugees on the road behind them. It was *fitna*, all *fitna*—chaos! Noor's throat tightened every time she remembered how they didn't—couldn't—stop for even a moment to tend the wounded, because the Stukas were circling back a second, then a third time.

That Hitler was shaitan in human form—prime cause of the world's troubles. Genghis Khan come again.

Reaching Bordeaux, the car bucked and bounced over tram rails as Kabir drove from the British consul's office to hotels and the docks, looking for any official who would evacuate British citizens. His British passport and Noor and Zaib's pathetic pleading got them a choppy ride on a rain-sodden fishing boat bound for safety in England. Abbajaan's Amilcar was abandoned at the docks.

Almost three years later, Mother, Dadijaan and Zaib were living on the unbombed side of Taviton Street, Kabir was posted at an airfield in Sussex, and here she was, standing beside Yolande. No longer Noor, eldest daughter of musician and Sufi teacher Inayat Khan, but an officer in His Majesty's Directorate of Air Intelligence, calling herself Leading Aircraftwoman Nora, taking her mother's maiden name, Baker, and stating her religion as Church of England instead of Islam.

Nora Baker, trained in the fine art of wireless operations and the craft of time-delay incendiaries.

Nora Baker, who shared with Yolande a dread of wasting time. At night in the dormitory, trading news and rumours about the war, both agreed life could end today, tomorrow—by random blast or fire from a German bomb. Something positive must be accomplished before that.

Through the Blitz, Noor was ashamed to feel she was safer than Armand, beloved Armand, lost somewhere in the recesses of conquered Europe. She couldn't be like Zaib, for whom London was one long party interspersed with air raids, lectures and lab work. Noor's pleasures were stunted by guilt.

If there hadn't been a war, she might have said she was Muslim just so the English might understand that Indian Muslim women were not as they imagined: weak, meek, stupid or spineless. But she adjusted like everyone else. An English accent wasn't required for wireless telegraphy at Edinburgh and Abingdon, but she acquired one to be understood, adding it to her French, Indian-English and American-English accents.

Amazing how much adjustment people could make, how cheerful people were. *Because* there was a war?

She was cheerful around the time she enlisted as Aircraft-woman 424598, back in 1940, when Armand's first letter said he and his mother were in Cannes. Cannes on the Riviera, at the time unoccupied by the Germans. He was free, he was safe. Noor's high spirits lasted almost a month. And she was cheerful for another week, almost a year later, when there was a letter from nearby Nice. But by the time Major Boddington's letter arrived, worry and fear for Armand were a ten-pound pole she carried across her shoulders, and no sooner did she read "an assignment that involves travel overseas" than she made up her mind. But there hadn't been any travel overseas. Not a single assignment, yet.

All through her toughening-up and training, she had been suspended in a semi-life, preparing, anticipating and waiting, waiting, waiting for her chance—insh'allah—to return to France. Twenty-nine years old and feeling her life had yet to begin.

More FANYs were emerging from the woods, their talk and laughter carrying across the clearing.

Be cheerful.

"Time for tea—race you!" she cried to Yolande, and ran across the clearing towards the triple roofs of Wanborough Manor.

Noor held the heavy oak door for Yolande and walked down the wainscotted corridor of the eighteenth-century manor by her side. The Special Operations Executive had requisitioned so many country homes like this one all over England that some wag said the letters SOE of the top secret agency, charged with Setting Europe Ablaze and all that, really stood for Stately 'Omes of England. Setting Europe Ablaze, Churchill's term for fomenting unrest, sabotage and uncertainty for the Germans in France, training and arming the French resistance for the day he'd give the command and they'd rise up against the Germans, had by now become more than a slogan for Noor. Here she learned to throw hand grenades, instantly identify German military uniforms, fire pistols, Sten guns and explosives, and evade anyone following.

"Miss Atkins?" said Noor to the compact figure standing in the gloom.

"Nora," came a flinty voice. "Colonel Buckmaster would like a word with you."

"I'll run along for tea, then," said Yolande, giving Noor a smile of encouragement.

Miss Atkins opened a door. At the far end of a large drawing room, two men in khaki standing at a desk looked up as Noor was ushered in. Both held plotter rakes as if they were billiard sticks. They'd been poring over a Michelin map dotted with markers.

She was introduced: ever-affable Colonel Buckmaster, head of the SOE's French Section, who always asked if she was quite sure her French was still fluent, and her case officer, Major Nicholas Boddington, code named "N."

Major Boddington, a flat-faced man with spectacles, had introduced her to the workings of the SOE seven long months ago in a little flat off Baker Street. After her interview he became for a time no more than an address to where she sent expense receipts for reimbursement. But over the last three weeks he'd "just popped in" five times. Twice she'd noticed him watching her at target practice, once Miss Atkins mentioned his requesting Noor's latest progress report, and a few days ago he had joined Yolande and her in the dining room for tea and inquired courteously about Mother and Kabir. He contrived to mention attending Oxford, said he'd been a journalist before the war. He could be charming but seemed a little preoccupied today.

A little red flag began to flutter in Noor's stomach. Was this the "sorting out" of which agents were warned? Was there something in that all-important English concept, her "background," that had been found unsuitable? It could be political; agitations for Indian independence hadn't abated. Perhaps the Brits had decided to reassign her—just before she set off to Manchester for her final week of parachute training.

Miss Atkins opened a file marked *Top Secret* and *Nora Baker*. Yolande thought Miss Atkins was about thirty-five, but the corners of her almost lipless mouth pulled downwards when she was tired, giving her an older look. Today she looked no more or less serious than usual. Still . . .

"Ah, Miss Baker. Do sit down."

Noor perched at the edge of a folding chair. When Colonel Buckmaster disappeared into an armchair with lace antimacassars, she could see Glory Hill framed in the window behind him better than she could discern any expression on his face. The Major leaned against the desk, polishing his glasses.

Miss Atkins gave the file to Colonel Buckmaster and said something inaudible.

"Up to twenty-four words a minute?"

"Yes, sir," said Noor.

"Excellent. In English, naturally."

"Yes, sir." Noor stared straight ahead past his shoulder.

"French accents would be difficult in Morse, I'm sure—a waste of time transmitting those silent verb endings."

Some answer was expected. "Yes, sir," Noor replied.

"Little trouble with a bobby, lately?" said Major Boddington.

A bobby in Bristol, where Noor was participating in a mock undercover exercise. How had the Major learned of the incident? Better not ask: such questions wouldn't be welcomed by a senior officer of the SOE.

Reassure him.

"Not exactly, sir. I rode my bicycle through a red light and he stopped me. I told him I wouldn't have if I'd known he was there—"

"You received a ticket for impertinence," Major Boddington interrupted.

"Yes, sir. Ten shillings."

"My word," said Colonel Buckmaster.

My word, indeed. Ten shillings was a sizable slice of £350 per annum, one she could ill afford.

"Well, you seem to have learned your lesson." Major Boddington seemed mollified by the punitive figure.

"Born in Moscow?" The Colonel was reading from her file.

"Yes, sir."

"Not Bolshevik, are you?"

"No, sir—we left after I was born. Before the Great War."

Noor didn't remember Moscow at all. Abbajaan was on tour, playing the veena and giving discourses on Sufism in Moscow, when she entered the world, and she was still a baby when the family returned to England.

"Wise move, wise move. Your father is—pardon me, was—a professor. Unpronounceable name."

The name Inayat Khan didn't seem especially difficult.

"Yes, sir."

Abbajaan—his constant absence was a different kind of sorrow.

"Of music and the philosophy of . . . Sufism?"

"Yes, sir."

"Mmm."

The Colonel didn't seem sure what Sufism was, but perhaps because Abbajaan's occupation didn't sound threatening, he moved on.

"Your mother is from Boston. An American. I see—hence the name Baker. Quite a popular lot, these days, Americans. Family moved around a bit, I'd say. England, France, India. But you"—he was consulting and calculating from the file before him—"seem to have spent most of your life in France."

"Yes, sir," said Noor.

Since her own displacement to England she understood how Abbajaan must have felt all through his sixteen years as an immigrant to France: duty-bound to someday return "home." For him, home was India. For Noor, home was now wherever Armand might be.

"A spinster?"

"I have a fiancé, sir." Far from the truth, but better than being called a spinster.

"Hmm. I did a stint in India a few years ago, trying to turn some natives into soldiers. Girl your age'd be married off years ago—willy-nilly, without so much as a by-your-leave. Count yourself jolly lucky you're not there now."

"And you too, sir." Noor kept her tone neutral.

Colonel Buckmaster glared at her, then recovered. "Quite a little Allied cocktail, aren't you? Yes. Let me see, just how long did you live in India?"

"Two years, sir."

A single week in India might rearrange anyone's understanding of the world, but two years living with Dadijaan and her Indian aunts and cousins had made India and Indians a constant point of reference and concern ever since.

"Only two years. Well. Under Causes for Concern, your escorting officer says here you were 'absolutely terrified' when they did the routine little stunt with you."

A residue of terror stirred in Noor. The "little stunt" was a mock Gestapo interrogation, complete with bright beams of light and an interrogator who abused, threatened and shouted just as Uncle Tajuddin once did.

If you were forced to flee your home in Paris because twenty-eight German bombs had fallen in your town just ten minutes after the sirens sounded, and the men in your family all carried British passports, you'd be frightened of those uniforms too.

"I was afraid, sir. But I'm much stronger for it."

Perhaps she shouldn't have acknowledged being afraid; Colonel Buckmaster had vanished behind her file again. But it was true—mastering the onslaught of memories stirred by the mock interrogation had given her confidence.

If, after these two and a half years of preparation and all my running up and down Glory Hill, you sort me into the wrong group, Colonel Buckmaster, if you reject me because I'm Indian and not good enough for the SOE or pack me off to the periphery where I'll never see Armand till the war is over, I'll find another way to leave your charming little island. I'll join the Maquis in France.

"You're not one of those colonials who're hoping the Germans win, are you? That chap Bose gave us the slip in Calcutta, went off and shook hands with Hitler—and next thing we hear he's gathering an army. Calls it the Indian National Army, if you please. Of course, a few chaps in the IRA have made overtures to Hitler too."

"Colonel," Major Boddington intervened, "she was referred by her brother. He's with Bomber Command."

"Oh. Well, then, she's the right kind." Colonel Buckmaster closed Noor's file, leaned his head back against the antimacassars. "Officer Baker, we have a special assignment for you, purely voluntary, you understand. We have an urgent request to send a wireless operator to France. Dropping you is out of the question as you have not yet completed your parachute training course, so . . ." He sounded as if Noor had been uncommonly slow and should have completed her jump training by now.

A glow spread within Noor, but with an effort she kept her face blank as a toy soldier's. She had worked for this, prayed for this for three years. France was in sight.

"If you are quite sure, then, not reluctant at all? You're willing to be landed there? And you fully understand we would much rather have dropped you by parachute to avoid Hun attention?"

To be landed rather than dropped by parachute! Before the war Noor had flown in Kabir's plane a few times in France, but she was not keen on jumping five hundred feet off anything, especially any moving thing. Now she didn't have to keep her many resolutions to face and overcome those fears.

"If you are sure, we can pop you in there to join our agents a few weeks earlier. But you must be sure—if your heart isn't in it, you'll do a bad job of it." Colonel Buckmaster was looking at her, then at her file, then back again as if expecting her to decline.

"Sir, I am ready to go when ordered."

Find out what they expect; perform better than they expect.

The Colonel closed Noor's file, passed it over his shoulder to Miss Atkins. "Miss Atkins will help you prepare. Cover story, that sort of thing. We are confident you will conduct yourself well. We will rely on you as we rely on the good conduct of all our colonials."

A glance at the documents from the Battersea Reception Centre in her file would have told the Colonel she was classified as a British Protected Person, not an Indian colonial; a refugee, like everyone else who had fled the Germans. Abbajaan was from the Princely State of Baroda, whose rulers had never been conquered in war by either the East India Company or the Raj. Baroda was a British ally, subjugated yet independent, and Noor could describe herself similarly. But Colonel Buckmaster wanted a pliable, eager woman, bilingual in French and English, with harnessable energy; he wasn't interested in the rest of her life, talents or languages.

The Colonel said, "Major Boddington will provide you with funds sufficient for your personal expenses and for members of your network."

The Major was gazing at Glory Hill, one hand tapping against his thigh as if he had more important things on his mind.

"Nick?"

"I'll keep an eye on her, sir," said Major Boddington. He turned and gave Noor a looking over. "I'll be out to see you as necessary. And may I say, my dear, you seem quite the perfect candidate for this important mission."

CHAPTER 4

Pforzheim, Germany
December 1943

ABBAJAAN USED TO SAY *every debt must be paid before one can set out on the path of realization, that obligations to every person must first be met.* I felt his words in the bone the years in England, and reproached myself every waking moment for being unequal to the obligations of love. And so my zikr, when I was supposed to be in remembrance of Allah, was a remembrance of Armand.

How should I describe my beloved—your father? He is more than the sum of his actions, his likes and dislikes; attributes give little of his essence. Taller than most Frenchmen, he has long arms and legs, supple fingers. His eyes—a soul-piercing blue. Hair lighter than mine, wavy brown. But describing his face tells nothing of his spark, his irrepressible humour or generous spirit. He delights in reading and chess, and is impelled to translate beauty and pain alike to boundless music. He always sees a larger world than the one we live in, and when I am with him, we are almost there.

Music chose Armand early, and he is gifted before the piano, whereas I am most comfortable behind the veena. Your father is that graduate of the Conservatoire de Paris whose every composition has an underlying swagger, whereas I passed my music examinations at the École Normale each year because not passing would have *disappointed my family. Like Stravinsky, like Abbajaan, Armand's prelingual rhythms are Eastern. Notes in groups of five, seven, ten-eight time. And he's a performer who brings life to each note. Once, he played a Brahms concerto and I felt he had reached through my ribs and taken my heart in his hands.*

Alone here in my cell I wonder why he never said I wasn't worth the waiting, the furtive meetings, the many lies. Many girls in Paris were less difficult to bed or marry than your mother, girls who might have converted to Judaism had he asked it, who would be better wives and mothers than I. Yet Armand—who could say when embarking on a new composition, "An artist can't wait for someone to give him permission, he must just take it"—spent years waiting with me for Uncle or Kabir to give his permission for us to marry. Love is inexplicable, but he did say once that, when he was with me, he felt close to something sacred.

The last time I saw your father, ma petite, was on May 2nd, 1940, two days before his thirtieth birthday. It was the last day of his leave, before he returned to the front.

Everyone knew German boots were marching towards us. Once Hitler had taken Austria, invaded Czechoslovakia and betrayed France by signing a pact with that other shaitan, Stalin, Armand's mobilization number was posted. By May 1940 he'd been with the 3rd Light Mechanized Division nine months, and was home on his second ten-day leave.

On that May day before he returned to war, we met in the Bois de Boulogne under the locust trees. He had made arrangements, he said, to evacuate his mother, your grandmother Lydia, if the Germans came too close to Paris. Madame Lydia was born Catholic in Russia but converted to Judaism when she married your grand-father. People who were Jewish had more reason to fear the German invasion than anyone else—and they still do.

"Just a precaution, Noor. The Germans aren't very well equipped, I'm told. They won't get all the way to Paris."

My uncle Tajuddin and Kabir were debating evacuation for our family each day, as both held British passports. I told Armand

I would remain in Paris waiting for him at Afzal Manzil even if my family left.

He would not hear of it. A shadow played over his face. "I never thought I'd say this, but I agree with your brother," he said. "We cannot be together without marrying — your reputation must be considered. And Noor, this is no time to marry a Jew. There can no longer be any promises between us. You are — you must be — free. Free to marry someone else."

He felt that what he was would harm me, that I would be safer without him. But he couldn't foresee the consequences of our separation. There were bombs in London too.

No one is safe from powerful men anywhere.

I said, "I will remain with you, I must be with you now," but he insisted.

"Je t'aime, je t'adore." He said those words as a reminder of all the love he had for me. He did say them. He held my hands to his heart, raised my lips to his, and we parted.

Oh Armand, forgive me for saying adieu. How bitterly I rue the word!

The next time Madame Lydia heard from Armand was on June 2, 1940 — a telegram from Dunkirk urging her, urging all of us, to evacuate. The Germans had overrun most of northern France. It was a miracle Armand was alive to send that telegram and that it arrived at all; in two weeks France had lost ninety-two thousand men. All I cared was that it said Armand was awaiting evacuation along with his regiment from the dunes of Dunkirk to England.

The Germans began bombarding Suresnes and the periphery of Paris the next day. In the morning there was no answer from Madame Lydia's telephone. By noon Kabir had packed our Amilcar for Bordeaux, and Uncle had gone in a car full of other Indians heading to Marseilles.

I thought Armand and I might, insh'allah, meet again in England, but when we got to London, I learned his unit had regrouped and returned to France.

And as soon as Maréchal Pétain formed his Vichy government to sign the armistice with Germany, the news turned worse: anti-Semitic edicts, confiscation of Jewish property. I didn't know if Armand was a German POW, or was in hiding, until a postcard from Cannes. For months preprinted postcards were the only communication the Vichy government would allow.

When I was training at Wanborough and saw bombers flying towards the Channel, I worried my Armand was in their path. Three long years without even our secret meetings, and only two postcards to Miss Noor Khan care of the Sufi Music Centre, London, and I had learned of myself that Armand was as water to the root of a plant, as necessary as sun for growth. There have been loves like ours over the centuries: Nizami sang of Laila and Majnu, the bards of Abelard and Héloïse. But our love was ours and, to me, unique.

Mother counselled never to love someone of another religion, someone different. She said nothing but confusion and pain come of mixing blood and religions, that she had often regretted taking the steamer out of Boston Harbor to follow Abbajaan.

But I did what my mother did before me, then deserted my love when he most needed me.

Abbajaan said we are being judged, all the time, by our Divine Selves. My Divine Self had judged me and already found me inadequate.

CHAPTER 5

London, England
Monday, June 14, 1943

UMBRELLA AND FANY CAP tucked beneath her arm, breathless from running up Clarges Street, Noor surveyed expanses of cream-clothed tables at Pinetto's. Too late to hope Miss Atkins wouldn't notice her being "on Indian time."

Miss Atkins was at a table in the far corner, sitting tall as if at her Baker Street desk. A cardboard-looking piece of whatever was passing for food today lay untouched on the plate before her. An overflowing ashtray and a mimeographed copy of *Tidbits*, the internal dispatch of the SOE, sat beside the silver cutlery.

Noor slipped into the vacant seat, smoothing her skirt over her knees. In England, being late was construed as disrespectful, much more than in France.

"Sorry, marm." She launched into explanation: the tube had come to a halt at an air-raid warning.

"You're here now."

Miss Atkins let a man limping on his cane pass out of earshot. A waiter hovered. Miss Atkins ordered for Noor.

"Well, Nora, still sure you're up to it?"

"Indeed, marm."

"I should tell you we have received some rather alarming reports."

"Alarming, marm?"

"In fact, two reports from your accompanying officers. Seems they don't believe you're quite the right material."

A flush warmed Noor's face. Being "the right material" could mean anything from the schools she'd attended to the shoes she wore. Miss Atkins seemed to be searching for flaws.

"May I ask why, marm?"

"Nothing specific, just that they feel you don't react quite as expected."

Days she'd spent on the range flashed to mind, hours before the looking glass—turn, draw, shoot. "I have very swift reactions."

But Miss Atkins didn't mean physical reactions. Couldn't any woman, Indian or French, experience the need to act, act against tyranny and injustice against all people, not just Europeans, not only Gentiles? Was she to sing "Rule Britannia" and wave the Union Jack? Rave that she had experienced a call of duty to the SOE or England? Even without a siren call, it didn't mean she wasn't the right material.

"Perhaps the problem is their expectations," she said.

A quizzical look came over Miss Atkins's face. She leaned forward. "Perhaps. They do say you were most keen to take a French assignment, which makes them wonder—why? Why not Holland or Belgium, where no one would recognize you?"

"I speak no Dutch or Flemish. I've always wanted to learn Dutch, but somehow—"

"There is also the little matter of your War Office interview."

Noor kept her face neutral.

Seven months ago, after the first interview at Baker Street, came a second before a board of bulbous-nosed, bewhiskered gentlemen—a retired Indian inspector general, a district collector and two deputy commissioners. What did she think about Indian independence? asked one. A vague question to which she answered that it was unconscionable that Mr. Gandhi, Mr. Nehru and thousands of others were wasting away in gaol, held without trial for months now. The eldest gentleman asked if she believed Indians should be armed. Yes, said Noor, for their own defence against the Germans and Japanese. If allowed arms, she said, India wouldn't have to pay the British government tons of rice and millions in sterling for its protection. India had numerous brave men and women who could defend its borders.

"They didn't like what I said."

"You must have sounded like a red-hot radical," said Miss Atkins. "As if you agree with those who say East Indians could govern themselves."

In fact, Noor's reprieve from the depths of their disapproval had come with the next question. Asked what she thought of Messali Hadj, the radical Muslim agitating for Algerian independence from France, she expressed admiration for any man who would spurn an offer of release from Vichy and remain in a French gaol—an attitude more in keeping with those of men who despised Pétain's Vichy government. She was warmly congratulated and passed.

A question mark seemed to hover over Miss Atkins's head.

"Everyone is capable of self-governance," said Noor. "Even Indians."

"Indians? Oh, don't be silly, Nora. They're not yet ready for freedom or democracy—haven't a clue. Really, do try being a little more politic. It surprises me the board approved you. But I've long resigned myself to working with flawed material." Her tone was turning ever more mocking. "Anyway, all your little outburst did was confirm Mr. Churchill's convictions: the naked fakir and that Nehru chap should remain in jail. Now, if you're going to take this assignment and survive, you must learn to lie, dear, lie convincingly about many things."

Noor could lie as convincingly as any other agent—why ever not? By the time she left France, she was skilled in the administration of a multitude of selves, not only her nafs, the base self that must be overcome. She could lie to her self as well as anyone else; had she not hidden her self from herself these many years? Thinking up excuses to circumvent Uncle Tajuddin's restrictions, hiding, meeting Armand in secret because she didn't want to disappoint or hurt her family. Once she imagined herself as she "should be," the right responses flowed.

"About your true identity, for instance," Miss Atkins added.

She was already lying about her true identity by calling herself Nora Baker instead of Noor Khan. She wasn't the only Indian ever to take a Western name. Still, it *was* a cowardly accommodation to England—and a lie.

As for cover stories, she'd be a veritable Scheherazade. How many consoling fairy tales she had created for Kabir and Zaib to explain Abbajaan's absence. Buddhist tales she translated had even been published as a book. She retold Sufi teaching tales, wrote her own short stories, managed the children's hour on Radio Paris. She could unfetter her imagination at will.

Miss Atkins continued, "Diplomacy, war and interviews require a modicum of, shall we say, prevarication." She paused to light a Players. "But I think you Indians have a native capacity for prevarication, so we shan't have to worry about that."

Noor felt herself flush. Fortunately, she was spared having to respond to these remarks by the arrival of a plate bordered in indigo blue. She had what Yolande termed "the curse," so she would eat, though it was Ramzaan. Besides, training exercises gave her a hearty appetite. Dadijaan, whose network of expatriate Indians extended into every nook of London, said, when serving small, tasteless rations after sundown, that so many in India were starving to support this war, everyone in England should be grateful for any food at all. But if the shrivelled island coated with cream sauce on the plate before her was pork, it would, taken with Miss Atkins's remarks, surely turn her stomach. Well, at least it wasn't soup.

She tasted it—fish of some kind.

It wasn't—it really wasn't—that she didn't like pork because it was taboo. Abbajaan hadn't exactly forbidden it; he advised his followers to elevate themselves by refraining from eating the base animal. She had scientific reasons, like avoiding trichinosis—not that there was much danger of trichinosis in London.

Miss Atkins continued, "We will overlook such insubordination. Your services are required."

The imperious "we" was not lost on Noor.

"And you've scored well in wireless operations." Miss Atkins flashed a rare smile. "I don't believe the board's opinion counts much in such matters. I'm confident your mother's blood will prevail. But it should be mentioned—some have their doubts."

Miss Atkins's caste system was blood-based enough to have been designed by Brahmins. A late-night story Yolande once told in a Nissen hut said Miss Atkins's father wasn't English either, he was Romanian; that, like Noor, Miss Atkins had taken her mother's English name. But Noor wasn't as determined as Miss Atkins to disavow the blood-echoes of Abbajaan's origins.

Change the subject.

"Do tell me more about the assignment, marm."

Miss Atkins inhaled, then puffed smoke from the side of her mouth. Her gaze locked on Noor's. "For some time now—since February, actually—an SOE agent we call "Prosper" has been operating throughout northern France, posing as a seller of agricultural implements. The usual sort of thing—arranging for arms deliveries to the Resistance, selecting locomotives to be sabotaged, trains to be derailed, aircraft or petrol tanks to be blown up. With excellent results, I might add: every time the Germans turn around, one of Prosper's cells has blown up a bridge or disabled an engine turntable or signal box."

Miss Atkins stubbed her cigarette out, but the ashes still smouldered. "He's built up a highly skilled network by drawing Frenchmen from many trades and professions. We trust they'll rise up and fight as soon as Mr. Churchill gives the word." She sounded a bit dubious about trusting the French. "You will be working with a select few. An engineer, code name "Phono"; "Archambault," a wireless operator assigned to Prosper's network; "Gilbert," who selects and secures the fields where agents and arms are dropped; a French businessman, a professor and a don—director, as the French say. You will be introduced—secure introductions are absolutely indispensable—as Anne-Marie Régnier, a nursemaid from Bordeaux."

Miss Atkins lit up again. Eye-stinging clouds accumulated about Noor's head.

"I will provide you with the necessary *carte d'identité*, ration coupons, a textile card and a certificate of Aryan descent. Your personal effects, wireless and code book will be sent once we receive word that you have made contact with Phono. As soon as Archambault has you adequately trained, you will replace him and he will return for training on the Mark II. Conditions have forced Archambault to transmit too often, and at times for too long. We fear it is only a matter of time before the Gestapo locates his transmitters. They're OSS-issue SSTR-1s. You will replace his transmitters with Mark IIs, and learn quickly."

"When do I leave, marm?"

"At the next full moon—that's tomorrow if the night is clear. Come to Orchard Court in Portman Square after tea, alone. Memorize this address. Tell no one where you are going. We will reach you if your flight is cancelled"—she consulted a card from her pocket—"on Taviton Street?"

"Yes, I'll be with my mother."

"'No one' includes family. They are not to know where you are being sent or when you leave. Your pay will be accumulated for your return or paid in the usual weekly dollops. Perhaps you'd like it paid to your mother?"

Noor dipped her head in a quick nod.

Money talk. Like dirty laundry. Sewage. Allah would provide. She didn't mind bargaining when necessary like any frugal Indian or Parisienne, but . . .

"We need your services—we don't expect you to starve."

A gentle reminder of the four weeks Noor went without pay when she first joined the SOE. Went without pay for four whole weeks because she couldn't bear to mention to Miss Atkins that His Majesty's War Department had mistakenly failed to pay her salary.

"I appreciate that, marm."

"Continue to use the code name we chose during training: Madeleine. In France, be most careful to avoid anyone who could recognize you from before the war or call you Nora."

None of Noor's friends in Paris would call her Nora. Miss Atkins had forgotten Noor Khan, though the name was on Noor's records; Noor had played Nora Baker quite well.

"Letters to your family can be sent in care of the War Office at Whitehall. Urgent personal messages are to use our prearranged code; these will be read over the BBC for you to receive. For instance, Prosper's team will be alerted to expect your arrival with the phrase *Jasmin is playing her flute*, and you will use the phrase *Jasmin has played her flute* to tip us off that you have arrived safely. You will identify yourself to Phono with the phrase *The sky is blue*. The correct response is: *But the bread will rise*."

"*Très drôle*," said Noor.

Gimlet eyes bored into Noor's. "Yes, very funny. Only, Nora, this is no game. All of France is occupied by the Germans now. SOE agents and the Resistance are risking their lives every day. It's quite possible you will be there when the invasion comes, if not on this assignment then on another. If captured, you know the rules: Deny all knowledge of other members of the network and the SOE. Hold out twenty-four hours before divulging any information so your contacts will know something is wrong and have time to destroy incriminating evidence and save themselves." Miss Atkins barely paused; she must have given the same instructions to other agents many times.

Could Noor resist for twenty-four hours? Of course she could. And they'd never catch her to begin with. And it was torture to be safe in England. And now to have this rare chance to be nearer to Armand, somehow get a message to him . . .

Out loud Noor asked, "Do members of the Resistance completely support the return of General de Gaulle, as the BBC says?"

"Pish, de Gaulle! Vichy court-martialled him *in absentia* for desertion, yet the BBC calls him General. He's not an elected head of state, after all."

To be court-martialled by Vichy sounded like an accolade. That Miss Atkins, weather vane of official opinion, was so disparaging could mean that General Charles de Gaulle wasn't as compliant as Mr. Churchill would like foreign leaders to be. His voice on the BBC, though—so inspiring. De Gaulle ran his own resistance networks too, the Free French.

"Miss Atkins, why have some French refugees joined the SOE and some the Free French?"

"Contacts, mostly. It's not always a matter of choice. If you ask me, de Gaulle's Free French are a ragtag lot, given far too much importance."

"Ragtag because they've lost everything," said Noor. "But they do inspire me, and each other. I mean people like Jean Moulin and others who refused to collaborate with the Germans."

"Oh, be very careful to use Moulin's *nom de guerre*—Max— in France. He's larger than life to the French resistants, perhaps larger than de Gaulle or his General Delestraint—but we don't mention that. He could become France's next president, if Mr. Churchill and Mr. Roosevelt so decide."

Miss Atkins pushed her chair back. Noor rose too.

"If you have a choice, the SOE is far more attractive. General de Gaulle doesn't have state coffers at his disposal to fund his little projects in France, you know. Anyway, your allegiance is to England and the SOE, my dear. But we do co-operate with the Free French. When we have to."

"Yes, marm."

The waiter held the door. Miss Atkins strode purposefully through. Noor followed close behind. On Clarges Street, Miss Atkins snapped a black umbrella open against a slow drizzle growing to shower. Noor did the same. Miss Atkins's umbrella bobbed away down the street. Soon she and Noor were far apart.

CHAPTER 6

Pforzheim, Germany
December 1943

MISS ATKINS NAMED US ALL. *Yolande was "Mariette" and I was
Madeleine. But the nom de guerre I wanted was Madelon.*

*Madelon from an evening in 1934, when I was twenty. Uncle
Tajuddin's lecture to the Sufi disciples closed with the Universal
Worship ceremony, and I slipped away with Armand to the Val
d'Or café. When we were sure no one who knew me was near,
we walked uphill, summoned by an old man's plaintive song,
"Quand Madelon vient nous servir à boire." A poilu from
the Great War sang of the girl Madelon who inspired warriors
like him.*

*The poilu stood on his wooden leg at the foot of Mont Valérien,
the cemetery where American soldiers lie. His accordion pleated
and unpleated, breathing that melody into the summer evening.
And before him on the ground he displayed his medals beside his
cupped beret.*

*Armand tossed a few sous in the beret and his arm encircled
my waist. In our special place, we lay down on his coat and the
tall chestnuts swayed above. We talked till we found ourselves still
speaking but without words. When I close my eyes in this dark
hole, I do not feel my chains but feel his lips again, lips on mine,
feel his hair between my fingers, dark hair scented with grass. The*

accordion music vibrates in me, a song from that war that was to end all war, from the poilu's days at Verdun.

We married, though no synagogue or mosque sanctified our nuptials. We married, though no one witnessed it but the stars over Paris. And for all that has happened as "the moving finger writes and having writ moves on," I would not lure that finger back to cancel that one line.

Of course we should have waited, of course he should have pulled away sooner. Suffragettes have secrets I should have known, but I'd never listened to them, never asked, never read a single pamphlet. Uncle's fears and restrictions had taught me to think of my body as a thing beneath my clothes, an evil thing to be tamed but never claimed. Armand explored it for me, with me. He played, read and described it to me as if reading a sacred scroll.

I never planned those long years of clandestine romance, and certainly not a secret marriage. I was travelling in two directions at once, and every magical hour with Armand became one hour stolen from my approved destiny as someone else's wife. Every hour I spent with him became tinged with the melancholy of probable farewells, yet every hour we were together we became more essential to each other.

But from the vortex of contradictions that led to this resumption of the wooden-legged man's war, from the eddying and rushing, from the headlong mix of suitable and unsuitable thoughts, there must have been a self-organizing moment in which thoughts cohered and glided to form a knot of flesh. Your body came into being in that instant, a particle of me became animate, waiting for you. Unensouled, and as yet without anger, defiance, sadness or fear. All that remained was for Allah to send you, light your life within me.

The girl I was then stood poised on the fulcrum of change. I follow that naive, idealistic girl as if watching another time, someone else's life. When she comes into view, I write, hoping one word will form the next, hoping a moving pen can translate thought, memory, love, grief.

I sit enchained, prisoner of the present, looking back farther and farther, letting collage develop to story. Events are connected like prayer beads on a string—Subhan-allah . . . Subhan-allah . . . Subhan-allah.

CHAPTER 7

Tangmere, England
Tuesday, June 15, 1943

NIGHT AIR PARTED before the nose of the Lysander, slipped around its wings. The shudder of the Mercury engine surrounded Noor, sitting in the converted air gunner's cockpit behind the pilot, facing the tail. Infinitesimal accelerations multiplied as the high-wing monoplane's propeller wrung and ripped at the moon-bleached night. The plane's wings rested on air flows as gravity strained to anchor the small plane to Surrey earth.

The drumbeat of the ground faded. A thump, and her stomach plunged. Excitement mixed with vertigo. The clearest thought since a motor car sped her away from Portman Square, London's buildings hulking past like old women shrouded in chadors of mythic black, since bumping down unmetalled roads to the cottage by the airfield: she was flying.

"Righto?" the pilot's voice blared through the intercom. Noor nodded, not trusting her own voice in the shuddering din. The passenger whose knee kept bumping hers, bull-necked, taciturn "Edmond," whose destination she didn't know, shouted a response for both.

The pilot had given Noor an appraising glance across the dining table. She knew the source of that glance; her features had tested his ability to classify. Not-English. French? Italian? Greek?

Once more her face had blended into context, becoming elemental, its differences from others around it becoming so minuscule as to make it unremarkable. Surrounded by other Indians, she looked and sounded Indian; by French agents, she looked and sounded French—a chameleon quality highly desirable for anyone in SOE's French Section.

She shifted her knees beneath the unaccustomed length of her reversible black and forest-green skirt; correct for current Paris fashion, old-fashioned by English standards.

Her own civilian clothes weren't too fashionable. Shown by the butler to a bedroom of the flat at Orchard Court, she had discarded them in the adjoining black-tiled bathroom. The French-made stays were stylish by contrast with her English ones, but the French tailor-tabbed blouse and skirt were drab and coarse in texture, to match Anne-Marie Régnier's circumstances.

In the bathroom Noor slipped into the white blouse provided, retained her wristwatch and gold stud earrings, and debated removing the gold chain and pendant she always wore.

The thin chain that was always tangling was a gift from Kabir, celebrating his first earnings. French-made; she could wear the chain.

The pendant—a tiger claw enframed in gold—was a gift from Dadijaan. Its gold frame had sheathed the claw's deadly hostility for nearly two centuries, turning it to ornament, and the strength of her grandmother and an unbroken line of noblewomen had seeped in, tinting it yellow. The claw was a bodily weapon, an amulet worn "for luck and courage." No German could ever comprehend the intrinsic value or meaning of the heirloom. Hand-fashioned by artisans in India, not England, to anyone unfamiliar with its origin it would appear a translucent seashell of little value. In dire emergency she could pawn the heirloom. It was so much a part of her, she even slept with its curve nesting between her breasts. If she concealed it beneath her blouse, she wouldn't have to regret leaving it.

She put on the jacket and reversible skirt.

Dark rushed past the dome above Noor's head. The drone of the engine was hypnotizing. She shifted gaze for a moment to the vibrating floor. Her low-heeled T-strap shoes were propped on a metal canister destined for the Resistance. She was at this moment probably perched on a load of live ammunition.

Noor gripped the seat, steadying herself.

Peculiar, being catapulted into the air then suspended in mid-air between departure and arrival—a little like the non-place and non-time of meditation. The wall at her back felt membrane-thin; anything could hit or penetrate this fragile, roaring space, not only German fighters.

The plane was a boat, just a little boat in the sky.

Feet resting on the canister.

She'd buckled those shoes in the bathroom, each shoe in turn on the onyx bidet. When Noor returned to the bedroom, there sat Miss Vera Atkins, primly, on the hope chest at the foot of the bed. She supplied the props that corroborated Noor's cover story: a postcard addressed to Anne-Marie Régnier of Bordeaux from a sick "Aunt Lucille" in Paris, beseeching her to visit; Anne-Marie's ration book, with a few coupons missing; Anne-Marie's identity card, issued in Bordeaux; a textile card; Anne-Marie's certificate of Aryan descent; a booklet of métro tickets; a signed and stamped pale green *ausweiss* that authorized her travel to Paris. Miss Atkins had neatly typed a one-page cover story, and Noor memorized the details quickly—names of Anne-Marie's "parents," an address in Bordeaux. Anne-Marie's lycée was a Catholic convent for girls like the one Noor had attended in Suresnes. Additional details were up to Noor. Miss Atkins pointed out that the travel pass was stamped "no expiration" with a signature, "Kieffer," beneath.

For emergency use there was a family photo featuring an old lady who might, by an India-rubber stretch of imagination, bear a familial resemblance to Noor. Miss Atkins showed Noor the *Made in Germany* mark on a miniature pair of Zeiss binoculars. A small parcel wrapped in brown paper and string was for Aunt Lucille if she were stopped at a German checkpoint. The parcel was really destined for Prosper. Lastly, Miss Atkins gave Noor the address of her safe house in Paris.

Noor touched the brass buttons on her new forest-green jacket. Miss Atkins had flipped one of the button covers to reveal a tiny compass within. And as a finishing touch Miss Atkins provided the large black leather handbag now resting on Noor's lap, showing her the twenty-six thousand francs sporting the face of Maréchal Pétain and mentioning, with a conspiratorial smile, that Pétain's images multiplied not from officially engraved plates in France but all the way from the basement workshop of an SOE counterfeiter in Toronto.

Miss Atkins also showed her the small slit in the satin lining of her jacket sleeve, a pocket just large enough for a tiny capsule. She secured the cyanide "L-pill" and sewed the slit closed. "Let's hope you shan't have to use it," she said, biting off the thread. "Or this." The cold snout of a French-made Mikros pocket pistol met Noor's hand. Noor drew back the slide to verify that the magazine was loaded. The thumb lever exposed a white dot; the pistol was on "safe."

Wound, don't kill.

Her instructors, former British heads of police and intelligence in India, were fond of pointing out that a wounded man absorbed the enemy's resources, a dead one did not.

The parcel, pistol and banknotes now lay swaddled in Noor's headscarf in the false compartment of her handbag. In the upper compartment lay a change of underwear bundled about her toothbrush and paste, a folded beret and gloves.

Waiting for the ground crew's ready signal in the drawing room of the little cottage at Tangmere, Edmond cranked up the phonograph and played "Just as Long as the World Goes Round."

"You have family in France?" Edmond was obviously speculating on her reasons for volunteering for a mission.

"Yes," she said, not allowing herself to say "my fiancé and his mother."

Sam Browne's baritone began to untwine Noor's tight-wound nerves.

"And you?" she ventured.

"A grandfather, uncles, aunts, cousins."

Miss Atkins went through Noor's pockets again, searching for telltale British cigarettes or a forgotten London bus ticket. Tucked low between her breasts, Noor's tiger claw went unnoticed. Then, as the sound of the Lysander's engines drowned out the gramophone, Miss Atkins turned to Noor and presented her with the parting gift Colonel Buckmaster gave all his women agents: a gold compact case.

"Made in France," said Miss Atkins reassuringly.

Noor thanked her, slipping it into the pocket of the oilskin coat folded over her arm. She had a tortoiseshell compact of her own, but it was kind of the Colonel.

Tucked in the sealed roar of the Lysander, Noor's palms tingled; she had been gripping the edge of her wooden seat. Ahead lay the Paris she, Mother, Dadijaan, Kabir and Zaib left three years and one week ago to fend for itself. England, with its sloping slate-roofed houses, its larks and hedges, that soot-grimed and war-besieged island, had fallen away and she was flying across its moat to plunge, like Alice down the rabbit hole, into the hexagon, back to the dark, silenced City of Light. Noor Khan alias Nora Baker was left behind. The code name imposed by Miss Atkins now compelled its alternate reality first on her life, then on the fictitious Anne-Marie Régnier's: *Madeleine*.

THESE MANACLES WEIGH HEAVY *on my wrists, but before the guard takes the pen Vogel allows by day and turns off the dim bulb by which I write, hear this: no postman delivered the letter I received three weeks before, nor had it stopped for the wide black nibs of eagle-eyed Englishwomen reading mail in their cabinet noir on the fourth floor of John Lewis department store. Like the two I'd received before—precious talismans I carried everywhere—it was addressed to Miss Noor Khan c/o the Sufi Music Centre, London, England, and had made its way across a France overrun with Germans in the hands of a Red Cross volunteer. The vellum note with it said, "Mademoiselle, a young gentleman in France asked that I deliver this by hand."*

Inside, Armand's flourishes filled one side of a postcard. Though black-lined by German censors, they were music to my eyes—such joy, such relief—your father was alive! But "Camp d'internement de Drancy" and "Bureau de la Censure" were spelled in the circle of the rubber stamp defacing the card. It meant everything I'd feared these three years, meant the worst— Armand was arrested. And Madame Lydia as well, since I deciphered the word "mère" on the card. The camp was somewhere close to Paris, I was sure, for the words "Département" and

"Seine" were barely legible on the second circular stamp above the address.

I would find it.

The first moment I saw your father practising in one of Mademoiselle Nadia Boulanger's piano rooms is engraved in my memory, from the dress I wore—Zaib sewed it for me from a pattern sent by our aunt in Boston—to the scratch of netted ponytail against the nape of my neck. Armand's lithe fingers drew Bach's Third Goldberg Variation from the grand, and our souls seemed to meet in the music. That day he played the way Indian musicians play—oblivious of audience.

He said he'd seen me once before, on the grounds of the 1931 Exposition Coloniale, that he'd followed me that day through the model Angkor Wat temple and the faux date and palm trees cele-brating the contribution of colonies to their colonizers. He'd hoped to learn my name, but I was with my friend Josianne and somehow he lost me in the crowd.

Something in his voice said I was expected, that he'd been wait-ing for me a very long time, and it made me give him my unequivo-cal trust, as if I were a bottomless well. I blushed, tongue-tied—you must understand, I was almost seventeen but it was the first time I'd been alone with a man who was not my relative.

Another day, still the summer of '31. I see myself at a corner table at Les Deux Magots with Josianne, and Armand approaching. Josianne had known me since childhood, and knew I expected my marriage would be arranged. So she was amused when my eyes lit up at the sight of Armand, and left us alone. Armand and I sat talking for hours and sharing silence as if we'd known one another always.

A week later I saw Armand sitting cross-legged among the dis-ciples in the Sufi school. He said he came from curiosity about Sufi music. When I knew him better, he said he'd been expecting micro-tones, superlative raags and complex rhythms because I'd described the school so lyrically. I had described what I loved—the school the way it used to be, not as it was under Uncle. Uncle's sitar whined the simplest of melodies in repetitive fragments; a gramophone recording might have shown greater emotion. Still, Armand listened with great attention. He listened as Uncle Tajuddin lectured for an hour on Love, Beauty and Tolerance. And another hour on the relationship between Love, Lover and the Beloved—Uncle Tajuddin always tried so hard to imitate my long-gone Abbajaan. But I knew Armand had come for me.

Three years later—how long ago it seems, though it was only 1934—when I delayed your soul from entering the world, I told myself the time was not right, that when Armand and I were married by law and in the eyes of our families, I could ask Allah to send you again. I was only twenty when Madame Dunet was enlisted to stop your soul from taking shape, twenty when I first promised never again to meet Armand. But I should have been stronger, should have stood by my dearest friend turned beloved.

Mother wanted me to marry one of the rentier class who dabbled in Sufism at the school in Suresnes, secure the family by alliance, no less than Uncle Tajuddin expected me to marry a nawab and secure the Indian branch of the family by alliance. How hard Mother worked to create the perfect package from her too Indian daughter—the right lycée, the École Normale de Musique, piano lessons with Mademoiselle Nadia Boulanger, riding lessons, art history and literature lessons—while Uncle countered with Urdu poetry, Arabic lessons and calligraphy. Everything but finishing school, which was far beyond our means.

Mother and Uncle never asked me to describe the life I dreamed of composing.

It was Mother who found out about Armand. Meeting Mademoiselle Boulanger one day on the Champs-Elysées, Mother greeted her and asked how I was progressing. Mademoiselle Boulanger replied that she hadn't seen me in months.

Confronted, I confessed to meeting Armand in secret. My family should have rejoiced with me that I had found the twin of my soul: I said to Uncle, "Didn't Rumi say the desire in a woman for a man is so that each may perfect the other's work?" But there was consternation, anger, accusations of betrayal; the inquisition began.

*I who wanted never to disappoint my family had, with a single deed,
succeeded in disappointing them utterly and irrevocably.*

*Mother said I was confused between love for the Divine—what
Abbajaan would have called ishq-i-haqiqi—and ishq-i-majazi, loving a man. Loving a man, she said, requires very different skills
from loving the Divine, though a man might believe he has something of the Divine in him. She recited everything she had lost or
given up to love and follow Abbajaan, and told me Dadijaan and
our Indian family had considered her his concubine for years—
until she bore a son.*

*I said Abbajaan told me love in any form, though it be for an idol
or another person, is sacred because it derives from love for the Divine.*

*"We make our choices," she said, and bit her lips closed as if she
couldn't allow herself to say more. She is from America, a place
where it seems one has choices unless a woman makes the wrong
ones, as Mother did. And so Mother proposed a quick courtship
with a large donor to the Sainah Foundation.*

*Why, I asked Uncle Tajuddin, did Allah allow love in the world
if marriages are to be forced by our elders? Allah could spare me the
yearning, the rushing in the heart at the sound of my beloved's
name, but instead he created passion in me, a woman, just as he
created it in men.*

*Uncle, knowing nothing of your body preparing itself within
me, blamed Mother's American example for the scandalous situation—I had allowed an ineligible young man's name to be linked
with mine. He proposed an immediate liaison with Allahuddin, a
poor, God-fearing cousin in Baroda.*

*Kabir preferred Uncle's solution though such exile meant he'd
rarely see me again. Eighteen that year, he was tyrant-in-training,
eager to assert his newly minted masculine authority, eager to pronounce my sentence first, verdict afterwards.*

*My Dadijaan wasn't living with us then, but she would have
been equally horrified. She came from a place where women had an
area of choice, a leftover area men didn't need. And she would have
blamed Mother too, if she knew.*

And all this when I felt already and forever married to Armand.

Embarrassed by my family, I telephoned my beloved, whispering, "Not now, not now," till I had only myself left to rely on. Only my trembling self.

I learned that my body belonged not to me but to my family, and it was my uncle's right to say yea or nay to marriage. Because I lived in Paris, he said, didn't mean I was no longer Indian and Muslim. He expected me to deposit my life in his care, and was so hurt and then insulted at my slightest hesitation.

Seeking to change me, he spared me no diatribe against Jews, no lecture about the degradation of Muslim women who shame their families by consorting with unbelievers. He forbade me to leave Afzal Manzil for one month, and I spent that month weeping, confined in the dead air of my room, your body growing inside me. Never will I forget that feeling of changelessness, of being held hostage by a strong man's will.

I was no better than a Montmartre prostitute, Uncle said, but because he loved me, he would keep my secret. His only condition: if I spoke to Armand ever again, everyone I loved—Mother, Dadijaan, Kabir and Zaib—would never see me or speak to me again. This for the sin of loving without permission; what if he had known of your body, that beautiful miracle Armand and I made the night of our clandestine marriage, growing within me?

I didn't fully believe Uncle's threat, for I still believed in my family's love, in my Abbajaan's teachings that all religions are equal paths to a Universal God, like many roads to the Ka'aba.

The very evening Uncle's sentence was lifted, I crept out and went to Armand's garçonnière, the tiny garret he rented so he could keep regular hours for composition; Madame Lydia's apartment was always full of cousins, mostly refugees from Germany. I looked up and saw candles shining in both windows. I had not imagined him celebrating Hanukkah along with other Jews. His family did not keep kosher, spoke no Hebrew or Yiddish at home, and only his father had read the Torah. How little I knew Armand, I thought.

And so I came away without telling him about you.

I felt abandoned by your father after that—I don't know why. It was I who kept you secret from him, but I felt that he, intuitive in so many ways, shouldn't need to be told of you. But even your father couldn't know what was in my heart as long as I was silent.

I never wanted Armand to feel he had been ensnared into marriage. He had commissions for new works for more prestigious orchestras. He heard an inner music, from his heritage of Russian folk harmonies, and it demanded to be rendered in concert music. He was introducing microtones, experimenting with "chain forms," jazz colouring and variations, reinforcing his personal style. How cruel to suppress his music with domesticity.

Even so, I planned to meet him as soon as I could—till Uncle mentioned casually, so very casually, one day that if I met him even once more, it would be my fault should something terrible happen to him. This time, I believed him. I didn't see balding Uncle who had banished himself from his respectable home to wear closed European shoes and live in fear of Parisians; to me, Uncle was vindictive, hate-filled and angry—and powerful.

So your mother was a coward, for my family made me ashamed of loving Armand, ashamed of love though there is never enough in the world. I had no confidence in our future, I had nothing to offer you in the present. I had not lived my own life enough to know myself—how could I be a mother?

At first I confided your existence to no one, not even my dearest friend, Josianne. But later, in desperation, I confided in your aunt Zaib. Zaib said I wasn't ambitious enough, that I could have done better than Armand, but she'd help me.

Armand and I met again, four years later. My Dadijaan had just unpacked her bedding roll full of gifts and spices in November 1938 when we heard the news of Kristallnacht. I telephoned Armand to ask if he had relatives or students in Germany, to commiserate, and most of all to ask for reassurance that he would be safe.

Armand was angry. After all, we had not met in four years. He told me of Jews forced to sweep the streets, of regulations, a cousin in Berlin and an uncle in Vienna who were missing. His voice was tender at the end; he was touched that I still cared.

I felt stronger after I spoke with my love, but burdened with secrets. So I wrote. I told him about you, ma petite, and I told him how I came to lose the courage to marry him. I didn't know what he would say, and I was ashamed to reveal my uncle's hypocrisy and threats, but I had to write. I waited and waited—it seemed forever. But he did write back—such a letter, ma petite! Your father wrote to comfort me. Half the blame was his, he said. He wrote that his cousins and refugee students had worse tales of anti-Semitism.

He wrote that he loved me—I must remember this today. He and Madame Lydia agreed, he wrote, that in these times when love has become so rare, our hearts must become our only compass. He promised we would marry one day in the eyes of the law and together bring you back. He wasn't afraid of Uncle as I was, nor did he believe Uncle's threats and bombast, but we lived in France, where, as in India, I needed Uncle or Kabir's permission to marry.

War came very soon after that, in 1939, and Armand left his students and the sonata he was composing. For almost a year he sat in the fortified bunkers waiting for the Germans to breach the velvet rope of the Maginot line. Or the Imaginot line, as Kabir and I called it later—the line that marked the limit of our imaginations, and through which no one, certainly not Hitler, could venture.

I wrote every day, I sent Armand parcels. I stole away to Madame Lydia's to share his letters. Madame told me stories about Armand—how his Jewish name was Aaron but he chose Armand himself as his French name to use in school. How he sang before he learned to speak, and would, as a child, borrow money to buy her flowers. I listened, wanting her tales to make up for all the years I had not known him. Shared love for Armand made us special to each other, as if we'd never been strangers.

I was almost twenty-six by then, and again I thought perhaps now I was old enough to make my own choices the way my mother had. I turned to her again for help, but Mother said I was making the very mistakes she made. After all the love she'd lavished on me.

I was betraying the entire life Mother planned for me to live.

Kabir was twenty-four then, and I hoped, if he met Armand, he would see, he would feel intuitively, that my Armand is a refined man, an educated, decent man. What more can anyone ask in a brother-in-law?

In the spring of 1940, Armand had but ten days' leave and was back in Paris. I persuaded Kabir to meet him. I waited in my room at Afzal Manzil, praying Kabir would be willing to share me with Armand and give permission for our marriage. But Kabir! He returned from meeting Armand and said he agreed with Uncle!

"It is impossible that you could love Rivkin," said he, assuming a deep voice of authority. "You've never been in love, you don't know what it feels like. But you're tender-hearted. Yes, you have feelings, deep feelings. But you feel pity, not love. That's all one can feel for a Jew—pity! But you—you care so little for this family that you can even think of marriage. Listen to me! If I marry an unbeliever, she'll become Muslim. But if you marry Rivkin, Jews will inherit Afzal Manzil. That's disgusting. Think how you would feel if I told you I wanted to marry a man. Wouldn't you be disgusted? That's how I feel."

He had begun to name my feelings on my behalf, tell me what I felt—so I would know what he permitted me to feel. Just what did he know of love at twenty-four? He said I'd ruined my chances of marriage to any wifeless Muslim; a marriage should be arranged for me in India—perhaps our cousin Allahuddin could yet be persuaded to take me as his third wife. He was playing head of the family again, posturing to show he could be a man. Scandal was to be avoided at all costs; we were dependent on donations to the Sainah Foundation.

Now that even Kabir, beloved brother who was to carry our father's teachings of tolerance forward, had turned against us, I lost courage a second time, capitulated again, setting off these years of separation and grief. Too weak to break my blood ties, too anxious to please, too frightened of penury, I did not protest enough that Kabir had excluded the man I trusted, admired and loved most from my life, in the belief that he was protecting me, preventing further "mistakes."

So I was given love, that rarest, most precious spark that can ignite between man and woman, and I had not the courage to accept its demands for fear of losing my family's love.

I had expected Armand to argue with Kabir, to fight like a knight for his lady. Instead, Kabir said Armand had agreed we should part.

When we said goodbye in the Bois beneath the locust trees, Armand explained why. Yes, I agreed we would part, it's true, but what I did was desertion. Unpardonable even though Armand wanted it.

Suresnes was bombarded a few weeks later. Uncle Tajuddin took a steamer from Marseilles back to Baroda while the rest of us escaped to England. Uncle could not threaten me now, and Mother, Dadijaan, Kabir and Zaib were safe in London.

The unpardonable can be neither forgiven nor punished, only atoned for by action. So as I flew towards Paris in the Lizzie from Tangmere, laden with admonitions, instructions and directions from the SOE, I also went determined to make amends. I told myself I was no longer a trembling kind of woman, that I claimed my life and body as my own. This time I would not fail Armand.

Three weeks in Paris for my secret mission, and if I could not touch Armand's cheek once more and hold him to my breast, I would find a way to tell him only this: that I will always love him, that if he should still desire, we will marry anew in the eyes of the law when the world finds peace.

CHAPTER 9

En route to France
Tuesday, June 15, 1943

Noor scanned the night sky, looking out as ordered, for patrolling German night fighters. Thankfully, for almost an hour now, only the silvered dark rushed over the clear cowl-roof.

Edmond pulled a leather-jacketed hip flask from his raincoat pocket, unscrewed the top and proffered it. Noor shook her head. She liked a glass of wine on occasion, now Uncle Tajuddin was too far away to sour it with his frowns, but tonight she needed every sense alert.

"Landing soon." The pilot's shout burst against her eardrum.

He must have identified himself by s-phone to the waiting resistance team and the air movements officer, the lieutenant code-named Gilbert. Now he'd be searching for the inverted-L-shaped flare-path from their torches. Strangers—but please, Allah, not the Germans—were standing below with upturned faces, right now.

Noor's stomach lurched as the Lysander began its descent. She was tipping backwards in her seat. She listed against Edmond's shoulder as the small plane circled to come down against the wind. There was a bump, a jolt, a rise and another bump. The plane taxied down the long leg of the L, turned sharp right along the short leg and came to a standstill. The pilot throttled back his engine, exchanged a challenge question for the password from the waiting reception team.

The roof above Noor slid back. The dark shape of a peaked cap appeared over the rim.

"*Venez—vite!*" invited a hoarse voice.

She rose quickly in the cramped space and swung herself out, feeling for each rung in the ladder leaning against the plane. Halfway, strong hands gripped her waist, then someone lifted her bodily from the plane, held her a moment against the vigorous thumping in his chest, and set her feet on spongy, grass-stubbled ground. Slightly winded, she looked up into a flashily handsome face under the peaked cap.

"*Bienvenue, mademoiselle,*" he said with a chivalrous grin. "Wait here."

A commanding overarm gesture marked him as the air movements officer. An experienced pilot, Edmond had said over dinner. Gilbert was trained by the SOE to select and arrange fields on which the cloak-and-dagger planes could land—nothing ploughed, no soft mud. The Loire was as the back of his hand, and, the pilot informed Noor, Gilbert was a walking Michelin guide to the best black market cuisine in northern France. Besides, since he had begun selecting landing sites, the squadron had not lost a single flight.

Three men carrying small valises and clutching their hat brims scurried past Noor to the foot of the ladder. Edmond lifted out Noor's coat and handbag, his own valise and, with some effort, the long drum-like canister. These passed down the ladder to waiting arms of the departing passengers. Other figures crowded around and carried the canister away in their midst. Then Edmond hoisted himself from the plane.

How could three men fold themselves into the tiny gunner's cockpit she and Edmond had just vacated? But they must have done so, and rapidly.

The roof of the gunner's cockpit slid closed. A hand emerged from the cockpit window and wiped a smudge of oil from the windscreen.

The engine gave a bursting howl loud enough, Noor felt sure, to wake every German from here to Berlin. Gilbert gave the thumbs-up sign. In sixty yards the Lysander was airborne, the roar fading to a distant drone in the sky. Gilbert signalled and two men ran from the clump of trees behind Noor and pulled the guiding torches from the ground. Noor read her wristwatch by moonlight—00:45 hours. Landing and takeoff had taken only three minutes.

Edmond tramped across the pasture to wait at her side, hands in his coat pockets, hat brim tipped forward, eyes on the ground, discouraging conversation. Noor pulled the winding pin on her watch and reset it to Paris time as decreed by the Germans—an hour ahead, to coincide with Berlin.

Gilbert appeared at her side as if dropped by parachute. "Come with me." He gave her the handbag and coat, his eyes darting left and right. Noor's too, searching for German uniforms or anything suspicious.

The night was warm, but nerves taut as telephone wire drew the warmth from her skin. She slipped her oilskin on.

Two men stood waiting, guarding five bicycles. Father and son, it seemed, one too old for military duty and the other much too young. No greetings were expected or made. Gilbert pointed to a bicycle minus a crossbar, for Noor. She put her handbag in its basket and fell in line, following closely behind the father and son. Gilbert and then Edmond brought up the rear.

They wheeled their bicycles stealthily through the moonlit woods.

"My wife couldn't manage for even one day with so little luggage." Gilbert came up beside Noor and nodded at the handbag bouncing in her bicycle basket.

Noor gave him a hesitant smile. Mindful of security rules, she said nothing.

Gilbert whispered, "Vol de Nuit. The perfume you're wearing—correct? The top note is there, I think. Very faint."

Noor shook her head, eyes on the road. Wearing perfume on a night mission would leave her signature wherever she went—the sign of an amateur.

"What is a woman without perfume? But don't worry, the pilot said he'll be back in a few days with your luggage."

"If there's moonlight," Noor said. No reason to be silent, since Gilbert seemed to know.

A few metres later he asked, "You're the new *pianiste?*"

She gave another slight smile, but said nothing.

"A courier, then? I must know, you see, because I select the airfields and then radio London. I have orders to take you to Paris."

"Yes."

"I must know where to find so beautiful a woman again."

"You will be told when you need to know," whispered Noor, somewhat archly. Beyond the excitement of clandestine danger, she was enjoying the underlying banter of their exchange. Three years in London and she had never come to understand the dry wit of English men.

"*Alors*, you will want to tell people in London that you have arrived safely. So have your letters ready next week," said Gilbert. "I'll give them to the pilot of the next landing."

"And where will I find you to give you letters?" asked Noor.

"I assure you we will meet again, and soon, mademoiselle. But in case you must send a message to someone in London about me, my code name is Gilbert. And yours?"

"Madeleine. But to people here I am Anne-Marie Régnier."

The small caravan plodded on, wheeling their bicycles now side by side, now in single file. Too loud crunch of footfall on twigs, over fallen branches, roots and stones along the muddy path.

"You speak perfect French with no accent, mademoiselle," said Gilbert. "Where did you learn?"

Only a Parisian would think her French was *sans accent*, so Gilbert was Parisian. The question was conversational, but again against the rules. SOE security precautions seemed to be ignored here, at least by Gilbert. But if she was to work with Gilbert and other resistants, she had to be accepted. She should make the first effort.

"I once lived near Paris," she acknowledged.

"Aha! That explains it. Which arrondissement?"

"No, just near Paris," she said, still guarded.

"Ah, the beautiful *banlieue*," he said with irony. Most suburbs of Paris were dumping grounds for refuse and factory waste; they could scarcely be called beautiful.

Gilbert now fell back and began quizzing Edmond, who responded with grunts. Noor took the opportunity to memorize local landmarks, as the SOE handbook taught, in case she needed to return this way. People and animals had left signs everywhere. Covert ones, like the glove hanging from a branch, the remains of a poacher's fire; overt signs, like the finger-post to a disused mine she had passed a few paces back, and a grotto of the Virgin Mary, her eyes shining like jewels. In India, Hindu idols dotted the land-scape like the Virgin in France. French Catholics kissed her feet just as Muslims kissed the Ka'aba, each calling the other pagan.

A dormouse whistled and clicked in a tree hole above. Noor flipped her jacket button open, squinting in the moonlight, not-ing the direction of the tiny white N on the dial of her compass.

A dog bayed faintly. Uncle Tajuddin would say it was an unclean animal, but Noor had loved dogs as a child—that is, until a dog bite followed by fourteen injections against rabies.

The dog bayed again, sounding huge, wolf-like and far too close.

Another twenty minutes' walking and a road broke across the dense woods. Here the father and son whispered low *au revoirs*, arabesqued over their bicycle seats and rode away into the night. She imagined the two cycling home in the dark. No one was pay-ing them to risk their lives helping British agents bring in arms.

Gilbert mounted his cycle too, and motioned to Noor and Edmond to follow him.

"Where are you taking us?" asked Edmond.

Noor didn't think he'd looked at his compass at all.

"To the railway station. At Le Mans."

Noor and Edmond mounted and pedalled after him.

Moonlit vineyards, fields and hedgerows stretched away on either side of the road, tranquil as if no war had ever disturbed them.

The jumble of medieval buildings marking the centre of Le Mans loomed against the moonlit sky. Not a single light glinted; curfew was total. Gilbert dismounted and again walked his bicycle. Noor and Edmond did the same. At a small tool shed by a field of freshly cut wheat, they wheeled their bicycles in and closed the door. They set off, skirting the city. Within an hour Noor's new shoes were chafing her feet.

A glow swung to and fro in the distance—a lantern. A *cheminot*'s lantern. Morning mist lifted, revealing tracks flowing through a station, wagons marked SNCF on sidings and then four being coupled near the station to a small locomotive. The first two were passenger carriages. At the third wagon a gendarme stood ramrod straight, overseeing the loading of wine bottles. The fourth was being loaded with boxes marked *bustes du Maréchal*—busts of Maréchal Pétain, Marshal of France, hero of the Great War, and now the Frenchman who had shaken Hitler's hand.

"We part here," whispered Gilbert. "Act as if we had never met."

Edmond gave Gilbert's hand a quick, grave tug and touched his hat in Noor's direction. "You first," he said. "I'll take the next one."

At the front of the station, a gendarme and a German grenadier were seated side by side at a desk beside the turnstile, a Thermos steaming between them. A quiver raced through Noor from head to toe as she approached the ticket counter.

It's a play. Play the part, play it well.

She was Anne-Marie Régnier, she was from Bordeaux, she had a signed *ausweiss* authorizing unlimited travel. Imitation Anne-Marie would be better than any real Anne-Marie.

"One way to Paris," she said to the official in his little cage, passing him a counterfeit note. She looked away as if impatient, while he grumbled about mademoiselle's not carrying exact change. A white strip licked forward to her waiting hand beneath the grille.

She approached the turnstile for the next test.

"*Papiers?*"

Her gaze fixed on her hand, her hand offering the forged *carte d'identité* and the pale green *ausweiss* to the gendarme. Not trembling—good. Miss Atkins said women were less conspicuous operatives, unlikely to have trouble with documents. Few women had any identity papers before the war. Certainly she, Mother nor Zaib was ever issued an identity card or needed a licence to drive all the years they lived in Paris. Uncle Tajuddin never allowed Mother, Noor or Zaib to hold a bank account either, and all women in France needed permission from a male relative.

The gendarme bent his black cap over her papers, studying them a long time. Had he scented her fear? What if the forged papers failed to pass inspection? An oblique glance told her Gilbert had stopped at the newspaper kiosk. The gendarme finally completed his perusal and passed her papers to the German, who gave them a cursory glance, yawned and motioned her through the turnstile.

Take a seat in the first compartment so you can jump out and run if need be.

The compartment's only occupant, a farmer in a jerkin, scarf knotted about his grey-stubbled neck, sat with legs crossed at the ankle, boots dribbling mud and clay onto the floor. He gazed at Noor from head to toe with frank curiosity—a young woman travelling alone, early in the morning. She clasped her hands in her lap.

He could stare as much as he liked. Anne-Marie Régnier was accustomed to making this journey every week. Aunt Lucille was very sick and would surely die if her loving niece failed to reach her today.

In a few moments a blank-faced Gilbert walked down the corridor past her compartment. The German soldier too mounted the train and leaned from the doorway. He gave a nod and it began chugging and clanging from the station. He passed down the corridor. Thin. Too young for a uniform. If all German soldiers looked like him, the war would be over soon. But of course they didn't.

Noor settled back in her seat. She had read and heard so much in England about the German presence in France, but experiencing it was another matter.

He is the Boche; he is the enemy. Men like him guard Armand at Drancy.

Rain slanted against the window, strengthened to fine rivulets. Clear tadpole shapes smeared a horizontal path across the glass, then dried and stilled as the sun rose. Outside, wind ruffled the tall grass by the tracks.

A newspaper, *Je Suis Partout*, lay discarded on the seat beside her. A few days old. How was the German-controlled press presenting France to the French?

The very first article she read touted the number of French prisoners of war who had joined the Pétain league — at least 80 percent, it said, in camps everywhere. A second described with breathless earnestness how many volunteers were heading to Germany, where work was plentiful. One unnamed writer preached the duty of all French women to have children. The editorial by one Robert Brasillach denounced writers for disputing the great boon of being occupied by the Germans, and issued fatwa after fatwa calling for their deaths. Along the way he mentioned that Jews who once thought themselves safe in the unoccupied zone were scattering in all directions "like poisoned rats."

A wave of nausea swept over Noor. Brasillach's hatred was more elegantly and eloquently expressed than any propaganda pamphlet issued by the German Propagandastaffl. However, Brasillach had accurately assessed the situation: Armand and Madame Lydia had been in the unoccupied zone in the far south when they were arrested.

The farmer was still staring. She lowered her head and read on.

An anonymous article inched its way into a long diatribe alleging that POWs in Germany were being treated like kings while British barbarians kept German POWs enchained hand and foot in defiance of every treaty and international law. The accompanying sketch even showed a poor wretch manacled, a chain running from cuff to cuff, leg-ironed, chains running between his ankles and another long chain connecting the two—worse than a creature in a zoo. An insult to anyone's intelligence! She set the paper aside, almost tossing it.

The farmer stood up, reached for the paper and, without a word, proceeded to tear it into strips. He used each strip to wipe his muddy boots, then opened the door of the compartment and carefully placed the whole wet mass squarely in the centre of the corridor. It was difficult not to give him a conspiratorial look. The German soldier would have to exit along that corridor. The farmer took his seat again, a pleased look coming over his face.

The journey continued in companionable silence over the plain, past the cream-painted brick stations of Beillé, Connerré, La Ferté-Bernard, Nogent-le-Rotrou, La Loupe, Courville-sur-Eure. Here the train was shunted to a siding and a long wait sorely tested Noor's already taut nerves. Then it set off again past the cathedral of Chartres, through Maintenon and Épernon, climbing a little to Versailles Chantiers, towards Paris.

A lump rose in Noor's throat as the train chugged into the great hall of the Gare Montparnasse in Paris. Memories surged like desperate fish rising against the nets of time. Whenever she came to this station, she felt twelve years old again, saw herself with one hand in Mother's, the other in Kabir's, waving Abbajaan goodbye. Zaib must have been too young to be with them that day. Noor and Kabir thought it so very exciting that Abbajaan was leaving for Bordeaux, to board a steamer to Bombay, then a train north from Bombay to Baroda. How they had pestered Mother that they wanted to go too, especially to anywhere in India. No one knew Abbajaan was leaving forever.

But perhaps Mother had realized.

Noor felt her hand slip from her mother's again, saw her rush to Abbajaan and clutch the sleeves of his black shervani as he walked down the platform. Before Noor, her mother wept and clasped her arms around Abbajaan's neck, begging him not to leave her. He had reached up and removed her hands, lips moving in his long brown beard. Noor and Kabir could not hear, but Abbajaan must have reminded Mother of where she was, in public, in a train station. He must have reminded her she could join him at any time, and bring his children to live in India, that it was by her own choice she stayed behind. Noor and Kabir waved to Abbajaan as the train hissed farewell, then turned to comfort their mother.

Noor's glance flicked left and right, looking for German uniforms moving towards the train. Everything just as she remembered it. Women with hat boxes beside them, men scanning newspapers, waiting for trains. A woman with feathers in her hat pressed her cheek against an old man's lapel, goodbyes lingering in the tears on her lashes.

Noor's shirt collar had dampened though the morning air was pleasantly cool.

Pretend you never left. Pretend no one would have any reason to look for you.

A twelve-year-old girl and a sad-looking, gangly boy of about ten stood with arms looped about each other, unaccompanied, pale as Noor and Kabir must have looked the day Abbajaan left.

That day. Yes, Mother had known. Known Abbajaan wasn't planning to return. She told them later that Abbajaan wanted all of them to move "home" to India. But Mother worried Abbajaan might be pressured into accepting more wives, and she didn't want to live in seclusion under Dadijaan's rule. When she opened the telegram announcing his death in India of pneumonia five months later, it was final, but over the years Noor realized that the moment of Mother's abandonment took place here, at the Gare Montparnasse. Mother's widowhood began the day Abbajaan left for Baroda in 1926, leaving her alone in Paris to look after Noor and Kabir and little Zaib, alone to tell the world of his Sufi wisdom, while he returned to the source of his music.

Perhaps on this very platform.

And other memories. Leaving from this station in 1927 with Mother, Kabir and Zaib to pay their respects at Abbajaan's tomb in India, and returning home to Paris two years later. And soon after, greeting Abbajaan's half-brother, Uncle Tajuddin, when he arrived from Baroda in 1929 to live with them and manage the school of Sufism. Uncle Tajuddin, who ran their lives after that, changing everything for Noor and Zaib. And Mother.

The train's bump and sway subsided. Noor stood in the carriage doorway and looked out over the crowd milling on the platform, trying to stop her pulse from racing.

Clothes were shabby, even drab—not very different from Londoners, who in the last few years had learned to "make do and mend." How different were they from Parisians of three years ago? Probably very different. Everyone had been altered by war. But something in the way they carried themselves was familiar.

People seemed self-conscious, as if they were performing for an audience, eyes straight ahead. This wasn't the normal sensual awareness of Parisians, but the self-censorious awareness she'd seen in Indians whenever an Englishman was present. The audience: black and feldgrey uniforms moving among the Parisians. Everywhere, French *milice*, German soldiers and military policemen, with their rifles, waited for trains, smoked, kept an eye on the citizenry.

Noor dipped into her handbag, unfolded the brown beret with an attached black hairnet for her ponytail, and withdrew a pair of black kid gloves. Then she joined the crowd on the platform.

Walk, don't run. Down the platform. Look straight ahead, purposeful as everyone else.

Gilbert had descended from the carriage behind hers and was making his way past her down the platform to a ticket counter. She followed, inquiring about the special line that ran between the Gare Montparnasse and Auteuil. It was not in operation; she would have to take the métro.

As she moved away from the ticket counter, her eyes met Gilbert's for but a second. A surreptitious wink and he was gone.

Lose any Gestapo agent who may have followed from Le Mans.

She went to the WC and stayed there about half an hour for safety, then exited past a ring of anti-aircraft guns. The sky had lightened to pale June blue.

Paris looked familiar as when she and Armand met in cafés and talked for hours. Familiar, yet strange; she was alone.

She joined a tide of pedestrians on the boulevard Raspail, up to the boulevard des Invalides. The Musée de Rodin advertised its opening hours.

If she met any of these people, would she remember their faces? Too many.

Avoid looking anyone in the eye.

Walk normally. Notice everything.

For instance, how, past the esplanade des Invalides, the afternoon sun was glancing off panes painted navy blue, that no chink of light attract the attention of Allied bombers.

Don't notice the hollow-eyed look those dark panes give the pale stone buildings.

She crossed the Pont Alexandre III. The usual *bateaux-mouches* slipped slowly beneath the bridge.

Ignore the swastika flags and banners adorning the Grand Palais. Ignore uniforms, and all the broad-shouldered, tall men.

Why had the Germans removed sandbags and scaffolding Noor remembered from 1940? But then, why should they care if French monuments were destroyed by Allied bombs?

Don't notice that American and British flags are absent from their embassies.

Noor doubled back to the boulevard Champs-Elysées and detoured through streets taking their names from generals, battles, revolutionaries who fought for freedom, stood for individualism and liberty.

Chairs stacked behind glass doors began to appear on *terrasse* cafés. Sun strengthened, turning sheer to shimmer. Readers lingered in minuscule bookstores, grey-haired men played pétanque. But everywhere, finger-posts pointed in German, and the rumble of traffic she remembered so well was stilled. Even the confused buzz of outdoor conversations seemed muted.

Late in the afternoon, a very footsore Noor hesitated outside a *pâtisserie*. Slices of National Loaf in London were a poor substitute for the round, fire-tinged loaves in Paris's *boulangeries*, and she was tempted to buy a *café filtre* and a brioche as she had before morning lectures at the Sorbonne. But did ration coupons need to be presented at a café or only at a grocer? A detail that her instructors had forgotten to include in her syllabus.

Hungry as she was, she could not buy food. But she went in, to rest her feet.

Allay any suspicions. Order a glass of Vichy water; they can't request ration coupons for Vichy water.

It looked like any other water, tasted like any other. The spa water wasn't responsible for the actions of Petain's government encamped there. No ration coupons were requested.

If any German was following, he must have given up by now. Didn't the Gestapo have more important things to do than follow a young woman from Le Mans all day? They should.

Head for the safe house.

Down a narrow wooden escalator into the *pissotière* smell of the métro. Noor showed her papers again at the checkpoint, and presented a ticket from the booklet provided by Miss Atkins. A train bound for the Étoile stood at the platform, the doors of its last carriage closing.

Squeeze in. Hurry!

She seized a hand-strap to brace herself. The métro began to worm its way into the tunnels. A burst of yellow caught her eye, then another and another. Her gaze leaped from star to yellow star patched to men's and women's clothing. Every one read *Juif*. The *étoile jaune!* She had been told Jews had to travel in the last carriage of the métro, knew about the yellow stars they were required by law to wear, but in her hurry she had forgotten. And only seeing the star actually being worn by people brought belief. The train picked up speed, and some glanced at her own lapel with its missing yellow star.

Oh, Armand, are you too wearing one of these?

The pungence of her fellow travellers' desperation rose around her as the métro flowed through the dark under Paris. She was kin to these helpless people; had her marriage to Armand been solemnized, she might now be wearing the star with them.

Brakes squealed. Noor alighted at the next station with a stab of guilt for not riding further with the star-branded group. But she could not attract attention from officials.

Wait on the platform. Find a bench till the next train arrives. Look inconspicuous. Watch for anyone in the crowd, French or German, who might be watching you.

Two uneasy hours waiting for another train. This time she was careful to board a middle carriage on the métro bound for the Porte Maillot.

Sit beside the old woman with the shopping bag over her arm.

In this carriage, passengers had their inviolate bubble, a cordon of private space. Only the German soldiers stared, their gaze occupying each bubble by ignoring it.

She alighted at the Porte Maillot and headed for the point where tramlines knit dense patterns against the sky and tram tracks grooved the street.

Stop! No, keep walking.

Two German soldiers sat on a bench near the tram stop, poring over a thick Guide Bleu to Paris.

Do not turn, do not walk away.

She sat at the other end of the bench, heart racing at this proximity to the enemy. The two were deep in discussion, unfolding and smoothing maps bound to the inside cover of their translated guidebook.

Inevitably, one looked across at her and asked in broken French for directions to the Hippodrome in the Bois de Boulogne.

If they walked around the station from which she had emerged, they'd find themselves facing the Bois, and if they joined her on the tram opening its doors before the stop right now, they would pass the Hippodrome they sought. But she turned to them and pointed north.

"Continuez tout droit . . ."

The two thanked her courteously and set off in the direction she pointed. It would be a long time before they realized their mistake.

She closed her eyes for a moment once the tram chimed away. Her first act of resistance—such a small one. Strangely, venting her anger on the soldiers by sending them in the wrong direction brought little satisfaction. Instead, her act of revenge conformed to the trait Hitler had instilled in Germans, that of identifying others by race.

The tram rattled and clanked southwards down the allée de Longchamp past the stately old trees of the Bois de Boulogne. In her teens Noor came to know every inch of the Bois from trotting down its paths with her friend Josianne at the École d'Équitation. Knees tight, she'd urged horses over its small jumps and streams, and cantered tight dressage circles near the polo field.

Now down the boulevard de Boulogne, past the bus stop near the windmill. There were the locust trees under whose leafy shadows she said *adieu* to Armand; that *adieu* that should have been *au revoir* till they met again.

Her throat—dry and empty box. Heart—incinerated rag fluttering in a body cavity. Hands—once more enfolded in Armand's. If only she had some small thing belonging to him.

It was still not dusk when Noor turned down the rue Molitor, though her watch said it was 21:00 hours—nine at night—Berlin time. She stopped before a window filled with mannequins as if to admire it. No one reflected behind appeared to stop. Still, she strolled up the rue Erlanger and back again before she began searching for number 40.

Forty seemed auspicious—the number of days Moses fasted, the number of days Hazrat Issa fasted in the desert. The Prophet, peace be upon him, was forty when the Qur'an was revealed, and forty was the number of years the children of Israel walked in the wilderness. But where was 40 rue Erlanger?

Number 41 sat just next to 36, and number 17 sat beside 24. Number 23 rue Erlanger was behind number 10. The second half of the rue Erlanger continued past the rue Molitor. She passed number 40 several times before she realized—a single-storey house crouching behind its garden far back from the street, crushed between two art nouveau apartment buildings, 41 and 40-bis. So close were the apartment buildings, their walls left no passage between them and number 40. The house seemed to match Miss Atkins's description of its owner. She'd said an old lady, Madame Garry, would be waiting for Noor, that she was the only one who knew Noor would be arriving from London today.

Miss Atkins should have said something about what to do if Madame Garry was not home.

If she isn't here, I'll make my own instructions and follow them.

A caramel-brown turban poked from the shutters of a window next door. Probably the concierge of the apartments, hair bound up for cleaning.

"Leave any packages for number 40 with me," said the towel-head.

Noor waved as if to say this wasn't the address she was looking for. The brown turban retreated. Noor walked away.

A few minutes later Noor returned, unlatched a scrolled iron gate set in the low grille fronting the garden and walked up the stone path.

A serious-looking man of about thirty-five with receding brown hair and a pencil moustache came to the door. Square-shouldered as a claret bottle, with the compressed energy of a pugilist.

"Oui?"

"*Madame Garry est là?* She is expecting me."

Large moss-green patches were sewn about the elbows of his well-pressed grey suit; there *had* to be a Madame Garry somewhere. But every house has its secrets. Was this a Monsieur Garry who didn't know his mother, wife, sister or daughter had agreed to shelter a radio operator from London?

"I am Monsieur Garry."

He did open the door.

Monsieur Garry led her to a drawing room, where a woman about Noor's age came forward from a stool at the piano.

"May I present my fiancée, Mademoiselle Monique Nadaud."

Burnished chestnut curls bobbed shyly at Noor. Merry-eyed Mademoiselle Nadaud was the same height as Noor. An hourglass figure made her worn burgundy dress and grey cardigan look positively chic.

Now a high-nosed woman in her late thirties with a cameo brooch at her lace collar left a game of solitaire spread upon a small table in a nearby alcove. She peered suspiciously at Noor, a single card held close to her chest. A streak of grey ran from the centre parting of her dark hair past her temples to join a tightly knotted bun.

"My sister, Madame Garry. Renée, you were expecting Mademoiselle . . . ?"

"Anne-Marie Régnier."

"*Mais non,*" said Renée. "I was not expecting anyone."

Noor stood disconcerted, looking at the three, till Mademoiselle Nadaud smiled at her. "I was about to prepare coffee," she said.

She and Renée left Noor alone with Monsieur Garry. How to force the issue or retreat gracefully? Noor was . . . mistaken about the house, had a poor memory for numbers—was really looking for number 44 . . .

No. Plunge in.

"The sky is blue," she stammered in a tight, desperate voice. Said to a total stranger it sounded childish, foolish.

But Monsieur Garry responded with a large, welcoming smile, *"But the bread will rise."*

Noor burst out laughing; after a second, Monsieur Garry joined her.

Soon Mademoiselle Nadaud returned with a tray of coffee.

"London doesn't always know what is going on in Paris, Monique," said Monsieur Garry. "Mademoiselle Régnier—Madeleine—was told I was a little old lady."

"Oh, *les Anglais!*" said Renée Garry. "How can they not know you, Émile, after all you've done for them?"

"Not for them, Renée. For us. They help all of us."

"Maybe. Excuse me, I must see if my Babette is still sleeping."

As her heels clicked down a passage, Monsieur Garry and Mademoiselle Nadaud exchanged glances.

"Have you dined?" asked Monique Nadaud as if to change the subject.

"No," said Noor. "Not since last night." She sipped the barley infusion Monique had called coffee, and told them about landing at Le Mans and how she criss-crossed Paris making sure she was not followed.

"Good—be vigilant. Be alert," said Émile.

Monique left the kitchen door open to listen as she goose-necked in and out of cupboards.

Renée returned to the drawing room just as Noor was telling Émile about her jumping into the last carriage on the métro. "You look Jewish," she observed from the far end of the room. She took a half-knitted scarf from a basket beside her chair.

"Mais non, Renée—how can you say that?" Émile asked.

Renée shrugged, stitches clicking rapidly. "She is dark-skinned. Perhaps it is her nose."

No one had ever remarked on the olive tone of Noor's skin or her nose the many years she lived in Paris. Perceptions must have shifted radically in the last three years to match official attitudes. But one person's opinion was no indication of everyone's; in Paris you always found a myriad divergent ones.

"Her nose?" Monique carried a steaming plate to the table in the alcove. "What is it about her nose?"

Disarm with charm.

"My nose smells wonderful French cuisine," said Noor. She took her seat in the alcove, opposite Renée's abandoned solitaire.

"I saw pictures of people who looked just like her at the Palais Berlitz last year."

Noor closed her eyes to say grace. Grace had returned to the family table in London once Uncle Tajuddin was back in India and could no longer protest the prayer as un-Islamic. The ritual touched Noor deeply during food shortages and whenever sharp hunger reminded her of the famine-hungry in India.

Bless us, O Lord, and these Thy gifts which we are about to receive from Thy bounty . . .

She left out "through Christ Our lord," ending with a mental *Ameen.*

"You went to the Exposition?" Émile was saying to Renée in a disbelieving tone.

"Oui, oui. I took Babette so she could see it too."

Noor opened her eyes. "Which exposition?"

"They went to Le Juif et la France," said Monique.

"Non, Renée," Émile was remonstrating.

"Sometimes London sends you Jews," said Renée. "Don't they realize how dangerous that is for you? And she rode in the yellow-star carriage. The Gestapo may already think we are hiding an unregistered Jew."

"The Gestapo may *think*? Gestapo men do not think!"

"Believe me, Émile, she has put us all in danger."

Soothe her—this is her house. And it's almost curfew—where can you go?

"I am not Jewish," said Noor. "And no one followed me here."

Why would they? A nursemaid visiting Paris to see her aunt. Only the truly egocentric believe they are so important.

She glanced at her plate—a pink, spongy slice of canned something on toasted black bread, and boiled vegetables. She took a bite of the vegetables. Delicious.

"Then what are you?" Renée fired at her. "You don't look French. You look different, somehow."

The expression on Émile's face pleaded for Noor to exonerate herself. Monique seemed more dismayed by Renée's discourtesy to a guest than concerned by the question of Noor's heritage.

What was she? The one question for which Noor didn't have a ready answer. Should she tell Renée the olive tone of her skin and the shape of her nose were East Indian and American, but not Jewish? But that would only increase the distance between Noor and Armand. It might also make Renée more uncomfortable; African Muslims were familiar to the French, but Indians might be far from her experience. Renée probably hadn't travelled much, probably considered Paris the cultural pinnacle of the world. She seemed already confused between religion and race; supplying details of many allegiances would only confuse her further.

"I am French enough," said Noor. "I lived here most of my life. And I am also British enough—the combination is common."

"Most of your life!" Monique smiled, striving for levity. "You look about twenty-one."

"I'm twenty-nine," said Noor with droll dignity.

"We care little about origins and ages," Émile said. "What is important, Anne-Marie, is what we can do to defeat the Germans."

"You're a *métèque*." Renée used the street term for a mixed breed.

"Hush, Renée!" said Émile.

The Resistance needed a radio operator; here she was—tired from walking all day, hungry, but very willing to work, even if she was a *métèque* or some other questionable thing. But there was no denying her hybridity, so Noor said only, "My transmitters will arrive soon."

"I will take you to meet Prosper the day after tomorrow," said Émile. "My headquarters is in Le Mans and I stay here with Renée when in Paris. All you need to know is I'm an engineer with the Société Électrochimie. I will call you Anne-Marie from now on."

"You live under your own name?"

"It is only you British whose names don't sound French," said Émile with a teasing smile. "I don't need a cover name. But of course in messages and transmissions I am Phono."

Renée stood abruptly and returned to the kitchen. Through the open door Noor saw her place a wooden crate on the table and begin filling it—socks, a scarf, glass jars of jam, chocolate, even bread.

Noor had finished the vegetables. Delicately, she pulled the bread from under the pink sponge and continued eating.

"My sister is sometimes hasty, Anne-Marie," said Émile in a low voice. "Never unkind, but hasty. Her husband . . ." He glanced at Monique.

"Her husband, Guy, is a prisoner of war in Germany," Monique supplied. "Renée is so alone. How she worries. I help with Babette, after my work, but each day is exhausting for her and she cannot sleep at night. Guy is allowed only two parcels a month and two letters—not really letters, small postcards."

Noor's empathy came naturally, for she too had written letters and sent parcels to Armand on the front during the year-long Drôle de Guerre, the "Funny War" of '39, and longed for him since the Battle of France. In London she had written him many letters in the last three years, but they remained unposted—she did not know a destination. Two postcards from Armand, each with no return address. Oh, for just a glimpse of him, some reassurance! Renée would never know how much she and Noor had in common.

"So many Jews have also become prisoners of war since 1940," Noor observed. "I'm sure Renée is sympathetic."

"*Mais oui*, Anne-Marie!" said Monique. "All of us are sympathetic—it is much worse for them. But what can be done? Every day more Jews are hunted down and rounded up and held in camps. Not POW camps but Jew camps. Émile, how long has it been since the mass roundup at the Vél' d'Hiv'?"

"A year, perhaps?" said Émile.

"And another huge roundup last February. Many are in hiding now," continued Monique. "I work in the Hôtel de Ville, in the office that issues identification cards and ration books. When possible I bring home blank ones for the Jews, for British airmen, for French boys trying to hide from the STO, and for people like you. But you cannot believe what is happening till you have seen Vichy gendarmes breaking into homes, taking old Jewish men, mothers and children, and forcing them onto TCRF buses."

Allah! Were Armand and his mother arrested like that?

The last postcard from Drancy. The blackened lines. Had Armand been subjected to such terrible treatment?

Could she ask Émile or Monique for directions to Drancy? Could she ask anyone? Anne-Marie Régnier couldn't go to a train station and ask for a ticket to Drancy unless she knew where it was and had thought up an acceptable reason to go there.

Could she go there? Could she meet Armand, send him parcels as Renée was doing? Patience! Her hosts were still strangers. Armand was her secret, the secret she'd kept from family and friends alike. After Renée's comments she couldn't confide she was looking for a Jewish man, a dearly beloved Jewish man, and his mother.

Twenty-four hours of involuntary fasting had left her ravenous, but she toyed with the pink sliver on her plate. Was it pork? She shouldn't ask if it was pork.

Ask more questions. Sound merely curious.

"Where do they take them?"

"To camps in France—Compiègne, Pithiviers, Drancy. Places of misery. Then, if one can believe what one reads in *Combat* and *Libération*—and I do—many are being sent east by train, some say to be resettled, some say to work."

"What if they refuse to wear the star?" she asked.

"It's true, some have escaped by not registering. They live among us," said Monique. "We remain silent—that is the best we can do for them."

Armand wouldn't have registered as required by Vichy law; he had an artist's wariness of edicts. Besides, he knew stories told by his refugee cousins and by students to whom he taught French at the Alliance Française. Yes, Armand and Madame Lydia would have relied on the silence of friends—that is, until someone they had relied on turned them in.

"With what are they charged?"

"*Rien!* Absolutely nothing. Yesterday, I was at a tailor's shop and a man was arrested because a book he was carrying covered his yellow star. And the day before, I saw a Jewish woman arrested for shopping at 15:00 hours rather than 16:00 hours," said Émile. "Surely they know of these crimes in London?"

Noor had heard rumours, read newspapers and seen French POWs in newsreels, but all rhetoric was passionate propaganda in England, as elsewhere. How could one know what to believe? Knowledge and power—they were inextricable. Hadn't English newspapers suppressed counter-knowledge of famine reports from British India? Meanwhile, they had published the fictions of India's British district collectors as news. But she had heard tales from escaped POWs at Piccadilly's Café de Paris, or from downed airmen of the RAF who'd escaped out of Marseilles, Le Havre or Spain—tales of repression and mass executions of dissenters, and of unprinted and unprintable German savagery.

For the sake of her own hope she had not wanted, still didn't want, to believe.

Noor's appetite suddenly vanished. Émile's words might apply to Armand. But she would not curb hope on her day of arrival.

Trust Armand. He's a resourceful man with many friends.

Renée returned. What was she looking at? Noor followed her gaze to the small pink tongue left on her plate.

Challenge sparked in Renée's eyes. Plainly, a test lay on the plate before Noor.

It's ham. Eat the ham.

With every disgusting morsel that passed her mouth, she felt Renée relax a little. By the end of the evening the older woman was almost civil.

Flowered curtains drawn tight for blackout, two beds, a dresser and a small cot where a dark-haired little girl lay fast asleep on her side, an arm thrown round a china-faced doll.

"Renée could rent out the other room and get three hundred francs a month for it," said Monique. "But she keeps it like a shrine waiting for Guy, and sleeps here in Babette's room. You'll sleep here too."

"It's difficult for her, I'm sure," said Noor. How many sleepless nights had she spent, thinking of Armand?

"Babette is just nine," whispered Monique, "but so intelligent. Émile is her godfather and like a father to her now. It's three years since she saw her own—she loves him very much."

"And you, I'm sure," said Noor.

"Of course. I bring her boiled bonbons—one needs no ration tickets for those. She says she'll love me more when I am her tata."

"And when will you be her aunt?"

"It was to be three years ago, after Émile was demobilized. Pétain said the war was over. But after the armistice, Émile said the war will be over only when the Germans are defeated, and I agreed we should postpone our wedding. But this year, on Palm Sunday, I said to Émile, I said: 'Émile, if we wait for the whole world to be at peace, we'll never marry. We don't know how long it will take to defeat the Germans. We should marry immediately and continue fighting together.' We have registered our intentions now. We'll be married on the thirtieth of June."

Cool slim fingers touched Noor's, and Noor sighed over each facet of Monique's briolette cut diamond. Armand had offered her a ring many times.

I could have been with Armand now. We too could be fighting together.

"Émile says I'm too young for him, but often I think I am the elder. Our old friends don't come to visit us any more. One's circle shrinks to those one can trust, non?—those who are committed, who cannot suffer by associating with us. And you—you have family in France?"

"No."

"*Bon!* You'll be freer to act. You are married? Non? Then you have a fiancé?"

"Yes." Noor's face warmed. "At least, I think so. I hope so."

"Is the gentleman here in Paris?" Monique's whisper had turned arch.

With Jews being treated as Monique had described, she couldn't say anything close to the truth.

"Oh, no," she said, adding vaguely, "overseas." Most young Englishmen, Frenchmen and many Indians were in the armed forces; why not a mythical fiancé?

There was a pause, then Monique whispered as if she understood the need for secrecy. "It is very difficult to be separated, even for a few weeks. But your presence cheers me, Anne-Marie. It means we are not forgotten, it means liberation will come."

"When did you begin working against the Germans?" asked Noor.

"'The work' as we say? Just after I saw the Boche march down the Champs-Elysées." Monique pulled open dresser drawers. "Not that much was possible then. Émile made leaflets, I made a few forgeries—I'm considered quite an artiste! Then last year I was ordered, along with the other women who work at the Hôtel de Ville, to the Préfecture to work on a card index file. Each card—and there were 27,400 of them—had to be duplicated and sent to Gestapo headquarters. All were foreign-born Jews. We worked for three days."

Noor swallowed, found her mouth dry. If Armand hadn't made evacuation arrangements for Madame Lydia to go south right away in 1940, both might have been arrested and taken to the Vél' d'Hiv' last year. Armand was born in France—but could the Germans redefine him as foreign? Madame Lydia was foreign-born, Russian. To be Russian and Jewish today in occupied France was ten times worse than being British.

"I came home and I said to Émile, I said: 'Émile, the Boche are going to do something terrible.' And they did, with the help of our own gendarmes. It took them a week to arrest fifteen thousand people—all Jews—and they crowded about seven thousand into the stadium with no food or water. I know because it took five of us to count and sort their cards. We still call it the Grand Rafle."

No food or water for so many! The card from Armand was dated April '43, so Armand and Madame Lydia had been arrested after the Grand Rafle. There must have been similar *rafles* in other cities. Or they could have been arrested individually. Which was worse?

"We tried to warn those we could the night before, but some don't speak French or, if they do, speak with accents. Most had no relatives in France. Where were they to flee overnight? Germany, Italy, over the Pyrenees or the Alps? The newspapers said they were all criminals and black marketeers—*c'est impossible!* Are we so stupid to believe that? Then why have they not been charged or tried? The chief of my department at the Hôtel de Ville calls it 'preventive detention'—*c'est incroyable!* Today the Jews are persecuted, and tomorrow we'll all be enslaved."

So obvious it didn't require comment, but it wasn't obvious to most Europeans. Monique's "we" meant France, but her words brought to mind the news buzzing through London's expatriate Indian community. Dadijaan's Urdu newspapers said the number of Indians gaoled in the past year of civil disobedience against the British Raj had risen to thirty-six thousand. Arrests and persecutions were continuing daily in every city. Those arrested had the comfort of knowing they were active protesters against the Occupation of India and, to her knowledge, their ranks didn't include children. But they were no less in gaol, without trial, and still wasting away there like her poor Armand and Madame Lydia. And without breadwinners their families had to survive on savings and charity, and the Brits knew it. Such repression and persecution had been carried out by Europeans with impunity for centuries in the East, but never had it happened in Europe. Had a karmic madness afflicted the continent?

"Can we help them in any way?" she whispered to Monique.

Monique pulled open another drawer, wincing as it creaked, but Babette didn't stir.

"Renée said we could bring our friends here and do the work so long as we don't bring any Jews or Communists. We wouldn't anyway—it is too dangerous to show interest in Drancy or Compiègne or any of the camps. It might attract attention of the Germans to this safe house, to the entire network. And there are Resistance groups working to help Jews. In fact, they have their own organization, the UGIF. They look after the children when the parents are deported." Another drawer scraped open. "*Attendez un peu!* I'm looking for a nightgown for you. I keep a few old clothes of my own here, for escapees and people like you.

"Anyway," Monique continued, rummaging through the clothes, "Émile was so shocked after that roundup, he contacted someone in London and said he was an expert in explosives. He didn't know anything about making bombs, only firing them, but he was in the military and an electrical engineer, so he bought books, went every day to the Bibliothèque Nationale and learned quickly. He even taught me!" She gave a bell-like laugh. "There should be a nightgown right here. Renée keeps every cushion and curtain in place, whereas I—*Voilà!* You're lucky we are about the same size. By the way, you're wearing a well-cut skirt—it's reversible? Maybe I can borrow it sometime to copy the pattern?"

She held up a gilt-edged red book: *Mein Kampf*, the French edition. "And look what else I found—a 'present for newlyweds.' From the German army, when we registered to get married. A present, but we had to pay for it!"

Monique's shoulders shook with repressed laughter at the old practical joke, the same that France historically played on its colonies, Britain on India. The Germans were selling the French whatever they wanted sold. And the French had to buy.

Babette stirred in her sleep; the china doll gazed unblinking at the ceiling. Noor put two fingers to smiling lips. Monique sobered. "You have a long way to go tomorrow, Anne-Marie. And it's late—Émile will take me home before curfew."

In the bathroom adjoining Renée's bedroom, Noor changed into her borrowed nightgown, washed, put on her headscarf and used the bath mat as a prayer rug. She wound her wristwatch, then got into bed and waited for Renée.

If anyone had followed her from Le Mans, Gare Montparnasse or the last carriage of the métro, she would have been arrested by now. She wasn't important enough to be followed—why would they bother?

Even so, vigilance was essential; the Gestapo habit was to come in the middle of the night.

But it had been such a long day. Let the Boche come knocking—she would deal with it then.

Noor thumbed through the magazines on the nightstand between the beds by the light of an oil lamp. *Pour Elle*, a magazine full of airbrushed photos and articles suspiciously similar to the old *Marie Claire*. One called *L'Illustration* had rotogravure photos. And here was one she had never seen: *Femmes de prisonniers*. An article detailed what France's million prisoners of war needed in Germany—tins of condensed milk, shoes, socks, soap, cigarettes, chocolate. Below it, an exhortation to wives of prisoners to keep themselves looking chic. On the next page a column of advice for wives who might have urges to be unfaithful, and in the middle of a column detailing how to refashion a jacket in these times of scarce fabric Noor fell asleep like a stone sinking into water.

CHAPTER 10

Pforzheim, Germany
December 1943

WHEN MONIQUE TOLD ME *about the Grand Rafle, my heart
flooded with anger against the Germans who held Armand and
your grand-mère Lydia in their grasp. Anger was the emotion with
which I was least familiar.*

*When I was growing up, anger in a girl was almost haraam—
forbidden. In its place I allowed myself to feel only hurt or sadness—cover-up feelings, the bomb shelters of the powerless. I never
acknowledged my anger when Abbajaan left us in Paris and died
soon after in India, when Uncle Tajuddin lectured on tolerance but
would not tolerate my marrying Armand, or even when I could not
become your mother, ma petite—you who would be little Babette's
age now.*

*But this time, when anger appeared on behalf of my beloved,
I found my hands trembling with it, could even name it. Every
moment of anger I should have spread over the years seemed to meet
and knot inside me.*

*In the years before the war I was, like everyone in France, all
acquiescence and conciliation and non-aggression. I admired
Monsieur Gandhi, whose non-violence was shaming the occupiers
of India, for he spoke of brotherly love and said that differences
between Hindus and Muslims will be honoured in a free India.*

With other followers of Sufism, I performed namaaz and zikr, meditating to heal the planet. We prayed for the miraculous enlightenment of Fascists everywhere—German and French, Hindu and Muslim. At the time, Monsieur Gandhi had not yet grown feeble from imprisonment, and the future of Muslims in a Hindu-dominated India still held promise. And the dictator in my family, Uncle Tajuddin, still quoted Abbajaan and Rumi.

But where did conciliation and appeasement lead? First to losing you, ma petite, then to losing the one man worth calling husband.

And so, my first night back in Paris, I swore to Allah: I resist all tyranny. Know this, little one, when your spirit returns from hiding in Al-ghayab, the great beyond. Say no to all oppression, whether it rise from those you love or from an enemy, for the shame and self-hatred your mother carries for not resisting when I was younger are worse by far.

It was now too late for doubts. If I had wanted to be protected from the consequences of love and anger, from risk of pain and death, I could have stayed in London, remained a nurse or become a chauffeur in FANY, and no one would have said I hadn't done my part for this war.

Abbajaan said the Sufi trusts his intuition, following it where logic cannot go. He said life's events lead you to encounter your nafs, your base self, and you must surmount it to find your true self.

So I held my anger close that night, and by morning it had turned to renewed resolve: I would reach Armand and tell him to have faith. We will be together again soon.

CHAPTER 11

Paris, France
Thursday, June 17, 1943

NEXT MORNING, Noor closed the door to the safe house behind her. Seven o'clock Berlin time, but a hesitant rose dawn was breaking over the grey roofs of Paris.

It must have been dark when Émile departed an hour ago. Their destinations were the same, but caution prescribed she leave and travel separately.

"Take this bag," Renée said to him. "If by some miracle you find sugar, milk or butter . . ."

Émile promised Renée he'd return with fresh eggs.

Once Émile was gone, Renée served Noor a vile-tasting ersatz coffee and day-old croissants while aiming a stream of admonitions at Babette. *"Ne mets pas les coudes sur la table!"* and Babette took her elbows off the table. *"Tais-toi!"* silenced Babette's shy stirring of conversation with Noor.

"Take the blue dress from the cupboard. Her socks are in that drawer. Give me the hairbrush," she said.

Noor's cover story about being a nursemaid seemed to have come true.

Though habituated to orders from officers, the implicit contempt in Renée's voice irked her. That haughty tone was reserved by Dadijaan for servants in India, and by Mother for the maids in

Suresnes, but it went unused in London, where war afforded no such luxuries.

She was unlikely to meet Renée often during her three weeks in Paris, so there wasn't much reason to object. Instead, as Renée sat before a mirror applying powder, Noor perched on the bed and peered into a jar full of *doryphores*, green locusts Babette had collected on a school outing. They plagued the crops, and the Germans enlisted schoolchildren to kill them.

Was it a sin, Babette asked, to kill the pretty creatures she'd captured? Noor said what she believed: every being deserved life unless it harmed another. That remark drew a snort from Renée. Noor moved on to comfort Babette over a page in her sketchbook where the big-eared, smiling Mickey she had drawn had been defaced with a big black X. The words "degenerate art" appeared below. Babette began to read a homework essay she'd written in her copybook: "Our führer is Adolf Hitler. He was born in Braunau. He is a great soldier who loves children and animals . . ."

Noor was tempted to recite a La Fontaine fable in response, if only to ensure Babette would learn something French, something of her own heritage that would be more helpful in life than the biography of Adolf Hitler. But would a fable recited in school be grounds for punishment? German repression went beyond British disparagement and suppression of the indigenous in India, or French disparagement of Muslim traditions.

Instead, Noor applauded Babette's efforts and began to read the slogans presented after the portrait of Hitler on the frontispiece of her schoolbook. One in particular caught her eye: "Common interest before self-interest." Under it the Victory rune mark of the SS, presumably capable of defining "common interest" for its colonized people.

Then Babette was back, with her sketchbook turned to a page with a large check mark and no comment at all. It showed a bearded man with squinty eyes, thick lips, horns jutting from his curly black hair and a beakish nose.

"That's a Jew," said the nine-year-old. "They have flat feet, they walk differently."

"*Mais non*, Babette. You don't believe that? Surely you don't?"

"Anne-Marie, you have to go now," said Renée. "Babette, *vas-y!* Time for school."

Babette turned Noor's wrist to look at her watch, then nestled into Noor's embrace. "*À bientôt*, Anne-Marie!"

Renée tucked Noor's oilskin coat in the closet by the front door and showed her the flowerpot where a spare key to the apartment lay in case Noor needed to stay in Paris again, a gesture that compensated for her sharp remarks on Noor's arrival.

Still, Noor was glad to be out of Renée's home, walking past beds of cabbage and carrots to the gate, breathing fresh morning air.

Following instructions, Noor avoided the obelisk at the métro entrance in the Place d'Auteuil. She passed signs in shop windows: *Pas de sucre. Pas de lait. Pas de beurre.* The Seizième Arrondissement was not as busy at this hour as she remembered.

Loud, angry voices.

She rounded a corner and came upon a crowd of women standing in a ragged queue outside a *boulangerie* waiting as the baker rolled open his canvas awning. A few doors away a shop bore a sign, *Entreprise Juive*, in red. The colour signified the shop was now under Aryan ownership. Black, gouged holes said it had probably been plundered, its contents sold.

Where are its Jewish proprietors now?

Three dark maidens lifted the heavy dome of the Richard Wallace drinking fountain above their heads—much like poor women in India labouring on construction sites, except that these were not women of flesh and blood.

On the rue La Fontaine she passed an art nouveau house with a medieval turret and cast-iron balconies, then a park before a neo-Gothic chapel.

Trying to take a circuitous route to her destination, as prescribed by her instructors at Wanborough, was boring, and she had blisters from all her walking the previous day. She headed directly to the avenue Mozart and the métro at the end of the rue Jasmin. She took the métro as far west out of the city as it extended, to the Porte Maillot. Following instructions again, she went to the Objets Trouvés and asked the man at the counter for a bicycle that was lost, and might now be found, giving the licence plate number specified by Émile.

The bicycle was wheeled out to her, along with a loudly delivered homily on the presence of thieves who would not hesitate to steal so fine a bicycle if mademoiselle wasn't more careful next time. Noor hoisted her bag off her shoulder into the front basket and rode away into the summer warmth of the country.

Sunlight strengthened as Noor pedalled down the black ribbon of road past fields of rapeseed and wheat. Her hair lifted like a warm cape against her shoulders till she stopped, took a rubber band from her handbag, tied it into a ponytail and pedalled on.

How unthinkable that this beautiful land could be invaded. How could Paris have fallen before Hitler? But it had, and the fall divided all of Noor and Armand's yesterdays from today.

When Armand came home on leave from the Maginot line early in the spring of 1940, he asked again, had Uncle Tajuddin agreed to their marriage?

"No," Noor said, "but he will, or Kabir will."

"Noor," he said, "we've known each other almost nine years—nine years of loving, meeting, parting and hoping in secret. How long can we wait?"

"I know, *chéri*. But my family is everything I know. How can I live and never see them again?"

Blue eyes looked into hers. "I don't choose for you," he said.

"Could you leave Madame Lydia and never see her again?"

"Noor, each of us has the right to live without fear. Your uncle, your mother, your brother—they hold you hostage but call it love. We could marry in Switzerland, in England or anywhere outside France, if you gave yourself permission."

It was true, Armand said, that Europe was regressing to chaos, but not as far back as some Neanderthal era in which men dragged away the women they wanted by the hair, or sweated the labours of Hercules to win the damsel of their desires. Nor was he a Svengali, as Uncle and Kabir seemed to think, casting Noor in the role of his feeble-minded dupe. They were, Armand said, civilized people in a civilized country with progressive ideas and relations that surely could be reconciled. But at the time, the stakes were higher for Noor than for Armand. Armand would gain a wife; Noor would lose a family.

"Someday," said Armand, "you'll choose whose life you'll live—the life your family planned for you or one of your own."

Hoping those two lives could be one, Noor ventured to ask Kabir to meet Armand. But Kabir . . .

Armand came into my life to free me from fear, to teach me laughter, generosity and kindness. Through his actions he taught me the principles: my life is my own, my soul and my body my own. But claiming my own life or body was just a lovely idea when Uncle Tajuddin was arranging to marry me off in India.

A firebud of hope bloomed within her.

What was impossible then might be possible now.

The only animals grazing today were sparse and scrawny. The fields she remembered—for instance, on that day Abbajaan took the whole family to Versailles in the Amilcar for a picnic—were full of dappled, cud-grinding cows, puffy black-eared sheep and powerful percherons.

At Versailles, Abbajaan had walked past foaming fountains, left Mother preening in its sumptuous Hall of Mirrors and the guide extolling the Sun King for spending sixty million livres to build that temple to himself. He didn't show his children the secret door where Marie Antoinette escaped from the revolutionary mob, or the diary entry where, on the day of the storming of the Bastille, Louis XVI wrote "nothing happened," but stood in the marble courtyard to show his children where the king greeted his subjects from a balcony. There Abbajaan explained the concept of *darshan*, how the sight of an enlightened being or the king, assuming him to be enlightened as the maharaj of Baroda, brings the one who sees—in the Sanskrit term, the *dixit*—a blessing.

Noor and Kabir dutifully tried to imagine a blessing from the chicken-legged Sun King.

"Try," Abbajaan continued, "to become people who see beyond what your eyes tell you. Use all your senses, and your *ajna*, your third eye. See the invisible—Al-ghayab."

Kabir and Zaib had played hopscotch in the courtyard as he spoke, but Noor was old enough to understand.

A wind-breaking row of poplars provided a cool patch of shade, then she was out in the open again. She took deep lungfuls of air with each wheel-whirring movement, but even so, her hands were soon sliding on the handlebars.

Boys walked the footpaths between hedgerows, carried rakes and hoes far too large for them. A man bending over a shrub straightened as she passed, the curve never leaving his back.

Where were the young men? In England, she, Mother, Dadijaan and Zaib had slept many a night in Mother's basement kitchen armed with pumps, buckets and Dadijaan's good luck amulets, and often said namaaz over the boom and smash of falling bombs and debris; but the sight of strong young men like Kabir in the streets, in small towns, almost all in uniform, was comforting. In Paris, and here, young Frenchmen had been spirited away—some, like Armand, to camps in France, some, like Renée's husband, to Germany.

She cycled past a couple of well-dressed women incongruously carrying *panier* baskets. City women; their expressions said they would rather be elsewhere. They must be on their way to pick their own fruits and vegetables. A snub-nosed truck with a crooked tail caught her eye—a *gazogène* tractor. A few fields away, a shapeless woman in kerchief and clogs whacked an emaciated horse straining in the traces of a plough. Both looked as if they were weathering the nineteenth, rather than the twentieth, century.

Sweat prickled at Noor's eyebrows, her eyes itched as if gnawed by the wind. Her thighs, strong as she was, were stiffening against her will, her calves threatening to knot into a cramp.

She dismounted, wheeled the bicycle to stretch her legs for a while till she came to an incline, then pumped up the low hill, riding the balls of her feet, crested the top and sat down, jarring on the husk-shaped seat, bruising her inner thigh once more.

Twenty kilometres had spun away behind Noor.

Only five to go.

Pforzheim, Germany
December 1943

Pedalling to Grignon, I had none of the hesitation that rises from knowledge; I had yet to come upon the peaks and troughs of circumstance. Yes, I had been told but did not comprehend how the war had made France a place where the ordinary and the dangerous could not be differentiated, like a desert where you cannot tell snake from rock, rock from cactus.

I thought of the sketches and slogans Babette showed me. If you were her age in France then, you too might have written such praiseful essays to a worshipper of Death, would have been asked to draw your internal demons and call them Jews.

But I put aside those thoughts. That day I was glad to be in France, nearer to Armand.

My captor Vogel wants me to write stories for his children. But every story I've written since 1934 has been for you, ma petite. In 1938, I translated Buddhist stories you'll read someday. My book is called Twenty Jataka Tales. *I wrote my own stories for you, too, and they were published in the newspaper* Le Figaro.

Nineteen thirty-eight. Dadijaan had just arrived to stay with us when news of Kristallnacht rippled through Paris. A Jewish man traced the German deporter of his parents to Paris, and shot him. In retaliation Hitler ordered "spontaneous" demonstrations against

Jews everywhere. In panic for Armand's family, I telephoned him again. Although four years had passed since our last meeting, it was as if we had parted the day before. I asked if he knew people, or was related to people, who were affected.

"Of course I do," he said.

Once a week, after his piano students or practice, Armand had begun volunteering at the Alliance Française on the boulevard Raspail. He taught French to refugees and immigrants from Russia and Germany, mostly Jewish, and many whose only crime was to disagree with the Nazis. Stories poured in from his students after Kristallnacht, and though your father is an explorer, open to all faiths, not only Judaism, he was incensed. "Two hundred synagogues, Noor! A licence to loot and destroy ten thousand shops! Five million marks' worth of shattered glass, and Hitler wants the Jews to compensate for damages, demanding a billion marks!"

In the piano room at Mademoiselle Nadia Boulanger's, we turned to music for comfort. Music cannot tell if its performer be Muslim, Jew or Christian; French, German, English or Indian. All afternoon we played duets, improvising snatches of jazz, my knee touching his as we reached for the pedals. Afterwards we stopped at a Boulant restaurant on the boulevard St-Michel and ordered one crêpe for two. Then upstairs to your father's apartment—bodies thirsting, clinging, desperate to love—but we were more careful this time.

With Armand, I was unconscious of being woman, unconscious of him as man. With him I could act, and he had liberty to feel. I loved him for what he confided to me, the glimpse of his forbidden inner core, for the things I could say only to him when he shared my body and was enclosed by me. In those moments there was nothing impermeable between us, no trivial differences to separate us.

His weight shifted above me and he said, "I am outside and inside you at the same time." Then he kissed me, said how much he loved me. I must remember this.

Joy and pain came together without distinction, joy in our inter-penetration so that active became passive, pain that I could not bridge the barrier of his skin to know how he felt—one day you'll find such pain is part of desire, ma petite.

"How does it feel," I wondered aloud, "to be a man?"

You see, I could ask him such things.

He gave a surprised laugh. I waited as his thoughts formed to the precision of words. "I was never anything other than a man— how can I answer?"

"But you must have thought about it." My fingers slid over his short beard, chest, then down, committing his shape to tactile memory.

"I've never thought about it," he said, as if realizing. "I'm a man—that's all." His thumb moved at the wedge of my clavicle, massaging my back, returned to my throat. His fingertips followed my gold chain to my breasts, traced the gold frame of my tiger claw.

"It's cut from the carcass of a great beast slain by my ancestor, Tipu Sultan, the Tiger of Mysore," I told him. "A tigress, perhaps. Maybe she was hunting or in defence of her cubs. I often wonder about the women who wore it before me for luck and courage. Armand, haven't you ever wondered what it would be like to be a woman? Today or perhaps in another time?"

"Never, chérie."

"Or another man?" I ventured.

He considered this, delving into childhood, adolescence, coming closer to now. "I have often wondered how my father felt when he arrived from Moscow after the famine."

Your grandfather came to Paris in 1892 because every university in Moscow had filled its 3 percent quota for Jews. He dreamed of being an engineer—but except for the Great War, laboured the rest of his life on the line at Renault.

"Did you ever ask him?" I said.

"No, and now that he's gone I can't."

Your father and I were both fatherless, you see.

Armand rolled away, cupped his hand over a match, lit an Anoushka. *That smell always reminds me of him.*

"My mother still has all his military decorations," he said.

I must tell you about your grandmother Madame Lydia, Armand's mother. She was born a Catholic, and sometimes went to mass. But she took the ritual bath and converted to Judaism, and joined your grandfather in France. When Armand was born in Paris, she learned to raise him as a Jew. Armand took me to meet her the very first Rosh Hashanah after we met, and she accepted me immediately. I was born in Moscow like her, she said. She told me about the first time she made challah, and showed me the slippers she wore to dance Raymonda under ballet master Petipa in Moscow. But all she could get, when after long waiting she received her permis de travail in France, were parts in Folies Bergères revues. Of course, she wouldn't take them; she preferred to manage the laundry department at the Hôtel Lutétia. She always had visitors to stay, and as I got to know her, I found they were ever more distant "relatives"— and so many came with children that Armand had to rent a second apartment, a garçonnière, where he could keep regular hours, composing. Someday, ma petite, you will taste her special kasha, her poppy-seed cakes, her borscht and blinis.

When he first heard of our love in early 1934, my uncle shouted that he had no objection whatsoever to Armand's religion and, not being Christian, had no tradition of hatred against Jews; that he objected only to Armand's mother's work "as a washerwoman." If that one fact were different, he said, he might have agreed to our marriage, if only to save my tarnished reputation. But since Armand could not change his mother or her past (nor wished to, being so proud of her), my uncle's impossible condition was just another way of forbidding our marriage; a way he could continue talking to his students about Sufi Muslim traditions of love and tolerance and the Universal God of all faiths, and at the same time continue promising my hand in marriage to my cousin Allahuddin in Baroda, even as he knew I wept in my room.

"And you—you plan to leave me and return to Moscow?" I asked Armand, pouting a little.

"I'll take you to visit Moscow one day, but if my family wanted to live as subjects of Moscow and remain Russian, wouldn't my father

have stayed there? Non, I don't like the thought of Moscow control-
ling France. Those who care for the French people should govern it."

"I have a Russian passport somewhere," I reminded him.

"That will save time when we visit—you won't have to apply for
one!"

We laughed together at bureaucracy then, never realizing how
deep its tentacles could reach.

I rose, wound a sheet around me and tipped the long mirror in
the corner of the room upright. I let the sheet fall like a wing veiling
me till he came close, put his arms around me from behind.

"Which do you prefer," I asked with the mirror before us, "me or
your image of me?"

"You," he said, resting his hands on my shoulders and kissing
the nape of my neck, understanding both the question and my need
to ask it. It would be the question I asked my brother a year later,
but though Kabir also answered "You," his actions showed he preferred the sister in his looking glass.

But Armand's answer reassured me, and we returned to the still-
warm sheets and held one another as we talked.

"Have you ever wanted to live as someone else for a while, just
to see if you could do it? Transcend your self, my Abbajaan used to
say . . ."

But your father was, as the French say, bien dans sa peau—
comfortable in his skin. More than I was, then.

"No. I am human and a Jew," he said. "Every day I hold fast to
that belief."

Armand didn't need to explain. Even before Kristallnacht, new
German restrictions for Jews were broadcast every day, wherever Hitler
ruled, restrictions Uncle and so many others in France didn't notice.

"Not in France," I tried to reassure Armand. "Kristallnacht
would never happen in France. France is different. Remember the
Rights of Man, and Liberté, Égalité, Fraternité, non?"

"I hope you are right," he said.

But I was wrong, so very wrong, for it did happen in France. The
things we thought could occur only in Germany happened.

Tolerance vanished overnight the moment war was declared the next year, and like many French people who had read articles about the "Jewish Peril," Uncle began to talk about Jewish conspiracies, even quoted the Qur'an. But I know my Qur'an—Abbajaan taught it to me very well. I didn't need Uncle to quote it, nor was there such hatred in it as he said, for Jews or any others. The unbelievers it speaks of are those who, professing Islam or not, have never yet touched the spirit of Allah. And for each concession I made to intolerance in my home, appeasing and placating Uncle Tajuddin and his campaign to keep our family's blood pure, the world conceded to and placated Hitler and his Nazi thugs. It wasn't long before your father sat in the bunkers warding off the disease of purism that would soon invade France.

When your spirit enters this world, ma petite, may you remember this: If you speak of tolerance while planting a hedge between yourself and your neighbour, as my uncle Tajuddin did, as many in France did, your hedge will one day be replaced by a fence, then a low wall, then a high wall, and finally fortifications.

Grignon, France
Thursday, June 17, 1943

A short distance past the train station and the swastika-draped front of the *mairie* building, through the market square, and the village of Grignon was left behind.

Every Hindu temple she'd seen in India had its swastika, a health charm—*swast* being Sanskrit for "health"—so common it was woven into the fabric of women's saris. Even in Europe the twisted cross was older than tyranny itself, ubiquitous, spokes bent right for male power, left for female. But for the Germans it meant one power only—male. What ego! Red for blood, white for Aryan purity and black for Hitler's intent to obliterate "others." Mr. Jinnah, the leader of the Muslim League of India, must feel the same terror of extinction as Noor at this moment, watching the power of the swastika rising in India. For the first time she understood Mr. Jinnah's fear of a Hindu mobocracy that could, if independence came, set out to annihilate Muslims in India, and why Mr. Jinnah was agitating for a separate homeland he called Pakistan.

More and more separation, bane of our very existence. What a terrible idea.

Rolling fields bordered a stretch of bumpy country road. Past the fields the road flowed into the gloom and the woody scent of a pine and oak game forest. The road behind her was empty; no one was following.

She set her shoulders and cycled on, arriving at high stone porticos marking the entrance to the Institut National Agronomique.

Inside, ancient trees swayed above her. A familiar scent whiffed past. Horses—a stable. Long dark blouse-coats—students walking by the road. Noor squeezed her brakes, stopping beside a pleasant-faced young woman wearing clogs and carrying a clipboard.

"The library? Straight ahead past the director's château you'll see the administration buildings in a horseshoe to your right. The classroom buildings are the long ones on your left. Pass them and turn left at the crossing. You'll be in front of the Grand Château. Enter at the far end, near the woods. The library is upstairs."

Noor thanked her, wiped her brow with her handkerchief and continued. Handlebars bumped beneath her sore palms as the road ran downhill past a large greenhouse and a shuttered shop. Past the horseshoe of the administration buildings her mount settled as the road widened into a crossing. Noor dismounted beside flower-framed, rectangular lawns and wheeled her bicycle across the expanse of a courtyard where, a few decades ago, horses must have pawed the ground in anticipation of the hunt. The brown-and-cream façade of the Grand Château of the institute towered above.

Allah! I'm late again.

She leaned her bicycle against the stone wall of the château, taking her handbag from the basket. Entering, she climbed wooden stairs worn concave over the years. A door creaked open, releasing the scent of yellowed paper.

At the centre of the high-ceilinged room lined with glass-faced cabinets, Émile Garry's elbow patches rested on a time-polished table. He was in hushed conversation with two older gentlemen, so Noor waited in the doorway, handbag clutched uncertainly before her, till he noticed.

He rose immediately, came forward to greet her with Gallic courtesy. "Ah, Mademoiselle Régnier. We were beginning to worry. May I present Monsieur Hoogstraten, director of the institute . . ."

Mr. Hoogstraten's smooth face, whose forehead rose all the way into a shiny bald pate fringed with silver, glowed in a wide smile of greeting. The military set of his shoulders relaxed. "Enchanté, mademoiselle."

" . . . and Professor Balachowsky."

The Professor rose with a slight bow. The unused end of his belt stuck out past its buckle at least a foot. A pipe rose to his lips. He came to Noor's side.

"So this is the mademoiselle from London?" Kindly brown eyes twinkled above a moustache and sparse goatee, like those of an Indochine elder. Beard and moustache were seasoned with grey, and he puffed at the pipe as if from habit, though no smoke rose.

"This is Madeleine," said Émile Garry. "Alias: Anne-Marie Régnier."

"Ah, Madeleine," said Monsieur Hoogstraten. "How is your Colonel Buckmaster?"

"Very well, monsieur."

"Please, be seated," said Monsieur Hoogstraten.

Émile held a chair and seated Noor as if she were made of blown glass. Monsieur Hoogstraten took Professor Balachowsky's elbow and whispered.

Professor Balachowsky nodded and took his pipe from his mouth. "Mademoiselle Régnier, could you wait for us for just a few minutes?"

"Certainly," said Noor.

He turned to a huge door that almost reached the ceiling. "*Tu viens*, Émile?"

Alone in the library, Noor drew near the windows. A black cat stepped gingerly below, balancing on the stone wall of a dry moat that separated the château from fields. Unlucky, according to Mother. Abbajaan always said they were lucky.

If I marry Armand again, it will mean black cats are lucky.

As she turned back to the room, a sparkle caught Noor's eye; a chandelier's prisms winked from the door left slightly ajar. Noor glimpsed the three men gathered around a long table with stark black shapes arranged on its white tablecloth. Émile was nodding as Monsieur Hoogstraten pointed—Sten guns, pistols, incendiaries, grenades, explosives.

Noor moved away. The weapons must be from the canister hidden under her seat in the Lysander, or one just like it. Émile, Monsieur Hoogstraten and Professor Balachowsky must be, under orders from Prosper, coordinating weapons distribution for safekeeping. Only Prosper would know how much had been secreted away till now throughout northern France.

Gilt lettering on the spines of the leather-bound books in the glass cases: Jean-Jacques Rousseau's *Du contrat social* and his *Discourse on the Origin and Foundations of Inequality in Mankind*, a few French translations of Trotsky and Freud, André Maurois's *History of England*, another about travelling in Germany by a Henri Bordeaux.

When Noor first met Armand, she needed to borrow something from him so she would have some excuse to see him again. He loaned her books from his bedchamber—distilled summaries of whole areas of his life before their first meeting. And Noor loaned him Rumi for his Rousseau, the Qur'an for his Old Testament, Tagore for his Tolstoy, the poet Kabeer's *Bijak* for a Balzac novel. Then secret meetings at the library in Suresnes, debates in passionate whispers.

Oh, Armand, how shall I find you? The country we knew and loved has grown strange.

Monsieur Hoogstraten, Professor Balachowsky and Émile Garry returned to the room. And as if on cue, a walrus-whiskered, leathery face appeared at the library door.

"Marius," said Émile, "I was just on my way to find you." To Noor he said, "Marius is one of the gardeners here at Grignon. We call him Master of the Greenhouse, *n'est-ce pas?*"

A light crept into Marius's black eyes. He stood, cap in hand. Émile showed Marius to the Grand Salle.

"Come, messieurs," said Monsieur Hoogstraten. "We have much to do, but at this moment Madame and my daughter are waiting for lunch. I invite you, mademoiselle, to see your new home."

CHAPTER 12

FROM THE COURTYARD before the library, Noor and the three men walked up the central path to Director Hoogstraten's château on the hill. Noor left them to wheel her bicycle to the shed at the back. At her knock, a woman in a black dress with a frilly white cap and apron peered from the screen door of the kitchen.

"Anne-Marie Régnier," said Noor.

The maid turned a latch, opened the door a crack, and a sleek black shape shot past Noor into the house and jumped up on the kitchen counter. A chef, hunched over an enamel bowl, started in surprise. *"Chat lunatique!"* The gloom filled with the whisked rhythm of judiciously chosen imprecations.

The maid scooped the cat out of his reach and held it close, crooning, "Ooh, Mignonne, Mignonne!"

Noor followed the maid through the dining room, where a long table was set for lunch, then a salon with Louis XIV–style furniture, to Madame Hoogstraten's sitting room.

Madame Hoogstraten, a kind-looking woman with sandy hair rolled fashionably high, rose from her escritoire and greeted Noor. A sautoir necklace of pearls flowed down her black dress, the tassel ending beneath her waist.

Mother's style, worn in a French way.

The cat sprang from the maid's arms into the open drawer of Madame Hoogstraten's desk, evidently her accustomed spot.

Madame Hoogstraten asked Noor conversational but probing questions. "How old? Married? Ah! Engaged. Your fiancé is where? Ah, Londres. I was there a few times before the war—I love Walter Scott and Madame Tussaud. You too? Ahhh. You lived here how long? Ahhh! Many years. Your father? A teacher of philosophy. Which lycée did you attend? Ah! Not far from here—and afterwards? L'École Normale de Musique? Six years of the piano—you must be quick-fingered on the wireless. And after that? The Sorbonne. Of course. *Vous avez reçu une bonne éducation. Vos parents vous ont bien elevée.*"

Well educated, well brought up. This being verified, Madame was welcoming, showing Noor to the WC so she could wash her hands before lunch.

Madame's questions had to be asked and answered, regardless of the SOE's training and instructions. Passwords and code names could not replace instinctive ways of building trust, forming friendships. And the first requirement in her line of work was the trust of her fellow agents.

Laughter pealed from an inner room. Madame Hoogstraten's brow furrowed. She went to the door and called, "Odile?" A laugh rang out once more. "Odile?"

A pixie-faced, dark-haired girl with striking green eyes came running, bubbling with barely contained mirth.

"What *are* you doing?" Madame Hoogstraten's voice sharpened.

"It's Monsieur Gilbert!" said Odile. "He told me to tie him up very tightly. What an ingenious agent he is—now he can't get free!"

Madame Hoogstraten's lips twitched. "Where is the monsieur now?"

"*Là!*" Odile gestured behind her. "I tied him to the chair. I took the rope and wound it round him. I even tied his hands together behind his back . . ." She broke down in giggles.

"Free him immediately. It's time for lunch."

"Yes, Maman."

"Young people!" said Madame Hoogstraten. "Excuse her, please—she's only seventeen." Responding to Noor's amusement, she said, "Odile doesn't act like a child too often. In fact, sometimes I think her father gives her too much responsibility—but these days, who else can he trust? You'll sleep in her room. If the servants ask who you are, say you're my cousin, visiting for a few weeks."

The men were now assembled in the salon. Professor Balachowsky produced a bottle of wine from his briefcase, opened it, and left it to breathe on the sideboard. Gilbert was a little rumpled but no worse for his misadventure with Odile, his grin raffish as ever. Behind him was a short, gloomy menhir of a man whom no one introduced. When they moved to the long dining table, Noor found herself motioned to a seat between him and Gilbert.

"Archambault." The code name for the radio operator she was to replace. She had the feeling she had met him before.

"Madeleine," she said.

The glare beneath his knit brows did not relax. A pause lengthened to the point of discomfort.

"She gave the correct recognition phrase, Archambault," Émile said, taking his seat across from Noor.

Now she was sure she had met the gloomy man, years ago. "Be most careful," Miss Atkins had said, "to stay away from anyone who could recognize you from before the war." But Archambault was a member of her cell; she couldn't avoid him.

"You were in my brother's class at the lycée," she said.

Archambault picked at his teeth with a toothpick. "Your brother's name?"

It was a challenge question.

"Kabir Khan."

"The Indian boy. How is it you remember me?"

"You were a tenor soloist in the choir, yes? You once sang one of my favourites, the Benedictus from Bach's B Minor."

His serious face lightened slightly. The memory of a time before the war made the difference, like the possibility of return to one who roams in a strange country.

"B minor—yes, key of passive suffering. For myself, I prefer his Agnus Dei aria. G minor, the key of tragic consummation. I have the record at home." He put the toothpick away. "We will work together after lunch," he said, as if according her a great favour. "We must tell London you have arrived."

"My transmitters are not yet here."

"We will use one of mine."

"Is Prosper here?" asked Noor. The package wrapped in brown paper in the hidden compartment of her handbag must be delivered soon.

"You will meet him."

Professor Balachowsky offered a first taste of wine to Monsieur Hoogstraten, and once the bouquet was pronounced acceptable, measured carefully into each long-stemmed glass.

"It's a Vouvray—1934," he said.

It was a gesture of welcome. Noor took a sip and smiled her thanks.

In London's social circles the war would be intentionally ignored, like an amateur's mural on the walls of a dining room, Hitler's bombing being considered in very poor taste. But it was not ten minutes before the group at the château was deep in passionate discussion about the war. This was no social occasion, but a meeting.

Monsieur Hoogstraten passed the cheese soufflé along with the latest developments. "Terrible, terrible news: the Germans have arrested General Vidal."

"Vidal" was a code name for the head of General de Gaulle's Armée Secrète, taking shape for a little over six months, since late 1942. Noor had heard more about General Vidal's second-in-command, Jean Moulin, the legendary *Max*, who had travelled undercover through France earlier that year, calling on disparate Resistance groups—Combat, Libération, Action Chrétienne and La France—to unite.

Monsieur Hoogstraten paused for a moment, then seemed to recover. "Judging from the large number of Sten guns, incendiary bombs and grenades we've received in the last few weeks, the Allies must surely be planning the invasion soon."

He glanced at Noor as if seeking confirmation from the latest arrival from London. She gave him a blank look. He continued.

"More than 1,000 Stens, approximately 1,800 bombs and nearly 4,500 grenades—we are storing arms from the drops as fast as we can, but it's difficult." Worry flickered in his eyes. "There isn't enough manure in the stables to cover it all—the Germans have taken most of our horses. Prosper tells me shipments will double this month, and double again in July."

"*Mon Dieu!* We'll have to double the manure, and double it again in July," said Odile.

Madame Hoogstraten's spoon tapped the table. A look of utter innocence came over Odile's face.

"Archambault," continued Monsieur Hoogstraten, "six more canisters must be disposed of tonight. Marius and two students will go with you."

Archambault nodded.

"Where will you dispose of them this time?" Gilbert's voice was worried.

"In the Seine," Archambault said with laconic simplicity.

Monsieur Hoogstraten focused on Noor. "Madeleine, you will send messages only from myself, Émile or Professor Balachowsky."

"And myself?" prompted Gilbert.

Monsieur Hoogstraten hesitated. "And Gilbert. Professor Balachowsky, please give us your report."

"Only good news from the Versailles region," said the Professor, chewing away at his unlit pipe. "From Rueil this time. On June 13 our saboteur blew up a barrack occupied by German troops. Thirty-eight German soldier casualties."

A low cheer echoed around the table.

"None killed, unfortunately. At Argenteuil, on the fifteenth of June, a charge set by Émile destroyed a detachment of German military, wounding thirteen." A second cheer fell away as the Professor added, "Unfortunately, three of them were French civilians, but . . . it's a war. Every French martyr is one more step in the fight against the Occupation."

He looked around. No one objected. He continued. "There is news from Dourdan that gives us courage. After exiting a cinema, spectators marched up and down the streets of the city singing the Marseillaise."

Madame Hoogstraten offered Noor a tomato salad garnished with chervil, then a platter bearing a wheel of desiccated brie. It was Ramzaan, but she was travelling; she'd make up her missed days of fasting when she returned to London.

"For July 14, we plan an operation at Houdan—resistants will take back the Monument of the Dead and observe a minute of silence. Of course, there are demonstrations planned in Paris, some at Versailles. Please be very careful in the next four weeks. The Germans know well the symbolic importance of Bastille Day, and will be quick to make examples of any suspicious behaviour. Last week one of my men in Paris was arrested, not for listening to Radio London but for listening to General de Gaulle broadcasting on Radio Alger."

"Ah, Gaullisme!" Gilbert rolled his eyes.

Odile said, "Then who shall we listen to? General de Gaulle is recognized all over the world."

"But not yet by Monsieur Roosevelt." Gilbert wagged his finger at her.

"Then Monsieur Roosevelt does not understand yet: Gaullisme is no longer incarnated in de Gaulle. It is no longer just a movement, a spirit, a tendency—but a spiritual force. One we can trust—unlike Vichy!"

"Mademoiselle Odile, neither your father nor I have elected General de Gaulle our leader."

"Monsieur Gilbert, when the war is over, everyone will vote for him. Give me a vote and I will too."

"Odile!" Madame Hoogstraten frowned.

Noor revelled in the rapid French flowing about her, surprised how deeply she had missed its melodic cadence during her three years in London. Not only French but the lively interruptions, the rapier thrusts of teasing between friends, and the tangential drift of conversations. Evidently the institute was better supplied with food than Renée Garry's little apartment in Paris, and even this wartime meal was served with an élan Londoners might envy. What a pity she couldn't belong to this group longer than her allotted three weeks. Their determination and dedication were contagious.

Gilbert was saying to Professor Balachowsky that when he was eighteen years old, he saw Lindbergh land at Le Bourget airfield. "The roads were jammed with cars, so my friends and I rode the métro all the way to the end, to Le Bourget–Drancy station."

Drancy?

"There we waited and waited in a muddy field well past dark with a hundred thousand others. Of course, I didn't know then that we were so many. All I could feel was the man before me and two more pressing on either side. Sometimes, while we're waiting for planes from England now, it reminds me of that night—that same fear of danger, the same rush of excitement at the daring of the pilot in his little plane. Then we saw tiny dots, lights weaving and circling in the night." A prone hand demonstrated over Madame Hoogstraten's Limoges. "With just one man." The hand wavered and descended slowly to the tablecloth. "And he landed! The first flight over the Atlantic! Thirty-five hundred miles in thirty-three and a half hours, with just a compass, an airspeed indicator, favourable weather and luck."

Drancy was near Le Bourget airfield. Noor knew the airfield was somewhere in the industrial suburbs of Paris, but she had never been there. She listened closely as Gilbert continued.

"We rushed past the restraining ropes so fast that those in the front could have been killed by his propeller, and we were all shouting 'Vive Lindbergh!' and clapping, and I was waving my hat as if I'd gone mad. None of us slept that night. We were raising glasses to Lindbergh in every bistro in Paris."

When Lindbergh made the first crossing of the Atlantic, Kabir was only eleven, yet that epic flight, and that of Bellonte and Captain Costes soon afterwards, had changed the course of her brother's life as it had Gilbert's.

"The next morning we went to the Hôtel de Ville, and I watched the president shake hands with Monsieur Lindbergh and give him the Orteig Prize. It was a great moment, a moment when I knew here"—he struck his breast—"that I would be a flyer."

"And Monsieur Lindbergh greeted you by name?" Odile snickered, setting off a bout of verbal sparring with Gilbert.

Noor could visit Armand at Drancy simply by taking the métro!

She would excuse herself that very moment, leave now.

But Archambault was looking at his watch. "Time to transmit."

Neither war nor Occupation had affected the midday ritual of her childhood milieu. This three-hour lunch would have lasted a maximum of an hour in London.

Monsieur Hoogstraten rose, saying to all and no one in particular, "I will be in my office."

This permitted all to rise.

"I have a meeting," said Professor Balachowsky, excusing himself with a small bow to Noor. "I am organizing a student expedition in a few days. We shall discover and classify many insects," he promised with touching enthusiasm.

"Anne-Marie," Émile Garry whispered, "Prosper will meet you tomorrow morning."

He took a leather-bound notebook and pencil from his pocket and drew a small map, wrote the password. He showed it to her and, once she nodded, tore them to pieces.

"I am expected in Paris," he said to all, putting notebook and pencil away. "*Mais, nom de Dieu!* I almost forgot—" He foundered in embarrassment. "Madame Hoogstraten, I was wondering, are there . . . perhaps . . . if you can . . . spare some eggs?"

Madame Hoogstraten nodded graciously. Émile brightened.

When again ready to leave, he whispered to Noor, "Tomorrow, 11:00 hours, Chez Tutulle. Take extra precautions. Be sure you are not followed."

Noor followed Archambault out of the director's château, across the wide drive leading downhill into the institute. He collected Marius at the institute's garden shop, then led her towards a greenhouse whose shining glass roof nestled beneath chestnut trees. Two huge desert palms framed the doorway. Noor hadn't seen desert palms this size since her stay in India.

"Monsieur Hoogstraten wants to grow one plant from each corner of the world at the institute," said Marius.

"Mind the nettles," said Archambault.

"*Enh!* No nettles here," said Marius. "Those grow in the ditch by the road."

Noor followed him into dim, glazed verdure.

Scent of humid soil, flowers . . . green. The fragrance of the Prophet's colour.

"We can't transmit from in here," said Archambault.

"Too much metal?"

Archambault nodded, continuing past neat rows of Latin-labelled plants, then stooping to exit by a small door. Emerging into sunshine again, Noor stood on a patch of unkempt grass in a courtyard formed by high surrounding stone walls draped with ivy.

Archambault turned to Marius. Marius stepped forward, clasped the ivy in two callused hands and held it back like a curtain, revealing the door to a small stone garden shed—so well concealed, Noor hadn't noticed it bulging the ivy. Archambault unlocked the door and led Noor across a wedge of sunlight into cool darkness.

The cabbage smell was Marius, the hint of Old Spice, Archambault. What did she smell like to them?

A torch clicked in Marius's hand and light spread over the plank floor to the legs of a desk and chair, swung up to a shuttered square—a window set in the stone wall—then back to illuminate a jumble of spades and trowels in the corner. Archambault lifted away some of the implements, revealing a suitcase. He placed it on the desk and thumbed the clasps. Marius opened the shutters. Sunlight streamed over the four compartments in the suitcase: the power supply dials, the short-wave transmitter and receiver, and a spare parts kit. A now obsolete OSS-issue SSTR-1 radio. She was more familiar with her own SOE-issue transmitter, a Mark II suitcase radio about half the size of this one, and considerably lighter.

"We can operate off the battery for these few messages," said Archambault. He reached over Noor's head to a shelf above the door and retrieved two exercise books—his code and message books. He and Marius strung the radio antenna out of the window, carefully hiding it in the ivy.

"I'll be on guard outside, on the road," said Marius.

Once Noor heard the ivy scrape across the door, she moved to the window. Outside stood Marius's hunched figure—hands in his pockets, a Gauloise drooping along with his moustache, standing watch for enemy uniforms beside the nettle-filled ditch.

"Encode, please." Archambault pulled the headphones over his ears and plugged the cord into the receiver.

Noor took a pen from her handbag and began referring to the crib sheet in his code book, writing down in the message book the resulting coded letters to be transmitted in successive squares of five blocks across.

"You must decide by reading the whole message before you begin if this one is worth your freedom. Some messages, they might be worth one person's freedom, *tu sais*, Madeleine?"

Noor nodded.

"Send quickly. We are the only radio operators left in the north now. The German mobile receivers located all the other transmitters by taking bearings on their signals. They are swift and deadly in triangulation. My colleague in Reims was arrested two days ago after transmitting for less than five minutes.

"Your double security check authenticates your transmission. If you're caught and tortured, you may reveal your bluff check when you can't bear the pain any longer, but try never to disclose your true check. If the true check isn't transmitted after each line, operators in London will assume this radio has fallen into enemy hands. But if ever you are in haste and have to dispense with the checks, as I have on several occasions, they should know your fist by now."

By "fist" Archambault meant her distinctive style. Yes, London operators certainly did know her fist; it had taken as long for women there to adjust to the rhythm of her dots and dashes as for Noor to improve to high speed. From years at the veena Noor's natural rhythms varied from five, seven, nine to ten-eight time. Like Abbajaan's, like Armand's.

Jasmin has played her flute.

The message squirted a thousand miles around and across the Channel in Archambault's rapid hand relay of dots and dashes to the attuned headphones of one of three hundred women in radio intelligence near London. A few seconds on the air, and Miss Atkins and Colonel Buckmaster would have the message on their desks in a matter of hours.

More messages, some over two pages long. This time Archambault encoded and Noor sent them in rapid succession. Afterwards, Archambault returned his code and message books to their hidden locations. Noor drew the antenna back and closed the shutters to signal Marius. Archambault stowed the suitcase, locked the shed door and led Noor back through the greenhouse. Marius was already back at work in the institute shop.

"Marius told me a white van was seen prowling Grignon village yesterday," said Archambault. "Grignon is becoming too dangerous—you must find other safe houses where you can transmit. I must teach you our safety precautions quickly. A moon plane is coming for me a month from now. London has ordered me to return for retraining." He straightened a bicycle leaning against the stable wall. "What made you volunteer for this assignment, Madeleine? Your father is a sultan, *n'est-ce pas?*"

Noor suppressed a laugh. Her family of courtier musicians were noble indeed, but several steps down the scale from all the maharajas, sultans and nawabs that populated the minds of Europeans upon mention of India. Should she exploit such ignorance, as Mother did? But denial would bring little illumination to Archambault.

"My father taught philosophy," she said. "And yes, he was from India—he is no more."

"I'm sorry," he said. "Your brother—he was named after an Indian poet, I think. Once, he said his sister was going to be a writer for children. Was that you? We were both little more than children ourselves, and I remember thinking how wonderful it would be if someone wrote stories for us. But then I grew up."

"I did too," said Noor with a smile. "But I still write stories for children."

"Pardon me, mademoiselle, but it does seem strange to see you back in France, and in the Resistance. I sent a message a few days ago about some Indian troops taken prisoner by the Germans. They wear patches of orange, white and green with leaping tigers. The patches say *Free Indians.*" He paused, waiting.

It was understandable that some Indians would join any enemy of their exploiters; but at the moment, either Archambault needed a radio operator or he didn't.

"Of course, I remember your mother—American, oui? The Americans are with us now . . . Well, you must have your reasons."

"I do," said Noor. "Probably similar to your own."

"I was in England visiting my father's family when the war broke out."

"Your father is English?"

"Yes, and my mother, she is French. They needed bilingual people, and I wanted the chance to learn about radios. Maybe, when things get better, I'll open a radio repair shop. But now . . . I'll be back tonight to help with the canisters. Have you been told the danger signals?"

"No."

"Ttt! Come, I'll show you."

They headed uphill along the drive leading out of the institute, Archambault walking his bicycle. Halfway to the stone porticos he turned around.

"From here you can see the top-storey windows of the director's château and the main château. If the curtains are drawn back in either one, it means danger. If it is dark and a candle is shining in either of those windows, that's also a sign of danger."

"Then?"

"Then stay away. Get away as fast as you can and warn others in the network. Use a public phone if possible. Then hide. Later, find out what has happened and transmit the details to London. You understand?"

Yes, she understood.

"*À la prochaine*, Madeleine." And he cycled away.

So many cautions! Necessary, but each administered a dose of contagious fear.

Noor wandered into the stable. Several empty stalls. Horses requisitioned by the Germans, Monsieur Hoogstraten had said. A few muzzles poked from the stalls as she walked past, and a roan with a white diamond on his forehead gave her shoulder a wet nibble. Too old for horsemeat, and he wouldn't have much speed before a cart. Cheek against his mane, Noor took in the scent of hay, horses and manure.

Armand, how I wish I could transmit a message to you as I just did to London. Tapping it out, knowing you are there to receive. A short message. How to encode it? To whom would I entrust it? What should I say? Perhaps: "I am near; have hope, my love. We will be together again." But anyone could say that. Some pattern you will recognize like a radio operator's fist, a message you would know could come only from me.

Beneath the slanting eaves on the top floor of the château, Noor faced the casement, clad in a borrowed frothy pink nightgown. The dark hand of blackout had spread through the village of

Grignon and lay across the woods surrounding the director's château. Grasshoppers, like small violins, began the staccato rhythm of mating calls.

"I used to go to the cinema to learn English. I will speak English with you. You like the cinema?" Odile's chatter in English mixed with French followed Noor in a steady stream. "Gilbert said *Gone with the Wind* was in the theatres in London—he told me the whole story. In French the book is called *Autant en emporte le vent*. It is a good translation. After I read it, I made a dress from my bath curtains, just like Scarlett. Then the BBC said Ashley Wilkes was shot down by the Germans—that is so sad, no? Gilbert says he was on a spy mission—ha, how does he know? But you can tell me, what is the *goût du jour* these days?"

Noor turned back to Odile, who had arranged her limbs in a languid pose, like Ingres's *Odalisque*, on one of the two beds. Odile burbled on, not waiting for an answer.

"Here we have mostly German films. *Ils m'ennuient!* And the Germans bore me too. You know the first time I saw the Germans? It wasn't from this front window but from that side window, the oval one. I looked out one morning and there were two planes chasing one another in the blue sky, a French and a German one. And *mon Dieu!* our horses were grazing below in the fields as if nothing was happening. Of course, I didn't actually *see* a German in the plane, so I should say I saw my first German many days later—on a motorcycle in Grignon."

Noor listened with interest as she took her freshly washed blouse and lingerie out of a basin and hung them behind the chamber door to dry. She only needed to prompt Odile with a nod, at most a word or two.

"But when I saw the planes, immediately I thought of Papa. You know why that was strange? Because he was at Verdun that very instant, and later I learned that I thought of him at the very moment of his capture." A second's pause emphasized so amazing a coincidence.

"He was captured at Verdun?"

"Yes. Maman fainted when we heard the news. But I got on a *vélo* and cycled to Verdun to find him."

"Cycled from here to Verdun?"

"Yes, three days, sleeping by the road. I had to find out if my papa was alive or not, you see. And when I got there, I found him in the prison camp, and he was so surprised to see me, he forgot to be angry."

"Did they let you see him? Did they let you bring him home?"

"*Mais non*, he wouldn't leave his men. But he gave me a letter for Maman, and all his men gave me letters for their wives and fiancées and mothers, and so many other men wrote to their families. I put all their letters up here in my dress—I had no breasts then."

Odile didn't have any breasts to speak of three years later, either, but Noor let this pass.

"Like this, I carried all their letters past the guards, smiling sweetly at them." She hitched up her dress at the waist so the top ballooned over her belt and she gave Noor an exaggerated smile, batting her eyelashes in demonstration, then lay down again on the duvet.

"That's how I carried them home. It took me months to send them, because of course all mail was censored by the Boche. When my father was released, he vowed: no matter how many years it takes, nor how many pay the price, we cannot allow France to be occupied by the Germans like a country of savages in Asia or Africa."

After only three years of Occupation Odile's passion was like Mr. Gandhi's when he spoke of the hundred-year British occupation of India.

"So ever since, I'm a courier for Papa, after school. I bring Archambault's messages, and probably I will bring yours too. Papa says I have a good memory—I only write down very long ones."

The seventeen-year-old slip of a girl had been risking her life almost daily for three years on every road, at every Gestapo checkpoint.

"*Tiens,* if I call you and say 'Keep in touch' like an American in the cinema, it means you must check for a message behind the milk bottles at Flavien's pawnshop in the Troisième arrondissement. And you can leave messages there for me."

"With pleasure, Mademoiselle Odile," said Noor gravely.

Odile paused only to draw a map in her copybook and mark the location of the letter drop, then her questions plunged off course. "You think Monsieur Gilbert is handsome?"

Noor hadn't thought about it. "Mmmm, not really. He looks a little like Maurice Chevalier."

"Oh, he has eyes for you."

"I don't think so."

"I think so. When he told the story of Lindbergh and how he wanted to be a pilot after that, he was watching to see if he was impressing you. But one can see you are not easily impressed."

This could be true. Students at Afzal Manzil, the Sufi school, were prominent in their fields; discussions of philosophy, history, music, art and literature were common. Even in London, everyone she knew had impressive achievements, not only Gilbert.

"He doesn't know me," said Noor. "Besides, I am engaged."

"Oho, you are engaged! Who is he? What is he like? Where is he?"

Noor sidestepped the entire flood with a spur-of-the-moment fabrication. "He's a navy officer in London."

"You have a photo?"

"No, Anne-Marie Régnier cannot carry photos of English navy officers."

"Oh, of course. But that is so bad! It's so difficult, no, not even to have one photo?"

"Yes, very difficult."

Noor had carried a photo of Armand for a long time, until Uncle Tajuddin took it away from her in 1934. In 1939 it was replaced by another she had treasured, of Armand in his uniform during the Drôle de Guerre. It was left behind in her bedside drawer in England. But she needed no photograph to recall

Armand's thick-lashed eyes, or the expressive tenderness of his octave-and-a-half-span hands.

To Odile she said, "You like Gilbert?"

"No, I detest him. I don't know why, I just detest him. Always asking questions about everyone. He's not well educated—his father is a postal clerk and his mother a housekeeper. You know his flat in Paris? Just now his wife had it renovated. I said to Papa, where did she get the money for new curtains?"

"What did your papa say?"

"Oh, Papa trusts him because London trusts him. And we have need of his *prouesse*, you know, his *spécialité*. In spring, when Prosper brought him here to meet us, it was once a week, then twice a week, now three times a week. He organizes landings, and boasts he has never once had an arrest at a drop zone. So many flights—Prosper says he thinks the invasion is coming very soon, maybe this summer."

"Prosper said that?"

"Yes, I heard him tell Papa—don't tell him I told you. Oh, but you must know anyway . . ."

Noor tried to look as if she did.

"You go to meet Prosper tomorrow, yes? He's a great man. Gentle and strong at once. And he doesn't trust Gilbert either."

"How do you know?"

"Because Prosper returned last night by parachute and Gilbert, the great Gilbert, knew nothing about it! *Rien du tout!*" She was obviously delighted by Gilbert's discomfiture. "Prosper arranged his flight with another organizer, 'Marc.' And he dropped in a field Monsieur Gilbert did not arrange." Her tone turned mocking. "*Eh bien*, I think maybe Gilbert's feelings were hurt, the poor man."

"It's late," said Noor. "Do you think Archambault and Marius came for the canisters?"

"I went to the stables to meet them after dinner," said Odile. "Actually, to meet one of the students."

Odile's rapid stream snagged, and the moment of silence drew Noor's attention as no words could have.

"Which student?" In a gentle voice.

"The most handsome, of course. Louis de Grémont is his name."

"*De* Grémont?" Noor emphasized the aristocratic appellation to tease Odile into confiding more details.

"Yes, de Grémont." A pause, then Odile said, "I had to tell him I can't marry him till Vichy falls. He said that could be years and years from now!" She sighed, looked away as if embarrassed. "But I had to tell him—I heard his family's factories are supplying the Germans every day."

"Maybe they have to," said Noor, intending comfort.

Odile shook her head sadly. "I could accept that. But I went to their home once and saw a portrait of Pétain on their mantelpiece. *C'est insupportable!* No, no, no."

"But Louis is not a Pétainiste, himself, if he is helping us."

"Non, but . . . it is too difficult."

Noor sat down on her bed, next to Odile. After a moment Odile's thoughts found a new outlet.

"What is your real name?"

"Why do you want to know?"

"I know it already. I heard you whisper it to Archambault. It's Noor Khan, correct?"

"So you know. Why do you ask?"

Odile abandoned one strategy midstream and took up another. "Will you go with us to church on Sunday?" The idle-sounding question seemed to have slipped out. It lay on the duvet between them, awaiting Noor's response.

"Certainly, if I am not required to transmit that day."

Noor had often attended mass with Mother and fellow students at the lycée, abstaining only from communion. Jesus Christ was a venerable prophet in the line preceding Muhammad, peace be upon them, just not the final one. Besides, as she and Armand often discussed, at church, mosque or temple one was praying to the same force: the spirit of creation.

"Oh, I am glad," said Odile. "I was so afraid you would say no."

"And if I said no?"

"Why, that would mean you're a Jew."

This was no time to try educating Odile; better to take her ignorance of the existence of religions other than the Judeo-Christian in stride. All his years in France, Abbajaan believed he could interest Europeans in his version of Sufism, a Sufism that included all faiths. He'd enlarged his ideas with French ones, but there was never any reciprocity.

"And then?" Noor prompted.

"It would be so dangerous for us," explained Odile. "London has sent us three Jews already, and Papa was so angry, he said they must be assigned to a separate network."

"Why was Monsieur Hoogstraten angry?"

"He said London was being careless. They do not understand that a Jew can jeopardize everything—we could all be arrested."

Noor seized the opportunity to probe further, and Odile confirmed the situation Émile Garry had described to Noor the night before.

"Can one visit a Jew in a prison camp, as you visited your papa at Verdun?"

"Oh, *mais non*, Anne-Marie! They find out who is writing to them or sending them parcels, they arrest them. Even the Red Cross cannot visit the Jews in camps, because they are not POWs. They are locked up by Pétain like criminals—and the Red Cross doesn't visit criminals in prisons."

Yet some intrepid social worker *had* managed to enter Drancy. Some Red Cross volunteer *had* taken Armand's censored postcard out of Drancy.

Bless that stranger.

"Have any Jews been released, as your father was?"

"Non, non. Jews are not prisoners of war—who knows what they are. All Jews are being sent east to work now, even the children."

"Even children? Why? What work can children do?"

A moue of ignorance. "Children, old people, all being—how

you say?—'evacuated.' Resettled. My Latin professor is glad—
Premier Laval says for every three Jews sent to Germany, Hitler
will release one French POW, and my Latin professor's son is captive in Germany."

"But Israelites are French—French-born Jews."

"Non, but Jews are *all* not-French. Monsieur Laval revoked
the citizenship of all Israelites naturalized after 1927. Now they are
just Jews again. *Émigrés.*"

"*Mon Dieu!*" said Noor, heart plunging. Wasn't nationality a
basic right? How could it be taken away? She didn't know if
Armand's father had been naturalized, whether Madame Lydia
had ever become a French citizen. Questions she should have
asked Armand, but she had never thought she would need to know.
"But if their citizenship is revoked and they become foreigners, the
Red Cross should be allowed to inspect their camps, no?"

Odile shook her head as if in wonder at Noor's naïveté. She
crouched by her bed and pulled. A wireless came into sight.

"I'll try to get Honneur et Patrie or Radio London," she said.
"Better than listening to Radio Vichy's propaganda."

The dial turned slowly. The needle passed hisses and whistles
till a cocksure voice announced each item of war news that
Churchill wanted Hitler to know, then cricket news for the rest of
the listeners.

They heard, "*Ici Londres. Les Français parlent aux Français,*"
and the personal announcements began: "The rabbit will nurse
the pig . . ." "Tonight the suspenders will find their buttons . . ."
Each surreal, nonsense-sounding phrase conveying vital information to resistants, triggering sabotage operations or a landing
reception, confirming departures and arrivals of resistants, arms
and intelligence dispatches.

And lastly, news of the colonies. "British field marshal
Archibald Wavell became governor general of India today . . ."

Lord Wavell on his way to New Delhi would find three hundred
million Indians who had been agitating for their independence
from British occupation for nigh on fifty years, exactly as the French

were resisting the Germans, but without arms drops, with no weapons but determination and their meagre flesh against British truncheons, machine guns and armoured cars. Had she been in India, carrying out the same actions as she was in France, Lord Wavell would label her a terrorist, not a resistant.

Maybe Dadijaan would be a little happier today. She might be hopeful that the next governor general of India would re-evaluate Mr. Churchill's boat denial and rice denial policies. Maybe Lord Wavell was different. Maybe he wouldn't consider Indian millions dying of famine "acceptable losses" in this, the war for the world.

Pforzheim, Germany
December 1943

I wish I had learned to fight oppression as early in life as Odile, but I didn't have her confidence at seventeen—and I couldn't imagine myself riding to Verdun all alone when I was fourteen. When I was seventeen, I cried all day after Uncle Tajuddin reprimanded me for opening the front door of our home for a man—as if I could have known before I opened the door that the man was not our relative. When Uncle shouted at me for wearing a pair of red shoes I'd borrowed from Josianne, I took them off and ran barefoot to my room, and cried because I wanted so much to please, wanted everyone, even Uncle, to love me.

Odile! So different. She reminded me of Mother—the most adventurous woman in our family.

A bricolage of images comes, each rising like a Poussin painting from a miniature tableau. The five of us around the table for the evening meal always served, American style, at seven; Josianne's family served dinner at eight. The light changes from image to image, streaming, swelling, decaying. But our positions never change. Practical, ambitious Mother at the head of the table, spinning yarns, a Yankee Madame Defarge knitting the threads of her narrative around our Indian blood till her stories fulfilled their

*Oriental promise. In her stories Abbajaan was transformed from itin-
erant court musician and dervish to "Pir"—Indian sage, preacher of
Sufism—a spiritual master privy to the mystical secrets of living
connection with the infinite compassion of Allah. Kabir was called
Pirzada Kabiruddin, the closest word to Prince that Mother could
tease from Abbajaan's repertoire of Muslim titles. Little Zaib loved
to call me Pirzadi Noor-un-nisa, for then she could play at being
Princess Zaib-un-nisa. And when the students came to the summer
school that year, Mother christened Abbajaan "Hazrat," his new
title of respect, and all the students were "mureeds."*

*Sometimes, ma petite, parents are captured in the web of their
own stories, and retell the past to match their times and needs.
That was Mother, Aura Baker, your grandmother from Boston who
never told the cover story of her lineage the same way twice. Only
to me would she speak of her first day in the orphanage a month after
her mother died. She was vague about where her father vanished—
something related to gambling debts. Sometimes she'd tell of her
life after the orphanage, living with her older stepbrother, our
uncle Robert and his wife, slowly becoming his unpaid domestic
servant.*

*I always believed Mother and I had a special bond, but later I
learned we never did. She was the teller of tales, I the listener and
her confidante. I kept my own hopes and dreams secret from
Mother from the time I met Armand, and she never knew, because
she never asked.*

*Let me tell you how Mother and Abbajaan met. It was highly
symbolic: Abbajaan was looking in one direction and walking a
different one, the way he often did, and their paths collided. He
could have collided with anyone, Mother said, but he'd collided
with Aura Baker on Maverick Street in Boston—she was fond of
retelling this. To Abbajaan such encounters manifested the laws
of life and Allah's undefinable aims, but to Mother almost every
person and every thing was Opportunity.*

*In the short version of their meeting, the one reserved for the
public, they met while he was playing the veena on tour in America.*

This version did not mention that she invited him home to dine, it being Thanksgiving, when the tale of the Mayflower pilgrims was making its yearly round at the schoolhouse and it was appropriate to invite a troupe of Indians to dinner, if only to mitigate the error of Columbus. But Abbajaan and his brothers were the wrong Indians for the story, and so Mother compounded Columbus's error instead of honouring tradition.

Mother eschewed both History and Geography, being prone, in 1910, to the American conceit that the world was in need of a demonstration of how to melt people in a large pot devised expressly for the purpose. I'm joking, of course. But really, she was overwhelmed by Abbajaan's dark strangeness, his respectful manner. She was enthralled by his lilting English and elevated him instantly to maharaja status, the better to introduce him to Uncle Robert. So Uncle Robert found an Indian from the Princely State of Baroda at his Thanksgiving table, a dark, intense, golden-turbaned man with praises for everyone flowering on his courtly tongue, in a fitted black brocade coat, strings of pearls dangling on his chest.

Uncle Robert immediately forbade Mother to have anything to do with Abbajaan ever again.

But Mother wasn't a trembling kind of woman, as I was. As soon as she was twenty-one, she ignored Uncle Robert's edict and followed Abbajaan all the way to London. And when they married there, Mother took a Muslim name, Rukhsana, to uphold Abbajaan's religion and traditions. She knew next to nothing about his religion or traditions, but she loved him so much, she was willing to uphold anything Abbajaan held dear. She went with him on music tours the first few years after they were married— that's how I was born in Moscow—but a few years after he moved to Paris, Abbajaan began travelling alone, returning to Paris in the summers to teach Sufism.

That was your grandmother—Mother before Abbajaan returned to India. When we returned to Paris, having paid our respects at Abbajaan's tomb and toured the major Sufi shrines, she learned a different courage. Every time Uncle made his dutiful offer of marriage to his half-brother's widow, she mustered copious widow's tears and Uncle Tajuddin's own traditions against all his gallant propositions of co-wifehood. She went into weeks of self-imposed purdah, emerging from her seclusion periodically to confront him with the courage of a squirrel facing down a Doberman. Poor Uncle Tajuddin! He's probably still bewildered by her rejection of his well-intentioned charity. For five years she was as a Shia waiting for the reappearance of the Twelfth Imam, as Penelope weaving by day and unravelling by night, and she was ever and also Aura Baker, always imagining the next story for her children to live.

Mother would have loved being undercover at Grignon.

In the lavatory at the château, after my ablutions, I slipped the cover off my jacket button, referred to the compass beneath and faced southeast towards the Ka'aba. I used my headscarf as hijab and knelt on cold tile in the first motion of my Tahajjud prayer. Abbajaan would tell us—your uncle Kabir, your aunt Zaib and myself—that if we couldn't find time for five prayers, a remembrance of Allah once a day was better than none. The Tahajjud prayer time, when one can speak one's mind to Allah, from whom all favours come, always refreshes me.

That night at Grignon, I dreamed that masked demons danced around Odile's room. One bore the face of Gilbert, which metamorphosed into a mask with the haunted eyes of Renée Garry. I thought such nightmares terrible then—but they shrink to nothing compared with the one I live here. Vogel and I are enchained together in a nightmare whose shared space has become this room no bigger than a water closet, ten feet by six.

I could pray five times each day in this cell, but I don't. How can I dare devotion, now I have lost my freedom, when I never thanked Allah on my knees five times a day for it before? Instead, I perform only the Tahajjud prayer late at night, and pray for Armand, your grandmother Lydia, Mother, Dadijaan, Kabir and Zaib.

Even so, Fajar, Zuhr, Asar, Maghrib and Isha—the prayer times—sustain me through each monotonous day. It was Fajar when the pale dawn mist filtered through the iron bars and the bell rang to wake all the women along the cellblock. The guard came to unlock my hands; she turned away while I used the toilet in the corner of the cell, then turned back to shackle me again. On pain of the dungeon, regulations forbid me to look directly at her or the other SS woman, who pours a foul-tasting liquid in my wooden bowl and gives me the wedge of bread I get once a day.

The clang of iron doors and shouts of guards said women prisoners were filing out of cells into the corridor and out into the freezing courtyard. I stood on tiptoe on my iron bed so I could see them walking slowly in circles, one behind the other, never touching. As for me, I am taken into the courtyard alone once a week for exercise, never allowed to speak to anyone except Vogel.

When the clinking of keys stopped, it meant the women had been returned to their cells, and I allowed myself half the bread, saving the remainder for its fragrance. Then silence as Zuhr began. When, standing on the bed again, I saw the barbed wire fencing above the courtyard wall become one with its shadow, I knew only a single hour had passed. And that it was time for warm swampy gruel: a second bowl of swedes, crushed peas and a paste of sour cabbage. When it came, I committed each morsel to memory. The guard collected my bowl and I returned to the odour of previous inmates permeating the thin straw of my mattress.

Some days, though not today, the guard brings me white paper tickets, string and a knitting needle I have to use to string them together. A purposeless task I barely manage with my chains. Zaib was always a better needlewoman than I.

Most days now, since Vogel authorized paper and pen, I manage to write to you.

When the shadow of my pen doubles, Asar will have passed. And with it, two, perhaps three, hours? Maghrib, earlier and shorter at this time of year, will begin at the last slotted rays of lukewarm sun. I will bang my chains on the door to demand an oil lamp or that the naked bulb be lit. The flap door will drop for a brief moment. There will be water for the basin, another bowl of the same soup. And when *a stray star winks through barred fog, it will be time for Isha prayers, and I will have outlived another two hours of captivity. Only then will I allow myself to chew the last of the hard brown bread, to help me through the lice-infested dark.*

When I came to this cell, I passed many days and nights furled into a ball as you were in my womb, dwelling on my multiple failures. But now I find I am not alone. With me are the reformers, anarchists, nihilists, the mad, the pacifists, the utopian Communists, the atheists, and devout women of all faiths. This is a zenana, an Auratstan, a place of segregation. Here we silenced women wring our collective hands at our state, and outside the world goes on with its killing.

Bombs crash in the distance. We call out in hope the Allies are coming closer.

As I write, a woman is singing the news in French. The guards cannot stop each teardrop note from carrying. "The Allies bombarded Munich and Dusseldorf again. Churchill, Marshal Stalin and Roosevelt met in Teheran and demanded Germany's unconditional surrender."

But the Germans won't surrender without an invasion on the ground. And it's too late this year, too cold now. Insh'allah, the Allies will come with spring.

It would be comforting if I could believe that Allah placed Vogel in his role as captor and I in the role of prisoner, that every feeling, every moment is predetermined, that the outcome of this charade with Vogel is predestined, but no strand of logic strains that far — the Allah I love cannot be so cruel.

Our conversations, when Vogel comes, eventually drown in his terror and mine — terror of the perverse violence and rage of which he is capable against his "Princess" for whom he professes only the deepest concern and love. But your mother has known the love of an honourable man, and so I recognize Vogel's "love." Like Uncle Tajuddin's, it is love of his own power, love of my dependence on his every whim. Out of "love" Vogel invokes German orders and says my bondage is for my "safe custody," just as Uncle Tajuddin once invoked custom and the Qur'an for my "protection," as the British "defend" India, starving millions while reciting odes to the white man's burden.

When I think of this war, I am glad I delayed your soul, for you would have entered the world Vogel and Uncle Tajuddin prefer, a world that wants its bloodlines pure, its people destructive or acquiescent.

Often, Armand comes to visit me, teasing, his voice smiling. Today I could swear he was in one corner of my cell, leaning with furrowed brow over a chessboard, Anoushka in hand. Another time he was at the piano. "Sing, Noor! Sing—with me, or alone—but sing."

When your father and I marry again, ma petite, there will be singing. Singing of love in many languages. I won't wear white. I see myself in the red-and-gold lehnga Dadijaan promised me. Armand will wear his black formal jacket and a red cummerbund as he does when performing with an orchestra. We'll stand beneath a chuppah, drink from the same glass and smash it; our valima celebrations will last till dawn.

Before we bring you back again, we must try to make this world a better place. You are the essence of our future, our future together. When you enter your body, let it be when your parents and others like us are free to marry, keeping our own faiths, and honouring one another's just as my Abbajaan taught. Armand and I will travel with you to the Kingdom of Baroda, to India, Russia and even Jerusalem—may the lands of our forefathers someday be free.

Soon millions of Germans will celebrate the birth in hiding of a Jewish child—Christmas is coming, ma petite. I remember Christmas with Mother when Abbajaan was alive. But once Uncle Tajuddin arrived, there were no more Christmas decorations.

Outside, the first light fuzz of snow must be growing on the fields. Westwards, in the Alsace, snow-fur will lie heavy on frozen stems. But here, these 360 degrees, the chains I wear and these words I write to you are changing me. So gradually, I scarcely notice.

CHAPTER 13

Paris, France
Friday, June 18, 1943

NOOR CYCLED DOWN the boulevard St-Germain. Too quiet. No cars, some bicycles. Queues of tired-looking women and old men. Shuttered and sandbagged shops with signs: *Rien à vendre*— nothing to sell. More signs in German. Two *milice* gendarmes standing outside a Monoprix. Streets marked *Germans Only*, like streets in India marked *Europeans Only*. Where was the jaunty energy of Paris?

How often had she cycled in from the periphery, pedalling purposefully as now, to attend a lecture at the Sorbonne, meet Armand clandestinely or see Josianne and other friends. Paris was like London then, believing itself centre of the universe, law unto itself, colonizing and subjugating people of other faiths and climates across the globe. She'd never imagined herself participating in its future.

But though the city was backdrop to every image of Armand in memory's eye, without him the romance of Paris was just a fable. Without his arms about her, what was Paris but row after row of sooty old grey-roofed buildings huddled about their inner courtyards?

What had become of Afzal Manzil, her family's home and school in Suresnes? Was the *British Property* sign—painted hastily as Kabir honked the Amilcar's horn, shouting that they must leave—still nailed to its imposing green gates? That house—site of fear, site of tears. She hadn't been sorry to leave it. Or sorry that Uncle Tajuddin bundled away his one pair of European shoes and went home to Baroda.

She dropped her bicycle stand before a restaurant with an all but unnoticeable label: *Chez Tutulle*. Inside, she wended her way through a few early diners populating the tables and chairs in the dark cavern. An aproned maître d' stood behind a hulking cash register, running his pencil down its ledger columns. Noor approached and asked in a low voice for Phono.

"I'm not familiar with Monsieur Phono, but if mademoiselle would like to leave a message?"

Noor rummaged in her handbag, contriving to drop a slip of paper with her password to the counter.

The maître d' made his way through the tables, greeting customers as he went. Reaching a window, he glanced out, left and right, checking if she'd been followed. Then he returned with a brusque *"Venez!"*

Into steamy heat where aproned chefs and sous-chefs chopped and sautéed and stirred. Through thickets of shouted orders aimed at small boys with red hands who were clattering and sliding plates into large vats of water. No one glanced in her direction. Then into sunlight and open air in a bicycle lane behind the restaurant. Across the lane he unlocked a wooden door set in a stone wall. Noor followed as he ascended two flights of stairs.

She quickened pace behind the maître d's long strides down a musky corridor in what seemed to be a boarding house. A dishevelled woman in a low-cut red velvet dress peered from a doorway as they passed.

All this secrecy was welcome; she wouldn't want Uncle Tajuddin to know she'd ever been to a place like this.

At room twenty-nine, the maître d' gave two knocks, paused, then two more knocks. A long pause.

Twenty-nine. I'm twenty-nine. Two plus nine equals eleven. Eleven is a one and a one, equals two. Two signifying man and woman together. Noor and Armand.

A glance at her watch. Seven minutes late.

The door opened a few inches to reveal the pencil moustache of Émile Garry. Noor slipped in, leaving the maître d' behind.

Émile—Phono—led her past a puff-pillowed four-poster and opened a large armoire. Three-quarters of the hanging space inside was occupied by a woman's colourful clothes. The rest—some shirts, a man's suits in shades of grey. Émile placed his hands, palms outwards, between a feathered black silk gown and the front of a man's shirt, and cleared a path. Somehow the back of the armoire slid magically away. Noor followed Émile into the cloying scent of Shocking from the gown in the armoire, to a whitewashed workroom lit by a skylight.

Archambault, Gilbert, Professor Balachowsky and a broad-shouldered man about five years older than herself broke away from an open wicker picnic basket. Each left his brown paper packet of bread, cheese and tinned sardines to rise from the table and greet her.

If asked later, she would have no difficulty listing everything in this room from memory: a carpenter's bench and lathe, a small trunk in the corner blocking a wooden door. Expanses of once-white stucco walls unbroken by windows, adorned only with a 1943 calendar. Today's date circled. Friday, June 18. Friday, day of *juma* prayers.

Gilbert swept back his forelock, came forward, took her hands in his. Noor withdrew her hands with a polite smile. She looked at Émile.

"Madeleine," said Émile, "*c'est* Prosper."

"Delighted, I must say," said Prosper in English, the welcome in his firm handshake reflected in his brown eyes. The right height to blend with Frenchmen. Right colour hair, too: brown. Ears rather prominent—jug-ears, the English would say. But other than that, he wouldn't stand out physically, even in England.

Prosper continued in French once she was seated with a packet of bread and cheese and a small measure of *vin ordinaire* before her.

Sunlight slanted into elongated rectangles on the wall. Prosper's rapid French laid out plans for another drop, this time at Rosny sur Seine.

"Expect seven parachutes if you hear the BBC announce *La route est belle* on the twenty-first of June."

"We need a reliable motor car. To be hidden in a garage near the field," said Archambault.

"Mine," volunteered Professor Balachowsky, chewing vigorously on the stem of his unlit pipe.

"What's the cargo?" asked Gilbert.

"The usual," Archambault replied.

"*Mais*, Archambault, can we make do with one motor car or do we need two? There will be seven parachutes this time." Gilbert had exaggerated his tone as if speaking to a child.

A precarious silence.

Noor said, "Perhaps there are seven as my suitcase and transmitters are coming? They're heavy but not very large. I want very much to get to work."

This seemed to refocus the men's attention on the project.

"We will make do with one motor car," said Prosper. "We can't risk two. Phono, can you obtain a permit for petrol?"

"*Absolument.*"

"Good. The reception committee will be Gilbert, Professor and . . . ?"

"Some of my students," said the Professor.

"*Bien*, Professor. Have them collect the cargo and hide it— just temporarily, till a secure location is identified."

"Temporarily where?" asked Gilbert.

"Why must *you* know?" Archambault was openly challenging Gilbert now.

Gilbert gave Archambault his usual grin, but his eyes glittered behind his forelock. Prosper seemed about to say something but thought better of it.

"At Grignon, in the greenhouse this time, not the stables," he said. It sounded as if he was voting to trust Gilbert.

Archambault stuffed his mouth with a huge bite of black bread.

Prosper continued, "Madeleine will courier a message from Phono to the Professor next Thursday, giving him the passwords for release of the cargo to a safer place."

"Next Thursday." The Professor consulted a small black book from his pocket. "I have an appointment with my tailor near the Jardin des Plantes that day—we could meet in the gazebo. Fifteen-hundred hours."

"A tailor?" said Gilbert. "Please, Professor, refer me to any tailor who can obtain cloth these days."

"Oh, it's just an alteration, Gilbert," said the Professor. "Too much room in my clothes. But you may certainly have his name."

"Don't give him any names," said Archambault.

The Professor shrugged. "My tailor is sewing more Gestapo uniforms than alterations for people like me, Archambault. How else can he survive?"

"Ça y est?" said Prosper.

Glances all around confirmed all the details had been covered.

"Next meeting?" asked Gilbert.

"You will be told," growled Archambault.

"I swear it will be my pleasure to put you on a plane to England," said Gilbert.

"I would leave tonight if I could."

"Yes, I'm sure you would," Gilbert sneered.

"But if I did, you couldn't send messages to England—like the ones asking for gin and brandy."

"Messieurs, messieurs!" said Prosper.

"Sunday night at the Jazz Club on the rue Pigalle, then," said Émile, supplying a distraction to break the tension.

Prosper's face lit up; plainly he loved jazz.

Émile continued, "I can introduce Madeleine to Viennot."

"Excellent. I thank you all for coming," said Prosper. "Leave one at a time. Carefully. You two: take the front exit. You two: wait five minutes, then exit through the alley door."

Professor Balachowsky gave Noor a small bow and stepped nimbly through the armoire.

Émile said, "Madeleine, it's too late to cycle back to Grignon today before curfew—tonight you must stay in Paris."

"Or she can be my guest. At my apartment," said Gilbert, giving Noor a flirtatious wink.

Archambault and Prosper exchanged glances. "No, Gilbert," said Prosper. "Madeleine will stay with Madame Garry."

Archambault jammed his hat on and bent to enter the armoire. Once his heavy footsteps stopped clomping in the wooden chamber, Émile drew a key from his pocket and squatted beside the small trunk.

"Put these two grenades in your handbag. Carefully, Madeleine. Take them to Renée's for me. Give Babette my love. Tell her I'll see her and Renée on Sunday. Tomorrow . . ." He looked up at Prosper. "For tomorrow I need thirty-two more blasting caps."

Prosper spread large empty hands, a gesture that, performed by an Englishman, should have been incongruous. That it came naturally said he had been disguised as a Frenchman for many months.

"And our target is . . . ?" Gilbert asked. He sounded almost too casual.

"We haven't yet received that information." It didn't appear Prosper was trying to evade the question.

Gilbert gestured at Noor. "Didn't Madeleine bring it with her?"

But Noor shook her head. London had sent no verbal message through her, only the package wrapped in brown paper. She was waiting to give it to Prosper in private, but maybe it contained the blasting caps Émile needed, or the name of their target.

"Just one moment." Noor stepped into the dark armoire and crouched between the clothes. She took the package from the secret compartment in her handbag and returned to the room.

"I'd love to see where you were hiding that, mademoiselle," said Gilbert with an elastic grin.

Noor ignored him and handed Prosper the package.

"Thank you." Prosper took a jackknife from his pocket. He cut the string and slit the brown paper to reveal a button-down leather pouch. "*Voilà!* A detonator magazine. One—not two, unfortunately, Phono."

Émile shrugged and took the magazine, which, Noor knew, gave him only sixteen of the thirty-two caps he needed.

"That's all?" Gilbert sounded as if he had expected much more.

"Nothing about the target, so we can expect that information at Archambault's next scheduled receiving time," said Prosper.

"Tonight," said Gilbert.

Prosper gave a reluctant nod at the deduction, and glanced at his watch. "You must leave now."

Émile retrieved a black device with trailing wires from the trunk, placed it in the picnic basket and covered it with brown papers from their lunch. Gilbert closed the lid over the picnic basket and fastened it, put his arm through the handle.

"Madeleine, wait here," said Prosper, buttoning the leather pouch.

After seeing Émile and Gilbert through the armoire, Prosper returned, pouch still in hand. "At this moment, Madeleine, what you've managed to smuggle into France will be far safer with you than with me." He'd relaxed into English as if he'd slipped on a pair of old slippers. "So put this right back in your purse and I'll collect it next week. Very valuable, and not explosive—that's all you need to know."

Noor nodded.

"Now, your first task is to find two rooms to let. New safe houses—we cannot use the institute at Grignon much longer. Try the *banlieue*. Rents are lower past the fort walls, and there are fewer Jerries on the prowl in the factory districts. Find a room close to a train or métro line. I expect you'll raise bloody little suspicion—you do look awfully French, if you don't mind my saying."

No, she didn't mind his saying. It quite restored her confidence after Renée Garry's comments and Archambault's questions.

"Excuse me again." She returned to the armoire, carefully removed the grenades from her handbag, stowed the leather pouch away in its secret compartment, then replaced the grenades and arranged her headscarf over the lot. She returned to Prosper.

"Too heavy?"

"No, sir."

"You're not French, are you?"

"No, sir."

"Archambault tells me your father was the leader of a cult. Had a big home in Suresnes."

"Not a cult, sir. He was a musician who taught religion and philosophy."

"A swami and a musician? A Gandhi with music?"

"Some similar ideas, sir, but my father was a Muslim."

"Not a separatist, are you?"

The word contained semitones Prosper seemed unaware of. In light of Britain's pilfering colonial commerce, she sympathized with a people wanting independence from their empire, but "separatists" wanted Mr. Jinnah's land of the pure, Pakistan—a paradise Uncle Tajuddin might appreciate, but no better than prison for herself.

She would live in France with Armand once war conditions improved, and never again fear becoming cousin Allahuddin's third wife in either India or a theoretical Pakistan. And surely Prosper was only asking for reassurance that she would be loyal for this mission.

"No, sir, not a separatist."

"Have enough money?"

"For now, sir."

"Right, then. Off you go, Madeleine, old girl. Quickly."

Prosper ran his hands through the close-cut hair over his large ears and resumed his seat at the table as if expecting another visitor. A beam of sunlight slanted over his head.

On leaving Chez Tutulle, Noor caught the tram bound for the Gare de l'Est, descended to the scarlet gates of the métro and presented a ticket from the booklet in her heavy handbag. Consulting a wall map, she caught a train going in the direction of Amiens. She had the afternoon for her first mission, to find a room to let. A room suitable for transmitting and as close to Armand in Drancy as could be. From there, Allah would show the way.

The underground train gradually emptied as it crept to the periphery, terminating at Porte de la Villette. Next came a train that chuffed along the surface at escargot pace. Noor was the only passenger in the carriage by the time it reached Le Bourget–Drancy.

The gendarme at the station would ask her to open her handbag, heavy with grenades.

Look confident.

Noor held her crumpled ticket and papers out for inspection. She came here every day; this was just another visit. The gendarme waved her through without a second glance. She climbed a stone staircase to a bridge that doubled back over the tracks. Below her, the conductor turned the sign on the engine; its direction now read *Paris* instead of *Amiens*. The long, soot-blackened train rumbled away beneath, leaving her standing on the bridge feeling suddenly lone and small.

She shouldered her handbag and walked purposefully towards some shops in the distance. A boy of about fifteen with a checked beret angled over curly brown hair cycled past, and Noor hailed him for directions to the village centre. He pointed straight ahead.

Where should she wait for an omnibus heading into Drancy?

"On the avenue." The boy adjusted a leather satchel about his neck and touched his beret in farewell. "Avenue Jean Jaurès."

Standing at the omnibus stop brought no omnibus, and impatience set Noor walking again. How far away was the camp? She had to find it, rent a room nearby if she could, and get all the way back to Renée's apartment before curfew.

Sometimes you have to trust strangers.

In a park, children swung and climbed under their mothers' watchful eyes. Noor chose a kind-looking woman about her age, cooing from beneath a purple hat into the wicker hood of a perambulator, and sat down beside her. She asked, as if it were the most normal question in the world, if madame could tell her the way to the internment camp.

The purple hat lifted from the pram and cocked in Noor's direction. Brown eyes looked Noor over, gaze resting pointedly on Noor's starless lapel.

"You have someone there?" the woman whispered, as if the Germans had listening devices everywhere, including children's parks in broad daylight.

Noor's desperate silence said yes, she did. She could only hope the woman loved someone dearly enough to understand.

The woman reached into the pram and adjusted her baby's bonnet. Out of the side of her mouth, never taking her eyes off the baby, she said, "Continue walking down the avenue Jean Jaurès. Take the right fork in the road after the *mairie*. You'll see the watchtowers. *Bonne chance.*"

Noor controlled her urge to run down the avenue, and set off at an even pace.

She was Anne-Marie Régnier on her way to meet her aunt. Aunt Lucille—Tante Lucille. Tante Lucille had a history of malingering illnesses. Tante Lucille had acquired a number of dearly guarded possessions that might be willed to poor Anne-Marie if Anne-Marie tended her well. Her dear old *tata* began to play the harp—badly—developed a dislike of strangers, a love of bone china figurines, and lived in Drancy instead of where she belonged, with Anne-Marie's family in Bordeaux, because her son was killed nearby at Meaux in the Great War, and she now refused to leave. It was like the game she and Kabir played as children, making up stories and motives and histories for people they saw on the métro.

A turreted watchtower came into view against the brilliant blue sky, looming over six parked German military lorries. Factory workers walked or wobbled past the camp gates on threadbare tires as if accustomed to its presence. For so many, as long as they were not within, Camp de Drancy was a place to cycle by.

What were the cyclists *thinking?*

At the lycée Noor's teachers often blamed the ills of the world on the inflow of immigrants, immigrants coming to France from anywhere, everywhere. Foreign-born people like herself who lived in Paris, and even those like Armand, born in France of naturalized parents. But for immigrant Jews they reserved a special distaste.

The words of popes, abbés, curés and pastors over centuries, not the words of Jesus, had paved the road to this camp. Artists, writers and politicians down the centuries re-enacted the crucifixion of Jesus "by the Jews" in paint, prose and palaver. Could one blame any one Frenchman for the anti-Semitism that created this camp? That one . . . or that one, beret pulled low over his brow?

Armand had been more afraid for Madame Lydia than himself, yet both were now behind the walls of Drancy. It might be worse for Madame Lydia: Russia had joined the Allies, and Madame Lydia had a Russian accent.

How could Maréchal Pétain and his premier, Laval, believe that the people behind those walls deserved such treatment? That someone like Armand, born in France, someone who composed music from the wind, whose every performance gave nothing but joy, posed a danger to France? Or to anyone?

When war was declared in '39, France incarcerated thousands of non-citizens, using amorphous words like "patriotism" and "prevention of terrorism." War, said everyone, required the imprisonment of immigrants and refugees from Germany, Poland, Russia — anywhere, especially if they were Jewish. People like Pétain said the French could no longer afford equal rights for citizens and non-citizens. Or even all citizens. People like Pétain said democracy's unending debates and strikes had crippled the country.

What had Armand and Madame Lydia done to the French, Pétain or the Germans? Nothing.

How often had newspapers said even "Israelites"—Jews like Armand, born in France, speaking French—were "unassimilable," and Noor had dismissed them because the French were wont to say the same of Muslims. The peeves and pettiness of the French rose from the same dark core as centuries of crusades and Christian hate-mongering against Muslims.

If the French didn't have Jews to blame, they'd have chosen the Muslims.

Yet how could she judge a single French man or woman harshly when her own elders, elders of the one family she had believed free of hatred towards any group, those who preached tolerance of all religions and spoke of the melding of East and West, rejected Armand when it came to marriage?

But what was that cyclist *thinking* about people behind those walls as he passed them by?

Noor was near Armand. Right now it was all she could do.

A bell sounded as she entered a *tabac* with standing room for two before its grimy counter. She asked the reedy proprietor leaning on his elbows from his stool behind the counter if he knew of any rooms for rent. He listened and allowed her to finish about Tante Lucille before remarking, "There are so many like you, mademoiselle."

Plainly he didn't believe in Tante Lucille, but by now Noor had convinced herself by the telling. "My aunt prefers that I live near her, you see."

The proprietor swept a rag over the counter with a gnarled hand. "Wait," he said. He opened a door behind him, barked out, "Claude!" then resumed his seat, folded his arms across his chest again and glared at her.

A checked beret poked through the door; it was the boy she'd stopped for directions to the village centre. The proprietor and Claude conferred about the possibilities for rental.

"Go with him on his bicycle," said the proprietor.

Claude brought the bicycle to the front of the *tabac* and held it steady as Noor hopped on the metal carrier, handbag on her lap.

She clutched at his coat, smelling rain and sweat and the acrid scent of his fear mingling with her own. The boy rode slowly past the lorries, the turreted watchtower, a long, long, four-metre-high wall topped with rolls of concertina wire, another watchtower fifty metres from the first, and another long wall.

For three years Noor had consoled herself in London by telling herself the incarceration of non-citizens and Jews in France was a temporary measure, but that now seemed terribly naive, too comforting, an idea these forbiddingly permanent camp walls and watchtowers did not support. These towers were built with French labour to inhibit foreign-born and Frenchman alike, with Vichy collaboration. Escape from behind those walls seemed impossible, even to her trained eye. What if the "temporary" measure became life imprisonment for Armand and others like him? But no, no—Armand and Madame Lydia would be released soon, certainly when conditions improved. The Germans had no reason, no reason at all, to keep them.

Past the last watchtower Noor looked back. Her mouth suddenly felt like a parched hole—a machine-gun silhouette turned towards them. She closed her eyes and took a deep breath.

Claude was approaching a five-storey red-brick building lurking behind a chestnut tree, a dilapidated structure that leaned in on itself, as if no one had entered it since the Great War. He cycled around the side, down a sun-variegated lane to a gate in a low wall. Noor jumped off as soon as his brakes squealed.

She followed him into a patch of lawn criss-crossed with lines of hanging laundry, past cabbage and potato plants, a vacant pigpen and an untended flower bed where tough little forget-me-nots braved the sun.

"Madame Gagné!" he called.

A woman in a sacklike dress came to the door, wisps of white hair straggling about her face.

"Have you a room for rent?" Claude asked.

"A hundred and fifty francs a week."

Claude whistled, glancing slyly at Noor.

Noor was elated enough to open her handbag and offer Madame Gagné the hundred and fifty francs immediately, but the bargaining instinct Mother complained she'd inherited from Abbajaan reminded her that one should show interest but not too much.

"It's expensive, but it's the best," said Madame Gagné. "With a view. It's occupied right now, but the tenant is moving. You could move in next week."

Noor looked at Claude. He gave an almost imperceptible shake of his head; too high.

"Seventy-five francs," said Noor, and held her breath. What if Madame Gagné refused? She told about Tante Lucille and how very sick she was, how she needed to be near the dear old lady.

Madame Gagné shrugged her complete disbelief. "*Sale Juive!*" she muttered. "I told you it has a *view*. One hundred francs and food coupons for your breakfast. That's my final offer."

Noor ignored the epithet; it was probably useless to protest she was not Jewish. At four hundred francs a month, the price was a hundred francs higher than Monique had mentioned for a clean room, but any safe house was good for only three or four weeks. All Noor cared about was having a room close to Armand.

She nodded, and the door opened.

"Return for me in half an hour," she said, pressing an SOE note into Claude's palm. He gave a quick grin, touched his beret in appreciation.

Madame Gagné wended her asthmatic way up seventy-two creaking stairs to a room on the fourth floor. Between wheezes she told Noor she was from the Midi but had lived in Paris twenty-five years—not long enough to feel or call herself Parisienne, but enough to long for Paris whenever she visited her cousins at home. Noor ignored the implied invitation to share her own origins and asked, were there any other rooms to choose from in the boarding house? Madame Gagné shook her head. The internment camp was excellent for business; every room was full.

"No one complains," she said, "even when the searchlights keep them awake at night. I serve breakfast from seven to nine.

Some men—probably Jews—have such an appetite, if you're not downstairs early, there'll be nothing left to eat."

She led Noor into an attic room, overheated from its proximity to sun. Its only furnishings were a cot-like bed and a desk. As Madame Gagné had emphasized, it had a view—one small window recessed into the slanted wall. And from it Noor could see over the camp's wall, see the U-shaped, five-storey concrete structure that was Camp de Drancy, see clusters of men, women and even small children in the central courtyard—prisoners all.

She was so close, so close. Yet too far to recognize one man among the rest.

"The children—wearing the yellow star."

"Of course they wear it." Madame Gagné coughed at her elbow. Her long ears had picked up Noor's involuntary whisper. "Jews who get caught not wearing the star are imprisoned and sent east to Germany." She looked pointedly at Noor.

Best to ignore the comment as if it was no concern of hers.

Noor studied the chestnut tree growing before the house. It offered a convenient branch that almost touched the window, a branch on which to string an aerial.

The sheets were clean, even if the duvet smelled of spilled wine and clandestine ardour. With some pride Madame showed Noor the timer light switch that would give a maximum of fifteen minutes of light, if there was electricity. Then she led Noor down the corridor to the lavatory.

"On this floor you share with Monsieur Durand, but often he is gone. He says he travels through France selling X-ray machines—but I think he only sells rabbits, that's what I think. I tell him what I told you: Jews caught not wearing the yellow star could be denounced. But he pretends he is hard of hearing."

Returning down the corridor, Madame Gagné pointed to another room. "This one is Gabrielle's room—she's a waitress at the Café Vidrequin—don't believe anything she says."

Rabbits are sweet and harmless. And anyone named for Angel Gibreel deserves a listening before judgement or dismissal.

"The bathroom is downstairs on the first floor."

Noor took the long iron key from Madame Gagné and counted out the rent in counterfeit francs. She must make contact with Armand. Insh'allah, she would think of something.

"I will stay three weeks," she said. "By then I'm sure Tante Lucille will be better."

Madame Gagné sniffed.

Noor sifted through the friable soil in the flowerpot, found the key and let herself in.

"Je suis seule ce soir avec mes rêves . . ."

Léo Marjane's mournful voice spun from the grooves of the record and flared from the gilded horn of the gramophone, amplifying the emptiness of Renée's drawing room.

"Renée?"

"J'ai perdu l'espoir de ton retour . . ."

A match scraped. Shadows danced a gavotte around a candle. Renée, in a chenille rose-vine print robe, reclined on a chaise longue, a framed photograph and a hanky on her lap. An abandoned game of solitaire was spread across the card table.

"Anne-Marie, Émile telephoned to say you would be coming tonight. Oh—hours ago!"

Renée sounded less peremptory tonight, or Noor had caught her at a vulnerable moment.

"Oh, Renée, am I late again?" Noor presented her with a posy of drooping forget-me-nots carried all the way from Madame Gagné's garden.

"Very pretty, Anne-Marie." Renée took a leather-bound ledger from the desk and pressed some flowers between its pages. "You really shouldn't wander about alone. Only prostitutes walk the streets so late. You almost missed the curfew."

"I'm sorry," said Noor. "Is Babette asleep?"

"My friend Madame Aigrain is looking after her tonight," said Renée. "Just nearby."

She arranged the rest of the flowers in a fluted vase, then brought Noor a bowl of carrot soup, a chunk of rye bread and a tiny slice of Camembert.

"Beautiful china," remarked Noor of the blue-flowered soup bowl and plates. It was impossible to compliment Renée on the soup.

"My grandmother's Gien." Renée joined Noor at the table.

"A lovely memento," said Noor, her hand rising involuntarily to the tiger claw beneath her blouse. Dadijaan's wizened brown face came to mind.

"Huh. I was not indulged," said Renée, "but my grand-mother did leave me this house as my dowry—and I promised her I will never sell it." She gave a great sigh. "It's going to fall apart around me."

Noor said, "My grandmother always indulges me. I wish every little girl had one like her."

"My mother pampers Babette," said Renée. "Too much—it's not good for the child. She must learn she can't have everything because she wants it." Her eyes gazed far away. Then a smile lit her face for a moment. "Guy—my husband—spoiled me. He did everything for me, everything I have now to learn and do myself."

"But now you are less dependent, non?"

Renée gave a sharp, sardonic laugh, lit a cigarette. "It's natural to be dependent. All these responsibilities—they are for men."

Whenever Uncle began another lecture about the "natural" dependence of girls, Noor and Zaib retorted that their father trusted women initiates in Holland, Belgium and America to carry his teachings forward, and he always said women's dependence had no basis in either nature or the Qur'an. But it would annoy Renée to disagree.

"If you had a child and an old house to look after, you might understand," said Renée. "Today I had to move that heavy chest in the kitchen and carry a sack of wood chips down to the cellar by myself. I planted carrots, cabbage and turnips in the kitchen garden—now I have to harvest them. Like a peasant, myself!"

The carrot soup was bitter. Only hunger and politeness allowed Noor to swallow it.

Work wasn't a burden; it was an opportunity to contribute to and participate in the world. Attitudes like Renée's were preached to Noor's cousin-sisters growing up in zenanas in India. How could Noor commiserate with Renée's helplessness?

"I always wanted many children," Renée went on. "But look—I'm thirty-nine. If my husband doesn't return soon, I will be left with but a single child."

Worse could happen to a woman than having only one child, and if Renée had travelled beyond Europe, she might readily imagine it.

But then, I didn't begin resisting dependence till I understood that being protected required me to forfeit a piece of my soul. Renée must not have realized that—yet.

The day she earned her Red Cross nursing certificate, Uncle had been furious! One would think she had joined a brothel instead of learned basic first aid. He roared that she would bring down her family in the eyes of the world, that a daughter of his *khaandaan*, the feudal House of Khans, should never be educated past her baccalaureate, should never work outside the home. His rage was so much grander than any potential earnings; her little certificate had threatened Uncle's fragile core. But Uncle knew, as she did, that with that certificate Noor would never be completely dependent on him or Kabir.

"I said you must have left at least three children behind in London if you are twenty-nine, but Monique said you are not married."

"My fiancé is in London," said Noor, for consistency with the story she'd told Monique.

"He gave you permission to work, then? Permission to leave the country?"

Noor kept her face pleasant but gave no answer. French law might still require women to obtain a man's permission to work, travel and marry, but not so in England. So Noor hadn't asked anyone.

"Your parents allowed you?" Renée suggested.

"My father is no longer alive," Noor replied.

"That is a pity," said Renée. "My father disappeared fighting the Germans. We were told he was buried alive while digging a tunnel near Vauquois. Émile was quite small, I was thirteen."

"I too was thirteen when my father died." To satisfy Renée's sense of propriety she added, "My mother gave permission." Knowing all the while that Mother knew nothing of her present whereabouts.

"You have sisters and brothers?"

"One of each."

"Your brother, he is in the army?"

"No."

"The air force?"

Noor didn't hesitate. "No, he's a teacher."

"And your sister?"

Renée seemed warmer tonight. Playing the enigmatic spy would only rekindle distrust.

"She's studying to be a doctor."

"A doctor!" said Renée. "I pity her husband and children — she has a suffragette mentality."

Be quiet. Be quiet.

Playing the veena, singing, horseback riding and writing stories for children, Noor had expressed herself far beyond the houseful-of-children terminus to which Uncle's marriage plans led; and insh'allah, Zaib would go further along that path, if Noor and Kabir could find the money for it. War brought opportunities as well as hardship, opportunities Uncle could never imagine. Zaib had Mother's drive: she wouldn't waste a single one.

Uncle would have approved of Renée as fit to befriend his nieces — one reason Noor would never have invited Renée to Afzal Manzil for his approval.

Perhaps Renée was simply bewildered and annoyed by choices and decisions. But no, it was more than that. Renée stubbed out her cigarette and lit another, saying, "I have no one but Émile. And with Guy captive in Germany, I am afraid for him. For every act of sabotage, the Germans execute ten Frenchmen. The guns are never silent at Mont Valérien."

"Mont Valérien?" Noor felt Armand's coat beneath her shoulders again, remembered their special spot under the tall chestnuts, the night of their clandestine marriage.

"The Germans shoot Communists and resistants there."

What desecration of a beautiful, sacred spot! Even without her memories of Armand, Mont Valérien was sacred to the memory of the soldiers buried there.

"I lived near Mont Valérien."

"Everything has changed." Anger born of crumbled expectations filled Renée's voice. "We are hostages abandoned by our men. They could have fought harder. Now the Germans will be here forever."

"Oh, no, Renée! It is not the fault of French soldiers. Listen, everyone says the Russians won at Stalingrad. That should give us hope. Even Napoleon couldn't conquer Russia, yet that insane Hitler believes he can! And so many like Émile are working to free France. The Allies have landed in Africa. The war cannot last forever."

"Allies in North Africa—huh! *Comme tu es naïve!* They've cut off supplies from our colonies. Today I paid eighteen francs on the black market for dates—a few months ago they cost four. I can't even find figs to fill our stomachs! You're too young to understand, Anne-Marie. Jews and immigrants led France into this war, and now the Germans imprison us all."

Change the subject.

"What work did your husband do?"

"Before the war? Guy was an engineer, like Émile. For years I told him he should get a government position, but he said private companies paid more. Maybe more when times are good, but when he became a POW, they stopped sending his salary. Now if he had been a civil servant as I begged him, the government would have paid it to me. You know how much is my allowance?

One hundred and forty francs per week and just half of Guy's army pay. Can any woman survive on that and buy milk for a child? Each parcel I send Guy costs me 250 francs—and does the government give me extra rations or textile points for him? No. Guy was saving to buy me a car, but now I've spent almost all our savings. I sold my mother's Daumier at an art auction for only sixty thousand francs—and this too is all gone. I might have to sell this house. In the Stalag, the Germans don't even give Guy clothes— I had to send him shoes in the last parcel. Oh, that was the worst! I told the social worker I know of wives who get much more. It's a disgrace." Renée held out her hands, palms upwards. "Are these the hands of an engineer's wife?"

Noor gave a sympathetic murmur as she rose from the table.

Prices and scarcities had dominated every discussion in London over the past three years too. But it did seem Renée wasn't being paid by the SOE. Miss Atkins hadn't instructed Noor to offer Renée payment for her hospitality, or said how much. Should she offer Renée money? Did she have enough SOE funds to do it? There'd be someone, insh'allah, to whom she could apply if funds ran low.

But Renée might be insulted by an offer of money. And Noor hated discussions of money; it received far too much importance.

"I won't be staying very long," she said, intending comfort.

In the bedroom, Noor carefully removed the grenades from her handbag, returned to Renée, and gave her Émile's directions to hide them till Sunday and his message of love for Babette.

Pforzheim, Germany
January 1944

The guard plays with me—she cheats me of bread some days, brings it late on others. There is no complaint department. I announce to myself I am a dervish living on bread and water. That doesn't stop me from remembering the taste of cardamon chai, a morsel of sweet jalebi, the scent of beef bourguignon—anything other than soup.

I drag my chains around my sealed cell in a stumbling approximation of exercise. I touch the walls—they feel warmer than me. I listen for patterns of explosions, patterns in the pulsing rush of nearby trains. I search for meaning in the scuttling of insects.

But I come back always to my paper, pen and ink. Why, and for whom, do I write? I fool myself, I pass the time. I add nothing to the world, I give no one pleasure or pain. Why render the past for you, spirit I never knew, may never see? But what else can I do? Sit here and look at the scratches on the plaster, worrying that I may meet the fate of those who've suffered in this cell before me?

A true Sufi would embrace this chance for solitude, meditation, silence. A true Sufi would use this time, focus on her beloved and the Divine Beloved, and pray for the annihilation of Self.

Abbajaan taught that separation from the Beloved, from Allah, is the greatest sorrow, that pain of which Rumi and other Sufi poets wrote. In my separation from Armand, I fathom an element of their anguish, for in the vast landscape of past emotions no pain is quite like this. The yearning for the beloved, human or transcendent, is its own pain and its own joy, varying in intensity, constant in its presence.

That night, in the small bedroom at Renée's, I searched my heart for sympathy with Renée for her similar separation from Guy, but her feelings were mixed with an anger I could not comprehend, an anger dwelling just beneath her suffering, waiting for direction. I had seen such anger mixed with sorrow and helplessness before, in Mother, your grandmother, left alone in Paris like Renée, without a husband and with children to feed. Mother blamed Abbajaan no less than Renée blamed Guy, first for leaving her, then for dying in India.

Yet how dissimilar were my reactions from Renée's, to the same events. The war and my escape to London freed me from Uncle Tajuddin's plans for my marriage to cousin Allahuddin, and taught me to rely on my own wits and actions, while Renée was defeated *at thirty-nine and blamed the enemy du jour for her unrealized potential. She seemed to experience every event as one more addition to a stream of affronts and inconveniences directed at her, and at no one else. She wanted security, safety—changelessness.*

Maybe because I am ten years younger, I still feel hope. My responsibility to you, ma petite, is to better the world before Armand and I ask your soul to return.

I had failed to say my prayers all day, and felt out of touch with Allah. So by the glow of a lantern placed between my bed and Renée's, I rested on one elbow and filled a sheet of onionskin with a letter to Kabir, asking him to pray to Allah on my behalf.

Bhaiya, brother mine, *I wrote:*

Allah has guided me to a place where hope and despair show their faces alternately. Pray that I have courage enough for this mission, and that we are united forever with those we love when this unending war dies down. I cannot write of the present, but since the present is but an echo of the past, I will write about the past.

Remember when we were children, Josianne and I would chase you and Zaib through dim rooms at Afzal Manzil after Abbajaan's students had gone home, how we played catch about the stone fountain at the end of the lane? And the garden where Abbajaan passed his mantle to you—you were only ten. I remember Mother sitting at her desk with her ledgers, frowning about finances, then putting on her bright smile to greet the students. Always she could play many parts, simultaneously.

And there were other actresses. Remember the time Zaib and I were at the cinema laughing at Arletty in *Fric-Frac* while you made excuses for us to Uncle. How glad I am to this day that he believed you!

Remember the shared times, brother of mine.

Say a *du'a* for me, forget me not,

Noor.

Kabir was flying missions over Europe; it was not the time to remind him that my memories of shared times were not all beautiful. I don't know all that was said between your uncle and your father when they met in 1940, only that Kabir refused to see what was special about Armand. Kabir's heart turned from me at the very moment I needed his love most, when he agreed with Uncle that marriage to cousin Allahuddin would be the best cure for my love for a Jew.

I signed that letter "Noor," but I could have signed Anne-Marie or Madeleine so long as I called him "brother." I have known your uncle Kabir a few years longer than he has known himself, but Kabir has never known Noor, only the role called "sister."

I sealed the envelope, put it in my handbag and returned to bed. Renée knelt beside the lantern and the small tongue of flame grew dim, then vanished.

She lay down and I lay awake, thinking long and hard of the white walls and gun towers surrounding Camp de Drancy. Armand's letters flashed before me as if on a cinema screen. The one from Cannes, saying only that he and your grandmother Lydia were safe. Then the one from Nice. Then finally the card from Drancy in April. No message sidled between the blackened lines, I could make out nothing that said he wished we were together.

And how, when I had said "Adieu," did I expect Armand would write at all, for was it not I, your cowardly mother, who agreed that afternoon in the Bois de Boulogne, agreed because Armand wanted it so, that we must forget one another, forget eight, almost nine long years of love and waiting?

Maybe his cards were but tributes to nostalgia for our friendship; he has always been my friend first, my closest friend.

Could I ask one wish of a genie, I thought, I would return to that moment in the Bois and say, "I do not want safety; we are only safe when nothing more can happen to us. I am your wife: I share your fears, your burdens; your people are mine. If they and you are not safe, no one is safe. I will be with you always."

Allah, my love had survived even our dashed plans for life together. I could not—still cannot—bear to think of Armand suffer-

ing, without adequate food, needing clothes, shoes. Was it possible? The night I wrote to Kabir, I still believed such suffering could not happen in Europe, could not be inflicted by Europeans on Europeans. Like Odile, I too believed that kind of suffering is only inflicted on the colonized in places like India and Africa.

I heard a sniff, then another; Renée must have thought me asleep. I wondered if I should try to comfort her, but some griefs and longings are private, like my grief for you, my longing for Armand. When these come upon me unpredictably, there is no bargaining with them. I hide them beneath distractions, resolutions and activity.

Eventually I fell into exhausted sleep and dreamed I was searching for Armand, when suddenly I began falling from a great height, that a man I did not know reached out to save me. Then I was suspended in mid-air with only a strange man's arms supporting me.

I woke sweating, wondering which of my countries I was in, and why my tears were still falling.

CHAPTER 14

Paris, France
Sunday, June 20, 1943

PIANO TRILLS TRICKLED into the summer night from the Jazz
Club on the rue Pigalle. Inside, knots of men and women clustered at tables before the crimson-curtained stage. Among them,
one . . . two . . . three Abwehr officers and one Luftwaffe. The low-
level danger alert resounding in every cell since Noor left England
transposed itself a semitone upscale.

Actually, a little danger and excitement were welcome. All
day Saturday she was learning procedures from Archambault in
the tool shed at Grignon. Encoding, tap-tapping in spurts to transmit, receiving and decoding messages — no time to return to
Drancy. In the evening she had roamed room after room with
ghastly decor in boarding houses beyond the perimeter of Paris,
searching for one suitable for transmissions. But each had its
flaws, and with less than half the métros and buses in operation
the search took hours she would rather have spent at Drancy making discreet inquiries.

And today — a long day. Early morning mass with Émile,
Monique and Renée. Noor left their church full of faith, trust and
hope in Allah, uplifted by the hymns she'd sung and the communion she'd taken to allay any latent suspicion in Renée.
Consuming the body and blood of anyone, leave alone Hazrat

Issa, left her feeling a bit like a cannibal, but at least she wasn't struck by lightning for being a non-Catholic yet taking communion. She'd said mental *rakats* while kneeling and standing for hymns—Allah would understand.

But then Émile and Monique left and Renée made it clear she expected Noor to mind Babette at a merry-go-round in the park, and peel potatoes and carrots for dinner. In mounting frustration Noor had even done Renée's mending—she, who had always detested sewing—and boiled cauldrons of water for Babette's bath in the evening. So she was glad to be here; one might think Renée had permitted her the evening off.

Where was Émile?

The foyer was dense with many hues of women's perfume. Despite the club's location in the red-light district, the women looked respectable, a few wearing real silk stockings instead of beige leg paint. Noor's white cotton dress, borrowed from Renée, was appropriate; so too the lemon silk headscarf that framed her tiger claw. Still, if Zaib were here, the sisters would have chanted the old line in unison, "Uncle Tajuddin would never approve!"

If I did only what Uncle Tajuddin approved, I'd accomplish nothing at all. But Zaib and I could have been kinder; all poor Uncle wanted was to do his duty by us, for his half-brother's sake.

Hitler disapproved of "schräge Musik"—he'd banned jazz from the airwaves. But here his officers were, enjoying its "decadence."

Paintings quilted every inch of faded wallpaper: a curvaceous nude knelt in her gilt frame beside a landscape in dabbed brush strokes, a Senegalese mask frowned cheek by jowl with an Erté-style drawing, an experimental abstract nudged a Surrealist rendering of some waking dream—so diverse, they must have been traded by artists in settlement of bills.

She sauntered past the hat stand like a regular patron, into a smell of vinegar pickles and burnt raclette.

The curtain rose, and a stoic, smoke-husky voice began an imitation of Piaf. Lights dimmed till a single spotlight constrained the sombre hope of the song. Cymbals clashed, gently marking phrases in the bass player's tempo pump-pump-pumping beneath the melody.

She had been to other jazz clubs—in Montparnasse, for instance. Surreptitiously, of course, for fear of Uncle. With Armand, with friends like Josianne. Before the war.

One moment, just a moment, of surrender to the music and her eyes began smarting. From the cigarette smoke? No. The lyrics. All about separation and heartbreak.

Three short weeks for this assignment, and here she was, five days after landing in France, two days after renting a room in Drancy—but no contact with Armand. She took a deep breath and focused on the shiny trouser knees of the clarinetist, the grey of the drummer's pre-war white shirt, the threadbare droop of the saxophonist's bow tie.

Fair hair stood out even in the gloom—German bureaucrats towering a head taller than the average Frenchmen. Earlier she had noticed only the Germans in uniform.

Look out for taller men. Be more observant, more aware!

Something else—

The musicians were all Europeans. In every jazz club she and Armand frequented before the war, she could not recall one such as this, where the band had not a single Negro musician. Most Negroes had probably fled France, and those who stayed must have been interned. *Bien sûr!* Many were American citizens, like Mother.

The singer circled back to the chorus, the song faded. Lights brightened in their sconces.

Noor approached the bar. Émile Garry—Phono—stood beside a glass of absinthe, nonchalant, acting as if he came here every Sunday evening and had no appointment with anyone called Anne-Marie.

"*Un café noir,*" said Noor.

The barman pointed to a sign: twenty-eight francs. An astronomical sum. "It's a dry day tomorrow, but not today," he suggested, meaning there were alternatives to black coffee.

At such prices her money wouldn't last three weeks. For a moment Noor reconsidered. But an aperitif would be more expensive. She repeated her request.

Émile's coat sleeve brushed her upper arm. The reassuring tightness of his biceps. Phono—just a name recited by Miss Atkins six days ago in London, now a friend pretending to meet her by chance.

Could she see the door from here? Escape if necessary? The escape route: through that kitchen door, into the courtyard behind and over the wall, Émile had said.

She spread her dress-skirt wide as she took her seat, to discourage anyone from sitting too close. No mistakes. Of any kind. A single mistake might bring arrest not just for herself but for her contacts. There should be a list of all the mistakes a secret agent shouldn't make.

Darkness spread across the club again. An instrumental stretch unfolded in accord with itself, notes improvising their way out of the spotlight to an unknown destination.

Abbajaan improvised on the veena for hours when she and Kabir were small. Music was his métier, his true vocation, but Indian instruments and music proved incomprehensible to Western audiences. Mother had urged him to simplify the music. Who could blame her for that? But eventually Abbajaan had refused. Making his music any simpler for Western ears, he said, degraded the devotion to Allah that underlay each note. By the time she was nine and learning the veena from him, Abbajaan could talk for hours about that devotion—people paid to hear him speak—but refused to play in public any more, and bitterly resented the loss of his art.

Instruments were incidental to Abbajaan and Armand; how they sounded was everything. If Abbajaan had been alive, he would have welcomed Armand, whatever his heritage, improvised with him, allowed his presence to enrich their family.

"May I join you, mademoiselle?"

Noor shrugged assent, as if Émile were a total stranger. Émile pulled a chair close enough to whisper in her ear without leaning, then almost deafened her by shouting.

"*Viennot, mon ami!* I haven't seen you in months!"

"Or at least since last week," said a wry voice behind Noor.

A pair of bushy black eyebrows, a mop of dark, curly hair and a half-sniggering grin installed themselves beside Noor.

"Please, do not insult the *patron*'s intelligence, Émile. And remember"—Viennot lowered his voice—"there are enough Gestapo here who know me quite well."

Émile seemed about to retort when a German officer in a black uniform entered. Silence swept across the table, in fact across the room. Noor narrowed her eyes. SS. Death's head on his cap. Sicherheitsdienst, or the SD—police officer of the SS. He joined a suet-faced German bureaucrat wearing round spectacles. People went back to their conversations.

Viennot seemed not yet thirty, an age where either employment or wits kept him from being sent to work in Germany. Instead, here he was, lolling back in his chair, moving one foot in time to the music, the ribboned tassel of a red beret bordered in checkered black and white dropping almost to his back. The ends of a long brown silk scarf knotted themselves like hands above the collar of his burnt sienna coat, a black onyx brooch winking at his throat as if holding the whole ensemble together.

"You ask me to come, I come," said Viennot. He sounded like a venturer down all avenues. "Mademoiselle——?" An eyebrow lifted in her direction.

"Anne-Marie Régnier," said Émile.

Viennot's remark about the Gestapo wasn't reassuring. Noor forced a smile.

"Jacques Viennot."

Viennot stared deeply into Noor's eyes, then fixed his gaze upon her lips, lingered at her neck, stayed a few seconds too long on her breasts. He seemed to think his admiration was a compliment; plainly he thought that about every woman. A little hijab would offer some protection against his barely repressed fantasies. Noor let her hair fall forward, obscuring her face.

Viennot ordered a Pernod, remarking that this was one of the few places you could still get one, and didn't count his change when the waiter returned with the green concoction.

"Mademoiselle is newly arrived," whispered Émile. "Code name: Madeleine."

This information elicited Viennot's undivided attention, though his foot never lost a beat and his eyes roved, watching other club patrons.

"*Bienvenue*, mademoiselle," he said. "Émile, I congratulate you—another war tourist to educate, shelter, shepherd around, hmm? Another prudish Englishwoman to protect till Mr. Churchill decides we've been punished enough by Herr Hitler."

Émile gave his good-natured smile. "He is not serious, Anne-Marie."

"Frenchmen should do the job of Frenchmen," said Viennot. "Placing women in dangerous situations . . . it offends my chivalry."

"Monsieur Viennot," said Noor, "hundreds—maybe thousands—of French women are in very dangerous situations. All of us, men and women, are in dangerous situations at every moment."

Viennot looked surprised, then nodded grudgingly.

He's unaccustomed to the idea that women can take action.

Émile said to Noor, "Viennot requires a *pianiste*. from time to time. He's well connected, often has advance information that can be very useful to our friends in The Firm. Odile or Monsieur Hoogstraten will convey his messages to you, but you should recognize him by sight."

Noor had no doubt she could recognize Monsieur Viennot by sight, about a mile away.

"*Voilà*, now you know your partners," whispered Émile. "Monsieur Hoogstraten, our chief, Professor Balachowsky, Gilbert, me and Viennot. Prosper, of course." He leaned back in his chair, tipped his glass as if sipping and spoke to Viennot from the side of his mouth. "Archambault will leave as soon as Anne-Marie's transmitters arrive."

Viennot's eyebrows met. "Is he marked in some way? Identifiable to them?" He half turned in his seat and looked away from Émile as if surveying the room.

"Archambault needs training on new equipment."

"I see. Have we experienced any new outbreaks of sickness?"

"Yes, we had more people taken ill this morning, near Dhuizon."

"Taken ill"—code for arrests.

Viennot took a larger sip, almost a gulp. "How did our friends on the avenue Foch find out?" He meant the Gestapo, appropriators of several mansions on that long leafy boulevard.

"I really don't know. Archambault swears we have a double agent. When Prosper came in last week, he requested Marc, the officer he has worked with ever since he first arrived—a true patriot, above suspicion. Yet they were waiting at a road block. They dragged two good men out of their truck and beat them unconscious."

"Did they find the supplies?"

"All nine containers, under the straw in the back. And worse: a courier was arrested on his way home after disposing of a load, and they let him go after questioning. You know why? They said they were looking for someone arriving *from London*. How did they know? Of course, right now, they could arrest every person travelling at night on the roads around Paris and down the Loire valley, and every man would be a member of some resistance group or a Maquis. Viennot, so many supplies—every day we ask more people to take more terrible risks. London wants us armed for a ground invasion, and it's our only hope—but it must happen soon."

"Émile, *tais-toi!* The Germans don't have to go down the Loire—someone will overhear you and arrest you right here."

Émile gave a sardonic laugh. "Here? *Moi?* I can say anything today—it's not a dry day. To them I am a stupid, drunken, lying, lazy Frenchman—all of us are. And these Germans are sellers, friends of yours, from whom you buy information every day."

Viennot made no answer, but cloaked himself in the smoke and scent of a Gauloise. He looked unabashed.

Across the room, an argument had escalated to a sharp slap and tears. A woman staggered into the night, shrieking maledictions. Unconcerned, an artist a few tables away carefully arranged the angle of his model's head and continued sketching her profile in charcoal.

"Did you have enough blasting caps last night?" whispered Noor. She had had no chance to ask Émile before now.

"Oui, oui—and we managed to find more. The German side of the hospital near the junction was very busy this morning," Émile whispered in a tone of cherubic glee. "I will give you a message to send as soon as I know how many Boche wounded, how many dead." He broke off. *"Voilà!"*

Monsieur Hoogstraten, Prosper, Archambault and Gilbert were doffing their hats and making their way past the white jackets and the soloist. Prosper and Gilbert absorbed the pulse of vibrating bass strings, but Archambault's deliberate gait remained unaffected by the deep booming beat. Monsieur Hoogstraten's military gait and silver-touched pate stood out in the room; most of the men were half his age. Chair legs scraped terrazzo as the men sat down at the next table. A bottle of wine made its precarious way from the bar.

Émile's furtive demeanour turned festive; his job of introducing Noor to her fellow agents was done. Now Noor had to look just like any other Parisian enjoying jazz.

Glasses clinked as signature to unwritten promises, in the press and hubbub of ongoing commerce. The musicians bowed to applause and left the spotlight briefly to a flamenco guitarist, whose minor chords and depressive lyrics of unhealed wounds matched his refugee eyes.

When they returned, they resumed without fanfare or drums. A slow piece that alternated between wordless resignation and sporadic creative buildup. Whispered cues caused new instruments to appear and change hands. A tenor saxophone launched an accelerando, the piano a glissando. The bass player's fingers danced an arpeggio. It was a gathering of effort that verged on the heroic. Clarinets and drums entered the fray now, heralding a vertiginous crescendo. Soon the walls of the small club vibrated with compressed expectation. Nothing intervened to offer release.

Just as Noor's temples began to pound with the tension, each instrument, every player, every note went silent. Mid-bar, mid-phrase, mid-note, suddenly there was silence, a jolting, brutal silence that dispelled the revelry with a final, shocking break, with not an isolated chord to cushion the end.

Just silence.

Clap, clap.

Clap.

Monsieur Hoogstraten had taken the sudden silence for successful conclusion. Younger French patrons accustomed to more satisfying musical dénouements followed his lead hesitantly, and Noor joined in.

The band must have been making an artistic gesture of valiant defiance.

German officers, unaware of the subtle symbolism, looked up from their champagne glasses and banged their fists on the tables in appreciation.

No Mad Hatter's tea party was ever so strange.

The Jazz club was becoming more crowded. Viennot and Gilbert departed in the direction of beckoning eyes. Prosper patted a vacant seat beside him, so Noor moved one seat over. Monsieur Hoogstraten made his way to the lavatory, and Émile to the bar for more absinthe. Archambault offered cigarettes to Prosper, then Noor. Noor declined; she only smoked occasionally, in surreptitious protest against Uncle's restrictions.

Prosper flicked his lighter. A tremor stirred the flame. Noor hadn't thought Prosper's hand could be unsteady.

"That's what will happen."

Was he speaking to Archambault or to her?

"Silence, just like that. For all fifteen hundred brave French soldiers in my network. Tell the Colonel. As soon as you arrive, say: there is a traitor in The Firm." He was speaking to Archambault.

"I say the traitor is right here," said Archambault.

Noor looked away but strained to listen; Prosper was now whispering.

"I know what you think. But we have no proof. All Gilbert's operations have been successful. Every case of illness has been elsewhere. I tell you, this network cannot survive three more months." Prosper leaned back. He glanced at Noor, excused himself and now included her fully in the conversation. "I moved today."

"Will you tell me where?" asked Archambault.

"The Hôtel Mazagran in St-Denis, room fifteen," he whispered.

"Back among your old friends the Communists." Archambault made it sound like a nasty flaw in an otherwise rational person.

"They are workers willing to unite against Hitler and the Germans, that's all."

Archambault backpedalled. "I meant it's a far cry from the comfort of the Seizième, n'est-ce pas?"

"It's bloody uncomfortable, but I think still safe."

"Who else knows?"

"Mademoiselle Anne-Marie needs to know," said Prosper with a slight nod in her direction, "because she must know where to reach me. And Gilbert. No one else."

"Why Gilbert?"

"Because if I have to leave suddenly, he will have to arrange a flight." Turning slightly to Noor, he said, "Mademoiselle, have you rented the new premises yet?"

"Only one. In Drancy."

"Bien. I will be gone for a few days. Use Grignon until your sets arrive, then leave a set at each safe house and move between them for transmissions." And to Archambault, "You heard what happened this morning at Dhuizon?"

"Yes. I sent a message addressed to Monsieur N. immediately."

"Sometimes I think everyone is oblivious to the dangers. We must be more careful, for the sake of all! I was with Monsieur Hoogstraten and Professor Balachowsky at Grignon today when I heard the news. I felt terrible, terrible. The Boche seem to know all our plans in advance. What is to be done?"

Archambault gave a noncommittal grunt and sipped his wine.

Order him to transmit a message, blow up a train or meet a plane and he can do it, but advising Prosper is beyond him.

Prosper looked so wretched, Noor's heart went out to him. But what comfort or assistance could she offer? She was too new to her cell.

Viennot, Gilbert and Monsieur Hoogstraten squeezed their way back through the crowd and sat down beside Prosper. Émile returned from the bar.

Time for a little gypsy guitar music or something like "Je Suis Swing," from the Drôle de Guerre days of 1939. But—remember the Germans!—swing was outlawed. The band launched a slow foxtrot, prompting a Wehrmacht officer to lead a French woman in a georgette dress of Prussian blue to the dance floor. The spotlight illuminated his uniform, never box-stepping more than a few inches off dead centre, stiff as a robot from the '37 World Exhibition. If this were London, Zaib and others would be on the dance floor doing the jitterbug.

Under cover of the music, Prosper, composure regained, launched into more orders, more plans. "Gilbert, bring the Canadians to Paris tomorrow morning. Meet me at the entrance to the Gare d'Austerlitz."

"Canadians?" said Viennot.

"Yes, two Canadians. Don't worry, they speak fluent French."

Viennot's eyes rolled, Noor smothered a smile. She fell silent with everyone else till the waiter refilled their glasses and departed.

"No sleep tonight—the Canadians are coming," grumbled Gilbert. "Then no sleep the following night either, because I must meet the plane at Rosny."

Archambault glared. "Sleep all day, then, but be there."

"Are we ready for Rosny?" asked Prosper.

Attention intensified around the table, though to any curious German it would seem there was no change in physical attitudes and everyone at the table was listening to the music.

Émile reported, "Professor Balachowsky has spoken to his students, I have obtained the petrol permit. Now I have to find the petrol. But have no doubt—I will."

Lights dimmed and the jazz players began to improvise from the first three bars of the Marseillaise, the musical quote recognizable enough for the solace of French patrons but moving away from its source rapidly enough not to trigger German suspicions.

Gilbert's arm sidled across the back of Noor's chair. "You have letters?"

Noor opened her handbag below the table. She whispered, "Please make sure this is delivered, Gilbert, it is so very important to me."

The lights blazed on and the jazz players retreated immediately from their dalliance with the Marseillaise to safer musical ground, "Lili Marlene."

Gilbert skimmed the address silently—*Kabir Khan, c/o The War Office, Whitehall, London*—and gave her a knowing wink as he slid it into his pocket.

Noor wasn't required to explain to Gilbert that Kabir Khan was not a lover or fiancé. Let Gilbert believe what he pleased. But that wink irked her. She looked at her watch. Half an hour to curfew; time to catch the last métro.

Shiny black automobile doors opened before the club and slammed squarely, amid the saluting of chauffeurs. Monsieur Hoogstraten and Archambault left, sandwiched in a group of tipsy Luftwaffe officers. Viennot muttered *au revoir* and slipped into the night. Gilbert said he was going home to sleep a few hours before the landing.

Noor walked a few streets away and waited on the corner.

A warm, clear night—an invitation to bombers. Stray dogs had collected around rubbish heaps to gnaw at gristle and bone.

A low laugh from a brothel window above her countered the stillness of the street. Light slanting from a chink between drapes illuminated a handbill from a long-ago Communist call to strike: *Venez faire de jolies grèves avec nous!* Beside it, bold black letters on a gargantuan yellow poster said BEKANNTMACHTUNG in German and AVIS in French. She read the French proclaiming that fathers of all "bandits, saboteurs and troublemakers," their male antecedents and descendants, cousins over the age of eighteen and anyone guilty of assisting them would be shot. Women relatives of the same degree would be condemned to forced labour, and children under the age of seventeen would be taken and put in homes.

Horrible. When did this begin? The date below the signature of someone designated *Leader of the SS and the Police in France* said almost a year ago. And below that signature some intrepid resistant had lettered a V for victory and drawn the Gaullist Cross of Lorraine.

Heartening, even inspiring.

A light tap on her shoulder. Noor spun around; she hadn't heard anyone coming.

"*Shhhhh!*"

Émile. Only Émile.

She slipped her hand through his crooked elbow and he escorted her to the métro — a most respectable couple going home after a summer evening of jazz.

CHAPTER 15

Paris, France
Sunday, June 20, 1943

A PENETRATING WHINE built to a moan then whipped itself to a centrifugal wail. People halted on the rue Erlanger as the code heralding danger swooped among them, splintering the flow of time. Dogs growled then yapped, snapped and broke into furious barking. Then everyone was shouting and moving again, at double speed.

Noor had stopped halfway up the stone path to Renée's home. She was behind Émile as he snatched the key from the flowerpot and shouldered in.

"Thank God you've come!" came Monique's voice.

Renée was in her dressing gown in the kitchen, moving with practised swiftness, stuffing tins, candles and blankets into a basket. Émile darted into the bedroom, came out carrying a sleep-tousled Babette against his shoulder, and a torch.

"It's only a test, I'm sure," he said.

"Tests are on Thursdays," said Monique, her clogs clattering after him. "Today is Sunday."

Suresnes, all over again. June 3, 1940. Noor had crouched for hours with her family deep in Afzal Manzil's wireless cellar among sacks of lentils and ceramic jars of Indian pickles imported from Bombay.

Get down to Renée's cellar.

In the kitchen, Renée had opened a linen chest against the wall and removed the tablecloths and serviettes. She leaned into the chest and in a second removed a false plywood bottom. Noor helped unwind a rope tied in a figure eight around a hook. With the restraining rope untied, the chest pulled away from the wall effortlessly, revealing an iron ring in the floorboards. Monique grasped the ring and heaved. A section of the floor came up in her hand. Below, a rusty corkscrew of a staircase bore down into darkness.

Émile put Babette down. The siren wail faded as Noor followed his bobbing light down the spiral. It was the Blitz again, the air raids on London again. Mother and Zaib ahead, and Noor holding fast to Dadijaan's hand, shouting instructions in Urdu for her—all descending underground at Euston Square station.

But now she was hiding from Allied, not German, bombs.

Above Noor, Renée and Monique pulled and strained till the trap door scraped closed.

A loop of rope dangling from the roof guided the way down. Noor reached for it.

"Don't!" Renée shouted, descending quickly.

Noor recoiled.

"That pulls the chest back against the wall."

"Renée, she didn't know!" said Monique. Pulled tight and looped about a hook in the cellar, the rope locked the chest in the kitchen back in place. Pulled from above, knotted in the false bottom of the chest, it would do the same.

"Welcome to our Scarlet Pimpernel room," said Émile, his torch guiding Noor past the foot of the stairs to a bench.

The cellar had the usual complement of crates and barrels neatly stacked in a far corner. The torch illuminated the square nub of a boarded-up well at its centre; the house predated Baron Haussmann and his sewer engineers. Past the well, through a narrow archway, stood two long tables. One was laden with wires, steel parts and small packets marked TNT. The scent of pigment dye, embossing ink and solvent hovered over the second.

Noor drew closer.

Stacks of identification booklets, blank ration tickets and rubber stamps of all kinds. So here was Émile and Monique's workshop.

"The house was rebuilt a few times since the aristos hid here to escape La Guillotine. They took a passage"—he pointed to a door recessed into the wall—"all the way from here to the Seine. It was sealed off when the apartments were built on either side."

Monique brought Babette her doll.

"So we may not have an escape route, but we do have camouflage. Monique and I made this together."

A match flared in Monique's hand. A candle appeared on a ledge set in the stone wall, beside the puddled wax of many others.

Émile moved to the wall and turned a crank. A pulley mechanism began a metallic creaking and rumbling. Something began to slide slowly from the ceiling—a canvas screen, painted to match the stone wall. Noor stepped back, and Émile bent before it cleared waist level. Once in place, the cellar was almost halved in size and the workshop was completely concealed behind the mural. In the dark, if you didn't touch the screen, it looked just like a wall.

"Monique painted it," Émile said, waving the torch. "A true artist."

Monique's temple rested for a second on his shoulder. "Save the battery," she said.

Émile clicked the torch off. A distant rumble and boom sounded above. Then another. The stone walls seemed to vibrate.

"*Sales Anglais!*" Renée hissed into the dark.

"It's not the British, Renée, it's the Americans," said Émile.

"Whoever it is, wish them well, Renée." Monique's voice was steady. "Think of every bomb bringing us a little closer to freedom."

"I wish I could believe that." Renée's voice sounded over the rumbling overhead. "Three years. How long can we go on living like this? We could all be killed, but I think it's worse to be wounded. You know the concierge next door? Her sister's leg was crushed in a bombing."

"Madame Meignot?" said Monique. "Poor thing! Her own knees are shaky from years of polishing floors. Pétain may have surrendered to Hitler, but she says she hasn't."

Noor shook her head, tried a yawn. Her eardrums strained as if a thousand kilos of steel pressed upon the small room. The cellar was close—too close—to the surface. They could be buried alive. But what choice was there? The métro was too far away.

Struggle not to think of what must be going on somewhere outside. Calls of "Aidez-moi! M'aidez!" The sputter and rage of fires, the crying of children. Running stretcher-bearers, nurses, doctors, bobbing gas lanterns, the desperate clang of shovels and pickaxes. Don't think of bombs falling on Drancy. Or bombs falling where the land has no bricks and mortar for armour. Don't think of London, Dunkirk and Coventry, and so many other cities bombed by German planes . . .

Renée had her arm around Babette, a wide-awake Babette quivering from either fear or excitement.

"Those bombers," said Renée. "Dropping bombs on us as they did to our fleet at Mers el-Kébir."

Fight had drained from her face. Noor stopped herself from a cutting retort; it would be cruel to defend Kabir and the British forces in the face of such mortal fear.

"Renée, that was the English navy, not the RAF," said Émile.

"The British scuttled our whole fleet, didn't they?"

"If they hadn't, Pétain would have placed every warship at the service of the Germans," Émile replied. He sounded unusually impatient; he must have explained this to Renée before.

"Don't worry," said Monique. "Sometimes the Boche sound the sirens to make Parisians believe we are in danger from the Allies."

Whistles, booms and the sounds of ack-ack guns above contradicted Monique's optimism. In all its years the house had probably never encountered such vibration and pressure. If it collapsed, they would all be sealed inside. If this were London, Home Guard personnel and bomb-diffusion experts would be dispatched to dig them out—but who was assigned this job in Paris? German soldiers? The *milice?*

"The trains. I know it—the British are bombing the trains. And almost every train is filled with Frenchmen going to work in Germany!"

"Renée, I said it's not the British, it's the Americans. From the direction, they must be bombing the Renault works or the diesel engine factory."

Émile was just trying to comfort Renée; he couldn't possibly tell which direction the bombs were aimed. But Noor's heart had begun to race faster. Renée's fear gave rise to her own . . .

What if my Armand is no longer at Drancy? What if he is one of those Frenchmen sent to Germany?

She had never considered this. Why had she not considered this?

Mais non, non! Allah is not so cruel. Armand must, he must still be held at Drancy.

The crash and thunder of falling debris shook Noor, even in the cellar. Somewhere outside, people were dying. Would it be better to die outside than be killed in this hole? She was a qualified nurse, she might be able to help. Should she go to their assistance?

"How can you call yourself patriots when Frenchmen are being killed?" Renée's voice ricocheted off stone.

"Renée, those who die are martyrs," said Émile. "But even if it takes a century, the Boche are doomed because the Occupation is wrong. Any occupation, *vous savez? Immorale!* Listen: we have survived the most terrible of years, building small networks while we squabbled. But all of us—even the Communists, the trade union federations—are now united. The whole Resistance is united. You'll see—we'll knock the Germans back across the Rhine."

Émile sounded as if he had met Max, General de Gaulle's liaison to the Resistance in France, who had clandestinely travelled all through France earlier in the year, uniting the Free French; who Miss Atkins said might even become president of

France if Mr. Churchill and Mr. Roosevelt decreed, and if there was a France left to be governed.

Renée pulled her dressing gown close about her thin shoulders and kept talking. "*Perfide Albion!* They make you promises to respect France if you support them, they tell you, 'Come, rise up against the Germans!' and then they will sit back and watch the repression. And if they rout the Germans, they will simply occupy France in place of the Germans and fold our empire into theirs."

Renée's reading of the British had some truth. They had fomented rebellion in Indian territories they sought to conquer, then betrayed those rebels who relied on their promises. Control of a threatened state's foreign policy in return for guarantees of independence—then they reneged on the independence part, as the Germans were doing in France. But usually Britain reserved such subterfuge for areas east of Suez, and for brown people like Tipu Sultan. They wouldn't do such things to fellow Europeans.

"If that should happen, I promise on the graves of our parents, dear sister, we will begin a new resistance against the English," said Émile.

Renée threw up her hands. "*Mon Dieu*, can you not see, Émile—while you hope and work for an invasion, fat Mr. Churchill devours roast duck every night. And we live on potatoes."

Noor interposed, "Madame, in London the posters say *Better potluck today with Churchill than humble pie under Hitler tomorrow.* Mr. Churchill has only one goal: to defeat Hitler."

Renée turned on her. "Mademoiselle—I too wish for the defeat of Herr Hitler, but I am no dreamer, and it does not mean I wish for the victory of the English, the Americans and some general who flees to England while his men are sent to prisons in Germany. And it is they who are, this moment, bombing France and Germany—" Her voice broke. "Bombing my Guy in Germany."

Was there some third path Renée could see between Allied victory and Hitler's defeat? Not for France, with its vanquished army. And meanwhile?

Renée said to Émile, "I have a child and no husband. Please, I do not want to lose you too. No one in our family has ever been a saboteur."

Can Renée believe collaboration, Vichy style, is acceptable? No—this safe house shelters me and other British agents, and harbours the work Émile and Monique do in this very cellar.

"I shall be the first, then," said Émile, unrepentant.

Renée shook her head and wiped her eyes.

"If I had a sweet child like Babette," said Noor, "I might also prefer safety to freedom. But I didn't come here to surrender to Fascist ways. You know why I'm here—it's all illegal, like Émile's work. But since free people do not recognize the laws of despots . . . *tant pis!*"

"So many laws—one cannot obey all of them." Monique's coaxing tone held a smile.

"You mock me?" said Renée. "We could at least try to obey."

"But remember, Renée, since I was a little boy I have been chronically unable to obey," Émile said in a jesting tone. "And now that I'm a vicious criminal, it's even more difficult!"

Babette put her arms about his neck. *"C'est vrai, Oncle Émile?"*

"Huh!" said Renée. "Don't let your uncle fill you with his ideas."

Babette withdrew.

The candle guttered in its own smoke. A second flame rose from Émile's cupped hand.

"Oh! What have I in my pocket for Babette?" he said. *"Tiens!"*

Babette's laughter warmed the cellar. Tension melted.

"Chocolate? Say '*Merci, mon oncle.*' Share it with everyone," chided Renée. "One piece for each of us."

Noor's body shouldn't betray her by enjoying chocolate when Armand could not share it. Under cover of the dark she slipped it back into Babette's hand.

Monique said, "I'll save mine for Odile. She loves chocolate."

Voices rose and fell around Noor, arguing the merits of dark chocolate over light, Swiss over Belgian. The best chocolate éclair she had ever tasted, said Monique, was from Madame Millet's *pâtisserie*.

"What's a chocolate éclair?" Babette interjected.

Startled silence all around. It was a question any child in India might ask.

Monique explained. Then, to Babette's giggling delight, she told a tale of a *mousse au chocolat* so light, it slid from its mould and floated right up into your mouth. Émile added one of a chocolate fondue from Fouquet's so creamy that each strawberry dived in of its own volition. Noor told Babette the adventures of a little poached pear in chocolate syrup searching for his love, a pear in vanilla syrup.

"*Très bizarre!*" came Renée's brittle voice. "Don't fill the child's head with such lies. She'll think everything she swallows has feelings like us."

Émile's cheek shone gold with sweat. Noor touched her collar—too tight. And damp. Dust trickled down over her head—another explosion.

Now Émile reminded Renée of the chocolate gâteau she had made for Guy, when Guy came to court her. No cake she had made since equalled it. Warmed by his compliment, Renée promised to make such a cake as soon as chocolate returned to the shops, or for Émile's wedding if that came first.

"I am a realist, my dear sister—our wedding will come first. Monique, tell me, is your wedding dress ready yet?"

Monique hesitated, then said, "*Non, chéri.* There is no material to be found for a wedding dress. But it's no problem, I have some very nice dresses."

"Oh, no, no. Tell the couturier she will have fabric. Tomorrow parachutes are landing at Rosny."

The all-clear signal sounded before dawn. Émile led the way up the spiral stairs.

Noor ventured out with Émile and Monique. Babette squeezed past, evading Renée's restraining hand, running to the rue Erlanger. People from the apartment buildings were gathering there, looking up, looking south. Orange and red sparks flickered like fireflies in their eyes—reflected, Noor saw once she was standing beside them, from fires gorging themselves on Paris.

A hot prong of smoke drove into Noor's lungs. A man beside her shook his fist at the sky. Behind her, a woman's moan rose to a cry, fell away to sobbing. Ambulance bells—far away, getting farther away.

The crying of babies and coughing of children in the crowd now rose above the distant crackle and hiss. Renée pulled Émile back indoors. Noor glanced at Monique, who shrugged her helplessness and went in as well. Noor followed, shutting the front door.

The chest was pushed back against the wall, its rope-lock pulled tight and knotted, the linen rearranged to hide its false bottom. Renée flounced to the card table to continue her game of solitaire; sleep, she said, was beyond her now. Monique and Noor helped Babette to bed. Then Monique curled up on the chaise longue under a blanket to snatch three hours of sleep before work. Émile was soon snoring in Guy's bedroom.

Noor stretched across the spare bed in Babette's room, but a gramophone needle seemed to snag on a groove in her mind, repeating Renée's words over and over.

Renée was at odds with herself, her hospitality at odds with her words. She said she desired Hitler's defeat, yet she was angered by Allied actions that could lead to eventual victory and a free France. But didn't Mother often say, after Abbajaan's departure, to appraise a person's actions, always, not words. Renée had opened her home to Noor and other agents. Such hospitality to strangers was part of life in places like India but not usually exhibited by Europeans.

Did the SOE reimburse people like Renée for board and lodging for its agents? She should have asked Miss Atkins, even if it meant discussing money.

Why did she distrust Renée's hospitality, paid or not? It seemed to rise from Renée's love for Émile, not from a conviction that resistance was critical or that the three-year German Occupation could be ended by an Allied victory.

She wouldn't stay with Renée again if she could possibly help it. But Émile and Monique needed her services as soon as the transmitters arrived; that resolution wasn't one she could keep.

Forget about Renée. What of Armand?

Armand might not remain for very long at Drancy but could be sent to work in Germany. Why had she not thought of this? Émile said, the day she arrived, "Many are being sent east by train—some say to be resettled, some say to work." But he had not said when. Odile's voice replayed: "All Jews are being sent east to work now, even the children." But Odile too had not said when. Did she mean immediately, soon after they were arrested or . . . when?

How long will the Germans keep Armand and Madame Lydia at Drancy? They have already been in the camp more than eight weeks. How can I know if they are still there?

Noor was as divided as she had judged Renée to be. There was Noor Khan who needed news of her love, fearful of making some terrible mistake that might send Armand and everyone in her network deeper into the clutches of the Germans, and who must not contact a single friend who knew her or Armand before the war; and Nora Baker, alias Madeleine, trained operative— detached, careful, logical, cool. Both would return to Madame Gagné's boarding house as Anne-Marie Régnier and somehow, insh'allah, find Armand before the Germans sent him away to work in the east.

CHAPTER 16

Pforzheim, Germany
January 1944

A KEY RATTLED in the lock, bolts drew back. I barely had time to hide these papers under the mattress before Vogel entered.

Gloves in hand, coat over his arm, gull-egg blue eyes squinting through round glasses. The same brown felt bow tie upon which I fixed my gaze through hours of questioning at the avenue Foch, a new suit of worsted navy blue wool. Leather boots wet with snow. In spite of myself, I welcomed the scent of pine and fresh air he brought to my cell.

I retreated to my cot. Rattle of chains as I sat down. Red-raw ankles extended, manacled fists in my lap.

The former bank clerk's pallid face loomed over me.

He rode in a staff car from Munich. Came out of his way just to see me, having told Kommandant Kieffer that more information was needed from Princess Noor. Was I not pleased to see him?

I closed my face and looked away. I don't know what I look like, but it can no longer be my "exotic" features that attract Vogel. My cheekbones have edged to the surface. And my hair! Its sheen is long gone. It's long, matted and crawling with lice. The clothes I am allowed to keep—two blouses, this skirt and a sweater—hang at chest, hip and thigh. My hip bones fit in the groove of my cupped hands. My stomach has flattened as if to meet my spine. What is my body, which the poet Kabeer called "but a skin sheet stuffed with bones," worth to this man? He sees something in me or what I represent that brings him here each month, longing in his gelid eyes. He never touches me and comes only to talk in measured tones to his audience of one.

"Writing paper is scarce, yet I authorized it for you. What have you written?"

"A children's story," said a rasp with little resemblance to my voice. I speak in French to Vogel; his English is not as fluent as he believes. So it was not really a lie, because the word for my "history" and my "story" is the same in French—"histoire."

He thought it a harmless pursuit, like a game of solitaire. Something womanly to while away my time. Maybe it is. When I write to you, I am no Scheherazade performing for her life. Forgive me for not telling a happier tale, the kind of tall tale of American cowboy derring-do Mother loved inventing, or some Sufi fable replete with turtledoves, fountains, talking animals in deserts imparting wise sayings we forget to follow.

"What stories were you told as a boy?" I asked, trying to imagine him smaller.

"The usual ones . . . Hansel and Gretel," he said in a musing voice. He was predictably flattered by my slightest curiosity about him. "Every night of '39 in the POW camp I dreamed I was Hansel and couldn't find my way home. I dropped breadcrumbs and the birds had eaten them."

Vogel spent almost a year during the phony war he calls the sitzkrieg with other German nationals in a French POW camp, until his countrymen invaded. I think that year changed him from a cosmopolitan francophile to a rabid follower of Hitler, fanatically German as only an expatriate can be.

He mused on in his soft voice. "I would search and search, believing I would find the end of a ball of twine that could be unravelled to lead me home. But I never found it—Why am I telling you this?"

Because I listen, I answered mentally. Vogel and I have met many times for my "interrogations," and if I begin by asking questions instead of answering, I learn more.

"I ask the questions. Kommandant Kieffer says compassion is making me soft." He stood over me—stood too close—cleared his throat and began with the usual ones. "State your true name."

"My true name is Noor. Princess Noor Inayat Khan."

You know I am no princess, but Mother taught me well to spin a yarn, though she could never teach me how to knit. My trumped-up title brought stupid Vogel, ignorant of the Orient, importance in his Kommandant's eyes, as if a little royalty rubbed off on them. Both are comically feudal, like so many Europeans once the veneer of National Socialism, Fascism, Communism or Democracy scratches away.

"Why don't you join us, fight against British imperialism?"

"I do not want to follow Germans into Fascism."

"But, Princess, the triumph of the Aryan can be yours as well—but if we cannot establish beyond doubt that you are Aryan, I have to regard you as non-Aryan. Perhaps even a Jew."

A hoarse hack of a laugh burst from me. I am Rapunzel, Rapunzel who can let down no blonde hair, nor can spin straw from my flea-infested mattress to gold, for the fair skin he perceives before him results from a tangled bloodline. Isolating the Caucasian blood of my mother would mean disavowing the Pathan and the Persian, the Dravidian, Maratha, even African strains in my past.

"There is no room in your Aryan heart for people like me. You said yourself: I am the ultimate threat, the mischlinge—the mixed breed."

"Listen to me—Germany was a great power until the Jews made us their target. Poor Germany! Jews in every country finance our enemies. But we will resist them, we will drive them from the world . . ."

On and on—words that sickened my soul, set my teeth chattering with anger. Who is victim, who the perpetrator, who is the oppressor, who the oppressed? Today his fulminations pinned me in a paradox: he sustains me in this cell even as he presses inexorably forward, turning my beloved to demon.

"Do you know a single Jew?" I said at last.

Vogel waved the question away. "You, the English, the Americans—I do not understand how you think. The Japanese bombed Pearl Harbor, not the Germans. Americans should be fighting with Germany, against the Bolsheviks. Why, why do you hate us Germans so much?"

Vogel asks about Germans, but he wants to know if I hate him. He wants my hate; he would like it better than my indifference. Fear and respect come parcelled with hatred. I answered Vogel once only—that it is not Germans who are hated everywhere but their rabid nationalism, their forcible occupation and rapacious plunder of other countries, their bombing of innocent people, their acts of barbaric cruelty.

Strange that I rely on Hitler's purist orders for protection from Vogel's ardour; I should have been silent, the way I used to be whenever Uncle shouted at me, years ago. But the peace of silence is only temporary; something reckless rose in me that moment.

I said, "I do not hate Germans, but I fear becoming like them."

"All Germans," he said in a calmer voice, "are not like Kommandant Kieffer—many are cultured—enlightened."

"Enlightened! Enlightened people wouldn't follow a madman."

Allah, what made me say that?

Vogel took a deliberate step forward. I braced for his fist.

"The Führer is no madman!" Rage reverberated in his voice. "He's brilliant. Brilliant!" And his ice-stiff gloves lashed across my face. "A cultured man. A lover of Wagner, Fauré, Gluck, Schumann and Bach."

The composers Vogel loves, the same Armand loved. Love of music doesn't ensure enlightenment or tolerance.

Hot blood oozed from my cut lip. I swayed like a reed. The walls closed in.

He persisted. "What do you gain by silence, so many weeks of silence?"

But why, ma petite, why could I not be silent now? My life depends on it. I am tired of silence, tired of listening to men like Vogel. Still, I wrapped myself in it again.

He offered to remove my chains. "I could take you to Munich. I would give you a hot bath, a soft bed, a candlelight dinner. The Residenz Theatre is performing As You Like It." *Like a guardian serpent, he'd protect me, interpret my rebellious "exotic nature" to his Kommandant, if I just . . .*

The sentence trailed away, but I could complete it: if I propitiated him daily, kneeling before him in adoration, offering my subordination, asking to be interpreted by him alone.

If I, of my own volition, called him Ernst.

I don't pretend to comprehend the home or society that grew a man like Vogel. All I can tell you is that his kind have been rewarded daily, have multiplied across Germany, Austria and even France, in a grotesque farce beyond any imagined by Molière.

I pressed a finger to my bleeding lip and looked away. I had no trouble fetching tears. It had the desired effect: my captor turned to penitent.

"Forgive me, Princess. I am greatly distressed. My wife and children—indeed all of Munich—are being bombed by the RAF by night, the Americans by day. Now I must get back to Paris."

He put the pages I gave him in his breast pocket without counting them, without verifying them against my guard's count. He put on his gloves and coat. He shouted and she came running, braids shining gold above her SS epaulets.

"Wie, bitte?"

"Place this prisoner in solitary confinement," *he said, then uttered the dreaded words,* "Pas de privilège."

The door slammed behind him. The SS woman has gone to prepare my punishment cell and I have pulled these papers from the mattress to write.

At this juncture where past and present meet, eternal child outside time, you are Hope. Without you, reason might desert me in the unknown geometry of the dark, where there is nothing to witness, nothing to comfort, but remembered images. Reason might give way to the terror Vogel wanted me to feel when he told me my file was marked "Nacht und Nebel." By his will I can disappear into the "night and fog" with no trace. Without you, terror would brand my mind, incarcerating it along with my body. Perhaps my story will remain for you—a mother's myths from which all others come.

I look at the wall. Blank wall with scratches.

I take up my pen and scratch five small words with no apologies to Descartes. Five small words that join the scratches of other women on these walls: "I resist, therefore I am."

Then the date, as close as I can speculate and calculate: January 12, 1944. Only days since my thirtieth birthday.

I sign it and this page with my true name, Noor.

Now I wait to be taken down to the dungeon.

PART THREE

CHAPTER 17

En route to Drancy, France
Monday, June 21, 1943

RUSTED GIRDERS, smoking chimneys and cavernous warehouses replaced the cream and grey buildings of Paris rushing past Noor's carriage window. Beneath nearly closed eyelids she studied her early morning travel companions: the worried-looking woman who'd asked if this was "the potato or the bean train"; the two younger women who'd responded in unison "the bean train"; the old man at her left with his empty macramé bag—probably on his way to forage for food; the German soldier about Noor's own age who gave up his seat for the old lady in mended espadrilles; the white-lipped little boy on her right who hadn't taken his eyes off the soldier since the journey began.

And if the little boy's mother didn't stop staring at Noor's bag, the soldier might notice. Was it too large, too expensive-looking? Perhaps too full?

Carry an empty basket next time.

This time, when the train stopped at Le Bourget–Drancy station, Noor knew her way to the *centre-ville*. But she had no plan. Gauzy blue skies veiled inspiration; she was a cavity of indecision. Inspiration, Abbajaan said, comes to those who prepare themselves. But how to prepare herself?

Get information. Use the tradecraft of secret agents.

Watchtowers of the internment camp loomed ahead.

Don't attract attention. Take the back streets.

But there was the *tabac* door, held invitingly open to cool the little shop. She stopped and asked the owner for Claude to take her to the boarding house again.

"Mademoiselle, a customer who returns is impossible to refuse." He went to the back and shouted for Claude. "It's the mademoiselle you said had such pretty eyes."

Claude's face popped around the door, flushed pink to the roots of his brown, curly hair. Noor gave him a bewitching smile, accelerating his tint to scarlet.

She hopped sidesaddle on Claude's luggage carrier, bag on her lap, and steadied herself with one hand about his waist. Claude began pedalling down the avenue.

Even his neck had turned beet red.

Don't laugh.

"How is your Tante Lucille?" asked Claude.

"Oh, the same, thank you. Kind when she has good days, unkind when she is in pain."

Claude was approaching the turreted watchtower. Claude had passed the watchtower.

Just another part of the landscape.

"Does your aunt take medicines for the pain? Laudanum, perhaps?"

"She should, but who can find laudanum these days," said Noor.

Past several lorries parked at the entrance gate like dogs sniffing for bones.

"Everything can be found, for a price."

His tone was meaningful. A new avenue opened before Noor.

Allah! Sometimes all one has to do is be present and not give up.

Careful. A hunter who traps a tigress tricks her with a branch-covered pit.

"Was that your papa?" she asked.

"No, he is not my papa. My papa is still in Germany."

"In a camp like this?"

"*Mais, non!* Not like this! A Stalag, widening roads, building irrigation canals in Germany. Drancy is for Jews."

How different were conditions for French soldiers who were now in POW internment camps and for Jews in internment camps? How should Claude know?

"And you are—how old?" He was tall but malnourished. Perhaps fifteen?

"Seventeen, mademoiselle."

Seventeen—only a few short months from being called up for the Relève and sent to make weapons for the Germans. Unless he was fortunate enough to be employed in an essential industry in France.

"You look older, Monsieur Claude," lied Noor.

His chest puffed at her compliment.

"Where is your mother?"

"Here, in Drancy," he said. "I carry messages from the *tabac* when I'm not working at the automobile garage—I'm apprenticed to the mechanic there."

Young Claude wasn't black marketeering for a fat pocketbook but to survive. Still, he could be working for the Germans. He could be trying to trap her, trap her into divulging her own interests.

Keep your inquiries general.

High walls passed the bicycle. And passed and passed. How very many people there must be like Noor, whose loved ones had disappeared into that camp.

Lorries, pedestrians, very empty shops on the other side. But perhaps she could find work close to Armand.

"There must be so many jobs that need to be done at the camp," she said.

"I've asked," said Claude. "But the prisoners are forced to do everything."

"And what about deliveries? Couldn't you help deliver food, clothing—letters?"

Claude grunted. "These days? Every camp gendarme who comes to our repair shop is trembling for his job. One of them told us a new director has been appointed. A German this time—SS."

"Why? Don't the Germans believe we can guard our own people?"

Sound casual! Sound indifferent!

Unwittingly she had used the first person plural *nous*. Using *nous* when her family's inclusion in France was tenuous at best had always felt inappropriate. But it came naturally with her outrage at the treatment of people with whom she'd shared her childhood.

"Oh, we guard them well," said Claude. "But we aren't deporting the Jews to Germany fast enough. The gendarme said the new Kommandant has vowed to change that."

"How long are prisoners kept here before their deportation to Germany?"

There—she'd asked it. A simple question, dropped easily into the conversation.

Claude shrugged. "It depends. Maybe a few weeks, a few months. The gendarme said the Kommandant was appointed because there have been no shipments from Drancy to Germany since March. The French director intended to, but they'd no coal allotment for prison transports. He said the new Kommandant was enraged that not a single convoy has left Drancy in three months."

Allah! If no one was sent to Germany since March, there was a chance that her Armand and Madame Lydia were still at Drancy. Armand's postcard was dated April. Hope brightened the sooty façades of passing houses and shops.

But hadn't Monique said fifteen thousand Jews had been rounded up in one week? Where were the Germans housing them? Suddenly the long walls of Drancy appeared far too short, the whole camp shrank in her mind.

Hold fast to hope.

"So, Monsieur Claude, tell me . . . what other things can be had for a price?" she murmured to Claude's back.

"That depends, mademoiselle"—the whir of wheels punctuated his voice—"on what your aunt Lucille requires."

"I will ask her," said Noor. "You can call me Anne-Marie. Anne-Marie Régnier."

The bicycle bumped along past the last watchtower and its machine-gun silhouette, and this time Noor looked back as it swung and became sure it wasn't aiming at her. Wasn't aiming at her at all. Claude turned at the chestnut tree waving its leaves against a warm, cloudless sky. When he stopped in the lane, Noor slipped off the carrier and opened her bag for a tip. He shook his head.

"Non, mademoiselle—I will take you again, for your pretty eyes. You can ask for me at the *tabac* or the garage on the other side of the camp. I deliver bread here in the mornings, too."

"Merci, Claude," said Noor warmly. "I will ask Tante Lucille what she needs." With Dadijaan in mind she added for greater effect, "You know old ladies—today it is one thing, tomorrow another."

Claude ran a few paces on his wood-soled shoes and vaulted onto his bike. He looked over his shoulder, beamed and waved when he caught her eye.

Inside, Noor greeted Madame Gagné.

"Oh, have you come, then? Too late—breakfast is over. You can have the last of the oatmeal."

Late despite her best intentions; the meal would have been welcome. Still, she had learned something. Noor ate the weak oatmeal and climbed to her attic room, a little wiser, much more hopeful than before.

Flashes of light resolved into patterns:

. . . dot-dot-dash . . . dash-dot-dash . . . dash-dash-dot . . .

Inside Madame Gagné's creaking house, Noor rose from the chair she had pulled to the window and raised her binoculars. Chestnut leaves, metallic in the moonlight, filtered a welcome breeze through the window. Mice or rats skittered beneath the floorboards.

Noor had watched the camp since mid-morning to acquaint herself with its routine. At noon, prisoners were herded into the central courtyard for a bowl of what she supposed was soup. An hour and a half later, prisoners were marched out, presumably to work again, leaving little activity in the courtyard. At 18:35 hours they returned to the courtyard for roll call and soup distribution, and at 20:00 hours a blast from a factory horn must have meant something to inmates. At 22:00 hours lights went out in the complex and, suddenly, perimeter lights above the barbed wire fence flashed on. Then searchlights in the central courtyard raised moonish faces to the night.

Again: dot-dot-dash . . . dash-dot-dash . . . dash-dash-dot.

Sudden, fleeting as intuition—the prisoners were using battery-powered torches to send Morse code messages from the camp.

Noor snatched up pen and paper and began to record the letters she was reading from the flashing lights. Who was the sender? who the intended receiver? She'd decipher it later. Receiving was the least and the best she could do. It would be beyond all possible coincidences if Allah were to allow Armand to be sending in Morse as she was watching. Like herself, Armand could have learned Morse in the last three years, but she didn't think he would. Anyway, she'd record and, if possible, send the messages from these unknown captives to their destination.

É—C—O—U—T . . . Wait, what was that sound? Aeroplanes buzzed in the distance. Sirens wailed and anti-aircraft guns in the camp's central courtyard thundered into the night. The still-life painting on the wall behind Noor quivered, drifted askew, then crashed behind the headboard. The walls were vibrating, shivering down to their timbers.

But the lights—the perimeter lights. They still blazed. Turn them off! Plunge the camp in total blackout! Instead, every light remained on, as if intended to guide the bombs.

Noor trembled for Armand as the bombers screamed and roared overhead. A camp this size, lit up as it was, would be a highly visible landmark from the air. Was it a target?

The bombers ploughed through the exploding sky in tight formation.

Madame Gagné was shouting from the landing, a clattering filled the stairwell. Noor should run downstairs, take shelter in the cellar. But she couldn't tear her eyes from the camp windows where the torches had been flashing.

Kabir, if you're above us in that bomber and you destroy this camp, I'll never forgive you. Never.

But then, if the camp were bombed, it might be possible in the ensuing chaos for Armand and Madame Lydia to escape. If the camp were destroyed, it would make it difficult if not impossible for the Germans and Vichy to incarcerate Jews and send them to Germany, or at least make it difficult for a long time. And meanwhile, if they had fewer Jews to slave in their armaments industries and help repair their bombed cities, perhaps they would lose the war.

Kabir, if you're above us in that bomber and you don't *destroy this camp, I'll never forgive you. Never.*

But the booming of guns and ack-ack quieted, and the flock of unseen arrowheads flew away to top priority targets in Germany. Noor sat waiting, watching beneath night-sifted starlight, but the torches did not flash again.

Drancy, France
Tuesday, June 22, 1943

"*Tickets, tickets, s'il vous plaît!*"

Madame Gagné was moving around her dining table, collecting rainbow-coloured ration coupons for meals served to the boarding house residents, when Noor came downstairs the next morning. Tickets for the bread ration, twenty-four hours old in accordance with German decree, bread she said cost her three hundred francs today. Tickets for the margarine, but not the saccharine jam.

The dining room lay at the heart of the house, adjoining the kitchen. Through an archway lay a cavernous drawing room where blackout curtains surrounded slip-covered furniture. Beyond it, a panelled corridor led to the front door.

Noor placed her bag next to a chair, murmured good morning and sat down beside a buxom woman in an apron. The waitress Gabrielle commanded the rapt attention of four others—two men, two women—as she described how to make an eggless omelette.

"Have you tasted one?" asked a grey-haired gentleman.

Animal smell. Monsieur Durand, the salesman who kept rabbits as pets in his room. Benares silk tie. A better-cut suit than these surroundings warranted. But those Degas eyes and unstarched shirt collar spoke of bachelorhood or a recent fall in circumstances.

"Non, non, but can't you imagine it?"

Each resident savoured his or her version of the imaginary omelette.

"Eggless omelettes! If there are no eggs, it's not an omelette. What did I tell you, Mademoiselle Régnier? Don't believe anything Mademoiselle Gabrielle says."

But Gabrielle's description must have called to the right elements in her audience's experience, for the omelette was no less wondrous to them for being eggless and tasteless. At Madame Gagné's comment Gabrielle shrugged muscular shoulders, from which, despite her name, no angel wings extended.

Having pronounced judgement on their culinary fantasies, and with the coupons dutifully submitted by Noor, Madame Gagné disappeared into the kitchen. Beyond the cast iron stove Noor spied Claude lounging in the open doorway facing the garden. He noticed her at once, straightened, smiled and blushed. Such amusing admiration; he was so much younger. Noor couldn't help giving him a coquettish glance over the rim of her coffee cup.

"You're across the corridor from me, non?" said Gabrielle. "Did you not feel the house shake when the guns fired last night?"

Noor nodded.

"I knocked on your door as we ran downstairs to the cellar, and there was no answer. You sleep too soundly—or you're very brave. Or very foolish."

"Thank you for knocking," said Noor. "It was almost over by the time I woke up."

She helped herself to a pat of margarine. A few seats away, a woman resident's eyes followed the pale smear through the air till Noor's knife touched her plate.

Noor continued, "They left the lights of the camp on. People in that camp could have been bombed!" Outrage in her voice.

Restrain yourself.

Monsieur Durand wiped his lips. "Of course they could. The Germans wouldn't care."

"Oh, they would," said a bald man at the other end of the table. "They need our imprisoned friends for German factories." And he left the table, stopping to take his hat and portfolio from the hat stand in the hall.

Gabrielle tossed her head. Golden locks brought her closer to her angelic name than her sharp tone. "We all know why *he's* here. He's a *missionnaire*." She leaned back, fingering the gold cross at her neck. Her expression said she'd just revealed a great secret.

"A missionary?" The bald man had neither cleric's collar nor priestly demeanour.

"Yes. He's allowed to leave the camp for a few days at a time, to find and collect families of prisoners. Women and children— I ask you, what work can children do in German factories? Then, when the families have been, as they say, 'reunited,' they are all sent to Germany together."

"Why does he return to the camp?" asked Noor. "Can't he refuse to gather up families?"

"Oh, don't blame him! He said once that if he failed to return to the camp when he was expected, the Germans would shoot someone in his stead and send a new missionary out the very next morning. But I tell everyone new: if you have anyone in the camp, don't breathe one word before him."

Deny you have someone in the camp.

"Oh, I'm here to visit my aunt—Tante Lucille," said Noor. "She's very sick."

"This is amazing," said Gabrielle. "So am I! Monsieur Durand here was just asking me about my aunt's health."

A wry smile came over Monsieur Durand's face. "And *my* aunt's name is Madame Frédérique Durand. She is very sick too. Sicker than your Tante Marie, Gabrielle."

The three looked at each other in a silence that restrained volumes of questions, not the least of which was the obvious one: where were these three sick aunts at this moment? No wonder Madame Gagné had smirked in disbelief when Noor told her about Tante Lucille.

The two women next to Gabrielle finished eating, stood up and nodded farewells. Their wedge sandals clumped through the kitchen where Madame Gagné was counting out ration tickets for Claude.

Three of us with sick aunts, at the same table.

This was no coincidence but a joint failure of imagination that might have been comical if it wasn't so dangerous.

Around the dining table, intuitive evaluations continued. Monsieur Durand's salted brows were drawn together in a frown. If he was Jewish, as Madame Gagné had implied, that probably said Noor and Gabrielle were not Jewish enough to trust. The pressure of Gabrielle's gaze intensified. She was evaluating Noor's features; perhaps Noor and Monsieur Durand were not Christian enough or not French enough for further confidences from her.

They aren't Muslim or Indian, but we certainly think alike. We who have invented similar lies may have similar reasons, similar concerns.

She kept her face unguarded and open. A subtle change came to Gabrielle's eyes.

Perhaps loving a single Jewish man deeply, without reserve, moulded Noor's eyes, nose or mouth in some friendly way others in Armand's community could sense; or perhaps shared fears, anger and loss could instantly create the first person plural *nous* without shared memories, for Monsieur Durand rose abruptly and with a slight bow began measuring out Noor's bread, cutting it evenly and finely till her fair share lay before her.

There was a sudden dyspeptic buzz.

A doorbell. At the front door.

Gabrielle looked startled, Monsieur Durand fearful.

Noor tensed in reflection of their attitudes. Her hands suddenly felt damp. She wiped them on her serviette and glanced at the kitchen door. In an instant she could be through it and into the garden.

She listened with the others. Madame Gagné went to the door and opened it.

"*Papieren?!*" came a German voice.

Papers? At this hour? Gabrielle and Monsieur Durand exchanged glances of panic.

But the Gestapo isn't here for them. They must have come to arrest me, the foreign agent, the spy. Run now?

Gabrielle was sitting very straight. Monsieur Durand shot his cuffs, popped the last of his bread into his mouth and waited, cheeks bulging.

Noor could do that too, appear normal.

A German soldier's large frame filled the dining-room doorway, Madame Gagné behind him.

What did "normal" look like? It didn't look like Noor. She leaned forward. She would just reach under the table slowly, as if reaching for her handbag to take out her papers. Her muscles flexed, ready to flee.

But the soldier took a cursory look around the dining room and said in guttural French, "Everything looks in order." He turned to Madame Gagné. "Is Claude here?"

Madame Gagné called and the boy entered the dining room, wide eyes already protesting innocence.

"You work at the garage, *ja?*"

Claude nodded, cheeks flushing red.

"There's a noise in my gearbox. Come outside and check my clutch."

Claude followed the soldier through the front door, and everyone at the table seemed to breathe again. Madame Gagné returned to tend her cauldron on the stove. Gabrielle jumped up from the table and disappeared between the ghostly furniture shapes in the drawing room. She opened the painted window a few inches and peered out onto the street.

"That soldier comes into the Café Vidrequin," she said. "Always has two beers—I serve him. He must have recognized me, that's why he didn't check our papers. No, wait—he's talking to Claude."

"Why here?" said Monsieur Durand. "He could have gone to the garage."

"It's too early—the garage isn't open yet."

"He could have waited half an hour. I don't like it."

There was a short pause, then Gabrielle said, "I think Claude has repaired his motor car."

Claude came back.

"Did you repair his motor car?" asked Monsieur Durand.

"There was nothing wrong with it," said Claude.

"Nothing wrong? These Germans are idiots." Monsieur Durand was nearly laughing with relief.

"Yes, well . . ." Claude hesitated. Then it came out in a rush: "He said he needed me to inspect his motor car for tomorrow—a convoy leaves in the morning for Germany. He has to drive the SS officers to Bobigny station."

All the air seemed sucked out of the room.

"I—I think he wanted me to tell someone, maybe everyone. But I don't know who needs to know. Besides, what can anyone do?"

Gabrielle sank into her chair with her face in her hands. The cross at her throat must be for costume, because her pallor said she knew someone in the camp. Could she be Jewish? Did she have a Jewish husband? A Jewish lover?

Don't show you have any reason to care.

Monsieur Durand blew his nose thoughtfully. "Have you met this German before?"

"No, never," said Claude. "But he's a Bavarian. Catholic— I see him in church."

Monsieur Durand gave a derisive grunt.

"Well, he isn't likely to attend a synagogue, you know!" said Claude.

So Monsieur Durand was Jewish, as Madame Gagné had suspected. And Claude knew it. Monsieur Durand's eyebrows rose, and Claude retreated in deference to Monsieur Durand's years. But then Claude shifted from one foot to the other and blurted, "The list of selected prisoners has been posted."

"Did your German say how they had been selected? Did he give you the list?" asked Monsieur Durand.

"He's not 'my German.' Anyway, he said nothing. And of course he didn't give me a list."

"You think he carries a photograph of such a list in his pocket just so he can tell you who is on it?" said Gabrielle, with a return of spirit that called to Noor's own.

Monsieur Durand shrugged. "If he was really trying to help, he would have brought us the list. What is the use of telling us there will be a convoy tomorrow? What can we do about it? And a German who can behave with humanity—it is impossible."

The soldier's action did not match Monsieur Durand's experience of Germans.

But strange things do happen when we ask Allah to help us be healed or complete. He reveals himself in signs and symbols, opening doors before us; then it's up to us to walk through. Is it not completely strange that though the war still rages, I have returned to France? That though Armand is not free, I am closer to him? Allah,

you meant for me to be here, in this room, this very day, to hear that
a convoy is being sent to Germany tomorrow.

Guide me further.

"I must go, I can't be late for work," said Claude. "I'll be at the
garage if you need me."

"Merci, Monsieur Claude," said Noor. She turned back to
Gabrielle and Monsieur Durand.

"And if he gave you the list, what then?" Gabrielle was wreak-
ing her anger against the Germans on poor Monsieur Durand.
"Can we take it to Vichy and say, please, Premier Laval, don't
deliver our little children into the hands of the Germans?"

Noor asked, "How do they select people for the convoys?"

Monsieur Durand raised heavy-lidded eyes. "The lawyer working on my relatives' case says the Germans have changed all the
categories since they took over the camp. Now not only foreign-
born, stateless and immigrant *Juifs* but any Israelites—French citizens!—can be sent east. A circumstance of war, it's called."

Perhaps she too could engage a lawyer, to fight for Armand's
release? But no lawyer could plead for release by the next morning. But if Armand remained at Drancy after tomorrow's convoy,
a lawyer might help.

But how? Noor had only two more weeks in France. Not
enough. And to seek a member of the court might endanger other
members of the PROSPER network. Besides, French society had
changed so much in three years, she was no longer sure of anyone's political leanings.

"Don't waste money hiring a *bavard*." Monsieur Durand had
almost read her thoughts. "The Maréchal's actions can only be
challenged in special courts. My advocate can't protest Vichy's
laws, only argue them—try to reduce the pillage. He's a liberal
with a turn of phrase much admired by his old school friends, but
completely useless. The Nazis and Vichy cannot be fought with
rhetoric."

"Which relatives is he defending?" Gabrielle asked. "And
please don't tell me about your sick aunt again!"

"My parents, my wife, my children. My brother and his family . . . Fourteen people."

Gabrielle threw up her hands. "*Mon Dieu!* How can this be?"

"I was away on a selling trip, and when I came home they had all been arrested and our apartment was taken over by the German soldiers. They showed me billeting chits. I showed them my Great War medal, and as professional courtesy they refrained from inviting the Gestapo to arrest me."

"I can't believe it!" said Noor.

"I too could not believe it, refused to believe it," said Monsieur Durand. "I went completely out of my mind with fear that I had lost my mind. What crime had my relatives committed? But let me tell you, Vichy and the Nazis can do anything they want. Do you know, I went to my bank to withdraw money and stay in a hotel, but they said the account containing all my savings was blocked. I went to my manager for assistance and he said, under some new law, all my commissions—about one thousand francs—had been deposited to my bank account, though it was blocked."

"Your manager should have refused to deposit it," said Gabrielle.

"Ha! He'd be at Fresnes prison right now. There was also a new Vichy decree, he said, that required him to deduct an annual tax of 120 francs from every Jewish employee, to meet the Jewish obligation to pay Vichy's new 'fine.'"

A jizya tax on unbelievers. How utterly medieval.

"He did allow me to stay at his home for a few days, so I didn't have to sleep on the streets. I went to every police station and the Hôtel de Ville."

"They could have arrested you too!" said Gabrielle.

Monsieur Durand shrugged. "Yes, but I had to inquire."

"But why was your family arrested?" said Noor.

Monsieur Durand gave a great sigh that told Noor he could not explain why, so he was answering the how. How it happened to his family. That was dispiriting enough, without searching for reasons for German and Vichy anti-Semitism.

"I traced my family here. I had a few shares in companies, but the bank dutifully blocked my safety deposit as well. I gave my manager my key and he went to the bank, told them he was joint owner and an Aryan—this way he brought me my share certificates. I sold the few shares of companies that hadn't yet been 'Aryanized' and came here. I cannot leave."

Gabrielle rested her elbows on the table, knit her fingers beneath her chin. "The gendarmes who come to the Vidrequin were saying the new camp Kommandant interrogated every prisoner last week. He must have been preparing for this convoy. They hold back those they need—doctors, cooks."

Gabrielle hasn't mentioned musicians.

"There's a railroad worker who stays a little later after lunch than others," Gabrielle was saying. "I think he has special rank or privileges. I could ask him if the Germans have ordered any third-class coaches to wait at Bobigny station. But what will that do? Oh, my little ones!"

All pretenses about sick aunts were gone.

"You have children in the camp?" Noor exclaimed.

"Not my own—my sister's. She was sent to Germany and the children are still here, still in the camp. Their father is a Polish Jew, but the children are both born in France, so they were left with a UGIF social worker. And then—*tenez, regardez!*"

She pulled a postcard from her pocket, one familiar in size and colour. Noor had left one just like it in her locker at Wanborough Manor, a card stamped *Camp d'internement de Drancy*. Noor took it from Gabrielle and read it aloud. "'Madame la Concierge, I am writing to you because I have no one left. Papa has been deported, Maman has been deported. Please can you write to my Tante Gabrielle and tell her I am looking after my little sister but she is always hungry.'"

Gabrielle's head slumped to her forearms. "He's only seven years old," she sobbed.

Noor's sympathy was beyond words. Her own cheeks were wet. Her own half-Jewish child might have written such a letter;

any one of the famine-orphaned children of Calcutta could also have written such a letter, if they knew how to write and had concierges to write to. She stroked Gabrielle's arm gently.

"It's bad enough my sister and brother-in-law are gone—I don't know where. The children are my responsibility—I don't know why the camp authorities won't release them to me. I went to see the director a few weeks ago—it was a Frenchman at that time. No, he said, it would be 'bad for discipline' if he were to release them, and that they would be better off in the camp than with an unmarried woman. So I got work here and I send them parcels on Tuesdays. When I was registering for ration coupons at the *mairie*, I told them I was here to care for my Tante Marie."

"But if Monsieur le Missionnaire or someone else reports you to the Germans—wouldn't you join the children in the camp?"

"Oh, Monsieur le Missionnaire reports as few people as he can—certainly not the people who give him tobacco ration coupons."

"How do you get tobacco coupons?" asked Noor. Her own ration book didn't have tobacco coupons—women weren't issued tobacco rations.

"From the café—sometimes the Germans leave them as tips. I told Monsieur le Missionnaire that my parcels to the children often contain cigarettes. He understood what I meant. You can get or barter about 200 to 500 francs for a pack of cigarettes in the camp. And on the day of a convoy, 150 francs for one single cigarette! I don't know how the prisoners pay, since each person can't have more than 50 francs."

"I give him rabbits," said Monsieur Durand. "He needs them to bribe his guards sometimes. I think he's a good man—we attended the same yeshiva as children. Twice since February he's taken letters in for me because I can't write a return address, but since the new Kommandant came, it's too dangerous. He said the penalty for any correspondence with the exterior that does not pass through the camp post is twenty-five strokes of a baton. Any communication with a Resistance group could get him hanged . . . And you?"

In the charged atmosphere of self-disclosure, the question from Monsieur Durand was inevitable.

"My husband."

Noor surprised herself with the word. She had forsaken "fiancé" and called Armand "husband" aloud, claimed him before strangers. But it was safe to say "my husband" before these two; these strangers would understand. And the moment the words were spoken, they felt true. So many years together. And if he was her husband, she was his wife.

I need at least to tell my husband I am near, that I love him always and forever.

An hour past breakfast, Noor and her new acquaintances sat around the dining table talking, debating, falling silent when Madame Gagné came in to clear away plates and cups. The conversation continued in low voices. Noor was intensely aware of each minute ticking past as they pooled and evaluated resources and options.

Noor could contribute money. It was counterfeit, but there was no reason to tell Gabrielle and Monsieur Durand that. And it was to be used to help the French as she thought fit.

"Money my dear sick Tante Lucille gave me," she said in a question-repelling voice that brought a rare smile to Monsieur Durand's eyes.

He wanted to bribe the bald man. Gabrielle said she could bribe a gendarme who came into the café. Perhaps Noor could bribe Claude.

"Yes, I can see he likes you," said Gabrielle.

But bribe any of them for what purpose? A gendarme might take a message into the camp, at most. Bribing the missionary with rabbits had kept Monsieur Durand out of Drancy; bribing him with money might get them a list of evacuees. The man was Jewish, after all, Monsieur Durand reminded them, and a veteran of the Great War. Perhaps he couldn't remove anyone from the list—certainly not fourteen people named Durand—but he might find out if a prisoner was or was not on the list for tomorrow's convoy. And then?

"That *missionnaire*," said Gabrielle. "I've been giving him cigarettes for months now, the least he can do is tell me where is the train going. I have to find my niece and nephew when the war dies down. You know how big is Germany? And what if they really do what people say, and send them along with all the other Jews to Madagascar. How will I go to Madagascar?"

Noor said, "We'll go together."

She was more confident she could take a steamer to Madagascar—halfway to India, after all—than that she could stop a convoy Hitler had ordered to roll out of Drancy tomorrow morning. Hadn't Mother done so in 1913? Yes, Miss Aura Baker had stolen away with one suitcase and a hat box and, against Uncle Robert's wishes, taken a steamer out of Boston Harbor. If Mother could cross an ocean to follow her heart, so could Noor. The difference was that Abbajaan was giving veen a concerts in London; he hadn't been locked up by Hitler in a camp in France.

There was not a moment to waste and here they were, still discussing what to do! Noor pressed cold fingers against her overheated forehead.

"We need to know where the train is going, which city or camp," said Monsieur Durand.

He offered, with no enthusiasm but by virtue of being the man in the group, to talk to Monsieur le Missionnaire—if the bald man returned to Madame Gagné's for lunch or dinner. But there was no assurance Monsieur le Missionnaire would return at all. Perhaps he was back in the camp. Madame Gagné said he wouldn't be returning that night.

Someone would have to find him now and invite him to return to Madame Gagné's for a rendezvous with Monsieur Durand. Noor suggested they telephone the garage and ask

Claude to courier the message to Monsieur le Missionnaire, offer Claude a reward to find the bald man quickly.

"Yes, but never trust a telephone for such delicate matters," said Monsieur Durand. "Persuasion is best done in person. The switchboard operator would wonder why we want to meet a man known to be from the camp, and she'd alert the Germans. Especially if you mention a reward. You will have to go there yourself."

Noor agreed.

Suddenly Gabrielle let out a wail. "How will I recognize the children if they are taken away to Germany and I don't see them for a few months? A year or two—or many years? What if they grow up and I can't recognize them?"

"Give them something," suggested Noor. "Something of your own that says you love them always and will be waiting for them."

"Something that will help them find me—a letter? Can we ask Monsieur le Missionnaire to smuggle it in so I can say what is in my heart?"

"Non, non," said Monsieur Durand in high irritation. "I told you, twenty-five strokes of a baton. In the centre courtyard before everyone. Letters must go through the camp post. Monsieur le Missionnaire can help us once it is inside the camp."

Gabrielle's opinion of the camp administrators was indelicate but to the point. "I won't send it through Monsieur le Missionnaire, then. I'll hide it in my parcel that passes through the camp post checkpoint. I'll take it there today as I do every week. But you must tell him to explain to the children that they must keep my letter with them till they return from Germany. Tell them forever, till I find them again. Oh, what should I write?"

"May I send some little thing to my husband in your parcel?" asked Noor.

"*Mais, bien sûr*, if Monsieur Durand can persuade Monsieur le Missionnaire to take it from the parcel and deliver it. We can't endanger the children by asking them to find your husband, you understand. But no weapons—the Germans take revenge for concealing weapons. They'd send my little ones away immediately and hang Monsieur le Missionnaire for delivering such things."

Everything now depended on arranging the conversation between Monsieur Durand and Monsieur le Missionnaire. Today, immediately.

What should she send Armand? The advice she'd given Gabrielle felt like advice she should take herself: an object that would say she loved him dearly and would be waiting for him. But unlike Gabrielle, Noor could not send a long letter with the parcel; she wasn't supposed to be anywhere near France. Signing it *Noor* or *Nora*, or supplying an address, would endanger her mission. Armand didn't know an Anne-Marie Régnier. *Madeleine* or, better still, *Madelon* might remind him of their evening of love at Mont Valérien. But—it might not.

Armand believed Noor to be in London. But he would recognize her writing.

Allah, guide me to the answer soon.

She glanced at her wristwatch. "It is now 11:00 hours. Everyone returns to the camp for roll call in the evening at 18:35 hours. Monsieur le Missionnaire has to be back then too, since he isn't staying here tonight."

Gabrielle went upstairs to prepare her parcel for the children; she had to be at the Café Vidrequin to serve lunch but would return after that. Noor took directions to the garage from Monsieur Durand before he went upstairs to feed his rabbits, "In case I have to say *adieu* to one of my gentle friends tonight. Now hurry back!" He raised the tips of her fingers to his papery lips.

Noor let herself out through the kitchen. "I'm going to visit Tante Lucille," she said to Madame Gagné over her shoulder.

"You want me to find Monsieur le Missionnaire?"

Claude looked as if he had been about to embrace Noor as an old friend but then, embarrassed, barely shook the tips of her fingers.

"Monsieur Durand asked if you could find him."

"Yes, but why did he send you?" He turned her hand over as if to verify he hadn't sullied her with grease. His hair smelled of pomade, *gazogène* and diesel.

"Oh, I was coming this way. Going to see my aunt, you know." Noor's attempt to smile turned into a desperate grimace.

Claude wiped the dipstick he had used to check the oil in the open mandible of a black Citroën. Cars at various stages of cannibalization were overcrowded into the garage. Spare tools lay scattered on the dirt surface. Light poured through clerestory windows, dispelling the dimness at intervals.

"He said it's very urgent."

"Mademoiselle, if you think it's urgent, then it is urgent for me. *Venez . . .*"

Noor let her hand nestle in the crook of his arm. Claude led her to a bench, wiped it carefully before allowing her to sit down. Someone shouted at him from the rear. He shouted in return but made no move to leave.

"Monsieur Durand asks for Monsieur le Missionnaire? Monsieur Durand should know that he should do nothing to attract Monsieur le Missionnaire's attention in any way. And you too."

His tone wavered halfway between brother and lover, like a puppy that paws and bites before it learns the power of embrace. Like Kabir. But oh, for Armand's sake, let him understand!

"Claude," she said, "about the news you gave us this morning? I think your German wanted to tell us more, but he couldn't."

"He's not my German."

Noor's shrug conveyed a mote of scepticism. "Good. Well . . . Monsieur Durand thought that with so many prisoners leaving the camp tomorrow, what that German wanted to tell us was that there could be jobs there soon. So—Gabrielle would like to know if they need help with the officers' laundry. But she must ask soon, before the jobs are filled by new prisoners. That is why I need you to find Monsieur le Missionnaire quickly."

Noor could see Claude didn't believe the story, plausible as it was. But she wasn't going to tell him any other. Where was the implicit understanding and trust she had felt in him from the moment she first rode on his luggage carrier?

Besides, she was ready with a one-hundred franc note to press in his hand.

He unfolded the note, looked at it, folded it up again and returned it. "Mademoiselle, I don't know if I can find him. He could be gone to Paris, he could be anywhere. But I will go cycling for one hour. If I find him in the village somewhere, I will invite him to meet Monsieur Durand *chez* Madame Gagné. But after an hour . . ." He glanced over his shoulder in the direction where the shout had originated. "More than an hour and I could get a beating. I'm just an apprentice here."

Noor leaned over and kissed Claude on the cheek. She fluttered her lashes ever so slightly. *"Merci, mon gallant chevalier."*

Claude blushed.

As Noor left the garage, she was tempted, very tempted, to pick up a pair of pliers, a spanner or a wrench and slip it into her bag. But Gabrielle had warned: no weapons. Endangering the children or Monsieur le Missionnaire was not permissible.

Leave this theft undone.

But what of Armand, of Gabrielle's little niece and nephew, of Monsieur Durand's fourteen relatives who might be on the list? She turned back.

Claude's back was to her. Leaning into the car, he looked as if he were struggling in the open jaws of a great black whale.

Pliers were tools, not weapons. Noor snatched the pliers.

Just in case.

It was past noon when Noor returned to the boarding house and climbed to her room beneath the eaves. In the skulking heat her blouse was sticking to burning, moist skin. Time was flying away.

Monsieur Durand poked his head from the room across the hall. "Has Claude gone to find Monsieur le Missionnaire?"

"Yes," said Noor. "We must hope he can."

"Gabrielle said she'll return after lunch," he reminded her. "She left you her parcel."

Monsieur Durand brought in a parcel the size of a newborn. He placed it on the desk near the window and stood looking at the camp for a minute, lips moving in soundless prayer. Noor busied herself with the parcel till he nodded and left the room.

A note from Gabrielle: *Add your message—the sardines.* Also a sheet of brown paper and a ball of twine.

The sardine tin must be fake. SOE had sent so many spy devices into Europe. The false bottom slid away, revealing a small compartment.

What gift should she, could she, send?

I need to tell Armand I am here, that I love him always.

Too many messages to fit in that tiny compartment. She was sorry for the seven years of waiting, for the intolerance of her family, she had never stopped loving him, she was as Rumi's separated reed without him, he must know they still had a task they could only effect together: the return of a child's soul in a better time to come.

But anonymity was safety—critical for so many. For Armand and for her mission. The sender must disappear into the message.

Allah, guide me.

The parcel must be ready by the time Gabrielle returned. Yet the message Noor had come so far to deliver must be the perfect representation of her love, their love; some shape so powerful it would swallow the need for words. It should say, "I am near you. Have hope, my love. We will be together again."

Anyone could say that. Her message must have some pattern distinctive as a radio operator's fist to be a message that Armand would know could come only from Noor. It must speak of the coexistence of beauty with the beast, and the hope of transmuting suffering to beauty. She must send Armand some very small thing that could carry the weight of this desperate love and hope that had her standing by the bed, looking into the half-composed package with brimming eyes.

The day she returned to Paris, as the tram shuddered onto the boulevard de Boulogne and passed the very spot where she had said *adieu* to Armand—the *adieu* that should have been *au revoir*—she had yearned for some small thing that belonged to him, something she could have held at that moment; something eloquent with memories of shared experiences, intimate times. Was Armand feeling the same at this moment? Could she give him a part of herself?

She peeked into the parcel again. Where had Gabrielle found wool to knit a scarf? Where had she found a second, real tin of sardines, one of condensed milk, even a jar of honey and another of jam? She must have been saving them for the children for quite a while. Each container compressed nourishment, and included so much more—assurance, hope, love, and Gabrielle's sadness and anger that she could not protect these little ones.

The attic room grew warmer from the fever of Noor's thoughts. She unbuttoned the top of her blouse.

Of course, of course.

What else was there? She had brought nothing of the past, Armand's and her past, to France but this.

She unfastened the thin gold chain, held the crescent shape of her tiger claw up to the afternoon light.

Some foreknowledge must have counselled her to keep the pendant upon Anne-Marie Régnier's person while divesting herself of every vestige, symbol and relic of Noor Khan. Armand knew its value—not only how precious it was to Noor, linking her always to India, her grandmother, Dadijaan, and the generations of women in her family who had worn it, but he would also know she gave him something to barter or sell, should his life depend on it.

For luck and courage.

Translucent yellow, smooth except for minute cracks, the power of the inarticulate but deadly beast restrained by its golden frame. Ancient relic of the pride, it flashed and shimmered, illuminating the dingy attic. She enfolded it in her hand.

Let the ferocious energy of this beast cross the barrier of its extinction.

She found a piece of white tissue paper in the desk drawer. She smoothed it carefully and wrote *Je t'aime toujours.* Beneath that she wrote *Adieu,* then crossed out the word and wrote beneath it, *Au revoir.*

She took a step back from her words, nodding as if Armand were present. That would reveal herself to him while still retaining a measure of purdah from the eyes of strangers.

Insh'allah, our past and future can be rewritten by these few words.

Then Noor wrapped the tiger claw and gold chain in the tissue. She wrote *Armand Rivkin and Madame Lydia Rivkin* in small, precise letters on the tissue, wedged the packet into the tin and slid the false lid over it. She shook the tin to be sure it wouldn't rattle, then placed it back in Gabrielle's package.

Every woman who ever wore that pendant would have done the same.

She wrapped the knitted scarf around the lot, then wrapped it in the brown paper left by Gabrielle. She entwined the whole package till it bulged like a four-chambered thing.

She knocked on Gabrielle's door, but she had not yet returned. So Noor took the parcel back to her own room, pulled her chair up to the window and raised her binoculars. She would need a telescope to find Armand in those cheerless soup distribution lines.

But she knew his face in memory. In memory, felt the curve of his chin graze her cheek.

Noor paced her attic room and the landing outside like a caged tigress. Monsieur le Missionnaire had returned. Monsieur Durand invited him courteously to come and see his rabbits. They had been in Monsieur Durand's room a long time. With the door closed.

Poor Monsieur le Missionnaire. What an existence! What choice did that poor man have but to betray his friends?

The missionary emerged from Monsieur Durand's room, ducked his bald head and sidled downstairs. In a trice Noor was at Monsieur Durand's door.

"Will he do it? Can he bring us the list?"

"He promised to try. Come in. Sit down."

Since there was but one chair, Noor sat on the bed. Monsieur Durand's room had a window but no view of the camp.

"I told him Gabrielle's letter to the children is wrapped in plastic at the bottom of the jam jar. He will explain to the children, as often as necessary. And he'll look for your packet in the sardine can and take it to your husband."

"He took the money?" Noor had given Monsieur Durand three hundred francs.

"Oh, yes." Monsieur Durand's eyes brightened for an instant. "And the pliers—thank you, mademoiselle."

He opened the rabbits' wooden cage and drew out the piebald one—scrawny by contrast with rabbits in England, but among the three, the rabbit with most flesh on him. Monsieur Durand stroked his black ears and sighed. He put the rabbit back in the cage and fastened the door.

"Where did he say the train was taking them?"

"'East.' That's all he knows. There are rumours about 'relocation in Poland' and other rumours that the destination is Metz."

"Why Metz?"

"It used to be in France, but it's in Germany now." His response fell far short of her question.

"Do you think he'll report us to the Germans?"

"Not yet." Monsieur Durand nodded towards the piebald rabbit. "I promised him I'd give him that one when he brings me the list."

Pain crossed his face fleetingly.

"Monsieur le Missionnaire doesn't think the list is final yet—avenue Foch prisoners are added last. I told him we don't need names of the Gestapo's prisoners, we just want the names of people to be sent from Drancy." He paused, then said in a musing tone, "He told me he doesn't eat the rabbits I give him. He sells them to a black market restaurant so he can buy baptismal certificates."

"Baptismal certificates?"

A knock at the door—Gabrielle. Punctual and full of questions. Monsieur Durand explained in a low voice.

What could his reference to baptismal certificates mean? If Armand pretended to be Christian, could it prevent the Germans from sending him to Germany? Once, long ago, Noor had asked timorously, intensely aware that it went against every tenet of Sufism ever propounded by Abbajaan's school, if Armand might convert to Islam to please Uncle Tajuddin. Armand replied in an instant, "We profess what we know. I couldn't be a converso. My mother converted to Judaism, but she has never felt it in every bone as my father did. She tries at Purim, at Rosh Hashanah, at Yom Kippur, but she didn't grow up with it."

Like Mother, joining in rituals while privately dismissing many tenets of Islam as superstition. Dadijaan had sniffed out Mother from their very first meeting—she could tell Mother had never truly converted, that her Christian notions had simply acquired a new label.

Some Jews were denying their faith, Armand had told her, because they found it inconvenient—but if he left his faith, it wouldn't be to acquire another equally inconvenient one but because he'd lost faith that any Messiah could save the world. She couldn't expect someone who had answered the question of conversion to Islam in such terms to now consider Christianity. Besides, neither he nor Madame Lydia had ever suggested Noor convert to Judaism. Like Abbajaan, their definition of secularism was the Gandhian one, which included rather than excluded all religions, saw all religions as worthy of respect.

Still, she repeated her question about baptismal certificates.

"You should tell Monsieur le Missionnaire not to bother," said Gabrielle. "I pawned my gold cross to buy baptismal certificates for the children two weeks ago, but when I realized all they have to do is check if my little nephew is circumcised and the certificate will be useless, I went and got my cross back."

The same was true for Armand. He and Kabir had this in common, besides their similar avoidance of pork. The baptismal certificate was futile but attractive, a logical answer to an illogical situation.

"He said each baptismal certificate is worth its weight in gold, but it's a good thing you got your cross back," said Monsieur Durand. "When the guards see you wearing it, they don't search your packages as much when you leave them at the camp post, oui?"

"Non, non, they search. But I hope it makes them treat my little darlings better. Oh, I didn't mean . . ."

"Better than Jews, yes."

"Anne-Marie, stop chewing your hair, you're making me even more nervous!" Gabrielle deflected Monsieur Durand's attention to Noor.

Startled, Noor looked at the end of her ponytail and realized she had indeed been chewing it. Her wristwatch said it was almost 18:00 hours.

"Can we do nothing more?" she asked.

"I don't know," said Gabrielle. "But I'm going now to deliver the parcel. If I see something or think of something . . ."

Noor and Monsieur Durand sat at Noor's window, watching the camp, waiting.

Monsieur le Missionnaire did not return with the list that evening. Noor brought in chairs for Gabrielle and Monsieur Durand and sat watching the camp with them. As darkness fell, the perimeter lights flashed on, their beams shooting into the night sky.

Gabrielle cut Monsieur Durand's tobacco ration cigarettes in half and re-rolled them. She smoked carefully, holding the smoke as long as she could, smoked them down as close as she could without burning her fingers. Noor found herself doing the same.

In a low voice Gabrielle told them her entire life story, showing no interest, thankfully, in Noor's. Monsieur Durand held his cigarette between thumb and forefinger the way Indians smoked bidi-cigarettes to appease their hunger. By dawn Noor's eyes and lungs were leaden, her attic room hazy grey as the dawn sky. Behind the lavatory door at the end of the corridor she turned the spigot and let her tears flow with the water.

What could they, what could *she*, do by watching the camp? Absolutely nothing. Then why did she, Monsieur Durand and Gabrielle watch all night? They needed to believe they were doing something. Perhaps they were there to comfort each other, especially Monsieur Durand; to have fourteen relatives in that camp was beyond understanding. What could Monsieur Durand's father possibly do in a German factory at age eighty-one?

Crying was useless too. Noor dried her eyes and turned back.

The door to Monsieur Durand's room was open, and both he and Gabrielle were crouched in the corner, looking into the wooden rabbit hutch.

There was nothing but straw in the cage. The rabbits were gone.

"But the cage is still locked," said Gabrielle.

"Look in the lavatory—" Monsieur Durand's voice was breaking.

"But the cage was locked," repeated Gabrielle.

"Maybe they got into your room," said Monsieur Durand to Noor.

"But I tell you, the cage door is not open."

Repetition finally penetrated Monsieur Durand's misery. He sat down heavily on the edge of his bed and said in a bewildered tone, "What do you mean, the cage is not open?" He made kissing sounds in the direction of the cage, but nothing moved.

Gabrielle sank to her knees, opened the cage door and reached in. She rummaged in the straw for a second, then let out a shriek. She drew back, wide-eyed, revulsion distorting her nose.

"What? What is it?"

Gabrielle was speechless. Noor had to see for herself.

A rabbit skin was almost plastered to the floor of the cage. The rabbit's flesh had been sucked out of its body, leaving only the head and a scaffolding of bones under its skin. Blood, sinew, entrails—all drawn right out of the poor animal. Smell of decay already permeating straw.

Noor pushed more straw away. Another skin. Blood soaked the floor, bits of flesh.

And when she pushed the straw away for the third, she could see the marks, the gnawed hole in the floor of the cage where rats had attacked. The starving creatures had chewed through the floorboards.

Why had the three of them in the next room not heard the rats attacking the rabbits? Why had the rabbits not made some sound— cries, screams—whatever sounds of distress a rabbit can make? But they had, yes, they had. The cage was nicked and scraped by their desperate death throes. Would that they had had pliers to escape from their cage, but they had no such tools . . . And meanwhile she, Gabrielle and Monsieur Durand had been right there in the next room, eyes fixed on the camp, waiting for Monsieur le Missionnaire's return.

Monsieur le Missionnaire! He would be expecting his rabbit, and there was now not a single rabbit left to give him: the rats had done the job neither he nor Monsieur Durand could bring themselves to do. Would Monsieur le Missionnaire give them the list now? Would he turn Monsieur Durand in to the Germans? No— he would see the distress in Monsieur Durand's eyes. Monsieur Durand was sitting on his bed, tie undone, grey hair rising in tufts about roving fingers. Perhaps Monsieur le Missionnaire would accept more money and give them the list.

The drone of motors rose from the street below. Suddenly Noor abandoned the carcasses of the poor rabbits. She, Monsieur Durand and Gabrielle acted as one: they hurried to Noor's room, crowded around the window again.

Buses were arriving at Drancy, the open gates of the internment camp sucking them in one after another like pastilles. More and more buses, like green locusts descending on the camp. Noor, now leaning from the attic window, could see that while they had been aghast at the fate of the rabbits, a roll call of prisoners had begun in the central courtyard. Women holding children in their arms, men shuffling forward, some leaning against each other for support, each clutching a suitcase or bag. She took out her binoculars, shared them with Gabrielle and Monsieur Durand in turn, but they couldn't recognize a single face from this distance even if the light were brighter. Quink-coloured clouds hovered, threatening rain.

Noor ran downstairs with the others behind her, no longer caring if she was seen or by whom. Into the street she raced, past Madame Gagné standing on her front steps; into the street, just as a black Citroën with headlights on led the first bus from the gates. The roar of engines must have woken others in Drancy. Hundreds lined the avenue where the buses would pass on their way to Bobigny station. Some from curiosity. Some must be like herself—related to the inmates. Angry murmurs rose and fell, but there were no shouts of protest. It was an alliance of the helpless.

Noor's fists and jaw clenched.

Allah, no, no! Not now, not when I am so close. Please, please, Allah, don't take Armand away! Why did you bring me here only to send him away to Germany before my eyes?

Take someone else, Allah, not my Armand, not him, not him . . .

She was weeping, running after the first bus, sobbing, Gabrielle beside her. She'd seen a man at a window, a man who looked like Armand. No, there was Armand standing—no, there—crammed among the old men and boys.

No—there! There!

No—there!

Oh, where? Where?

"Armand, I'm here, look, look!"

Please, Allah, let me speak to him first. Let me tell him. Oh, tell him for me . . .

Then came the headlights of another crowded, lumbering bus and she began running beside it, looking, throat soon rasping, lungs gasping, legs beginning to drag. Gendarmes moved into the crowd with their batons. Gabrielle was howling.

Monsieur Durand was left far behind.

Was that Madame Lydia's face? No, no.

White birds fluttered in the smeared windows—hands, large and small, waving.

A third bus thundered by, listing with the weight of its passengers, and she was running, running, but couldn't keep up. Gabrielle was left behind.

Another bus, and another.

Suddenly there were more birds, grey birds, flying from the windows of the buses. Square birds that fluttered to the sidewalks, then skittered and blew like dry leaves.

Legs heavy as if wading through water. A biting pain entered her side, she stumbled, had to slow . . . walk . . . double over . . . stop.

Vision was liquid, spilling over. She looked up, fighting for breath, fists still clenched over emptiness. The sky was an inverted bowl moving impotently above. Houses and shops were shuttered all around. How could it be that the din and cries of prisoners leaving Drancy at this hour had disturbed no one along this road? Had the convoys become so familiar a sight?

On the pavement before her lay one of the grey birds. It was a letter. She picked it up as if it were injured.

Addressed in pencil, but not to her.

She had run all the way to the *tabac*. Closed this early in the morning. There was an old half-barrel to rest against till panic subsided and reason returned.

She hadn't seen Armand. She hadn't seen Madame Lydia.

She examined the address on the letter and put it in her pocket. She would post it, as a kind stranger had done for Armand—for her.

Noor walked back—a long way back—soft-boned, insides jangling.

Monsieur Durand was standing among the dwindled crowd by the camp gates. He stood empty-handed, looking very old. Gabrielle's head leaned on his arm, she patted his hand. No letters in sight; they must have been scooped up and pocketed quickly.

"God will look after them," Monsieur Durand said to Noor.

A blade pierced her side again.

"He saw his father, his wife . . . everybody," whispered Gabrielle. "I didn't see the children, thank God."

The three began walking back to the boarding house.

"We did see Monsieur le Missionnaire," she said to Noor. "He was on the last bus, poor man."

"He's a good man. God will look after him," said Monsieur Durand. "And your husband, Mademoiselle Régnier?"

"I didn't see my husband."

Alhamdulillah.

Self-loathing welled and Noor's eyes dampened. How could she rejoice for Armand even as other prisoners were being sent to Germany? But then—had she missed Armand? Perhaps he had been on the far side of a bus.

Banish the thought. Believe your eyes, only your eyes. You didn't see him. So he's not gone, he's still alive, he's still in the camp.

She joined Gabrielle in helping Monsieur Durand up the stairs. At their urging he lay down on the bed in Gabrielle's room. Gabrielle kept up a steady stream of fantasy as comfort.

"Don't worry. People in Germany live like kings—they take our wheat and coal there because they have to feed prisoners of war in the camps. Don't worry, the Red Cross inspects German camps for foreigners—they can't be all that bad."

Noor contributed one too. "Remember the Geneva Convention. Please don't worry . . ."

Gabrielle brought a bucket from Madame Gagné and water from the lavatory. Noor helped her clean, swab and scrub till all traces of the mauled rabbits were gone. Gabrielle took the skins away to sell, the cage to be repaired by Claude and the bones to bury in a flower bed. Then Noor led Monsieur Durand back to his room.

The problem struck her as she stood gazing at the camp again from her window. With Monsieur le Missionnaire gone, how could she know if Armand had received her tiger claw, or that he was still at Drancy?

Noor stood in the doorway of the garage, caught in the abrupt change of light from bright afternoon to murky interior. Smell of grease and acetylene welding. A light shaft from the clerestory window lit a table beside the automobiles. One of the two figures with lunch packets and bottles of cider open before them looked like Claude. The other was an older man in overalls.

"Salut, Monsieur Claude!"

The boy came towards her, a lopsided grin adorning his face. A muscular arm rubbed against her shoulder, leaving an odorous dampness. He stood a little closer than she liked, but she let him.

"I have one more favour I must request." She spoke softly enough that he bent closer.

"Mademoiselle, what is it?"

Noor twiddled her watch about her wrist. It was too difficult to make up a tale after the events of that morning. She would begin from the truth and diverge a little for the sake of persuasion.

"Claude, Gabrielle delivered a parcel to the camp for her little niece and nephew—and I took the opportunity to send a small gift to a friend there."

"Oho." Claude stroked his beardless chin. "A friend?"

"Yes, a family friend."

Another lie; her family had never considered Armand a friend. Perhaps Anne-Marie Régnier's family considered him a friend.

"And so?"

"I must find out if he received my gift."

Claude gave a low whistle. "*C'est tout?!*"

"Yes, that's all."

Claude's guffaw began falsetto then cracked to bass register. "Ask Monsieur le Missionnaire."

"Regrettably, he was sent on one of the buses this morning."

"*Mon Dieu!*" Claude hunched his shoulders and stared at the ground. Then he said, "Mademoiselle, I can sell you Pall Mall, Brut champagne, Algerian wine, Scotch whisky, apples, quinces, truffles, tripe, even oysters—but only a Resistance group can get a message in and out of the camp."

"You must know someone in the Resistance? *Enfin*, you look like a man who would be fighting in the Resistance—even the German officer suspected so."

It was unmistakably a compliment; she hoped he would take it as one.

Claude stood a little taller but said, "Non, mademoiselle, my mother says if one is going to fight, one should be in French uniform, not creeping around doing sabotage in the night or hiding in the hills like the Maquis. And if I were caught, who would look after her?" But he did look disappointed to be left out of the adventures.

"Yes, your mother is right," said Noor. "But this is not to help France or Germany. Nor is it anything illegal. It's just to find out if a small packet was received. And it's not as dangerous as selling whisky and tripe on the black market."

Claude looked away, half his face in shadow. A shout came from within the garage; Claude's break was almost up. Noor let a questioning silence lengthen.

Claude looked back at her. "You know, mademoiselle, it is a strange thing."

"Yes?"

"Last week, the curé was so tired of hearing me confess my sins about the black market that he didn't give me novenas as penance. He said I must do one deed that did not benefit myself, and remember the feeling. And when I asked which deed, he said it would present itself to me. He didn't say it would be something so difficult."

"I know it is difficult. But you will try?"

He jerked his head in assent.

Subhan-allah!

Noor touched Claude's hand lightly, then pressed the hundred-franc note into his palm a second time. This time he put it in his pocket, mumbling about possibly having to pay someone.

Noor showed him a small card with Armand's name. "Memorize this," she said.

He nodded after a second. She put the card back in her pocket and gave him a look that said they shared a secret. A bell rang. Claude touched his beret and loped off into the gloom.

Pforzheim, Germany

January 1944

Metz, Madagascar! I must forget what I have learned since that day at Drancy about conditions in German concentration camps to remember how we felt then. As long as we—Monsieur Durand, Gabrielle and myself—continue to believe the Germans took the Durands and others to work in Germany, we can hope to reunite with them when the epidemic of destruction has passed.

But now, here in my prison cell, I am not so sure. They could be starving my beloved—how can I know? What work is a musician fit for but to create music?

And there are stories I cannot believe, frightening stories.

But I still believe there are deeds an educated populace cannot do, that literate people will not countenance. I think of French friends I grew up with—our neighbours, Josianne Prénat and her family—polyglot, self-critical. Josianne with her bantering sense of humour, helpful, willing to learn from the world, not only France. Can Germans be so different?

Europeans living in their not-Asian and not-African fortress are a people who had an "Enlightenment" and ever since call themselves "civilized."

I must continue believing this.

I wrote to Zaib that night at Drancy. I know it was a Wednesday, and it was June 23, 1943:

My dear sister,

Writing brings us closer, if only on the page. How much suffering has this world experienced—still experiences—one person's suffering is nothing, and yet it is everything.

I may ask you, Zaib, what I may ask no one else, for you held me through the long night at Madame Dunet's, when fear of shame overcame my courage. Little sister, you comforted me when Kabir refused to give permission, permission our Abbajaan would surely have granted. Yesterday I sent a message to A. Pray he forgives me. The German Raj and Vichy cannot outlast my hope, my love—still, say a du'a for me.

Avec love, avec pyar. Forget me not,

Noor

PART FOUR

CHAPTER 18

Paris, France
Thursday, June 24, 1943

THE MOSAIC DOME of La Mosquée pressed into milky sky. The café nestled in the shadow of the grand mosque seemed to wake, as a few people entered its cedar-trellised courtyard. A fezzed *garçon* brought tea in a cone-lidded pot. Noor poured it into a demitasse and glanced at her watch.

Early, for a change. At 15:00 hours Professor Balachowsky would be waiting in the Jardin des Plantes, a short walk from La Mosquée.

A fine mist rose from the marble baths within the mosque compound and scented the summer air with an attar of rose. In the distance, the sound of oud strings joined the slow rhythm of a *zikr ilahi*. It was past Zuhr, but even if she had intended to say her Asar prayers, Noor couldn't enter the mosque, mindful of her orders not to return anywhere she might be recognized. The café close to Allah was her compromise.

Snatches of Moroccan Arabic, close enough to Urdu and Qur'anic Arabic for her to piece together meaning: old men were passing a water pipe along with stories of their years of resistance to the French Protectorate. A few tables away, a calligrapher bent over his ink pot and paper, labourers hunched over a chessboard. A group of men talking in French bemoaned the difficulty of sending money to Tunisia and Algeria. Curious glances flicked in her direction from time to time.

Probably wondering what kind of woman she was, and what a girl of Noor's age, alone and unclaimed, was doing here in public. With only a headscarf as hijab. Like Uncle Tajuddin, none of them would find Noor "Muslim enough" for their liking. Still, there was an unspoken bond she could rely on with Muslim strangers, even disapproving ones, and it was ingrained in them never to call a gendarme, German or French, for any reason.

Because of Ramzaan, only travellers were dining. Maybe she shouldn't have ordered tea? But even without fasting, Noor was faint from lack of food. Worry for Armand and Madame Lydia had dulled her appetite at Madame Gagné's table that morning. The tea might settle her stomach.

Monsieur Durand hadn't come down to breakfast. Gabrielle said she would check up on him later. She scooped up Noor's share of jam and threw two tobacco ration tickets across the table at her, saying anyone could have them, she didn't need them; what good were they to anyone with Monsieur le Missionnaire gone?

Gabrielle had second thoughts this morning—like Noor. She might not have seen the children on the buses because they were sitting or because they were too small. Because they were facing the other side, because they were going too fast, because . . . because . . . Gabrielle would present herself at the gate today and ask for the children's laundry. If the guards gave her any, the children were still within.

Such a simple and effective verification, that laundry request. Couldn't Noor do the same? But wilfully presenting herself anywhere identification would be scrutinized more carefully than at street checkpoints was dangerous to her mission, to the network—no, she couldn't.

Mint tea stung Noor's tongue, burned all the way down.

Her clothes smelled of the tobacco-filled night of waiting, muscles remembered her panic-stricken running beside bus after bus. The rabbits' blood had washed off her hands, but the image of skins tented over bones was indelible. Worst was the memory of Monsieur Durand's eyes, his empty hands and his faith. "God will look after them."

His dignity guided by example, guided her through the not-knowing.

Allah, you who know the suffering of Al-Hallaj, let not my Armand suffer hunger, wound or pain. Allah, if he has been sent to Germany, don't let them treat him harshly. I would take his place, Allah. Let them take me, not him.

Now, more than ever, she must trust Allah to keep Armand safe, and hope Claude would confirm Armand had received her message. She took smaller sips and distracted herself with memories.

So many visits to this grand Moorish-style mosque when she was a child. There were so few Muslims in France in those days, and so few from India, that a glimpse of another Indian in the café at La Mosquée crinkled the tributary lines at Abbajaan's eyes. Brimming with questions, he'd invite perfect strangers to his table and in mellifluous Hindustani or Urdu say, "Where are you coming from? Near Bombay? We are coming from the Kingdom of Baroda."

Uncle Tajuddin, on the other hand . . . Uncle, whose duty to his half-brother's legacy compelled his presence in this land of infidels, compelled him every day to wear his one pair of European shoes. Uncle was far too haughty to chat with Indian Muslims who frequented La Mosquée. To him Maghriben Muslims from North Africa were entirely beneath his noble station. And as for non-Muslims of all kinds—they were *dhimmis*, redeemable only by conversion.

All Abbajaan's inclusionary ideas were "non-Muslim" for Uncle. He was shocked to find Abbajaan teaching that Islam was one way but not the only way to God, shocked that Abbajaan permitted his daughters, wife and women followers to dress and "express themselves" as they felt, and to imbibe wine. While Abbajaan searched for seven levels of meaning, deep metaphors and symbolism behind the words of the Qur'an, his half-brother was a Qari, a reciter for whom the Qur'an was a set of sounds and commands with a single interpretation—his own. For Abbajaan, Islam laid down unattainable ideals that everyone could aspire to; for Uncle, it was not simply a religion but an ideology from which there was no dissent, only heresy.

Allah would be merciful, but his representative in the Khan family was not.

Oh, she should be kinder to Uncle even in memory. He banished himself from his home and family and the comfortable life of a *raees*, a landed gentleman in India, to be exiled in France—a country with ways he didn't comprehend, speaking a foreign language he considered crude; to run a school of Sufism preaching in English about tenets he didn't believe, all to feed and care for his half-brother's family. Thankless family, too. Each resenting him for not being Abbajaan, resenting him, poor man, for not even coming close.

"Duty! Honour!" he'd remind Kabir each morning, in a melancholy voice.

Mother put aside her own yearnings for casseroles, peach cobblers and the like, tolerating Uncle's need for goat curry and Surati lentils—but then, she couldn't survive without him even so far as to write a cheque; and without his guardianship and lectures there would have been no Sufi school. But no amount of experimentation or employing of immigrant chefs helped her prepare pilau or okra the way he liked it. The only "Indian" cookbook Mother had in those days was by an Englishwoman who gave recipes for mulligatawny soup and "keggeree." When Noor or Zaib tried to help, it only extended Uncle's lengthy lectures on cooking—though he couldn't even boil an egg for himself. Nine years of those lectures, till Dadijaan's arrival in 1938.

Dadijaan's cooking soothed her half-son's culinary cravings, but Mother had to live with her constant disapproval. Still, Dadijaan was a fount of fascinating stories of when Abbajaan was young, stories Noor translated for Mother. And Dadijaan's faith in Allah called to Noor's as Uncle's never could.

Mother and Dadijaan will see one day they had someone they both loved, in common.

The calligrapher was fanning his ink dry. The labourers finished their chess game, traded colours, lined up their men again and began anew. If she weren't concerned about attracting notice, she might have moved closer to watch the nuances of play. But the men might be like Uncle—so unaccustomed to the presence of unrelated women, they'd be highly uncomfortable if she so much as took a step towards them.

Noor glanced at her watch. She would wait ten minutes more.

Uncle Tajuddin's reactions were extreme and individual, unique to him. The chess players might be quite unlike him.

Uncle couldn't see much individuality in the French. "What is individual about these bourgeois Parisians?" he would ask. "If they questioned themselves 'why?' before they bought a new dress or coat, instead of 'why not?,' wouldn't they have more for the poor? Women buying long jackets one season then short the next, all at the same time. Women with finger curls today, no finger curls tomorrow, as if they shared one brain among them! Men taking mistresses instead of helping indigent women by marrying them! French women willing to live out their lives in *ménages à trois* but gasping in horror at polygamy. The challenge," he said, "is to find happiness within the constraints of your society, not to throw off all restraint. Creativity," the courtly old gentleman would pronounce in his flowery Urdu, "requires the constraints of form to find expression."

But the constraints Uncle spoke of were those of his childhood in Baroda, not Paris, and the customs he wanted to re-create were the idealized feudal life of the fifteenth century, customs no longer practised even in India except in the courts of nawabs. By twelve, Noor had read and discussed the Qur'an enough with Abbajaan to know that restraints on women's conduct and marriage were inventions not of Allah but of the mullahs who succeeded the Prophet. And so from the age of fifteen, when Uncle arrived, Noor's creativity, and that of Zaib, lay in finding detours around his limits.

Noor sipped her tea almost to its dregs.

For instance, when, to Uncle's horror, Zaib "expressed herself" on her eighteenth birthday, in the *hammam* behind this café, by henna-dyeing her hair auburn, Uncle promptly punished Noor for "allowing" it. Reprisals were always his way. But the corner of Noor's mouth rose recalling how Zaib stubbornly kept to her auburn hair, even in London, long after Uncle had returned to India. Putting it in Christian terms for Mother, Zaib said her disobedience was a sin but one Noor had already redeemed on her behalf.

Noor and Zaib would chat for hours in the steamy women's *hammam* and afterwards order tabouli, lamb kebabs and flaky honey cakes. None were available today—not only because of the war, but because of Ramzaan.

Noor swirled the tea leaves gathered at the bottom, then decanted the dregs into her saucer. The clumped, dark leaves were supposed to guide, but assigning meaning to their random shapes required a gymnastic imagination. Letters referred to names of people. Was there an A? Not that she could find. All she could see were flags or squares—warnings. But warnings of what? When? All in a clockwise spiral: events were coming towards her, around her.

Noor glanced up. Everyone seemed to be engrossed in his own work or play. Too quiet, perhaps, but quite as normal as she remembered.

Zaib would interpret happy endings from her tea leaves; Zaib was so much better at adjusting to the world the way it was. How matter-of-fact Zaib had been the day she accompanied Noor to Madame Dunet's home. Four years younger, the sixteen-year-old took charge. Somehow she had five thousand francs, all counted and ready in an envelope, for the midwife. More money than Noor had ever seen in her life. Zaib held Noor's hand all the way across the Bois de Boulogne, held her close as Madame Dunet applied the suction, washed her clothes afterwards.

Strange how my secret, shared at Madame Dunet's, brought us closer.

The warnings, the warnings. What could they mean?

The red-fezzed *garçon* who took her order—was he a collabo? Or were the chess players? What if the place she felt safest was the one place she wasn't?

Stay alert, stay vigilant!

Abandoning her attempt to decode the tea leaves, Noor paid the *garçon*, arranged her headscarf about her neck and made her way across the street, through the tall gates of the Jardin des Plantes, past a wooden signboard that announced *No admittance to Jews.*

Inside the Jardin des Plantes, regiments of riotous flowers from all corners of France and many other countries stood upright in their oblong beds, neatly classified and separated beneath the sculptured trees. The Germans had yet to invent a method of transporting these fragile beauties to Germany.

In the distance, starched white plumage—a nun shepherding a line of girls in neatly pressed, pleated skirts. Noor slowed for a long-eared white rabbit mincing across her path, its leash, then a very old gentleman in a top hat, his face like Monsieur Durand's abject one. Then past a couple who, oblivious to a barbed wire blockade beside their bench, were entwined in a passionate kiss.

A pair of cocky young men with slicked-back long hair, long coats and drainpipe trousers passed carrying a bundle: a cat wrapped in a small straitjacket. The poor animal would soon be passing for rabbit in black market bistro tureens. *"Lapin rôti au four . . . au poivre . . . au fenouil."*

Professor Balachowsky was bowed over a bed of *pensées*. Noor murmured the all-clear password as she walked past. The Professor straightened, put his pipe in his mouth. In a few minutes he joined her in the privacy of the gazebo.

The exchange was to be quick. The map, marked with an X to show the burial spot for the arms canisters dropped two days earlier at Rosny, passed from Noor's hand to his. She whispered the code words that would authorize release of the smuggled canisters for transfer onwards from Grignon.

Quickly, Noor pulled the letter she had written to Zaib from her jacket pocket. "I would be obliged, Professor," she whispered, "if you would give this letter to Gilbert before the next landing."

But the Professor was pale behind his unlit pipe. Sweat beaded above his worry lines.

"What is it, Professor?" said Noor. "Are you not feeling well?"

He jerked his head. "Max was captured by the Gestapo in Caluire, near Lyons. Go to Phono immediately and tell him. Say it is very possible the great Max is no more." He turned away, slump-shouldered.

Max. Jean Moulin.

"Wh-when was Max captured?"

"Three days ago—June 21. *Hélas!* He was tortured horribly. Horribly. But I know he did not speak—why would he speak now? The first time the Boche tortured him, three years ago, you know he slit his own throat with a splinter of glass rather than sign his name to lies. But it is too much to expect that he will resist and survive a second time. Or escape again."

Noor laid her hand on the Professor's arm; a bone-deep tremor went through it. She helped him to a bench in the corner of the gazebo.

Professor Balachowsky seemed to struggle to master himself. "*Je suis fou!* We all know this happens but never think it will happen to someone like Max. I only met him once, but . . ."

He sat up straight. "When the Germans came, I thought, 'I'm just an old professor teaching about insects—what can I do?' Then I heard of Max and I thought, 'My grandparents came from Poland and bought a vineyard, but I'm as French as Monsieur Hoogstraten.' Monsieur Hoogstraten's grandparents were Dutch, you see. So as soon as he returned to Grignon from the POW camp, I asked, 'Director, what shall I do?' Little did I know Director Hoogstraten had been in the Resistance for more than a year, since the Battle of France . . . But it was all because I heard the story of Max."

"But you're not sure Max is dead."

"I hope so, for his sake," said the Professor, looking away. "The Gestapo chief in Lyons put him on display for fellow prisoners — all with the Resistance, so they smuggled out messages as soon as they could. They said he was in a coma. Swollen lips, head in bandages. Knuckles broken, face beaten to an unrecognizable pulp, eyes dug in as though they'd been punched through his head — Oh, please excuse me, mademoiselle! *Enfin*, it was the last time our Max was seen alive."

A cold sickness crawled over Noor.

"The Germans must be delighted," Professor Balachowsky said after a silence. "Without Max, the Free French groups will return to sporadic sabotage. Well-meaning, but scattered and uncoordinated."

"But it is all fighting the Germans — isn't that important?" Noor hoped to lead him back to hope.

The Professor gave a ruptured sigh. "Anne-Marie, it is only in the past few months we began to benefit from working together. If we derailed a train, the network with a well-placed worker made sure phone lines were cut so there was more time to get away. If we planned to blow up a building, another network might verify it would be full of Germans. It's taken three years to create what we have today — codes, supply lines, maps of secret passages, courier lines, workshops, escape routes and safe houses."

He glanced right and left, then spoke even lower. "In the beginning we were just schoolboys playing with matches. Printing newspapers, pouring water into German petrol tanks, making grand symbolic gestures, risking our freedom and our lives just to paint V-for-Victory signs on street corners — pinpricks to the Germans! It's only now that no German feels safe anywhere in France. Every time they climb aboard a train, mount a truck or a bus, they fear the Resistance will call down English bombs upon them — or set their own charges."

"By Resistance, do you mean networks like ours, or the Free French?"

"Both. I was at a meeting where we all agreed to co-operate — the only time I saw Max, standing there with his white scarf covering the scar. Heard that strange voice."

Miss Atkins had said the SOE only co-operated with the Free French "when we have to."

"Why would The Firm co-operate with the Free French?" asked Noor.

"*Vous savez*, the Free French have gathered information for General de Gaulle that The Firm could only dream of gathering for Churchill. Free French networks extend everywhere in France, and know the right questions to ask and whom to ask in every village, and because they ask it on behalf of a Frenchman, General de Gaulle, people are glad to help. But when people know their answers will be sent to Churchill and the English, they think twice." The Professor sounded almost envious of the rival intelligence group.

A sooty pigeon fluttered into the gazebo and pecked about, searching for crumbs.

Noor reached into her pocket for the tobacco coupons Gabrielle had given her, and held them out to the Professor.

Professor Balachowsky's gloom lightened for a moment. Without a word he pulled his pipe out of his mouth and pointed to a tiny hole at its tip.

A miniature poison dart gun.

She nodded, still holding out the coupons.

He took them with a grave "Merci," then straightened, wiped his brow with a large white handkerchief, then his moustache and grey goatee. "First Vidal, now Max. But we carry on. There is nothing else to be done. We'll come through this, Anne-Marie."

He stuck his thumbs in his vest pockets and took a deep breath. "Archambault said your transmitters and suitcase arrived. It was so amusing . . ."

In a teasing whisper he recounted that one parachute got caught in a tree, breaking open Noor's valise and festooning the drop zone with her white lingerie. Archambault and the others had to hunt all over for the clothing. The valise was now strapped shut and taken to Grignon.

Noor might have been embarrassed except that the jovial tale of her unmentionables was so obviously told to mask Professor Balachowsky's greater woes.

"I'm most thankful that the delay didn't give the Germans time to reach the drop zone," she said. She and Émile would make separate trips to Grignon to move the transmitters and her personal belongings. Noor would conceal one transmitter at Madame Gagné's boarding house at Drancy, the other in Renée's cellar. The last would be transferred from Grignon to the boarding house behind Chez Tutulle.

The Professor seemed recovered now. Noor kissed him on both cheeks as they parted.

"*Haiya-'alas-salah! Haiya-'alas-salah!*"

The *azaan* was ululating from La Mosquée's minaret as Noor left the Jardin des Plantes. As she hurried down the rue Monge, the full import of Professor Balachowsky's news rippled up inside her. A tidal wave chased her down the métro stairs and crashed against her solar plexus.

Allah! If the great Max, the one man who knew every leader of every Resistance network in the country, has been arrested and tortured by the Gestapo, how long can our network last?

CHAPTER 19

Paris, France
Saturday, June 26, 1943

AT A LITTLE PAST 18:00 HOURS, Émile returned from the couturier with Monique's white gown of Indian parachute silk looped over his arm. Monique draped it across the card table in the drawing room so Renée, Noor and Babette could admire its delicate lace.

Suddenly, four pairs of knocks sounded on the front door of the little house on the rue Erlanger. Then again. And again.

"It's the right signal," said Émile.

Hard and loud enough to be the Gestapo.

Monique said, "*Chéri*, were you expecting anyone tonight?"

Émile shook his head. Forefinger to his lips, he pointed towards the kitchen.

In a trice Monique had bundled up the wedding gown and was following Renée and Babette through the kitchen, down into the cellar. Noor seized the knob of a cupboard door in the foyer and joined the brooms and buckets inside. The door wouldn't quite close behind her; she could see through the slit.

Émile took his time putting on his jacket, deliberately straightened his tie and reached for the latch.

It was Odile Hoogstraten, a breathless Odile, who flung herself in, leaving her bicycle sprawled on its side on the stone path behind her, wheels still churning.

"Message for you." Her whisper verged on tears.

Noor left the cupboard and joined Émile and Odile.

"Papa sent me to tell you: Prosper and Archambault have been arrested by the Gestapo."

The cupboard burst open behind Noor. An avalanche of brooms plunged into the foyer.

"Prosper captured? Archambault arrested?" repeated Émile when all the crashing and drumming on the wood floor stopped.

"When? How?" Renée had come out of the cellar and was standing in the passage, Monique and Babette behind her.

Noor began picking up fallen brooms and mops and putting them back in the cupboard.

This was not supposed to happen. Arrests happened to others, theoretical agents who didn't study the SOE handbook carefully, or agents with code names like Vidal and Max. Not to people she knew, people in her cell. Not to jug-eared Prosper, who moved in time with the jazz and called her "old girl," or Archambault, who sang in the choir at his lycée, smelled of Old Spice and was to leave for London as soon as Noor's transmitters were operating.

Odile took a deep, gulping breath. "Prosper—yesterday morning—they were waiting for him when he returned to Paris from Trie-Château. Plain-clothed, in black Citroëns—definitely Gestapo. Archambault after him, at midnight—but Papa didn't learn of it till today."

Odile's shoulders began to shake. Renée guided her into the drawing room, where the girl dropped into a chair. Though Noor had met Prosper only twice, she shared Odile's instinctive esteem for him—a man of integrity, responsible for a very large family.

Odile caught her breath and went on in a more coherent flow. "It started on Monday morning. Gilbert didn't come to meet Prosper at the Gare d'Austerlitz with the two Canadians. So Prosper thought they must all have been arrested. He came to talk to Papa— he was so agitated . . . Papa agreed he should get out of Paris, till he could find out what happened. Prosper went to Trie-Château. But when he came back . . ." Odile's face sank into her hands.

A suspicion crept into the back of Noor's mind—something Odile had said. "Why didn't Gilbert meet Prosper at the station as planned?"

Odile looked up. "He said the Canadians arrived late and he was delayed. There's more. An agent who landed at Rosny the next night was also arrested, but I don't know where or his name. Another agent left a message at Flavien's saying all of them are now at the avenue Foch."

"They won't talk, you know they won't. However they are tortured." Émile smoothed his hair but only succeeded in tousling it further. He turned to Noor. "We must send a message to London at once. The entire network is compromised. London must inform the other cells, other networks . . ."

Noor nodded. Since her rendezvous with Professor Balachowsky at the Jardin des Plantes two days before, she had concealed one transmitter under her bed at Madame Gagné's boarding house at Drancy and one in Renée's cellar, but the third, destined for transfer to the boarding house behind Chez Tutulle, still waited at Grignon.

"They will hold out twenty-four hours. But wait—when were they arrested? *Mon Dieu!* We have only a few hours left and they can speak," said Émile.

Noor had her own questions for Odile. "Where did the Gestapo catch Prosper?" she asked. "In Trie-Château, on the train, at the station in Paris or at his apartment?"

Odile took a glass of water from Monique and gulped it down. "At his apartment."

"Where?"

"Gilbert said it was at the Hôtel Mazagran in St-Denis."

Gilbert. Archambault was right.

At the Jazz Club last Sunday night, Prosper said only Archambault, Gilbert and herself knew his new address. Archambault had been captured after Prosper. That left Gilbert and herself as informers. And since she had not committed such a crime herself, that left Gilbert.

Tuck away the information. Tell Émile later.

Aloud, she said, "How did the Gestapo know he would be there?"

"I—I don't know," said Odile. "They were waiting for him when he returned, that's all we know."

"From Gilbert."

"Yes, from Gilbert."

"We must send a message to London," Émile repeated with an edge in his voice.

"You can't transmit from here," said Renée. "The Gestapo might already be watching us."

Noor could receive without detection, but German vans were on the prowl night and day in hope of intercepting radio traffic to England.

Renée left the drawing room. "Come here, Émile!" came her voice.

She was lifting a corner of the lace curtain above the kitchen sink and pointing. Émile joined her at the window. Renée pointed into the darkening courtyard behind the house. Émile put his arm around her shoulders and their voices sank to a murmur.

Monique placed a bowl of soup and a piece of chocolate on the dining table before Odile.

Babette looked back and forth from one adult to another, then curled up on the chaise longue, lips puckered to match her china-faced doll. She stroked its rose-patterned silk dress and wound a lace scarf about its neck.

Renée returned to pace the drawing room, Émile behind her.

"I don't think anyone was watching us—you were mistaken, Renée. It's nothing, just a shadow."

"If you are not careful, you too will be captured," Renée said to Émile. "You just go anywhere this fiancée of yours leads you."

To Noor, Émile's fiancée seemed to follow more than she led.

"Our wedding was only three days away." Monique's voice held tears. She caressed the white silk gown, draped again over the card table.

"Oh, we will have our wedding," said Émile. "The Gestapo isn't going to stop us from getting married!"

"You've risked so much for her wedding dress, you may as well marry," said Renée, sitting down at the card table. "But I think *she* must move." She pointed at Noor. "Your involvement is dangerous enough. Having this woman from England here with us now—*Écoutez!* We may as well ask the Germans to come and arrest us."

Renée might be right, but Noor couldn't go to Madame Gagné's and hope to arrive before curfew.

"*Pas de problème!* I will arrange for you to go to Madame Aigrain," said Émile. "Her apartment is just a few minutes from here."

"I will go with Anne-Marie to Madame Aigrain." Babette was looking up from her doll.

"*Shhhht! Tais-toi!*"

Monique prepared a packet with a cheese sandwich and a bottle of cider for Noor, and Noor packed her transmitter and a few clothes into her valise. It took no more than a few minutes and Émile was back to take it from her hand. Swiftly, he gave Noor directions to Madame Aigrain's.

He thumbed each side of his moustache. "The Germans are frightened of cemeteries, especially at night. Our information is that they find excuses not to patrol there. The Claude Lorrain cemetery here in Auteuil is too close. Meet me at the Cimetière de Montmartre at 21:00 hours. The sepulchre of the Famille Ginot on the avenue des Polonais will be left open. Remember, Famille Ginot." Then he left.

Fifteen minutes later, Noor stood at the door with her transmitter suitcase in hand. She looped her lemon scarf about her neck and put on her oilskin. She took leave of Monique with kisses on both cheeks.

"I must see you at our wedding," said Monique, almost in tears.

Babette kissed Noor formally, then threw her arms around her.

Renée's rouged cheek was cool against Noor's. "A *bientôt*," Renée murmured, as if she would have preferred to say *adieu*.

Pforzheim, Germany
January 17, 1944

A few minutes ago I woke up fighting. The dungeon has not even the straw mattress from my cell, and I had dozed off on the damp stone floor; by now I can sleep with insects crawling over me. This was no nightmare. My chains whipped my shins as I kicked and flailed against a clawing thing. A rat gibbered and squeaked when my clog hit its hide. The sight of Monsieur Durand's rabbits at Drancy still haunts me; starving rats in my cell and my heart races like a Spitfire engine.

In the absence of light I no longer read the world, scan its symbols and hidden meanings. I squeeze my eyes shut then open them to know if the blackness lies within my eyelids or is the inside of my cell. Invisible colours surround me, all absorbed into black.

I can no longer trace the anatomy of letters. I am bereft of pictographs, icons and signs. With no paper, no pen, I commit words and phrases intended for you to memory. For you, ma petite, my unborn audience of one, I rearrange and revise words in my mind. Perhaps I will never see paper or pen again. If so, this is the letter you will never read, letter from my spirit to yours.

I feel my way across the cold floor to the door, lie down and press my nose to the line of light at its base, suck in a small current of fresh air. I hear moaning and find it comes from me.

Sometimes I talk to Armand too, but to imagine my beloved for an instant in circumstances like mine, or worse, is to near the dread abyss of insanity; my thoughts flee from the brink. That any of my friends in the Resistance might be in dungeons like this is horror enough.

Let me remember something beautiful — the sustained strength of breath in a khayal, Debussy's Afternoon of a Faun. *I try to* whistle a Chevalier song, then a Piaf lament, but their words elude me. I play a sonata on the damp, slimy wall, but that reminds me too much of Armand. Then comes defiance. I sing out the Marseillaise, then "Quand Madelon." But this too reminds me of Armand, and my voice breaks down. I recover after a while, sit up in a corner and sing "We're Going to Hang Out the Washing on the Seigfried Line" till my throat is sore.

Light blazes from the open door. I squint. A shadow looms across the walls. My gaoler's face comes close, face like a Frankish battle-axe. Wordlessly her hand draws back.

A sharp crack to my face and I am silenced.

Much later she brings a cup of water, cool and pure as if drawn from the well of Zamzam, and a cup of cold mangel-wurzel soup.

I try to meet her eyes, imagine her smiling, breast-feeding a child. No image comes.

She turns away. The metallic slam of the door reverberates behind her.

The dark is the danger zone where distinctions fade to black and nothing has a name. Here day and night, logic and clairvoyance, reason and madness, objectivity and subjectivity, dream and reality, positive and negative energies are one. Here past and future become present, become visible.

My leg cramps, I vomit a thin stream of burning stomach juices, vomit out of sheer rage.

Rage at Vogel for reducing me from the sublime importance of action in service of love and ideals to the scatological—that bucket of feces in the corner whose vile odour keeps me light-headed and nauseated. A few short months ago I had what every woman needs—dignity, vanity, modesty. I want them again, to look and feel and be my best for Armand. I want Armand back. I want the prospect of our life together again.

Pacing, pacing, on legs jellied in fear of the return of the rats, I measure this dungeon cell. It's the same size as the room Émile arranged for me at Madame Aigrain's the night Prosper was captured. Eight paces long, four paces wide. I know these dimensions well; I spent many hours there, in hiding.

Leaving Renée's home the night we heard Prosper and Archambault had been captured, I took a circuitous route to avoid a checkpoint and a Mercedes parked before an épicerie. The concierge took a key from the pigeonholes behind her desk and led me up two flights of stairs to meet a wisp of a woman with a very large face.

Madame Aigrain—oh, c'est incroyable! Madame Aigrain was the improbable made probable: Tante Lucille come to life. She was old, sickly, and moved with a cane. She had a history of malingering illnesses. She was born in Bordeaux, had lost a son in the Great War. Yes, at Meaux. An old harp stood in the corner of her drawing room, and later I found that her callused finger pads gave it a harsh, edgy tone; each piece sounded like a chorus of insects.

I felt almost guilty for my preknowledge of her.

It was so disconcerting to meet a person I had created from a name given by Miss Atkins. I kept comparing, comparing, the way Mother had compared me always to her idea of a perfect daughter, the way Uncle had compared me always to his idea of a perfect niece.

I had no right to compare Madame to any pre-existing template. She was herself, she was unique and, above all, she was kind.

Awkwardly I asked her prénom and was relieved to find it was not Lucille, but Solange. And that she collected Lalique perfume bottles, not bone china figurines; and she didn't mind, indeed positively enjoyed, a new face in her home.

Madame Aigrain lived alone but for her Siamese cat. She managed a perfumier—which explained her strange smell; she resorted to eau de cologne to mask the scarcity of soap. Her daughter was the couturier who had sewn Monique's wedding dress, and we became friends when I said her daughter had what every seamstress boasts: "les doigts d'or"—fingers of gold.

The thimble-size room where Émile had already deposited my valise was windowless and airless, no more than a cupboard. The transmitter I'd brought in that valise was useless here. A folding cot, *a coarse carpet, a folding chair, a bookshelf. Madame Aigrain brought a pitcher of water and a basin, and set them on the bookshelf above leather-bound volumes of Proust's* A la recherche du temps perdu, *pages still uncut. Some comfort; at least Madame Aigrain was storing, if not reading, the works of banned Jewish writers.*

A second shelf held a row of well-thumbed Simenon detective novels—Simenon, author of the Jewish Peril *articles, whose name I'd heard on the blacklists aired by both the BBC and Honneur et Patrie, the clandestine Resistance radio station.*

On the third shelf lay a French–English dictionary and a set of Dickens novels in English.

In English?

Tucked under the carpet I found a map of France. I held it up to the light and found pinpricked holes at Marseilles, Barcelona, Lisbon. They confirmed my guess: Allied airmen shot down over France must have hidden in this room before me. Madame Aigrain was helping smuggle those downed airmen back to England.

With Madame Aigrain, I was as safe as I could be; my confidence bounded back.

I sat on the crocheted coverlet and looked at my watch—19:00 hours as the French say, or seven P.M. as the English say. Two hours till my rendezvous with Émile at the Cimetière de Montmartre.

How quickly things had changed. Chance rather than choice had staked its claim again to direct my life, just when I was becoming an asset to the network, ready to relieve Archambault. I was now the only radio operator left to the Resistance in the north; the Germans had captured all the others, and their transmitters as well. With Archambault arrested, other Resistance cells would need a radio operator to contact London.

Suspended from a nail hammered into the fleur-de-lys pattern of the wallpaper, a chain held a lattice-framed blond Hazrat Issa, rays emanating from his dark heart. "Heureux ceux qui aiment Dieu," said the Jewish prophet Jesus— "Happy are those who love God."

But do you mean the tri-form God of Christ, Yahweh, our Allah, Brahma–Vishnu–Shiva, or the Universal God that Abbajaan believed in, or a self-styled God named Hitler? Always the question, non, Jesu?

Jesus was smiling. And he was silent.

The rat came back and I killed the gibbering thing. From my fear and loathing I killed, following its sounds and beating at it in the dark with my chain till its squeals went silent and at last it was still.

Killing made me feel better, but it didn't take away my terrors.

I could confess and be pardoned of so many things if I were Catholic. But I have no Jesus who, like a switchboard operator directing calls, comes between me and the creative spirit of the universe. I am personally and irrevocably responsible for my actions. If I deserve hell, so be it.

Not that I can't respect Christians. I think Abbajaan would say: if one man, Hitler, can ruin the whole world, why is it inconceivable that one man or woman can save it?

The guard drops the flap door and I place the rat's body on it. She recoils with what sounds like swearing.

Now I wait and wait for soup.

How does she justify her cruelty today? I read somewhere—was it in The Times?—that a third of Hitler's SS men remain Christian. And the women? Christian too, I presume. But which God can it be—the Christian God or the Universal God of us all—who forgives them their cruelty because their Führer ordered it?

That guard probably believes she is doing right. We all have to believe we're doing right or we'd kill ourselves. But then, some people know when they are doing wrong, and even enjoy it.

Gilbert.

If Gilbert betrayed Prosper, I don't believe any God will forgive him. Because if he did, it was not only a betrayal of Prosper. How many others did Gilbert betray by this one betrayal?

Will Allah strike him down in retribution?

But what if Abbajaan was wrong and there is no Allah? I'm sure my father never conceived of that possibility, but it was a question that worried Armand. He believes in any God or force that would *send him music, with an apprehension that if he doesn't, the music he composes could go elsewhere. I never doubt Allah exists and creates for us, but oh, ma petite, we who follow the Prophet's teachings are so flawed. Someday your father and I will talk about this again. I wish I could talk with him now.*

I no longer believe as the Sufis that our suffering through this war is caused by ignorance. Ignorance is no plea when educated people—men and women alike—allow themselves to be swayed by Hitler to believe compassion is a weakness.

I sound like Kabir. He had his doubts too. We discussed it endlessly.

My doubts here are not about Allah. I wonder if I should have told Émile the very night we learned Prosper was arrested that I suspected Gilbert of betraying Prosper. But if I had and Émile had confronted Gilbert, Gilbert would have denied any betrayal and he would have accused me of betraying Prosper. Gilbert didn't know that I knew he was the only other person who knew Prosper's new address. I had to be sure before making such a grave accusation, for I had no desire to sign an innocent man's death warrant. The Resistance shows no mercy for informers; they would surely kill him.

So, while waiting at Madame Aigrain's till it was time to meet Émile, I decided to say nothing at present, and do what I could to help Prosper and Archambault. I recalled the brown leather pouch I held in safekeeping for Prosper. Was there something in it that could help poor Prosper and Archambault? Perhaps something Émile, Monsieur Hoogstraten or the Professor could use? I took it from my handbag. It was flat, like a wallet. From it I pulled a tiny brown brocade purse like the one in which Dadijaan brought my tiger claw from India. I spilled the contents onto the coverlet.

Five large baguette diamonds winked up at me. The most compact way to transport money to the Resistance. A small fortune that would doom any Frenchman searched by the Gestapo. It was best for all if they remained with me; I could declare they were my jewellery.

Quickly, I returned the diamonds to the silk purse, put the purse back in the leather pouch, the pouch back in my handbag. The fewer who knew of their existence, the better.

I poured water from the pitcher and washed. Then, covering my head with my scarf, I knelt to implore Allah's strength for Prosper, for poor Archambault and for all who suffered in the cells of the Gestapo on the avenue Foch. I added a prayer for all the downed airmen, for Kabir not to be one of them, a prayer that they might find their way back to England.

Have I been locked in this dungeon for three weeks or four? Perhaps more—I cannot tell. The sweep, whistle and slam of Allied bombs is almost inaudible down here.

Allah, do not fight on the side of tyrants!

Do I remember for the sake of shedding my past or to hold on to it? Do I truly remember my actions or do I tell only the stories I wish you to know of me? Only Allah knows. For myself, I set aside such questions, conjure up whole scenes from the past, and conserve my strength for some crucial moment I feel sure is coming.

CHAPTER 20

Paris, France
Saturday, June 26, 1943

SACRÉ COEUR LOOMED LARGE on the Butte Montmartre under a bitten moon, the neon signs and street lamps of Pigalle made extinct by war. A clock tower's hand pointed three minutes past nine. Noor walked quickly from the métro near the Place de Clichy towards a bridge. Her transmitter suitcase pulled at her arm as she descended a stone staircase to the avenue Rachel.

Beyond the large iron gates of the Cimetière de Montmartre, mausoleums crowded beside the path. Tall and narrow, like the checkpoints she'd encountered on the way.

Slam, bang, click. She closed and locked all the doors that must remain closed for efficiency—doors to imagination, worry, fear. But no door could be slammed on memory.

If there had been a cemetery like this one for Muslims in 1926, Abbajaan wouldn't have been buried so far away, and she, Kabir and Zaib might have tended his grave. But at the time, Christians didn't allow Muslims to be buried beside their kin.

When this war was over, she'd go to India with Armand. Introduce them.

The avenue des Polonais was a short climb up the hill past a bed of tulips, their purple brilliance dimmed to lavender by the moonlight.

Here the rich and famous slept together. Abbajaan lay alone in his marble dargah in a high-walled compound. By the time thirteen-year-old Noor went to India with Mother, Kabir and Zaib to bow her head at his tomb, Abbajaan had been buried three months. And no matter how much Noor had wept for that tomb to be opened so she could see Abbajaan's body, she was hushed, soothed—and denied.

The fragrance of woodsmoke wafted by. She was a dark wraith slipping between mausoleums, invisible to any German.

Don't think of Germans, think of something else.

To thirteen-year-old Noor, Abbajaan had joined the *farishtas*, become an angel. Later—all paths to Allah being valid— Hinduism, idol worship and all, brought the comfort of a temporary belief in reincarnation. But as for the Hindu custom of cremation, the very idea wrung Noor's stomach like a sponge.

A half-uncle had once willed that he be cremated instead of buried like other Muslims, setting off a huge family conclave that eventually overturned the dead man's will. The cremation of one man in the family could mark all of them as subject to Hindu law in the eyes of the British Raj, and while the Khan men didn't mind honouring the dead man's request, every woman in the Khan family was adamantly against losing her Qur'an-guaranteed right to inherit a fourth of her husband's estate. They said respecting all religions was one thing, but practising all their contradictory customs and rituals at once was impossible.

A breeze, cooling after the hot day and the stuffiness of Madame Aigrain's apartment, soughed and sighed amid the branches of old trees. Noor crept behind a stone bench and peered into the dark.

Mother brought Noor and Kabir here one wintry day when Abbajaan was giving a veena recital with his brothers at an Oriental revue in Montmartre. Mother turned up her collar and tugged at her single-breasted coat to double-breast it. Here, on this stone bench, she sent Noor with Kabir to search out the graves of famous composers Abbajaan said were Sufis who didn't know they were Sufis.

Kabir found the grave of Hector Berlioz; Noor found Adolphe Sax, inventor of the saxophone. She came back to tell Mother and found her with a handkerchief to her eyes. But Mother got up gamely and soon found Jacques Offenbach, the comic opera genius. Too bad Uncle wasn't there to be scandalized; the idea of respecting the grave of the creator of the cancan!

But it was soon after those tears that Abbajaan began teaching Sufism and his music began its diminuendo.

Past the stone bench now, stone sepulchres looming on either side of the street. The iron grille gate of the Famille Ginot hung open as Émile had promised.

Checking to see no one was following, Noor slipped in, the door creaking closed behind her. Inside, an exquisitely carved statue of Mary leaned over two ragged cushioned kneeling pews. She hefted her suitcase up on the altar, flipped it open, drew aside the chemise she'd thrown over her transmitter, removed a torch, her code book and message book. She was about to thumb the switch on the torch when a phantom loomed from the shadows.

Noor froze. Her heart hadn't drummed like this in training or even when working at Grignon with Archambault.

Only Phono!

In silence, he helped her string the aerial through the broken stained glass window behind the Virgin. The tomb, barely three feet wide, wasn't built for two agents formulating telegraphic sentences. Émile held a torch steady as Noor coded and pencilled the resulting message into the squares of her message book. The page began to look like a fragment of Suleyman's magical shirt.

A few minutes later the Morse sequence bearing the terrible news propelled itself into the moonlit night. Then the final sign-off, *Madeleine.*

"Madeleine," directed Émile, "go into hiding for some days. I will tell Monsieur Hoogstraten, Gilbert and Viennot we have warned London. London will stop sending arms and agents."

"You will continue without London's help? How?"

Émile reeled in the aerial and returned it to the suitcase. "We can continue cutting phones, derailing trains, bombing warehouses and stealing factory job sheets, whether the Allies invade or not. Viennot will get us information from German officers— he's in touch with the Free French."

Noor tossed her code and message books on the transmitter, threw her chemise on top, closed the lid and secured both clasps.

Émile's furious whispers continued. "Not a single German occupying France must be allowed to sleep easy in his bed while they billet themselves in French homes, steal our coal, grain and wine and 'resettle us' somewhere in the east."

Noor put a finger to her lips.

Émile was not finished. "The tanks and guns may be with them, but we have no recourse but to fight, for our families, for the future."

Carefully, he opened the mausoleum door, looked to left and right, and slipped out. Noor pulled the door closed and stood sweating, mentally counting to a thousand.

Émile is right—the French must shake off their chains. As long as the Occupation continues, resistance must continue.

For three days after Prosper and Archambault were arrested, Noor remained in Madame Aigrain's spare room, lying low, following Proust's self-absorbed characters through their jaded existence.

Her only respite from Proust was another quick evening foray to Drancy, back to the garage. Had Claude determined if Armand was still in the camp? Had he received her message? Was there any news?

"Non, mademoiselle, je suis desolé." But he promised he would tell her immediately he learned anything. "I have my contacts," he said in a conspiratorial whisper.

A dispirited Gabrielle served dinner at the Café Vidrequin and, when her German soldiers were gone, showed Noor a postcard on which was printed, *Je serai transféré dans un autre camp. N'envoyez plus de colis. Attendez ma nouvelle adresse.* "I will be transferred to another camp. Do not send any more parcels. Wait for my new address." Gabrielle's little nephew had signed the printed words.

Gabrielle had presented herself at the camp gates and asked for the children's laundry. "They said there is no laundry. They said, 'They have been deported.'"

She looked straight before her; it was Noor whose eyes brimmed.

"I can't say how I felt when I heard that," said Gabrielle. "I'll tell you another time."

Then she had requested an appointment with Herr Brunner, the new Kommandant; it was refused. No one would tell her which camp the children had been sent to. Her letters were returned by the camp post.

"The railway workers who come in here say those cars were bound for Metz," she told Noor. "But after that they don't have one single idea where the boxcars will be switched. Idiots! Don't tell me they don't know, *enh!* They have friends down the line, they could find out for me, if they wanted."

Gabrielle's anger at the Germans had deflected to people who were trying to help her.

And Monsieur Durand—poor Monsieur Durand. Madame Gagné said she had told him to leave. Her voice turned self-righteous, tinted with the certainty of a fortune teller gazing into a crystal ball. "If he'd told me where he was going, he'd be behind the camp walls by now."

Back to Madame Aigrain's little room in Auteuil, where she couldn't think of anything more she could do for Armand but pray. She had to rely on Claude now.

By the third day, the forced inactivity was making her muscles crawl; her body was accustomed to hours of exercise. So when Monique insisted she attend their wedding, Noor gladly accepted. She needed a ceremony that celebrated love even as she yearned for her own.

CHAPTER 21

Paris, France
Wednesday, June 30, 1943

"OH, YOU TWO! Look where you're going!" Renée's re-soled wooden heels teetered down the street behind Émile and Monique. "No more kissing!"

War-weary Parisians stopped to smile as Émile's curly head obscured Monique's eyes, radiant beneath white netting.

A photographer's lens might have lingered on his tenderness, her joyous smile, brown ringlets and floppy hat brim, the white silk gown edged with lace, bare shoulders and forearms, might have focused on the white kid gloves beaded with pearls that encased her small hands, and missed the swirls of Renée's hair, swept high into a pompadour decorated with flowers and fruits, more colourful than any turban Abbajaan ever wore for performance.

Noor, walking in their wake, Odile's chatter in full flow beside her, wore a pink-ribboned flowered muslin, the only formal summer dress she had brought from London. It didn't match her black handbag and gloves, but that couldn't be helped. The sun's heat was welcome upon her shoulders after the past few days in Madame Aigrain's apartment.

Lovers with enough confidence in their future to celebrate a wedding in the middle of war lifted everyone's spirits. German soldiers sweating under their steel helmets waved the laughing little group through a maze of checkpoints with only a cursory glance at their papers.

Only three years of Occupation and the Germans have become unremarkable, as if they have always been here.

"Babette!" Renée called.

Babette was skipping ahead, past a *salon de thé*, a *boulangerie*, a flower stall, heading for the wedge-shaped block of buildings rising over the rue Erlanger. She stopped before the rows of boxed red geraniums limiting the crowd on the sidewalk terrace of La Gargote, turned and called, "Maman! Maman! It's Madame Meignot."

"*Ne fais pas l'idiote!*" Renée sailed forward, artificial fruit tinkling and bobbling. "Madame Meignot wouldn't leave her *loge* for a minute."

"*Maman, vraiment!* I see her cane."

It was indeed the concierge from the adjoining apartment building, hair bound up in a sky-blue turban, coming towards them.

"If I were a director, I wouldn't give her even a bit part in my films," Odile whispered at Noor's shoulder. "Anyone can see she's trying to find someone but pretending she's not looking."

Émile continued deep in banter with a couple at one of the sidewalk tables, everyone raising their glasses in congratulation. Monique's laughter pollinated everyone else's.

Madame Meignot couldn't be a Nazi sympathizer, given Monique's comments about her during the air raid, but after General Vidal, Max, Prosper and Archambault . . . anything unusual was a danger warning. Madame didn't seem to be looking in her direction, but Noor's palms were suddenly damp. She moved into the shadows beneath the bistro's awning.

Madame Meignot went up to Renée and grasped her by the forearms. Steadying herself, she shouted, "Congratulations!"

Noor could see that wasn't all she said.

Renée turned to Émile and suggested they take a table inside. Her smile looked forced, and terror filled her eyes.

"A table—here?" Émile's arched eyebrow warned of expense. "*D'accord!* It's our wedding day."

Renée steered him through the arched doorway with *La Gargote* wrought in iron. Monique followed quickly.

Inside, white-aproned waiters smoothed and straightened, recommended and served their patrons—Germans and French, elbow to elbow. Odile and Noor helped Madame Meignot to a seat at an empty table. She was quite out of breath. Émile, now serious, ordered a *pichet* of white wine to go around.

"Several men—at least five—came to your house," said Madame Meignot to Renée, eyes large as the dinner plates. "I heard the Citroën and then smashing sounds, so I left my *loge* to investigate. I thought they were *zazous*. I was going to beat each boy with my broom and tell him his mother would be ashamed of a son who stole. But then one spoke German with a French accent. He called the pale one with little round glasses Monsieur Vogel instead of Herr Vogel, and I thought, 'Pah! A traitor.' The pale one gave the orders: 'Cartaud! Check the dining room' and 'Cartaud— the kitchen.' So I put the broom away, slipped out and came to look for you. I knew you'd be coming from the métro . . ." She took a shaky sip of wine.

"Were any in black?" asked Émile.

"Non, no black. All plain suits. Like yours—but no patches."

"Tante Monique and I sewed Oncle Émile's patches," Babette objected.

Renée speared Babette into silence with a single glance.

"And trench coats," added Madame Meignot.

Too hot for trench coats. Definitely Gestapo.

"You can't go back. There's a Citroën at the end of the street, patient as a mule."

"What shall we do? Where can we go?" Renée's trembling voice rose.

Émile hushed her.

"They'll have us in a minute, dressed as we are," said Monique. "I just wish we knew if they have found . . . what they have found."

"They will find nothing," said Renée.

Not upstairs. But they will downstairs, in the cellar. We must destroy evidence that could lead the Gestapo to others.

A coy look came over Madame Meignot's face. "I don't want to know what you've been up to, but I'll tell you a way you can enter your home. Just for a few minutes, then out, oui?"

"How?" asked Émile.

"There's a passage. All the way from the courtyard behind this restaurant to Madame Garry's cellar."

Noor remembered the door to the hidden passage, the one Émile had shown her during the air raid.

"That old passage? Wasn't it blocked up? I thought it was full of water," said Émile.

"Locked up, not blocked. I have keys. But—you will have to be quiet and very quick."

"Oh, madame! That is most kind."

Madame Meignot's turban bobbed back as she quaffed her wine. A waiter came, took her glass and offered Émile the bill.

"*Combien?*" Émile asked Madame Meignot, as if studying the bill.

"Four hundred and eighty francs for Jews, nothing for patriots," said Madame Meignot, as if Jews and patriots were mutually exclusive. "And you both just married. My father died when the Prussians came last time, and I lost my husband fighting the Boche at the Somme—I have no love for Germans."

Émile took a deep breath, then nodded. "No time to waste. I'll go with Madame—you all stay here."

"I won't let you go alone," said Monique. "Besides, I must change. Renée, too. Perhaps Babette can stay here with Odile and Anne-Marie."

"No one can stay here and wait," said Madame Meignot. "It will look strange. The Gestapo could be watching the café right now."

Émile nodded reluctantly. "What shall we do?"

"Ask to speak to the owner," said Madame Meignot. "Say you would like a private room."

Émile snapped his fingers and, when the waiter came, followed Madame Meignot's direction. The owner, tapered as a penguin in his black jacket, soon approached through the tables. He wore a questioning look till he spied Madame Meignot. Her turban leaned close to his ear for a second.

"This way."

Noor followed, moving through the other diners in the brasserie with the same braggadocio as when they arrived, Odile chattering again beside her with desperate bravado. Every detail of the day seemed to have sharpened. She quelled an urge to run, and kept pace with the dignified procession following the owner.

At the back of the restaurant he opened a door to an oval courtyard dotted with empty tables. At the far end of the courtyard a flight of stairs led down to a nondescript door.

"We will return within half an hour," Madame Meignot said. "But if anyone asks, you saw us leave."

The owner nodded and slid his key into the lock.

Down a stone spiral this time, with Noor and Odile holding up Monique's white silk train. Cool air breathed from the earth as they descended into a large, cobwebby cellar filled with crates of wine-glasses, barrels, casks, chests, trunks, hat boxes. Madame Meignot took a lantern from a niche, and a molten glow filled the room.

"The passage goes all the way to the Bois. Sometimes I take Jews through here," she said.

At 480 francs each. Four times the jizya, the 120-franc annual tax levied on Jews to pay their "fine."

In a corner of the cellar Madame Meignot paused before a gilt-framed painting two metres high, leaning with its face to the wall. She motioned to Émile to pull it back, revealing a low door set in an archway. Noor crowded with the others in the entrance.

A ghostly apparition glided before Noor in the afterglow of the lantern—Monique's white silk gown. Her fingertips grazed damp limestone in the chilly passage. Tiny rough stones pitted the path. Soft little fingers—Babette's—slipped into her hand. Shadows leaped and danced with every movement of the baubles in

Renée's hair. Madame Meignot's voice echoed back, telling Émile her husband had been an *égoutier*—a sewer worker.

"When he was alive, we grew mushrooms down here and so I learned the tunnels. Now I come here during air raids, and the restaurants pay well for my mushrooms. This stretch runs all the way from the métro to the Seine. They build new buildings above, but everyone leaves the tunnels alone." She pointed to the support pillars leading to a larger tunnel. "That one runs under the rue Molitor. They intended to build a station there, but it was never completed aboveground. My husband maintained its tunnels till he died, but we're still waiting for the day it will be built."

Snap! Noor started like a high-strung foal. Renée had stumbled on a fissure. Every black shadow in the labyrinth held a German about to spring from his Minotaur's lair.

"The Boche think they've sealed all entrances to the catacombs and the sewer tunnels inside the city," said Madame Meignot. "North of Paris they even use some of them to make rocket engines for Hitler, safe from English bombs. But they'll never find all of them."

"Let's hope so," whispered Monique, tucking her white veil into her hatband.

Noor was in a *fête macabre* complete with costumes, Moët et Chandon, and violins, such as debauched aristos held in centuries past. She looked back: only black. No cellar door.

Try to breathe regularly.

Past a few blocked side tunnels, Madame Meignot stopped as solemnly as if in church, to light and plant a candle at a brick-walled intersection. They turned to follow gas pipes, air tubes connecting mail drops for the Paris Pneumatique, and telephone wire sagging from the irregular ceiling till everyone but Babette had to crouch while walking.

Someone who lived centuries ago had carved friezes into the walls here. Ancient inscriptions they couldn't stop to read passed beneath Noor's fingertips. Wet gravel crunched underfoot.

For once even Odile was quiet.

Noor was losing track of direction. How far had they walked; surely they should be near or under number forty by now? Air pressed at her eardrums, she could almost hear ethereal music. This was how Abbajaan's buried soul-energy must feel.

Just then Noor trod on Monique's white satin heels. Madame Meignot had stopped suddenly. Émile held the lantern as she unlocked an arched wooden door. A groaning creak echoed down the passage to Noor, and the lantern showed a glimpse of Émile's workshop.

Madame Meignot whispered, "I'll go back through the passage and enter through the front door. If those Boche bastards are hiding inside, waiting for you, I will say I came for cleaning."

"Wait!" Émile whispered directions on how to find and enter the cellar from Renée's kitchen.

Noor crept into the cellar behind everyone else, and straightened. Émile moved past his workbench to the wall, lit a lantern and turned the crank to raise the camouflage canvas screen.

Noor's gaze swept the cellar with the boarded well at its centre. The workshop was intact. The rope-locked chest had fooled the Gestapo—or they were waiting upstairs for Émile to return and be caught with the incriminating evidence. If so, Madame Meignot had volunteered to test the trap set for Émile.

Minutes passed, interminable minutes of silence, waiting for Madame Meignot. Renée took to the bench, her head in her hands. Odile whispered to Babette, stroking and re-braiding her hair. Émile and Monique moved around the work tables, deciding which items to leave, which to take. Noor helped collect and classify.

Her dress felt as if it were sliding over her skin. She dashed her sleeve across her forehead.

A creaking and scraping above, and the rope-loop loosened then began to descend. Madame Meignot had returned. The trap door slid back and Madame's sky-blue turban nodded above. "*Vite! Vite!* The Boche aren't up here, but they could be watching the outside."

Noor was last out of the passage, behind the rest, as a low, doleful sound broke from Renée.

"What happened, what happened?" Odile wriggled forward.

Cast iron pots and pans were scattered everywhere in the kitchen. A shelf of crockery had been thrown to the floor. Blueflowered white fragments were everywhere.

Renée sank to a stool. "My grandmother's Gien! *Sales Boche!*"

Noor reached instinctively for her own grandmother's memento, her tiger claw—then remembered where it was now. Broken china didn't cause Renée's tears; it was the wanton destruction of her final link to her grandmother.

"And my cake! They took the cake."

"Which cake?" said Émile. "Is this the time to think about cake, Renée?"

"Renée made us a chocolate wedding cake," explained Monique.

What barter, wheedling, saving and sacrifice it must have taken Renée to find chocolate, eggs and flour for that cake, and yes, it was a terrible waste; but there was no time to cry for a missing cake, not now.

"*Vite! Vite!*" hissed Madame Meignot.

Émile sidestepped stealthily to the front window and parted the blackout curtains a crack. "Black Citroën. Yes, at the far end of the street."

Noor peered into the ravaged drawing and dining rooms. Houses in London had looked like this during the '40 and '41 Blitz when they took a direct hit. But bombs didn't pull open every drawer in the sideboard, slit the flowered chaise longue upholstery down the middle, pull the stuffing out of cushions or tear back the green felt of the card table. And where there were bombs, there were clouds of plaster dust. Here, the ceiling was intact.

Black Bakelite circles were strewn around the room like platters; each gramophone record had been taken from its jacket. Even the curtains over the side windows overlooking brick walls had been torn down, their hems slit. A hard object had split the telephone receiver and its cradle in two. A decapitated lamp had rolled off the table in search of its shade. Babette, lower lip trembling, held up her china-faced doll—face smashed, eyes rolled back in its head, ribbons of rose-patterned silk hanging from its waist.

A frisson of fear rippled through Noor, despite the summer heat, at the thought of what could have happened had the wedding party returned earlier.

Speculating about Gestapo motivations led rapidly nowhere, but Renée headed in that direction. Monique had wanted white silk for a wedding dress, which had caused Émile to meet parachutists at Rosny, which had attracted the Gestapo.

"*Non, non, non!*" Émile said.

"Then they must have been looking for Anne-Marie's transmitter," reasoned Renée. "When they didn't find it, they became enraged and destroyed everything."

Highly improbable as there was no receiver, English or German, that could detect the presence of a transmitter without it sending, and Noor's transmitter had never been activated at Renée's home. But it was no time to correct Renée, not when she was so upset.

"*Vite! Vite!*" Madame Meignot stomped her foot in the kitchen.

Émile snatched up a cardboard suitcase and dashed back down into the cellar. Monique and Renée began filling another: a photograph album, a jewellery case, a wallet, Renée's ledger book and ration coupons, a few clothes, tins of food.

"Hurry up! Change!" Monique threw Odile a powder-blue dress and tossed a pair of black slacks, a maroon blouse and a beret at Noor.

"I can't decide what to take!" Renée's cheeks were glistening. "We go too fast, too fast—I'll leave something important behind."

Noor fumbled with the side zipper of her slacks and her blouse buttons, but changed in record time.

"You look like a man," Odile said with a nervous giggle, turning her back towards Noor.

"And you look ten years older," Noor whispered, zipping her up.

A severe-looking Renée met Noor in the drawing room—all the pins, fruit and flowers out of her hair. Monique had changed into a black dress and flat ballerina shoes.

Noor followed down the spiral staircase as everyone joined Émile in the cellar. Émile's upper lip was rash red, his moustache gone; he did look different. He was closing the suitcase full of wires, welding torches, trigger devices, rubber stamps and forged papers. He cranked the mural down. Madame Meignot was already waiting. The passage door squealed shut behind them.

"Monique, Renée, Babette and I will leave immediately by train for Le Mans." The lantern illuminated Émile's worried face. "We'll be safe there for a few days."

"Do we need new identity papers?" asked Monique.

Émile hesitated, then said, "We have blank ones if necessary, but I don't want to rouse suspicion. We're on our honeymoon—*c'est vrai?*"

Monique managed a wan smile.

"Now leave singly, and meet at the Gare Montparnasse," said Émile.

"*Vite! Vite!*"

The lantern swung and bobbed away down the passage in Madame Meignot's hand, but Émile stayed the little group for more instructions. "Odile, you return to Grignon immediately and tell Monsieur Hoogstraten what happened here. Tell him to move every bomb, gun and bullet from Grignon—I don't know where, just somewhere else. And warn Professor Balachowsky."

"Didn't the Professor take his students touring for new insect species?" asked Monique.

"Yes," said Odile. "Waste of petrol—he could have brought his students here and they would have found a new Boche species of insect right here in Paris."

"Shhhh! Make contact with his wife, then. Warn her."

Odile was nodding like a marionette.

"Warn Gilbert," continued Émile.

Warn Gilbert? Of what he knew already? He must have led the Gestapo to search Renée's home. Intuition? No, logic. Should she warn Émile?

"Viennot must be told—maybe he can find out what made them search here."

But maybe it was Viennot who had led the Gestapo to Renée's home. Noor wasn't as comfortable with the idea of Viennot's Gestapo contacts as Émile seemed to be.

Wait.

"Monsieur Viennot has a telephone—I'll call him," said Odile.

"From a call box," Monique reminded.

"And leave him a message at Flavien's," said Émile.

"Anne-Marie," said Émile to Noor, "Gilbert has urgent messages to be sent to London tomorrow. I said I would be meeting you today and would ask you to transmit for him from Grignon tomorrow. So, meet him at the institute at 10:00 hours. But tell him this will be the last time—it's too risky now. If the Gestapo came here, they may know about Grignon. Remove Archambault's transmitter and your own. Take them with you after your transmission."

Noor followed as the little group, stumbling, suitcases bumping against passage walls, retraced their steps all the way to the *brasserie* cellar. Here, Madame Meignot embraced Renée and Monique quickly and patted Babette on the head. She waved to Émile and Noor in silence.

The pre-arranged sequence of knocks on the door to the courtyard brought the owner. He did not ask where they had been or if their mission was successful.

"Follow me. A man who finished his lunch has not moved from behind his newspaper. I can't believe anyone finds the newspaper interesting these days."

Émile, Renée with Babette, Monique, Odile and Noor headed for a side door in the courtyard. The owner motioned each person through, singly, carefully.

In her turn Noor peeked through the side door into a carriage lane. To her left, a parked vélo-taxi like the bicycle rickshaws in India. Brightly coloured, though. A horse hitched to a cart, feeding from its nosebag, swivelled his eyes at her. To her right, a few bicyclists and some children running away, chasing a bicycle wheel. She slipped into the sun-washed lane, feeling more agile in her newly acquired slacks and blouse.

A woman darted out behind the horse. Noor shrank back against the wall. The woman collected the horse's dung in a dustpan, like fuel-gathering women in India. Noor waited till the woman took her pan back inside.

Noor drew in a lungful of fresh air, looped the handle of her handbag over her arm and set off on a circuit that would eventually take her to Madame Aigrain's, back into hiding.

CHAPTER 22

Grignon, France
Tuesday, July 1, 1943

A TRENET SONG blared from a megaphone as Noor cycled past the toylike train station of Grignon and the swastika-draped *mairie* building and rode into the village square.

Two weeks before Bastille Day, the town was celebrating the feast of Saint Martin under a sunny sky embellished with a few puffs of teased wool. And under the eagle eyes of Marktpolizei circulating and watching the crowd. In one corner of the square, balls clicked in games of boules. In another, painted horses whirled children about a carousel. Puppet knights slew infidels on the Guignol stage; a little girl tugged at her mother's sleeve, begging to join the watching crowd. A young man snapped his suspenders, flexing his biceps for the oblique glance of a passing shopgirl. Stilt dancers whirled like dervishes. A rag man cried, "Chiffons! Chiffons!" extolling the merits of his well-used wares. Girls and women carried baskets, buying and selling unrationed apples, turnips and Jerusalem artichokes at trestle tables, talking, listening, walking, their elders resting in the shade of willow trees. Boys in short pants dodged their mothers.

On any other day Noor would have stopped before the glove puppets or bought an apple for Babette. But after her narrow escape with the Garrys the day before, it seemed a dread flood was rising to drown everyone. The tightness in her chest said England, the SOE, friends she'd trained with, agents she had come to know in the PROSPER network, relatives of whom she was always aware—everyone she knew seemed more remote than India.

Monique's borrowed slacks and blouse were more comfortable for cycling than any skirt.

If only there were some way to know that Monique herself, Émile, Renée and Babette had reached Le Mans safely.

And if she could have received one, just one, word of news from Drancy, just one word that Armand had received her tiger claw and message; but there was none. If it was selfish to think of Armand when Prosper's arrest had endangered more than fifteen hundred resistants across northern France . . . so be it. Each of the fifteen hundred resistants in Prosper's network had a raison d'être. Armand was hers.

Crossing the square would attract the attention of the Marktpolizei, so she detoured through a web of streets and alleys that predated Cartesian geometry; and each turn delayed her further. At last she was out of Grignon, pedalling down the bumpy country road towards the Institut National Agronomique, standing as she pedalled as if straining to remain above water.

A quarter past ten—Gilbert, wait for me!

Sparrow hawks chattered—*kyow-kyow*—from fir branches. Wagtails *tchik*ed, flicked their white tails and fluttered away as she rode by vineyards. Her blouse clung to her back, her hands slipped on the handlebars. She stopped, took her beret from her handbag and tucked her ponytail into it. A welcome breeze cooled her neck.

Rolling fields bordered the roadsides for a mile or so, giving way to the gloom and woody scent of oak from a game forest. The stone wall and porticos of the institute came in sight.

Behind her, a shiny black shape roared and reared up. Noor swerved sharply as a Citroën swooped within an inch of her left knee. But her hands refused to surrender the handlebars, and down she went in a great jangle of metal to bone-jarring gravel.

Elbow-searing, hand-grazing gravel. Glimpse of a *milice* kepi on the driver's head.

A pale face with round spectacles turned towards her. It flicked past as the Citroën swished away, leaving her bruised and winded with the bicycle coiled above her.

Noor scrambled to her feet, dusting off hands and slacks, searching for her beret, tucking her ponytail under again.

What satisfaction did they gain by frightening French people for sport?

But annoyance gave way to dismay as she saw the Citroën turn at the stone porticos and enter the institute.

Allah, don't let this happen!

No need to look for any covert signals. The Gestapo had come to Grignon.

If she hadn't been late, if she'd been minutes earlier, as Gilbert ordered, she would have been caught in the act of transmitting!

Noor pulled her bicycle erect, ready to mount. Émile had told Odile last night to warn the Hoogstratens, Professor Balachowsky and Viennot. And Gilbert—assuming there was any need to warn Gilbert. Following Émile's instructions, Marius and the students must have hidden or moved every bomb, gun and bullet by now.

Archambault had told her to stay away, to use a public phone to warn others, and hide.

Out of the question. She needed details of what had happened or was happening at the institute to determine the damage and transmit the information to London. She had seen only one Citroën, but there could be more Gestapo coming, or Gestapo men already at the institute. She had to risk that.

She tried to advance her bicycle, but the front wheel was bent, so bent it mimicked a melted Dali clock. No time to straighten it.

She shook dust and pebbles from her clothes.

Steal through the woods, come around behind the green-house and the administration buildings. She'd seen the

Hoogstratens' cat walking the wall of the dry moat; the institute's stone wall didn't continue all the way around. Insh'allah, she could find her way.

No time to lose.

Noor lifted the front of the bicycle, with the basket and her handbag, balanced the weight on the back wheel and rolled it into the woods. A few metres from the edge she glanced back, searching for landmarks to orient herself. Then she retrieved her black kid gloves and binoculars and, from the concealed compartment of the bag, the loaded pistol.

She slipped the binoculars into her pocket and drew her gloves over scratched palms. The bicycle would be safe on its side beneath the toothed leaves and spiky yellow flowers of a mignonette bush. Noor piled ferns and underbrush, hiding it from sight. Then, inserting the pistol in her waistband, she set off stealthily through the woods.

Twenty minutes later, as Noor crept between trees under leaf-filigreed light, a man's voice boomed through the woods.

"*Attention! Attention!* Every student and professor of the Institut National Agronomique," it said in imperative tones, "must report immediately to the courtyard before the Grand Château."

Noor drew closer. The megaphone repeated its directions louder.

At the edge of the woods, trees gave way to the grounds of the institute. Noor tensed into a squat behind large, hairy burdock leaves. Where the drive from the entrance of the institute flattened to join the courtyard, three private omnibuses stood side by side, doors open.

Professor Balachowsky's expedition.

With the torso of an oak tree at her back, Noor raised her binoculars. The courtyard before the Grand Château swarmed with swastika arm bands, Gestapo police—the dreaded SD—and the black jackets and kepis of Vichy's *milice*. She focused on a ring of rifles surrounding a bewildered, heat-wilted group of about two hundred young men and women dressed in the familiar blouse coats of the institute.

Parked at right angles to the buses, blocking the exit, were two German lorries on the drive. Two lorries holding about twelve SS men each: some could be searching classrooms or posted on exit roads leading to the fields. Noor adjusted her focus, swept the woods behind her, but saw no uniforms.

She let out her breath—even that seemed unnaturally loud—and sank down further behind the bush, inched into a cross-legged position as if seating herself before a veena.

Control your thoughts. Calm. Calm.

An open Mercedes with a swastika pennant on its front fender stood before the carved double doors of the Grand Château. Behind it was the Citroën that had knocked her off the road—and there was the *milice* kepi of its chauffeur. Below it, a sandy brown moustache and beard moved into the circle of her lenses.

A breeze ruffled the flower beds and lush green lawn between the Grand Château and the director's château on the hill. Odile's room in the director's château was out of Noor's line of vision. Insh'allah, the intrepid young courier was safely at her lycée at this moment.

The chef's tall white hat and the maid's frilly apron stood out in the crowd of students. Professor Balachowsky? Not in view. But there was a large hat and veil, then a chartreuse chiffon dress and pearls—that would be Madame Hoogstraten. Too far away to see her face.

But she could see Director Hoogstraten's face. He was standing very erect before the wrath of a man tightly buttoned into the full regalia of an SS Oberstürmbannführer. Looking force-fed as a *foie gras* goose, the Gestapo captain shouted into his megaphone in German, in language obviously deafening but incomprehensible to Monsieur Hoogstraten. And to most in his audience.

The pale-faced man with the round spectacles approached Monsieur Hoogstraten and the Oberstürmbannführer. Taking over the megaphone, he stood a little behind the Gestapo captain and added French shouts after each shout in German: "We have been too patient with you. It is enough."

Monsieur Hoogstraten looked mystified but unapologetic.

"You are the director of this institute. You will be held responsible."

An SS man stepped forward, holding a stack of books to his chest. The SS captain read aloud, *"Du contrat social."*

The leather-bound book flew from his hand like a white-winged bird and thudded onto the sandy courtyard.

"Discourse on the Origin and Foundations of Inequality in Mankind."

The volume skittered across the ground and stopped at Monsieur Hoogstraten's feet.

"Trotsky! Freud! Thomas Mann!"

Books—precious books, rare books—flew through the air.

"André Maurois. Henri Bordeaux."

More books flew, slapped and smacked to hard ground. Noor squeezed her eyes shut, seeing other books, books that, when she was sixteen, flew from her bedroom window on the third floor of Afzal Manzil the day Uncle Tajuddin decided all books by writers unknown to him were to be banned, destroyed or thrown out.

"Banned books! Jewish authors!" said the megaphone.

Books about other religions, even ones bought by Abbajaan, were the first to land in the garden below, over Mother's cries of outrage. Then Uncle enlisted Kabir to take down paintings from every wall of Afzal Manzil and stack them in dustbins. Soon these were joined by a tubby little Ganesh statue, memento of an elephant ride with her cousins in India. Noor felt Mother's arm around her shoulders again, saw Mother's clenched fists unclenching. Saw herself standing with her arm around Zaib.

Noor forced herself to look as the megaphone voice persisted. "In defiance of explicit instructions from the Ministry of Information, you have not removed these works from the institute library. This is why, Monsieur Hoogstraten, we no longer believe you know nothing about English arms and ammunition on your premises."

The pale-faced man rested the megaphone on his shoulder after translating, and Monsieur Hoogstraten's voice could be heard quite clearly. "We have been co-operative, Herr Kieffer," he was saying. "We have invited you to search every classroom and sleeping chamber for yourself. Four hours and your men found nothing. Perhaps you have been misinformed."

Herr Kieffer shot back via the interpreter, "The SS is never misinformed. We have always very good information."

Good information from Gilbert or had the SS tortured it out of poor Prosper and Archambault?

An SS man ran up to the SS captain, stopped, gave the Nazi salute, said something in German. Herr Kieffer turned back to Monsieur Hoogstraten and shouted louder. The interpreter relayed the message in turn, shouting in French.

"You said we should check the stables. There is nothing in the stables."

Be still.

Odile had warned her father in time.

Monsieur Hoogstraten took the megaphone and a deep breath, as if about to make a statement or exhortation to the students. Then he looked up at the interpreter as if suddenly struck by a bright idea. "Did you check the pigsties?"

The innocent-sounding question boomed over the crowd. The image of Gestapo men mucking in the institute pigsties, checking under offal and ordure for British weapons, was alluring. The students thought so too; snickers and laughs surfaced here and there in the encircled throng.

The pale-faced man snatched the megaphone back from Monsieur Hoogstraten. Even without her binoculars Noor could have seen Kieffer turning crimson. Sunlight glinted off the silver death's head on his black cap. Kieffer turned to his interpreter and told him what to say.

The interpreter took a deep breath and shouted into the megaphone. "The director and students of this institute harbour terrorists and their weapons. Weapons that have been supplied by foreign powers for use against innocent Germans stationed here to protect France from its enemies. We have given you every opportunity to surrender these weapons peacefully, but we now have no choice but to show you what happens when you continue to support violence, sabotage and illegal activities."

At Kieffer's order two husky SS men reached into the crowd of blouse coats and dragged a young man of medium build from its edge. A young woman—perhaps the pleasant-faced one who had given Noor directions the first time she came to Grignon—cried out, but her friends held her back.

Noor went cold in the humid warmth of the undergrowth.

People who can throw books to the ground are capable of anything.

The SS men forced the young man's hands behind his back and cuffed him.

Kieffer spoke, and his interpreter continued. A soft voice, calm, as if explaining the rules of Monopoly. "We hear that suicide holds traditional fascination for Catholics. Our scientists say this has become part of your psyche, a reaction against the modern world and full participation in the New World Order that the Reich is bringing to Europe. So, we will test your fascination by executing one student at a time. The choice is yours: if you wish the executions to stop, tell us, where is the cache of foreign weapons?"

A threat. A trick. Surely no one would execute innocent people at random.

These are students, civilians, citizens of a friendly power, a conquered power. A German ally—Vichy. Don't give in, monsieur, don't agree.

The interpreter held the megaphone out, inviting Monsieur Hoogstraten to call students forward by name or give them orders. But apparently Monsieur Hoogstraten had come to the same conclusion, for he shrugged and said clearly into the megaphone, "I cannot tell you what I do not know, Herr Kieffer."

Upon hearing this in German, Kieffer shrugged too, and barked an order.

The two SS men shook the poor student. He attempted protest till a gloved fist smashed into his mouth and a knee into his groin.

They dragged him around the side of the château, out of sight.

The young woman began screaming. Someone shouted, *"Salauds!"*

Kieffer's eyes were on Monsieur Hoogstraten. The director looked into the distance. Kieffer nodded to the interpreter.

The colourless man's eminently reasonable voice began again, its undertone setting the leaves surrounding Noor quivering. "We have asked you to set an example for your students. If you do not condemn terrorism, you support it. By not co-operating, you are sending this young man to his death just as if you pulled the trigger. For the last time, where are the arms?"

Monsieur Hoogstraten shook his head as if completely baffled.

Everyone expected the shot, yet no one expected it. When it rang out, Noor almost left her skin. A commotion of birds rose to wing. A horrified murmur rippled through the milling, sweating students. The young woman gave a howling cry and fell to her knees.

Noor's eyes blurred momentarily. But her trainers had said: "Every army holds mock executions to get information. We do it, they do it. The rounds are blanks. Don't be deceived."

They didn't shoot him. Allah, let him live and I'll read my Qur'an again from cover to cover.

Monsieur Hoogstraten looked unperturbed.

He isn't deceived.

The poor young woman, who knew nothing of mock executions or blank rounds, continued her low weeping.

Kieffer spoke, and the pale face and megaphone turned to the students. "Your director is willing for all of you to forfeit your lives and your futures to protect terrorists and saboteurs. Perhaps he does not know any students who are secret terrorists, but you know who these are among you. You must speak now before you meet their fate."

Monsieur Hoogstraten shook his head, and no one volunteered to betray his fellows. So a second student was hauled unceremoniously from his comrades.

Peasant stock, well built. Awed by the SS men.

He tried apology and pleas, and for a moment both Kieffer and the interpreter seemed to shift stance and consider him, as if both drew confidence from the man's self-abasement. But then Kieffer jerked his head. The student fought, kicked and shouted, but he was handcuffed and gagged. Noor's binocular-enlarged gaze followed as he too was dragged around the side of the Grand Château, out of sight.

It's a charade. Please, Allah, don't let them shoot anyone. Allah, let it be so and I promise to give a month's salary to immigrants at La Mosquée.

But a second shot fractured the stillness.

A hare scampered into the underbrush. A kite gave a high-pitched squeal and circled above.

The crowd of students was separating into stoics and lamenters. The SS men had the guns, but the few rebels in the crowd were becoming desperate. If every student was at risk, they had nothing to lose by trying to break away. But trying to escape would only justify the Gestapo in more deaths.

Please, Allah, no more!

Kieffer and his interpreter conferred. The wide circle of the megaphone eclipsed the interpreter's face again. "It is possible you have trouble believing your senses. Perhaps you are superstitious enough to believe the two men whose deaths you heard can be resurrected by a little journey to Lourdes. We did not wish to execute people before the ladies . . ." He bowed slightly in the direction of Madame Hoogstraten. "But perhaps you will only tell us where are the arms if you see a man die here, before your eyes."

Noor felt the words as if they ripped her in two.

Monsieur Hoogstraten must have felt the same. He was mopping his face with his handkerchief. He appeared to be pleading.

The interpreter pointed. Two *milice* gendarmes tore a third student from the crowd.

Noor scanned the student from head to toe in the bounded vision of her binoculars. This one was tall, his blouse coat tailor-made. Leather shoes, available only on the black market. A haughty carriage—no peasant here. He shook off the restraining hands of the *milice* gendarmes as if they soiled him, stepped forward himself.

Kieffer and his interpreter looked a little nonplussed. But the *milice* gendarmes were ready with cuffs, and soon the young man's hands were manacled behind him. Kieffer gave an order and a gendarme stepped forward with a blindfold.

Students in the crowd backed away. Someone fainted from the heat and tension.

Oh, Allah, send your farishtas! Send all your angels now!

Now the bourgeois young man was refusing the blindfold. The *milice* gendarmes shoved him to his knees on the sandy surface of the courtyard.

A Luger appeared in the SS captain's hand.

Monsieur Hoogstraten's hand reached out and grasped Kieffer's swastika-banded arm. The SS Captain shook him off. Monsieur Hoogstraten was now gesticulating, thrusting himself between Kieffer and the kneeling man. German and French were being shouted everywhere at once, and the anger of the French students was rendered powerless by the sight of the guns.

A gloved hand pointed the semi-automatic at the young man's temple.

Noor couldn't hear what Monsieur Hoogstraten was saying, but she could see his resistance crumbling, see it in the droop of his shoulders and the slight fall of his chin. Suddenly he raised his hands, then held them out.

A gendarme stepped forward and clinched the cuffs on him.

The megaphoned voice announced, "This student is pardoned. Your director has confessed to participation in sabotage and terrorist plots. He is a criminal. He is under arrest. He will show us the weapons. Until all the weapons are found, this institute is under Gestapo supervision. No one is allowed to leave the grounds."

Monsieur Hoogstraten was a respected, upstanding citizen, not a criminal. He was a fighter in the legitimate, necessary jihad against the Occupation.

The young man was standing up, rubbing his wrists now, as Monsieur Hoogstraten was marched to the Citroën. There was no sign of the two students dragged out of sight.

Before getting in the car, the director turned and met his wife's eyes.

More discussion and orders in German and French, and the Citroën's chauffeur left the car. He escorted the maid uphill at gunpoint to the director's château.

The SS men still ringed the students, administering a rifle butt where needed to assert control. What were they waiting for? Was the maid leading the SS man to the arms? No—if the arms weren't in the stables any more, Monsieur Hoogstraten had probably told Marius to hide them somewhere off the premises. And for maximum humiliation, the SS captain would make Monsieur Hoogstraten lead them to the cache himself.

Did Monsieur Hoogstraten tell them the whereabouts of Gilbert or Professor Balachowsky?

Non. Pas possible.

A black-and-red widow spider was slinging sticky threads on a branch above Noor. She shifted carefully, quietly; its bite could be poisonous. A hornet buzzed past. Mosquitoes hovered over the burdock. Minutes dragged by with no change in the tableau in the courtyard. Noor checked the woods behind her again. Movement, uniforms?

Clouds had swirled into arabesques, readying for rain.

The maid and the *milice* chauffeur came back into sight,

walking downhill from the director's château. The chauffeur's sandy brown hair and moustache centred in the circle of Noor's binoculars. He carried a leather suitcase in his left hand, held the maid's forearm in his right. He thrust her back into the crowd of surrounded students and took the suitcase to the Citroën.

With the suitcase stowed, the black car started, turned around and headed up the driveway.

Madame Hoogstraten's tearful supplications had broken through the cordon of SS men. She intercepted SS captain Kieffer and his interpreter as they walked towards the Mercedes. The gendarmes, the soldiers and everyone in the crowd was watching her too.

Noor could steal away now. She had the information she had come for, and would send it to London right away: Monsieur Hoogstraten had been arrested. He had agreed to reveal the location of the arms. Gilbert and Professor Balachowsky were still at large. Archambault's transmitter and her own were likely to be discovered soon if they hadn't been already; she would tell London both were likely in enemy hands. In any case, they were useless without the security check known only to Archambault and herself.

Madame Hoogstraten's pleading was now directed at anyone within hearing.

Noor slipped her binoculars back in her pocket, adjusted the pistol in the waistband of her slacks and crept from the bushes. Behind her, words of the megaphone became indistinguishable, then faded. Every rustle and crunch reverberated among the lofty trees. She drew close enough behind the institute's administration buildings to look through the windows: the Germans had emptied offices and classrooms of people. Crouching, she moved swiftly through the shadow-patterned woods on a course parallel to the institute driveway, heading back to the road.

She could cross the unpaved road past the courtyard wall surrounding the tool shed she and Archambault had used for transmissions. The squat shape of the greenhouse lay beyond it. Was Marius still free?

Two SS men stood on guard at the corner, backs to Noor, rifles slung over their shoulders, watching the drama in the courtyard at the bottom of the hill. She could steal across the road and the nettle ditch and continue into the woods—they would never notice.

But just in case . . .

She drew the pistol from her waistband and moved quietly, keeping her eyes on the SS men.

Halfway across now.

Suddenly, a black shape darted between the Gestapo men. The Hoogstratens' cat was streaking right towards Noor. An SS man was turning, and she was galvanized into a dash for the cover of the woods. A yell, then another, and both were running down the road towards her. Noor jumped a ditch just as sound-burst stole the peace of the woods.

They'll split up, to cut you off before you reach the institute wall.
Cover? Cover? Low land. Rock? Tree?

She dropped behind an uprooted tree and turned in one movement, thumb flicking the safety catch off, the heavy steel finger of the gun steady in both gloved hands.

Wait, wait till he's closer.

The death's head wouldn't stop coming.

Point—shoot.

Noor squeezed.

The recoil knocked her clasped hands upwards and to the left. The SS man suddenly went down in the ditch among the nettles, a look of disbelief on his face. His rifle flew from his hands, through the air, landing a short distance away.

A second shot, this time from the direction of the greenhouse. Not too far away.

Take his rifle. Now!

She jammed her pistol into her waistband and, without knowing she was going to, bounded in a single fluid movement to the rifle, scooped it up and away.

Then she was off and running again, the rifle grasped tight across her ribs, lungs pumping, heart slamming. Heels jarring against ground, wind whipping her hair against her cheeks, and a huge darkness opening its mouth behind her.

Run faster, run before darkness.

Crashing thud of jackboots to her right. Coming closer, closer.

Muscles flexed, blood rushed. Danger heightened awareness: she wouldn't reach the road alive. Was that the rat-a-tat-tat of her imagination or a gun firing?

Not in the back. Not to be shot in the back like prey run to ground. She must turn, turn and face her enemy, look him in the eye.

So she turned, dropped to the ground, to face the second death's head. On her stomach and barely breathing, the rifle stock wedging into her shoulder. The bolt drew back with a loud click, the bullet sprang from its magazine, slid into the chamber. It waited—she waited—till he came crashing through the woods. And when he was in range, the rifle came up by reflex. Steady. The bullet cracked and flew.

The death's head grabbed his chest, went down.

A man with no compassion forfeits his right to mine.

The shots would soon bring other SS. A massive hunt would begin. And if either of the two she had fired on remained to describe her . . .

Run! Run!

She threw the rifle into the undergrowth and was scrambling over rocks and roots, then running crouched between trees, taking cover behind bushes and too-slender trunks. Leaves and branches flicked and scratched her face, tore at her blouse.

Seconds later, Noor reached the edge of the woods. And the road. She took a deep, gulping breath.

Get your bearings.

The porticos of the institute jutted up to her right.

I am not a trembling kind of woman.

But she was trembling like a sheet of foolscap.

She knew very well what happened to anyone in France who shot a German. Even if you missed. The same that happened to Indians who shot Englishmen: arrest and execution. More immediate here, that's all. But contrary to Herr Kieffer's speculations on the suicidal desires of people he wanted pliant or dead, she would stay alive. For Armand.

She hadn't shot a man; she'd shot a Nazi who stood by and watched innocent students executed.

Had she killed one or both of the SS men? If she had killed one, could the wounded one describe her? If so, Kieffer would have soldiers stopping every train, bus, automobile or bicycle between here and Paris, searching for a woman in a white blouse and black slacks.

She hoped she had killed them both.

But then she'd have two deaths to atone for on the Day of Judgement, not just one.

Merde!

Keeping the road in sight but staying within cover of the woods, Noor retraced her steps to where she'd hidden the bicycle. She retrieved her handbag, hid the pistol in its secret compartment and covered the bicycle again. She would tell Odile where to find it.

Noor peeked around the side of a tree, looking up and down the country road. Empty. But now what? Run from the cover of the forest in her buckled two-inch heels, all the way back to Grignon? She hadn't seen any dogs with the Gestapo, but if they were searching, dogs would be let loose very soon.

Stucco clouds advanced in a solid line on Grignon. The starchy brilliance of the day wilted before their marshalled prowess.

Think!

Thinking didn't help.

But then, in the distance, came a blustering, popping engine sound—thankfully, not the purr of a Mercedes. As if ordered up by Allah, a fat, rusted *autobus* approached.

It could have Gestapo men on board, it might be stopped by the Gestapo along the way. She'd worry later; this was the best and fastest way away.

Noor stepped from the cover of the woods and waved. The bus drew closer, came up to her and trundled past. Noor shouted after it, ran behind it.

Now it stopped, waited till she caught up. Noor flung herself on and clung to the rear railing, searching the forest and each passing vineyard for pursuing men in black. She glanced down the centre aisle: too few passengers to hide between and too many to make a quick exit possible.

An unmarked stop beside a field. No Gestapo.

A woman moved past Noor. "*Excusez-moi, monsieur,*" she said.

Monsieur? Of course, monsieur! The Gestapo and the *milice* wouldn't be looking for a woman in black slacks with her ponytail netted in a black beret. They'd be looking for a man in a beret wearing a white shirt and black trousers.

The *autobus* coughed on—much too slowly for the pulse racing in Noor's temple—spewing wood-fuel fumes over passing vineyards. Dogs barked in the distance, but no roadblocks barred the bus. By the time it listed to a halt, depositing its passengers on the outskirts of Grignon village, Noor was controlled and purposeful, if a little queasy from *gazogène* fumes mixed with nervous tension.

She drifted casually from the bus stop to the fair. She mingled with the crowd, marvelling that they could not hear the bounce and judder of her heart.

Scan the area.

Nothing out of the ordinary.

Noor rummaged through the rag man's wares, counted out francs, sous and centimes, and in the water closet of a café wiped her muddy shoes, sent slacks and blouse down the towel chute, let her hair tumble down and changed into someone else's brown flowered dress.

The disguise released her from herself; she was calm again.

As she left the café, there was a shout—"Mademoiselle!"—and it almost set her running. But instead, she assumed a madonna face and turned. A lean, lined face—the rag man. Gypsy features—as brown as Abbajaan.

"A soldier asked if I have seen a man in a white shirt, black pants, black beret."

A hot floodlight seemed to centre on Noor.

"And have you?" she asked, voice low and quite steady.

"I said there are thousands dressed like that, but one such man came to me not five minutes ago and asked if I knew the time for the next train to Versailles. They seemed glad to know this."

The Gestapo would probably round up every man so dressed in Versailles.

"Merci!" Noor's eyes met his for a second of thanks, then she walked quickly away from him, realizing he had mistaken her for Jewish—why else would a woman buy a dress and change on the spot?

She would have to wait for a train. On a secluded bench beside a cluster of cypress trees, she devoured a lunch she'd never have found in Paris: a sliver of Camembert, a hunk of black bread and a wedge of *tarte tatin*. Swallowed without tasting, as if filling a dry well.

An hour later, she mingled with a crowd of revellers returning to Grignon station, and presented her papers to the German soldier at the checkpoint.

Fragile threads of rain turned to a shower. Noor kept her eyes on the soldier's helmet, trying to convey by stance and posture that she fully expected to be waved through and onto the train. The soldier stood dry in his sentry box, and kept her and five others waiting just because he could, till Noor's hair was plastered to her scalp and her brown dress clung. Till rivulets ran down her calves and her socks squelched in her shoes.

Her staged confidence must have been convincing; her papers were returned. She put them back in her bag and mounted the carriage ladder.

The train set off. Every compartment was full but one. She could sit opposite two stern-faced old women or stand where she was, in the corridor.

Another soldier swaggering down the corridor towards her. Another identity check.

Noor pulled out her headscarf. "Again you want my papers?" She made a show of wiping her hair and patting her face and neck with it. "They'll get wet . . ."

His gaze slithered over her. Noor darted a glance of mute appeal at the two old women. Both leaned forward, frowning and staring at the soldier as if he were no bigger than a toddler. Abashed, he moved past Noor.

She entered the compartment and took the seat opposite the victorious women. "Merci, mesdames." She smiled. They nodded back.

Noor closed her eyes and feigned sleep.

Agonized faces rose before her: two students dragged away to be shot—was that mock or real? were they alive or dead?—the student who refused to be blindfolded, Monsieur Hoogstraten's brave face, Madame Hoogstraten's tearful one, and faces of two Germans crowned with death's head caps. Were they alive or dead?

The train sped back to Paris.

Pforzheim, Germany
February 1944

My hip bone grates against plank; throbbing in each stiff limb. I can feel my intestines moving, scouring their emptiness. Sour spit in my mouth—juices demand something to digest. Soon they will turn on the lining of my stomach. How will it feel to consume myself?

Perhaps every crucial moment has come and gone and your mother is forgotten.

But this is still happening.

Night is unending in my dungeon chamber, darkness packed above me. Pungent sealed air, eroding me, single occupant of its vacancy.

Faces shuffle. Kieffer, Ernst Vogel, Pierre Cartaud. It was at Grignon that I first saw them. Vogel the interpreter and Cartaud the French milice chauffeur—men who would pursue me, each for his own reasons.

Nerves at knife-edge, I returned, waterlogged and shivering, to Madame Aigrain's. On the corner, a sleepy German soldier sat in his sentry box. A band of street urchins scampered by—children of the deported? orphans?—none of them taller than me. I matched their gait and passed the sentry box in their wake. Then I melted into the shadows, my eyes lowered to the strips of black tartan rain running in the gutters.

One thought above all others: I must have killed a man today, perhaps two.

High above the street, a double window slid down—shuk!—like a guillotine.

At Madame Aigrain's, the concierge stood waiting, the telephone receiver cradled in her hands. It was a taut-voiced Odile telephoning from a call box.

"Anne-Marie? You wanted to meet Papa tomorrow? But he has gone away—we don't know how long he will be gone. Several people at the institute have been taken ill—it's highly contagious. Monsieur de Grémont was asked to go into quarantine, but Papa said he didn't need to—yes, the same de Grémont whose father loves Pétain so much."

Her voice dropped to a bare whisper on the line. "Papa went in his stead."

After a time she said, "I think Professor Balachowsky has gone to the hospital too. When I called his apartment, a strange voice answered. Madame Balachowsky telephoned and said he had no chance to smoke his pipe, but has taken it with him. Quite a few have already succumbed to the sickness—at least twenty or twenty-five friends. Maman? She is well, as well as can be."

All the information I required was conveyed in her innocent-sounding chatter.

She ended with "Uncle Gilbert is quite well—he says 'keep in touch.'"

So I should check for a message at the letter drop behind the milk bottles at Flavien's pawnshop. I could leave Odile a message there, too.

"He is making arrangements, but you must wait till Saturday to find out the surprise. Uncle Viennot is well and sends his regards— you must telephone him, he misses you. Oh, I must tell you, I received a postcard from Phono—when I have my honeymoon, I will go to the Loire! What beauty is there!"

I wondered what "arrangements" Gilbert could be making— until that night, when, like a ghoulish noctambulist, I crept through the streets to the cemetery. At my appointed time, kneeling within the sepulchre of the Famille Ginot, I transmitted details of the Grignon roundup to London.

I waited, crouched among the dead, till Major Boddington responded. He would send a Lysander for me on Saturday.

I radioed back, "I cannot leave. I am the only radio operator left in northern France."

My muscles ached, my head felt larger than La Mosquée's dome. I was aflame, in a fever of anger at the Germans who had my leaders in their grasp, yet chilled with fear. I diagnosed my own symptoms: I was becoming sick, sick at a time when I so desperately needed all my faculties about me. Thought fragments collided; I fought for equilibrium.

At last Major Boddington replied. I received, and quickly left the cemetery, taking the message back to safety at Madame Aigrain's. There I decoded the first lines:

"Madeleine must leave. This is an order: Le Mans. Saturday 16:30 hrs.–."

How could I leave, not knowing if Armand had received my message? I needed to be at Drancy, close to my love. But how could I stay if ordered back to England; it would be an act of insubordination, even desertion. I could volunteer for another assignment, though. As long as the war lasted, London would need radio operators. I could return.

Would I help anyone by staying?

Tethering loyalties asserted pulls in every direction.

I could no longer transmit from Grignon, and there was nowhere to string an aerial from Madame Aigrain's apartment. How often could I use the Cimetière de Montmartre for transmissions? I had moved one transmitter to Madame Gagné's boarding house in Drancy, but now I was afraid to go out at all for fear of arrest—I had killed a German, maybe two.

And I was in terror of myself, having learned the violence of which I was capable. Once more I had shattered the looking glass and seen the beast within.

But I might endanger others if I stayed.

I decoded the last line:

"Meet Gilbert at the Landowsky monument at La Place des Jacobins."

Meet Gilbert? I was almost certain he had betrayed Prosper and led the Gestapo to Grignon. London just wasn't aware of it yet.

But surely I was wrong to believe a Frenchman would betray his countrymen to the Germans. It was just coincidence that Gilbert had told me to come to Grignon at ten A.M.

Yet, why was he not present when the Gestapo searched every chamber of the institute?

What if Gilbert had me arrested at Le Mans? It would confirm my suspicions, but that would be small comfort. But London could not risk a Lysander and pilot for one agent—other agents must be returning with me. Gilbert couldn't betray us all and remain above suspicion.

I had to obey Major Boddington and travel to Le Mans on Saturday.

Duty would separate me from Armand, separate us once again. But, I told myself, I was trained now. Madeleine, perhaps even Anne-Marie Régnier, would return to France.

And I could do one last service to the shattered PROSPER *network. I could meet Émile in Le Mans to warn him about Gilbert.*

Someone in a distant cell is singing "The Partisan's Song"—notes of mournful longing. The other prisoners join in until the guard silences all of them with shouts and threats. It is not only my orthodox uncle who cannot tolerate music, but those who proscribe every moment of another's life. I return to my imaginary pen and ink.

I felt no moral pain that those SS men might be dead, though they were beings of Allah like me. Why was I not in anguish from self-recrimination? Was it because they were German? Was it because they were Christian unbelievers? But no. Over and over I returned to the thought that flowed through me in that instant when I waited with the rifle and shot the second time:

A man with no compassion forfeits his right to mine.

Are my beliefs that simple? It explains how I find it in me to play the heartless princess before Vogel. Yet he is capable of love and kindness for his tribe. He carries his wife's picture in his wallet. His children were both born in France, and could be French; he loves them still. So, blood supersedes borders when he wishes. I do not try to understand how men can come to be like him; but, as with Uncle, to be shunned by Herr Vogel would mean dire consequences.

Once when Vogel came to see me, he showed me photographs from his wallet. Alongside pictures of his smiling wife and children he carried photos of Nazi doctors' experiments on Jews, gypsies, homosexuals, Communists, POWs, criminals—dissidents of all kinds, he said.

A prisoner buried vertically up to his chin in a hole, an SS man pointing his rifle at him. A naked woman suspended upside down with metal clamps about her ankles, her eyes gouged and bleeding. A man who leaned against his cage, legs folded, knees under his chin. With no trace of outrage Vogel said the man had received electric current to his testicles.

I had to believe it happened: the camera certified the existence of what it recorded.

Vogel thought I would be repelled by the sight of suffering. I was not repelled, but appalled: someone revelled in another person's suffering. Someone must have held a Leica and coolly taken a photograph instead of rushing to the assistance of the tortured. Someone with a Roman blood lust.

Blood pounded through my heart till it threatened to explode, imagining my Armand or your grandmother Lydia in such a hell. Vogel said such "experiments" have a purpose: to care for German soldiers who contract diseases on the Russian front. But I do not believe him. It is he who needs the suffering of others, he who needs persistent images of utter powerlessness to feel potent.

Vogel lingered over each pitiful photo with lascivious perversion to demonstrate what my fate could be if I were not subservient. He reminded, "You are designated Nacht und Nebel—a Night and Fog prisoner who has disappeared. I need not account for you to anyone." But for him, he wanted me to understand, I could disappear without trace into the laboratories of these Doctors of No Conscience, sacrificed "to preserve the Aryan race."

Like Uncle Tajuddin, my captor poses as my saviour, my protector . . .

"I must verify your identity as an Aryan, Princess," said Vogel. "The Reich has recognized all Indian POWs as honorary Aryans."

If this is what it means to be Aryan, I thought, I want no taint of it. But I dared not say this to Vogel.

"You are a spy. I could have had you executed. Instead, I treat you as a POW."

"But of course I am grateful, Herr Vogel," I said, avoiding the issue of whether I am Aryan. I aim for graciousness, and never to give in.

Instead, I tried to interest Vogel in my mother's blood, because it is more powerful at present. Euro-American blood. He called it Caucasian, though Mother's stories of her lineage could not be more distant from the Caucasus. I warned Vogel the Americans are coming, that he must keep me alive to barter when the Reich falls. Mon Allah, let him never know what I learned in 1940 when I contacted the American embassy in London: Mother, having married an "alien ineligible for citizenship," is no longer American.

But this is a technicality; Mother remains American in the lies I tell Vogel.

Images from the past fade; the present must be borne again. In the finite space of my cell I vacillate between despair and liberation. Is this madness, this edgy feeling that the abyss of non-being yawns beyond the next thought? The connective tissue between intent and action is wearing away. Imprisoned here, without even the solace of knowing the writer of my lettre de cachet, speculations multiply . . .

Did Gilbert betray me? Could Prosper have done so? Or was my betrayal planned by Major Boddington and his comrades? Someone else?

Trolley wheels on stone. My stomach churns in hope of food. A chink of light shines at eye level and someone shouts. A bowl of cabbage soup comes towards me at the end of a woman's arm. I fall upon it like an Indian denied rice since '41. I try to imagine the SS woman's eyes, her nose, what she believes she does and why.

What choices did she make that caused our paths to cross? Without German, I cannot ask her, and she wouldn't respond if I did.

I begin a zikr, silent of necessity. The recollection of Allah from the heart, from the bottom of my heart. "Huwallah-ul-lazi la ilaha illa huw-ar-Rahman-ur-Rahim-ul-Malik-ul-Quddus-ul-Salam-ul-Mu'min-ul-Muhaimin-ul . . ." When I come to the eighth name, al-Muhaiminu, the Preserver, I can go no further. "Al-Muhaiminu, al-Muhaiminu, je me souviens de toi, je me souviens de toi."

Ma petite, what if I am too late in begging Allah to be delivered from the troubles I've created? What if even Allah can't rescue me?

CHAPTER 23

Le Mans, France
Saturday, July 3, 1943

WAITING FOR ÉMILE in the gilded chinoiserie of the foyer at the
Hôtel du Dauphin in Le Mans, Noor daubed her streaming nose
with a hanky. Miss Atkins should have warned how much waiting
and worrying espionage entailed. Her note at Flavien's requested
this meeting—but had Émile received it? No confirmation before
she left Paris.

A cough hacked from the base of her lungs. She was light-
headed, her muscles ached.

In the two days since the executions and arrests at Grignon,
she had thought it only a summer cold, but these symptoms felt
closer to influenza. Just influenza—not pneumonia, TB, cancer
or typhoid. Influenza, the disease Abbajaan had suffered alone in
India, that malady that progressed to pleurisy. He wasn't the only
Indian to succumb to the dread disease; twelve million Indians
died of it in the epidemic years after the Great War. Had anyone
from the Red Cross nursing school said Indians were more prone
to it than others?

Whatever the Red Cross said, Abbajaan's disease was the psychic cost of his assimilation, pleurisy rising from the slow suffo-
cation of his spirit in France, and the loss of his music. Her own
sickness was similar—the dis-ease of her soul over the probable

deaths of two SS men. This was no time to worry about it, but she couldn't stop. How long should she fast in expiation of her shootings at Grignon, how long for her continuing unrepentance? She had done as she was trained, but no one had mentioned one could feel guilty even for not feeling guilty.

Would Armand ever accept her again, knowing she had killed? He had forgiven her once, years ago. Could he whose love always called to her best and highest self forgive her again?

Allah, I don't care if Armand cannot forgive me, so long as he survives this time of terror, lives long and free.

A tranquil breeze passed through the sunny lobby. Here she was, sitting alone waiting for a man in a *hotel;* Uncle Tajuddin would never approve. She took her new sunglasses from her handbag. Expensive, but an excellent disguise, offering an element of purdah; she could see without others knowing the direction of her gaze.

She'd be flying to England tonight. She'd find an army doctor immediately. There were miracle medicines available there that weren't available in France—that new one, penicillin—she'd be cured.

Wait, wait—she hated waiting.

Gilbert was the one she should fear, the one everyone in the Resistance should fear. Where was Émile? Would he come or was it too dangerous to meet? Had he been arrested?

Eyes everywhere, even in the furniture.

A man signed the register at the desk and looked in Noor's direction. Her tongue went numb till he picked up his suitcase and disappeared behind the brass scissor-grate of the lift.

She slid her sunglasses to the tip of her nose.

She hadn't been dressed as now, in black slacks, a white cotton blouse and green cardigan, when she entered the front courtyard of the Hôtel du Dauphin off the avenue Thiers two hours earlier. This morning, when soldiers checked her papers at the station and she passed her valise and oilskin coat to the helpful bellman, she was "Madame," looking like a schoolteacher on vacation, complete with straw hat and sensible paisley skirt. A schoolteacher who glanced into every mirror and shop window as she passed.

The lunch menu in the hotel read *Soupe aux légumes*. Soup. Day in and day out in London, Paris and now here. Enough of soup.

She left her coat and valise in the care of the bellman, and avoided a checkpoint by wandering back streets behind the Notre Dame de la Couture church. Through the place de la République she went, down to the river.

In a quayside café open to the breeze off the Sarthe, she ordered an omelette, even buttered bread, saving the cheese sandwich packed by Madame Aigrain for dinner. No reason to save her counterfeit francs; she was leaving.

A carved doll with a dress of yellowed lace for Babette. Four inches high, it couldn't compare to the beautiful china doll the Gestapo had smashed, but it was pretty. A shocking amount, but no matter—she paid in false coin.

Gifts caused embarrassment, Mother said, placed a burden on recipients to reciprocate. But Noor enjoyed giving.

Monique had mentioned wanting the pattern for Noor's reversible forest-green skirt, so the skirt was left for Madame Aigrain's daughter to copy. Noor would use it again, insh'allah, on her next assignment in France. But a promise of the skirt pattern as present for Monique wouldn't suffice. Noor couldn't meet her empty-handed. Or Renée, or Émile.

A peach for each.

Tart green apples and a couple of Anjou pears for Mother, Dadijaan, Zaib in London—and Kabir, though she didn't know where he was stationed at the moment. A glimpse of fresh fruit would raise their spirits.

Returning to the hotel, Noor retrieved her valise from the bellman and, in the ladies' lounge, quickly exchanged her straw hat and paisley skirt for the black slacks, cardigan and sunglasses, tying her hair in two ponytails. She returned to the bellman's desk with her coat and the handbag containing the gifts over her arm, as if going for a long walk.

He addressed her as "Mademoiselle" this time, as he took her valise for storage.

Amusing.

Please, Émile, please walk through that door.

An Abwehr officer passed through the lobby.

Émile must have been arrested. She was sure of it.

She was poised at the very edge of her chair, handle of her handbag in hand, when Émile came into sight at the door. He sauntered as if looking for but not finding someone else, and as he passed, whispered an all-clear. His moustache hadn't grown back to its slender line in the three days since his flight from Paris. His hair seemed to have receded further; he looked older.

She took a deep breath, held it as long as she could and exhaled. Then a second breath. With the third exhale she calmly adjusted her sunglasses, picked up her handbag and coat, and followed him from the hotel.

Down the avenue Thiers to the checkpoint. Noor allowed a man with a wheelbarrow full of bricks and a woman shouldering a dachshund to queue between them. Émile passed through and continued walking down the avenue.

The little dog licked at the woman's earrings, and the soldier reached out to stroke its ears. The woman jerked the dog away.

"He bites B—" The word bitten off unspoken was "Boche."

The young German's face hardened beneath his helmet. "Next!"

The now grim soldier examined Noor's *ausweiss*, verifying its expiration date. Sweat varnished his hairless upper lip. Her own had beaded from the heat, yet she shivered and shivered. He would notice. In a moment he would notice.

"*Danke!*" He returned her papers and motioned her through.

Émile wasn't leading her to his home? Of course he wasn't—too dangerous. Moss-green elbow patches flashed like semaphores down cobbled streets, into a park neatly structured as a Mughal garden.

Her head was swimming. Noor sniffed.

Émile dropped back. "*Salut*, Anne-Marie! I didn't recognize you at first. I like your hairstyle, but you are quite pale."

Renée, Monique and Babette sat on a blanket spread under a canopy of cherry trees, a picnic hamper open before them. At the sight of Noor, Renée set her book aside, and Monique her sewing. Babette jumped up and ran to Noor.

Noor kissed the air wide of the little girl's cheeks; if she had influenza, she didn't want Babette to catch it. Babette grasped Noor's hand, laughing, eyes sparkling as she discovered the doll.

Monique moved the hamper, making room for Noor and Émile. Exclaiming over the peaches, she lifted out sandwiches, even wine.

Renée commanded and Babette skipped away, taking her new doll to a grotto in the far corner of the park. She began bathing it in the stream spouting from a gargoyle mouth.

"What happened?" said Émile. "Why are you here?"

Noor whispered details, recounting events since the Garrys fled Paris: the sudden arrival of the Gestapo at Grignon, the executions, the bravery of Monsieur Hoogstraten.

"This is terrible," said Renée in a fear-constricted whisper. "Even worse than before—we can never return home."

No mention of the arrests of Monsieur Hoogstraten and Professor Balachowsky. But it was possible Renée didn't know them.

Émile was close to both men, of course. His eyes dulled with pain-filled shadows.

"*Quel bordel!*" he said.

It certainly was a mess.

Should she mention the exchange of shots? She was trying to snare butterfly thoughts—so little time—it was best Émile know.

Renée looked shocked. "You shot two Germans?"

Noor should have taken Émile aside to tell him. Too late.

"I did as I was trained," she replied. "But I am most grieved since. The men may be wounded, not dead."

"I would have done the same," said Émile. "You are a true patriot."

"*Sales Boche!*" said Monique. "I hope they are dead—I wish you'd killed more."

Renée looked from one to the other. "What children you are! The Englishwoman has confessed to murder, and you applaud? You want to be her accomplices! I want to return to my home, not join her in a Gestapo cell!"

Noor was wretched enough without Renée calling her a murderer. If she could change what had happened at Grignon, she would. But she couldn't. And she wasn't answerable to Renée or the Germans for her deeds.

"No one is going to prison," said Émile. "In Paris, Fresnes is full to capacity with resistants. As are all the prisons in France, Renée—they won't have any place to imprison us!"

It was a valiant effort to make light of things, but Renée brushed it off. "*Mais vraiment,* Émile, we too are implicated. We can never return home now."

Monique tossed her chestnut curls. "Anne-Marie didn't begin this, Renée. We've all been implicated for three years. None of us are innocent. We don't tell you everything, but Émile and I are not machines that, when the Gestapo or Vichy throw a lever, change purpose and motion. Émile, you remember I said to you, I said: 'If we don't refuse, what will our children learn but Nazi brutality?'"

She took up her sewing and pulled her needle through a pleat—she was smocking a baby's gown.

"Anne-Marie did what had to be done," said Émile. "*C'est tout!*"

His voice challenged his sister. He held Renée's gaze till she looked away. Monique continued sewing. It was up to Noor to break the silence.

She blew her nose. "Any news from Guy?" she asked Renée.

"Still in the Stalag." Renée seemed a bit mollified by the question. "I don't understand it. Other soldiers have been exchanged for workers and Jews, and have returned—why not Guy? The exchange program is working, but not fast enough. Many are hiding from the STO in the hills, not far from this very park."

"Patriots," said Émile.

"Outlaws," said Renée. "Playing soldier games in the Maquis, to avoid work. Young people don't know the meaning of work."

How many years had Renée worked? When Noor was thirty-nine, she wouldn't feel old enough to say "young people" as if they were a new species of insect.

"Those young men are trying to stay alive, Renée," said Monique. "Trying to fight with few weapons and fewer provisions."

"We'd be completely disarmed if we followed every law the Germans pass," said Émile.

"Have you written to the Kommandant of the Stalag?" asked Noor, remembering that Gabrielle was able to meet with the Kommandant at Drancy.

"*Naturellement!* He wrote back—a very courteous, correct letter. He said it takes three French volunteer workers to release a French prisoner of war, but the ministry here says it takes six. Others say it only takes one Jew. I haven't written to Guy or sent him a single parcel since we arrived in Le Mans. How am I to tell him we can't go home because the Gestapo is waiting outside our door? And if I write to him now, I'll lead the Gestapo here, to Émile's home."

Yet another dilemma of war. What could Noor say beyond commiseration? Renée deserved better. Many women like her in France, and indeed everywhere in the world, deserved better. Renée needed something to cheer and distract her, but Noor couldn't think of anything.

She draped her oilskin over her arm and a round flat shape came to hand—the gold compact Miss Atkins said Colonel Buckmaster gave all his women agents. Extra, as Noor had her own tortoiseshell compact in her handbag. Made in France, Miss Atkins had said. A bright little thing, a conciliatory gift to express Noor's gratitude to Renée—Renée who had given grudging but essential hospitality to an agent torn between two secret missions, Renée whose heart was as full of longing for her Guy as Noor's was for Armand.

Noor held the bright disc out to Renée. "Please accept this. A parting gift. From me."

Surprise registered in Renée's eyes, then reluctant pleasure. She opened the compact, looked solemnly at her reflection for a moment, then snapped it shut.

"You are leaving, then," she stated and questioned in the same breath. Noor's gift was interpreted as partial reimbursement; Renée uttered no word of thanks.

"Yes."

She could tell Renée found the news reassuring.

"Back to Paris?" asked Monique.

"No." Noor took a deep breath. "I am leaving for London tonight."

"Tonight? So quickly?" Monique sounded genuinely sorry.

It was too quick. After all her training and preparation, Noor had, in her short time in France, sent fewer than twenty messages for her cell. Important, some critical, but still . . .

"Gilbert made the arrangements?" Émile was asking.

"Yes."

"I thought you distrust Gilbert," said Renée.

"I do, but I have my orders."

"The danger of betrayal is far more for Frenchmen," said Émile. "Will they be sending another operator to take your place?"

"I don't know."

"I wish we didn't need a radio operator from London, Anne-Marie, but we do. A radio can be a better weapon than any gun, *tu sais?* It calls down destruction. I know Morse, but the Germans would detect me before I finished the first sentence."

"My transmitters remain in France, but no one can use them without security codes and encryption keys," said Noor. "One is left at Madame Aigrain's. The one at Grignon was probably discovered. When London sends my replacement, you will need this to locate the third." She showed him a piece of paper—the address of Madame Gagné's boarding house.

He nodded once he'd memorized it, then said, "Once you leave, the Allies will bomb France without fully understanding their targets. If French civilians are killed and not German military, you know what will happen: the support of the people will wither. And the Allies desperately need French support on the ground when they invade." A pause, then disconsolately, "*If* they invade."

"What do you suggest? I should not leave? My superior officer said it was an order."

Émile bit into dark rye. "No, of course you cannot disobey." He held the sandwich at arm's length. "What's in this, Renée?"

"Cauliflower."

He made a face and waved it before Noor.

"I've eaten lunch," she said. "But, Émile, don't you think the English understand this? They will send in a new operator soon. No need to explain this to my superiors."

"Yes, yes, I know. They will send a new operator when it is a hundred percent safe," said Émile with uncharacteristic bitterness. "They keep out of harm's way, the English, the Americans, they think dropping explosives from the air will defeat Hitler and Vichy. Oh, I know they're waiting for Stalin and Hitler to exhaust one another. But explain! A second front is needed. Now! Explain to the Colonel and to Churchill—eventually they will have to invade and fight him here. On the ground, not from the air!"

Noor laughed shortly, but Émile was quite serious.

"Émile, I can explain to the Colonel, but don't think I can request an audience with the Prime Minister."

"You cannot?"

"No. You overestimate my powers, my rank. I'm a radio operator, *c'est tout!*"

Émile shook his head vigorously. "*Mais non!* Prosper met him."

"Met whom?"

Émile whispered, "Monsieur Churchill."

"No!"

"*Si, si!* Archambault told me."

Mr. Churchill was reputed to be fascinated by his SOE agents. Some agents she knew had met with him before their missions, but . . .

"Ah, well, Prosper is Prosper. He outranks me many times." But then her curiosity prompted, "What do you think Monsieur Churchill discussed with Prosper?"

"The invasion."

"*Mais oui*—but that's a very big subject."

"I think not. I think Prosper was told something specific. You've heard what Monsieur Churchill said on the radio? Four days ago he said the invasion will come 'before the leaves fall.' But I think Prosper knows something more specific than 'before the leaves fall.' And the Germans want it."

Perhaps Émile's hope for an invasion, the hope of everyone in France, had drawn him into the realm of astrology.

"Oh, be sensible, Émile—" said Renée.

A man in a suit approached. Noor raised a forefinger.

Renée began to tell about something cute that Babette had said. Émile and Monique nodded and smiled as if they were listening.

Had they been speaking too loud? How long had the man been there? What had he heard?

The man passed by without looking in their direction.

Renée resumed in an even softer undertone. "Prosper knows your name, where you live, details of your 'work.' Isn't that enough?"

"*Our* work," Monique reminded her. "But they won't get it from Prosper. He's very proud, very strong."

"He has not been tested," said Émile. "All of us are not as strong as Max."

Would Noor find the courage to resist if captured? How could she know—how did anyone know? She wouldn't be arrested; she'd never find out. She fought the image of Prosper under torture, drove it from her mind.

"Anne-Marie," Émile said, getting to his feet, "time is short. Would you like to walk in the gardens?"

Noor began to rise, but Renée said, "Brothers and sisters have no secrets. Say what you need to say."

Émile and Noor sat down again. She'd already told Renée what shouldn't have been said. Best to fulfill her reason for meeting Émile in Le Mans. So Noor told them her suspicions of Gilbert.

When she was finished, Renée looked affronted instead of grateful. "Gilbert is French. Frenchmen are not traitors."

One would think she knew every Frenchman personally.

"But Renée," said Émile, "I have the same suspicions."

"*C'est impossible!*" said Renée in a voice of certainty. "A Frenchman betraying Frenchmen? Foreigners betray Frenchmen, Frenchmen do not betray Frenchmen."

Noor was the only foreigner present, accusing a Frenchman. Renée didn't wonder if Gilbert was a traitor or not, or what information might have led Noor to such a conclusion. What she disputed was Noor's right to comment on the proclivities of a single Frenchman.

"Renée," said Monique, "Maréchal Pétain and every minister in his Vichy government are Frenchmen, so how can you say Frenchmen do not betray Frenchmen? I have witnessed it myself: every day at the Hôtel de Ville in Paris, Frenchmen denounce other Frenchmen. *Écoute!* the Boche pay ten thousand francs for each arrest."

"Those are denunciations of Communists, Communist Jews and Israelites by Frenchmen," said Renée, "not denunciations of *French*men by Frenchmen."

Respect for her sister-in-law seemed to restrain Monique from pointing out that Renée had completely sidestepped Monique's mention of Vichy.

"Most Jews living in France are French," said Noor. "It's a religion. And they are not all Communists."

"I'm sure you would know, Anne-Marie," said Renée.

Should Noor address the implied accusation? If she did, the conversation would turn to her beliefs and religion, something she had not the time to explain. Better to let it slide.

Back to Gilbert. "So Gilbert is safe in the ever smaller pigeon-hole labelled 'Frenchmen' and you cannot see his potential for treachery." Her passion sounded muffled by the handkerchief held over her nose. "How many more arrests will it take before you believe it?"

"Someone," said Émile reasonably, "alerted the Gestapo that there was a house on the rue Erlanger that should be searched."

"I feel it was Gilbert."

"You feel? You have no proof," said Renée. "I agree someone did, but not a Frenchman."

"It was a warm, beautiful day," said Monique. "It was our wedding, and I'm so glad you were with us, Anne-Marie." She bent over her smocking. Obliquely, she had delivered the reminder that Noor could not have betrayed them without walking into the Gestapo's trap herself.

"You told me Gilbert said to meet him at Grignon at 10:00 hours," Noor said to Émile. "But had I been on time, I would have been arrested. And Gilbert must have been there, but he was not arrested."

"Coincidence," said Renée.

"Perhaps," Noor conceded. "We have not considered: what if Monsieur Viennot informed the Gestapo?"

"Oh, no," Renée responded for Émile. "His grandfather and ours were brothers. He's our cousin."

"Even if he were not," said Émile, "Viennot has been buying information from the Gestapo for a long time. He cannot want Prosper arrested — there are hundreds, maybe thousands of people in that network, all his best customers. And I never described to him the extent of our work at Grignon."

"Gilbert gets a big salary from London," said Monique, "so why should he want Prosper arrested?"

"He could be well paid by Berlin as well," Noor pointed out.

Émile's lips twisted in wry acknowledgment of this possibility, but Renée and Monique seemed surprised by the idea. Noor sneezed as if she'd sniffed pepper.

I'll be here till next Id without convincing them.

She rose. The garden undulated around her.

"Believe what you will," she said. "Pray there will be no more arrests, but we cannot be too careful. I had to warn you. What are your plans?"

"Émile telephoned Madame Meignot's *loge*," said Renée, "and Madame told him a Gestapo car parks every morning at the end of the street and another takes its place at night. But we cannot stay in Le Mans forever, Babette must return to school in Paris in September."

"She could go to school in Le Mans," said Monique. "And under the circumstances, perhaps it would be wise—"

Renée looked down her nose at Monique and gave a firm, "Non!"

"We'll find another apartment in Paris before September, then," said Émile. "We have to stay hidden for some weeks. They'll tire of watching the house. I don't mean we can return and live there, but . . ." The sentence trailed away.

Noor's glance prompted Monique. "I have two weeks' leave for our honeymoon. After that I will write to my superiors at the Hôtel de Ville saying my *grand-père* has died and I must go to Marseilles for his funeral. So if the Gestapo comes to search for me, they would send them to Marseilles. *Voilà!* That will keep me away from work this month. Next month, August, is a month of vacation. And then the Allies will come. If they don't . . ." She stopped. "I must return to the Hôtel de Ville. Especially if we rent an apartment here and another in Paris."

So vast a gulf between those who can leave and those who must stay.

"I will return to France as soon as I can," said Noor.

Monique took Noor's hand. "I can see you now. At the front of the invasion, the Maid, Anne-Marie Jeanne d'Arc!"

Everyone laughed, even Renée. Babette was called to say goodbye. Renée's admonitions to the little girl faded as Émile escorted Noor back to the Hôtel du Dauphin.

A new soldier was stationed at the checkpoint. The heart-thudding humiliation of identification must be endured again. Three streets away, Noor caught up with Émile's stride.

"Each year, I think I am now used to Occupation," he muttered. "Then they search and manhandle us, and it infuriates me again. Monique and I were walking in the gardens yesterday and a soldier came and asked what was I doing there. What am I doing in my own country? Where else should I be? We're second-class in our own land—they call us chimpanzees."

The British used such tactics in India, and Indians were called "brown monkeys" in London. The French had like terms for Algerians, Moroccans and Tunisians—personal indignities trivial compared with arrests and torture, distractions from the colonizers' plunder.

"Can you imagine, we French are reduced to living on cauliflower sandwiches," said Émile. "Renée complains she has no kitchen garden here but insists on cooking, and Monique is kind enough to let her—but one of these days I'm going on a hunger strike! But then I think, what can she do when the Germans give ration tickets for just 1,200 calories a day?"

Earlier in the century, Algerians under the French had made do on 1,500 calories a day, two-thirds of what Europeans lived on. And Dadijaan said Indians in Calcutta were trying to stay alive under the British Raj on a mere 850. The Germans had learned the colonizer's tactics well.

"Since you're leaving, you could give me your ration tickets?"

Noor fished in her handbag and came up with the booklet of ration coupons. Keeping three for her dinner that night, she handed the rest to Émile.

"*Merci bien!*"

Émile slowed to let other pedestrians pass, and detoured around a tarpaulin-covered car.

"Renée—she is carrying too many burdens," he said in an apologetic tone. "She refuses to understand the times, the France we now live in. She sees only the distance between what she expected and what she has become."

Noor was silent. Émile continued, "You know, some of Guy's clothes were stored at my home, to be used whenever Renée and Guy visited in the summer. She is helping Monique refit them for our boys in the Maquis, the same she called outlaws."

Parting with some of Guy's clothes has to be Monique's idea, not Renée's. How uncharitable of me to think so.

Émile gave an indulgent laugh. "Oh, Renée, Renée! She is a pure patriot, above all. She taught me to shout '*Vive la France!*' when I was a boy."

But Noor had heard Renée exhibit her patriotism. Genuine and pure, but that didn't make it any more attractive. France for the French, as defined by Renée. None of them—Armand's family, Noor's family—none of them could assimilate into Renée's ever-shrinking circle. It was possible that Monique and Émile were so accustomed to her anti-Jewish and anti-foreign remarks that they simply didn't notice them any more; they assumed she was like them at heart, forgiving her for the sake of preserving their family. Perhaps it was Noor who was acutely sensitive to words undergirded by hate, feeling their cruelty as Armand might, responding with greater anger than he could at this moment.

A little further, Émile said, "Madeleine, do you still have the pistol?"

Noor hesitated. The incriminating pistol was with her, concealed in her handbag. She could guess why Émile needed it.

"You have Sten guns and Bren guns, grenades and bombs, buried all over the Loire," she whispered.

"A pistol is easier to hide. *Tu sais*, I believe you about Gilbert. Maybe you do not know, but it is not only Prosper and those in our cell who were arrested. All through northern France, hundreds of men and women have been marched into Gestapo headquarters with one suitcase. Here is a list. I typed it for you to transmit, so no one would recognize my writing if it fell into enemy hands. All code names, of course—but since you're going to London, take it with you. Agents arrested in the last three days. Eighteen people." He pressed a leaf of foolscap into her hand. "And only this morning I learned of one other. Wait, give me the paper—I'll add his name." He took a pencil stub from his pocket and wrote at the bottom.

Nineteen! No wonder Émile looked so haggard.

They had entered the Square Lafayette. Émile guided her towards the Monument aux Mortes.

"I come here for inspiration. My mother used to bring me here every Sunday. She'd sit on this bench and talk to that stone monument, and I was too small to understand she was really talking to his soul—to me, that stone *was* my father. She'd tell it all that Renée and I'd been doing, things I'd already confessed to in church and some that I still wonder how she found out. She'd ask his advice as if he were alive, till the very end of her life."

Mother and son, both earnestly engaged in what Uncle would call "Hindu idolatry."

"Renée said your father died in the tunnels at Vauquois," said Noor.

"Blame that too on the Germans. He's still buried somewhere in that mountain—we never received his body."

Under other circumstances, or if Émile had shown reciprocal curiosity, she might have mentioned her similar grief for Abbajaan.

She took a seat on the bench beside him. A couple of disconsolate pigeons flew away.

"Renée used a pigeon in *poule au pot*—I had to hold my nose to eat it! I'm told they taste better with a bottle of Moulis or Margaux. But *hélas!* even those wines are loaded on trucks and trains bound for Germany. It's not only the wine—I hear there's bromide in our coffee . . . and I'm a newlywed man."

He made a comical face. She smiled.

"*Alors*, we were discussing Gilbert. I believe you even if my sister will not, that's all. And if he leads the Germans to us— should I lead them to an arms cache while I go to find a pistol? The solution is—*Merde!* I don't have to tell you."

That solution was why she hadn't voiced her suspicions before. That solution was the one she had used at Grignon. It saved her life, but today it felt like no solution. The reminder of her violence, held constantly against her body, was affecting her health. She wanted never to see that pistol again.

But she didn't want Émile to kill anyone.

"Leave a packet for me with the bellman at the hotel." Émile had sensed her hesitation.

Noor had the pistol with her, but this gave her more time to decide. She agreed.

"I've been thinking," said Émile. "Gilbert knew the location of the safe house. Two reasons. First and foremost, I remember when we were at Chez Tutulle, Prosper told Gilbert you would not stay at his apartment but at Madame Garry's home. Second: I have information that other agents strongly believe they were followed immediately after landing."

So the Gestapo could have followed Noor the many hours she had wandered through Paris. Maybe Renée was right: the Gestapo had noted that Noor travelled in the last carriage of the métro, and followed her and discovered the safe house. It wasn't egocentric to believe she was important enough to be followed; it was her part in the larger game that was important.

"And if Gilbert knew about Madame Aigrain's home, the Gestapo would have searched it by now."

His words transposed the images of destruction at Renée's home to old Madame Aigrain's apartment.

Noor said, "My father said one can bring about events one fears, just by fearing them."

"Maybe. But at present, fear keeps me alert, anger keeps me from despair. I never go into a room with only one way out. They don't even need to arrest me—I would live in fear even if I wasn't doing this work. If I lose my job for any reason, Renée, Monique and Babette will have no one to support them. Three years ago I thought all the time about getting away to England. But then I thought, 'Who will look after them?' so I couldn't leave. But now I wake up angry, go to sleep angry. I, who was going to be a great inventor—huh! You know, I have a better design for an automatic washing machine, another for an electric shaver. And what am I thinking of every day? How to destroy a plant or derail a train. It's no way to live!"

In an undertone he said, "Don't tell Renée, but if you are a murderer, so am I. Germans, mainly. French, sometimes. *Merde*, it's war! You know how easy it is to destroy? Far easier than to create and invent. I have destroyed trains and sabotaged factories, but . . ." He stopped and glanced away. "Never have I killed someone I know, someone I trusted. But when I think of poor Madame Hoogstraten, Madame Balachowsky, Odile . . . what they must be feeling at this moment! I think of Prosper and Archambault suffering, tortured as Max was. And not only them. German reprisals against relatives—women and children! All held collectively responsible! Oui, oui, oui—I would kill Gilbert to save others from that."

Noor opened her handbag and put her sunglasses on to veil her eyes from Émile. Had she added to all the wrongs she had hoped to oppose by coming to France? She'd have to wait till Judgement Day to find out. Meanwhile, she would live with her actions, and Émile must live with his own.

She was about to close her handbag when she remembered the leather pouch and five diamonds. The pouch was concealed with the pistol. Quickly, she explained to Émile and suggested he take the gems—use them to help the families of those who were arrested.

"Sell or barter them," she said.

"Yes, but where? The jeweller in Le Mans is a Nazi sympathizer, and in Paris diamonds are assumed to come from the Resistance. Any offer to sell would be immediately reported to the Gestapo. And if I were caught with them . . . would I be free a single day? *Jamais de la vie!* And I could not let Monique or Renée hide them, after what has happened. No, no, it's far too dangerous." He plucked anxiously at the stubble of his moustache with thumb and forefinger.

Émile was right. There was a better way.

Noor drew the last of her counterfeit money from the hand-bag and offered it to him, retaining only a few francs for dinner that evening. "I won't need this now. *Bonne chance!*"

Émile's face relaxed for a moment. With a grateful nod he slipped the bills into his pocket.

"It is easier to fight when you're alone, Anne-Marie. I would be a bolder man if Renée, Monique and Babette were in England."

"You are very brave," Noor assured him.

A sharp laugh. "To be brave, one must learn to ignore reality."

"Renée might be safer in England, but I doubt she would be happier."

"Better unhappy than dead or at the mercy of the Gestapo," said Émile. "*Tiens*, ask Colonel Buckmaster if he can send a Lysander to take them to England? Tell him Marc will be our air movements officer, the same Prosper used last time he landed."

Odile had said Prosper chose not to land at a field picked by Gilbert when he arrived two weeks ago.

"I will go to the Colonel immediately," said Noor, rising. Her legs felt like water, the touch of her garments chafed her skin. "Now, we'll need two phrases." She paused. She couldn't think of a nonsense phrase in the condition she was in.

Émile waited expectantly.

She would rely on Rumi, translate lines familiar to her, unfamiliar to others. "Listen to the BBC, and if you hear *The angel's wings are tied to the donkey's tail*, it will mean London has agreed to send a plane for Renée, Monique and Babette. And when you hear, *Open the prison door with keys that spell joy*, the Lysander will arrive the next day . . . But without a radio operator, how will Marc tell London where the plane should land?"

"He will have to send a courier to a Free French network with a radio operator of its own. There is one cell still operating. Of course, they don't use that *salaud* Gilbert."

The pigeons fluttered back to the bench.

"Meanwhile, be strong," said Noor, as much to herself.

A woman of about sixty, dressed in black and clutching a bunch of flowers, approached the monument. She looked harmless—but an informer *would* look harmless.

The woman laid the flowers gently before the inscription—*La Sarthe a ses enfants. Morts pour la France 1914–1918*—and stood with her head bowed.

Émile stood and took Noor's hand. "I must leave you here. *Mes hommages.* Thank you for all you have done." Then he whispered, "I will ask the bellman for a package. Remember about the aeroplane. And tell London: one more arrest or incident and I swear Gilbert will be no more."

With that, he turned and walked away, elbow patches swinging, fists punching backwards, punching air.

Noor lifted her heavy head to the breeze percolating through the sunny cobbled streets of Le Mans. Her forehead was burning. A clock tower chimed 16:00 hours.

Almost time to meet Gilbert.

The flying buttresses of Le Mans cathedral soared on the hill above Noor. She had knelt to make a *zikr* there, lit a candle before the Virgin and admired the stained glass in the rose window, but dread still lay leaden in her stomach.

Across La Place des Jacobins, a bird man struggled from the peak of a dun-coloured obelisk. Noor sat in the shade of a chestnut tree, keeping the monument in sight. So far, no Gestapo in sight, no uniforms, no one hiding behind a newspaper.

A pregnant woman rested her *panier* on a bench, an old man pushed an earth-filled wheelbarrow across the square. Laughing children ran about. Pigeons nodded, fluttered and preened.

Almost 16:30 hours. Would Gilbert come, or would the Gestapo?

A man with a magazine under one arm approached, a swagger in his step. Around the monument he went, as if studying the workmanship, then took a seat at its base. His hand passed over his brow, flicking back a lock of glossed hair. Gilbert.

Wait, wait. Watch. Do his eyes dart anywhere?

Gilbert shook open his magazine and began flipping pages.

After a few minutes Noor stood up and walked past the monument. In a moment Gilbert was at her elbow.

"Monsieur, monsieur! Oh, it's a mademoiselle. You forgot something," he said.

"Thank you," said Noor, taking the magazine from his hand.

He fell into step with her. "The slacks—very American. And the two ponytails. *Mais, très chic!* Almost I didn't recognize you."

"Thank you."

"Have you ever seen such a monument! Can you see Messieurs Wright in Ohio, flying twenty-four miles at thirty-eight miles an hour? How amazed they would be to see me in a modern flying machine! They were like you: only in France were they truly appreciated."

"I am appreciated, monsieur."

"But not enough, mademoiselle. Englishmen only prize women's ankles. We French, on the other hand, we appreciate women completely. But you know that . . . *alors!*"

He led her to a bench in a corner.

"What news of Prosper?" she whispered. "Archambault? Monsieur Hoogstraten and Professor Balachowsky?"

Eyes looking directly into hers—camouflaged eyes. "It is very sad."

"Sad?"

"They were careless."

"Careless?"

"Oh yes, careless."

"And you are careful?"

In response, a look like that of a hurt puppy. Gilbert flicked back his hair. "*Mais oui.* Did I not escort you safely to Paris when you first arrived?"

Émile's remark that many agents were sure they were followed from the landing field flashed to mind.

"Yes, you did. But where were you while the roundup was taking place?" She kept her tone merely curious.

"I was waiting for you. In the garden shed behind the greenhouse. You were late."

She ignored his accusing tone. "How is it you remain free?"

"I'm lucky! I've always been lucky. My profession was aerobatic shows before all this sneaking and secrecy, you know. You are very lucky too, it seems."

Was she being warned? Gilbert's tone was innocent enough.

"Yes, it was fortunate I was late," she said.

Silence stretched a beat too long.

"I will take the messages you wanted sent with me tonight."

"I have them," said Gilbert. "You are happy to leave all this danger, *non?*"

Happy to leave with her Armand at Drancy, or exiled in some worse place? Happy to leave without even a chance to see him, or to find out if her message reached him? But before Gilbert she must not be Noor. Anne-Marie wouldn't feel so empty an ache in her belly.

Remember how many women have had no news of husbands and fiancés for months, even years now—not only me.

She blew her nose. "My valise is at the Hôtel du Dauphin." A trace of emotion still clouded her voice.

Suddenly, Gilbert was all business.

"There is a reading room in the hotel. Behind the lobby, beside the courtyard. Continue walking. Meet me there at 20:00 hours."

CHAPTER 24

Le Mans, France
Saturday, July 3, 1943

IN THE BOOK-LINED READING ROOM at the Hôtel du Dauphin, Gilbert's brown head bowed over ivory pieces dotting a chessboard. Shadows drifted across his face.

Where could she sit and observe his game? On a sofa between a faded man reading a French translation of the third volume of *War and Peace* and a well-preserved lady moving her lips silently, deep in the private debates of a novel.

At the far end of the room, the pendulum of a mahogany grandfather clock swung like an elephant's trunk, chimed a study in eight repeated notes and returned to loud ticking.

Gilbert reached across the board, moved a walnut piece. A painted white knight jumped a few squares and captured it. He leaned across again, moved a walnut rook. The white knight captured it, and the rook vanished into Gilbert's fist for a moment then reappeared on the sidelines with its mates.

Noor drew closer to the board.

Chess and mysticism—just beyond human mental ability, but not so far that she ever lost hope of mastery.

Everything was conspiring to remind her of Armand on her last night in France, the very night she was to leave for England. Armand waiting for her at Café Zola in the fifth arrondissement.

"I have the men, did you bring the board?" Armand following and re-creating the champion Alekhine's tournaments, discussing alternate moves and defences against the Dragon opening. Why hadn't they discussed the possibility of the situation each was faced with today? But life couldn't be reduced to sixty-four squares and thirty-two pieces. How could they possibly have foreseen Drancy?

The painted white knight had advanced within a few moves of the walnut queen.

"It isn't a game when you play against yourself," Noor sniffed into her handkerchief.

"But when you play against yourself, you always win, mademoiselle. You can relax the rules, even invent rules."

Noor took a seat opposite, put away her handkerchief, rubbed her hands, blew on them, rubbed them together again.

Sick or well, I can play this game.

He placed the pieces in rank and file, white before himself, walnut before Noor. A notebook appeared from his vest pocket to write down each move. A white pawn slid forward. Noor replied with an Indian opening, moving the walnut horse immediately into the fray. Gilbert arrayed a good classical defence.

The grandfather clock ticked, chimed, ticked on. The faded man marked his place in *War and Peace* and tiptoed off. Noor looked up from a move to notice the lady had vanished as well.

Gilbert was playing to win with the strategy of capturing the most pieces, carefully noting every move as he went. Noor searched for the best move in light of changing circumstances, playing fluently, with analysis and intuition, using supporting pieces behind one little brown pawn advancing, advancing to an end square, to transform itself to a queen.

The end-game was soon in sight—win, lose or draw.

Calculating moves, Noor's transformed pawn would soon check Gilbert's king. And *voilà!* checkmate as well.

Abruptly, Gilbert stood up. "I'm hungry. We'll finish the game after dinner."

And I predict we never will.

The hotel dinner menu repeated *Soupe aux légumes.* Good thing she had saved the cheese sandwich. Gilbert went to have a word with the maître d'hôtel.

Noor examined the moves he had recorded. What was Bc6x? The notation was not correct, but she'd seen it before somewhere.

Alekhine vs. Rethy, Munich.

A poorly translated German news report of that championship game had confused readers of the *Herald Tribune* by recording moves resulting in capture with *x* at the end.

Bc6x.

German style. This Frenchman records his moves German style? He must play chess with Germans. Regularly.

Was this evidence? No. But circumstantially, yes. Still, there could be other explanations. France was occupied; French chess clubs couldn't refuse German members. Perhaps the Germans had introduced their notation rules for chess clubs?

"Do you belong to a chess club?" she asked when Gilbert returned with the maître d'hôtel.

"No, but I play as often as I can with friends." He put his notebook back in his pocket.

German friends?

But she didn't ask that. If Gilbert had no compunction about betraying old comrades, what was there to stop him from making a quick ten thousand francs by luring her down to the nearest checkpoint or to Gestapo headquarters in Le Mans? If she could not reach Armand on this assignment, Noor wanted only to return to Mother, Dadijaan, Kabir and Zaib in England.

The maître d'hôtel looked down his nose. "This way, monsieur, this way, madame."

"Mademoiselle," said Noor. And added sweetly, "And my uncle."

Oh, the pleasure in seeing a look of discomfiture dart across Gilbert's face. And the pleasure of ignoring it as she followed the maître d'hôtel.

But instead of leading her to the hotel dining room, the maître d' moved across the reading room and pushed down on a lever beside the grandfather clock. An adjacent bookcase creaked, then swung open into a stone passageway. With a wink and a finger to his lips, he led them through a short dark passage. A door slid back and she was in a second dining room, this one furnished in *belle époque* style, in colours of mauve, Pernod green and mustard, dim mirrors reflecting urns filled with fresh flowers.

The Lysander pilot had been right: Gilbert certainly must know every black market restaurant in the Loire.

By the time they were seated at a candlelit table, Gilbert had recovered his bonhomie. In an instructive undertone he pointed out the local wine bottler, *négociant* for many wine growers in this area, and the wineführer with whom he was dining. And another private niche where a sawmill owner clinked glasses with a German buyer.

The colours of flags can be less important than the colour of money.

Could the other guests detect Noor's desire to be miles away, out of danger from Gilbert? If they thought him a German sympathizer, they might think Noor was an informer at best, a prostitute at worst. But his presence was, she must admit, better than dining alone.

Think of Mother—she would have summoned the requisite flair. But then, Mother hadn't grown up with Uncle's rhetoric about loose women, a term that definitely included unmarried women who waited for men who were not their relatives in hotels and then dined with them in secret dining rooms.

Not respectable. Armand would laugh at the word. Musicians—indeed all artists, he said—had to unlearn being respectable.

The plat du jour offered oysters, a paté Mother would have called meat loaf, a delicious partridge *en casserole*, a dish of potatoes boiled with peas, four kinds of cheese and a Grand Marnier crème brûlée.

Noor dined, comfortable with silence.

But silence was unendurable for Gilbert. "This room—in fact, the entire hotel—it reminds me so much of Château d'Iffendic. I grew up there, you know . . ."

Stranger and stranger.

"The decor, it was like this?"

"Oui, oui, just like this. The walls were a soft blue, not green, and the chandeliers were pewter with toile shades."

"And where is the Château d'Iffendic?"

"Very close by."

Odile's voice trickled through Noor's mind: "He's not well educated—his father is a postal clerk and his mother a house-keeper."

"You grew up there?"

"Yes. We had a cordon bleu chef who always said 'timing is critical' for cuisine. I should send him here—he could teach the chef a little haute cuisine."

"You live there?"

"Oh, our château was requisitioned by the Boche, like so many other châteaux."

He didn't seem at all upset by the requisitioning. He hadn't exactly said he or his family *owned* a château, but his silk-smooth voice certainly implied it. He hadn't mentioned his parents or their occupations, but why should he provide her with such details? His hands on the tablecloth before her—too large and wide to pass for bourgeois hands. Was this tale evidence of betrayal or bad faith? No more than Mother's stories. Mother always dismissed questions of genealogy or made up some new tale of her lineage. Europeans and Indians, she said, gave their bloodlines far too much importance; one should be judged by deeds. The château could be a detail in Gilbert's cover story, as Bordeaux was for Anne-Marie Régnier.

She had not quite convinced herself when Gilbert snapped his fingers. "*L'addition, s'il vous plaît.* And my niece and I would like a room for tonight."

"Yes, monsieur."

Noor travelled from surprise to anger in two seconds.

Dissemble, act, pretend.

She shook her ponytails. *"Oh, non, Oncle Gilbert!"* Assuming a little girl voice, "You must get to Chartres before curfew—I promised Tata you'd return home this evening. We shouldn't make her worry."

The maître d's "Yes, mademoiselle" remained between them like the Cheshire cat's grin as he vanished. Gilbert's glowering look said he had not spent the tremendous favour of his presence with her for an hour playing chess and bought her a very complete meal to be denied the next few moves.

Noor widened her eyes to juvenile innocence.

Gilbert's look of insult gave way to a knowing smirk. *"Merde!* I've heard of women like you, but I've never met one. No desire, no passion—you have lived in England a few years. That is why you are *célibataire.* You have only a pen pal at the War Office, but no husband."

Heat rose to Noor's cheeks and an unsought longing stabbed her heart.

Yes, I have desire and desires, and no, that is not why I have no husband.

Fidelity might be out of vogue in Gilbert's milieu, but it wasn't too difficult for Noor; Gilbert was no Armand. The thought of being subjected to his touch . . .

Other guests were rising to leave before curfew. Gilbert began to draw in his notebook—a map.

"Take the bicycle in the shed behind the hotel—*ici."* He drew compass points and marked the direction of the landing field from the hotel with arrows. "The landing is at 02:00 hours. Take the turnoff here." He marked an X. "It's marked with a netted pole. Meet me here—it's a woodcutter's cottage. He was a skilled mechanic at Le Bourget, but he didn't want to repair Boche aeroplanes, *et alors* . . ."

Noor took the map, oriented herself, made a mental picture and returned it.

"I must meet two other agents at midnight," Gilbert said curtly. "I had hoped to spend the time more pleasantly, but . . ."

"We could finish our chess game," Noor suggested. She went into a coughing fit but let her eyes blaze at him over the handkerchief masking her face.

Gilbert flicked his forelock, obviously annoyed. He accompanied her from the dining room, through the passage and lobby, then departed, without a backward glance, into the warm night.

Noor borrowed scissors, needle and thread from the bellman and, seated on a chaise longue in the ladies' lounge, cut up the brown flowered dress she'd bought at Grignon. She wrote to Émile, a single line informing him that she had noted Gilbert used German chess notation and had no affiliation with a chess club.

Written down, it was such a small thing. Too small to mention? She nibbled the end of her pencil.

It wasn't small if she thought of Professor Balachowsky describing Max's torture, and the fear that had invaded Renée's home, causing an entire family to flee, or Monsieur Hoogstraten's anguished face during the shootings at Grignon. Her heart and pocket were burdened with the code names of nineteen men and women arrested by the Gestapo as terrorists for protesting the Occupation, nineteen names on the leaf of foolscap she was carrying to London.

No detail was too small if it would save a single resistant from the Gestapo.

Write without expressing an opinion. Let Émile form his own conclusions.

Should she tell Émile about Gilbert's Château d'Iffendic story? But Gilbert hadn't claimed to own a château. Whether someone was high-born or low should make no difference, since everyone was a fragment of Allah. Suppose Gilbert was the son of a postal clerk and a housekeeper, as Odile said; he might be a parvenu and a war arriviste trying to polish his past, but it didn't prove he was a traitor.

He had invited her to bed. Also irrelevant. When she was about sixteen, she remembered arguing it was men's lust that should be controlled and men kept in seclusion, not women. Uncle Tajuddin had been so terribly hurt, so very insulted by the idea!

She wound fabric around the pistol and her note and painstakingly sewed the entire package tight. If she was wrong about Gilbert, the pistol might kill an innocent man, but instinct said she was right, so the pistol might save the lives of other agents. Émile wouldn't act on it unless there was another arrest. Small comfort in that, so long as that arrest was not her own or Émile's.

Her head—feeling immense as a barrage balloon. Her eyes— red and half closed in the mirror. She locked the door to the ladies' lounge, took her headscarf from her handbag and used the Isfahan carpet for namaaz. Insh'allah, the landing would go smoothly, with no arrests tonight.

She put on her green jacket, took her coat over her arm. She would leave long before curfew, arrive well in time.

The bellman exchanged her valise for the package for Émile, bobbing his kepi at her parting tip. When he was back behind his desk, Noor slipped out, circled behind the hotel to the shed Gilbert marked as her starting point.

The bicycle was a racehorse caught in the traces of a bullock cart—a ten-speed fit for the Tour de France fitted with a pedal generator that powered a headlamp, a luggage carrier with a rope to fasten her valise, and a wicker basket for her handbag. She fastened finger-curl pins to hold her slacks away from the chain, and had a little trouble getting her leg over the crossbar. She took the back streets again, to avoid the checkpoint. Soon the cone of light from her headlamp began bumping over cobblestones in the Gallo-Roman ruins of the old city and descended to the riverbank of the Sarthe.

The swish, creak and bump of tires began to reverse the route she and her fellow agent Edmond had taken only two and a half weeks earlier.

Noor cycled past darkening fields, manure smells. The moon had subsided to a pale crescent since the silver night of her arrival. She gauged the roadside by the glint of porcelain bulbs atop telephone poles.

By 02:00 hours a pilot would be unable to see trees in the dark. London must be concerned in the wake of so many arrests, to risk a landing on any night with less than a full moon.

Slow down.

If she wasn't careful, she'd land in a ditch instead of taking to the skies.

There was the forest—where was the netted pole? A partridge poacher's netted pole at the mouth of a game trail. She dismounted and wheeled the bicycle about a hundred metres till she found it.

Along the game trail, trees creaked and popped in the cool night breeze. Small animals scurried through grass. The path snaked through heavy undergrowth interrupted by felled logs and stalwart trees. Fine hair on Noor's arms stiffened; her skin felt moist and cold.

There was the stream she had to follow, a small backwater with spinning eddies, disturbed as her thoughts. What if? What if? What if an angry, rejected Gilbert went to the Gestapo?

Beyond the banks of the stream, all shapes faded to black.

Stop those thoughts.

But they returned, incessant as raindrops.

Watch those thoughts pass, let them go.

Meditation techniques were useless; every shadow hid a German shouting, "Halt!"

The stream riffled over its gravel bed, poured short curtains over cobbles. Piles of rocks altered its flow and direction.

Tamas, Abbajaan called it, chaos of the mind. She was light-headed with it.

Noor stifled a cough and wiped her nose.

She came to a wood-slat bridge. Pul-Sirat—*"baal se bareek, talwar se tez"*—slender as a hair, sharp as a sword-edge. She would fall on one side or the other, into the ravine below; not from the balance between her good and bad deeds, but because she felt so unwell.

Allah, send your farishtas to me.

She led her cycle along the trail and came to the X on the map in her mind—the woodcutter's cottage.

At her knock, a woman with a knitted shawl covering her head as if for namaaz took the bicycle with no comment. Noor put on her coat and crept out, carrying her valise and handbag through an area of long grass into a newly cut field.

No Germans arrayed for her arrest. But they could be lurking in the dark.

This wasn't where she had landed two weeks earlier.

A lantern placed on a tree stump illuminated Gilbert and someone in overalls—probably the woodcutter. Gilbert held a torch tied to a stick. He brought the flat of his other hand down lightly on its unlit face, demonstrating planting it in the soil. The woodcutter took up an armful of torches and disappeared into the dark. He would be forming the L-shape to guide the landing.

Halfway to the tree stump, Noor recoiled. A strange object hovered before her eyes.

"Bonjour!" said a voice.

Bonjour with a German accent? Where was the "Halt!"?

Then another, "Bonjour."

Where were the boots? The swastika? That smell—what was it? Chocolate.

Fragrance steamed into night air from the hovering thing. Only a flask cup.

Two fair-headed men of college age wearing jackets with sleeves ending halfway up their forearms stood before her. They whispered at her in Dutch that was double dutch to Noor and held out strong right hands.

Don't let Gilbert see you were frightened.

"Vous parlez français?"

Both shook their heads. They gathered around the tree stump, and since they spoke only a few phrases of French or English, all Noor could do was nod, smile and pantomime.

Gilbert greeted Noor, cocky as ever and very much in command. He spoke no Dutch either.

Torches in place, there was nothing more to be done till 02:00 hours but wait.

The aeroplane mechanic turned woodcutter spread a blanket over the nubbly ground, placed the Thermos flask upon it, blew out the lantern, rolled over on his side and fell asleep. The heat coil of Gilbert's lighter glowed beneath a cupped hand. He drew deeply on his cigarette, yawned, lay down on his back and patted the blanket beside him.

Disregard him.

Noor sat down cross-legged. The gourd base, bridge and strings of an imaginary veena lay between her and Gilbert. A yawn came, but she wasn't sleepy; she was wound more tightly than her wristwatch. Cold seeped through her oilskin coat.

Tweedledum and Tweedledee lay down, leaning against their duffel bags, and whispered to each other.

"They're agents of Queen Wilhelmina's WIM," said Gilbert.

Noor had heard of WIM, a Dutch resistance network. Its leader, a Belgian code-named *Rinus*, had been recently arrested. These two agents must be escaping to England.

"I wish I could speak Dutch," said Noor.

"What for?" asked Gilbert. "You want me to believe you prefer Dutchmen to Frenchmen?"

"Non," said Noor, stung into reaction despite herself. "But I would like to know who betrayed their leader and his network, and what advice they have for smelling out traitors."

"Some networks don't need traitors. They can betray themselves by carelessness."

"Carelessness! Someone told the Gestapo where to find their leader, and when. And the same with Prosper. That kind of man is a traitor."

Gilbert shrugged. "Traitors can be women also. My wife, for instance . . . I just paid two million francs for a parcel of land in the Midi and now she says she doesn't want to leave her lover in Paris."

Two million francs was a large sum. A huge sum. How could an air movements officer afford two million francs? But someone who owned a château could afford it.

"Men or women traitors, both are despicable creatures," said Noor, having no desire to discuss the dalliances of Gilbert's wife. She gritted her teeth to keep them still.

"Have more chocolate—I laced it with rum," said Gilbert. "No? Then I'll have some. How quickly you judge others, Madeleine—but then, you're so young, so naive. 'Traitors!' We're in a war. *Enfin*, some people get involved more deeply in the Resistance than they meant to, or circumstances force them to compromise, leaving them no choice but to betray."

She had pitied Monsieur le Missionnaire at Drancy for such a dilemma, and she had to agree. But Monsieur le Missionnaire was truly forced; his family was hostage at Drancy. What circumstance forced Gilbert to betray Prosper? Money. Provide the Gestapo with information and get paid.

Perhaps over a friendly game of chess.

Gilbert hadn't once mentioned the messages for which she had almost been captured at Grignon.

"Do you have the messages I am to take to London?" asked Noor.

"Those messages? I sent them."

But a few hours earlier, when he met her at La Place des Jacobins, had he not said, "I have them"?

"How?" asked Noor. "Do you now have another radio operator in northern France?"

"No. I sent them by courier over the Pyrénées. He should be in London by now."

There had been no messages to send from Grignon. There were no messages to carry to London. She had been lured here.

You're not being fair; suspicions are not proof. You mis-remember what he said.

A sound like a steam engine startled them—only the wood-cutter's snore.

"Dream!" said one of the agents. He shook the woodcutter.

Noor's head seemed to be moving through its own dream. Sharp fronds interlaced themselves around her heart, squeezing it tight.

"Aren't you at all sorry for those who have been arrested?" she asked Gilbert.

Gilbert slowly expelled a sigh. "Madeleine, the stupid cause their own problems. If you ask me, Prosper lost his nerve in the last few months. I've seen it happen to pilots."

"Losing your nerve is not *stupid*. It's unfortunate, unlucky. Often sad. If a pilot lost his nerve after seeing his comrades fall, I would call him human, not stupid."

"*D'accord, d'accord.* But you have, I'm sure, had some long night when something overcame your courage. For you, it may have been fear of shame, for Prosper, fear of capture."

A warning bell crashed in Noor, sounding all the way to her womb. Those were her own words, "the long night at Madame Dunet's when fear of shame overcame my courage."

Mais non! Impossible. Impossible.

"What do you mean?"

"Only that it is impossible to judge men—and women—who play many parts simultaneously. Like Arletty in *Fric-Frac*. She's still playing many parts."

Her own words again. "*Mother showed me how to play many parts simultaneously. Remember the time Zaib and I were at the cinema laughing at Arletty in* Fric-Frac?"

Why would Arletty come to Gilbert's mind? And *Fric-Frac*? An old film, a little-known comedy. How?

Gilbert had read her letters. To Zaib and to Kabir.

Did her blood run cold from night chill or the implications? If Gilbert had read those letters, he had read others, letters with much more confidential information. It showed a malevolent curiosity, a quest well beyond casual interest. He could have collected an arsenal of information for the Gestapo. Simply horrifying to contemplate.

She had no proof Gilbert had read the letters of other agents, only her own.

But why had Gilbert quoted her words now? Was he not afraid she would report to London that her letters had been opened by him, or was he so confident he could spin a tale to justify his actions?

She would tell her fears to Major Boddington on arrival. He would take action.

But suddenly Noor didn't want to be on an aeroplane arranged by Gilbert. Maybe there were no Gestapo men on the ground because that plane, Noor and the two Dutch agents would never survive the crossing.

A mosquito-drone became a buzz. Gilbert and the woodcutter ran into the field to switch on the torches. By these and the tiny lights below the black plane, the resistants gathered on the ground could intuit its silhouette.

Maybe Gilbert quoted her letters to her in petty revenge for rejecting his advances. And with impunity, knowing she would never carry the information anywhere but into the waters of the Channel.

The stars rotated in their sockets above.

How many farishtas must Allah send with signs before I heed his warnings?

The buzz became a pulsing roar.

"Lysander again, not a Hudson," said Gilbert.

Noor scrambled to her feet, her handbag looped over her arm.

Torch in hand, Gilbert flashed the Morse code signal into the sky. The landing lights sparked briefly and the heavy-footed plane touched ground. Noor felt the earth-shaking bump, and the Dutchmen seized their bags and ran past her, following the propeller's slipstream.

Gilbert flung the torch onto the blanket and picked up Noor's valise. But Noor tugged at his grasp till he dropped it and turned with a look of irritated surprise.

"I'm not going," she shouted over the roar. "I'm not going."

"What? Get on, get on!"

"I'm not leaving."

"*Merde!* What are you saying? *Allez-hop!*"

The pilot leaned out, so close she could see his scarf. The woodcutter had the ladder up against the side of the plane. She yelled to the pilot, "Stop! Don't—"

She was about to shout, "Don't let those men get on the plane, don't take off! Don't, don't . . . !" But Gilbert clapped his hand over her mouth and dragged her nearer the flutter-roar, nearer the propeller, overpowering her voice.

The woodcutter came running. One of them had her by the forearms. She was shaking, shaking till her head lolled. It was Gilbert, teeth clenched at her eye level, rum on his breath. He was thrusting her so close . . .

He wouldn't dare, not before so many . . .

The woodcutter had retrieved Noor's fallen valise and was clinging halfway up the ladder, handing it to the mystified Dutchmen.

"She's hysterical! Hysterical!" Gilbert yelled over her head. "Afraid of flying!"

The pilot threw up his hands. Gilbert dragged her past the wing, closer to the ladder.

At the base of the ladder Noor went limp. She slipped through Gilbert's grasp to the ground, as if struck unconscious. Gilbert backed away. But a second later his hand thumped down, grabbing her arm through her coat. Away she rolled, shedding the oilskin, retaining her grip on the handbag.

She found her feet. And ran, ran into darkness.

Out of range of the landing lights, into the cover of the long grass at the edge of the woods.

Breathing like a piston, running, she glanced over her shoulder. On his feet again, Gilbert had started across the landing field towards her, but then he stopped, turned on his heel and ran back, up to the cockpit.

Lungs burning, Noor hunkered down and watched. Gilbert cupped his hands and shouted something at the pilot.

The overhead canopy slid closed. Gilbert waved the plane forward.

Don't go, don't go!

But the Lysander pumped its throttle till it roared, and began to taxi. Then its nose lifted and it was soaring into sky. The wood-cutter picked up the lantern and blanket. Gilbert began helping him remove the torches planted in the soil.

And she watched, helpless, as German flares lit up the sky and night fighters zipped down from above. No one could see the black monoplane any more. Gilbert, too, watched. And he didn't point, didn't make any move, no sign of alarm or shock. The woodcutter ran up and stood beside him, and both looked upwards.

What chance do they have? It's a slow, unarmed plane!

Beneath the howl of Messerschmitt engines, the Lysander's pulsing roar dimmed to a buzz and went silent.

Imagine, imagine that little plane searing the stars as it fell from the sky.

The night fighters circled.

The sound—they were diving. No, climbing. Now they were leaving, whizzing away.

Noor sat still, looking up.

Night noises—breeze in leaves—filled the tense silence.

Noor dashed her nose on her sleeve and moved stealthily into the forest. She was only a few feet in, proceeding at erratic angles through complex thickets and skin-snagging thorns, scuffing over leaves and tilted stones, bushes lassoing her feet, when a shooting pain in her shoulder said she had rammed into bark.

She sank to earth with a groan, and went limp. This time with no pretense.

A cone of torchlight bobbed towards her. She sank lower to the ground, moving deeper into the brush. Leaves rustled, so loud they would surely hear.

A second yellow cone stopped at the edge of the woods, lifted, then described a long slow arc. Low voices; Gilbert and the wood-cutter were conferring.

Back and forth went the light cones, for what seemed like hours. They seemed to be walking a path—so there was a path, and not very far away. The lights came together again. More voices ampli-fied by a breeze flowing in her direction, but incomprehensible.

The torchlight divided, cones moved in opposite directions.

No more torchlights. Noor rose to tensed thighs, then upright.

Take the opportunity now.

Fallen branches and twigs cracked as she moved away from the tree.

Too loud, too loud!

Was Gilbert armed? He must be. And if he found her . . .

Move, move. No one can rescue you but yourself.

On a cow path now, trodden about four feet wide. The com-pass in her jacket button gave her north. Le Mans lay northeast. She must avoid the route Gilbert had mapped for her.

She set off, walking and stumbling across fields and through vineyards, losing her way several times.

She came upon a grotto to the Virgin Mary, a familiar patch of flowering hogweed, a finger-post pointing to a mine shaft and, rain-faded but still discernible, a quail poacher's painted X between the sweeping branches of an ancient oak.

Coincidence or the hand of Allah? It didn't matter; the famil-iar reassured.

Noor walked on through the night, shins scraped, shoulder throbbing, till early dawn, when the town of Le Mans loomed above the plain.

She must tell Émile what happened. But where was he in Le Mans? Even if she knew, she couldn't go there. Too dangerous for her and Émile. Besides, that would make Renée even more frightened and angry.

She couldn't walk into the Hôtel du Dauphin at any hour looking like this: wet, muddy, scratched — a bloody mess. And with only diamonds left for payment, there was no question of getting lodging at any hotel.

She rummaged in her bag, counting the francs she had saved by dining with Gilbert. Enough for a ticket to Paris; not enough for a room in Le Mans.

Madame Aigrain's safe house was closer than Madame Gagné's boarding house at Drancy. And Émile said Gilbert didn't know of its existence.

Gilbert might assume she'd take the first train back to Paris. So Noor let the 04:00 train depart, and the 04:30, before she entered the station. She ate one of the pears that wouldn't be going to London after all, and composed her features to match the blank expressions of other waiting passengers, queuing with them to present her papers.

A German soldier took and returned her papers in square movements, his gaze never touching her face. On the platform now. About twenty people waiting, and no one looked like Gilbert or Gestapo. To her right, two boxcars marked *Hommes 40/Cheval 8* — forty men or eight horses. Empty. To her left, first-class compartments filled with glum-faced German soldiers. No doubt going to Russia, setting out for the front.

German eyes boring into her back. Shouts in German. They might be shouting at her.

Slowly. Count carriages: one, two, three . . .

Almost to the end of the train, now.

. . . nine, ten.

She boarded the single second-class passenger carriage for French civilians and collapsed into a seat.

CHAPTER 25

Paris, France
Sunday, July 4, 1943

NOOR ARRIVED at Madame Aigrain's door chilled to the bone, an hour before the lifting of curfew. The sentry had been snoring at his post, and the concierge's *loge* was Sunday-dark. Between sneezing and coughing, Noor managed four pairs of knocks. Despite the signal, Madame's eyes were roundels above the restraining chain. But the chain fell away. Madame took Noor in.

"How is it you have returned, Madeleine?"

A steaming cup of milk Noor knew Madame had intended for the Siamese appeared on the table before her. Madame Aigrain almost disappeared into the sofa.

I must look like a stray, and smell terrible.

"There was a problem," said Noor. "I will try to leave again soon. Émile must be informed as soon as possible."

With no hesitation Madame agreed to leave a message for Émile at the letter drop. Sacrificing details, Noor wrote a note: *To Phono: Madeleine is still in Paris.*

He might imagine there was serious trouble or might read nothing into the statement at all. Planes developed engine trouble and had to turn back to England. Sometimes resistants found the Germans had planted stakes on landing strips. She couldn't tell what Émile might imagine. She needed to meet with him and discuss Gilbert's reading her mail. But meeting with Émile came with Renée in tow—Renée who didn't want Noor to come near Émile. A rendezvous would be too dangerous now.

Besides, the room was sliding sideways, even as she presented the fruit she'd intended for her family in London to Madame.

"Thank you. Now rest, Anne-Marie." Madame Aigrain's soft hand brushed Noor's forehead. "I would call a doctor, but mine was sent to Germany. I don't know one who will come on a Sunday, and the concierge has locked away her telephone. We need someone who will not ask questions, who will not mind a little deviation around the law."

"But I have no money left." Noor discovered her eyes were streaming.

"*C'est ça?*" said Madame Aigrain. "I have a little—enough for a doctor." She lifted a cigar humidor standing on the mantelpiece. "Here—"

Sparks struck up inside Noor's head as she shook it no.

"It's a loan. Take enough for the doctor and so you won't have to ask me again for at least a week. Then, if you are still here, still in need, I will arrange more. *D'accord?*"

Still Noor hesitated, then said, "A loan. And I will pay you back as soon as I can."

Madame Aigrain counted out five thousand real francs, wadded them up and held them out to Noor. She replaced the rest in the humidor and put it back on the mantelpiece, evidently quite confident of Noor's honesty.

In the cupboard room, the forest-green skirt she'd given Madame Aigrain's daughter to copy for Monique lay neatly folded on the bed. Noor changed from her slacks, shook out her damp hair and lay down.

Madame Aigrain dipped a lace-trimmed handkerchief in eau de cologne and placed it on Noor's burning forehead. Then she bustled about the apartment squeezing the netted balls of atomizers till heavy, soft, sharp, bright, resinous and animal scents dissolved and combined. In a lavender Sunday dress, black shawl and black fishnet gloves, she took her cane and left for church.

Noor closed her eyes, but every nerve was on edge. With each breath she smelled the cologne of Gilbert's betrayal. Now he had many reasons to pursue her.

She saw the pilot throwing up his hands, believing her hysterical. Once again the plane rushed past and roared away. Then the flares, the fighters, the silence. She could imagine what must have happened: three men cremated alive.

If only she could have warned the Dutchmen or the pilot. Luck or Allah's *farishtas* had now saved her from Gilbert and the Gestapo three times. How many more times would be too many?

Waking sleep. What day was it?

July Fourth, a day so important to Mother. The one day Dadijaan was civil to Mother, conceded her approval of any country that fought for and won independence from the British, even a Western power. Sunday morning: Dadijaan would be standing at Speaker's Corner, silk sari *paloo* billowing about her, giving her weekly speech in Urdu about the starving in India to passing churchgoers. Mother, believer in everyone's right to free speech, would be her only, long-suffering, uncomprehending audience, and the two would garden their allotment in Hyde Park afterwards.

Mother required everyone to be home for dinner on the Fourth and, being from Boston, would tell the story of the Tea Party. The first time the story was translated for her, Dadijaan had winced at the waste of that much fine tea, even to protest British taxes. "You know how long it takes to pick and dry one shipload of tea?" she said. "And why did they dress up as Indians? Everything, every time, blame it on Indians!" But pressed by Noor and Zaib on July Fourths since, Dadijaan would launch her own tale of how the Mahatma passed through Baroda on his Salt March in 1930. Dadijaan had joined his procession, walking for days, also to protest taxes, those on salt—but never destroying any salt, never wasting a single grain. After dinner the family would come together around the phonograph, listening to recordings of Abbajaan.

And if things had been different last night, Noor would have been with them, playing the veena.

She rose and lurched from her little room. Perfume hung in vaporous puffs in Madame Aigrain's sitting room. In the dining room the fragrance of roses mixed with lemon. Lalique bottles released a musky patchouli that combined with a scent reminiscent of raspberry.

Each hybrid fragrance begged for an open window, a single breath of air.

I never felt such nausea since mon petit problème.

Siamese eyes of unblinking blue reflected her own. A little motor purred as she lifted the cat from the windowsill. All Madame's windows were locked, hermetically sealed with blackout tape; Madame's fear of draughts ran deeper than her fear of bombs.

Noor stopped struggling with the windows to cough into her handkerchief. A spot of red in the palm of her hand—she was spitting up blood!

She could not stay in the airless rooms a moment longer. Not an instant longer. All she needed was a prescription for some medicine to cure influenza quickly. But how? She couldn't approach a doctor at an office or a hospital. Madame Aigrain had gone to church and then Flavien's pawnshop; it would be hours before she returned.

At this moment she didn't care if she was seen by one, two or fifty Germans.

Get some air.

Noor picked her handbag off the bed and slipped down the stairs, past the concierge's empty *loge*. A moment later she was out on the sunny street, gulping lungfuls of fresh air, and coughing again and again.

Five thousand francs in her handbag and Madame Aigrain's words echoing in her mind: ". . . someone who will not ask questions, who will not mind a little deviation around the law."

One step forward. She knew immediately where she needed to go. Knew to whom she might go again.

CHAPTER 26

Paris, France
Sunday, July 4, 1943

LEAFY BRANCHES OBSCURED the curlicued iron gates of shabby houses lining the rue de Jolivet. The tiny brass nameplate still read *Dunet*. Feverish and wool-headed, Noor took the stone-flagged path and knocked at the arched wooden door she remembered only too well.

What had possessed her to return, like a criminal to the scene of a crime? She was making an exception to SOE rules, but Montparnasse was a long distance from Suresnes and other areas where she might be recognized.

Some events in one's life stay forever.

And she had a problem again, a problem that needed a practical though illegal solution.

The woman framed in the doorway had faded a little in nine years. The mane of coarse hair falling to her elbows was greyer and sparser, but her face was the same, harsh with disappointments. Madame Dunet was a *sage-femme*, a midwife. Once a nurse at the American Hospital, she was competent as a physician.

Noor gave her name as Anne-Marie Régnier, and beyond noting that Mademoiselle Régnier was *sans rendezvous*—without appointment—no flicker of recognition came to the midwife's eyes.

"Sunday is a busy day," said Madame Dunet.

She was with a patient; Noor would have to wait.

A few copies of *Pariser Zeitung* in the dreary waiting room; Noor hadn't known Madame Dunet spoke German. Four-year-old copies of the *Herald Tribune* and *Vogue*. No picture of Pétain on the wall. That only meant Madame Dunet was not a Pétainist; it didn't mean she was a Gaullist or would sympathize with Allied secret agents.

Madame Dunet ushered a pale, middle-aged woman to the door and returned.

"Don't ask me for a medical certificate for someone in a camp—I can't give it to you. And if you're Jewish, you can go to the Hôpital Rothschild. When was your last period?"

Madame Dunet showed Noor into her kitchen.

The same table at its centre.

"*Tiens*, now I remember you, girl! You asked if I could make the bleeding start again. You came with your sister—she wanted to be a doctor, oui? I remember her, because I too once wanted to be a doctor . . ." Madame threw back her hair and gave a rueful laugh. "And because you wore a long dress—a ball gown, maybe? Indian."

That summer evening in 1934, Noor had worn a sari. Not because going to Madame Dunet's was any celebration, but because Uncle Tajuddin, as soon as he discovered Noor's love for Armand, decreed both his nieces must wear only saris and ghaghras. He didn't order complete *burqa* as he didn't want them mistaken for Arab girls, but a few months of Indian traditional garb, he said, would repel the desires of men like Armand.

"Maybe to hide it?" Madame Dunet demonstrated with her hands clasped low around an imaginary belly.

No, Noor's stomach had been flat as ever that day. Although, if Uncle had kept her in her room much longer, she might have begun to show.

"You are still in France, girl?"

So Madame Dunet had no idea she had left France, ever been in London. Convenient; no explanations necessary.

Noor gave a heavy-lidded nod. "Oui, madame."

"Have you come on behalf of your sister this time? Maybe a friend? Ah, the German soldiers are handsome, non? *Eh bien, ma fille—vous avez encore un petit problème?* Are you in trouble again?"

In trouble. A fist clenched about Noor's womb again at the words.

"Non, non," she assured the midwife. "I came to you because I knew you would be discreet. It's dangerous to be a foreigner in Paris these days. You were always more concerned about helping your friends than with the law." She sneezed.

Madame Dunet inclined her grey head with a knowing wink. "*Mais, bien sûr*, girl. I am discreet—you remember."

As if she could ever forget.

A fabric screen stood at one end of the kitchen, a screen like the one that separated praying women from men at La Mosquée. Madame Dunet motioned Noor behind it and pushed a garlic-smelling apron after her.

"Can a medical certificate help someone escape a camp?" Noor asked. Every button seemed to have grown larger than its hole.

"Sometimes. Britishers and Americans in Vittel and Besançon camps have successfully used them, but it only gets POWs and Jews into more trouble." Madame Dunet continued talking. "Bombs and air raids—I barely slept last night. The Allies should invade, have their battles and let us all go back to normal. The cosmopolitans who used to come here when their daughters were in trouble have deserted Paris. But you are still here, girl . . ."

Madame Dunet's kitchen table was cold beneath her thighs, the way it was on a night nine years before. The midwife made Noor breathe deeply, tapped her breastbone with two fingers, listened to her lungs, her cough, nodded when she said she was spitting up blood.

"Influenza," she confirmed. "Maybe pneumonia."

"My father died of influenza," Noor blurted.

"He was a guru from India, yes? Your sister told me. Medicine is so backward in India—he probably had astrologers for doctors. Susceptibility runs in the blood."

When Abbajaan caught influenza in 1926, it was an equal scourge in France, one that couldn't be healed simply by faith healers. But the midwife was unlikely to comprehend any similarity between Indian astrologers and the *guérisseurs*.

Madame Dunet gave Noor a dose of belladonna and a vial of smuggled American Prontosil to be taken morning and evening. She directed Noor to gargle with bicarbonate of soda and drink an infusion of linden flowers.

"I gave you tisane of linden after your operation. It was effective, non?"

"Oui, madame," said Noor, though nothing Madame Dunet had given her nine years ago had helped mitigate the shame draining her heart, weakening every limb.

What was torn from me that day was only flesh, less than love. No child asks to be born or to die; ours was no exception.

Madame Dunet was speaking again, lecturing. She should listen politely.

" . . . Midwives who help women deliver fine offspring understand the science of heredity. The arranged marriages of our ancestors produced a strong French race. But nowadays people do not acknowledge the value of blood."

Heredity was the highest value of the Germans and Vichy. How could Madame Dunet still feel it was unavowed in the public mind?

"Madame Dunet, I thought you were a romantic," said Noor with an effort.

"Romance? Romance led us to defeat by the Germans. Romance led to decadence, softness. We French alone among all of European colonists committed miscegenation with our colonials, tainted our blood with the black man's and the Arab. Nothing like this would be possible in America, girl. When your mother married an Indian guru, in all of Europe the only country that would countenance their household was France."

Her tone held shame rather than pride. Noor had never told Madame Dunet anything about Mother or her antecedents, nor had Madame Dunet and Mother ever met. Had Zaib told her? Before, afterwards, while waiting?

Anyway, it wasn't true, for there were many other countries to which Abbajaan and Mother could have gone, but they didn't. Where to begin correcting Madame?

Yet Madame Dunet didn't appear a Pétainist, or a collaborator. Maybe she was simply someone categorical, accustomed to her categories.

She had come to Madame Dunet to be treated for influenza, not to be reminded of that painful day in 1934. It was highly indiscreet to mention a "stomach operation," a crime for which midwives could be sent to the guillotine; Madame Dunet could still be arrested. The Vichy slogan *Travail, famille, patrie* glorifying work, family and country meant her operations were less acceptable than ever before.

"So when your mother came to see me, it was clear I had to help you."

Noor had never told Mother about her "situation." Surely there was some mistake.

"Mother came to you? Met you—here? Non, non. You mistake me for someone else, Madame."

Mother, if she had known, would have begged Uncle's permission for Noor and Armand to marry. And Noor didn't want Mother begging Uncle for anything on her behalf.

"My sister made all the arrangements."

Madame Dunet threw back her grey mane and laughed. "Your mother. A shrewd lady. Oh, she knew you'd never come if you knew *she* wanted you to do it, so she said she would give your sister the money. She said you'd never ask where it came from."

Oh, Zaib! Though sworn to secrecy, Zaib had told Mother. Anger swept Noor. Anger at a previous version of herself—such ignorance!—such stupidity!

Madame Dunet was right, never once had Noor asked Zaib to explain how she collected the five thousand francs. And Mother, who always held the family purse strings, knew her eldest well. Knew Noor loathed discussing money, how she trusted Allah would bring it forth when necessary, never asked where money came from nor cared much where it went. How could she have been so juvenile, so very naive?

Madame Dunet's hair splayed across her back as she hunched over the kitchen sink to wash her hands. The last time Noor saw her turn to that sink . . .

"I—I had no other way," stammered Noor. She was back in that time of terror and clandestine inquiry.

She should not have come here today.

Soapy water slithered like mucous between the midwife's hands. "Nonsense, mademoiselle. I tell all my Medeas there are alternatives. I told your mother what else could be done."

That's what Madame Dunet thought of Noor? No matter that it was her hands that performed the operation, Madame Dunet judged Noor a Medea. For Madame Dunet she was no longer Noor, with her own motives, constraints and love, but sorceress Medea. Armand was no longer Armand, who had affirmed her possession of her own body and stood by Noor whatever her decision, but a Jason abandoning his unborn child. But there had been no revenge or anger in Noor as in Medea, only sorrow.

What alternatives did Madame Dunet mean?

"She could have sent you to a convent. The nuns often raise 'foundlings.'"

Noor's head bowed into her open hands. No one had offered her such an alternative. Certainly Madame Dunet had not, nor had Mother.

"M-mother? She knew this?" Nine years ago Mother must have thought her not old enough, not intelligent enough, not worldly enough. Nine years ago Noor was not a person, just a problem.

"Of course. I discussed it with Madame Khan."

Why would Mother have forgone such an alternative? Could she not have provided money for the nuns instead of money for Madame Dunet's stomach operation?

"And Monsieur Khan."

Noor looked up. Her tongue almost refused to obey. "With Uncle? You met my uncle?"

"I don't know any uncle, non, non."

Uncle would have shown Noor to the door immediately, had he known. Mercifully, Noor's shame must have been kept from him.

"You met my brother then?"

"Oui, oui. A young man, very handsome. Your brother Monsieur Khan."

"And what did my brother say?" She hoped to hear that Kabir had argued with Mother, argued to allow Noor to marry Armand immediately.

But Madame Dunet said, "Your brother was adamant—he didn't want any niece or nephew of his baptized."

Words like blows.

"But our mother was raised a Christian!" She was reeling; how little had she known Kabir.

"Oh, I was there when your brother reminded Madame Khan she was now a Muslim, even if his father had permitted her to go to church."

Permitted? A thunderclap in her heart as anger and sorrow came together. How could Kabir say that? Abbajaan always encouraged Mother—and everyone else—to go to any house of worship that inspired awe. If she couldn't comprehend the motives of a person with whom she shared two parents, was it possible to understand any other being?

We are all doomed to be exotic, each to one another.

Madame Dunet wiped her hands and made a sucking sound against her teeth. Then, as if revealing the intricate arrangements of a great practical joke, she said, "Your mother and I understood one another. She understands blood too, you know? I told her, not one more Jew should be allowed to enter the world."

No anger any more; nausea washed through Noor. Mother was not present to be confronted with Madame's revelation, Mother who always criticized Europeans and Indians for emphasizing bloodlines. Madame Dunet could not have stated such bigotry nine years ago as openly as today. As with Renée, Vichy had loosened the midwife's tongue by sanctioning and blessing such statements. Her words were supplied by editorials in *Je Suis Partout*, maybe they had even altered the midwife's memory of her own actions. She had arrived at a surreal defence of at least one of her operations, one of the few defences that would be acceptable to Vichy. How many more would she explain the same way?

And Madame Dunet was implicating her in a vile hatred of Jews, a hatred she presumed Noor and Mother shared with her.

Why did Madame Dunet need to tell Noor this, so many years later? Knowledge worming its way beneath Noor's skin. Madame wanted her to acknowledge that if she had a half-Jewish child or had simply been married to a Jew, she could be deemed a Jew under current Vichy laws, laws more stringent and anti-Semitic than the Germans required. Wanted her to understand that the gates of Drancy and Compiègne and Pithiviers would stand waiting to devour her today had Madame not saved her.

No feeling of gratitude stirred in Noor. At this moment she wanted above all only to be with Armand, in his arms—man and woman in a phalanx of two.

Madame Dunet's lips moved in a silent, carnivalesque movie. The dreary kitchen was dissolving into pointillist frames.

Was she Medea, or was she Noor? Was she but the effect of her family and its decisions for her, or was she Noor? She had not challenged their desires years ago. She had taken the safest route—name the crime, for crime it was then and now: to have Armand's child aborted before it could come into the world. And Madame Dunet was correct, without her ministrations Noor might have been interned today, with Armand.

Distance, I need distance.

"Stay in bed for a few days, Mademoiselle Khan. See me again in a week if you still have fever or delirium." Madame Dunet opened a cigarette case, removed a cigarette. A lighter flicked. A flame leaped and burned in the gloom.

In a waking, walking stupor, somehow Noor was outside, back on the path, then in the street, almost running before the evening blush of the sky, under the pooling shadows of deep-rooted trees.

Pforzheim, Germany
February 1944

Here in the dungeon, where night follows night, I toss in a fever-dream as I did for days in the little cupboard at Madame Aigrain's. No sound, no paper comes between us at this moment; my spirit speaks to yours across Al-ghayab.

A taste like the medicine the midwife gave comes again.

Talking to Madame Dunet battered my senses. I searched for false notes, but Madame Dunet had never claimed to be tolerant; her actions were consistent with her political beliefs, distasteful as I might find them. But as for Mother, and Kabir—the hiatus between discourse and actions astounded. I can say it to myself now where no one hears me, to myself if to no one else: I was ashamed of them, and ashamed for them. Their actions showed coinciding reasons to see me as a woman but never as Noor. Mother: her aspirations to bourgeois respectability. Kabir: the newly won masculine authority of majority.

Of course, they must have felt they did what was right, but . . .

The most important decision I ever made was chosen as they willed. Then, was it mine or theirs? They were munafiqs—hypocrites, talking and preaching tolerance while acting from prejudice.

Allah, I pray for hidayat: guide them to narrow the gap between their beliefs and actions.

Madame Aigrain brought lace handkerchiefs dipped in eau de cologne and damp linen towels, and plied me alternately with soup and hot milk. I wandered, delirious, in an inscape of anger mingled with remorse. I have no memory of that time till the twenty-seventh day of Ramzaan. Last year it fell on July 12.

On this day one should pardon those who have wronged us.

I who could not pardon Mother and Kabir implored your soul's pardon for me. You were silent all day; there was only Hazrat Issa faintly smiling from the wall, his sacred heart open and bleeding. Then came the Night of Destiny, when the Qur'an was revealed. The night all fates are sealed, the night one waits for angels. Madame Aigrain had retired when suddenly I sat up in bed. I heard a baby.

A baby crying alone.

It had to be you, the part of me that comes from the creative chakra of the cosmos. Meri jaan—the part of my self that is truly alive. You cried, you screamed, and I could not console you. Did you weep for the clay of the body I denied you, or for the world?

Forgetting the curfew, I ran downstairs and stood in the doorway. The dark, glistening street was illuminated by a single torchlight from the sentry box on the corner.

There was no baby, no baby crying there.

I turned my face so Madame Aigrain might mistake my tears for rain. She led me back to bed.

Tell me, what should I have done ten years ago, ma petite? If, as Madame Dunet said, there were nuns who would look after a foundling—I did not know them. I swear.

But to have you, touch you, then renounce you forever. Would not that have been worse, worse for both of us?

I tell you, I was never afraid of the pain of your birth. Love and fear, rather than chains or bars, bound me when I stopped your soul. In 1934, I imagined you entering your body in the sixteenth week, imagined your heart pumping, taking shape within me. I imagined you forming eyes, lungs, a spine. I thought I felt the long rope of a placenta growing between us, sending nourishment from my inmost recesses to yours. I talked to you as I'm doing now, and you could not express any reason why you needed to be.

Why does any child need to be?

Was it a homicide I did that day, or an act of love for you and Armand? The divine and demonic met in me; years have blurred memory and left only what I wish to remember.

What I wish to remember is love.

Had I let your soul arrive, what would you have seen in my womb? A darkness as deep as the dark in this cell. What would you have heard? Sounds like I hear now: pipes gurgling, the exhalation of the tall building breathing around my trapped body. You would have been as dependent on the cord that fed you as I am on that single outstretched arm with its bowl of soup.

On the Night of Destiny your crying no longer permitted my evasions: I stopped my child's soul from entering the world by taking away its defenceless piece of my flesh. At twenty, I was capable of deliberate destruction.

My lips are bloody as those of Kali, who gives life and takes it away.

Would I make the same decision again? I lay shivering beneath the coverlet and thought about this for many hours, as if I were playwright, director and actor in my own story.

Enfin, the answer was yes. To bring you to a world in which a woman must have permission before she may love—that was, to me, a sin beyond any the Prophet, peace be upon him, had foreseen. To disallow your father from knowing you because he was Jewish—this would have been an injustice to him and to you.

In that answer I found some peace. You must have understood my thoughts, for by dawn you no longer cried.

I have this time-away-from-time to think, ma petite, think about what makes a human. It is not merely being born, or surviving, but being cherished, receiving love in enough measure that it becomes our obligation to pass it on. Love, caring—these are the true signs of life, not only flesh. The capacity to feel as others feel. To suffer, even vicariously. By this measure, you were not human.

By this measure, none of us have yet become human, for we are numb to pain that is not our own.

Hope is a dangerous luxury in this place that has killed so many of my illusions, but one illusion remains: I will be ready to receive you next time. The twin angels, Kiraman Katibeen, will record better deeds in the Book of Judgement to balance against the harm I inflicted on you, on myself. If not, my jihad-al-akbar, that war I fight against the forces of destruction within me will be lost.

When Armand learned of you, he said, "We'll have a little girl, we'll call her Shekinah."

Shekinah—feminine spirit. Ma petite ruh—yes, that will be you. I feel his smile tug at my heart. I grow from inside.

But do I hear footsteps and muttering? Was that a hollow bucket crashing against a wall?

"Is someone there? Is anyone there?" I call.

There is no answer, no human who answers. The war could be over, but no one would know I am here. Vogel is not required to account for me. By Hitler's command, he doesn't have to keep any record of me and other Night and Fog prisoners. Armand, Mother, Dadijaan, Kabir, Zaib—no one will ever know I am here. I'm just a combatant who has disappeared, an enemy forgotten in this stinking hole.

Is the world destroyed, and no voice but mine left in the universe?

Everything is collapsing.

Allah, my heart is breaking once more.

CHAPTER 27

Paris, France
Friday, July 16, 1943

NOOR REASSURED THE PROPRIETOR of Chez Clément that she wouldn't be dining alone, and was shown to a small round table in the corner beside an engraved glass window. Back to the wall, face in shadow, with a view of the Germans and French dining beneath the chandeliers, and of the tin-surfaced bar past the WC—just the seat she'd have chosen herself.

A dozen days since she escaped being shot down with the others in the Lysander and today was the first time since her encounter with Madame Dunet that she had emerged from Madame Aigrain's apartment. An anonymous message left at Flavien's directed Noor to meet "Monsieur N." here at 13:30 hours.

Green velvet half-curtains on the brass rail beside her smelled of tobacco and smouldered candles. Outside, Parisiennes with luxuriant headdresses sported baskets and bags for foraging. Each looking far more chic than Noor, whose green skirt was now feeling more like a uniform. She raised her copy of *Paris Soir*, and from time to time, looked over it at people entering and leaving. They couldn't see her whole face—effective purdah.

She had pictured herself in the seedy elegance of this restaurant often—not incognito, but with Armand. Celebrating the début of his sonata, an award, or yet another invitation to conduct or teach. Armand leaning across this peach tablecloth, tapering fingers lovingly slipping a ring on hers.

But without Armand, Chez Clément held little charm.

"If it is not my portion to meet thee in this my life . . . let me not forget a moment . . ."

Quell those lines.

Still no news from Claude. He had promised to telephone; she must not lose hope.

The black market plat du jour featured spaetzle, sauerkraut and pork in every guise—bratwurst, schinkenwurst, liverwurst, knockwurst, blood sausage. Amazing aromas of chicken, beef bourguignon, onions and cheese drifted from the kitchen. Major Boddington would pay for food and wine, but Noor wasn't hungry. Despite Madame Dunet's medicines she still felt weak. And "the curse" was upon her again.

Yolande called it the curse, when they were toughening up in England. What mission had Yolande volunteered for, and where was she transmitting from now? She could be with a different cell only a few kilometres from here and Noor wouldn't know. What of Edmond, who landed with Noor?

The windfall of a good meal and a long hot soak at a bath-house would, she was sure, restore her body to normal. Her spirit— that was another matter.

A brief article in *Paris Soir* said that at Houdan, on Bastille Day, "terrorists" had captured the Monument of the Dead. Professor Balachowsky's bold scheme had been successful. His last words repeated in her mind: "We'll come through this." Insh'allah, the Professor was still alive.

An editorial shrilled with indignation: the peaceful suburbs of Paris had been savaged by Allied air raids. On Bastille Day, it said— an outrage. It didn't mention that German orders had restricted Bastille Day celebrations to a few firecrackers. No mention, either, that Ramzaan had ended, and that Algerians, Tunisians and other Muslims of Paris celebrated Id at La Mosquée. Since it wasn't a Christian celebration, Id was of no interest to *Paris Soir*.

Id. She had so ached to be home for it. With Mother. With Kabir. Even though, if Madame Dunet's story was true, they were now proven hypocrites.

Family love — that myth she had maintained and bowed to for years, believing in their concern for her. Now she had no family but Armand and others who fought tyranny, fellow resistants.

But today was Friday, when *juma* prayers were usually followed by Dadijaan's delicious dhokla and kachoris.

And it was half an hour past the appointed time for lunch with "Monsieur N."

Major Boddington must have been arrested. Gilbert must have betrayed him too.

One last glance over the curtain rail and she reached for her handbag, stood up.

A pincer gripped her elbow. A man with a steel-grey raincoat over one arm loomed over her. "Mademoiselle Régnier! How is your dear mother?"

Brown hair now black, his attire bland. But that flat face and spectacles were Major Boddington's. How had she missed seeing him enter?

He slung his coat over the back of the chair opposite Noor, and forgot his cover only to shake hands instead of kissing her on both cheeks. A carafe of muddy-looking wine and two close-to-clean wineglasses arrived. A clink of his glass against hers, and the Major got down to brass tacks.

"Had a spot of trouble lately, haven't we, then?"

"A spot of trouble" for certain torture, instant executions or deportations of hundreds of agents? Major Boddington sounded like those in London who still referred to a massacre of unarmed Indian civilians as an "error in judgement."

But the Major had braved a covert mission to France to meet her, and no doubt other endangered agents. Capturing him would be a coup celebrated in Berlin, and he undoubtedly knew it.

"I've arranged a new safe house for you." Suavely accented French issued from the side of his mouth. "Secure place. You even have your own telephone. Seventeenth arrondissement—my agents must have a few perquisites, I always say. Memorize this number." He dictated like a ventriloquist. "Sablons 80.04. I haven't given it to anyone else. And the address: 3 boulevard Richard Wallace."

Noor warmed towards Major Boddington. Officious but well-meaning; perhaps he just didn't know how to express his concern. And she did need a different safe house. She couldn't transmit from the pocket-sized room and hated to burden generous old Madame Aigrain much further. Major Boddington was being considerate, making the arrangements.

"Rent's paid for four months. Here's the key."

He passed it to her under cover of the tablecloth. Noor slipped it into her handbag.

"You need more francs and ration tickets," said the Major. "Make them last awhile."

Beneath the table, a fat envelope nudged into her lap. A weight she hadn't realized was bearing down inside her lifted; she wouldn't have to ask anyone for money.

"Not as much as I give our young gentlemen, but then, you aren't paying for two at meals, are you?" He smiled away.

She'd sound rude and ungrateful if she pointed out his illogic. It didn't matter. Now she could reimburse Madame Aigrain. And she'd be most frugal after that.

"And this time they're real francs, so do be prudent. Oh, and I left some messages in an envelope with the concierge. Do send them on as soon as your transmitter is operating."

The maître d' passed, conducting a couple through the conversational hubbub to a table in the opposite corner.

Noor raised her voice a little for their benefit. "How is your family?"

The couple looked threadbare and gaunt. The woman held the man's hand tight.

"Well as can be expected." He lowered his voice. "Keeping Mr. Hitler on his toes." Major Boddington sounded like a news-wire telegram. "*Je Suis Partout* and *Paris Soir* aren't giving the facts here. In a snit about the Paris air raid—typically self-centred. Not a single mention of our bombers raiding Cologne again."

"Any news of my family, sir?"

"All's well. Miss Atkins said to tell you some amazing news: your brother's got himself promoted to flight lieutenant. My, that means he's captain of his ship, you know."

Amazing only because the Major never expected it. Kabir's record would have brought him a promotion months ago but for his Indian blood.

"I'm so very sorry about the Lizzie, sir. Did anyone survive?"

"Survive what?" Major Boddington gave her an inquiring glance.

"The crash, I mean."

A momentary silence, and then the Major said, "Oh, they did-n't crash, no, no. Good man, that pilot. Cut his engines, dived like a Spitfire. Evaded two Messerschmitts. Got home safe, and the two Dutchmen are, I'm sure, properly grateful."

"I'm much relieved to hear that, sir." She was relieved the Lysander had escaped the predators, but delighted to find Gilbert's plan had failed.

The Major's eyes narrowed behind his spectacles. "Now. You seem to have been up to a little mischief, my girl? Heard you balked at the fence, came right up to the Lizzie, refused to go home? Fall for a handsome young frog, then?"

Major Boddington assigned a narrow range of talents to Noor; reasoning was not one of them.

"No, sir," said Noor carefully. She would pass over explana-tions of motives and state what she required at once. "I need to be with people I can trust. I will no longer work with Gilbert. I mean, I do not wish to work with Gilbert."

"You *are* exhausted, old girl."

She wanted to shout, "Don't ever call me 'old girl'"—it sadly reminded her of Prosper. But the Major was her superior officer, so she kept quiet.

"You've been awfully brave." The Major was all tender commiseration. "And quite alone. We kept you in play far too long. And then your refusal to return, becoming hysterical—I must say, I was surprised."

He was waiting. He hadn't addressed what she'd said about Gilbert, but had adroitly turned the conversation. Clearly, an explanation was required.

"You might have refused to take any aeroplane arranged by Gilbert too, sir, if you found out he had read your letters. While we were waiting for the Lizzie, he began alluding to the contents. And he didn't accidentally read them, he deliberately opened them!"

"You don't say!" Major Boddington clasped the edge of the table and leaned forward. "So that's what caused this little rumpus. Dear girl, you're quite right to be upset—caddish thing to do. Reading a lady's mail. Quite unforgivable."

"A serious infraction, sir," said Noor. "Against the rules."

"Ah yes, the rules. Come, come, love, Gilbert isn't the only one not playing strictly by the Marquis of Queensbury. If you want to stay within the rules, I dare say you should be fighting in uniform rather than—uh—what we're up to."

"Why did he read my letters?" Noor kept her voice low.

"My dear girl"—Major Boddington gave her a head-to-waist glance—"have a look in a mirror. You just don't realize, do you? Believe me, it's more than curiosity about your *je ne sais quoi*, your enigmatic Indian eyes. It's the exotic element, that's it. Gilbert's a good sort, but you know the French—Gallic urges. Introduced him around at my club and the rascal was winking at the barmaids the next minute."

"Sir, what you're saying is, boys will be boys?"

Major Boddington looked mystified by Noor's indignation. "Well, yes, as a matter of fact—what other explanation can there be?"

"If he read my letters, he must have read the letters of hundreds of agents," Noor whispered furiously. "And agent after agent has been arrested, and you don't believe Gilbert has something to do with it? Who led the Gestapo to Prosper's new apartment? And to Archambault? How did they find out where Renée Garry's safe house was? How did they find out about Grignon? And since then—" She pulled Émile's list from her pocket and smoothed it, keeping it below the tablecloth. "Phono gave me this list of agents on July 3. These are just the ones he has confirmed, but hundreds have been arrested. I don't know how many more of us have been taken away to the avenue Foch since he wrote the last name."

She glanced around, then down before slipping the paper into the major's hand.

Oh, merde! Edmond. The last code name Phono wrote on the list is Edmond. Merde!

Major Boddington scanned the names. His jaw tightened for a moment. Then he put it away and looked up. "My dear, it's unfortunate. Quite awful. You're not under the mistaken impression that we're unaware of the tragedy? Miss Atkins and I have been up night after night writing to the family of each captured agent, letting them know how concerned we are. Indeed, we're all praying for their safe return."

"I'm sure you are, sir. But today my name should be on a list of lost agents. Gilbert expected the Lysander to be shot down by the Germans—we're just very lucky it got home."

"Very lucky, indeed. The pilot was cool as a cucumber. You say Gilbert *expected* it to be shot down?"

"I believe so, sir."

"How do you know?"

"He showed no alarm, surprise, or fear when German night fighters suddenly appeared."

"He was on the ground, they were in the air—what did you want him to do? Turn into Superman? Your kind might wail and dance over calamity in India, Madeleine, but it's just not done here."

A waiter, Chaplinesque in a too-large suit and bulbous shoes, hovered and recommended. Major Boddington ordered *Poulet à la King* for two in passable but accented French.

"You could be mistaken for an RAF crew member, sir. Perhaps I should have ordered."

"Allow a lady to order? Nonsense. He understood me perfectly. Now, where was I? Yes—my, my, what a lot of questions! One gets quite feverish from thinking sometimes, and it can make one think one has all the answers, and worse, that all questions have the same answer." Major Boddington loosened his collar a little. "Each could have different answers," he continued in a fatherly tone. "And a single outcome can have multiple causes."

This seemed enlightened; she was willing to listen.

He set his glass down, looked directly into her eyes. "First, Prosper. Quite possibly the Nazis didn't know he had anything to do with us. I warned him to stay away from Communists, but he took a flat in a Communist neighbourhood. The Germans are executing Communists in droves—by the thousands. And when they got him, it must have been obvious, after a while, that he's one of us. Slight Cornwall accent, I do believe."

"But how did the Germans know when he would return from Trie-Château?"

"Have you been to Trie-Château recently? No, I thought not. There is only one train left, one train a day. Not too difficult."

"How did they know he was going there?"

"By following him, naturally. Thinking he was a Communist, you see."

"And Archambault?"

"We're convinced Prosper held out for at least twenty-four hours, then talked. No one can predict how an agent will react to torture."

Prosper tortured—please no, Allah!

But it did seem plausible.

"As for how they learned where Renée Garry's safe house was? I took an evening amble down the rue Erlanger and, I must say, that's an old cottage, an eyesore stuck between those lovely new buildings. Any neighbour looking down from the apartment buildings on either side might have taken note of the unusual number of strangers entering and leaving. The Gestapo could have received a denunciation from any opportunist."

This too seemed plausible. Monique had remarked on the hundreds of denunciations received at the Hôtel de Ville each day.

"And the Grignon roundup?"

Major Boddington sighed. "I'm sure Miss Atkins told you why we needed you to take over from Archambault. We needed a fresh radio operator, fresh codes, more secure transmitters. Archambault's had been in play for a dangerously long time. Old science—it was inevitable."

Miss Atkins discussed this with Noor. So had Archambault.

"Why not just arrest Archambault? Why a roundup?"

"We think when the Gestapo couldn't quite pinpoint the source of the signals, they decided to solve the matter with a roundup, a roundup that would frighten any students thinking of joining the Resistance. I have visited Mesdames Hoogstraten and Balachowsky, and the gardener showed me the greenhouse and shed. The metal roof of that greenhouse must have foiled German interceptor vans for quite some time, but time ran out."

"And this list? Nineteen arrests *after* the roundup at Grignon."

"We received messages from Archambault's transmitter for several days after Archambault was arrested. It could be Archambault being forced to send or someone using his code books. So it's quite possible those nineteen were arrested if Archambault carelessly allowed his code and message books to be found with his transmitter."

The wrong person is being accused of carelessness.

"Sir, you know Archambault had—all of us have—double security checks to authenticate his transmissions. There's a bluff check and a true check. If either is missing after each line, it means the transmitter is in enemy hands. And even if both checks are missed because we're in haste, the operators in London know our fists."

The Major's expression was inscrutable.

Noor plunged on. "Phono and I radioed The Firm to notify

you the day after Prosper and Archambault were captured. That should have told you transmissions from his radios could not be trusted. Two weeks ago I sent a message immediately, reporting the Grignon roundup and probable capture of his radio set and one of mine. Do you mean you have still been responding to messages from Archambault's set?"

"The messages were nothing out of the ordinary."

"The ordinary means requests for arms and money. We could have been responding to transmissions from the Germans asking for arms and money?" Noor was aghast.

"I suppose we may have. I brought a few canisters of explosives with me when I landed last week."

"But why?"

"'Yours not to question why,' my dear," the Major misquoted. *'Theirs but to do and die.'* Noor couldn't help thinking of the nineteen code names on her list.

"But we do have matters under control. The Hun doesn't know we know they have our transmitters, which is quite all right. All I want you to understand is, we need Gilbert—we need landing fields."

Major Boddington's half-revelations had the ring of raving lunacy. Noor wasn't calmed by his assurance that the SOE was in control of events, and of Gilbert. Wasn't calmed at all. The Major was suspiciously cheerful. But then, he hadn't fled Gilbert, dashed through a forest while escaping in the middle of the night, felt the terror of presenting false papers at checkpoints or gone underground for twelve days.

A bone china plate appeared before Noor. A chicken breast in a pool of sauce, like a ship run aground. Wet ashes, that's what each bite tasted like.

She glanced around at the other diners. The couple at the table in the opposite corner sat with a single omelette between them. They raised their glasses to one another and the woman leaned forward and cut it in two. They began to share, holding hands across the table.

Prosper, Archambault, Professor Balachowsky, twenty-five students, the eighteen poor souls on her list—nineteen with Edmond: they'd all be tortured, then taken to Mont Valérien and shot.

Why was it important that the Germans *not* know that the English knew it was the Germans operating captured radios? It could only mean that London wanted the transmitters in place for the Germans to receive and trust information, or misinformation, when the English sent it.

The couple who had shared an omelette began to count out money and ration tickets. The woman searched through her purse a long time.

It didn't take a genius to deduce what information Germany needed above all: information about the event that every resistant in England, France, America and Russia was so anxiously awaiting, the event for which canister upon canister of munitions and weapons was being dropped to resistants across occupied Europe, the event Germany had to avert and destroy, what Churchill had promised Stalin—the Allied invasion of the Continent. But why would the Germans be foolish enough to trust a single message received on any captured transmitter? Why did London think the Germans *would* trust messages they sent to those transmitters?

Too few tesserae to form any image of the unifying mosaic.

The couple was paying for the omelette. The woman's eyes followed each coin as it dropped into the waiter's pouch. They departed, and Noor continued probing.

"How could Archambault have prevented his code and message books from being taken with his transmitter? We leave our books hidden with the transmitter. Being caught with them at a checkpoint or in a search would be a disaster. And even if the transmitters were discovered, the Germans would need our encryption keys to decode the messages. They would need to know our code names and true names to know who was being discussed in the messages or to transmit and receive. And besides, they'd have to know our addresses so the Gestapo could arrest us. All this requires someone like Gilbert. Gilbert who meets us as we leave the plane, asks question after question and escorts us to our safe houses."

"A most interesting speculation, Mademoiselle Régnier. Quite the *roman à clef*. You write fiction, am I right? *Children's* fiction? Aired a story on the BBC, as I recall? I'm told you're quite accomplished. But I assure you, HQ has done its own thorough background check on Gilbert, and we are quite satisfied."

How the imperial "we" or Major Boddington could investigate Gilbert's actions when the transmitter beneath Noor's bed was the only remaining secure radio transmitting from northern France was the question. No messages concerning Gilbert had been received or sent by her. No, London hadn't investigated Gilbert. At most, Major Boddington had asked an acquaintance at his club if Gilbert was a good egg.

Major Boddington waved his fork. "This *poulet* would cost a fortune in London. That's if you could find one. Do you see, old girl? There are alternative explanations for every allegation you've pinned on poor Gilbert. Keep in mind that, thanks to the Luftwaffe, skilled pilots are scarce. Gilbert can assess a field in an instant, make sure there's enough taxi length, persuade each farmer that he should allow a foreign power to land its planes on his property. We can't sacrifice Gilbert on the hunch of a young miss." He dabbed his mouth, but a few morsels had already dropped on his tie. "And may I remind," he added, "it would do your brother's career no good if you were to do something disruptive."

Noor blinked, surprised. "Sir, there's no need to threaten."

"Not at all, my dear, not at all. Making a prediction, nothing more. We need you here—right skills, right time, right place and all that—but do me one favour, old girl: do curb your curiosity about the larger scheme of affairs. We absolutely must operate on a need-to-know basis."

The word "dismissed" seemed to dangle somewhere overhead, for having disobeyed Major Boddington's direct order to get aboard the plane. "Dismissed" was a good word, as was "discharged," a great deal better than "deserted." Life would be simpler; leave her here in Paris to begin a life of her own, forget the betrayals of her family, become mistress of herself. She'd return to Drancy, find work as a nurse, make Anne-Marie Régnier a permanent being. But Major Boddington didn't seem inclined to dismiss her.

"Try the Black Forest cake," he suggested. "Tell you what: I'll suggest to HQ, just so you don't become hysterical again, that you be set up with Marc. He'll be your air movements officer when you return."

Relief.

But Major Boddington hadn't mentioned when she was to return.

It was all right, really. He would continue to send money to Mother, and he'd have to provide francs for her survival expenses during the remainder of her mission in France.

Should she mention the diamonds? Tell him Prosper didn't have them when he was arrested, and that meant the Gestapo didn't have them either? She had transferred the leather pouch to the lining of a new valise; the diamonds were safe at Madame Aigrain's home. But something about the Major wasn't right. The syrup-shine eyes behind his glasses as he perused the menu?

Major Boddington wished to operate on a need-to-know basis. He didn't need to know, and she didn't need to tell him.

"Oh, and Madeleine—you may as well know, to show our appreciation for his courage and loyalty to the Crown, I've recommended Gilbert for the DSO."

The Distinguished Service Order? For Gilbert?!

His finality closed the subject.

"Please excuse me," said Noor. She shoved her chair back and picked up her handbag.

With the door of the WC shut tight, she gripped the sink as if to pull it from the wall and gulped back sobs. Anger flashing—no, rage. A decorated Gilbert would be trusted with more agents. So many more would be captured, many more tortured. Their beloveds wouldn't even receive censored postcards smuggled out of Drancy. Spies disappeared, spies were executed; all her warn-ings couldn't prevent it.

There would be no change in policy towards a man Major Boddington had introduced at his club and recommended for a DSO. Certainly not on the basis of accusations by a radio operator, a mere girl with colonial antecedents.

When the pale oval in the mirror had composed itself to mask the disturbance within, Noor drew herself to her full height.

Return to the table. Smile and thank Major Boddington for lunch, the francs, the ration tickets, the new safe house. Think.

Even if Major Boddington didn't intend to investigate Gilbert further before pinning a DSO on his chest, surely Colonel Buckmaster and Miss Atkins would.

Gilbert's duplicity would be discovered, his treachery exposed. Allah would see to it.

This game was being played with rules she could never have anticipated. She would adapt, move accordingly.

Pforzheim, Germany
June 1944

I have not had strength or will to write to you again till now, ma petite, though I have had pen and paper since February. From the tapping in pipes that pass between the walls, I learned it is the first day of June, and the autobahns are still choked with refugees from air raids on Munich.

I spent three weeks in the dungeon, fed soup once every three days and water each day. By the time I was carried back to my cell, I had lost most of my strength, but the words I'd scratched on the cell wall renewed my courage — "I resist, therefore I am."

Vogel came to visit me. He was travelling back to Paris from Munich, having attended the tenth anniversary celebrations of the Nazi organization for Mothers and Children. He brought more paper, a new fountain pen and ink. He was shocked by my state,

*though it was caused by his orders. He ordered soap, a toothbrush,
a larger ration of soup, toilet paper, even sanitary towels should I
need them. And weekly changes of prison uniform, weekly exercise
in the courtyard.*

*The governor of the prison approved. He came to inspect me with
Vogel, and I heard him mutter in French, so he meant for me to
know, that he'd never kept any woman in the dungeon before, never
kept anyone enchained, not even a murderer.*

The guard had to comply. I could see she didn't want to.

*And today another of Vogel's monthly visits, more regular than
the curse. He sat beside me on the cot, and I wondered how he could
stand my odour. He put his arm across my shoulders. I wished my
lice would crawl into his black uniform.*

"Your new uniform looks very smart, Herr Vogel."

*I couldn't say he looked smart, so I said the uniform looked
smart. He looked pleased.*

"I have been appointed an honorary member of the security
police. I can arrest anyone for defeatism."

"There is defeatism in Germany, Herr Vogel?" *I said sweetly.*

"Call me Ernst," *he replied automatically.* "No, no defeatism,
except from the weak—there are severe penalties for it."

*Vogel should try selling pork sausages to hadjis! Hitler can't out-
law his people's feelings. Even Vogel's certainty wavers these days, or
he wouldn't keep me as a hostage to be traded for his safety if—
when—the Allies are victorious.*

"How is your wife, Herr Vogel?"

*I emphasized the word "wife" slightly. He grew immediately
morose.*

"I found an apartment where she can live temporarily. The
entire building crumbled. It was the only one left on Rosenstrasse
after September's bombing—and after this raid it fell as if something devoured it from inside. How some suffocated and others were
crushed! We are still searching for bodies. I am lucky my children
are alive. Schwein! Flying above, dropping bombs on civilians! The
Führer should come and see us, see for himself what is happening."

"You started it," I wanted to say. I had been one of the civilians on whom the Germans dropped their bombs during the Battle of France. But I didn't. The man who had sent me to the dungeon for a small remark seemed to be criticizing his führer for ignorance, though absolving Hitler of any responsibility for rapacious aggression.

Vogel can show anger about injustice to Germans; they alone upon the planet are "people." Perhaps the bombs that destroyed his home were from your uncle's Lancaster. I do not know, but the possibility made me culpable for his family's homeless state. I am the eldest and always feel responsible for Kabir, for the actions he has committed and those he may have.

Vogel drew a picture of his wife and two children from his pocket. I have seen them before—his blonde wife who looks as beatific as a student "discovering" Sufism, his cherubic boys in short pants. Twins. Ten years old, as you might be today, ma petite. He said the one who looks like him is a naughty fellow, while the other is doing his part in the Hitler Youth.

"How can you tell them apart?" I asked.

"Sometimes it's difficult even for me to know which is which," he acknowledged. "I'm sending the younger one east to stay with a cousin, for the summer till we parade to Buckingham Palace. He'll be safe there. They had a small raid last February, but that must have been a mistake—there's nothing worth bombing in Dresden. The elder must stay to protect his mother from looters. They are everywhere now, many of them but a few years older than my son. Orphans of the war, most of them."

He showed me a copy of Munich's National Zeitung.

"We do not need more of Herr Goebbels's fairy stories, Princess. Here the Führer himself says soon London will be ashes."

"What will you do after that?" I asked, feigning concern for him, trying not to think of London in ashes.

"Return to Munich. The bank where I worked was owned by Jews, but now, Heil Hitler, it's back in German hands. They will give me a new position when we win the war." He had been listening to Nazi speeches again.

He said "Heil Hitler" the way I say "Peace be upon Him" for the Prophet, and to him there was nothing blasphemous about it. He believes Hitler is another messiah, whose only problem is the quality of his apostles. Fearing the dungeon again, I said nothing.

He said roughly, "Gilbert sends you his regards," and waited, watching my face.

I wanted to scream "Gilbert is a salaud! Un vrai con! Une ordure!" but I couldn't admit to knowing him. I turned a waxwork face to Vogel.

He slapped his gloves on his knee. "Read aloud, Princess."

I began reading the stories I'd written on onionskin. Vogel closed his eyes and I felt the one-second lag as he translated from English to German. It was a retelling of el-Rifai's "Wayward Princess," in which a king imprisons his daughter in a small cell to prove his will and law sufficient for justice and happiness to prevail.

"Gutt, gutt." Vogel swayed.

I wondered, as I told it, if his twins will ever understand the meaning of that tale.

Then I read a fable of my own, in which caged rabbits avenge themselves on rats, and another in which an Indian princess turns into a tigress and slays all the trappers who hunt her tiger for his claws.

Vogel listened, purblind to allegory, metaphor and symbol. He didn't count the sheets before he took them.

What fable will he fashion about his actions in this war?

Locked in my cell, once again I cannot celebrate Id-ul-Fitr with my family. I thank Allah he told the Prophet there need be no fasting for the ill. For I am ill indeed.

I should be celebrating—the Allies have invaded at last. The news came hidden in a basket of laundered clothes brought to a prisoner by her daughter. Tapped in Morse, it crossed lead pipes between cells. Whispered down air vents, it must even have percolated to the poor woman now consigned to my dungeon cell. Emboldened, we shouted the news from one cell to the next. We *sang, we hooted, we spat at the guards. My chains were of gossamer that day. The Germans feared we'd riot; the food trolleys didn't come that day. By nightfall we sobered.*

The English, English colonials and once-colonized Americans invaded on June 6, 1944. D-Day—our Dream Day. I don't know where they landed, but it is not, as the Germans expected, at the Pas de Calais. Messages racing in the walls say the Germans were surprised, overwhelmed; we hear they are retreating. I think of Prosper, of Archambault, of all the agents who gave so much for this day. Of Émile, who begged me to tell Colonel Buckmaster and Churchill that the Allies would have to invade and fight on the ground, not from the air. Is this Allied landing the crucial moment I felt coming?

No, it is only the beginning of a new phase of war.

News comes so slowly here. Our Morse messages say the Japanese invaded India two months ago, in March, using an army of Indian resistants led by Subhas Chandra Bose. Once upon a time Bose came to Afzal Manzil, to raise money to fight the British from "rich émigrés outside India." But Bose was an idol-worshipping Hindu, Uncle said, so Bose left him empty-handed.

Can we last till the Allies reach us? Where are the children of the mother who weeps for them each night? What will happen to the woman who worries for her old father, and the one who, like me, longs for her husband's arms?

Ramzaan should be the month when forgiveness is implicit in embrace, the month of repair, when wayfarers return home for Id, when one's load is shared with others by action or telling, and nightly the Tarawih prayer heightens the force between us and our creator. It should be a time when the weary stop to remember how it felt to be safe, when hope in humanity is replenished. At this time last year I took the Lizzie from Tangmere—so full of hope, I might have been flying a magic carpet.

By Id, that carpet had landed.

The third-storey apartment on the boulevard Richard Wallace was light and airy, with waxed parquet floors. A candlestick telephone

stood on a marble demi-lune table in the vestibule, an empty side-
board graced the dining room, a chandelier denuded of its crystal
swung in the grand salon. One chair and a Bokhara foot-carpet
remained. Major Boddington had omitted to mention the apart-
ment was otherwise unfurnished.

Thanks to Major Boddington, German officers and soldiers
lived above me, below me, walked the corridor between my apart-
ment and the lavatory. Yet he accused poor arrested Archambault
of carelessness, Archambault who was probably being tortured by
the Gestapo even while Major Boddington dined at Chez
Clément. I remembered Archambault not as the man of quiet effi-
ciency who trained me to transmit messages and watch for danger
signals but as a solo voice in the choir when Mother took us to
church in Suresnes.

A walnut tree grew past the window facing the Bois de
Boulogne, its limb close enough to string an aerial. This apartment
was no more than a transmission location and a letter drop.

Then I thought: perhaps it was part of London's plan that
I should be surrounded by Germans; no one would suspect me. I
wanted to trust Major Boddington — he was my superior officer, he
was privy to more than had been told me.

Today, I burn to know where I made my fatal mistake. The only
person who knew the telephone number at the Richard Wallace
apartment was Major Boddington, apologist for Gilbert. Could he
have told Gilbert and Gilbert told the Gestapo, who then traced the
telephone number?

When I ask Vogel, he says he'll tell me the day, the very
moment, I call him Ernst. So I may never know, unless the answer
comes some other way.

Downstairs, the concierge said the building was comman-
deered to billet German soldiers, but my apartment became vacant
when many of them left Paris to fight at Stalingrad. Later, it was
deemed too small for an officer, too large for a soldier. The German
who'd occupied it sold everything — paintings, sculpture, furni-
ture — before leaving. To whom did the apartment and its contents

belong before the Germans came, I asked. The concierge's eyes slid away. "*Je ne sais pas.*"

How could she not know?

From the tale of Monsieur Durand at Drancy, I knew the apartment must have been owned by Jews before the war.

Where are they now?

Two days later, Madame Aigrain's concierge called me to her telephone. Claude said Gabrielle had given him my telephone number.

And he said another convoy of buses left Drancy that morning, the morning of July 18. Nineteen hundred and forty-three years after the great Sufi master Jesu came to enlighten the world, organized Christian terrorists took more than a thousand people and loaded them on boxcars at Bobigny station because they were infidels.

Fear, my Abbajaan said, comes from oneself. If one expects harm, harm will come. He said you can bring about events not merely by wanting them but by fearing them. Had I brought about the very event I feared, by fearing it so deeply?

Claude couldn't tell me if Armand was one of the passengers on the convoy. He couldn't tell me if Armand was still at Drancy. He couldn't tell me where the train was going.

He just didn't know.

His tone was changing; the task he'd undertaken in a moment of sympathy was proving far beyond his powers. He had tried to impress me, but he was realizing how difficult it was, perhaps even impossible. The boy had wanted to be given the respect accorded to a man, had hoped to show a man's achievements. And now he really didn't care what happened to my "family friend"—he felt used. From my calls and inquiries he sensed, I'm sure, that this family friend was dearer to me than any in my family, and his enthusiasm seemed to ebb away.

I had used Claude—but for a good reason. Allah give me tauba, a good reason.

I sank to my knees in the foyer. The concierge made me sit down, dabbed water on my face.

Could Allah have brought me all this way only to send Armand away to Germany? Was there nothing more I could do?

One long year later, here in my cell, I continue to believe, believe stubbornly in the impossible . . . I refuse to believe Armand is in a place like this . . .

Armand, where are you now? Are you hungry, like me? Maybe you have found new friends, a new love because I said adieu. Maybe you have forgotten your Noor.

Still, be protected, surrounded, nourished by my love.

The guard served me oversalted soup and now ignores my cries for water. She's trying to break my will, will that grows more bloody-minded by the day.

My shackles have rubbed deep pink rings about my wrists and ankles. The ceiling leaks. I feel my hair growing, growing, my nails growing long and brittle.

Water. My tongue is a Persian slipper in my mouth, and she doesn't bring water.

I shout for water, a scrubbing cloth, soap, a tweezer, fishnet stockings, lipstick and perfume. I laugh, laugh like an idiot.

Now I write to keep myself from crying, begging.

I am descended from the Tiger of Mysore. Tigers do not beg.

Move into memory—where was I at this time last year?

Last year, both July 4 and Id came and went and I could not celebrate them with Dadijaan, Mother and Zaib, nor congratulate Kabir on his promotion. There was no news of my beloved; he and your grand-mère Lydia had disappeared. Almost every member of the network I had come to assist was in the clutches of the Gestapo at the avenue Foch, or imprisoned elsewhere. Major Boddington reassured about Gilbert, but I still felt like an actor who had rehearsed for the wrong play.

Weakened from the influenza, I had the curse. I cramped and bled as copiously as when Madame Dunet sucked your un-ensouled flesh from my womb. I was miserably angry at Madame Dunet's revelations. How could I have been so foolish as not to see

Mother's hand holding sixteen-year-old Zaib's, giving the money for my operation? I had not dreamed Madame Dunet's bigotry might coincide with my family's intentions. I was but a holder for my family's expectations.

What would I say when I met Mother and Kabir again, now my trust was shattered? Would I embrace them, kissing the air wide of ears that once heard my endearments? Perhaps I'd shake hands; both had shown themselves to be strangers to me. So just who were they when they weren't playing their roles? They meant well, I'm sure, but by what right had they chosen for me?

Everything was mixed up, everything going wrong.

I had volunteered for a supporting role. Suddenly I had become primary, even essential. What did I say to Miss Atkins? "Everyone is capable of self-governance." If that was really my credo, why was I now so terrified of operating alone, without someone to guide me, counsel me, lead me? All my life, elders and superiors had told me how to live, who and what to like, what to do, how to do it. And even if I didn't obey every injunction, my rebellions were small, mostly verbal. Always, I had seen myself as I "should be" not who I was.

Could anything Uncle taught guide me, anything help me to survive now? He had never foreseen his niece landing in occupied France, working for the British, tapping Morse messages to London about the plans and effects of battles.

What and who should I be now?

My first day in Paris, I thought I could "make my own instructions and follow them." How simple it seemed then to give myself advice. No one had taken innocent people away on buses, no one in my network had been arrested, no one had torn apart Renée's home, people had not been rounded up and—possibly—executed before my eyes, I had not wounded or killed any SS men, aeroplanes had landed and taken off again without being shot at. And through it all, I never believed my own mother or Kabir could betray me, choose for me, to serve their own purposes.

After all that, what instructions could I make for myself?

Who should I become now?

The unmitigated present, with all its possibility of meeting the Archangel of Death at any moment and living in separation from my love forever, was far from my idealistic ideas of "doing my bit" for the pursuit of justice, with a preordained "happily ever after." I had longed to hold Armand again, talk to him, tell him I love him, and instead I was all intention with no hope of success, all resolve without execution.

What use was anything I had done? I didn't even know if Armand still cared for me. How foolish to believe he would recall my tiger claw, or that my note would convey meaning, should he receive it. My beloved deserved that I write him a book, not just a few words.

Allah was asking too much of me. Much too much.

I could not help it; I lay alone in Madame Aigrain's room without Armand to hold me and I became a child again, weeping, weeping all night. I wanted the mother who would brave the world for me and Zaib when we were small, the one who hadn't cared if she and Abbajaan lived on bread and water, the one who read me fairy tales she'd read as a child. I wanted the loving, generous-spirited brother I once had, the Kabir I once knew. I wanted Dadijaan's teaching tales, her fighting spirit. Even Zaib—anyone of my own.

I cried a pool of tears. They let me cling to my troubles for a while.

Then at dawn each motion of my Fajar prayers reminded me to praise and thank Allah I was alive, healthy again, having recovered from the influenza that had claimed Abbajaan. I was not in want, not fighting in the jungles of Burma or crossing an African desert. Though I had been forced to flee my home I was not forced into hiding as Armand, Monsieur Durand, Émile, Monique, Renée and little Babette had been.

I was not being starved in India, I was not deported.

I was not the only woman—or man—whose beloved had disappeared. When his master disappeared, Jalaluddin Rumi was transformed into love itself and, though far from the physical form of his beloved, became sure they were one single light. So too, I became stubbornly sure my love, my husband, was alive. And that he, who called me to my highest self yet loved me even after learning of your body's destruction at my hand, who loved me dearly for almost nine years though we could not be married in the eyes of the world, still cared for me. That I was bleeding meant my body was sound, that Armand and I can re-create ourselves in you, despite Madame Dunet's ministrations and intentions.

That morning I did a zikr of gratitude that I had not been arrested by the Gestapo, gave thanks that Allah had saved me from their clutches, saved me from execution, not once but three times. How dare I still fear death?

When Kabir and I were small and grieving for Abbajaan, Mother explained death in a comforting way. Endless sleep, that is death, she said.

Your father said once that the world will never finish arguing if there is an afterwards. To him, there is no such thing. He is no Café de Flore existentialist, but a seeker for the source of his creativity. He said it could be that we live and vanish like music into air. He loved the idea in the Zohar that one's body is a kinnor, letting a divine melody vibrate through it till one day the melody comes to its end.

As for me, life is an obstacle course like the ones Josianne and I rode in the Bois, and death the final jump to which I am riding my body headlong against time, a dark wall hiding a great trench, and just when I say "Un, deux, allez-hop!" my horse will balk, pull up short, digging its front legs into friable soil. And I'll go over the wall, into the trench, alone.

When I was afraid—of heights, of dogs, of any man who shouted at me—Abbajaan would remind me he had named me Noor, Light of the Soul. The light required to dispel the world's fear. But I never aspired to dispel the world's fear, I just needed to dispel my own. When that fear was gone, Armand said, I could compose my own life and live within its music.

My mind shifted like a restive horse. All night I moved and retreated from my options, like mercury. My neck and shoulder muscles were taut as veena strings.

By dawn in Madame Aigrain's closet room I began to think more clearly. I realized something I must remember here in my cell today: as long as I live, I must use every advantage Allah has given me.

I could not yearn for the mother and brother I once had when the Noor they knew as daughter and sister was no more.

If every man or woman dies only at an appointed hour—then of what use is it to fear? The Sufis say we should "die before we die," facing the world without renouncing it or declaring it all illusion, so that when the Archangel of Death comes, we will be ready and eager.

I reminded myself the greatest of Sufis, Al-Hallaj, suffered nine years of torture and trial, suffered his hands and feet to be cut off, and then was crucified. Execution at the hands of the Gestapo is not the worst that can happen.

What is worse is not resisting injustice. What is worse is denying that Allah created suffering that we may learn.

If I could not reach or help Armand directly, I could help the Allies overthrow the Germans who held him. If I could not prevent Gilbert's betrayals, I could at least ensure that this agent wouldn't be turned in.

My future was racing to meet the present, but now there was work to be done. Émile had said that a radio is a better weapon than any gun. I would use my radios. I was trained and eager. They would stave off helplessness.

Jacques Viennot was the only member of my cell still at large. I would offer him my services. I'd tell him I could operate radios for the Free French. Gilbert would expect me to contact other SOE cells, so the more I worked with the Free French, the better my chances of evading him. And Miss Atkins had told me, "We do co-operate with the Free French, when we have to."

Even with these precautions, Gilbert might still find me. Might still turn me in. But I could pretend to be brave; how can anyone tell the difference?

Madame Aigrain's home was just a cachette, not a true maison cachée—a real safe house from where I could transmit. I could transmit from the new safe house Major Boddington had rented, but I couldn't sleep there. I could transmit from Madame Gagné's boarding house in Drancy and sleep there; only Émile knew that location.

I'd have a better chance of evading Gilbert and the Gestapo if I transmitted from the boulevard Richard Wallace and Drancy but turned nomad, sleeping at a different location every night. I needed one more safe house not far from Madame Aigrain's, somewhere I could receive, code and decode in safety, and sleep at night.

I had said to Major Boddington: "I need to work with people I can trust." If he could not recommend any beyond Gilbert, I would have to find my own friends. I would step off the stage and write my own script, find fellow actors, direct our own play.

No matter what Miss Atkins had told me in London, no matter what the SOE *handbook said, I could see only one choice: to find people I could trust, I must break cover.*

I would return to Suresnes and contact someone with whom I shared my earliest memories—Josianne.

With Josianne, I never had to explain origins or allegiances. Josianne understood the premises of Sufism though she was Catholic. She had learned of Islam, having travelled in Algeria as a child. She understood and respected that I tried never to disappoint my family. She never thought of us as "different" and "exotic"; we were a part of her childhood. Though she had never travelled to India, and probably never will now, she took epicurean delight in Dadijaan's sweet daals and kachoris. A beneficiary of colonization—but then, so were most of the French bourgeoisie—at least Josianne always acknowledged it.

I felt sure of Josianne's sentiments, but Josianne could have married and moved away in three years. If she still lived with her mother, Madame Prénat, in Suresnes, I would need to gauge where Madame's political sensibilities might lie. I knew Madame almost as many years as my mother—but that, I now felt, meant little. A friendship from another time, an era of plenty, with no war, no real dangers to test Madame's principles. But she was proud. She wouldn't have become resigned to the Occupation. She wouldn't be afraid to offer her home. But what if she had placed her trust in Pétain and truly believed his surrender had averted France's complete destruction? Then I wouldn't ask for shelter. I'd say I was back to check on Afzal Manzil, and in private, ask Josianne to help me find another safe house.

With this plan, I would return—return to where I began.

PART FIVE

CHAPTER 28

Suresnes, France
Monday, July 19, 1943

NOOR ALIGHTED at the Val d'Or trolley stop at a little past ten in the morning. Fear currents flowed from the nape of her neck and branched across taut shoulders, down to the hand gripping the suitcase transmitter and the other looped through the handle of her handbag. Her sunglasses were slipping; she adjusted them.

See and do not be seen.

She wore Monique's slacks again, because she had never worn slacks all her years in Suresnes. And a chignon; she'd rarely worn one while living at Afzal Manzil.

She could have walked directly up the rue de la Tuilerie to the green gates at the top of the hill, but in case Gilbert or anyone else was following her, she detoured through the coil and branch of Suresnes streets.

Read the landscape, read every lane.

Everything familiar must be seen with a sceptical eye. Poplar leaves jangled SOE handbook warnings at every corner: someone would recognize her, someone would notice she had returned. She paced streets that ran at forgotten purposes, and intersected seemingly at random, trying to understand herself as foreign even to this, the peripheral town she once called home. Foreigner. Foreign-born. She could be deported to a camp in a minute.

She turned towards the central square.

The *mairie* should have had swastika banners draped over its façade as at Grignon—but all that remained of the stately old building was a gaunt, skeletal outline.

Past a hedgerow at the corner of the square, helmeted heads and shoulders glided with not a single bob above some imaginary plane—German soldiers marching past.

She doubled back and forth through the little town. Bombs, German or Allied, had damaged the locks on the Seine, but the Pont de Suresnes, rebuilt after the 1870 war, was intact. Little girls wearing bows in their braids swung bare legs from windowsills of shell-pocked apartment ruins. The Coty *parfumerie* was busier, sleeker. Employees came and went from the Radiotechnique buildings. Little boys got their knickers wet in the stone fountain at La Place du Marché, as mothers and grandmothers scolded.

Surprising that Émile Zola's bust still stood before the municipal library; he should be alive today to defend more falsely accused Jews. Avoid the library—many an hour spent there, with Armand. Avoid the shops too.

In the *buvette* on the rue de la Huchette, a few German soldiers were gathered around a radio, but only a few—some messages she sent mentioned entire divisions being sent to fight Russia now.

At the Café Val d'Or, where she had so often met Armand in secret, waiters were wiping tables and polishing wineglasses, readying for lunch. Scarlet tablecloths ballooned and flowed from deft hands, as if to enrage bulls. Outside the *tabac*, men discussed the odds on favourites at Longchamp. Not one gave her a second look as she passed—but why should they? They weren't looking for her. Everyone was engrossed in their own affairs.

Afzal Manzil was still carved into the marble slab beside the green gates of her family home. Was this really where a little girl, then a young woman, called Noor had lived?

The rue de la Tuilerie was now Neu Rosenstrasse. In place of the hastily painted *British Property* sign, nailed to the green gates in 1940, was a black-and-white sign saying something in German.

She should have expected this. Renaming was ever the colonizer's way in India too; the Germans were simply extending the "favours" of colonization to Europe. But she hadn't expected it, and it irked her that she hadn't, and a "little thing like that," as Londoners would call it, was suddenly meaningful, sinister, one more example of German inhumanity.

The Sufis say one's true home is a place with a name but no precise address. How many times did you say that to yourself when you lived in this "house of peace" that became your House of Grief?

She must try to imagine the homesickness of the German bureaucrat who had renamed rue de la Tuilerie. Imagine a civil servant far from home who longed for his family living in, say, Berlin, Hamburg or Munich on a street called Rosenstrasse.

Too charitable. The German bureaucrat was probably now living in Paris, might even be billeted on Neu Rosenstrasse, in Afzal Manzil, occupying her old home with other Germans.

Circling back on Neu Rosenstrasse to the top of the hill, Noor stopped before a modest red-brick house sitting beside its enclosed garden, patches of ivy climbing the stone walls. The wall was a costly endeavour and a nuisance to maintain, but Josianne's father built it because his father had built one and his grandfather before him. Behind it he kept his wife and children, before it and its buffer space of garden, the world. Josianne's father, a colonist in Algiers, died a year after Abbajaan, and at the lycée teenage Noor offered Josianne the comfort of a Petite Beurre biscuit at break time, and listened as Josianne talked about her father's liver disease.

With no elder brothers, only younger sisters and a brother who left at eighteen to run the family vineyards in Algeria, Josianne was the one friend approved by Uncle, the only one Noor was allowed to visit in her home. To Josianne, then, Noor confided all the restrictions placed upon her. And Josianne endeared herself to Mother, obtaining permission for Noor. Together they had cantered through the Bois, attended open-air concerts beneath the metal girders of the Eiffel and roamed the Louvre. Later, it was Josianne who noticed, well before Noor herself was aware of it, that in the daily tide of Sorbonne students, Noor's face glowed only for Armand.

Since her family's flight from Afzal Manzil, the "next-door neighbours," as Mother called them, had installed louvred windows and heavy curtains for blackout. Was anyone within?

Kneeling as if to adjust her shoe buckle, Noor glanced over her shoulder. No one on the street seemed interested in her. No one on the street resembled Gilbert. She straightened, unlatched the low gate in the wall. Beyond it, all the doors would be open; this was, after all, Suresnes, not Paris.

Josianne's rusty bicycle with its painted wicker basket leaned against the wall. Noor let herself in. From an open window she spotted bony Madame Prénat, under a veiled hat in the back garden, supervising a gardener raking the prongs of a *binette* into soft earth. Noor wandered into the drawing room to wait.

Josianne's oil paintings, still on every wall. The same three chairs in the drawing room: the armchair for Josianne's departed father, Madame Prénat's straight-backed chair and Josianne's.

Josianne's chair felt just right.

Josianne entered, carrying a porcelain bowl. Bobbed hair— three years ago it was long. A crisp pastel-blue linen dress, real stockings and platform shoes.

Josianne looked, and looked again. Then dropped the bowl with a great crash and let out a scream.

Noor jumped up and clapped her hand over Josianne's mouth. But Madame Prénat came running, casting back her veil. She turned Camembert-pale and sank into a chair.

An electric rush of sheer gratitude and relief came over Noor as Josianne's arms tightened around her. She came to tears, embracing Josianne and Madame Prénat in return. She was no longer alone.

A great mess of shattered porcelain and oatmeal had to be swept away and mopped up, the linen dress had to be spot cleaned and powdered. Twenty minutes later, all the exclamations hushed and questions began to flow.

Madame Prénat said she'd lost all respect for the Germans after their invincible General Rommel was routed at El Alamein. Their Thousand Year Reich wouldn't last another year, she scoffed. "And you and others who escaped to the Riviera after the bombardments cannot imagine how humiliating life has been here."

Emboldened by her words, Noor said, "We didn't go to the Riviera, we escaped to England. Kabir and I joined the airforce. Now I'm with the Résistance Service des Renseignements."

The Information Service. Madame Prénat's face, all planes and angles above her lace collar, wore a look of amazement mixed with agitation as she took this in.

"That's all you need to know." Noor sounded determined, sure. Like a woman, not a girl, as she asked if Madame would take her in, give her a place to sleep, understanding the dangers involved? And a place to transmit?

"And no questions," Noor added.

There was a weighty silence. Josianne's hazel eyes gazed at Noor in wonder. Madame Prénat was hesitating. It was plain she really didn't want to get involved; the Occupation had probably rearranged every person's relationships as if they were anagrams.

Pretend to be brave; no one can tell the difference.

"There have been many executions, Noor," said Madame.

From Madame's expression Noor could tell she still thought Noor the trembling young girl she used to know.

"At Mont Valérien," added Josianne. "They began soon after the old town crier came on his bicycle, rapping his double-faced drum, with the Ortskommandantur's instructions for Suresnes. Fusillades sound almost every morning now."

"Mostly godless Communists, *je sais*," said Madame Prénat. "But the guns! If we are caught helping you—"

"Godless Communists, Maman?" said Josianne. "Each condemned man spends his last night before he is shot *in the chapel*. The Germans just call every resistant a Communist."

Josianne's sense of justice—strong as ever! But Madame Prénat must make her decision. To her generation Noor was not French, British or American, but Indian—via her very brown, bearded and kaftaned Abbajaan. Indians might be subjects of the British Raj, but to Madame they were not allies but from a not-Europe area, like Algeria, an area marked "Past here there be monsters" as on maps of old. Indians, whether living in or out of French Pondicherry, were subject to the European *mission civilisatrice*.

But Josianne's sense of justice stemmed from Madame Prénat's; Noor waited hopefully.

"Don't chew the ends of your hair, Noor," said Madame. "I still have to tell you that, or is it just because your maman is not here? *Attends!* Does Madame Khan know what you're doing?"

Madame Prénat was susceptible to Mother's ingratiating charm, a charm Mother had lavished on her, for Madame, a widow with a steady income from her husband's well-invested Algerian fortune, epitomized Mother's social aspirations. So much so that, years ago, Madame Prénat (completely ignoring that Mother was Christian) said that if *she* could live peacefully side by side with Muslims in Paris, French *colons*—colonizers— in Africa could live in peace with Muslims. If Noor said that her mother was aware of what she was doing, Madame Prénat would open her home.

So Noor said yes, Mother knew. But quickly added, "Madame, I insist on paying rent. Then you can deny knowing me at all. I will be a stranger who came to rent a room—nothing more."

With Josianne nodding her bobbed head vigorously, Madame Prénat sighed yes.

And she would accept a token rent. She had been considering renting a room to a student, anyway. Every day, Madame said, she inquired at the post office, but no letters or money were coming from Algiers since the Allied defeat of Vichy forces. "Perhaps you can radio your superiors," she said, "tell them to wire my son; perhaps they can find a way to send me my money?"

Noor offered her a maybe-smile.

She carried her suitcase transmitter upstairs to Josianne's room. Josianne leaned against the windowsill, lit a cigarette and crossed her Dietrich legs.

"How long since you returned to France?"

"About a month and a half," answered Noor, surprised by how much she had missed Josianne.

"And this is the first time you've come to see us? For shame, Noor!"

Noor laughed—the first time she had laughed freely since she left England.

Josianne was delighted that Zaib was studying to be a doctor, and not one bit surprised to hear of Kabir's flying in the RAF and his promotion. Where were the friends they had known at the lycée and the Sorbonne? Josianne checked them off: married, married, married. As if marriage cut each girl's life short. Which girls supported Pétain, which were secret Gaullistes? What of their husbands' political leanings? Were any still single? Very few.

Few girls ever meet a man who can enlarge the soul, so they make do with a man who can enlarge their stomachs.

One had become a nun. And there was Josianne.

"I'm teaching, but only till I can get married . . . Sometimes I think my resistance is simple: I refuse to be sad, angry or unhappy. . . *Écoute!* I have one special proposal that interests me . . . You don't know him, but he is the son of a *colon* family . . . I'm considering it, but I would have to live in Algiers—can you imagine leaving Paris? Oh, of course you can, because you had to. But voluntarily? Ah, but London is also the centre of the universe, non? And also, poor Maman, how can I leave her alone?"

The young man's great-grandfather and Josianne's had together cleared their three hectares of land (confiscated from Arabs, Josianne wryly noted) in the days when the French government was giving Frenchmen 1,200 francs, aid, free grains and free passage; and the young man was very eligible, having turned the property to viniculture.

"Maman says if I marry him, it won't be for long—I'd be a supporter of Ferhat Abbas or some other radical and he'd send me home to live with her. But until recently he sent me postcards and letters from Algeria, always asking . . ." She turned a little, cigarette in hand; smoke gusted from the window.

Tremendous fighting had taken place across Algeria, but Josianne didn't seem particularly anxious for her *colon*. For Josianne, all men were flawed but alike in their need for Josianne; she was still single because her difficulty lay in choosing. Whereas Noor found her Armand at seventeen, and ever since needed and wanted no other.

"*Et toi?* You have a new amour? English, perhaps?"

"Yes, he's in the navy."

"Oh, I must hear all about him."

Noor would have to invent a whole fantasy Englishman, but later.

"And Armand?"

Noor told her about the cards she had received in London.

"*Mon Dieu*, at Drancy!"

This stopped Josianne as if Armand were one of their school friends who had married. So Noor wouldn't tell her she had been to Drancy or say anything about sending Armand a message and her tiger claw. She would be silent about her morbid fears, her anxiety, her waiting, hoping to learn if Armand was still there or deported to Germany. She had put Josianne and Madame Prénat in enough danger without revealing details of her connection to an internment camp.

Josianne tucked her hair behind her ears, as if demonstrating how Noor should listen. "Anyone can be arrested for any reason, and without reason. Even Henri Sellier. He's still at Compiègne."

Something shrank within Noor. The mayor of Suresnes—popular, progressive, even powerful. The similarity to Armand brought no comfort. Unless—

"When was he arrested?" she asked.

"Oh, about this time last year—no, the year before. Yes, the summer of '41."

"And he is at Compiègne? Still there? Not sent to Germany?"

"Oui, oui. You remember his wife? He sends her a label every month, and she sends him a parcel."

Someone Jewish was still in a camp, still able to send word to his wife.

Noor felt light enough to dare anything. She placed her suitcase on Josianne's bed and thumbed it open.

"This is what women are wearing in London? It looks just like our lingerie," said Josianne, holding up a frothy satin slip.

"It's French. A soldier ordered me to open my suitcase on the métro this morning. I told him it was a cinematograph—he believed me! *Mon Dieu*, when I thought what could have happened, I was so nervous! I stopped at Galeries Lafayette to buy this as camouflage—my own went to England by mistake a few days ago. Josianne, may I borrow some clothes?"

"*Toujours, mon amie.*" Josianne pointed to a chest of drawers in the corner.

She gazed at the dials and wires of the transmitter, then looked up at Noor. "*You* know how to make this work?"

Josianne declined, positively refused, to understand anything with levers, dials or switches. She probably still couldn't drive a car, and even had trouble using a telephone. The transmitter was of no interest, but the code books and encryption keys intrigued her. Noor explained they were like the Rosetta stone.

"You want to learn how to decipher the messages?" said Noor. "I could teach you—it wouldn't take you more than a few hours to learn. You could assist me."

"*Bien sûr!* You remember, non? I love secret messages."

"Shhh!" said Noor, as if Uncle Tajuddin had some special hearing device that could listen all the way from India.

But yes, Josianne had carried messages between Armand and Noor, to and from Afzal Manzil, right under Uncle's nose. What would Josianne, her closest friend, say today if she knew the truth about Noor's "stomach operation"? If she suspected it, she had never said so. What would she say if told of Madame Dunet, and five thousand francs, and Noor's years of shame and pain? Josianne would no doubt keep her secret, but—

"Shhh!" said Noor again, more for herself.

Josianne moved her nightstand against the window. Noor placed the transmitter on it, stringing her aerial out, twining it through the ivy. The fragrance of quince at the edge of Afzal Manzil's garden mingled with Josianne's Chanel.

Afzal Manzil was just her house, not really a home.

Mother often said of Afzal Manzil: when people give you gifts, you have to live with their choices. It had wounded Dadijaan's pride to learn the house was donated by a benefactor, a bourgeois woman who found peace in Sufism and the comfort of a direct relationship with a universal God.

Branches and weeds tangled on the stone walls between the adjoining gardens. A rusty barbed wire was strung along the top—by the Germans, Josianne said. A riot of colour clustered around the oak tree; Abbajaan's transplanted flowers were holding their own.

The garden grotto. Abbajaan standing there again in a long cream-and-gold kaftan. The guests were there again. The music, the clapping. Abbajaan unfolded a man-size pashmina shawl for everyone to see. Embraced ten-year-old Kabir. Drew back. The shawl remained, draped across Kabir's shoulders. Twelve-year-old Noor sitting in the audience between Mother and Zaib. Kabir looking down at her, his changed expression. Something had reversed who was elder, who was younger, who gave permission and who must ask.

Behind her a chair scraped, distracting her momentarily.

Back to looking at the garden. But Abbajaan, Kabir and all the guests had vanished into the present.

Her gaze climbed to the door set at the top of its walrus-moustache staircase. She saw herself at thirteen, fourteen, seventeen. Standing again at the mouth of its darkness.

Noor closed her eyes and let imagination turn the walls of Afzal Manzil to glass. On the ground floor the rooms flowed around a central courtyard.

Remember happy times.

She was back in Abbajaan's recital room, sitting cross-legged on frayed kilims as Abbajaan taught her to play the veena, though he'd long since given up performing and composing himself. "*Dil mein Ali, mere man mein Ali Ali.*" She was listening to Amir Khusrao *qawallis* sung over the ripple and pulse of the harmonium by visiting singers from India. She was at the chess table across from Abbajaan, she was playing hide-and-seek with Kabir and Zaib, she was learning namaaz along with Mother, she was pulling on white stockings and gloves to attend church with Mother.

But other memories came unbidden. She had opened the front door for an unrelated man and she was confined in her room, crying. She was wearing a pair of red shoes borrowed from Josianne; Uncle was shouting, she was kicking them off, running to her room. She was reading in an upstairs room and Uncle Tajuddin was standing at her bookshelf, and her books were flying like birds from the window, fluttering, slapping down into mud.

Discovering love, perhaps not enough love for Allah but certainly love for Armand. Like Dom Pérignon discovering champagne—as if she were drinking stars. She was tiptoeing downstairs to sneak out without Uncle seeing her, she was slipping in unseen, she was standing by the telephone, whispering. She was standing in the bathroom looking into the mirror, wondering what in the world to do, where could she go, how could she start the bleeding again.

Back through Madame Dunet's recent revelations, back to now. Noor's eyes opened wide.

Downstairs, the gardener came in with a basket of newly dug beets, and the same mouse of a maid who had worked under Madame Prénat's thumb for years greeted Noor as if she had never left, and washed the beets for lunch.

In honour of Noor's return, Madame now took over the kitchen. Josianne helped her cut the tops and bottoms from the purple bulbs, and a caramel fragrance filled the house as Madame Prénat roasted them over a gas flame, then tossed them in sour cream, dill and lemon juice to balance sweet and sour. Once grace was said, they tasted like the concentrated sweetness of the earth. Josianne declared the bread a little dry and paste-soft in the middle—the firewood could have run out beneath the baker's oven, she said—but when served with wedges of Camembert and a bottle of Domaine Suresnes, it was delicious.

Neck and shoulder muscles relaxed, breathing came easier. Gilbert didn't know she was here, no one of the SOE knew either. She could receive and transmit here. She could trust Josianne and Madame Prénat—far more than Gilbert and Major Boddington, anyway.

She had made the right decision to contact Josianne, though it ran counter to Miss Atkins's instructions. It felt right, even if the SOE handbook might someday list contacting old friends while on assignment under "Where Operatives Go Wrong."

CHAPTER 29

Paris, France
Tuesday, July 20, 1943

A MESSAGE LEFT FOR ODILE, asking her to "keep in touch with Uncle Viennot," arranged a rendezvous at Madame Millet's *pâtis-serie*. Here, Viennot pointed out, the three tiny tables were wiped clean every hour and it was still possible to find sugar cubes with one's *café filtre*, and even sometimes—though not today—a cup of Ceylon tea. A few streets away, afternoon light played on tea-brown waves, and bridges hunched, catlike, from Left Bank to Right. Over the embroidered half-curtains Noor could see but not hear a restaurant tout outside, tantalizing passersby.

"The food may be expensive, but you can talk freely—as freely as you can anywhere in Paris." Viennot laughed as if amused by lunatic times.

He had addressed her as *tu*, a familiarity she did not reciprocate.

A honey-coloured toy poodle rested its head on its paws and listened to an animated discussion between its owner, an elderly gentleman in a polka-dotted bow tie, and a little girl of about five sitting with her mother at the table beside Viennot. The poodle's leash lay in artistically arranged coils beside the gentleman.

A sailor or a retired navy man.

The gentleman closed a leather-bound copy of *Candide* to show the little girl his knitted purse.

A scholar of the Enlightenment.

The girl danced around Noor and Viennot to ask her mother if she could knit one like it. The prospects of holding a whispered conversation were nil.

Noor pulled a fringed lace stole close about her shoulders and sat erect, responding to the finery she'd found in Josianne's dresser drawers.

"I remember this *pâtisserie* when ribboned bonbons perched on every shelf and filled baskets, when white, dark and milk chocolates clustered on trays. Madame Millet made the best chocolate éclairs in Paris. But now!" Viennot's bushy black brows wagged; he shrugged his disgust. "Everything is just beyond reach."

She wasn't sure whether he was discussing prices or the prospects for liberation from the Germans.

"Why couldn't they invade France?" he muttered.

He meant the Allies, who, instead of invading France "before the leaves fall," had invaded Sicily. The BBC was now using the word "conquered." *Paris Soir* had reported German "difficulties" in Russia, while the BBC said the Germans were almost in retreat from Kursk.

"I want this war over soon," he said.

Noor had an urge to suggest his schedule for the war be published in *Paris Soir*. "They could still invade France," she said.

"It's enough. Too many celebrities in Paris—the Abwehr, the Wehrmacht, the STO, the Gestapo, the Gestapistes. And you, Phono's celebrity from London. Anne-Marie, code name Madeleine."

Madame Millet patrolled the passage behind the counter like a German sentry on guard, though the labels—*pâté de canard à l'orange, fond d'artichaut saint-fiacre, pâté de veau au jambon, ballottine de lapin au foie gras et aux pistaches*—all described empty shelves.

"It's too difficult," said Viennot. "I can't remember real names, and now everyone who is anyone has a code name the British call a *nom de guerre*. If a writer has a *nom de plume*, does anyone try to remember his real name? Forget your real name, I'll call you Madeleine."

Noor ordered only a café noir because Viennot said the heart-shaped palmiers and the few petits fours on display looked far better than they tasted. Her SOE funds had dwindled now that she had reimbursed Madame Aigrain and begun paying rent at Madame Prénat's.

"And it's not only names! Every project has fifteen passwords, and if I forget one, I could be shot by my own friends. I'm going to change my business after the war, Madeleine. If it ends by 1950, I'll give some money to the Church. Maybe I'll even go to confession."

After eating a hundred mice, the cat makes a hadj to Mecca.

"And I'm going to have fewer customers," Viennot continued. "I'll still be an intermediary—but for cars. Bugattis, when the Italians return from their holiday with Herr Hitler. Monsieur Bugatti never sold to just anyone, *tu sais?* He interviewed each potential customer before he sold a single car. I'm just like him. Very discriminating about my customers—and the resistants I work with. No English—except for working with Phono."

Viennot, in sultry July, still affected his trademark brown silk scarf, black onyx brooch and beret, complete with ribbon tassel. Noor's soapy coffee arrived, and for him a crème caramel with a biscuit planted in it like a sword in stone. He removed the biscuit and presented it to her with a *"Mange bien, mademoiselle,"* urging her to eat.

"You've lost weight," he said with a disapproving look at her breasts.

Viennot knew of the arrests of Prosper, Archambault and Professor Balachowsky. And he had received a message from Odile about the Gestapo search of Renée's safe house, and later another about the Grignon roundup.

"I thought by now our pretty little war tourist would have gone home."

"I have not, though I was ordered to leave."

Viennot's bushy black brows rose into question marks. "It is one thing to know events, another to be told the details." He drew his chair closer than she would have liked. *"Alors, commence!"*

Noor lightened her coffee with a powder of substitute cream and began speaking low, trimming and editing her analysis of events as she went. The story of the roundup at Grignon was told without the shooting but with her suspicions of Gilbert. She told of her meeting with Phono without mentioning she had given him her pistol. In telling Viennot of her refusal to return on the Lysander, she had to discuss Gilbert's suspicious chess notation habits and his reading her letters, but she didn't mention foiling Gilbert's post-dinner plans in case Viennot decided on plans of his own. What she left out was almost as important as—perhaps more important than—what she told.

Cigarette in one hand, spoon in the other, Viennot asked only a few questions.

The gentleman at the next table produced a pack of cards, shuffled and fanned them out, and the little girl selected a king of hearts. The mother left her table and joined them, to watch as the magic began.

"Odile tells me you are anxious to resume transmissions. For us. One question: why?"

Beside them, the little girl began counting to ten.

"You need a radio operator. I have a radio. I'm trained for it. And I have a safe house from which to transmit."

"Where?"

"In Paris," she said, deliberately vague. Her current addresses at Mesdames Aigrain, Prénat and Gagné's would remain secret, along with the location of the apartment at the boulevard Richard Wallace.

"Is it secure?"

"As secure as any other place."

"We need money."

"Yes. My information is that London has resumed drops." She told Viennot of her meeting with "a highly placed man from London" and his reassurances, without mentioning that she was almost positive the Germans, with full knowledge of the British, were using captured transmitters to request arms and money from the Allies.

"Do *you* have enough money?" His tone seemed to hold genuine concern.

"Yes." She wouldn't say how much. If she really needed a loan, she would ask Josianne.

"Then buy yourself some clothes. Dowdy clothes make any woman your age look German or English. The Gestapo will pick you up and send you either to Berlin or Besançon if they see you walking around dressed like *that*."

Noor flashed him a look of annoyance. "This is a new hat. New slacks. Both are French."

"The hat is *très chic*. The slacks make you look American. The blouse—too masculine. You need some jewellery. Perhaps it is your hair—you should get a permanent. Put on more powder. Your lipstick is a shade too light for your colouring. *Ma fille*, when you need money, you come to Jacques Viennot, *d'accord?*"

She would throw her hat at him. But no. Instead, she wouldn't say a word about the diamonds she had secreted in her valise at Madame Aigrain's. At this rate Viennot might tell her to sell them and use the money for clothes and a permanent. He'd tell her to go shopping as her contribution to the welfare of the country.

Viennot puffed to the left, licked his spoon to the right.

"Never mind my hair and clothes," said Noor. "You haven't commented about anything I've said. Is it not terrible?"

He gave a great sigh. "Everyone knows what can happen. In my experience one is usually suspicious of the wrong person."

"In your experience! You're only a few years older than me, I think."

"Yes, but I have a lot more experience, mademoiselle. You're a little too beautiful to be intelligent as well."

She opened her mouth.

He held up his spoon. "Oh, *excusez-moi* if I hurt your tender feelings, but as for me, I begin from not trusting a person, and then he—or she—must prove to me that I should trust him—or her. We tend to trust those in our tribe, but from what you say,

I begin to believe Gilbert is a tribe of one. If you're arranging drops, make sure you don't send my money to him!"

Said as a joke, but Viennot was perfectly serious.

"Well, I never trusted Gilbert," said Noor.

Viennot waved his cigarette at her. "No, no. You wouldn't be so angry if you hadn't trusted Gilbert. Why shouldn't you? He is handsome. Like Maurice Chevalier—the same smile."

"It wasn't his smile. London trusted him, Prosper and Archambault trusted him. And I only trust you because Phono does—he said your grandfathers were brothers."

"It's true our grandfathers were brothers, but my Garry relatives don't invite Jacques Viennot to their homes. My mother's relatives only remember me when they have a task that might soil their hands. Always I have a perverse desire to tear down their complacency. But Phono—he's different. He hasn't changed from the cousin I admired. Every time Phono has said he will do a job for the Resistance, it is done. Done well, too. And it will be done exactly when he says it will be, or under the conditions he specifies. Prosper is—was—the same. The two of them along with Archambault are the reason the Germans can no longer sleep at night."

"'Was'? You think Prosper and Archambault have been executed?"

"Or sent to a prison camp, if they are lucky."

The little girl gave a curtsey, clasped her hands and began to sing "*Savez-vous planter les choux*."

"When we were children," said Viennot, "Émile would fall down and never cry. Renée—oh la la! She cried and complained about everything. *Tiens*, I just remembered Archambault knew you at your lycée."

"Yes, but not very well. He was in my brother's class, I was in the girls' school. He sang in the choir."

"So? That makes him holy? He told me some things about you."

She gave in to an urge to tease. "Why did you want to know?"

"I wanted to know how much he knew. He said you're yet another kind of celebrity—an Indian princess."

He sounded intrigued. She wouldn't deny it; what did it matter who or what he thought she was if it meant she could rejoin the fray?

"What else?" She tweaked her hat brim. Reflected in the window overlooking the busy alley, the hat resembled a cockeyed lampshade—not quite the right effect. She tried a Mona Lisa smile.

"That your mother is American—I only had to find out if you are a Yid."

"Does that matter? Why should that matter?"

He seemed to hesitate. "Anne-Marie, it matters little to me, but it would be very dangerous for you if it were true, you know?"

He leaned across the table and grasped her elbows. She pulled away.

"You should be in a palace." He made a U-shaped gesture across his chest. "With strings of jewels. And elephants. You should be in a scented harem, wearing the . . . the pantaloons. I see another Mata Hari—the spy who dances the dance of the veils."

Noor gave a soft laugh.

Viennot looked wounded. "Tell me, why did you not join the Free French under de Gaulle—why the English?"

"I am a British subject."

"*Bon!* Some British subjects are better than others. Your Colonel Buckmaster prefers his agents to operate only with each other and keep away from de Gaulle's."

"Oui, Professor Balachowsky explained this to me."

"He and Hoogstraten are probably executed by now—they would be no use to the Nazis."

This brought Noor back from her momentary flight of play-acting. Exciting intrigue. Harmless banter. But the stakes—one's life. Émile had said, "You have to deny reality to be brave." And right now she was pretending to be brave.

Viennot carried on. "Messieurs Churchill and Roosevelt have not yet made up their minds who should run France after the war, and believe they should decide. That's their idea of democracy, *tu sais?* They too, no less than the Nazis, have a New World Order in mind for Europe. But me, I work for the Free French and seldom for London. Now, if the Londoners are compromised, I will work only with the Free French—but we have to have money, even if it's from London. So, if you work with me, you will have to co-operate with Gaullists. But it's good information. Accurate, because a German talks freely to my little women, and what he doesn't tell them, he tells Viennot for money . . ."

So this was the kind of man she was dealing with. She stopped the question that was about to claw its way out of her. She had been about to ask if Viennot had contacts who might find Armand.

Don't ask Viennot, Viennot who doesn't like "Yids." He will have conditions. Or he won't let you transmit. There must be other ways.

"*D'accord,*" said Viennot. "If you are agreed . . ." He froze in mid-sentence.

Two black kepis had stopped outside Madame Millet's *pâtisserie.* They were talking with the tout across the lane. Now the *milice* gendarmes paced back and forth, carbines slung over their shoulders. A couple came out of the restaurant and one of the gendarmes gestured—the lane was closed off.

The poodle raised its head. Madame Millet went to the screen door to look.

Noor jumped up and got around the tables to the windows. The alley was emptying. She glanced back at Viennot. He now had his wallet out. He pulled out a fifty-franc note, placed it on the table, stood up. Far too much for their light repast, it lay suggestively across the path of any *milicien.*

"What is happening?" The little girl ran to the window and asked the question for all of them.

"A *shanghaillage,*" said the gentleman. The poodle quivered on his lap.

Madame Millet and Viennot exchanged glances.

"What is *shanghaillage?*" asked the little girl.

"A roundup of men for work in Germany."

"But there aren't enough young men outside," said the mother.

Viennot was the only man present who fell within the ages specified by Premier Laval.

"We must leave, Monsieur Viennot," urged Noor. She tensed to run behind Madame Millet's counter, out of the back door.

But Viennot shook his head. "No, look!"

A Hasidic Jew emerged into the lane, arms raised in surrender, squinting as if the sun scathed his eyes. The *miliciens* surrounded him, shouting "*Dépêche-toi!*" and "*Allez-y! Vite!*"

A torrent of blood rushed like a train through Noor's head. The poodle began to bark, its coiled leash unravelling.

Behind the black-garbed man came two women and three children, arms raised, heads lowered, blinking. A blue prison van reversed into the narrow lane. Its back doors swung open.

The sweet-faced old gentleman quieted his dog. "Probably criminals," he assured everyone with Panglossian equanimity. "Terrorists."

The mother nodded. "Black marketeers."

The little girl crept onto her mother's lap and sat very still.

"Strange—usually they come at night. Those Jews must have been in hiding," said the gentleman.

Viennot had returned to his seat.

A groan escaped Noor; she looked around wildly. The future was the past: she was running after buses again, green buses from Drancy, grey birds flying, she was running, searching, crying, the same pain in her side, that pain that arced out, reaching all the way to her womb.

"No, oh no," she said in a voice that wasn't her own. "No more!"

She reached for the doorknob, but Madame Millet stepped before it, loaf-like arms crossed upon her apron. Her *pâtisserie*, said her expression, didn't need attention from gendarmes.

Noor stopped, remembering where she was, her role, whom she was with, why she was here. She backed away. She joined the others, watching in an anxious daze.

When the *milice* began to prod the Hasidim into the blue van, Madame pointedly drew all the curtains.

"Where are they taking them, Maman?" The little girl's question rose plaintively around them.

The little group returned to their tables. It was very quiet.

Soon the poodle rested its head on its paws again. The gentleman removed his polka-dotted bow tie to loudly demonstrate mysterious techniques of knotting it. But the little girl was no longer enthralled, and began to cry.

"*Tais-toi!*" the mother hushed her. "Have they opened the street?" she asked Madame Millet.

Noor took off her hat and put it on the table. She stood looking down at Viennot for a long moment, then resumed her seat. Nothing could be said.

Eventually, Viennot fanned his fingers and met her accusing look. "It's war that tells the truth, Madeleine. We're all in tribes, no different from the Moroccan or Algerian in his souk. All of us, the Allies and the Axis, fighting for our fizzling utopias. But you care—care too much maybe?"

She looked away; let him not see her eyes had filled. "I'm a member of every tribe. At least, many tribes."

"Ah," said Viennot, taking a long drag on a newly lit cigarette. "I had that feeling once, the first time I fell in love. I loved everyone in the world—but you can't do that. It's very dangerous thinking. One must know very definitely to which tribe one belongs. That's why I don't do it any more—fall in love, I mean. Desire, yes—love, no!"

"And those people had the misfortune to belong to the wrong tribe? It's not something we choose!"

Viennot ignored her outburst and continued low-voiced and deliberate. "Madeleine, you wish to have your talents used, I can use you. In fact, I admit I *need* you. But I have rules. Listen carefully." His speech slowed as if he wanted her to memorize. "If you show any interest in Yids as you just did, you will attract the attention of the Gestapo to you, to Phono, Odile—any of us left in the network. Can you understand that? I will not work with you for one instant if you even try to inquire what happens to them, you understand? If you do—that's it! *Finis!* This is no place for tourism, Madeleine, nor a place to become a heroine or a saint. Do you understand?"

"*Je comprends.*" Yes, she did understand. Only too well.

"Now—what are your scheduled transmission times?"

"Wednesdays between 17:00 and 17:30 hours."

"Odile will courier you messages, or you will find them at Flavien's."

When Madame Millet drew the curtains back, the gendarmes and the Hasidim and the blue van were gone. A man with a broom bent over a dustpan. The lane had opened, and the tout was stopping passersby again. The little girl waved to her temporary friend before her mother pulled her away. The gentleman put on his hat, tucked Voltaire under one arm, the poodle under the other, and nodded "*à tout à l'heure*" to all.

A bell pinged as two German soldiers entered, their presence curtailing further conversation. As Noor left the *pâtisserie*, she heard Viennot order another crème caramel.

CHAPTER 30

Pforzheim, Germany
July 1944

NOTHING IN MY CIRCUMSTANCES *has altered since the Allies landed but my capacity for acceptance, my perception of my own adaptability. I am as Sleeping Beauty waiting for her prince; all of us are waiting. Rumi could have been speaking to the Allies across the centuries: "Open the gates of the prison with the keys that spell Joy."*

Today the guard gave me so many white tickets to thread on strings, I barely have time to write before my light is extinguished. The tickets have tiny holes through which I thread cotton, then make a knot. She supplies a single measured thread with the ball of twine, and I have to bite each thread to that length. Finished, they look like price tags for hats and clothes. Though I've always disliked sewing, sometimes I look forward to this useless work—it keeps my hands busy and dulls fear, regret, loss, yearning, self-pity and anger, and the stench of the toilet in the corner.

Forty tickets an hour—that's how many I can thread if I cut all the strings first and thread the tickets after. If I cut a single string and thread its ticket, I thread only thirty an hour. So I cut each string and thread its ticket, using inefficiency as my protest device. But today the guard's eye was at my peephole at least five times, and I got no soup at midday till I had threaded enough to satisfy her. So I tried to concentrate on threading, threading tickets all afternoon.

This is how I felt once I made contact with Viennot and began to work in earnest. The first static and whistles as I turned the dial were as the greetings of slow-turning planets, a cosmic noise of jangled intentions, but after a few days my concentration returned, skill and speed improved. I was back to that incredible feeling of lightness as thought projected from my tapping finger to ether, and I became Madeleine. Night after night, my finger on the key, translating French to English, then to Morse dot-dash-dash-dot, and I could not know if the information meant anything to the receiving women in London, Miss Atkins, Major Boddington or Colonel Buckmaster. After transmitting, I came back to being Noor, Noor who must, as Anne-Marie, live with the consequences of her communications. Once Josianne and I had finished decrypting and deciphering, we had messages and instructions to courier all over Paris.

I made contact with Odile again. Since her father's arrest she had become a little quieter, but had not lost her confidence.

Sometimes I thought all I was doing was waiting, waiting for messages, waiting for appointments in unfamiliar cafés with strange men and women from every occupation, every origin — people I might never have met in quiet Suresnes, or even in Paris, but for the war.

I felt connected to all my countries in this work — England and India, America, Russia and France. For once I was part of them all, necessary to the survival of nations, a finger-tapping sender connected to Colonel Buckmaster's women radio receivers, and because I was working with people who needed my skills, no one would call me foreigner any more. But every minute I lived with the thought that my love had become foreign in his own country . . . the one we had called "our" country.

For both belonging and non-belonging, there's no place like a war.

I disobeyed Viennot's rules, of course — adding one more disobedience to my stream of disobediences — and renewed my lease at Madame Gagné's boarding house in Drancy. Gabrielle, bartering more than tobacco ration coupons now at the Café Vidrequin, served me larger portions of food than she should have and took larger portions of drink than she should have. Her eyes were always puffy.

We never—I never—saw Monsieur Durand's sad eyes again, though I went to Drancy every week and transmitted from there. Poor Claude continued to call me at Madame Aigrain's, but now he called to say he had no news, just to have an excuse to call.

There were more transports, each of a thousand people. Each of a thousand Jews and resistants, some that left from Drancy station, some from Bobigny.

Once, only once, I was even angry at Armand. Why had he allowed himself to be captured? Why did he not resist more? And once he was at Drancy, why did he not try to escape? If he found his name on the list of deportees, could he not pretend to be sick, or fight legally not to go? But then Gabrielle explained what Monsieur le Missionnaire had told her, that the German quota of a thousand per transport meant if Armand found an acceptable excuse not to go, he would be condemning some other Jewish man to be transported in his stead.

The world is a barbaric place at present, ma petite—wait a while to enter it.

Gabrielle was there to comfort me if I ever saw your father, but I never did, though I stood by the gates and watched each convoy leave:

July 31

September 2

October 7

I watched unblinkingly. I watched to remember. I watched as if through the crocheted eyepiece of a shuttlecock burqa. Then back to work, after angry tears.

The work consumed me the way these tickets help to eat away time. All through August and September, Viennot attempted to meet me at his apartment, always mentioning that his wife was absent on vacation. He said he could fix my transmitter if it ever broke—and once upon a time I would have pretended to be very stupid, pretended I didn't understand his advances, or that he was *waiting for complete impoverishment to steer me down the road to selling my body. Instead, one day I explained that all I wanted from him was information. Information about the war as it was, not as I or Monsieur Churchill wanted it to be. And that if he expected to continue being paid by London, he should keep his suggestions to himself.*

To my surprise Viennot took rejection well, merely saying, "You know I had to try," as if a point of masculine honour had been at stake.

In England, I was trained to be a conduit, only a conduit. Told to ignore the content of messages—details about the movement of supplies, trucks, trains carrying tanks, troops, troop morale. But Archambault had taught me to grasp the significance of a message before sending. So I became familiar with the code names of Viennot's sources, and their motives. Germans were paid well, and some of the French will live like colons once the Allies liberate Paris. I sent signals for entire power plants and engine factories to blow up. My messages caused patrols and sentries to be blown to bits, horses to stampede, mail to burn in acid, food and forage to be poisoned, time bombs to detonate in cars and trains, stocks of petrol to burn. And it was not that I hated, but that I had no alternative. And I wanted German destruction in proportion to the cavity that yawned within me.

I felt then as today that I will prove to them, to myself: ours is a love their bombs can't shatter, that bullets can't kill, even if they have deported my beloved.

I wonder if it made any difference that I, Noor, was hiding in Paris and from my purdah behind a radio was telling the Allies where to bomb, when to hit, provided damage assessments and reports of roundups.

But it was not only me—Josianne was at my side, decoding. Odile was my courier, thinking up a million excuses any time she was stopped after curfew. One night she had gone out to call her German soldier from a phone box because her mother wouldn't let her call from home. Another night she was going to her sister who

was having a baby and the doctor had no gas for his car. And my surrogate mothers Madame Aigrain and Madame Prénat supported,
sheltered and fed us. The power and anger of our zenana steamed
like an engine to its goal.

Every day, I dispossessed myself of self to find some characteris-
tic, any small thing, in common with my assigned personas, Anne-
Marie and Madeleine. Translating to English, encoding, transmitting, receiving, decoding, translating to French again—for all of us
it was theatre without the drama or applause. This dance of pseu-
donyms carried me through to autumn.

In a few months, when the Allies release me and things are better,
ma petite, I will work for Radio France. I'll tell you stories on the
air, using my own clear voice in place of code. Armand always said
I have a beautiful voice, untrained but beautiful. I'll take singing
lessons, we'll write a children's newspaper together—we'll call it
Bel Âge.

Silence in my unaired cell now. In the distance a woman
screams, "If there is a God, hear me!" Another responds with the
Lord's Prayer. The Latin words return us to our atavistic urge to
believe, believe the crucial moment will come.

I hear the guard tramping towards my cell.

Allah hafiz for now, ma petite.

CHAPTER 31

Paris, France
Tuesday, October 12, 1943

THE QUEUE OUTSIDE LA PAGODE, the cinema designed like a Japanese pagoda on the rue de Babylone, was short. A matinee show—and who had money for cinemas these days? Or maybe the interest of Parisians had run its course, but the Germans still considered *The Life of Mozart* required viewing. The film did have a foreign following; a few callow-faced soldiers stood before Noor in the queue talking loudly in German. An accordionist serenaded French and Germans alike with "Sous les ponts de Paris." A few voices joined the chorus, but only one bought the sheet music when the song ended.

Noor's coat, tailor-made green jacket and skirt were the same she'd worn for her landing in France, a reminder that her three-week assignment had now stretched to seventeen. What must Mother think had happened to her—no more letters since the ones she'd sent to Kabir and Zaib in mid-June. And Gilbert probably hadn't delivered those.

The early afternoon air was chill and dense on her skin. Soon she would need to borrow warm clothes from Josianne. To engage a *petite couturière*, even Madame Aigrain's daughter, would be too expensive.

Before her in the queue, Odile Hoogstraten's strained young

face turned to the afternoon sun. Odile's eyes were her meter of suspicion; she could proceed.

Daily fear and tension were now as familiar as the ten-pound pole of worry and fear for Armand she'd carried across her shoulders in London and all the way to Paris. She had become like Odile and the Parisians entering the theatre, asking every moment: Who was listening? Who was watching? What would she find behind a locked door? When she received or delivered messages, who might be there—the Gestapo?

She chose an aisle seat with a pillar at its back; Odile slipped into the one beside her. Shadows danced across the blank screen and the walls as people took their seats. A German soldier clumped past, his stride muffled by the carpet but still sure.

A few polite inquiries in case anyone was listening, then Odile began whispering.

Noor cautioned, "Wait till the lights are switched off."

"They won't be," said Odile. "Sometimes they switch them off after the newsreel, but now they're too afraid, they want to watch us all the time."

"What can we do to them here?"

"We can applaud when they show the damage to hospitals bombed by the RAF. We hiss when they show Hermann Göring. It means we can't see the film very well. But," she sighed, "still I love the cinema!"

The assurance Noor had felt moments earlier siphoned away. She should have known the Germans wouldn't allow films to be shown in the dark so people could actually see them. She should have expected it; perhaps someone had mentioned it in training and she had missed it. How easy it was to make mistakes!

What could be so important that Odile had decided they should meet in person? And in a well-lit cinema?

The propaganda newsreel began and Odile twittered at Noor's shoulder.

"Phono and Monique have returned to Paris. With Renée and Babette."

Muscles tightened in Noor's neck. "Returned? Not to Renée's house?" she whispered.

"No, of course not. But it was *la rentrée* last month and Babette had to return to school. Phono said I should tell you he has taken an apartment in Neuilly. He said not to tell you the address, but I think he only said that because Renée doesn't want you to know where they are."

Too penetrating an observation; Odile had only a few opportunities to experience Renée's attitude towards Noor.

"Why do you think that?" Noor asked.

"Because when I went to meet Phono in Neuilly, she was arguing with him. She was so surprised to know you are still in Paris, and so angry. And you know, she is *never* angry at him! But she found out he was going to contact you. She said if you had returned to London, the Allies might have stopped their bombings."

Noor sighed. "She must believe I have great power. I assure you, Allied bombings will continue with or without my transmissions. Is there any good news?"

"Of course—here is good news: Renée said she was going out for a walk, to calm down after all her shouting. I was going to leave, because I'd picked up my messages for you, but Monique suggested I stay for lunch, so I did."

"And then?"

"Then Phono and Monique were at the card table playing *belote*, I was playing with Babette—it was a few hours. And then Renée came back. She had some good news. Guy—you remember her husband, Guy?—Guy will soon come home."

"*Magnifique!*" whispered Noor.

"Shhhh! Yes, it is. But . . ."

"But what?"

"She came back after walking in the Jardin d'Acclimatation and said she had a feeling. How do you just have a feeling?"

"When you love someone so much, you can have a feeling," said Noor. "It happens."

"You get a feeling about your fiancé—the navy officer?"

"I feel sure he is alive somewhere. I have faith."

"Maybe that's the feeling I get for my friend—you remember I told you about de Grémont? I don't know if he has the same feeling for me. But this feeling like Renée's—without even a letter, a telegram or a telephone call—I want to have it about Papa. Maman is desperate, telephoning everyone she knows. She even went to the avenue Foch to see the Gestapo. We heard he was sent to Fresnes, so we went there with clean laundry and a parcel. But now they told us he is no longer there, and they will not tell us where he is gone."

"Poor Madame Hoogstraten! I wish there was something I could do . . ."

"Maman should try and get this 'feeling.' Papa has to be alive, he has to be. I had a feeling, remember, when he was at Verdun and I learned later that I thought of him at the very moment of his capture? Even if he did smuggle arms from England, they can't just execute him. Don't they have to appoint a judge, then prepare for a trial?"

No, they don't. Occupiers—German, English, French, Dutch—consider trials for the colonized a singular favour to be suspended at will for civil disobedience. And your papa, Monsieur Hoogstraten, was planning armed resistance.

"We have news about everyone but Papa. You know the students we believed the Germans had executed at Grignon? They are at Fresnes! A translator and a prison chaplain smuggled their messages out of the prison—their families were so glad."

Subhan-allah!

Noor renewed the vow she'd made while watching the roundup at Grignon, to read the Qur'an from cover to cover and give a month's salary to the immigrants at La Mosquée, now it turned out the two students were alive. How much might she need to give at La Mosquée to pay for the two SS men who might be dead from her bullets? And for not feeling guilty enough about it?

"But the messages also said their punishment is to be sent to a work camp in Germany. What have they done? Nothing. *Quel dommage!"* Odile stopped for a passing uniform and then resumed. "Maybe the translator and the chaplain are behind bars too, by now. But at least those students' families now know they are alive. Whereas we . . . I told Maman we must get a lawyer for Papa, and send the lawyer to Vichy."

A liquid shine appeared in Odile's eyes. She looked straight ahead at the screen.

Monsieur Durand's comments about the uselessness of lawyers came back to Noor. Vichy was a marionette of the Gestapo . . . but it would be cruel to kill hope in Odile or Madame Hoogstraten.

"I told her I'll volunteer to work in Germany—they can trade me for Papa."

Noor held out her handkerchief. Odile took it.

Ushers in feldgrey moved past, the projector whirred and *The Life of Mozart* began.

Why did anyone come to see a film about a person whose life story was so well known? Rumi once said any tale, fictitious or otherwise, illuminates truth, but what could *The Life of Mozart* offer Odile and Noor in a cinema in 1943, with the whole world at war, with husbands and fathers disappearing into prisons and camps?

When you love someone so much, you can have a feeling. But at this moment the feeling of which Noor had spoken felt like some half-remembered dream. She should be glad for Renée, believe her intuition might be right. But Renée hadn't shown any respect for Noor's intuition about Gilbert.

Mozart's incomparable music. Phrases washed over Noor like a stream of coded personal messages from Armand. Eyes closed, she saw his fingers roaming the keyboard till the piano stormed and breathed.

She checked from beneath her eyelids; the uniforms had moved out of sight.

"*Alors,*" said Odile. "These messages must go to London tonight. The first one, unfortunately, is not good news."

A folded paper met Noor's fingers.

"A list. More arrests, all over the north."

Black-and-white images from *The Life of Mozart* blurred before the intensity of Noor's sudden anger.

Gilbert again! This is all Gilbert.

She pulled her jacket close as if blown into a draft.

"But there is another, more urgent."

"More urgent than this?" Noor was still taking in the news, her mind racing ahead.

"Oui, to Phono it is. He was very particular that I memorize this and say it to you: 'Monique needs, as soon as possible, to hear the messages we arranged in Le Mans.'"

Noor knew the messages meant by Émile, the BBC messages that would signal that his family would be flown out of danger, to England. He could have left such a coded message at Flavien's letter drop, like all the others, but by requesting Odile to deliver it in person, he had raised its urgency above the rest. Even above the list that lay folded in Noor's hand.

"Would you like me to be your lookout?"

Odile was volunteering to perform the service Marius the Master of the Greenhouse had provided Archambault before—well, before. Another signal of urgency.

Noor whispered, "No."

"A telephone number is written on the back of the list. Call me as soon as you have transmitted, so I can confirm it to Phono."

"Tell him I understand," said Noor, slipping the list into her handbag.

The film seemed to raise Odile's spirits. Afterwards she chirped away about the newsreel, decoding its propaganda statements to assess events for herself: the Germans had retreated from the Russian steppes—*bien*, but then they occupied Rome—was that *bien ou pas bien?* good or bad? And their omissions! They hadn't reported any *real* news, for instance that resistants had, a few days ago, killed the head of the forced-labour organization, the STO; that one second the man Ritter was alive and the next he was dead, bang-bang, falling down dead just like a Red Indian shot by a cowboy in a film. And his wife was probably crying in Germany. Oh no, they wouldn't show that, because people would be glad someone had done something about the STO. Odile was so very happy the Italians had come to the side of the Allies, but did Noor think the Holy Father was in any danger from Hitler? Surely not! What had really happened in Naples and Corsica, did Noor know?

"What can it mean, what will it all mean? What will it mean to *us*?"

On her way back to Suresnes, the omnibus took Noor as far as Le Moulin overlooking the racecourse in the Bois de Boulogne, where it stopped for the good reason, announced its resigned conductor, that the *gazogène* cylinder had run out of *gazogène*. Noor disembarked with the other passengers to wait for the next bus or a new cylinder, whichever came first.

The conductor tramped away.

Noor unfolded the scrap of paper Odile had given her. Her eyes travelled down the list—twenty-three code names this time. Mariette. Oh, no! Mariette! Yolande of the tweezed eyebrows and late night stories was arrested. Yolande with whom she had run up and down Glory Hill.

She bit a trembling lip. If Yolande had been arrested in the last twenty-four hours, she might be undergoing torture at Gestapo headquarters on the avenue Foch by now, perhaps at this very moment. And then . . . prison at Fresnes, like Monsieur Hoogstraten? Perhaps even Drancy or some other camp? Something large seemed lodged in Noor's throat.

Bon courage, chère amie!

Émile must be as angry about these arrests as she was. Of course, one could not be one hundred percent sure they resulted from Gilbert's disclosures to the Gestapo; they could also have resulted from torture of agents already captured. But Émile wanted his family to leave the country as soon as possible, and she knew why—so he could deal with Gilbert. Renée might not have been as angry with Émile if he'd told her *why* he was contacting Noor;

not to sabotage or derail more trains, but for Renée's sake, so Renée could be sent to England. That implied Émile hadn't told Renée he was sending her to *"perfide albion"* for the rest of the war. Mentioning an idea like that to Renée would have sparked a different argument altogether. Renée wanted to go home.

We all want and need to go home, Renée, not only you. But no place can be called home any more. We're all together in an expanding prison camp, and you'll only be home when nothing more can happen to you.

A few people who had descended from the bus set off on foot. Noor took a seat on a bench with others waiting either for a second bus or for the return of the conductor. Beside her, a woman with lips painted Kiki-style began to knit vigorously.

Coaxing Renée to get on a plane to England would be Émile's difficulty, especially if Guy was coming home. What were Émile's exact words? "Monique needs to hear . . ." Not "I need" but "Monique needs." So he had persuaded Monique to leave him and accompany Renée to London. And it sounded possible that Émile planned to act very soon, leaving Monique to listen alone for the BBC messages that would alert her to contact Air Movements Officer Marc instead of Gilbert at the next full moon.

How utterly torn Monique must feel. Here in the shade of the locust trees in the Bois, Noor once made a similar choice. How could she have known how deeply she would regret agreeing to leave Armand and escape to safety in London? How often she'd thought of that farewell, how much she'd wished to change it.

An autopiano drawn by a scrawny mule in the custody of a jaunty man in overalls came to a stop before the stranded passengers. When its owner bared the keys, "La Romance de Paris" rolled from punched paper, bringing a few sous of appreciation.

Once Émile killed a Nazi asset like Gilbert, his difficulties would begin. He'd have to join the Maquis and take to the Jura. At least there were bands to join; three years ago, when Armand and Madame Lydia left Paris, there were no Maquis. At the time, people believed only Jews and foreigners were at risk of persecution.

A murmur and roar behind Noor said a race had begun. She turned to watch jockeys and horses shouldering, gathering and extending as they came around the track.

Her immediate task was to encrypt and transmit Émile's request to London, and the list of arrested agents; not to wonder how her Armand and Madame Lydia had survived almost three years in hiding. Not to wonder if, when they were arrested, Armand's deep blue eyes had been like those of the poor old Hasidic Jew, squinting into sunlight. Not to wonder where Armand might be now, not to remember his unique scent, his limbs wrapped around her, or kisses gentle as afternoon rain.

Twenty-three arrests: chances were now very high that her transmissions were being monitored and traced. She could receive anywhere, but as for sending—no. To transmit from Madame Prénat's house any longer would be to wilfully place Josianne and her mother in jeopardy. Tomorrow, at her scheduled time of transmission, she would send Émile's request and the list of names from boulevard Richard Wallace.

No second bus would be coming. Instead, the conductor returned carrying a new cylinder on his back.

Far from the people in the stranded bus, hundreds of pairs of German and French hands were clapping for the winner. The drum of hooves began again, a fresh set of horses arced and leaned around the track.

Noor stood up to resume her journey.

No way out of this war but forward. The work must go on.

CHAPTER 32

Paris, France
Wednesday, October 13, 1943

THE OCTOBER AIR was so crisp and dry that, as she made her way down the boulevard Richard Wallace, Noor regretted wearing a skirt instead of her slacks. If Armand had been there, he would have teased about her thin Indian blood and offered his coat to wear over her green jacket and roll-neck sweater, his hand to cup her shoulder. Was Armand cold right now? What clothes was he wearing? Her T-strap shoes were wearing down from all her walking. In what condition were Armand's shoes now?

Soon, please Allah, let these messages help them invade soon, before any more of us are arrested, so Armand and Madame Lydia can be free and safe again.

The clock on the wall behind the concierge chimed half past four as Noor arrived, half an hour before transmission time. Five Wehrmacht officers no older than Kabir leaned against the concierge's counter as if at a bar, overwhelming the too-small salon with gusting laughter and loud camaraderie. They stepped aside courteously enough for Noor, but the scent of their boot polish followed. She let the brass-grilled lift rise without her and climbed a carpeted spiral to the third storey.

Silence and the smell of mould weighed heavy in the empty apartment; she hadn't completely closed the front window overlooking the Bois after her last transmission. It hadn't been this cold when Major Boddington first gave her the key, only three months ago. How annoyed she was he'd ignored the handbook: "Every safe house should ideally have one escape route, preferably two." But outside the handbook, everything had to be done under less than ideal conditions.

She placed the candlestick telephone on the floor, dragged the marble demi-lune under the window. Retrieved her suitcase transmitter from the bottom drawer of the sideboard and placed it on the table. Delved back in the drawer for her code books, then into the suitcase for the coiled aerial wire. She plugged the transmitter into a wall socket.

Cold air whooshed as, with a little effort, she slid the window upwards. She leaned out of the window. The window ledge had to be why Major Boddington selected this apartment—broad enough to hold the suitcase should anyone come to the door.

Below, on the boulevard, vélo-taxi drivers sweated and coughed, plying their pedicabs like cycle-rickshawallahs in India. Pedestrians raised their collars, nursemaids and mothers pushed prams or walked with children in the Bois. A German officer gave a stiff-arm salute and shouted a final "Heil!" as he left the building and stamped through the front courtyard and away down the street.

No white or grey vans. No one looking up. Safe to thread the aerial along the ledge now.

Back at the table, she opened her message book. First the most urgent message, requesting a Lysander for Renée, Monique and Babette. It might save lives of free people, whereas the second was to notify London about those already captured.

A small yawn was permitted after spending the early hours of the morning sheltering from bombardment in Madame Prénat's cellar. And she had worked with Josianne all last evening, composing and revising the message to be sent for Phono. Together they revised each word for utmost brevity, utmost clarity. The message had to explain to Major Boddington how imperative it was that Renée, Monique and Babette be flown to safety in London, from a field organized by Marc, not Gilbert. It reminded Major Boddington that Renée's home had been searched and watched, was no doubt still being watched. Deliberately ambiguous, it also explained that Émile—Phono—needed to be freer "to work on Resistance activities."

"Resistance activities" could mean more sabotage operations or the dispatching of Gilbert; Major Boddington didn't need to be told everything.

Afterwards, Josianne used Noor's code book to garble each word into clear text blocks, incomprehensible to anyone without a corresponding code book.

Noor placed her wristwatch beside the transmitter. Right forefinger ready to tap, like a horse at a starting line, the message copybook open like sheet music before her. Her left hand touched her throat. Habit. Habit of touch for luck and courage, though it was more than three months since she had worn her tiger claw.

Deep German voices outside the apartment door. She tensed, listening for tone, threat, a change in mood. Closer, then boots thumped past on the landing. A laughing response moved past. She took a deep breath.

Centre your mind.

At precisely 17:00 hours, she opened the channel between her pre-assigned kilocycles and identified herself as Madeleine. Then into the dream-space of transmission.

By 17:15 she had finished requesting the Lysander.

She waited with intense and total focus, transmitter set to receive. Wiped her brow, flexed her fingers, listening for a crackle. At last the acknowledging letter sequence came.

Noor moved to the foyer and lifted the earpiece of the candlestick telephone off its hook. The switchboard operator came on the line. Noor asked for the telephone number provided by Odile.

"Odile."

"Tell Phono to keep in touch with Uncle Marc," she said in a calm, friendly voice. She depressed the telephone hook.

Back at the transmitter, her hand was steady. The second message was longer than the first. *Tap-tap-tap*, the bass crackle sounding inordinately loud in the still, empty rooms. Pounding at the single key like the pounding in her heart, because the apparent randomness of the letters she was transmitting was not random at all. Pounding in her heart because these blocks disguised the fate of flesh and blood. Excepting Yolande, she didn't know the true identities of these captured resistants any more than they knew hers. The code names she was beginning to send stood for the complexity of each life, connections with friends and relatives and fellow resistants, their past, all reduced to a name on a list saying they'd failed to remain in play, saying they had been at the wrong place at the wrong time.

What would happen when London received these code names? Would they now stop sending agents and munitions into the open arms of the Gestapo? Émile had thought they would stop after the arrests of Prosper and Archambault, yet London kept sending more. And this was the result: five names, ten, fifteen, twenty code names, including Yolande's.

One *du'a* with each name, to ask the comfort of Allah for wives and husbands who would receive we-regret-to-notify-you letters from the War Office. Sending, sending one block of encrypted text, then her double security check, then another block and the security check again, sending as fast as she could possibly tap.

Almost finished now. *Tap-tap-tap.*

Finger turning to icicle, just three names to go. Noor glanced at her wristwatch: 17:27 hours.

Too long, too long on the air.

The round dish above a German detection van might be turning at this moment, cocking like an ear in the direction of the one transmitter it couldn't recognize, now all others were German-controlled. She tried not to imagine it, but once that dish had flashed to mind, there was no stopping its image . . . She transmitted the last three names.

The operator came back with "Security check not received. Be more careful, Madeleine. Re-send please."

Some schoolmarm, probably. With a pince-nez on her large, sniffy nose. Now she'd have to repeat her transmission of the last three names. But at least someone was minding security.

Footsteps creaked on the floorboards outside.

Noor's tapping stopped. The pace of the footsteps didn't alter, then faded away.

Back to the last two names, and Archambault's words streaked across her mind. "Some messages, they might be worth one person's freedom, *tu sais*, Madeleine?"

The pounding in her heart turned to a machine gun firing in her head, then an artillery barrage at the door. The door burst open. Over her shoulder, it filled with the contour of her ever-present fear: a trench-coated man beneath a large fedora, moving towards her with feral speed.

PART SIX

CHAPTER 33

Pforzheim, Germany
July 1944

BRAIN, HEART AND PEN — *not one will rest. My hands were occupied all day today, stringing tickets and more tickets. Thoughts rushed like the trains that set my cot vibrating at night. When I finished stringing tickets, my pen called me to you.*

A piping mezzo-soprano swells and ebbs down the corridor. I stop and listen: someone tried to assassinate Hitler, but our newswoman sings in French that he still lives. Stuttgart has been bombed, she sings. Paris is still waiting for the Allies, poor occupied Paris.

What do these events mean for Armand? What do they mean for me? Tell me, if you know.

The song communiqué begins again, this time in Polish. I hear the guard's baton strike the newswoman's cell door.

Screams, weeping.

Must my heart harden to survive? To feel deeply about a stranger when I can do nothing about her pain takes its toll on my courage. I write, trying not to wonder what our newswoman's silence means.

I go back to the instant my own transmissions fell silent, the last that London operators heard from Madeleine.

The man standing in the doorway — to how many had he come, in warning, in nightmare or in person?

Agile with fear, I overturned both chair and transmitter and made a dash for the open window. My feet met the ledge and I was out in the cold, hair whipping into my eyes, sidling out on stone, plaster wall against my back.

The man stopped at the open window. "Fais gaffe!" he shouted. "Tu vas tomber."

His accent: French as French can be. A milicien dressed in a Gestapo trench coat, a Gestapiste. He lit a cigarette and sat down on the sill to wait till I fell as he predicted, returned to the room or jumped.

Jump! Jump! I urged myself.

Three floors—I might have survived with a few broken bones, maybe even run away. But I looked down and my legs turned to stone. Grey mansard roofs stretched down the boulevard on one side, and on the other the milice gendarme sat smoking at the window.

Even had I a parachute, I couldn't have jumped. Even if I had completed my parachute training, I couldn't have moved a muscle. Your uncle Kabir might have flown like Superman, your aunt Zaib might have laughed in the milicien's face. Mother would have offered the Gestapiste fifty francs or a bottle of cognac to disappear, Dadijaan could have fed him an earful that would make him remember his own grandmother. But your own mother's legs turned numb. My chest heaved with angry tears, with anger at myself for cowardice.

Terror pushed me out on that ledge, but a far greater fear stopped me from letting go that day, from plunging down for the instant it would take to embrace death.

Do you know what it was, my darling? Today I see the reason, though I couldn't then.

I saw myself teaching you enough Arabic to read the Qur'an, Armand teaching you enough Hebrew to read the Torah for yourself. I felt myself drawing a tiny hand through bangles, dressing you in a vest with appliquéd flowers, presenting you my tiger claw to wear, as Dadijaan had worn it before us. I was picking peonies for your hair, singing for you, teaching you the veena, writing nonsense stories to make you laugh. I was learning to laugh again. Armand's blue eyes came before me, piercing my soul. He held you in the crook of his arm. I pressed my lips to his cheek and yours.

All this in a flash, looking down.

Do you see how powerful you are, ma petite? You, the hope of your return, stopped me from jumping. Then as now, your need to use my body gives it an obstinate desire to live.

Jump! I urged myself forward an inch.

But I couldn't.

I hated my body for being so weak, for clutching at life so greedily. For fearing death, reuniter of all souls.

The moment passed and I understood myself anew, understood I was the sum of my every obligation and attachment. If I jumped, I'd never know if Armand still loved me. I had failed your father twice, I could not fail him again.

If I jumped, I'd never know: would Émile really kill Gilbert? Would Monique, Renée and Babette be lifted to safety? I'd never meet Mother and Kabir again to ask why they betrayed the tolerance our family preached to others. I'd never know if the Allies would arrive to liberate France, never see Zaib become a doctor, see Kabir become Pir.

So when a man who was my enemy reached out to save me, I gripped his hand. For a moment I was suspended in mid-air, with only a strange man's arms supporting me, then I climbed back over the sill.

But once back on firm ground, I didn't leave that apartment without a fight. The scuffle brought Wehrmacht soldiers onto the landing, cheering as if betting on a cockfight. More milice gendarmes came and overpowered me. They called the man in the trench coat Cartaud. Pierre Cartaud.

Arms jerked behind my back, my hands were cuffed. I stumbled downstairs, out of the building, into twilight. Cartaud sucked his hand where I had bitten him and said to his men, "This one is a desperado, a dangerous terrorist."

I recognized that sandy brown beard and moustache now—he was the chauffeur at Grignon, who knocked me sprawling into the ditch, who stood by the Citroën as the megaphone blared. I had focused my binoculars on that face all the way down the hill when he led the maid back with Monsieur Hoogstraten's suitcase.

A Black Maria rolled up, took me away. It wasn't far to Gestapo headquarters at the avenue Foch. A cinema reel reverses and I see myself entering a mansion without invitation from its true owners.

CHAPTER 34

Gestapo Headquarters, avenue Foch
Paris, France
Wednesday, October 13, 1943

NOOR SAT BOUND in a chair in a *chambre de bonne*, a maid's room on the fifth floor of the Gestapo-occupied mansion, Cartaud's unbandaged hand clenching the tangle of her hair.

"Where are the arms dumps? Tell me! Where are your other transmitters?"

Shouting, shouting.

Mock interrogator. Mock interrogator with Uncle Tajuddin's face.

Neck jerking, scalp distending, follicles screaming.

Cartaud's hand twisting again. "Locations, passwords? Guardians? Names?"

Gargoyle face; interlaced capillaries on nose. Half an inch closer and she'd sink her teeth in him again.

Hair releasing, rope-bite saying she couldn't rub her head.

"Everyone talks. Prosper, Archambault, Hoogstraten—whatever their names are. All of them screamed, 'Enough!'"

Left shoulder exploding beneath his truncheon.

Eyes opening, opening wider than their sockets. Never forget, never forget his snarl of enjoyment.

Nose trickling blood yet registering his sour breath over her as he loosened the ropes that bound her. Testing communication with her left arm—the truncheon had stopped just short of break or shatter.

He wants screaming; I will not.

I am more obstinate than I knew, my body tougher than I thought.

Cartaud's head blocking the ribboned light from the barred skylight sloping above, his eyes colder than vichyssoise. Lips barely moving though his voice filled the tiny room.

Pain ejecting her from observation. Sensation demanding attention, excluding reason. Maggots seething in her head.

Falling, falling a great distance to the floor. The racket of sound as both chair and she hit the floor.

Remember Al-Hallaj, Jeanne d'Arc, Max, soldiers who have fought their way across the deserts of North Africa, the jungles of Burma, men at sea.

A snap inside her. The cavern in her shoulder pleading for the ball of her arm. Ligaments snagging on a bone crack in her collar.

Swelling, swelling ridges of oncoming agony. Flying towards the wall like a husk blown on the wind, ground falling away.

Colliding with a crack that resounded in her skull. Brain rocking like a vessel at sea.

A blow to the belly. Noor folded in two.

Drowning, drowning in air.

Chin rising, lifting on the tip of Cartaud's boot.

Blink, blink swollen eyes. See. See suited figure slanting from the floor at an obtuse angle. See corpse-pale face, round glasses, words falling from slash in face.

Kick-start of memory: the voice on the megaphone at Grignon. The interpreter's voice. Voice pulling Cartaud away, releasing the ropes that bound her hands.

Palm on solid floor. Trying to rise. Everything crumbling, even the walls.

"You interrogate, I'll hit, Herr Vogel," said Cartaud, as if proposing a compromise.

The maid's room turned uterine red. Then black.

———

Ting-chck-chck-chck-chck . . . ting.

A man with a swastika arm band hunched over a skipping red-and-black ribbon. The typewriter bell tinged again as it approached the end of the line.

A jigsaw resolved into the interpreter's face. Grey suit coat, white shirt, brown felt bow tie. All wallet-scale by contrast with the oversize portraits—Hitler, Goebbels and Göring—behind his gilded desk.

Al—inwards—*lah*—outwards. *Allah.*

Breath, separator of the living from the dead.

Noor struggled upright from her slump in a chair. Pain raged from her neck down her shoulder, down her left side.

Hands and feet no longer bound. Wet, wet—face and neck wet. Skirt chilling her thighs.

Cold like a sock to the face.

The interpreter set an empty carafe on his desk.

Vaginal muscles clenching, testing—no pain there.

Her gaze dropped to her blouse—bloodstained, rumpled, but yes, it was buttoned. The fractional movement jarred every ounce of brain. The back of her head was larger than it should be.

"My colleague is sometimes overzealous. Cartaud's emotions overcome him. He was unemployed so long before he joined the militia—now he tries very hard to please. But it takes time to train Frenchmen in German security methods."

Chords crashed in rhythm on a faraway gramophone. *Tannhäuser.* Chair legs grated on floorboards as if they grated in her head. The typist was gathering his papers, closing the door behind him.

The interpreter rose and came around the desk. He flicked a lighter, lifted a cigarette to his lips, lit it, held it out to her.

Noor turned away.

"We have not been introduced, it's true. I am Ernst Vogel, SS interpreter for you and Herr Kieffer. I have been asked to translate certain questions we have for you, and the consequences if you do not answer. Let us begin."

He wasn't shouting. He sounded more like a disappointed schoolteacher.

"I want your true name."

"Anne-Marie Régnier." Voice unwavering as a single note struck upon a piano.

"That is a lie."

The next questions, according to the ritual scenario visited upon her, should have been her rank and serial number, the only information she was required to give under the Geneva Convention as an officer. She was ready to deny she had either.

But Vogel led away from these with "A Mark II suitcase radio—that's SOE. But you don't look English. So—how long were you taken to England? A month? A year?"

Speech sealed itself tight in her cranium.

"To whom do you report in England?"

Silence.

"At what hours did you transmit? Name your accomplices."

Silence.

"Your accomplices have already confessed—we know who you are," he said in a you-weary-me voice.

Anger flooded in. "Then you know more than I," she mumbled.

He stopped and gave her a long look. She hadn't reacted as he had expected. "You are a British spy, a foreign terrorist. An officer, I hear—*Grüss Gott!* The SOE has learned to inflate its titles in the hope that we will treat its captured agents better. And your true name is Noor."

His tone said he had solved a riddle that led to another.

She said nothing, mind racing. This man knew the SOE's internals. He knew she was an officer; that could have come from torturing poor Prosper or Archambault. But how did he know her name? Prosper? Archambault? But if Archambault had revealed her name, Vogel would have learned the surname Khan as well. But he hadn't said that; he said, "Your true name is Noor." Could he have read her letters to Kabir and Zaib?

That *salaud Gilbert!* Fool, for trusting him with her letters! Such a fool, for not urging Émile to kill him straight away. What had she written to Kabir and Zaib?

Her brain was a bowl of mashed lentils. Vision shifted and blurred.

"Now"—Vogel shot Noor a glance like chilled metal—"if I am to help you, I must first establish your nationality and origins. What kind of name is Noor? I do not recognize it, but it is not a Jew name. I can smell a Jew for a mile—I see very well you are not a Jew."

He was waiting. Noor let silence lengthen.

He shrugged and continued. "Then I must know why do you fight for the Communists, the capitalists and the Jews? Do you need martyrdom? Is it ideology? Money? Out of fear? I can only represent you to Herr Kieffer if you help me understand you."

The obstinacy of love, anger at tyranny, concern for the world her child would inherit—such reasons for a woman to gird herself for battle were off Vogel's list. Noor's shoulder throbbed with anger.

"I think we will find that you are an innocent victim of terrorists, pressed into service by foreigners—the British."

He was suggesting an extenuating excuse, one that pride would never permit her to use.

"You must understand, Fräulein Noor, friends who have used you are troublemakers. You are young—heed my counsel. I've seen tactics like theirs for years. People like your friends carried a burning torch through the windows of the Reichstag and set it on fire. Can you believe—the Reichstag! That day the world changed. It was a day no civilized person can ever forget. I was visiting my uncle in Berlin. We celebrated when the Chancellor, now our Führer, declared a state of emergency and vowed war on terrorism everywhere."

And that first emergency decree has made arrest on suspicion, imprisonment without trial in camps, and executions possible in Germany and beyond ever since. That "law" has turned the whole world into a place of everlasting war.

"I joined the NSDAP that very day, mademoiselle. And since the war began, I have interrogated extremists, terrorists, guerrillas, militants, separatists, rebels, bombers, killers and murderers—call them what you will, they all do the same thing: deliberate attacks against unarmed civilians."

In Noor's jarred memory, stukas bore down upon the Amilcar as she and her family joined the refugees streaming out of Paris, bullets began to rip into unarmed civilians under deliberate attack. Against a dark veil of night in her mind, the Luftwaffe's Molotoff breadbaskets spewed clustered incendiaries that popped like starbursts from skyrockets, firemen ran through roaring flames searching for civilian victims in the debris-littered streets of London. Émile began to say what she wanted to say to the pale man: "Not a single German occupying France must be allowed to sleep easy in his bed while they billet themselves in French homes, steal our coal, grain and wine, and 'resettle us' somewhere in the east. The tanks and guns may be with them, but we have no recourse but to fight, for our homes, for the future."

"Their goal," Vogel was saying, "is continual fear. Which makes me curious about you, mademoiselle—or is it madame?"

"Mademoiselle," muttered Noor.

"Mademoiselle, then. Young women with features as delicate as yours, women as refined as you, don't usually join terrorists. Jews and Communists do, yes—but no woman like you."

Noor couldn't reply with the words Émile had said. Instead, when Noor thought of Armand in Drancy, Anne-Marie Régnier pouted. As soon as Noor thought of Armand probably in that green bus leaving Drancy for Bobigny station, tears leaped to Anne-Marie's eyes. And when she thought of him somewhere, starving as a poor man denied rice in India, his musician's hands callusing to build roads for tanks and Volkswagens, Anne-Marie's eyes brimmed over and she began sniffing. "Monsieur, I don't know what you're talking about—I want my mother."

"Your mother—she is a British hostage? Is that how they induced you to spy?" He reached over the desk. "You see only the war before your nose. You must realize that everything in this world is connected to everything else, connected to all that has happened in the past and to what will happen in your future. We have a duty to fight the war at all possible points, on all possible fronts."

"Then why don't you go and fight Russia?" Anne-Marie wailed, before Noor knew it. But it was time Vogel was given a seemingly innocent reminder of German casualties.

Vogel ignored her. He came around the desk and took his hand from his pocket. A folded square of white cotton came towards her. Vogel's handkerchief. He dabbed at her face, wiping away tears. She let him—Anne-Marie Régnier would let him.

Nothing like the SOE's mock interrogation.

Vogel returned to his seat and continued. "We must guarantee our safety against ruthless killers who move and plot in shadows. We never aim to kill innocent people. We may have to do it in reprisal, after we have been attacked, but we don't *intend* to do it. Whereas Jews and Communists who are the French 'resistants' intentionally kill innocent German soldiers placed in France to protect and defend the French. So much hatred! They kill priests, nuns, civilians—babies! Let me explain to you the consequence, mademoiselle: we have to target the family, friends and neighbours of terrorists to stop these miscreants. We're following terrorist activity, we're disrupting terrorist plots, we're shutting down Maquis camps from the Jura to the Alps, we're hunting down one person at a time. Many terrorists are now being interrogated. Many have been killed. And what thanks do we get for liberating the French people so they can join the New World Order? None. Ach, we now understand the nature of our enemy—you all hate us because of what we love—freedom for the Fatherland."

For the Fatherland only—what about everyone else in the world?

He came around the desk to her side. "Try to understand us instead of giving in to your hatred: we are only defending our freedom, our interests, searching for *lebensraum*—how do you say it in English?—living space."

"I don't understand," Noor said in French.

"Yes, you do. Your message book is in English."

Noor gave him a look of blank innocence she'd perfected for Uncle Tajuddin's benefit. But pain erupted at the base of her neck; Vogel's cold fingers were shaking her gently.

"Anyway, mademoiselle, France and Germany will prevail over our common enemies."

Pain drummed and muscles spasmed, but at least Vogel had returned to French.

"We must become better acquainted, you and I. You have an accent or an air, perhaps a scent, that is different. You don't look English, you don't look Jewish. A Spanish revolutionary perhaps? Where did you go to school?"

"Bordeaux. I am from Bordeaux, I want to go home," she wept.

This brought a derisive snort. "Every second agent sent by the SOE is from Bordeaux, because identification records at Bordeaux were destroyed. You think we don't know that? So, if you are from Bordeaux, tell me the name of the lycée you attended."

"Saint-Éloi Convent." Noor fixed her eyes on Vogel's brown felt bow tie as she provided this detail from her cover story.

"I can verify this with one telephone call, mademoiselle, but I won't. Because you see, I lived in Bordeaux for two years before the war, and in 1939 the French put me in a POW camp near Bordeaux, and I can tell you without telephoning anyone . . ." He shouted suddenly, "There is no Saint-Éloi Convent there!" Then quietly, "There is a Saint-Éloi Cathedral, but no convent."

"No convent? You bombarded it?" cried Noor, surprise and distress in her tone.

"No, Fräulein. There never was a convent. Ach! They should have taught you better lies."

His steady gaze brought a flush to her cheeks.

"Perhaps you can be put to some good use."

He will crack the whip and I am to perform. For him.

"*D'accord!* About England: Were you sent to the SOE's school for agents? Who was with you during your training? Names, descriptions! We must and will eradicate troublemakers, hit the terrorist organizations and their caches of arms. Their leadership has to be on the run, and all communications with each other and the terrorist state of England where they are given safe haven must be terminated. We will do this if it takes house-to-house searches. We will target everyone to whom you are connected, everyone with whom you have associated. Reprisals will happen—it is the only way to stop terrorism."

Professor Balachowsky seemed to answer for Noor: "Every martyr is one more step in the fight against Occupation."

"I want my mother," repeated Noor. And Anne-Marie dissolved into tears.

Pforzheim, Germany
July 1944

That night, I took one-handed the plate of cabbage and gristle meted out at the avenue Foch. All day my shoulder throbbed in tabla rhythms, though I tried to immobilize it by inserting my left hand in Napoleon pose between the buttons of my blouse. I had to wait till my body recovered in other areas before I attempted the procedure for a dislocated shoulder—one I'd memorized but never tried on any patient, certainly not myself.

Sitting on the maid's bed near the wall, I probed the hot, tender tissue of my shoulder with my fingertips, slowly rotating my arm, raising my elbow. When sweat beads stood out on my forehead and I could not move a millimetre more, I knew I was almost in the position in which the dislocation first occurred. Now I jerked my elbow up at an angle, throwing my weight against the wall. A firestorm coursed into me, like magma pouring from elbow to shoulder to chest. I fell back on the bed, sobbing.

The ball still protruded; all that pain and it hadn't moved.

I lay waiting for the pain to subside, wondering what to do.

I thought of another diagram in my Red Cross textbook. I lay face down upon the bed, with my injured arm hanging vertically. But I needed a weight to attach to my dangling wrist. I had no weight.

I lay, wetting the crook of my good arm with tears.

Another diagram entered my mind like a slow revelation. I needed a chair.

I had no chair.

But the headboard of the bed was steel, a roll bar like a hospital bed.

I wiped my tears. Was the bed too heavy to move? It was indeed too heavy to move with one hand. Quietly, I kneed it, nudging, pushing till it pivoted just a little away from the wall. I climbed up and knelt, dangling my arm over the headboard, letting it wedge into my armpit till I gasped. I reached through the bars with my good arm. I wanted to pull my dislocated arm slightly downwards, but I couldn't—too much pain.

So I remained kneeling on the bed, waiting, shaking sweat out of my eyes, biting my lip to keep from crying out. An hour passed, I think, until the head of my dislocated humerus moved, returning to its place in the joint capsule.

I rested awhile, then tore away the base of my blouse to make a better sling for my shoulder. Then I lay down, trying to quell the pain with deep yoga breathing. But the two-way signals raced up and down from my shoulder to my brain, reminding me of doctors who would tell me all pain was in my head. In my body there was no separation of mental and physical pain, as they taught, none at all.

I bargained with Allah. Is this enough pain, Allah? Or is this no more or less than the pain of others? Allah was too busy comforting needier people, the starving, the sick, and people like my beloved taken away in a bus to Bobigny station.

Late that night, I thought pain made me hallucinate Archambault's face in my room, but no—there was Vogel behind him, ushering him in.

Incredibly, Vogel said, "Explain to her."

Then left us alone.

Archambault leaned against the wall for support; how much more broken he was inside than I.

"Madeleine," said a saw-rasp in his throat.

I drew away. Vogel could have been watching through a peephole or listening at the door. There could be a listening device somewhere in the room. The pain in my shoulder burst forth again.

"I do not know any Madeleine."

He straightened, swinging his arms slightly, crossed the room to stand at my side. "Listen well," he said in French, near my ear. Prosper, he said, had made an agreement with the Gestapo.

"Who is Prosper? What kind of agreement?" I said through a cloud. Perhaps pain was causing me to hear voices.

"We said we will tell them what they want to know, provided they agree not to execute our agents and treat each arrested agent from our network as a POW."

Pierre Cartaud's voice flooded the tiny *chambre de bonne* again, shouting about arms dumps.

"You told them where they could find arms? Arms sent by the Allies? They'll use them against the French!" I whispered, abandoning caution. I had to understand more.

Archambault held out his hands. Fingers that had tapped Morse as fast as mine looked like ginger root. Deformed, blood-crusted where his fingernails should have been.

"Agents are more important than weapons," he said.

The SOE always taught this, even though they gave us L-pills full of cyanide. Mine was still sewn into the lining of my jacket sleeve.

"Archambault," I said, "is it true your transmitter was found at Grignon and the Germans used it to request more arms?"

He confirmed this with a nod.

I was shocked again, though Major Boddington had all but told me this.

"But, Archambault, how can this be? Even if they found your code books, we had security checks, encryption keys, and each of us has a distinctive fist. I transmitted news of every arrest . . ."

"*All useless.*"

"*Maybe so, but why would England continue to send arms when they knew the Germans were receiving them, arresting agents as they parachuted in?*"

"*They wanted the Germans to trust the transmitters when they called to the Resistance to rise up at the invasion.*"

I had thought so too.

"*Why should the Germans trust any messages about an invasion?*"

"*They didn't, until they caught and tortured Prosper. He confirmed it. Prime Minister Churchill had told him personally that the invasion would come on September 12.*"

I recalled Émile saying Prosper had met with Mr. Churchill.

September 12, 1943, was by then a month past; no Allied invasion had occurred. If Vogel and Kieffer had believed Prosper, they now knew they had been fooled. By now Hitler knew he had been duped.

Archambault, that menhir of a man, was in the throes of a pain so deep it was resistant to speech.

"*You cannot believe it, Madeleine. Neither Prosper nor I could believe it for so long . . . but after September 12 we had to admit Monsieur Churchill had fed Prosper a lie. It's now too late for an invasion this year, too cold.*"

That face—deflated as if he'd lost all his illusions.

"*Prosper was—we were all—we are all—doomed spies, Madeleine. Don't bother taking your L-pill, for both Prosper and I took ours and we are still alive. That's when we knew we were all doomed.*"

I had read enough of Sun Tzu to know what he meant by doomed spies: Mr. Churchill had given Prosper and thousands of agents false information—lies destined for the enemy. Assuming Hitler believed the false invasion date, Berlin could have moved military resources from the Russian front, giving Stalin a much-needed respite. The timing was critical, even if Hitler had no idea where the Allies were landing.

And if Prosper was a doomed spy, we were all doomed with him when Hitler took revenge; and now that we had done our jobs, succeeding by failing to stay out of Gestapo clutches, we were expendable as far as Mr. Churchill was concerned. I was destined to die as if Churchill had strapped bombs to my back and bid me walk into Germany.

Could it be that despite all my intentions I had been a marionette for the Raj? And was it now that I must abandon stubborn hope and look to Allah, admitting finally that nothing, but nothing in these last months of fear, running and hiding had been within my control? That all choices, actions and decisions had not been my own, but designed by men in London?

Unlike Archambault, I did not struggle to believe the worst of Mr. Churchill or the English. For had not Mr. Churchill denied rice and boats to poor Indians, diverting food from the poor to war industries, deciding that millions in India were expendable for this war?

And Miss Atkins gave me a cover story, a story with the specific detail that Anne-Marie Régnier was a student at Saint-Éloi Convent—when there was no Saint-Éloi Convent.

On my mission to France I had learned so many ways to be betrayed.

Even so, I knew from seeing Drancy that my life or death was but a tiny part in Christianity's Oedipal crusade against Jews. If I was expendable, it might be so that Hitler's jihad against the world was defeated sooner.

The last time I saw Prosper, at the Jazz Club, he said silence would be the fate of fifteen hundred brave French soldiers in his network. He meant the penalty for spying: execution. None of us wore uniforms. If we were French citizens, we would be treated as traitors to France; if foreigners, our execution chambers were already built and awaited us.

Unless—

And here I began to understand Prosper's thinking. Unless he could persuade the Germans to treat his agents as prisoners of war, in exchange for information about the arms dumps.

The doorknob began to turn; we thought Vogel was returning. Time for masks to slip back in place. Agony everywhere in my body, it was easy to weep and wail, "I want my mother."

"Anne-Marie," said Archambault quite loudly, "where is your suitcase?"

Archambault's sudden solicitousness for my suitcase penetrated my fog of pain. He wanted something, or Prosper wanted something.

The diamonds. Of course, they wanted the diamonds. Diamonds could be bartered with Kieffer, Vogel and Berlin, bartered for lives.

"I have none," I said, weeping loudly, copiously. "I have nothing from home."

It was not Vogel but the Russian guard who entered. Archambault's smashed, swollen hand patted mine with a shake of his head—he was telling me the Russian could not understand French.

"It's been more than twenty-four hours," he whispered. "Our people should have taken cover by now. Speak to Vogel. Hide what you can behind the sink in the lavatory. Bon courage, Anne-Marie!"

The guard pulled Archambault from the room before I could ask if he believed Gilbert had betrayed Prosper, indeed betrayed us all.

Requesting my valise meant giving Vogel Madame Aigrain's address. He could arrest her, execute her—I'd never know. And I was beholden to Madame Aigrain in so many ways, not only for shelter, for the loan she had given me, the way she had nursed me, the care she had lavished on me. Every day, she had been in danger of possible arrest and execution for harbouring me.

Her life balanced against the lives of hundreds of agents in the PROSPER network.

My dilemma was far smaller than Churchill's. He weighed the lives of millions starving in India against all the people like himself in England; he weighed the lives of fifteen hundred agents against the freedom of a continent. But I cared about Madame Aigrain, *cared deeply, as Churchill never cared about faraway brown men, women and children, or his legion of secret agents.*

Caring or not caring did not absolve me. I had to choose between tragedy and disaster.

It was past twenty-four hours. By now, Madame could have moved the English books, the maps and my transmitter to her daughter's home. But what if she had not? I had warned her, explained what she must do if I did not return—but what if she had done nothing?

For two days, I said the Istikhara prayer so many times, pleading with Allah for guidance. Then back to Vogel's office.

Saturday, October 16, 1943

Noor sat before Vogel's desk, hands in shackles. "Für Elise" played on the gramophone in the corner.

"You have indeed impressed me—why resist more?"

Vogel seemed to believe he was the natural and only audience for her actions.

"You see, my dear, at heart I am an idealist, like you."

"We believe in very different ideologies," said Noor. And regretted the word instantly.

Would Anne-Marie Régnier say "ideologies"? No. The vocabulary of a nursemaid from Bordeaux wouldn't stock such grandiloquent words.

"Mademoiselle, we know exactly who you are now. You are an Indian princess."

Indian princess—where had he heard this? Archambault.

Trying to help, no doubt.

She kept her face completely without reaction.

"I am Anne-Marie Régnier. I came to Paris to find work as a nursemaid and"—here she broke into tears—"I want to go home. I don't know any princesses."

"Archambault," said Vogel, "tells us you're a princess."

"You believe someone who tells you I'm Cinderella? That man—I met him for a few minutes, once in my life. *Il est fou!* He should go to Pigalle and indulge his fantasies."

"The time for lying is past, mademoiselle—although we know you do it well. Archambault went to the lycée in Suresnes—not Bordeaux, mademoiselle, but Suresnes—and he knew you there. He says you became an accomplished, though charming, liar by writing stories for children. You live, he says, in a fantasy world, in which you may fancy yourself a secret agent working for all kinds of foreign powers, but that is delusion."

Noor blinked at him but said nothing.

"In fact, I believe *some* of what Monsieur Archambault has told me is the truth. Because he didn't tell it without pressure, Mademoiselle Khan. Almost as much force as it took to find his real name—what does it matter?—we'll call him Archambault. Perhaps Archambault thought your German-sounding name, Kahn, would save you. But most interestingly, he says we are detaining a woman who has no desire to see the British win. A colonial completely unengaged in this war."

Archambault might have revealed her origins to Vogel, but had she behaved stupidly enough, Vogel might not have believed him. Anne-Marie Régnier from Bordeaux would have been humble, acted stupid, shown more fear.

"I am glad you can now see I could never spy for the English."

Vogel's face cracked in an approximation of a smile. "Non, non, non. You see, that is where I stop believing Archambault. You're a spy—you fought so hard, you bit Cartaud's hand! I wish I'd been there to see it. And," he added, "Archambault said your father is a maharaja and it was therefore even more impossible that you would collaborate with the British. This information explains many things."

She gave him a baffled glance.

"It explains your posture, your bearing. A certain flash in your eyes."

His gaze stroked her from head to toe. Vogel had mistaken her anger at herself for aristocratic imperiousness.

"And if you aren't a spy, just what were you doing with a transmitter? Using it to listen to the BBC? Even if you could use one for that, it is forbidden."

Everything is forbidden unless permitted by you.

"I found it," said Noor. "Someone left it in the apartment and I was trying to understand what it was. I thought Monsieur Cartaud was a thief."

"In an unfurnished apartment? What was there to steal?"

"I had just rented it, I didn't have money to furnish it yet."

"Non, mademoiselle. A princess can afford to furnish any apartment she chooses. You are a British subject living outside a detention camp, not obeying orders to report to the Kommandant every week—you're a spy. What other interpretation can there be?"

Armand. Not a single hint about Armand or Drancy.

A woman in a feldgrey skirt, jacket and high wedge heels entered—quiet, deferential, functional. She placed an armful of manila files at Vogel's right hand. A stenographer, perhaps.

Wet thumps alternated with the stamp of rubber on paper.

Grignon, the day of the arrests. Vogel standing beside Kieffer in the sandy courtyard before the main château, threatening immediate execution of the third man, Odile's aristocratic amour, Louis de Grémont. A moment of hesitation—the only such moment either had shown in the entire event—when they saw de Grémont was no peasant who could be labelled a Communist once executed.

Yes, she could perform like an aristocrat. She wasn't a princess, but Abbajaan's family was noble enough, a courtier-artist clan. Vogel wouldn't know the difference between her performance and the airs and graces of actual Indian royalty. He wouldn't know Baroda was ruled by a Hindu raja, not a Muslim nawab. He wouldn't know a Hindu from a Muslim. And wouldn't have any way to verify it. But to employ the same tall story Mother had invented so long ago—Oriental mystique . . .

Allah is showing a way; take it.

Give Vogel's small mind a large, unfamiliar idea with which to grapple.

Vogel recapped his fountain pen. The stenographer collected the files, closed the door behind her.

Noor gave an exaggerated sigh and switched to English. "Herr Vogel, your intelligence is indeed excellent. I can no longer deny I am Princess Noor Khan of the independent Kingdom of Baroda. My father and my government will be anxious for my return."

Electric daring crackled in every nerve. She held Vogel's eyes for a very long moment.

Vogel stood up and gave a slight bow, as if they were meeting for the first time. He came around his desk.

Her wrists—so heavy on her lap. She tried moving her fingers.

The scent of kerosene changed to a burning smell as Vogel flicked his lighter, cauterized a cigarette and held it out to her.

She turned her head away.

He shrugged, then switched to English. A new phase had begun.

"I don't understand why you work for your conqueror," he said. "Millions of Indians are fighting for independence. Your Mr. Gandhi has been imprisoned many times for attempting to unite Hindus and Muhammadans."

Mr. Gandhi, Mr. Nehru and thousands of others had not been imprisoned for attempting to unite Hindus and Muslims, but for exhorting the British to quit India. Correcting Vogel's grasp of reality or politics wouldn't help Prosper, Archambault or anyone else. So she lifted her good shoulder a little and said, "Baroda is independent, a British ally, neutral in this war. I request diplomatic immunity."

Vogel waved a hand. "It's subjugated by the English, I'm sure—no immunity. As for you, perhaps you believe the English have come to understand your colonial resentment. But they are not Germans—I assure you they understand only themselves."

Mr. Churchill didn't understand Indian resentment despite

their continuing, thirty-year independence struggle. But Vogel was implying the Germans would have had more empathy. He'd be convincing if she hadn't experienced the rule of both colonizers.

No matter who the colonizer, no matter who the colonized, there is no such thing as benign occupation.

Aloud, she said, "Many English people now sympathize with India's need for freedom from tyranny. The British have promised India freedom once Hitler surrenders."

"Herr Hitler," corrected Vogel. "Once Herr Hitler *surrenders?*" He crossed his arms on his chest. "Oh, *mein schatz*, the Führer is just falling back a few times to make the Allies believe he is being beaten."

Had he called her his darling? Perhaps she could use it.

"It is all part of his plan, don't you see?"

"Ah," she said, matching his tone with one of inscrutable Oriental omniscience.

She couldn't tell if she was hollow from hunger or fear.

Could her sudden elevation to princess help Prosper and Archambault? She had to try—but try while protecting Madame Aigrain.

"Herr Vogel, I need a small favour."

"Prisoners do not receive favours, my princess. And prisoners captured in combat without insignia are entitled to no favours at all. You are an illegal combatant—an enemy soldier who does not follow the civilized rules of war. You should be shot! Shot immediately!" His right eyelid drooped into a long, slow wink. "But all the same, you may ask me a favour."

Noor pouted for effect. "I know all prisoners are allowed one suitcase. I was unable to bring mine. Monsieur Cartaud would not allow me." Then she held her breath.

"My apologies, Princess, I will ask Monsieur Cartaud to collect it. You will give him a letter for your rentier, with a list of your requirements." He sounded pleased with his own magnanimity.

Noor took a deep breath and inclined her now regal head ever so slightly. "I was living incognito as Anne-Marie—the press, you know. They can be so insistent. My rentier is an old lady who would never have rented me a room had she known I was a foreigner."

"The very old and the very young are of no use and no importance to us. Give me her name, Princess. I assure you she will not be arrested."

A Nazi's assurance that old Madame Aigrain would be spared was no assurance at all, but it was all the assurance she would wring from him.

"Thank you, Herr Vogel."

"Princess, I understand you now."

He understood nothing.

"Please, call me Ernst. Soon I hope you will understand me."

Vogel would expect any Eastern woman, even a princess, to be submissive as a fantasy odalisque. Let him think so while she searched for a way to escape.

"Come, we will dine."

He snapped his fingers and the stenographer stepped in. Vogel's directions in German darted at the woman till she came forward and unshackled Noor's hands.

Noor stifled a scream of pain, let the waves pass. The stenographer led her to an adjoining windowless bathroom, handed her brush, comb and—wonder of wonders—soap! A creature with wild eyes stared at her in the mirror, cheeks patched black and blue. The woman waited while Noor washed her face and used the toilet, then helped her brush her troll-cloud tangle of black hair.

Back to Vogel.

A trolley nosed the door open. A few minutes later, silver cutlery shone beside gold-rimmed porcelain plates, and cut-glass goblets stood waiting for the first swirl from a bottle of wine at the centre of the table. Steam wisps curled from a covered silver gravy boat sitting on Vogel's desk like a just-rubbed genie lamp.

Some meat that didn't smell like pork, petits pois, baby potatoes, spaetzle.

Vogel snapped his fingers again and pointed at the mantel. The stenographer took the pair of silver candlesticks standing on either side of the gilt-framed mirror and placed them on the desk. Vogel flicked a lighter and two flames plumed the candle wicks.

Dinner for two, with her captor.

Noor picked up the fork in her right hand, speared a potato and forced herself to eat. No telling when she'd see a meal such as this again.

Tuesday, October 19, 1943

Under the splayed glow of the green-glass-shaded lamp beside Vogel lay Noor's identity card, ration book, certificate of Aryan descent, tortoise-shell compact, and *ausweiss* from her handbag. The valise she had requested three days ago in her note to Madame Aigrain sat open and rummaged on a table in the corner.

A sidelong glance told her the leather pouch had not joined the items on Vogel's desk.

This time she stood with her left arm in its makeshift sling and the guard chained only her ankles.

Could she leap from that window, the one slightly ajar? Only if she could leave her skin behind. She had lost count of the number of escape plans she had made and discarded in the last few days. Even with bound hands, she had tugged her heavy bed to the centre of the maid's room and jarred her shoulder again by attempting a jump. As if she could seize one of the bars beneath the skylight! Too high, even if she had two good arms.

"Forgeries. Excellent forgeries." Vogel looked up and straightened his bow tie. "The English are becoming more and more adept. However, I have learned something that confuses me. I need your help in understanding it—" He broke off. "Princess, I like it when you lift one eyebrow."

Vogel had moved from the familiar *tu* to the more respectful *vous*. Her princess performance was proving convincing.

Then Vogel went back to his prepared speech. "Princess, we now know more about you. You see, we have Monsieur Viennot in custody."

Viennot as well!

"It's unfortunate, as he was an old friend of ours—used to be a buyer for our Bureau of Requisitions. He too tried very hard to save you. From him Cartaud learned a very important piece of information. Would you like to know what it is?"

"Since you already know everything, how can there be anything left to learn, Herr Vogel?"

Vogel looked at her askance, but proceeded. "We have determined that you are not only an Indian princess and a British spy, but you are a *mischlinge.*"

"I have admitted I am Princess Noor," said Noor with a confidence she did not feel. "I repeat I am not a spy for any country. And since I don't know this Viennot or understand your language, you must enlighten me: what is *mischlinge?*"

"Mixed blood—offspring of an Indian prince and an American mother. Princess, why did you not tell me your mother is American?"

This was said as if she'd been a very naughty girl.

Viennot had probably given Cartaud this information under torture, and in the belief it would help Noor. Should she deny it? The Americans were coming—and they had tipped the scales against the Germans once before, in the Great War. If she denied it, would that mean more torture for Viennot?

"You didn't ask. I didn't think it important."

Vogel stopped and glared at her, then said as if to a child: "The Americans are our enemies." He pulled a chair behind her. "Sit down."

Behind his desk, he paced back and forth. Was Vogel moving, or was his backdrop of Hitler, Goebbels and Göring?

"Ach, they call themselves the Allies, but it is really the Americans who control. Since the Great War they have poured money into warfare, using England as their surrogate. Always clever, lending Germany money for reparations to France, and then . . . But that is history. I don't think you understand the position in which you have placed me, *ma princesse*. Each *mischlinge* is a deadly danger to the Reich, and if you are not to be executed as a spy, my duty is to deport you immediately. Those are the orders. Without delay, *vous comprenez?*"

A cold blade of fear entered Noor. Those buses, people crowded like cattle, the old, the sick and the children . . . Yes, she was afraid. In France she stood a chance, even now, of talking her way out of the avenue Foch. But if Vogel sent her to a camp or prison in Germany, she'd be closer to Armand but imprisoned indefinitely, with no hope of communication or reunion with him.

Vogel was still pacing, talking. "But American blood . . . this confuses the picture. It is not so easy to deport you . . . American blood. It could be useful. But tell me—how did your mother come to be pursuing happiness, as they call it, in France? I find this difficult to believe."

Noor's eyebrow rose involuntarily, then lowered; she wouldn't make a single gesture Vogel liked.

Evade his question.

"You said you lived in France for many years before the war. Did you not come seeking happiness?"

"That is *tellement différent*," said Vogel. "Very different. I live in exile here. I had to leave Germany long before the Führer came to power. Twenty years ago I was your age—about twenty-four? Those were difficult times, *très difficiles*. You know, I had to stand in line three times a day at the factory where I worked to get paid? My money was worth half its value by the end of the day. No, I didn't come to France to seek happiness—I left my home and my family to find work. And where did I find it? In the Rothschild's bank. I was a clerk in a cage, counting Jewish money all day. Now that Jew is in a cage and my office is in his home. That is the kind of justice I wanted, and the Führer made. The Führer understands—he is my megaphone. But *happiness?* I never pursued happiness, or expected any—"

His tone, like Uncle's, placed the word "happiness" in quotes. It was true Mother had pursued her own happiness, by running away to marry Abbajaan; but she hadn't pursued it at the expense of everyone else in the world. Whereas Nazis like Vogel . . .

Vogel went on, "—and not the state's happiness, but their own—so frivolous! Now in Germany, we aim for greatness, the grandeur of all Germany. America aims for mediocrity in the name of individualism. Fascism is like democracy—it expresses the will of the majority, *nein*? We have so much in common—even the eagle as our symbol. The tidal wave of Fascism is rising in America too, you know. They appear to worship Herr Roosevelt, they too would like to deport all foreigners—Germans, Japanese, Jews, Gypsies, Negroes, Indians—leaving just enough of other species and races to do the labour that soils their hands."

The world reflected in a funhouse looking glass, a mirror-world.

"I wouldn't know, Herr Vogel, I have never been to America." This, at least, was true.

Vogel came around the desk and stood before her. A little too close, especially at hip level. "Tell me, how does it feel?" His voice had deepened. He breathed from his mouth, shallow and quick. "To be a *mischlinge*, I mean?"

His accent had thickened.

"It must feel terrible," he said in a musing, intimate tone, "not to belong anywhere, to be a rootless cosmopolitan, never to be satisfied anywhere, to always be comparing one place to another."

Noor turned her head away.

"When I was with other Germans in the camp for a year before the fall of Paris—the one the French call the Battle of France," said Vogel, "I remember being afraid." He laughed. "Yes, I—afraid. I was afraid not of the French or martyrdom, but that the Fatherland might abandon me in France. My Führer might decide I no longer belonged to Germany. Do such thoughts worry you, *mischlinge*?"

The scent of his desire, words of tender concern—so long as he had her sitting before him with chained feet. He was calling to the fear she had in common with women of all nations. Using it. The only surprise was that he'd waited till now. But there was something holding him back. It would be foolish to believe it was conscience.

Noor sat up taller. "Herr Vogel, you are a most astute gentleman. I can only say you have made a terrible mistake. I am no spy, just a visitor to Paris caught in the war, unable to return to the Kingdom of Baroda. Forgive me for lying to you, but I was afraid you would send me to a concentration camp, where many foreign citizens have gone. I belong in India." She tossed her head. "There, someone like Cartaud would not be allowed in my presence."

"Oh, why do you play with me, Princess? I can interpret you, better than you interpret yourself. *Écoutez*, when it's better for you to be French, you say you are French, when it's better to be Indian, you say you're Indian. When you wish to be American, you will say you are American. And if it is ever advantageous to you to be German, I'm sure you will not hesitate."

Vogel was accusing with dreads she had always had, of discovering Mother's opportunism in herself, of being seduced by a need to belong.

"Not true," she protested.

"But have you ever thought, *mischlinge*, that the reverse is true as well—that when it is advantageous for the British to call you British, they will, and when it is advantageous for Americans to include you, they will, and when Indians wish to claim you for a while, they will."

Of course she had. But she wouldn't admit that to Vogel— Vogel who was casting a covetous glance over her.

"I understand, you see, because I am a linguist. People who know many languages have many selves, just like *mischlinges*." He lit a cigarette and pulled in smoke. "You're so lucky I have been allowed to interrogate you without Herr Kieffer present. He interrogates by domination. I have different methods. You see, people are like words—they have meaning only in context, so I ask myself what does your context and that of the others have in common? I mentioned to Prosper that Colonel Buckmaster was more likely to be found in a club than in a pub, and to Archambault I wondered why Colonel Buckmaster of the SOE wasn't sitting in the interrogation chair in place of his agent. But with you . . ."

Smoke puffed. He let the sentence trail away.

"For your interrogations, Princess, I have changed nuance and weight when I reported the answers you gave to Herr Kieffer. For your benefit I made tiny substitutions, supplied alternatives for a turn of a phrase."

Which answers? Vogel must have conducted entire interrogations in his own mind. If her few words were five percent of the story, his imagination had to supply the remaining ninety-five. But at least her "princess" story had one advantage: Vogel had made no move to touch her.

"Why do I do this? I cannot say. It is not what I have done for any other terrorists, even women."

He moved to the window and gazed down at the avenue. Ash grew on his cigarette. When he turned back, he seemed to have lost the thread of his thoughts.

"Language, separator of all men! To know even a single other language is to have a mistress to whom you cling in times when your wife and children only ask for bread at table, never how it got there. Language introduces you to men you would never have met but for her."

He tossed the cigarette end into the fireplace. "French has a passion wholly lacking in our German life—it refuses to obey even its own rules. Its syllables are as sirens seducing my ear. I taste them like fine champagne." He paused. "I am glad you are not French, little princess."

If Frenchness could be measured by how much one resisted all who threatened France, Noor had never before felt quite so French. But which performance did Vogel wish to see? To be Indian was important at this moment. But being Indian was also being English. How long could she meet Vogel's need for illusion?

She drew herself taller, summoning every ounce of majesty. "I appreciate your requesting my valise, Herr Vogel."

"Not at all. It enabled us to arrest yet another dangerous miscreant, a saboteur, a bomber of some repute. You may know him, mademoiselle? He is notorious—he goes by several names, but his file is labelled *Phono*."

Émile Garry! Oh, no, not Émile. Twenty-four hours! Émile had twenty-four hours to hide . . . Vogel is lying. What was Émile doing at Madame Aigrain's home?

"He was waiting for you," Vogel supplied, as if reading her mind. "He had a pistol. He was seated at your rentier's dining table with a pistol before him."

Noor kept her face self-assured and expressionless. Vogel was conducting her through an inferno of the lost souls of her friends. Chance had brought all Renée's prophecies to fulfillment. Hadn't Renée believed Noor would somehow, someday, lead the Gestapo to Émile? And she had, albeit unwittingly. She knew the pistol Émile had before him—the pistol she gave him. He had been waiting, but not for Noor. There could be only one reason Émile had been waiting at Madame Aigrain's with a pistol: he was expecting Gilbert. A message from Émile signed "Madeleine" would have lured Gilbert to Madame Aigrain's.

And Noor had sent the Gestapo to Madame Aigrain's at exactly the wrong time.

Before her was a picture that might have been fixed in black and white for all time: Émile and Monique kissing, walking down the street kissing, Renée's face, smiling for once, at their wedding. How terrible for Monique, bride of a few months, perhaps by now a mother-to-be. For Babette, who loved her uncle and godfather so dearly. Most of all, Émile's arrest would devastate Renée. Renée was waiting eagerly for Guy, but right now she had neither husband nor brother. And beyond love and concern for these men, Noor knew that Renée, untravelled, dependent as she was, could not imagine anything worse than this.

"I don't know this man Phono," she said aloud. "It's just your excuse to kidnap another Frenchman and send him to Germany. It's a *shanghaillage.*"

"If so, you have only to volunteer to work in Germany along with two others and Phono will be returned to his family. But how could I forget?! That applies to prisoners of war, not to spies and terrorists like Phono. Monsieur de Gaulle is funding all of them with money from the English and the Americans. He can stop the attacks whenever he likes. But he does not condemn the violence."

He was behind her chair, probably checking his reflection in the mirror.

"All we want is to stop the violence," he said in a quietly aggrieved tone.

He came before her again.

"Where is Madame Aigrain?" cried Noor.

"I kept my word, Princess. Your rentier was not arrested."

Blood pulled away from every extremity. Relief washed through Noor.

"I said to myself, 'English women like a man who keeps his word.'"

English woman? An English subject, yes, but not many in England would think of her as an English woman. No matter, if it made Vogel keep his word.

"Since I don't know this Phono, that is all that matters to me," said Noor. "The rest is between you Germans and the French. We Indians have nothing to do with it."

Vogel sat down behind his desk. "But you have American blood—now I have to treat you as an illegal combatant." He opened a bulging manila folder. "Perhaps your soft heart has persuaded you, my captive Indian princess, that being against us means you are *for* France or Frenchmen. I assure you, Frenchmen are never who they say they are. Ach, they all look alike, they are all alike—treacherous, mademoiselle, treacherous! Yes, every day I translate orders from German to French, but also

I translate letters from *corbeaux*—people who write anonymous letters denouncing and betraying fellow Frenchmen."

There was a pause. Then, in a voice of gloved steel he said, "If you're not with us, you're against us."

No tears. Don't let him see you cry.

The guard carried her valise and handbag as he pulled her down the corridor back to her room. With the door locked again, Noor sank down on the maid's bed and allowed herself to feel the full force of guilt and sorrow at Émile's arrest. The should-have-dones, the could-have-dones, the what-ifs. And all for naught—Gilbert was still at large.

She opened the valise and felt in the lining. Where was it? Had they found it? She scrabbled and tore. There. The little brocade pouch was there. And inside, the diamonds—all five.

That night, when prodded down the corridor to the lavatory, she slipped the pouch beneath the enamel triangle of the sink.

CHAPTER 35

Gestapo Headquarters, avenue Foch
Paris, France
Thursday, October 28, 1943

MAN. WOMAN. Man. Men, women. More men, more women.

The animal screams and pleadings Noor heard from other cells each night for eight nights were in French, the shouting sometimes in German, sometimes in French. She strained to recognize a single voice—Prosper, Archambault, Monsieur Hoogstraten or the Professor? Émile? Viennot? Not Odile? Not Josianne? Distance blurred words but retained the anguish of the sounds. At the end of each disturbed night came real coffee, rye bread and cheese for Noor. She ate it. Another beating might be coming. Interrogation scenes played over and over in her mind. Her cuts and bruises were healing. Every day, she had yet another wild plan for escape. But not a chance.

Now a guard was pushing her down the hall past closed doors of other rooms, down a servants' back staircase to Vogel's office. He shoved her into the chair before Vogel's desk.

Sit up straight. Don't cringe.

Rain ribboned the French windows overlooking the *contre-allée*, the side road that buffered the mansions from traffic on the avenue Foch. Outside, trees baffled and channelled an earth-musked breeze.

Vogel offered himself a smile in the mirror.

"Something to show you," he said in English.

A manila folder slid across the desk and opened before her. Some kind of report stamped *U.S. Board of Economic Warfare.*

"Read it," he commanded. "Read aloud where I have underlined."

Noor read, "'The average person in India is eating 600 to 800 calories per day. That is only a few ounces, consisting chiefly of starches. The average Englishman or American consumes between 3,500 and 3,800 calories daily . . . The minimum subsistence diet is 1,000 calories a day . . . Registration records show an increase of 47,000 deaths over the previous five-year average for the month.'"

"What does it recommend? Read the conclusion, underlined in red."

"It recommends immediate relief shipments."

"Yes, don't you see, Princess? These are your Allies."

"These are the occupiers of India, just as Germans are the occupiers of France."

He took off his spectacles and stared at her. Then he put them back on and said, "Read the clipping from *The New York Times.* It's dated August 1943. Read it aloud!"

"'The mayor of Calcutta has sent a telegram to President Roosevelt. It reads: *Acute distress prevails in the city of Calcutta and province of Bengal due to shortages. Hundreds dying of starvation. Appeal to you and Mr. Churchill in the name of starving humanity to arrange immediate shipment of food grains from America, Australia and other countries.'"*

Noor's cheeks grew warm, but she remained quiet.

"And this one." He picked up another clipping. "Dated August 30, see—not that long ago. Read it aloud."

Keeping her voice optimistic as that of a newsreel announcer, Noor read, "' . . . at a meeting of the Combined Food Board, the U.S. representative raised the issue of food with the British representative. He was told it is a matter of shipping, not of supply, and that Australia can supply India.'"

"Do you understand for whom you are fighting, now, Princess Noor? Allow me to read this one to you myself—top secret, intercepted from a consul general's dispatch to the U.S. State Department. It says, "'The problem of disposal of corpses from the streets of Calcutta is severely overtaxing the facilities available.' Don't you understand? Your countrymen are being exterminated, and the excuse is this war. See these—"

Her tongue turned heavy and helpless in her mouth.

Don't let him see any reaction.

Clippings spread across his desk: "Bengal Food Crisis!" cried the London *Times*. "Famine in Bengal" proclaimed the *Manchester Guardian*. "Hospitals receive 5,000 cases of hunger-related diseases" said *The New York Times*. And finally, one dated today, October 28, 1943, from the Associated Press: "100,000 men, women and children are dying of starvation each week in Bengal and the figure is likely to rise weekly till December."

Dadijaan's teak-brown face in 1940, the day they fled—old Dadijaan refusing to return to India with Uncle Tajuddin because she had "a lot of work to do in London." Dadijaan making her speeches at Hyde Park every Sunday.

Maybe, just maybe, someone who could understand Urdu had begun to listen. Dadijaan said, often and loudly, that the British-owned *Statesman* had been censored, barred from using the word "famine," yet the *Manchester Guardian* actually used the word.

The clippings showed some progress, a capacity for self-correction. And though they would never bring back those starved for this war, maybe these reports would pressure Churchill to request UNRRA grain and famine relief from President Roosevelt.

Swallow back tears, or he wins.

"At least," stammered Noor, "the English papers are freer than yours. People could be starving and enslaved in German camps and your Propagandastaffl's newsreels would never report it."

Vogel threw up his hands. "Now you don't want to believe what your 'free' press is telling you? Usually there are so many conflicting points of view, one doesn't know what to believe." He glanced at himself, then came back to Noor. "You are Indian, but you do not care?"

Noor frowned at the clippings before her and willed her voice steady. "I do care. Not only because I am Indian, but because I am human."

Vogel looked at her as if she had spoken in Urdu. "I have been so patient with you. Understand me: I report to Herr Kieffer every day how much you know. I tell him you have intimate knowledge of the PROSPER network, since all messages went through you. But you have to, you must, give me locations of hidden arms."

How long could the illusion Vogel had created last? She didn't know any locations. Vogel would never believe her, but the last time she had seen arms was in the library at Grignon. And the Germans must already have found those after the Grignon roundup. What she knew of the Free French networks for whom Viennot had enlisted her services was code names, addresses of safe houses. Resistants didn't have any need to inform London where arms were hidden in France.

"It's taken days, but we have deciphered Archambault's messages and yours. Very interesting. *Très intéressant!* But only code names have been used in every message. We have some information from other sources, but you must help me with the code names we don't know."

Other sources. "Ask Gilbert!" she wanted to shout. But she couldn't admit to knowing him. Gilbert would know only the names and addresses of SOE agents; he couldn't help Vogel with names of Free French resistants. Viennot would know those details. Insh'allah, Viennot had lasted twenty-four hours to let his contacts go underground. Silence was her only defence.

Vogel's face had actually reddened. "Herr Kieffer expects me to send you to Fresnes prison. Do you understand? That is no longer a prison—it's a prison camp! Don't oblige me to obey him. If not Fresnes, he commands that I send you to some other prison camp, as I have sent everyone in Prosper's network."

They haven't been executed! They must have used the diamonds to bribe someone in the Gestapo. Probably Vogel.

Though Émile was caught, at least some benefit had come of requesting her valise, some good for many others.

"If you give me nothing I can use, I will be forced to send you away. At present, I've told Herr Kieffer I can't find a prison or camp that isn't full."

Seeming unaware of the implications of his statement, he gestured at the clippings on the table. A throbbing ache returned to her shoulder, radiated through her.

"Think, Princess, think what Churchill is doing to your people, for this war. We'll have dinner together again when you're ready to talk to me."

The guard stepped forward, took her by her good arm and led her back to her cell.

CHAPTER 36

PIERRE CARTAUD came for Noor after midday soup and bread, two Gestapo thugs behind him.

Fear swarmed in her stomach. She backed away, glancing up at the sloping skylight as she had every day, since her last interrogation. Too high.

"Where is Herr Vogel? I demand to be taken to him."

"Herr Vogel," sneered Cartaud, "is wounded. In hospital—one of your Canadian spies shot him."

The two Canadians had landed in June, were escorted by Gilbert to the station and dispersed for their missions. They had disappeared soon after. If they hadn't been interrogated till now, that could mean they'd been shut away in Fresnes prison for more than four months.

"Nonsense!" she said, pretending to be brave. "Tell him Princess Noor wants to see him immediately."

This time he will rape me, without Vogel to stop him.

She was boiling and freezing inside.

Cartaud surprised her by explaining, almost politely, that he needed her room. "The Canadian must be kept under observation—he fired eight times. He threatened to shoot me too if I told him one more time how bad is his accent. And I only told him once—*quelle barbarie!*"

So, said Cartaud, he needed the room Noor had occupied for six weeks in the avenue Foch. Herr Vogel had found a prison that had a cell for her. Cartaud would move her tonight.

"You'll be a Special Prisoner," he said, as if offering her a special treat. He made it sound as if she had a choice, but she didn't. Not with three men exuding power, sweat and obvious relish, who cuffed her flailing hands before her.

"No fighting, now!" said Cartaud. "I'll shoot you right here and tell Herr Kieffer you tried to escape."

I should have bitten your hand much harder.

Her neck jerked. A bandage wedging her upper lip against her teeth, its snaffle forcing an unnatural grin, stanching her furious questions, threats and invective; both nostrils blocked. She worked facial muscles, jaw and tongue till the bandage slipped a few millimetres, granting air to straining lungs.

Welcome scent of new air: the door to her room had opened. Noor took a deep nasal breath, to scream. But the scream gagged in her larynx, going up up up, reverberating into her skull.

The thugs held her between them. German orders and *jawohls* flew over her head. Down, gun-prodded down, step by step. Eyes on the carpeted spiral. Five storeys she couldn't remember climbing.

Into the vestibule, out into chilly November sunshine. She was being shoved down the short driveway towards a black staff car waiting in the *contre-allée*. If she let her body go limp as she had with Gilbert, they'd have to drag her through the iron gates.

Those filthy hands would roam all over her again.

No. Struggle harder.

"You want me to tell Herr Kieffer how dangerous you are? He'll keep you in chains."

Five fingers and a giant palm on the crown of her head, pushing down. A blow, knocking her sideways into the back seat. Leather scraping her cheek, shoulder scraping leather.

Aim for Cartaud's groin.

She kicked out. Pain shot up her jarred ankle. Cartaud gasped like a pricked balloon. Behind him, a man laughed. The door slammed closed.

The door at her head opened. Glimpse of a husky SS man. He grabbed her.

Choking, choking.

She was folded into sitting position easily as a doll, nothing she could do. The SS man got in beside her, the trace of a smile on his face. Outside the window, Cartaud was still doubled over.

The SS man's side arm gleamed in its holster, just to frighten her; she refused to be frightened. With her hands shackled, escaping was a rope trick she couldn't do.

The car swung away down the avenue Foch.

Villages of cream stone and red tile, points of steeples rising in their midst. Plough-combed fields and periodic glimpses of the Marne flowing away to join the Seine. Solid stations resisting the motion of scurrying trains, woods swamped in water, nests clumped like lookout posts at the tips of branches, piles of firewood, the chug-a-chug of wheels on the track and the occasional toot of an engine. Wagons on sidings. A station—Chalons-sur-Marne.

How easily they had transferred her from the Gestapo staff car to this train compartment. Like a sack of grain. No chance to escape, and though her gag was removed, her feet were now shackled as tightly as her hands. Two SS guards, one short and pig-faced, the other tall with a sad-dog face, glowered at her from their seat opposite.

She turned to the window, pretended she didn't notice them.

A fountain spouted from stone, sheds of grain, sweet-faced cows at pasture, power lines uncut by saboteurs, covered wagons of the SNCF, shuttered windows of a *boulangerie*, bales of hay, milk-chocolate earth, a bridge, sun slanting through the green lace of trees, weathercocks on steeples.

Paris was left behind. Where was she going? East, since the sun was setting behind the train.

Undulating hills, a canal. Bar-le-Duc station.

A train swung by on the adjoining track, bound Parisward. Mountains in the distance offered sanctuary to Maquis bands. If only she could run away, join them.

Under a bridge now, then into a valley. A few bicycles moving on a thin thread of road. A hamlet, a square steeple, a road curving beneath the track, a rise of hill, puffy trees obscuring hard blue sky. In a hollow between hills, signs pointed to destinations—too far away to read.

Sunrays slanted further now, mirroring the still surface of a pond, teasing shadows from a line of trees. Patchy shapes of Holsteins should have been visible against the darkening earth, but animals were long slaughtered to supply the army.

Trees lay felled against each other, branches snapped, a crater before them. Lérouville station. A cemetery, scruffy shapes of woodpiles. A château brooded on a craggy hill overlooking the river. Who lived there—did they agree or disagree with Hitler and Vichy?

Sunlight moved away now, birds flew homeward, horses nuzzled one another in a paddock. A railway crossing, then the spread-eagled red roof of another railway station.

A canal flowed alongside the train. If she could work herself out of her bonds, maybe she could leap from the train and roll down the bank into the canal . . .

The windows filled with the echoing darkness of a tunnel. The light returned. The canal had veered away.

The train slowed but did not stop at Foug station.

Rust-orange mounds of scrap metal. A store of sandbags stamped with something illegible at this distance.

The train sloped in the direction of its turn, straightened. *Toul Poste* 1.

Double steeples rose from the grimy, rundown town into twilight. Storm clouds gathered over hostelries and turreted mansions. Noor squinted to read Pig-face's watch upside down.

Dwellings dotted across a hill. "Nancy," said Sad-dog to Pig-face.

Try not to need. Remember the taste of water. Turn off need, try not to need.

How, how to get out of the compartment? German soldiers everywhere.

Sad-dog stepped into the corridor. Pig-face stretched his legs out before him, stared at her with expressionless eyes.

A fricative whistle; the train began to chuff forward again. Desperation spread like an ink blot within Noor. Everywhere, windows were blackening for the night, shutters closing.

The train hooted past a petrol refinery.

Sad-dog returned with two enamel cups of soup, one for Pig-face, one for her. He didn't release her wrists. Mild taste of potatoes, brackish and lukewarm.

Drink it slowly. Look outside. Drink slowly.

The slope of rooftops changed, houses broadened at their base.

Nervous fluid rushing in her ears. This must be Germany.

And the landscape revised itself, colouring the sunlight red, heightening shadows, torturing shapes into metal objects and monsters, turning the flit of birds to ferreting movements.

Vineyards, sheep, railyards, empty stables. Horses, carts, night blue spreading. Footpaths wending their way into fields. Dark everywhere, not even a peep of light.

Low blue station light. Strasbourg.

Kehl. A Wehrmacht officer with a burn-disfigured pink face passed the compartment, gripping a valise with a bandaged hand.

23:00 hours on Pig-face's watch.

Karlsruhe.

23:30 hours.

A tambourine moon shivered in an unseen hand above a tiny station.

Pforzheim.

The tall guard rose to his feet and jerked the chain between Noor's wrists.

"*Raus!*"

———

One strong push opened the door, another sent Noor stumbling into an oblong cell. Iron bars sliced pale moonlight pouring through the high window.

She had entered this cell before, without manacles or leg irons. The walls of whitewashed plaster weren't familiar, nor the straw mattress on the metal frame cot. Nor the toilet, the only item out of the direct line of vision from the peephole. This dead air was familiar, its changelessness. The feeling of being hostage.

The month she spent confined for the sin of loving Armand, confined weeping in her room.

Limbs flailed in every direction. Two prison guards shouldered their way in and stood watching her, expressionless. Her hands were manacled, a chain running from cuff to cuff; she was leg-ironed, chains running between her ankles; and another long chain connected the two—worse than a creature in a zoo.

Anger flared to a scream that hadn't crossed her lips for pain, hadn't surfaced in torture, a shriek that mustered all her strength then exploded all around her.

A blow to her head brought darkness.

CHAPTER 37

Pforzheim, Germany
December 1943

A THIN MIST chilled Noor's cell. She used a knitting needle the guard had given her for stringing tickets, to carve hash marks into her cell wall, one for each day. The seventh, slashing across the rest, was Friday.

But she might have made two hash marks one day. Or she might have forgotten to make a hash mark.

Strange how Vogel simply appeared in her cell—like other ghosts and memories that gusted in with first snow. He lifted his shirt to show her the bullet wound inflicted by the Canadian in his left side, as if looking for comfort. He said he had to see her.

"I saved your life by reserving this cell. Instead of sending you to a camp, you know," said Vogel. "And your shackles, mademoiselle—they're your own fault. Cartaud told me how he caught you escaping through the skylight. Said he wrestled you down among the chimney pots. *Gott!* How I wish I'd been there to see it."

Her word against Cartaud's.

Silence. The only suitable response.

Vogel was looking as pleased as a sultan with a harem of one. A non-Aryan harem of one. There must be some huge fissure within him, some very basic need, carnal and beyond, for him to come here at all. Why had he? And what could she gain from his visit?

His hand moved towards her like a serpent arcing on its tail, then hesitated, fell. Serpent hand, serpent guardian, serpent who must be propitiated, satiated with milk, stroked and delighted. Had he come looking for a thank-you note? She wasn't thankful.

Writing things down should make men like Vogel nervous.

Play a little of the part he wants you to play. Play along just enough to be spared, Scheherazade.

Noor's shackles clanked as she leaned close to him for a moment. "Such ennui to be here, Herr Vogel. Especially for me. My world is so different! Durbars, tiger hunts, elephant parades, jewels, servants." She stopped as if struck by a thought. "Oh, the fables I could tell!" She looked up at him, gave an exaggerated sigh with a catch in it. "If I could write, it would pass the time."

"Fables?" Vogel cocked his head. "You write stories, *ja?*"

"If I had paper, pen and ink," she said, "Yes, I could write beautiful stories."

"It shall be provided, *mein liebchen*, it shall be provided. You shall write stories for my sons. And I will come to get them every month. See? I allow you everything in my power. In a few months, when the Jews and Americans are defeated, I promise we will be together."

My heart is sandbagged against you; I promise we will not.

When he was gone, Noor lay down on her filthy mattress. In waking dream she swam up Vogel's bloodstream, all the way to his heart, yet had no trouble breathing. A corroding substance flowed from her at will, and at last that heart was dehusked and laid bare. Cold, cold, cold in Vogel's heart, almost as cold as this cell, denser than night. Up she swam, looking for—what? A hidden chamber. There—what was inside?

A hunched shape, a small, woebegone face. A little boy sat in the bloodless chamber at the core of Vogel's heart. Little boy with a grotesque, too-large head, with great big hands and feet bulging from tiny limbs. Little boy who cried, sans intermission, covering his face with those huge hands. Genitals small and soft, penis receding, he cried from fear of the world, fear of anyone unlike himself, cried from terror because he would eventually die.

Almost, she felt sorry for him. But the wound from her dislocated shoulder had awakened, throbbing. Noor wakened too.

December moved in, taking up residence with Noor in her cell, and freezing the radiator.

Cold coiled in the bowl of her pelvis, turning shiver to quake as she lay beneath her blanket on the cot. Above, snow drifted against glass and bars. Shreds of thoughts, speculations, obsessions . . . some glue still held her fragments together.

The flap door clanged down.

"Herr Vogel . . ."

The rest, in rapid German, was senseless.

Silly hope reared inside; she reined it in.

The guard placed something on the thick, jutting tray, something invisible in the dingy half-light. Soup, probably. She didn't care.

She heard a clunk and a small swish.

Yes, she did care.

Noor rolled onto her stomach, chained wrists before her, supported her weight on her elbows and knelt. Then shifted to extend the chain running between her wrists and ankles far enough for her to be seated. The clanking weight of the leg irons pulled her bare feet to the floor.

She slipped into prison clogs, shuffled across the cement floor.

A pad of onionskin. A scrawl that filled the whole first page. It said in French, *For Princess Noor—write children's stories only.* Signed, *Ernst V.*

She had asked Vogel for paper, pen and ink, but had never expected to receive them. "Everything in my power," Vogel had said.

She tucked the pad under her arm, then tested the pen nib against her thumb. She reached for the glass jar. Dark blue ink. She opened it, inhaled its metallic fragrance.

She carried the writing materials back to her cot. She lay down, eyes open to the gloom, gritting her teeth to stop their chattering. Mosquito thoughts buzzed.

Do it. Shouldn't. Do it. Shouldn't. Do it.

Use initials, think the names, use false names, code names.

She caterpillar-crawled to the edge, turned on her side to block the vision of any guard and examined the leg of the cot. A pipe welded to the metal frame. Hollow pipe with a steel cover.

If I can hide some of my writing, I will write what I want.

She pressed a chain-link against the steel cover. Was it welded? Cold-numbed fingers exploring. No, not welded. Screwed on tightly.

Push, push with the edge of her manacles. Then with a chain-link. She wrapped her chain around the cover like a vise. It didn't move. She pushed and turned in the dimness for hours, till she was wiping sweat from her eyes. She froze whenever she heard— or thought she heard—a movement at the peephole.

Deep breath. Attack the hollow leg again.

Night blackened the cell. Baying and barking outside, beyond the stone walls of the prison. Twice, the rush of a train passing very close. Noor grimaced and grunted on.

Finally, the steel cover moved a millimetre along its treads. By dawn, it loosened. She lay back, exhausted. Then, with her back to the door, she rolled up half the onionskin, poked it down the pipe-leg and, with an effort, screwed the cover on again.

Above her, the window brightened.

The guard was at the door. She unchained the manacles so Noor could use the toilet. Did not glance at the bed. Did not shout.

The flap door dropped for Noor's morning bowl, sawdust bread. A single bulb lit the cell.

Begin, "Once upon a time there was a war . . . ?" No. She would write *une histoire,* not the kind her captor had in mind, for someone who might read her words in a time to come:

I am still here.

I write, not because this story is more important than all others, but because I have so great a need to understand it. What I say is my truth and lies together, amalgam of memory and explication. I write in English, mostly, English being the one language left in the ring. Other languages often express my feelings better — French, Urdu, Hindustani. And perhaps in these languages I could have told and read you stories better than this, your mother's story. But all my languages have been tainted by what we've said and done to one another in these years of war.

When the flap door dropped that evening, Noor dragged her chains to it and placed two sheets on the open tray. On one she had written the Sufi tale about the attraction of a moth to a flame, on another the one about the young man who came knocking at his teacher's door and when his teacher asked, "Who is there?" cried, "It is I," and was told, "Come back when you are nobody."

She could see the guard glance at the English writing then thrust the sheets in her pocket without examination. The pad of onionskin lay upon the cot behind Noor, but the guard didn't enter to count its remaining pages.

So, the next day, Noor wrote another paragraph, and another:

With that first creation of Allah — the pen that Vogel has allowed me — poised over the ink pot, then over the page, I wonder what to call you. Little spirit never whispered into this world — une fée. In Urdu I would call you ruh. Feminine. Ma petite ruh. We all begin feminine in Al-ghayab, the invisible, before we enter our nameless bodies.

I imagine you, ma petite, nine years old, looking much like me and as much like Armand, expectant and still trusting. Encourage my telling as any audience encourages a teller of tales, though I may tell what you may not condone, what you may not believe, or what you cannot bear to know. I write so you can see me, so Armand will appear again by the telling.

PART SEVEN

CHAPTER 38

Pforzheim, Germany
August 14, 1944

VOGEL GAVE ORDERS *for me to resume weekly exercise, but
today was the first time I was granted it. The guard took me past
other women's cells into the courtyard. There, she took the chains
from my feet and, truncheon in hand, led me around the compound. Fresh air on my face! Though I stumbled, I could have
thrown my arms about her.*

*I thought I had learned what prison means, but today I learned
I had no idea what prison means, no idea at all.*

*The walls and barred windows hulking over the courtyard
looked alien, though they have housed my body since last
November. A hand waved from a window a few cells from mine,
a white handkerchief from another. Women I may have glimpsed
in passing but never spoken to, never met—how kind! How very
kind!*

*I squinted, looking for any movement at my cell window. The
guard has never matched her count of pages given to me with the
pages I give to Vogel, but she could, or Vogel could. What better
time to search my cell?*

*Suddenly, I couldn't wait to be returned to my cell. I, who a
moment earlier wanted to be outside forever, now wished for nothing but the sight of these walls.*

When I shuffled back, the guard didn't push me in and walk away—but came into the cell. To my amazement, she removed the shackles from my hands as well. She left me the knitting needle and more tickets to string, and then was gone.

I held my hands out before me, tested each digit, massaged my wrists. I feel sure I was unshackled by order of the prison governor. He said he'd never kept a woman enchained as I was, not even a murderer. I don't know if my unshackling is a respite for a few hours or whether I dare hope for a more kindly regime.

I waited at least an hour before opening my khazana, my treasure chest in the leg of my cot. The sheets were still there. I write so small, using initials for code names; they reveal a tenth of my thoughts, but enough.

Ma petite, I must not write any more.

Yet how can I keep these pages? Keep them for you?

The pipes that bring me news in Morse run between two brick walls. Hands free, I worked all night, all night in the white-hot haste of desperation. By morning I had scooped a hole in one corner with the knitting needle. A hole no larger than the circle between thumb and forefinger, but enough to poke my papers one at a time between the cell walls. When I get some soup, I'll make a paste of all the plaster chips I've saved and it will camouflage the hole. The Germans will have to tear down the walls before they find them.

We are still together, ma petite. I continue speaking to your spirit as I did in the dungeon, only in my mind.

My manacles and leg irons were replaced this morning. I was unenchained only for a single night. And in the afternoon the governor himself brought my paper and ink. He stood looking at me a long time in silence. I cannot imagine how I looked to him.

"I telephoned Herr Vogel in Paris," he said eventually, struggling to find the right words in French. "I asked if I could remove your chains after so many months. I told him I never kept women in chains. *Sometimes in the dungeon, but not in chains. But Herr Vogel said there is a punishment order in your file. For attempting to escape, ja?" He shook his head regretfully. "He said already he has made too many exceptions in your case."* Here he gestured at the pen and paper. *"Remember, children's stories only,"* he said — and gave a little bow.

Even the Nazis cannot fully eradicate compassion and kindness.

I disobey him and write to you once more, against all resolutions, against all caution. I want you to know somehow — I don't know how or when — all I have said, all I have thought, all these months.

Talking to you distracts me from my daily fears, but leads me back to open questions. I want to know, I need to know: who told Cartaud and Vogel they would find a radio and an operator at the boulevard Richard Wallace apartment?

Was it my phone call to Odile? To trace it, the Gestapo had to know "Sablons 80.04" before I arrived for my transmission. The switchboard operator could have had it on a list of numbers under surveillance. How did they get it?

Major Boddington? Perhaps, when he told me in July that he had not given anyone my number, he meant "no one so far." He could have given Gilbert my telephone number afterwards. I can't believe he would tell it to Gilbert after I had refused to work with that salaud, but maybe he did.

The Gestapo could have triangulated on my transmission from detection vans, but how had they known the area a van should roam that day? Chance? I made my decision the night before and told no one, not Odile, not Josianne, that I would not be transmitting as usual from Suresnes.

Odile knew the address at boulevard Richard Wallace, but she would never have given me away — intentionally. But oh, she is such a little chatterbox. To whom might she have spoken? Viennot? Viennot knew my transmission times, but none of my addresses. Émile? Monique? Renée? They didn't know the new apartment either.

I have no proof, only suspicions. Polygamous conjectures that lead to more confusion.

Did Armand feel as I did when he was arrested? I felt panic, like a cornered animal; anger, like a wounded tigress.

August 16, 1944

Noor lay beneath her blanket, back to the door. A bolt drew back; she looked over her shoulder.

Sheen of sweat on that pale face, eyes bloodshot behind Vogel's spectacles. Perhaps some internal dialogue was in progress, finally.

"I walked from the station," he said, taking off his jacket and wiping his brow. "I couldn't get a motor transport to bring me here."

No internal dialogue—how foolish to expect it.

"The Gestapo headquarters are moving from Paris. Temporarily, you understand. *Befehl ist befehl*—an order is an order. We're sending everything to Berlin by car. Herr Kieffer could get petrol for that, of course."

Noor struggled to her knees, sat up, shook matted locks.

A small submarine began to bubble upwards in her stomach. If the Gestapo was retreating from Paris, the Allies must almost be upon them.

"I, however, am returning to Munich, Princess."

Change in pattern. Vogel usually came to see her on his way from, not to, Munich.

"Why not Berlin?" Noor asked.

"Herr Kieffer doesn't need an interpreter in Berlin. He may need an interrogator later, but at present he is not even taking Cartaud."

Of course, Cartaud would want to fall back with the Germans, even fleeing all the way to Berlin. Retribution was coming to the occupiers and their collaborators. No pity for Cartaud—he had felt none for her.

Vogel took a step towards her. She shrank away.

He sat down beside her and his shirt-sleeved arm looped around her shoulders. Cleared his throat. "I left Munich when I was seventeen . . ." He cleared it again. "I went back one summer and my wife . . ." He looked away. "She wasn't my wife at the time, but we . . . she became with child. So I had to marry her. But after the twins were born, I could never touch her again. You know I visit them dutifully, I provide for them. But, Princess, even now I feel nothing, though she is worn by war, sewing swastika arm bands. And then I saw you, a warm-blooded filly . . ."

Speech delivered, he began to flounder.

"When I come to see you, I am reminded of camp—nineteen thirty-nine. The year I last felt anything. Hope, pain, sadness, anger, shame—anything. It was safe in camp. No obligations, no women laughing at me if I couldn't . . ."

He didn't finish his sentence, nor did it seem he was going to.

"And now, to return to Munich . . . I'm going back to prison, a German one this time."

How dare Vogel compare this prison, this very real prison, with an abstract prison of rules willingly inhabited! Vogel should experience a real German prison camp, worse than Drancy if possible; he had sent so many Frenchmen—maybe even Armand—to German camps. A German prison camp would cure him of all nostalgia for Germany, make him truly appreciate his wife.

Vogel continued, "I have lived in Paris too long. I am accustomed to being served well in restaurants, having the right of way, interrogations, authorizations, reports. Munich has no need of me. I could be conscripted for military service, sent to the Eastern Front."

The hand resting on Noor's shoulder clenched a little, reawakening the ache of dislocation.

"I'm returning to a strange country. People don't require my translation skills, or if they do, no one wishes to pay. I think: what if I could take you with me? Call me Ernst, Princess, and I will get you a hot bath. You could do your hair. You would look as you did the first time I saw you—an exotic, beautiful thing."

Thing.

Cold fingers caressed the nape of her neck, his hand moved down, down, finding her breast. Did the Führer no longer prohibit sexual relations between Aryans and non-Aryans?

The pressure on her shoulders increased. Did it no longer matter to Vogel what the Führer prohibited? She leaned away, as far away as she could, sensed his biceps tensing beneath his shirt sleeve.

Then, suddenly, he released her and stood. She scrambled away to the corner of the cot, her back to the wall.

"Wouldn't you like a lovely silk dress? A pair of patent leather shoes? I can arrange a room for us at the Regina Palace Hotel—it has the most secure bomb shelter in the world. The Pinakothek is destroyed, but we don't need art. I prefer to take you to the opera."

She stared down at her ragged lap, manacled hands and feet before her. Yes, of course she would love a hot bath, a silk dress. But she was not Cinderella, Vogel was not her Prince Armand, and no glass slippers Vogel could buy for her would fit her feet.

Don't let him anger you—you have too little strength.

She was so tired of Vogel's games. So tired of being told who she was, who she should be, what he wanted her to be, how she should behave. Her half-starved body kept her almost in stupor these days, tired all the time.

He was over her again, grabbing the chain between her wrists. Pulling, as the iron rubbed its way into flesh. His hand was on her knee—the closest he had ever come.

"Please," she said, "please," but heard no sound emerging from her mouth. Heard only the cascading roar of fear within her.

Vogel held her shoulders in a vise.

"For once, call me Ernst, Princess! It's such a little thing!" He rocked her back and forth, crooning, begging, "Call me Ernst! Call me Ernst . . ."

She turned from his paleness, his decomposing breath, closed her eyes.

"You want something? I'll give you something. Here—" He let her go to fish in his pocket. "I was taking it for my wife, but I'll return it to you."

Noor opened her eyes, and a jolt went through her.

There on Vogel's palm lay a bright gold disc. The compact Colonel Buckmaster gave to all his women agents. How could this be? Yolande had been captured; it could be hers. But he had said, "I'll *return* it to you."

"It's yours, take it."

"What do you mean, it's mine?"

"I mean, I'll give it to you if you call me Ernst."

"It's pretty."

Lying on his palm like a third eye, reflecting a circle of light on the wall.

"A friend of yours gave it to me. Actually, it cost some money, not my own of course. It cost our department ten thousand francs, to be exact . . ."

"A friend of mine?"

"Call me Ernst and I'll tell you."

She didn't need to be told which "friend." She had given Colonel Buckmaster's gold compact to Renée Garry. If this was her compact, no one else could have or would have given it to Vogel. But Renée couldn't have betrayed Prosper and his whole network, she didn't have enough information—addresses, names—to do that. To have led the Gestapo to her brother, and her own safe house.

Vogel must be lying.

Wheedle, coax, cajole.

"How did you get it?" Noor insisted. "Tell me. I have given you so many stories, tell me this one. Maybe I will call you Ernst."

As he spoke, Noor saw with her third eye: Renée taking her walk in the Jardin d'Acclimatation, walking further and further, all the way to the avenue Foch.

"She asked for someone who spoke French," said Vogel.

And she sat where Noor would sit a few days later, before Vogel in his office, talking about an agent from London code-named "Madeleine," offering him the stranger she wanted out of her life in exchange for Guy, offering him a foreigner to bring her Guy home.

For ten months Noor had speculated and conjectured: who had denounced her? Anger and hatred would be normal. Anger and hatred—not anger mixed with pity, unexpected pity churning at the base of her stomach.

Renée! And all this time she had blamed Gilbert. Viennot was right—one is usually suspicious of the wrong person.

"Renée Garry said you were a Jew," said Vogel. "But I didn't believe her, once I saw you. And you didn't smell like a Jew to me."

Anger and pity somersaulted in her again as Vogel related how he asked Renée to bring him proof, something belonging to Madeleine.

"I had other compacts like it from other women agents. I believed her," said Vogel.

What a choice was offered Renée. What might Noor have bartered for the chance to feel Armand's breath upon her cheek? The first time she ran after buses at Drancy, had she not begged, *Take someone else, Allah, not my Armand, not him, not him.*

"She told us you had a transmitter. She didn't know where to find you, but my good friend Gilbert had a telephone number. And we waited till you used it. So you see, I always knew you were a British spy, but I couldn't help myself . . . wanting you. Now call me Ernst, just once, call me Ernst."

The compact sat upon Vogel's palm like an offering. She took it.

A scalding feeling at the back of her throat.

Do not cry.

Vogel's arms enveloped her again. Rocking. Would the guard come if she screamed? Any second now he would rock her back onto the cot; his weight would be upon her.

"Shhh! The guard will see you."

His grip loosened. She wriggled away.

"If you were convinced I was the spy, why arrest innocent people? Viennot and that man Phono." Her voice was angry again.

Be conciliatory, less confronting.

"Viennot is no innocent. And you *do* know Phono, Renée Garry's brother. Can you imagine what Herr Kieffer would do to you if I told him? You would be dead now, dead with Phono."

Émile executed! Good-humoured Émile—square-shouldered as a claret bottle, Émile of the grey suit with the elbow patches so lovingly sewn by Monique, the godfather Babette loved almost like a father. May Allah show his mercy.

A sly look came over Vogel's face. "I have stored two hundred litres of petrol, Princess. We could run away together, go to Switzerland."

Go to Switzerland with *Vogel?* Even had he not been a Nazi, how dare he think of abandoning his wife and children?

Vogel's look turned even more sly. "But for me, Princess, you would be dead for another reason. Renée Garry told me you killed two soldiers. Not even French—two German soldiers. *Ja,* she told me."

A numbing current of fear coursed through Noor.

"*Moi?*" As if completely surprised. A hangman's noose seemed to dangle above her; she reached out her toe, feeling for solid ground.

"*Ja,* but when I saw you, so dainty, so petite, I realized immediately you couldn't commit such crimes. Madame Garry swore you were at Grignon when we rounded up the terrorist Hoogstraten and his accomplices. But if you had been there, I would have seen you—and I would never forget you. I didn't bother to tell Herr Kieffer her inventions, because Madame Garry didn't know the facts: a man was seen running from Grignon after the shooting. We will find him."

You won't find him. You'll never find him.

She was savagely glad. But then—

Will he try to rape me without removing my chains? Keep him talking.

"The murderer could have been Phono. Was Madame Garry trying to protect him by blaming you? Phono was her brother. He has no need of your protection now—he's dead. Confess it, now—you knew him."

"I don't know anything."

"Remember I told you Cartaud found Phono when he went to get your valise from Madame Aigrain's apartment, and arrested him there? I told you Phono was lying in wait for *you*, waiting with a gun?"

Something was inhabiting her, crowding and pushing her organs against her ribs.

"Cartaud brought me to arrest Phono, and when he took Phono away, his wife—what is her name?"

"I don't know."

"Monique, that is her name. Monique came to Madame Aigrain's apartment looking for Phono. And Phono begged us for her life. He didn't know I had already promised you Madame Aigrain was not to be arrested, so he bargained for Madame Aigrain's as well. As if he had anything to bargain with!"

"These people are just names to me."

"No, not just names. I know everything. Everything! What is the use of denying it? Cartaud took Phono away and I began to interrogate Monique Nadaud and Madame Aigrain. Both were guilty—I knew that. And so was that Renée. Because she arrived too, looking for Phono."

Again, pity instead of anger. Renée arriving, seeing Vogel with Monique.

"She screamed, 'Where is Émile? What have you done with Émile?' And Madame Monique Nadaud said, 'He's gone, *ma belle-soeur*, the Gestapo has arrested him.' So you see, Phono was Renée's brother."

Renée's high-nosed face was before Noor, contorted with dismay and horror at where her actions had led her. If Noor were Renée, learning that she had gained her husband but lost her brother, she would wish the ground to open and swallow her. How would she feel if the Germans sent her Armand but took away Kabir? Even if Kabir had been tyrant-in-training, refusing to give permission for her marriage, even if he had been an intolerant *munafiq* who preferred her exile in India to her happiness, he was still her little brother to whom she told stories as he fell asleep at night. And Renée was so with Émile, whom she'd taught to shout "Vive la France!" Renée had offered hospitality to her brother's friends though vehemently disagreeing with his politics, and scoured all of Paris for chocolate for his wedding cake.

Vogel's spectacles drew close to her face, diminishing his eyes. His putrid breath chilled her skin.

"I've told you the story you wanted, Princess Noor. Call me Ernst. Now!"

His weight shifted, rocking her back. Crushing weight. He was rubbing himself against her, mumbling in German, pushing, snuffling, nuzzling into her left shoulder.

Old pain wakened.

This man, who had felt nothing since 1939, felt nothing even as he sent Émile to his execution, Prosper, Archambault, Professor Balachowsky, Monsieur Hoogstraten and Monique to camps, was pleading for her to help him, help him feel again.

To call Vogel "Ernst" would betray all the love she'd ever felt for Armand, that precious love that bombs could not shatter nor bullets kill. To betray that love would be true *zina*, betrayal of her husband.

And to call Vogel "Ernst" would invite his touch, and worse.

Corpse-pale lips parted. A grey serpent appeared, wet her cheek, then moved to part her lips.

Think. You are his weakness. Think!

The Allies were near, even the Gestapo was in retreat. If Vogel wanted a hostage with American blood, he'd have to keep her alive. He could confine her in the dungeon again, he could rape her, even execute her, and she would resist till her appointed hour.

She must love, continue to love. No other resistance, no other cure for Vogel's perversions of love. Hold fast to real love, the potential of love, that love that will outlast all the Vogels of this world.

Noor turned her head and shrieked, "Non!"

The tongue snapped back behind the cage of his teeth. For a long moment Vogel's eyes clenched shut. Then slowly his weight lifted off her chest, his hands released her body. He stood up, plucked the bright disc off the cot. Transparent blue eyes looked down on her.

"*Befehl ist befehl.* I have my orders, Princess, and believe me, I will follow them."

PART EIGHT

CHAPTER 39

Munich, Occupied Germany
October 1945

READERS OF *Paris Soir* might believe that once Hitler's body was found, the six-year-long night of war was over. But like so many other brothers, sisters, mothers and grandmothers, Kabir, Zaib, Mother and Dadijaan would have no peace till Kabir found some trace of Noor. General de Gaulle had returned to Paris and paraded all the way to Notre-Dame. And in Nuremberg, the Allies were charging Nazis with crimes against humanity.

Kabir longed to be above it all. His squadron went on alert when the Allies prepared for the invasion of Japan, but was not deployed. Younger pilots were required, with training for advanced planes—he was assigned to flight instruction.

And still no word from Noor. Not one telephone call, not a single Red Cross message.

In August, American pilots, army and navy men one and all said the A-bomb had saved their lives and gave thanks to Mr. Truman. Did the crew of the *Enola Gay* have more trouble sleeping than Kabir? No one at the flight officers' mess raised such questions. His mates had affection and awe for the bomb; one said its cloud rose "like a huge vase of flowers." Men—maybe women too—had lost their reverence for the mystery of death. His mates didn't mention nightmares filled with landscapes of desolation and ruin, the kind Kabir had had ever since that July motorcycle ride from Paris to Munich. He resolved to atone with better actions all the rest of his days for those his bombs had killed, but millions of dying curses continued to babble through his dreams. And in dreams his sidecar never came back empty — Noor looked up at him laughing, her black hair covered by a lemon silk headscarf that fluttered behind her like a pennant.

Then Zaib's letters and trunk calls from London to any and all American authorities who might have records seized in August 1944, after the Gestapo retreated from Paris, brought an answer. Forms, paybooks, passes, ration cards, reports, communiqués, directives and dossiers seized at the avenue Foch had moved several times. They had now arrived at the Office of De-nazification in the American sector. Yes, in Munich.

And yes, one of the SS men who had worked at the avenue Foch had been traced. A low-level interpreter. His name: Ernst Vogel. He was assigned a cell in the barrack for Special Prisoners, the one called the Bunker. There was no lock on the door; he was free to come and go from the camp during the day. A meeting could be arranged, near the camp.

"Which camp?" Kabir yelled into the mouth cup of the telephone.

"It's a place called Dachau," said Zaib.

After several telegrams Kabir boarded a couchette car in an "overnight" train from Paris, and alighted five days later at the Hauptbahnhof, Munich's central station.

Above him, cubist designs of bomb-blackened wood, iron and broken glass pierced the October morning sky.

Here was where the damn war began, Munich, with Chamberlain, Mussolini and Daladier giving the Sudetenland to Hitler, agreeing to give away land that wasn't theirs to give, someone else's land, regardless of the cost in life and blood. The very tactic now being considered by the British for Arab Muslim land in Palestine; the divisions and schisms of this war would reconfigure there.

From the station, umbrella held almost before his face against a pelting rain, Kabir walked full tilt through the rubble and remains of the city, past the twin towers of the Frauenkirche and the golden statue of Mary, back to the Rathaus.

A blonde-braided woman a few years younger than Kabir approached, thumb-sucking child in tow.

"You haf *schokolade?* I gif you one diamond, you gif me fifty Pall Mall? *Haben sie zigaretten?*"

Kabir shook his head, walked past and up the stairs. Inside, he was directed by a very polite German with no name badge to a large, ornately carved door. Inside, Kabir came upon the same American captain from Chicago, as boyish as before, but sitting behind a new, file-laden desk that filled half the room.

Kabir waited as the captain read telegrams and shouted messages at adjutants, clarifying American occupation forces policy on collecting firearms and cameras from "denazified Nazis."

"Here again, Flight Lieutenant Khan?"

"Yes, sir."

"I'd do the same, in your shoes. You know, your sister has one real nice voice on the phone. And she's persistent."

"It runs in the family."

"Swell." The captain searched through the files on his desk. "Don't get your hopes sky high, OK? We have no idea if the man we have at Dachau—name of Vogel—ever knew your sister. I gave him all her names: Madeleine, Nora Baker, Anne-Marie Régnier, Noor Khan. He keeps saying the Noor Khan he knew was a princess. But all these krauts say they know some big shot who'll get them out of trouble."

"Princess" could only have come to this man Vogel's European mind if he had somehow learned of Noor's Indian blood.

"Vogel says he had no rank at the avenue Foch; he spoke English and French so they made him an interpreter. Spent a year in a French prison camp from '39 to '40, then says he had to work for the Nazis, had no choice. Following orders—that's what they all say—I remembered you when I ran across his records, though.

Meant to write to you right away. Good thing your sister Zaib called a few days ago, so I didn't have to." He grinned. "I'm not the best letter writer, my girlfriend says."

Kabir nodded his appreciation.

"You ready, then?"

"Yes, bring him in."

Minutes ticked by, then two white-gloved, helmeted MPs led a man who was surely Vogel into the room. He wore a navy worsted suit and brown bow tie. No handcuffs.

A rush to avenge came over Kabir such as he had never experienced. He stood up, swaying on his feet a little. If he had had a bomb to drop at that moment, he might have vaporized the man. This man who might not be guilty of any crime at all. Who just might have information about Noor. Who was willing to share it with Kabir.

Kabir sat down again, forearms on his knees, fists clenching and unclenching. The captain cracked his knuckles.

Vogel peered at Kabir through round, wire-rimmed spectacles, like a schoolteacher. No trouble meeting Kabir's gaze. Not as tall as Kabir had expected.

A limp hand came towards Kabir. Kabir ignored it. His own was cold with sweat.

"So I meet the brother of Princess Noor," said Vogel in French.

He had the voice of a mild-mannered academic.

"Speak English," said the captain.

Vogel gave a slight bow. "You do not speak French?" he said to the captain with exaggerated puzzlement. "Or German?" He turned to Kabir. "I see the resemblance," he said. "Prince Kabir Khan, correct?"

"Not exactly," said Kabir. "I'm a Sufi master's son. A Pirzada, *vous savez*?"

"But Noor, she was a princess."

Kabir wouldn't argue the point, in favour of a far more important question. "'Was'?"

Vogel shrugged. "Was, is—who knows? I was the only one she could turn to in the last months of the war."

"And how did you meet her?"

"She was arrested as an enemy agent. She was transmitting strategic information to England."

"The date?"

"I can't be sure—wait, October 1943. Exactly two years ago."

"Did you torture her?"

"Oh, non, non, monsieur! She was interrogated. Many times. I was merely the interpreter. I found your sister charming."

"And from the avenue Foch? She was sent to prison?"

"Yes, but I visited her, to verify her health."

"When was the last time you saw her?"

"August, last year."

"August 1944. Where? Fresnes?"

"No, no. The Princess wasn't sent to *Fresnes*. She was sent to the prison in Pforzheim, Germany."

A slight pause. Kabir readjusted his thinking.

Agents and resistants captured by the Gestapo in Paris, debriefed by Miss Atkins, spoke of being sent to the prison in Fresnes, France.

"Why Pforzheim?"

"I found her a cell there—it was on my way to and from Munich."

"Pforzheim is not 'on the way' between Munich and Paris."

"True. But each month, when I visited my wife and sons, I would visit the Princess and return to Paris."

A Nazi who went out of his way to visit a spy in prison "to verify her health"—Kabir hadn't heard of any like Vogel. He was relieved, as Vogel probably meant he should be, by mention of a wife and sons; both gave a man respectability, were signals that his sexual urges were satisfied. Kabir's own women should be safe before him.

"I meant: why was she sent there?"

"It has a section for Special Prisoners. Excuse me, I mean *had* a section. I don't know if it is still there today, because"—he looked directly at Kabir—"the RAF bombed Pforzheim last February. She was sent there because we agreed to treat all the agents in her network as POWs. If we hadn't, she would have been executed."

Vogel was editing and deleting information as he went; Kabir could feel it. He was being presented with the *crème de la crème* of selective recall. Why would Vogel and his superiors agree to treat British agents as POWs? But Noor might still be alive—that was all that was important.

But for what reason had this man visited Noor every month? For how long? What had he done to her? *Refuse to think the word "rape."* But it came to mind anyway.

"May I sit down?" asked Vogel.

"No," said Kabir. "You may not. Continue."

"I kept Princess Noor at the avenue Foch as long as I could. I reserved the cell at Pforzheim, but I told Herr Kieffer she was injured—too weak to travel. Conditions were better at avenue Foch, she had a comfortable private cell. Food was plentiful. Many of her friends from the SOE were there . . . Even sometimes I would order dinner for her in my office."

He made it sound so benign, but Kabir had heard tales of La Gestapo at the avenue Foch. Too many to believe him.

"Which 'friends from the SOE'?"

"They called themselves Prosper, Archambault, Phono, Jacques Viennot . . . who knows what their real names were. All partisans and revolutionaries."

Kabir tucked the names into the mezzanine of his memory; he would ask Miss Atkins's help in contacting them.

But then Vogel said, "Prosper and Archambault went to Sachsenhausen. Phono was executed at Buchenwald, by Herr Kieffer's orders. Phono's wife was equally dangerous, and she was sent to Ravensbrück. Viennot—wait . . . I can't remember."

Kabir wrote in his notebook. The captain was also writing. Miss Atkins would tell the families of Prosper, Archambault, Phono and Viennot, whoever they were.

"And my sister? Why Pforzheim?"

"She had tried to escape—a punishment order was placed in her file." Bureaucratese sheltered the doer of the deed beneath its passive voice. "I was wounded and in hospital, and when I came back, Herr Kieffer had sent her to Pforzheim. You must understand, I felt terrible. I had tried to protect her for as long as I could—"

"I don't believe that for a damn minute."

"Non, non, Prince Khan. I went to see her, I couldn't stay away. I wanted . . ."

"Yes?"

Vogel squinted as if peering through a membrane. "I wanted her to call me Ernst. It was such a little thing."

A silence. Something had been blurted, something Vogel hadn't meant to say.

Noor would never have called him Ernst. No sister of Kabir would allow herself to be on first-name terms with someone like Vogel. He was beneath her. The way the Jew Rivkin had been beneath her.

"You wanted more than that," Kabir almost spat. "Admit it, you . . . you fornicator."

The word was archaic, anachronistic, Qur'anic, but it was the one that came to mind.

"No, no. What are you saying? It was against orders to touch a non-Aryan woman. And she was a *mischlinge*—a mixed breed— I don't know the word in French. Do you know that I could have been sent to a camp myself for that?"

Kabir felt he was flying into the centre of paradox. Vogel called Noor Princess, yet by Nazi definition considered her a menial. If the non-Aryan and the *mischlinge* were equivalent to the *dhimmi* of Islam or the untouchable of Hinduism, it meant millions had become subhuman to the Germans.

"I told Herr Kieffer I was just about to break her. I said one more visit and she would reveal whole realms of spies. Believe me, I tried to protect her, save her by visiting her."

"You were going to use her as a hostage."

Vogel seemed to consider. But was he trying to recollect his motives or to evaluate the possible consequences of admission or denial?

"Yes, I was," he said, as if the words wormed through a dyke inside him. "She was a princess and her mother was American — I was sure someone would want her badly enough to make an exception for me. Hitler had betrayed Fascism, and I could see we were destined to lose the war by then."

If Hitler betrayed Fascism, then Allah save the world the next time it surfaces.

"I gave her pen, paper, ink. I allowed her to write stories. Children's stories. I asked her to write children's stories for my sons."

"And she did? Where are they?"

Vogel took off his spectacles, leaving his face curiously vulnerable. He polished them with his tie and put them on again.

"Yes, she did. But I no longer have them."

There was no way to prove it, but again Kabir knew this was a lie.

"Why not?"

"Because my house was bombarded, sir. By the RAF. When the Gestapo office closed in Paris, I returned here. I discovered my wife had moved from the apartment I had arranged for her. She put our older boy in an orphanage, took all our possessions — to this day I don't know why. Even now I can't find her. And she doesn't know, yet —"

"What doesn't she know?"

"One of my sons . . ." Vogel gave a deep sigh. "We had sent him to Dresden for the summer in 1944, for safety. But then eight months ago, his legs were crushed from the bombings." A light-beam glanced off Vogel's spectacles and hit Kabir squarely between the eyes. "He didn't survive the amputation."

He appeared to be waiting for some expression of sympathy. Kabir couldn't find a single phrase in his repertoire of standard responses.

"So I now live alone at Dachau. Temporarily, you understand. I have become dependent on the Allies." He gave a small snort. "But then, they need me for interpretation."

"We have to translate five tons of documents before the Nazis get their trials next month," the captain interjected. "We wouldn't need his kind if we didn't have thirty thousand arrestees awaiting trial at Dachau."

"The victor shows his justice," said Vogel.

The captain shot him a deadly look. "Fuck you and every Nazi, Vogel. In the last few months I've toured enough camps and met enough people like you. If we said screw all this legality, just gave all of you a taste of your own justice, you bastards wouldn't suffer enough for the misery you've caused."

"The United States has set an example that will, I'm sure, be followed in future wars," said Vogel's smooth voice.

The captain said to Kabir, "We've brought in interrogators from the United States, but reports and evidence are coming in faster than we can translate them. We don't have time to prosecute thirty thousand krauts and be home by Christmas, so we're only bringing the camp director and his henchmen to trial. And we're leaving the crimes committed by Germans against Germans to their own courts, though how we're going to figure out the nationality of corpses, I have no idea."

"When did you say you last visited Mademoiselle Khan at Pforzheim?" Kabir asked Vogel.

"Shortly before we evacuated the avenue Foch."

"August of 1944."

"Yes."

"And your home was bombed—when?"

Vogel shrugged off the question. "Orders from Berlin were to send all prisoners to camps. We had kept no record of her, so she could have remained at Pforzheim—but I happen to know she was sent to a camp. And I do know where she was sent."

"Where, damn it, where?!"

"As it happens, I'm occupying her cell."

"Occupying her cell?" Kabir must have misunderstood.

"Yes, I've been living there for a little more than four months. Sometimes I feel a trace of her spirit. At Dachau, I mean."

This man who had wielded power over Noor's food, clothing and shelter, perhaps even her life, was now occupying the cell where she had been held at Dachau. And he "felt a trace of her spirit"? Words with a connotation of worship. It made no sense.

An MP entered with a note for the captain, who excused himself for a meeting.

Kabir's questions became louder. He began shouting. Ended up wheedling. Vogel gave him nothing more. Two hours later, Kabir was hoarse and feverish, red-rimmed eyes alternately burning and brimming with barely contained rage.

Everyone is part of God. Even Vogel. A fragment of the universal divine spirit, even if he tortured Noor and was part of the Nazi machine.

But Abbajaan's philosophy was never more distant than at that moment. There was no possibility that he and Vogel could have anything in common.

How many men and women like Noor had Vogel interrogated, tortured—killed? How many of those who passed through the avenue Foch headquarters of the Paris Gestapo had been sent to concentration camps? True, those men and women were not in uniform, but every enemy combatant, secret agent or spy had relatives who loved them, who worried about them; surely all of them did not deserve to vanish without trial or trace? How many orders for roundups of Frenchmen—Jewish or otherwise—had this man translated at the avenue Foch?

No one comes out of war without betraying his humanity in some way. There are no prophets, angels, pirs, gurus or messiahs who can keep us clean. But there are degrees of destruction, and trained killer though I be, I may not be cursed by as many dying breaths as you.

Clearly, Vogel didn't accept any role Kabir assigned him. Pressured further, he unfolded a cream-coloured paper and waved it beneath Kabir's nose.

A certificate issued by the Allies. The Persil Certificate, named after a bar of soap to show how very clean its bearer was. This one, countersigned by each Occupation authority—British, French, American, Russian—announced that its bearer had been cleared of all charges and was not wanted by the Allies in any of the four zones.

Kabir handed it back. Certificates like it could be easily forged for a few hundred occupation marks, perhaps a pound of butter.

He continued questioning, but it was of little use. Vogel had explained his participation in the machine to himself, persuaded himself he did all he could for Princess Noor. He said several times that if she had not been an escape artist, she would never have been sent to Pforzheim. And if she'd only done as he told her . . . Vogel sounded like Uncle Tajuddin.

Noor must have done or said something that annoyed this Nazi bastard, for Nazi he undoubtedly was. And she had been sent to Dachau. But there must have been something more that made this bastard request a billet in Dachau and live in Noor's cell.

Needles of anxiety flowed through Kabir's veins.

Where is Noor now?

What happened at Dachau? Has she been repatriated from there?

Vogel took off his spectacles. "One question, if I may, Flight Lieutenant Khan?"

"What is it?"

"Was your sister married? Or did she perhaps have a fiancé?"

"Why do you ask?" The man shouldn't be given any information at all.

"She wrote a letter, sir, a letter I happened to read."

How did you happen to read it?

"She talked about 'A' and said she had changed her *adieu* to *au revoir.*"

"Did you ask her?" said Kabir. "A" was for Armand. "A" spelled mistake.

"I didn't want to know her answer then. And she did say to call her mademoiselle."

If Noor had changed any former *adieu* to *au revoir*, perhaps she had contacted the Jew again. After he'd *told* her! But that was Noor—never obeying his explicit directions. Who knew what it had cost her to contact the Jew?

Kabir would have to find Armand Rivkin.

"No," he said, "she is most certainly not married. No, she does not have a fiancé."

"I didn't think so, sir. Well, if there is nothing further, I will wish you good luck."

"Nothing, except—here, write down where I can find you again."

Vogel said as he wrote, "I'm working as a cowhand on a farm. But I hope to return to my former position—I used to work in a bank."

The captain came back, looked pointedly at his watch. Kabir nodded wearily. The MPs escorted Vogel from the room.

"That's progress," said the captain, when Kabir brought him up to date. "There should be some record of her at Pforzheim. Maybe Dachau too. We're just piecing some of this together. Write down the date he said she was deported—I'll have my assistant look into it."

Kabir reached into his shirt pocket for his pen. Not there. He crossed the room—perhaps he'd left it on the captain's desk.

"Lost something?"

"My pen—it's one of those new ballpoints they give us pilots."

The captain gave a sardonic laugh. "That's three hundred marks the S.O.B. just got from you."

PART NINE

CHAPTER 40

Pforzheim, Germany
September 11, 1944

A REEL CROWDED with familiar faces from the past whirled around Noor and blurred to an end. Abruptly, she was back in the solitude of her cell. Here she was, *seule et toute-seule.*

Alone and all alone.

Above her, the small window dimmed as if disturbed by cloud.

How much time had she lost in reverie? Where would she be a month from now, a year from now? Still here, still waiting for freedom? When would she join Armand? How long would it take?

How much lay before her? She was growing weaker by the day.

Noor shuffled from her cell, the butt of a guard's rifle pressing into her ribs. The iron gates to the next bank of cells screeched open, bowls banged against bars, women's voices called.

This guard—she had never seen him before. Where was the woman guard? It was too late at night for exercise. Why was she the only one being taken from her cell?

A pincer held her upper arm, jerking her along. The main door to the women's cellblock was before her. She stopped, undecided, drawing fluent curses.

Sound of women screaming, shouting. One yelled, *"Au revoir!"*

A prod sent her staggering through the door. A desk, a lamp.

Slam of the door; no more shouted messages for loved ones, no more shouts of encouragement.

Where are they taking me? Is this my chance to escape?

Another guard came around the desk. He sat down, wrote something in a large ledger and swivelled it towards Noor's captor. Releasing her arm for a moment, her guard signed the ledger. Then the date: *September 11, 1944.*

He sank to one knee before her and her ankle irons clanked to the cement floor. She held out her hands as he rose. But he avoided her eyes, unlocking and removing the connecting chain but not the manacles.

Something small and white in his hand. Paper. He wrote on it—perhaps her name or number—then it disappeared.

A grab at her wrists and a string slipped around the right one. He stepped back, leaving a tag dangling from her wrist. Familiar-looking tag. Before she could examine it, she was shoved forward again.

Down another corridor slowly; swollen, raw ankles still feeling the weight of the absent chains. Another door. The guard signed another ledger here and took a lantern from the corner. An impassive orderly pushed open a heavy iron gate set in the wall.

Open air. Warm night. Crescent moon. Tiger-claw moon.

Was this freedom? What of the women she'd left behind? Freedom for herself alone felt like no freedom. This wasn't real freedom—handcuffed hands folded on her breast.

Hollow boom of anti-aircraft fire in the distance. The rifle-butt jabbed her side, energizing fear. A swinging lantern light led away from the prison. She was pushed after it. Watery legs, knees wobbling.

Move uphill. Breathe.

Slow burn of hope, no matter if disappointment lay in wait.

At the top of the ridge, rail tracks—source of the train sounds by which she had marked time. She wanted to lie face down, smell the earth. Instead, she stood motionless; her captor waited for something. Above her—stars.

A shriek filled the night. An engine puffed past and its carriages slowed to a stop before her though she saw no signal or station. Pain in her wrists crescendoing, smell of beer and sweat; the guard had looped his arm through her manacles and drawn her closer.

He extinguished the lantern, placed it on the ground and straightened. She was jerked and pulled down the length of the train to the very last carriage. A latch lifted, exposing a deeper darkness.

Jellied knees bumped the ladder. Hands grabbed her by the waist, lifted and tossed. She hit the carriage floor, went sprawling, then still. Straw grazed her face.

The guard climbed in behind her. A hollow thump — the door sliding shut. Then a low whistle.

She drew her bruised limbs close and squatted against the rough plank wall. The guard threw her a glance, said something unmistakably menacing. Leather boots strode past her into the next carriage. More slamming, steam built to energy and the carriage began to move.

Escape now, before the train picks up speed.

She steadied herself against the side of the carriage and crawled to the door. Felt for the handle and used it to pull herself upright. Then, with her weight against it, tried to slide it back.

Locked from the outside. She slumped to the straw, panting. She dashed her sleeve across her eyes. She couldn't help the tears overflowing; the sway and clash of the train said escape was impossible now.

Cold air on her face, dry breeze as from an air shaft. She found the slit that was the high barred window and stood with her eyes glued to the passing Black Forest. But to her mind's eye, unbidden, came Vogel's face with a fixed, sardonic smile, eyes blinking behind his spectacles.

The *quibla* at her heart's compass said she was travelling east, closer to Mecca, deeper into Germany.

Abbajaan, ma petite, anyone—say a du'a for me.

The tag still dangled from her wrist. So many hours spent threading tickets like this one, thinking the work useless, not knowing the purpose to which her efforts were directed. Thirty tickets an hour for eight, ten, sometimes twelve hours a day—an average of 300 tickets per day. Today was September 11, 1944, and she had been imprisoned from November 25, 1943. She had spent 292 days at Pforzheim. Say she had threaded tickets for 200 of those days—that came to 60,000 tickets threaded by her alone. Multiply by even a hundred women in this and other prisons for the same length of time and the number of tickets threaded went into millions.

Allah! How many had worn tickets like these to be sent to Germany? What were the Germans doing with so many people? Where were they putting them? There couldn't be room enough in Germany for so many millions, there wasn't food in Germany for so many, no matter if the entire harvest of France were sent there. And even if she couldn't care about and didn't know every single person sent to Germany, if Armand and Madame Lydia had been sent there, if Armand were deprived, she did care.

The ticket on her wrist was reality; the hours she had spent threading tickets was reality.

Émile was right: "Bravery requires that we deny reality."

Pretend to be brave; refuse reality as long as you can.

But there was no denying she had unwittingly contributed to the deportations. How could she have known? If she hadn't threaded tickets to the guard's satisfaction, she would have received no food.

Trust. Hope, as she had never hoped before, that Allah would forgive.

"Huwallah-ul-lazi la ilaha illa huw-ar-Rahman-ur-Rahim-ul-Malik-ul-Quddus-ul-Salam-ul-Mu'min-ul-Muhaimin-ul . . . al-Muhaiminu, al-Muhaiminu, je me souviens de toi, je me souviens de toi."

———

The door between the carriages opened. A figure loomed above her, shook her bruised, aching arm.

"*Rauss!*"

Through the swaying corridor to the next carriage, a troop car with windows. Empty but for two German soldiers playing cards at the far end—they barely glanced up. But one of the three ragged creatures seated on an iron bench beside the door turned towards Noor. Blonde roots at the base of dark hair; it was a woman. So were the other two. A lift of a thin eyebrow.

That's not Yolande. You don't know her, you have no idea who she is.

The guard pointed Noor towards the iron bench. Yolande moved to make room for her. Noor's breath lodged in her throat—such a battered, gaunt Yolande, far from the strong, nimble woman with whom she'd raced up and down Glory Hill.

A fleeting shadow crossed Yolande's face; Noor too must look very different.

A chaos of questions: *How, when, where? Who betrayed you?*

At the opposite end of the carriage, the soldiers and Noor's guard hunched around a table. The cards in a hand facing her: a three, an ace, a king, a *D* for a queen and *B* for a joker. The prison guard shuffled the deck "Hindu" style, inserting stacks between others without fanning. A soldier took a long pull at a bottle of Kupferberg, wiped his mouth on his sleeve.

Noor's temple touched Yolande's shoulder. Yolande rested her head on Noor's and her hand found its way into Noor's. Dot-dot-dot-dash, Yolande's forefinger began to tap into Noor's palm.

Concentrate. Feign sleep, but beware. Be aware.

The train swayed, chugged on.

A greyish dawn broke over balconies and fenced gardens backed up against the railway tracks. Weathercocks turned on steeples. Mossy hillsides. Mühlacker station. Orange-brown roof tiles, no different from French ones. The train rounded the western edge of the Black Forest, moving northeast.

Bietigheim—Bissingen.

Garden sheds flattened—by bombs? Dandelions dared raise their heads.

Kornwestheim.

Beneath an arched bridge, into a tunnel, out of a tunnel. A clock tower in the distance read 08:35 hours. Tracks knitted, trains passed, indifferent to one another's destinations.

Wooden watchtowers loomed over dark fields. Flowers clustered on graves.

A pond, fields, small canals, open sewers.

Low grain barns. A forest of steadfast pines. Now fields again, undulating. Weeping willows. Ivy-covered walls of larger houses.

Ulm.

Soldiers with Mausers slung over their shoulders stood on the platform—troops who had moved at night.

"Prost!" said the prison guard, passing a bottle of Warsteiner.

One of the soldiers smacked his lips and said, *"Die Königin unter den bieren."* She recognized the slogan from posters in Paris. He pulled a packet from his pocket, unwrapped it.

Odour of ham like a pain in each nostril. She might have killed for one bite of pork.

The prison guard unfolded a packet of cheese. A penknife passed between the men. A soldier took a large bite. The other women too gazed ravenously at the munching guards.

The game resumed, with only the occasional click of cards on the table.

The train rocked and pulled, thumping gently over the tracks, whistling past deserted stations. Noor stared from the smeared carriage window across the flat, dark German countryside. An occasional light peeped gently.

Morning light grew from stars. The tar ribbon of a road ran parallel to the track, ribs of earth bared by a plough. A palomino grazed at the edge of a bomb crater, and a single sheep grazed in a paddock. Two very thin cows.

The train pulled into Augsburg, slowed, stopped.

Minutes turned to an hour, perhaps more. Had it run out of coal?

Yolande's tapped translation said the tracks were blown up—Noor thanked Kabir and his comrades, mentally—but the SS had ordered them to be repaired immediately.

Try to escape. With three Germans sitting before me? Yes. Try anything.

Noor told Yolande she needed to use the WC and made a summoning gesture. Yolande explained to the guard in German, pointing at herself as well.

Yolande first. If anyone could find a way to escape, Yolande would.

But after a time Yolande came back, shaking her head a little.

Noor's turn. Down the compartment corridor. She held out her manacles, but her guard unlocked only one, averting his face as he held her enleashed. One-handed, she crouched to use the toilet with the door slightly ajar.

Anything heavy to hit him with? Anything sharp to cut off her manacle? Or even her own hand?

But should she, by intervention of some *farishta*, cut herself from her steel leash, the stamp-sized window above the flush-pull wouldn't allow exit.

Back with the others, seeing her own disappointment reflected in Yolande's eyes.

At the very next station she'd jump up, run down the corridor, out of the train. And, if she didn't take a bullet in her back, run right into the German soldiers on the platform. . .

The train slowed to a stop, and a large man in a singlet with suspenders opened the far door between cars and looked in. The guards started to their feet, guns in hand.

"*Nein! Nein!*" came giggles from girls in the next car. The large man turned back. The door closed again.

Moving again; moment of escape escaping. It had been only a two-minute stop.

Air pressed on Noor's eardrums as the train flowed into a long tunnel, emerged and continued its centipedal journey. A sign flashed by: *München.*

Munich.

From Laim, the train turned north. Slower now, dark puffs of trees framed by the carriage window. Tendrils of smoke from chimneys. At Obermenzing, houses grew more imposing.

Schlosses. German for mansion, château, haveli. This is no time to play multilingual parlour games.

Allah, what can I do?

Crabapple trees turned stunted here, fields sped away behind her.

At Karlsfeld, more red roofs peaked from fields, and row upon row of greenhouses. How far she had come since that day in the greenhouse at Grignon, the greenhouse fragrant with the Prophet's colour.

Do a zikr of them: Armand, Lydia, Prosper, Archambault, Monsieur Hoogstraten, Professor Balachowsky, Viennot . . . If you remember them, they still live.

Dark brown slate houses now. Carriageways. A station of three-storey stone with a sign: *Dachau.*

The station passed.

Beyond a tunnel of foliage a woman walked arm in arm with a soldier—dark-haired, like Armand. A girl with a feather in her hat wobbled her bicycle to a halt and let the train pass.

Noor's whole body thought of food, escape, food, escape.

The prison guard began to slap segments of the deck upon one another.

Breathe. Al-lah, Al-lah.

The train jolted, nudging the cards out of his hands. They slipped, shot in all directions.

The guard let out a roar. He would take his eyes off her—she would run with the others. But his eyes didn't leave her for a second as the soldiers began picking up the cards.

If she was dreaming like Alice, the cards should now fulfill their purpose: the falling house of cards should be the signal that called her to wake.

A sudden rush of hope; she pinched herself.

It hurt.

This is happening.

Ten minutes had passed, maybe fifteen. A smell, no, a stench unlike any other.

Sunlight poured through the carriage door. Hollow pulse of bloodhounds barking a few yards from the train. The soldiers rose.

"Rauss!" They motioned her with the others following to the door.

Before Noor, letters wrought above an iron-barred gate inset beneath an archway spelled *ArbeitMachtFrei.* Perhaps the name of this place? The prison guard pulled her from the carriage, sending her sprawling to skin-searing gravel. He leaned over, unlocked her handcuffs where she lay. The soldiers were shoving the others out of the carriage, too.

On one elbow, to her knees, to her feet. Hands dropping to her sides, swinging free.

Awash in gratitude—abject gratitude.

No reason to feel gratitude. Why feel any gratitude at all?

The guard's thumb and middle finger met upon her humerus. Pincer hand clamped about her arm, he tugged, dragging her, with Yolande and the others following.

Noor stumbled on swollen ankles, past a sign, *Jorhaus.* A gloved hand pushed. The barred gate halved. Agitated shouts of guards, a baying and barking as of wolves.

A room in the gatehouse. Guns all around. A woman guard inside. Folded towel thrust at her, then at Yolande and the other two. Not a towel, a uniform. The woman guard miming they must change. Watching, just doing her job.

Faded blue stripes and a single patch pocket.

No Schiaparelli gown, this.

Behind Yolande now. Being led away, not to the rows of hulking grey wooden barracks stretching away as far as she could see in the diffused light, but past a huge open space. Moving in the sights of guns from the watchtowers, she shuffled with the others past a whitewashed, horseshoe-shaped building.

Before Noor and the ragged little troop of women stood a long white barrack with barred windows.

"They're calling this the Bunker," came Yolande's whisper, translating the rapid German passing between the camp soldiers and the guard from Pforzheim. "For political prisoners only."

CHAPTER 41

Dachau, Germany
September 12, 1944

ON HER SIDE in her new cell, wondering if her blood was still flowing. Her teeth had chattered all night as if possessed by djinns and the six-rung radiator against the wall wasn't turned on. Breeze stirred a fine black dust, blew it through the barred window. Noor's eyes were smarting.

Dawn now, and a click at the door. A scarecrow with hollow eyes set deep in his stubbled face slipped in, a finger to his lips. He placed a battered suitcase on her cot and thumbed it open quickly, a pulse throbbing at his temple. Two planks of wood hinged out and a tiny crucifix and candles appeared. A portable altar—no need to explain at what danger to himself.

The priest's unexpected kindness penetrated her more deeply than any pain from her chains, bruises, hunger, shouts endured. She kneeled, ready to pray, trying to understand his textbook French through his German accent.

Was she Catholic or Lutheran? He wanted to know.

"I follow Sufism," she said. "I'm a Sufi Muslim."

He frowned, baffled. Then his brow cleared.

"Gypsy?"

She shook her head.

"You have been given this chance, mademoiselle. Repent of

paganism and accept Jesus Christ as the true messiah, forsaking all others, and you shall be saved."

What should she say to the scarecrow figure before her? She didn't want to hurt this large-spirited, sincere man who had risked his life to bring her his sacrament. But she could not accept his gift. His Christianity came at the price of rejecting all other faiths, but to deny the Prophet or any one of the prophets before him was to deny them all.

Could Hazrat Issa have wanted to save some and not all of humanity?

My soul is part of Allah; I don't want or need to be saved.

Could she explain that, in rejecting conversion, she meant no disrespect, no personal affront, merely a choice freely exercised? She was Christian, Muslim, Jewish, Buddhist and Hindu if she was a Sufi. But she was so tired, so tired—where could she begin to explain?

Why was it necessary to explain what should be so obvious?

And there was no time for explanations. Every second the portable altar remained open on the valise was one of terrible danger for him, for herself. All she could do was whisper, "Non. Merci, mais non—I can't say the reasons now. Perhaps some other time, when we meet again."

His expectation for her was in his elegiac eyes. She would not believe it.

I have claimed but never yet lived my life as my own. How can it be time to die? What have I learned of existence that qualifies me to knock on the door of non-existence?

"Give me your blessing instead, *mon père*."

Giving might make him feel worthy of his jealously guarded, exclusive God.

His palm scraped her forehead. "Bless you, my child."

Alone again but for the cold metallic odour inhabiting her cell, she pressed her palms to burning eyes. Had she imagined him? Sincere priest with the face of Azrael.

Imagined or not, when one has seen the Archangel of Death, the appointed hour has come. There is no time left to repent or change anything.

Blood slid through vein and artery, distributing the acid pain of bruise through tissue, to the bone. Heart rate, temperature, movement—thought—slowing.

A bowl of cold soup helped for a while, then she had to lie down.

I might as well be in India, starving, beaten or imprisoned without trial. Or confined to my room in Afzal Manzil, confined at the avenue Foch or confined at Pforzheim. Someone always regulates my surroundings, affecting the air I breathe. Other people's decisions have governed each moment of my life, limiting each choice by past decisions, decisions made by others before they ever met me.

Maybe I suffer from the illusion that I ever had choices. Perhaps my expectations of my family, my leaders and myself were too high.

If I surrender to these thoughts, does it mean I give in?

I have no tears left to cry, so I dream: On foot through a low fog, and I am following someone, gasping, panting. I'm in a field clotted with red poppies, dark hearts at their core, and I, running from light-swallowing darkness, wade in knee-deep. Bare knees feel the brush of petals, my shoes crush flowers. If I cross the field, I'll be safe, but there'll be no coming back to find out what lives in the darkness and why it chases me. I look over my shoulder—dark shapes following me again, running through dense trees, the skull and crossbones branded on each man's cap.

I am with child again. Large and unwieldy with your weight, ma petite. But the fingers that hold my own are strong, the voice deep and urgent, the eyes blue. It is Armand.

"It is time," he says. "I am with you."

I look down; my lap is soaked with life water. Desperately, I search for cover, but the pain in my enlarged womb is too great. I drop to my haunches behind the trunk of a felled tree. There, in Armand's arms, what should take hours happens in a flash in dream time. And this time I am ready. I experience it fully, genuinely and without fear—experience with my husband the sacred moment of your birth. This one moment is my own, a moment of my life no one may pre-define or permit. From it I become a mother. From it I know my own mother and my grandmothers, leaving the Noor who could not be Noor and mother together.

Afterwards, your father and I hold you and you give your first cry. But oh, ma petite, this is no cry, for I hear you laugh, a clear, spontaneous laugh.

A laugh!

And though I know I dream, some part of me learns what you came to teach me: that Allah, God or principle that created you, can also, if we wish, restore this war-weary planet.

"*Rauss!*"

A key clattering in the cell door. An SS guard prodding her awake.

I am just being moved to another cell, perhaps this is when they feed prisoners here . . .

In the narrow hall, three other cells opened. Yolande's familiar face, her lifted eyebrow. Noor answered with a weak smile, as if they were out in the Surrey woods again. The guard motioned her and the others down the length of the Bunker, out into the dawn. Pebbles speared her shoes, her legs were stiff as wood. But the guards were behind, so she stumbled forward. Around the side of the building, back towards the gatehouse.

To her right, between the Bunker and the rows of barracks, stood a legion of wretches in faded grey camp uniforms. A loudspeaker barked names and orders at intervals.

How often had she watched such roll calls at Drancy, through binoculars. But at this lesser distance she could see faces, see how gaunt and emaciated were the travesties of shaven-headed men who leaned against one another; see that there were old men and a group of women. Some little boys. Girls. One looked barely four years old.

Wardens moved among them, pushing and shouting.

Noor hung back, stealing oblique glances. Did someone call "Armand Rivkin"? Could he be here, among these men? Names came in a never-ending stream.

Yolande whispered, translating the shouts, "Road-building commando . . . stone-breaking commando . . . Krupp commando . . ."

"*Rauss!*" Behind her. A sharp twinge at her kidney—the barrel of a gun.

She tried to meet the guard's eyes, to make him truly see her, but he looked away.

Noor held her hand out to Yolande and gripped firmly. Slowly, past long grey barracks, more and more of them. Perhaps one of them was a women's barrack intended for their billeting. Were any from her network here—Prosper? Archambault? Monsieur Hoogstraten? Professor Balachowsky? Viennot?

A two-wheeled horse cart with a man in its traces came down an alley between the barracks and halted at a guard's challenge.

"The night's dead—under the tarpaulin," came Yolande's whisper. "He's taking them to the crematorium."

From the watchtowers, gun barrels swept in a slow arc. Where were they being taken? The far wall of the compound was in sight now, razor wire billowing above it.

Again, that stench from yesterday.

Opposite the last barrack, a double gate opened in the compound wall. The smell grew stronger, the barking closer.

Her legs belonged to someone else.

Pretend to be brave; no one can tell the difference.

Smoke belched from a chimney poking through the trees. Now they were at its source, a low red-brick building, smaller than the barracks they had passed.

The guards prodded her and then Yolande, then the others, past it, down a path to a gravelled clearing. There, Noor saw a brick wall, a trench running before it.

Dark wet trench. Blood trench.

Yolande's hand, cold in hers. Run! Run—where?

Dogs! Closer. They came into view. Two Dobermans straining and slavering, restrained by leather leashes. Two SS officers waiting, pistols drawn.

Noor's eyes caromed to Yolande's—nowhere to run.

Guards were pushing the others to their knees, one by one. No charges, no trial, no sentence? No blindfold offered? Nothing left to barter for treatment as a POW. No saviour in sight. She gripped Yolande's hand in her left and met her eyes.

Together to the end.

Noor knelt in the fawn-coloured sunshine, the nape of her neck exposed to an SS officer's Luger.

Allah, for which country do I die? Be with me now. Let me be true to you, now and always. Send my father to meet me in spirit, send my child to greet me.

Not in the back. Not to be shot in the back like prey run to ground. She must turn, turn and face her enemy, look him in the eye.

This is the moment, the crucial moment, in common with every being who has been or will come. The moment to which I was riding my body headlong against time. This is the trench; from here I go forward alone.

She heard the light coming, light behind her, light before, light above, light beneath.

Heat stiffened each muscle, every nerve. Before her, a light that excluded nothing, including her in its largeness, holding her in a munificent wholeness as skin turned to porous shield, let fire in.

Armand, I wait for you always. Allah! I evolve to spirit, withdraw from known to unknown.

Time splintered what glue held together fragments of Noor. She tasted hot breath leaving. A million other events could have happened at this moment. But there was only the sharp report that precluded all other events, the slow fall of a broken body to hard gravel. A confluence of betrayals no one could have foreseen.

Then the continued fight until her body knew action could no longer bring effect . . . that nothing could hurt . . . nothing hurts any more.

PART TEN

CHAPTER 42

Paris, France
December 1945

RELENTLESS RAIN drove Parisians underground to the métro, scoured monuments, washed away paint, dirt, tears, six war years. General de Gaulle was now President de Gaulle. Gas lamps hissed on smaller streets, electric lights had returned in several arrondissements. The better-off were buying marrons glacés and Christmas presents at Galeries Lafayette, trying to believe the years of war were over, that nothing was scarred, no walls bruised by ripped-away German posters, German signs. The barricades that had blemished streets during the Battle of Paris were gone, motor car taxis were back on the streets, ferrying Allied soldiers to the Louvre and the bordellos of Montparnasse. Some Frenchmen were heard muttering about an American occupation. Banners— *Vive les Alliés, Merci pour la délivrance*—were fraying.

The restaurant on the rue de Sèvres near the Hôtel Lutétia once had the best *tarte tatin*, but the menu chalked on the blackboard offered Kabir no such delicacy today. He consulted his watch, ordered two café filtres and waited.

It was time, American pressmen in Paris were fond of saying, to "move on."

But how could a man with no news of his sister "move on"? Every day, he lost a little more hope, hope he didn't even know he had to lose. He had sought Noor across Europe as his obligation as a member of the Khan family. But he did miss her, too.

He missed the Noor he remembered, wanted her back exactly as he remembered her.

After questioning Vogel, he had gone to Dachau, but in all the tons of documents translated for trials, there was no mention of Noor, Nora Baker, Madeleine or Anne-Marie Régnier. She was a Night and Fog prisoner, one of an unknown number of the disappeared.

Pforzheim prison was still standing, though a mound of bones and little else remained of the town. The governor, when de-nazified and reinstated to his job, could only confirm she had been there from November 1943 to September 1944, and his prison ledgers said she was sent to Dachau. He led Kabir down the women's block, now full of Nazi men, to an empty cell. There he pointed to the inscription, *I resist, therefore I am.* A date almost two years earlier, and her signature, so small, *Noor.*

The governor was delighted by his discovery and eager to please. He promised to contact Kabir if any further information ever came to light. But the discovery only raised more questions. What did Noor mean? What resistance could she effect despite imprisonment? Where was she now?

So many questions, how could a brother move on?

Even France couldn't just move on. First, said Frenchmen, the *épuration* of "national sentiments." Some said, "I resisted, why didn't you?" Others said, "I didn't resist, therefore it was impos-sible to have resisted," and discounted tales of resistance as wild exaggerations of Communists. What was resistance? Which acts were collaboration? Which acts of collaboration were simply nec-essary for survival? Old scores had been settled in the first few weeks of liberation when those deemed collaborators were brought to the rough and ready justice of the gun. Things had improved a little: now there were trials.

Kabir looked up as a tall, thin man with the unmistakable shuffle and sepulchral eyes of the returned deportee came through the door. A spectre reappearing, he looked around the room as if inquiring who had summoned him. The few diners in the restaurant fell to a silence in which discomfort was mixed with horrified compassion. Kabir rose to his feet.

No beard. But those blue eyes were unmistakable.

Kabir started forward, holding out his hand, then faltered when Armand Rivkin didn't extend his. Rivkin's hand, indeed his whole right arm, was bandaged. Awkwardly, Kabir closed the distance between himself and Rivkin with a half-embrace.

Bones knocked beneath the shoulders of Rivkin's wet tweed. Kabir resumed his seat. Rivkin sat down.

A glass partition seemed to rise between him and the Jew. All they had in common was Noor—and loving the same woman, as sister or girlfriend, wasn't grounds for friendship. Would Rivkin remember Kabir saying so in 1940?

Cigarettes were all Kabir had to offer. Rough fingers took one; it vanished into Rivkin's pocket. Two steaming cups were placed on the table between them—coffee served with almost palpable triumph.

Rivkin shook his head.

What had Kabir been thinking of, ordering coffee? He had heard, then forgotten, that coffee was vitriol in a deportee's stomach. Someone might be offering Noor coffee at this moment . . .

He ordered crème brûlée instead, and began.

It was less difficult than he'd expected, as if he had some obligation to tell Rivkin the scant details he had. Tie facts together. Perhaps draw conclusions, ask if Rivkin was worthy of this war, of Kabir's sorties over Germany. The warrior in him and the part that was American was proud. We saved you, we liberated you, he wanted to claim.

But he couldn't. How many sorties had he and his crew flown in formation over concentration camps, using their brilliantly lit perimeters as landmarks, never thinking, never thinking . . . War required that, required the suspension of independent thought.

He'd done it as well as any other skipper. Bomber Harris didn't think bombing rail tracks into the camps was a priority, so Kabir and his crew hadn't thought so either. Much as Churchill might solemnly aver today, the war now christened the Second World War wasn't undertaken for humanitarian reasons, but for survival. And for the import of tea, cotton, silk, jute, sugar and all the other luxuries Empire made possible. Revenge, too. Bombing of German civilians as revenge for Dunkirk, London, Coventry— never forget revenge.

He couldn't be accusing, facing Rivkin today: *You didn't leave her alone as you agreed. I heard she wrote to you. But not to me. Now she is missing, may have been tortured, may have died for your sake.* It would sound as if he'd given up, leaped to a premature conclusion that Noor was dead.

Rain twisted and pressed against the windows.

"Have you heard from Noor since your return?"

"No."

No, when Kabir wanted to hear yes. Yet he was glad. Glad Noor hadn't called Rivkin, hadn't written to him. If she was alive, she'd reach Kabir, yes, she would.

"Do you have any news?" asked Armand.

"No."

Maybe she wasn't dead, but she haunted him in his dreams. Last night she came dressed in slacks with a breastplate, like Jeanne d'Arc. He couldn't say this to Rivkin either. Any comparison to Jeanne d'Arc of the voices and braggadocio would ring overly facile. Heroines from before the war didn't seem to apply as models, cinema actresses played heroines who were nothing like Noor, and he couldn't recall hearing of any Muslim woman quite like Noor. Anyway, why should Rivkin feel moved by Jeanne d'Arc? Today, Jeanne d'Arc symbolized a France that had rejected him and his community. Rivkin's eyes said he and his kin had now prepaid for all assistance received or to be received from France.

He should tell Rivkin what Vogel said, that Noor had written to "A." Should, but the words wouldn't come. Rivkin might ask if

Noor had also written to Kabir. Then he'd have to say no, not one letter since she was sent to France.

Insh'allah, Noor would return, and if it was important, she'd tell Rivkin herself.

He took a sip of coffee.

He should express an interest in the camps. But living, life itself, in the kind of death camps shown in newspaper photographs was past his Imaginot line; he couldn't formulate a question.

"How . . . how were you saved?" His voice sounded unduly loud despite the clatter of spoons and plates behind them.

No answer for a long time. Kabir sensed Rivkin's mental scan of millions of words in French, English, Russian, Yiddish . . . sensed the successive failure of adjectives, adverbs, nouns, verbs.

"There were no reasons with the Germans," said Rivkin. "At Auschwitz, we called those who smoked their last cigarettes and became ready to die Mussulmans—a misnomer, of course. No one wants to die when he has something left to live for. Even hatred gives one a reason to live, not to die."

Another silence.

"I'll tell you someday. Not now."

The man across the table was harder, more obstinate—and, yes, stronger—for having been rejected in so many ways by countries and communities. Kabir too felt harder, harsher, older. But Rivkin had been tested to the limits of human endurance, a test that must have allowed him a glimpse of his true self. Kabir envied Rivkin that glimpse, but he was very grateful—*alhamdulillah*—that he had not experienced the same.

What if the true self is not as beautiful as the Sufis believe? What if it is shamefully amoral? Rumi said the soul is here for its own joy, but what if the outcast and the outcaste souls are here only for their own survival?

"Your hand?"

Rivkin dug it deeper into his coat pocket. "It's ruined. I cannot play again."

A statement of fact.

"And your mother?"

"You remember, do you not, that my mother was a washer-woman?"

The emphasis was unmistakable, linking "washerwoman" to Uncle's objections to marriage between Rivkin and Noor. Kabir's turn to maintain silence; words would only wound further.

"The Germans found out my mother was born in Moscow and they wrote 'Russian spy' in her file. At Drancy she was transferred to the laundry to wash typhus-infected clothing, and I thought she had been deported or was dead. Washing clothes saved her from Auschwitz—she was quarantined and could not be sent away. She never contracted typhus, either . . . she boiled her own clothes every night. But then . . ."

Eyes that had seen too much met Kabir's.

"She died last week."

What to say? Rivkin's suffering, his mother's suffering, Jewish suffering, set a new standard by which the suffering of all people would be measured. Every colonial not called upon by his occupier to report for annihilation with one suitcase could now be told his suffering was not commensurate.

"I'm sorry." He was sorry, and he was not responsible. Not for this part of Rivkin's suffering.

Silence lengthened, weighted with unspoken memories.

The crème brûlée arrived and for no reason reminded him that Rivkin had once attended Uncle Tajuddin's lectures. That he'd been a seeker, a self-styled agnostic.

"Perhaps it may help you to meditate? Look for the hand of Allah—God—in all things?" The kind of suggestion Abbajaan would have made.

"God!" Rivkin's laugh was like the rubbing of dry bones.

A godless man. Kabir was curiously unsurprised, as if he'd known the moment he sat down. He'd never talked with a godless man, really.

"Were . . . are you a Communist, then?"

A trace of a smile crossed Rivkin's face. "That's the American in you, always worried about Communists. No, I may be an atheist, but I'm no Communist. I sympathize with Communists—how could I not?—my father was a worker at Renault. But I rethought Communism in the camps. I rethought so many things."

Kabir had an urge to agree in some way—a minor point would do.

"It's classless, much like Islam," he said.

"Classless? From Auschwitz, the Russians sent me to two camps. And even there I found that even when everyone is dressed the same, fed the same, made equal by suffering, there is no such thing as a classless society. Stalin doesn't want a classless society—he wants a society of workers. Wants to banish complexity, just like the Nazis. And where there's no complexity, there can be no art—only propaganda."

Maybe Rivkin was right. Abbajaan had banned Indian music from his life rather than simplify it for his Western followers. Later, Uncle had banned complexity, killing any hereditary urge Kabir had to compose music.

"So, I think it may be difficult to truly love an art—any art—and also be a Communist. Or a Fascist. But"—Rivkin's voice acquired an edge—"Communist or not, a rational human being can realize God is but a human creation, a myth constructed to control and comfort the poor, the powerless and the dispossessed of the world. So—I have no faith at all."

"I see," Kabir said.

But he didn't. This would really hurt Noor; in fact, it might be the one thing that could finally sever her from the clutches of this Jew. But why, Allah, why was she who had so much faith the one still missing, feared dead—while ever-doubting Kabir, and Rivkin, agnostic turned atheist, were alive and here today?

"When did you . . . I mean, why did you lose faith?"

He asked for comparison with himself, though losing faith in Yahweh and losing faith in Allah might be two quite different things.

Rivkin's face gave Kabir nothing, for a while. Then he said, "I used to believe in that force that sent me music. But now . . . I hear no music. Another loss, beginning with that first loss—Noor's loss, our loss."

Eleven years ago—the child.

If only he could explain to Rivkin: A much younger Kabir had felt besieged, excluded from full participation in France. He had attempted to conserve his religious community.

Rivkin's spoon scraped the small dish.

It wasn't that you were a Jew. I was raised to respect your religion—we are all People of the Book. It was that my eldest nephew could have been Jewish, not Muslim, and Afzal Manzil might be inherited someday by Jews.

But those words, those unsaid words, were a half-truth at best. Kabir offered Rivkin another cigarette, struck a match for his own. Held it out to Rivkin, but the cigarette was already in Rivkin's pocket.

A carafe of house wine he didn't remember ordering appeared.

"Will you be at the Lutétia for long? It looks crowded with returnees."

"As long as I can."

"It is difficult to find an apartment in Paris. Soldiers everywhere . . ."

"Very few wish to rent to Jewish deportees," said Rivkin.

If Noor had married Rivkin in 1940, she too might be searching for an apartment now. Some moral consolation. He should invite Rivkin to stay at Afzal Manzil, just for a while. But he'd have to explain to Mother and Zaib, explain reversing his own adamant decision. Thank heavens Dadijaan and her Urdu orations had returned to India—he wouldn't have to explain who Rivkin was. Anyway, he wasn't going to weaken and invite Rivkin now; Rivkin wouldn't accept.

Rivkin was looking at him, through him. "Will you return to India?"

"India?" All the urgings of Dadijaan, the English and the Anglo-Indian press hadn't persuaded Mr. Churchill to request grain shipments for his brown subjects from Mr. Roosevelt till three and a half million Indian civilians had swelled the population of the dead. And two and a half million Indians had returned to their villages by now, taken off their British Indian Army uniforms and probably joined the ranks of independence agitators. "Return to *India*?" Kabir said.

"Home. To live there," said Rivkin. "You once told me how very Indian your family was, how important your traditions are to you."

Indeed, he had said many such things to Rivkin in 1940. But today . . .

"I'm a European Muslim," said Kabir. "I *am* home."

He might visit India again now the Suez had reopened, but the thought of living there had never entered his mind. He wouldn't know how.

"I will return to Afzal Manzil," he said. "Take up my father's mantle. Teach."

The irony. Inheritance, that fossil remains of feudalism in capitalism. What opportunity was left, now the war was over, would come from aligning his fortunes with the memory of Abbajaan and trading on a few slender, half-remembered associations with that starving subcontinent still locked in struggle against its occupier, a place he had visited but once for two years as a boy.

Life—Allah, kismet, what you will—required Kabiruddin Khan to become Pir Kabir, an expert on all things Indian. Oriental Thought, Sufism in particular. Mould and wrap ancient wisdom for consumption by the West.

Other people's half-baked mystical experiences would haunt him all the days of his life, and every day he would have to find French and English words to spark his inherited disciples' souls. Try, like his father before him, to dilute the fear of death that haunted them, haunted him too. Becoming Pir Kabir would never offer the ecstatic rush that came from wavering on the cusp of death, but it was a profession, like any other. He would wait for Judgement Day to begin the real atonement.

"Will you go to Palestine?" he asked, to deflect thoughts of his own future.

"Palestine? I hear it is beautiful. And being with other Jews for the first time, all together like that, no longer being in the minority—it's a powerful thing."

Rivkin stroked his chin. His beard was returning, Kabir noticed. Completely white.

"But how Jewish will I need to be for acceptance in Israel? If it ever comes about, the Zionists will make Israel a Jewish theocracy even if they call it democratic. Then how long before people with fantasies of God-given rights to land begin 'resettling' Muslims and Christians? They too will exclude those they need to hate to survive. Noor and I—"

Kabir stiffened, but Rivkin didn't pause.

"—if she returns and chooses to go, then maybe. But without Noor, with only French, Russian, English and a smattering of prison German and Yiddish—no. I'd only exchange the watchtowers and barbed wire of Auschwitz for the watchtowers and barbed wire of the kibbutz. And now, with the bomb—I don't want Gentiles to have us all in one place."

"I'm sure you won't find peace by going to the Middle East," said Kabir. "Muslims in Palestine won't accept becoming refugees in their own land. If they are pushed out by the British and the Jews, they'll run into the open arms of the fascists. Hitler may be defeated, but his Nazis are not gone, nor is their ill-gotten wealth." He extinguished his cigarette and poured himself a glass of wine. "How Muslim would a Palestinian Muslim have to be then? The first casualty would be Sufism, we who preach a Universal God, write odes to wine, sing and dance in devotion."

But how could Rivkin remain where he was unwanted?

"If not Israel, will you go to Russia? I read in the *Herald* that Stalin is offering amnesty to all who left during the Revolution."

Rivkin gave a mordant laugh. "Yes, poor powerless France would agree to a second deportation for me, to Russia." Unvarnished pain and reproach had thickened Rivkin's voice. "But I am a born

French citizen. So, now that they cannot send my mother back to Moscow, I will fight to stay here."

Rivkin was angry, not for his own suffering but for the suffering of those he loved. His mother, Noor. And, Kabir had read, he was one of only three thousand returnees; only three thousand of the three hundred thousand Jews in France before the war.

Living proof, a surfeit of it.

For a moment Kabir saw as Rivkin did: Gentile inhabitants of houses near the Jewish areas in nearby Montparnasse and in the rue des Rosiers should be drowning in the blood of thousands whose cries were ignored as the gendarmes kicked doors down, as buses and trains trundled away. The symphonic cries of the absent were notes played out of hearing range of listeners, though today's newspapers were full of the trial of Xavier Vallat, the Vichy administrator responsible for their deportations. Rivkin was a walking accusation. Yes, it was necessary for the French that he remain.

"Many are being brought to justice," Kabir felt it necessary to assure him. "Laval has been executed, Pétain sentenced to life in prison."

All year long, since Robert Brasillach, editor of *Je Suis Partout*, was denied pardon and executed, the trials of artists and other intellectuals had drawn press and spectators. Following some obscure logic, the French were holding their writers, musicians, actors and artists more culpable under Article 75 for putting their skills in the service of Fascism than black marketeers or war profiteers, more culpable than themselves.

"Yes, and France is découpaging its war years."

"I mentioned when I telephoned you at the Lutétia that I know who betrayed Noor," said Kabir. "Renée Garry is her name."

A silence. Then Rivkin said, "How do you know?"

"A woman named Monique Nadaud working in the Hôtel de Ville denounced her to the Allies after the liberation. There was evidence: she found a ledger where Madame Garry recorded receiving ten thousand francs for denouncing Noor."

Rivkin was staring out of the window at the rain. Was he listening?

"Madame Garry is at Fresnes now, charged with treason. The committee chose four jurors—all women! I have still to accustom myself to the idea of women jurors. All members of wives-of-POW organizations. They will have to accustom themselves to the idea of a Muslim woman as a resistant, then convict a European woman for denouncing her . . ."

A combustible anger burned inside him. He couldn't say the rest: chances of Renée's conviction were low.

"Will you attend her trial?" he asked Rivkin. Kabir planned to attend. Meditation and prayer might help him through it.

"I don't think so," replied Rivkin. "Today, all forty million liberated Frenchmen say they were in the Resistance. But the facts persist: My mother and my Noor were here. They are not here now. Me, I long just once more to hold Noor—"

He looked directly at Kabir. "What did you fear would result from my beliefs?" An inner energy seemed to drive each word.

The past, that insurmountable wall. Kabir's visit to Rivkin's apartment in 1940, days before the fall of Paris. The weight in his pocket. "Leave my sister alone." The packet of money that never changed hands.

"Nothing. Nothing at all."

Deep blue eyes that wouldn't let him look away. Mirror eyes.

The moment passed. Rivkin lit one of the cigarettes; smoke clouded Kabir's vision.

"What shall we do, then?" He discovered his voice was bleak with unshed tears.

"Continue," said Rivkin. "She still lives."

EPILOGUE

Suresnes, France
April 28, 1995

IN THE GARDEN at Afzal Manzil, people were taking their seats beneath the quince tree before a stage enveloped in red, blue and white. The men hatless, the women clutching handkerchiefs. Amid the dark suits and coats in the rows of folding chairs, Pir Kabiruddin Khan's kaftan of ochre velvet trimmed with gold stood out like a beacon.

A faded golden head leaned towards Pir Kabir's right ear.

"It's Armand Rivkin again," said his wife Angela.

A tall, stooped man in a dark hat and coat, silver showing at each temple, had entered the garden. He leaned on a brass-headed cane, kept one hand in his pocket.

Kabir glanced at his watch—a little past five o'clock.

Rivkin. Distracting him again.

The Jew would be at least eighty-five by now. Thin as only the survivors living in their rest homes were, yet he had a stringy resilience about him.

Kabir never thought when Rivkin attended the first ceremony, in 1946, that he would come every year. But he did. Always entered just when Kabir was mentally preparing his eulogy. Always stood at the back, never took a chair. Always left early. Kabir hadn't spoken to him since they met at the restaurant on the rue de Sèvres.

"Why does he come?" whispered Zaib in his left ear, auburn hair licking the shoulders of her navy blue cloak. "Noor was never really going to marry him, for heaven's sake."

"He thinks she was going to marry him," said Angela in his right.

Zaib sniffed. "If she had really wanted to marry him, wouldn't she have done so years before the war?"

Leave my sister alone—Zaib didn't know about that. Zaib, younger than Noor and himself, could no longer imagine the times, sixty years ago, when it was his and Uncle Tajuddin's duty to arrange Noor's marriage. Since no one ever suggested an arranged marriage for Zaib, and Kabir had married Angela despite the explicit disapproval of every Indian family member including old Uncle Tajuddin, Zaib probably didn't remember Kabir having anything to do with approval or disapproval of Noor's fiancé. The very idea was anachronistic in modern Europe, an immigrant practice. And as for giving permission— why, many women of Noor's station in India didn't need permission to marry these days.

Zaib, Kabir noted, had conveniently forgotten her own role in ridding Noor of Rivkin's bastard.

So long ago—why dig it up now?

The annual commemoration ceremony was Kabir's reparation to Noor; no one should mar it. Certainly not Rivkin.

"Ignore him, he'll leave soon," he murmured to Angela.

But he kept an eye on Rivkin as the ceremony began.

The mayor of Suresnes drew aside a length of purple velvet, unveiling a plaque resting on an easel. He read, "*Mémorial Noor. Ici habitait Noor Inayat Khan . . .*" He dedicated the plaque destined to be mounted on the gatepost and placed a wreath beneath.

Then came Colonel Buckmaster, spry at eighty-five. He solemnly placed another wreath and smiled for the clicking cameras.

People like Buckmaster and the official historians of the SOE were excellent at what they were paid to do after the war:

proclaiming that all 1,499 agents betrayed by Gilbert were deplorably lax in basic security, that the exigencies of war necessitated recruitment of agents like Noor, "not overly gifted with brains," excessively honest, and unfortunately incapable of the basic quality required of spies—prevarication.

Now came old Miss Atkins, who, despite her years, remembered to mention that Noor had been awarded the Croix de Guerre by President de Gaulle and the George Cross by England in 1948.

While she spoke, Kabir's memory sped away in reverse, to the envelope that arrived from Germany in 1975—twenty years ago now—addressed in a hand he did not recognize. Inside, a letter from the retired governor of Pforzheim prison. The prison was being repaired. A bundle of papers had been found squirrelled away between two walls, the same where he had shown Kabir Noor's scratched words. The prison authorities had contacted the governor, the governor had remembered Monsieur Khan from Paris.

Oh, the flaky lightness of those fragments of onionskin! Kabir had spread them over a table by the window and raised the blind. Faded, minute writing, situating itself carefully between invisible parallel lines, her f's and q's making quick forays over the baseline and back, downstrokes angled back as if dissenting. Vessels in Kabir's fingertips constricted as he imagined Noor's pressure on the pen, her leaning deep into the paper.

Could he but tap into the psychic source behind the pen, interpret hidden signs, he might one day understand the fragments better. He tried to find some beginning, searching for his own name or initials among the fragments. Surely, if Noor wrote, she'd write to him? Reordering the fragments, searching again: Zaib's name, Mother's . . . ? Only initials. There was an "A," but she didn't seem to be writing to Rivkin.

Wafer-thin strips threatened to disperse and recombine. He found the largest and began to assemble the others around it. *Love* was the first word he pieced together, and though it took him weeks, months, some fragments did fall together. A foolish thing to do; her life might have been even shorter if the Germans had found those papers. What strange things she wrote—a woman's hallucinations.

Hindsight impeded Kabir's empathy, raising questions Noor was not present to answer. If he had been in her stead, he might have been less foolhardy, made more compromises. Been less trusting. But the SOE had made Noor a character in a story, and hadn't Noor loved stories? She'd walked right into their hands and become *aleph-null*, the first number past infinity.

He had read Noor's papers every year since, but he never had understood the whole. But what happened happened. Kabir should have enough faith to believe it happened just as Allah willed.

Oh, but go back further: Kabir should never have introduced her to that blackguard Nick.

Nick. The mayor, Colonel Buckmaster and Miss Atkins standing on the dais before him hadn't mentioned Nick. Or how Major Nicholas Boddington came to Gilbert's trial by the Free French and testified on his behalf for acquittal. Allah had not acquitted Gilbert as easily, however, sending him to living cremation while flying for Air Opium in Laos. There wasn't a more terrible way to die.

And neither the Colonel nor Miss Atkins mentioned names like Prosper, Archambault, Phono, or the sacrifice of so many lives for the sake of misinformation.

And for the sake of a free Europe, one might say.

The ambassador of India was mentioning his great pride that an Indian woman had been of use to the French resistance, cementing "ancient ties" between their two countries, ties that went back to a French treaty with Noor's ancestor, the great Tipu Sultan. He carefully omitted mentioning Noor was Muslim, for she might then inspire other Muslims fighting Hindu fascism resurging in India.

Then the British ambassador emphasized his great pride that an Indian woman had worked loyally for the British. The phrase "example to Indian women" recurred. He omitted to mention that Madeleine was considered a British colonial at the time, and had, over these fifty years, inspired a few English women as well.

Someone lent an arm to help him up from his chair. Pir Kabir's turn to speak. He mounted the three steps of the dais. As in past years, he was intensely aware of Rivkin's presence.

"Today is the fiftieth anniversary of Dachau's liberation," he said. "My brave sister, the first Sufi saint in the West, was martyred there . . . We have no other date on which to mourn, no body or grave at which to pay our respects. She was as *za*, the rarest letter in Arabic. Were it not for women like Noor, whose very name meant 'light,' we would live in a world corroded by a constant darkness of the soul. Join me in prayer now . . ."

He drew his reading glasses from the pocket of his kaftan and began with the Al-Fatiha, then led the recitation of Surah 36: "In the name of God, Most Gracious, Most Merciful. Ya Sin. By the Qur'an, full of Wisdom, Thou art indeed one of the apostles, On a Straight Way . . ."

He came to the twelfth verse: "Verily We shall give life to the dead, and We record that which they send before and that which they leave behind, and of all things have We taken account in a clear Book of Evidence . . ."

He looked up, across the garden to the grotto where Abbajaan had placed his mantle on his ten-year-old shoulders and initiated Kabir as his successor. It came to him as he recited: the fifty years he'd lived between the dream in which he saw Noor writing his deeds in the Book of Judgement had been years of another man's life, a life charted by Abbajaan's dreams. Kabir had asserted himself after the war, assuring Uncle Tajuddin he was appreciated but that Kabir, Mother and Zaib would run Afzal Manzil and the Sainah Foundation themselves.

Too late to wonder what shape a life of his own design might have taken.

He continued all the way to the comfort of the fortieth verse: "It is not permitted to the Sun to catch up with the Moon, nor can the Night outstrip the Day: Each just swims along in its own orbit according to Law."

The surah reassured; the path itself would lead him to overcome himself and experience the Almighty. Perhaps he would never outstrip Abbajaan as a thinker, leader or dervish, but at least he followed the same *tariqah* as his father, the Sufi way.

Dadijaan, Uncle and Mother were long in their graves, and perhaps Kabir had created his own orbit, slightly modified for his own times, just as Abbajaan had modified his practice of Islam — validating all paths in hope of integrating East and West, skimming over the dire consequences to unbelievers mentioned in this very surah. He had even followed Abbajaan's practice of including women as carriers of his message of tolerance, though it was equally difficult for them to practice. Noor's story had made the Sufi school quite famous, sacrosanct in spite of the anti-Muslim rhetoric of conservative and fascist French politicians, notably Monsieur Le Pen.

He continued to the end, the eighty-third verse: "So glory to Him in whose hands is the dominion of all things: and to Him will ye be all brought back."

The *mureeds* broke into muted clapping. A representative from the U.S. embassy said a few words and presented Kabir with a tri-folded American flag.

Then Zaib spoke of how loving and gentle was her sister Noor. She quoted Noor's favourite verses from Tagore's *Gitanjali* and her favourite Sufi tale, the *Wayward Princess*. Strange-sounding remarks after other speakers had described Noor's role in sabotage operations, how she had fearlessly killed two Nazi soldiers, evaded the Gestapo for months and survived six weeks at the avenue Foch and ten months confined in chains on minimum rations. Kabir strained again to believe all this of Noor, his sister Noor.

The dignitaries entered the house to be served cardamom chai, saffron kheer, wine, cheese and petits fours. Kabir returned to the lawn; *mureeds* from many nations stood awaiting his blessing.

He had become what his followers wanted him to be, and brought comfort where he could. No more solitary quests for confirmations of faith; the community his father left him to guide was his responsibility. A woman came before him from the queue and said her son committed suicide three years ago. He placed his hands on her forehead with confidence after all these years, the way Abbajaan used to, and turned to the next follower, a man who confided that his daughter was mentally ill.

And there was still time. Time enough to make his private connection with the Divine before the Day of Judgement.

A tall figure approached the memorial plaque. Rivkin hadn't departed early this time.

Long, slim fingers touched the embossed inscription, as if reading Braille. The hand that could no longer play the piano rested in Rivkin's pocket.

Fifty years . . . maybe silence can be, should be, broken after fifty years.

Kabir motioned to his followers to go ahead. His ochre kaftan swept the lawn. "I'm glad you came," he said to Rivkin. "You look well." And almost added, "by the Grace of Allah."

The older man leaned his cane against a chair and took his hand from his pocket. "It's time I showed you something," he said.

Misshapen fingers opened, revealing a packet of yellowed tissue paper.

"You asked once how I survived when so many did not," Rivkin continued, as if there had been no intermission between their conversation at the restaurant on the rue de Sèvres in 1945 and this moment. "Look. See this—"

He unwrapped the packet and there, lying on the tissue, was a gold chain and a pale, curved charm, a tiger claw enframed in gold. That of his long-gone Dadijaan, the grandmother who so loved Noor. And it came—for luck and courage—from his ancestor, Tipu Sultan. And that chain—the one he bought for Noor from his first earnings as a pilot. The last time he saw Noor, in London, she was wearing them.

He looked up at Rivkin.

"Someone brought this to me in the camp at Drancy, the night before I was deported. I don't know how or at what cost Noor sent it. I thrust it between the layers of bandages on my hand and held it close all the way to Auschwitz. Read it. Read what she wrote on the tissue."

Kabir put on his glasses and leaned closer to the faded ink. *Je t'aime, toujours,* he read. Beneath it, the word *Adieu* — struck out. And on the third line, *Au Revoir.*

Maybe the *Au Revoir* was not from Noor. It could have been written by Rivkin himself, desire turning to fantasy. But no. The writing — definitely Noor's. And Vogel had said Noor wrote to someone whose name began with "A."

"When I believed I had no one, nothing to live for, I felt her love, her spirit urging me to live."

Rivkin rewrapped the tiger claw. With that pendant in Rivkin's hand, Kabir and Zaib could no longer say that Noor never loved him, that pity for a Jew had moved Noor to associate with him. Resting in Rivkin's hand, it became instead proof of a love so great she would brave a world war to reach him, a love that had outlasted Vichy and the German Raj. Kabir had never given or received such love.

Deep blue eyes, young in Rivkin's gaunt, lined face, met Kabir's.

"I told you I would tell you someday."

Revenge by silence. For fifty years Rivkin had kept this trace of Noor to himself, for himself.

"Why did you not show this to me all these years?" Kabir's voice sounded accusing. But he had no right to be accusing. He hadn't asked Rivkin for his interpretation of Noor's papers or offered a glimpse of them in twenty-five years.

"You might have asked it from me," said Rivkin.

This being true, there was nothing Kabir could find to say.

Maybe the time had come to tell Rivkin about Noor's papers, if only to share a memory of Noor.

"Will you join us for tea?" he asked, as if a ritual cup of shared cardamom chai could help them begin anew.

Rivkin shook his head and returned the tiger claw to his pocket. "It's a little late for that," he said.

Light faded over Mont Valérien.

Nothing finishes, thought Kabir. *It's fifty years and he hasn't forgotten.*

But then, how can he?

Rivkin hadn't shared the tiger claw with Kabir; Kabir wouldn't share Noor's papers with him. Yes, it really was too late now—Rivkin's stooped figure was already receding, crippled fingers hidden in his coat pocket.

In these fifty years, explanations of Noor's actions had multiplied, amoebic in their overlappings. Myths were stretched to clothe the first skeletal narrations: Noor was the colonial spy fighting bravely for the mother country. Then Jeanne d'Arc on a mission to crown de Gaulle her king. After Renée Garry's trial she became a female Jesus, betrayed for ten thousand francs without the Judas kiss. Later still, after half the SOE files were destroyed in a fire, some information surfaced: she was a doomed spy, an innocent, slaughtered for the unworthy cause of imperialism; very naive, extremely idealistic. People debated in print and Parliament if Madeleine was braver than other agents or a trusting, unwitting pawn. No wonder Noor had been captured, they said—she had ignored security procedure by returning to Suresnes. They tut-tutted that she had been captured with her code books, as if no other wireless operator was ever arrested with code books in hand; that she'd asked for her valise from Madame Aigrain's home and caused the arrest of Émile Garry, as if no other agent took a suitcase to prison. That *salaud* Vogel, now a retired bank clerk in Munich, was asked his opinion, interviewed several times to answer if Noor had failed as a soldier or had succeeded by failing.

The whole damn war of competing nationalisms was the first failure.

If Mother were still alive, she would have invented a common version of Noor's story and assigned it to her children for the telling—but she was not, and Kabir had spent years speculating about Noor's possible motivations at every step. Today, Rivkin had presented proof Kabir could not refute, proof that changed Noor's story yet again.

The actress Odile Hoogstraten and her husband Louis de Grémont were sitting under the trees deep in conversation with Josianne Prénat and her fourth husband. And there was Monique, survivor of Ravensbrück, whose husband, Émile Garry, had been executed yet who came every year to commemorate Noor.

Monique brought Renée Garry to mind. Renée Garry, whose husband Guy had returned in time for the shock of attending his wife's trial. By the time Kabir found it in himself to meet the acquitted Renée, she was a grandmother of ten, but having learned of Noor's Indian heritage during her trial, spent the entire meeting lecturing Kabir about overpopulation in India. When she heard Kabir now had two sons, she began lecturing on Muslim overpopulation in France. And she who had run a safe house for resistants had become proud to mention she'd voted for fascist Le Pen.

Renée Garry must live with her deeds, Kabir with his.

Other guests had gone inside, so Kabir followed. Thanks to Zaib, every corner of Afzal Manzil was decorated with vases full of Noor's favourite forget-me-nots and burning scented candles.

In Abbajaan's recital room, guests greeted him, bowing. A woman took her seat cross-legged on a carpet, drew a veena before her. Her *zikr* rose over the drone of the veena as if she were breathing through sound. Zaib's idea too, no doubt—it wasn't his.

Too reminiscent of Noor.

More would happen. What was yet to be written would supplement the spoken stories, the spoken would bring sound to the written, and memory would twine itself about the stronger of the two. Truth was buried somewhere in and between the scraps of Noor's words, truth as only she knew it. But Pir Kabir Khan would tell the story of Noor the rest of his days. Re-create Noor that she might live on in the world's memory.

Imagine that.

ACKNOWLEDGMENTS

THE SUPPORT and contributions of many people brought this book into being.

In France, I thank members of the extended family of Noor Inayat Khan for their hospitality, hours of discussion, and correspondence. To Anne Freyer of Editions du Seuil France, my gratitude for her encouragement, travel companionship to Le Mans and guidance as the book matured. My thanks to Florence Libert for her coordination of travel and research interviews, and translation assistance. Thanks for the kind assistance of Madame Semence, librarian at L'École Agronomique de Grignon, the personal memories and research of Madame Vanderwynckt, the guidance of Monsieur Trouvé and the memories imparted by Monsieur de Ganay.

In Germany, Susana Fernandez and Hede Mettler of Pforzheim's information bureau made it possible for me to visit Noor's prison cell. Christian Milankovic of the *Pforzheimer Zietung* accompanied me, providing translation assistance and discussion of context.

In Canada, I was privileged to attend the Banff Centre for the Arts Writer's Studio, a residency made possible by the Adele Wiseman scholarship fund and a travel grant from the Canada

Council. Grateful thanks to Bonnie Burnard and David Carpenter, who were generous enough to read and comment on the manuscript in progress; and to Greg Hollingshead and Edna Alford, who believed it possible, sometimes more than I did. I warmly acknowledge the financial support of the Canada Council for the Arts during the writing of this book. Thanks very much to writer Corie Johnson for sharing research documents and speculations. Many thanks for the support of my agents, Bruce Westwood and Nicole Winstanley, who believed in this book from raw text to publication. I appreciate my editors Diane Martin and Louise Dennys whose questions challenged me to go deeper, tell the story more fully. I am indebted to John Sweet and translator Barbara Collignon for their excellent copyediting.

In England, intrepid Andy Forbes provided research assistance and companionship for my visits to museums and sites in Noor's life. His Web site 64-Baker-Street.org describes the fifty women volunteers who worked for the SOE Thanks to the late Group Captain Hugh Verity and to Mrs. Audrey Verity for their hospitality and candidness. My thanks to librarians of the Public Records Office at Kew and the Imperial War Museum.

In the U.S.A., many thanks to Gaston Vandermeersche for sharing vivid memories of his incarceration at the avenue Foch both in interviews and in *Gaston's War*. Holocaust survivor Edel Ullenberg shared her memories of her time in Dachau; Marc Collignon his memories of life in occupied France. Werner Juretzko gave me details from his memories of incarceration in Germany. I am grateful to Nighat Kokan for her patience and meticulous research for meanings and transliterations from Urdu. The Ragdale Foundation in Illinois supported me for a five-week residency. This project was supported in part by a grant from the Wisconsin Arts Board, with funds from the State of Wisconsin. Sincere thanks and appreciation to Tim Baker, reference librarian at the U.S. Holocaust Memorial Library in Washington, D.C., and to the librarians at the Milwaukee

Public Library and Marquette University Memorial Library for their patience in filling my incessant requests for international interlibrary loans. Many thanks to Elaine Bergstrom (pen name Marie Kiraly), Beatrice Armstrong of the Alliance Française de Milwaukee, Amy Waldman, Pegi Taylor, Judy Steininger and members of my novel writers' group, who read the manuscript at various stages. Thanks also to the Safe House espionage theme restaurant in Milwaukee, a haven for meetings and interviews.

In India, my cousin-sister Ena Singh assisted with research travel and interviews in Delhi, and commented on the manuscript. I greatly appreciated Sardar Shamsher Singh's memories of the Princely State of Baroda (now Vadodara). Dr. Kimberley Chawla acted as Noor's long-distance medical consultant. Many thanks also to the Indian members of Noor Inayat Khan's extended family in Vadodara, who gave me a tour of their home, Noor's ancestral home.

Michael Sell's translation of the Al-Fatiha surah from *Approaching the Qur'an: the Early Revelations* is used by permission of White Cloud Press, Oregon. Quatrains in the epigraph are from *Unseen Rain*, translations of Jalal-ud-din Rumi's poetry by Moyne and Barks. They are used by permission of Threshold Books. Lines from "Je suis seul ce soir" are from the album *Les Chansons sous l'occupation: French Songs of WW II* published by Arkadia Records. The line from Rabindranath Tagore's *Gitanjali* was translated from Bengali by the author, and is used by permission of Macmillan India. Allusions to the *Rubáiyát of Omar Khayyám* are based on Edward Fitzgerald's rendering into English verse, published by Collins Press, London. Quotations from the Ya Sin are from *Holy Qur'Aan: Text, Translation and Commentary* by Abdullah Yusuf Ali, and are used by permission of Wordsworth Editions UK.

I owe too much to mention to my husband David Baldwin, always game to discuss, edit and burrow through his collection of espionage and history books for yet another arcane detail. He hauled and shipped research books to my writer's residencies, and accompanied me to Paris, Pforzheim, Munich and Dachau. His patience, love, humour and understanding help me daily in every way.

SHAUNA SINGH BALDWIN was born in Montreal and grew up in India. The story that was to become her bestselling first novel, *What the Body Remembers*, was awarded the Saturday Night CBC Literary Prize. *What the Body Remembers* received the Commonwealth Writers' Prize for Best Book (Canada and the Caribbean region). *English Lessons and Other Stories* received the Friends of American Writers award. *The Tiger Claw* was a Giller Prize Finalist in 2004. She is the co-author of *A Foreign Visitor's Survival Guide* to America, and presently lives in Milwaukee, Wisconsin.

A NOTE ABOUT THE TYPE

The Tiger Claw is set in Electra, designed in 1935 by William Addison Dwiggins. A popular face for book-length work since its release, Electra is noted for its evenness and high legibility in both text sizes and display settings.